RAKE I'D LIKE TO F...

NICOLA DAVIDSON   ADRIANA HERRERA

EVA LEIGH   JOANNA SHUPE   SIERRA SIMONE

The Last Crimes of Peregrine Hind, Copyright © 2021 by Sierra Simone

Two Rakes for Mrs. Sparkwell, Copyright © 2021 by Ami Silber

A Rake, His Patron, & Their Muse, Copyright © 2021 by Nicola Davidson

Monsieur X, Copyright © 2021 by Adriana Herrera

Sold to the Duke, Copyright © 2021 by Joanna Shupe

Cover Design: Natasha Snow Designs

Cover Image: Regina Wamba

Editing: Sabrina Darby

Copyediting:

The Last Crimes of Peregrine Hind and *Monsieur X* by Michelle Li

Two Rakes for Mrs. Sparkwell by Kelli Collins

Proofreading:

A Rake, His Patron, & Their Muse by Liz Lincoln

First Edition of All Titles: November 2021

Print Edition ISBN: 978-1-949364-19-4

Digital Edition ISBN: 978-1-949364-18-7

THE LAST CRIMES OF PEREGRINE HIND

SIERRA SIMONE

1

Peregrine

1710

THE ROAD WAS A RIBBON OF HORSESHIT OVER THE PURPLE MOOR.

Peregrine Hind sat atop his horse at the crest of a cragged Devonshire hill, staring at the distant gleam of Far Hope nestled into its valley. He couldn't imagine the number of candles it took to light the Dartham family seat, but he also wasn't surprised by the sheer waste of it all. The Darthams were like that—careless and prodigal.

But tonight they would pay for it, and ironically enough, it would be their own extravagance that would undo them. It was the week before the annual Michaelmas ball, which was why the manor house was glowing so merrily into the dark. It was also why the road was covered in horseshit, which had accumulated under the constant traffic of visitors coming from everywhere across the kingdom. In any other circumstance, so many coaches creaking their way through this wild and lonely landscape would be like a river of gold to a highwayman like Peregrine Hind.

But he only cared about one coach tonight.

With a soft cluck, he turned his horse back east to where the road from Exeter dipped into a steep, wooded valley. His friends were waiting at the bottom, their mounts already hidden deep in the trees.

"Well?" Lyd asked as Peregrine came to a stop. She was pacing while the others sat checking their pistols. Her jaw was tight, her normally pale cheeks flushed. "Anything yet?"

"No." Peregrine looked up at the moon through the trees. "The innkeeper did say it would be late."

Peregrine paid innkeepers all around Devonshire to give him information when he needed it. Even the keepers of the finer establishments were susceptible to bribery, so long as they were never connected to any crimes that came of the information given—and Peregrine was careful never to let those connections be known. It served his purposes to be thought unnervingly omniscient, his movements and motives shrouded in mystery.

It had given him the reputation of the most infamous highwayman in England, but after four years of terrorizing the roads, Peregrine could conclusively say that the recipe of infamy was much simpler than people seemed to think:

Half preparation.

Half indifference to death.

Peregrine no longer cared very much if he lived or died—and really, when stealing a mere twelve pence could get someone taken to Tyburn, a highwayman was already a dead thief walking. At thirty-four, Peregrine was already older than most in his profession ever lived to be, but the thought rarely bothered him. He'd come from the war, after all, from the bloody, desperate fighting in the Low Countries, where death stalked every man regardless of age or station. He never thought he'd live this long, had assumed from the moment he signed his name to the rolls of the Queen's army that he wouldn't make it to twenty-five, much less the age he was now. He'd joined the army anyway in order to send his much-needed wages to his mother and siblings, but when he'd returned, he'd found his family and their farm in ruins. Anyone he'd ever loved—any purpose he'd ever had after his career as a soldier—was gone. Dead and cold in the ground.

Now he only drew breath to destroy the Dartham family, and tonight, at long last, that destruction would begin.

"I hope she's with him," Lyd said, her voice shaking a little. "I want to see her face." Lyd had her own reasons for hating the Darthams—and the duchess in particular.

"The innkeeper said she would be with him," Peregrine replied, staring at where the road broke through the trees at the top of the hill. They would wait for the coach to work its halting way to the bottom and then begin its ascent up the other side. That way, they could free the horses without worrying about a rolling coach injuring them. Peregrine didn't hurt horses—or people—if he could help it, and he usually could. While he paid his army of innkeepers to spread stories of his bloody cruelty, he had no interest in dealing pain or death these days.

He couldn't even shake the nightmares from the war he'd left four years ago.

And what did I get for those nightmares? Peregrine asked himself as he watched a cloud drift over the moon. *What did I get for killing all those strangers for some other stranger's crown?* A dead family and a farm that had been enclosed for the Duke of Jarrell's sheep.

Which was why tonight, he'd make an exception to his usual rule about hurting or killing; why tonight, he'd embrace whatever nightmares may come. Because tonight, he was going to kill the Duke of Jarrell. Peregrine was going to kill him in the chilly, lonesome dark, the same dark in which Peregrine's pregnant sister had died as she'd waited outside of Far Hope's doors for help. Help that never came.

A distant creak and clack announced an approaching coach. The rest of the band—three thieves plus Lyd—got to their feet.

"Last chance to leave," Peregrine told them. They were brave, but the murder of a duke and the robbery of a duchess was a Rubicon. They'd be wanted criminals forever; they would be given a more vicious death than the usual Tyburn jig if they were caught. And while Peregrine and Lyd had revenge on their minds, the other thieves were here for money, plain and simple, and there was no telling how much the duke would have with him. It could be enough to set them up for life, or it might only be enough to buy them a pair of secondhand boots.

But even knowing that, none of them left. With nods at Peregrine, they melted into the trees near the spot where he'd confront the coach, ready to swarm the conveyance and disarm any guards or passengers. Peregrine urged his own horse up and into the trees too, deep enough that he was hidden from moonlight, but only a few seconds away from the road itself.

Then they waited.

As he'd known it would, the coach made its way slowly down the hill, using blocks under the wheels to temper its descent. As it came closer, the moonlight gleamed along its ornate trim and illuminated an image painted on the outside of its door: two stags framing a shield, which was adorned with a sun and moon and topped with a single golden key.

The Dartham family crest.

The coach made it safely to the bottom of the hill, and then the two footmen stowed the blocks and walked alongside the coach as the horses began to pull it up the hill. Peregrine's friends would take care of the footmen; his role would be to stop the coach's progress and prevent the driver from arming himself.

Flooded with a grim sort of excitement, he pressed in with his calves and surged forward on his mount, breaking through the trees and charging in front of the coach.

"Stand and deliver!" Peregrine cried.

All hell broke loose.

The Dartham horses shied—the driver lurched as if to reach for a gun—the coach came to an ungainly stop as the footmen raced to the door, almost certainly to arm themselves with a gun stashed inside. The thieves slipped out from their hiding places, and Lyd dissuaded the coachman from any heroics with a pistol aimed steadily at his heart.

Peregrine was already off his horse, and as his thieves subdued the two footmen, he flung open the door to the carriage and lunged inside, knowing that brashness and speed would be his only defense if the duke was armed.

It was dark inside the cabin, and before he saw the single occupant scrambling for the opposite door, he detected an oddly lovely scent.

Like cloves and orange peels, maybe. Like Christmas.

Then he saw the duke, and all other observations left his mind. He seized the murderer of his family by his coat and hauled him bodily out of the coach, sending him sprawling onto the damp dirt of the road.

Peregrine hopped easily to the ground and took two long strides over to the duke. "He was alone," he told Lyd, and she swore in response.

Lyd had wanted the duchess. Badly.

The duke was just pushing himself to his hands and knees when Peregrine pressed a boot to his shoulder and shoved the duke back onto his rump. Peregrine then raised his pistol, already loaded and primed.

He was grateful for the bright moon tonight. He hoped the duke would see enough of Peregrine's sister in Peregrine's features to feel thoroughly haunted by his sins as he died. But then the man on the road lifted his terrified face, and Peregrine froze.

Yes, those were the extravagant clothes a Dartham would wear; yes, there was the skin that seemed to shimmer the palest gold. Yes, there were those dark eyes, which Peregrine knew would be a deep sapphire if he peered closely enough. But this was not the duke.

This was not the duke.

Peregrine swore to himself as he studied the man's face, but there could be no doubt. Reginald Dartham had narrow eyes set closely together, a thin mouth, and a scattering of pockmarks across his jaw. But this man had an entirely different look to him: wide eyes fringed with long lashes, a full mouth, and a jaw carved in a fine, unblemished line. And while Reginald was well known for his elaborate periwigs, even while traveling, it was this man's real hair which tumbled darkly around his shoulders as he scrambled to his knees.

It gleamed like silk in the moonlight.

"Stop," Peregrine ordered coldly, his pistol still raised.

The man stopped, his face tilted toward Peregrine. There was no doubt now that Peregrine had gotten a better look. While the duke was in his forties, this man couldn't be more than twenty-five.

"Please," the man breathed. "Please. I have money—there's money in there—"

"We'll be taking that as it is," Peregrine interrupted. "Who are you, and why are you in the Dartham's coach?"

"I'm S-Sandy—Alexander. Alexander Dartham." The young man swallowed, and then breathed again, "Please. *Please.*"

An unpleasant stab of empathy followed the man's pleas. How often had Peregrine heard those words on a battlefield? Or after the smoke had settled, when all they could do for the wounded was hold them down and hope the surgeon could amputate quickly?

But then Peregrine remembered his sister and the little niece or nephew he never got to meet. He remembered the cold graves of his mother and brother.

Likely they had pleaded too.

Heart once again hardened, he stared down at Alexander Dartham. He'd heard of the duke's younger brother—a notorious rakehell who gambled and swived his way through London. They said no man or woman was safe from his charms, and Peregrine reluctantly admitted to himself that he could see why. Alexander was very beautiful, and on his knees like this . . . also dangerously stirring.

"Where is the duke?" Peregrine demanded, tamping down the flare of heat he felt looking at the brother of his enemy. "He's supposed to be passing through here."

"He took a horse and rode to Far Hope," Alexander said. "This morning. He was worried about being any later than he already was to receive his guests. Please. *Don't*. I can give you anything you want. Anything."

"No, you cannot," Peregrine informed him.

No one could bring back the dead.

One of the thieves relieved Lyd on coachman duty. She climbed down and came to stand next to Peregrine. "You should kill him," she said bluntly. "Hasn't it been your design to destroy them all anyway?"

It had been—although he hadn't intended to *kill* anyone aside from Reginald. After the duke's death, the plan went, he would rob the duke's widow and the new duke of everything that could be carried off, and then he would burn Far Hope to the ground.

And then what, he didn't know. All his careful preparations ended with Far Hope in embers. Maybe he'd retire.

Maybe he'd keep roaming the roads until he was inevitably caught and even more inevitably hanged.

But this was an unexpected difficulty. If he let this younger Dartham live, then Alexander would tell Reginald that he was being sought by a highwayman, not for money, but for murder. Peregrine's opportunities for revenge would shrink further—not to mention that Reginald would no doubt make sure Peregrine was hunted by the law more than he already was.

Which would be...inconvenient.

Peregrine looked back at the young lord, his pistol steady in front of the man's face. He hadn't killed anyone since the war, and even then, the battles had been volleys of smoke and mud and screams, utter chaos, impossible to tell who he'd killed or if his musket had struck anything at all.

Never had he killed someone like this—in stillness and in quiet, with them unarmed and helpless in front of him.

But his sister had died in stillness and in quiet too, she and her unborn child, and Peregrine didn't know what else to live for if it wasn't avenging her death, along with the deaths of his mother and brother. Why not start here?

Why not make Reginald Dartham feel part of what Peregrine had felt when he'd lost his entire family?

He curled his finger around the trigger.

2

Sandy

"WAIT, WAIT!" SANDY BLURTED, LIFTING HIS HANDS. HIS MIND RACED. He'd been in worse scrapes than this, surely—that time he was caught with a Bohemian princess in his bed came to mind, or perhaps the time a Spanish ambassador realized Sandy had been cheating at cards and was ready to fight a duel over it.

Sandy was very used to people wanting to kill him—honestly, it was starting to become something of a Friday night routine—but never had anyone seemed so emotionless about it. Usually, they were howling with indignation or livid with rage, and all Sandy had to do was remind them that he was the son of a dead duke and the brother of a living one, and then whatever it was went away.

But he'd have to do more than charm his way out of this one, especially if Reginald was involved. He had no doubt that this person had a very good reason for wanting to kill his brother, since Reginald was a miserable shit of a man. Not to mention that he was also a *very wealthy* miserable shit of a man, so his robbery or murder would brand any thief deep into tavern songs and fireside stories forever.

"You can kill me, I promise, you can kill me whenever you like," Sandy said quickly, still thinking of a plan as the words tumbled from his mouth. "But if you kill me here, you'll only get whatever valuables are in the coach."

The highwayman standing in front of him didn't react, and Sandy rushed on. "But if you abduct me instead, you can force my brother to pay any ransom you want, and *then* you can still kill me after you get his money. See? You'll get what you want, plus money! Everyone wins!"

The woman standing next to the highwayman was tall and slender, her long limbs displayed in the breeches and tailored coat she wore. She looked familiar, but Sandy couldn't quite place her, although her voice reminded him of . . . someone.

"He has a point," she said. "But Sandy is slippery. He'll try to escape."

Hmm. She talked about Sandy like she knew him. That probably didn't bode well.

Sandy put his hand over his heart like he was swearing an oath. "I'm not slippery! I won't try to escape!" He was definitely planning on escaping. The first chance he got. "And how do you know me again?" he asked her.

She didn't deign to answer, instead turning toward the highwayman. "We might have to kill him, Peregrine," she said quietly.

Peregrine.

Sandy's blood ran cold—well, colder—and then suddenly and fitfully hot. Peregrine Hind was, depending on whom one asked, either a devil who tortured his victims and then left no survivors, *or* a gallant thief who never hurt his victims or their horses and who gave most of what he robbed to needy families in nearby parishes.

Either way, Sandy was currently at the mercy of a legend, not a man, and that didn't feel like a safe place to be. Even if Peregrine Hind was a very tall legend. With very powerful thighs. And very broad shoulders.

And pale, eerie eyes that glittered in the moonlight.

"You can still kill me," Sandy volunteered helpfully. "I'll be your captive the whole time. And you'll get a ransom on top of it. And also, it will really, really incense my brother. Like really." Reggie wouldn't mind so much that Sandy had been kidnapped, but he would hate the paying part. Sandy already cost him plenty of money simply by existing. Well, and existing so lavishly, but Reggie could afford it.

Peregrine studied him, his face betraying nothing. In the stories, highwaymen always had masks and wide-brimmed hats. The other thieves had some variation on the uniform, but Peregrine Hind wore none of that. His black hair was tied back in a simple queue like a soldier, and his face was unmasked, revealing dramatic, ivory features: a high forehead, a strong nose, and a grim, sharp-edged mouth. His clothes were simple—dark breeches, dark coat, dark boots—nothing trimmed or fine, even though it all looked clean and of decent quality.

Nothing about him suggested he was a man used to treating himself with the finer things. At that, Sandy's heart sunk a little. Maybe money wasn't an effective lure after all.

Given the lack of mask and hat, and his overall cold, efficient demeanor, Sandy suspected that Peregrine Hind wasn't after melodrama or notoriety either. That meant Sandy could think of only one other reason a man would want to kill his brother, and that was revenge.

Which was not ideal.

He could work with a craving for money or fame—those urges were mollified easily enough. But revenge? He'd seen enough of it at court and in the Second Kingdom to know its bitter effects well. Revenge was a flame that burned without air, a sword that cut without a blade. It listened to nothing but its own counsel, and it had no master but itself.

A man bent on revenge was not a man easily persuaded.

But Sandy had cheated at cards long enough to read infinitesimal cues, and so he didn't miss the quick flick of Peregrine's eyes over to his band of fellow robbers, who had tied the footmen and coachman to a tree and were now standing by the road as they watched Sandy's desperate ploy unfold.

Peregrine cared about them. Or at least cared what they thought.

Sandy shifted his strategy a little, pitching his voice so the others could hear him better.

"The duke wouldn't think twice about paying five thousand pounds," he said loudly. "Maybe more. I'm his heir, you know, and he'd pay anything to get me back."

Sandy was fairly certain that Reggie would have his limit when it came to paying for a brother he despised . . . but the thieves didn't need to know that part. Not when they were casting each other round-eyed looks and mouthing the words *five thousand pounds*.

Peregrine seemed aware of this, aware of every murmur and glance that passed between his friends, though it all happened behind his back. "That's a princely sum, indeed," Peregrine said after a minute.

"I'm a princely man," Sandy replied, but Peregrine didn't smile, didn't respond at all, except to look over his shoulder at his fellow thieves.

"It *is* a lot of money," one of them, a short and stocky man, said. "Even split between us all, it could last the rest of our lives."

The others chimed in with agreements. Peregrine looked to the woman, who stood between him and the other thieves, her pistol still ready in her hand.

"What do you say?"

"That much money would set the duke well on the road to ruin," she said thoughtfully. "And you could still kill Sandy after you got it, if you needed to."

Sandy again. This woman must know him, but how? He mentally flipped through wine-soaked memories of London and Oxford while outwardly he tried to look sweet and pliant and like he'd be a very docile captive.

After a long, breathless moment, Peregrine gave his lieutenant a crisp nod. He shoved the pistol in his belt. "As you say."

"*Thank you*," Sandy breathed. His relief was entirely genuine, no playacting there whatsoever. "I'll be the very best captive, I promise. I even like being tied up!"

That part was also entirely true. He did like being tied up. And he had to say, as disagreeable as it was to be a captive of a man who planned to kill him, the thought of this stern-mouthed legend lashing his wrists together sped Sandy's pulse in a way that had nothing to do with fear.

Or maybe *something* to do with fear, but the fun kind.

"I'll take him to the priory," Peregrine was telling the woman. "Free the horses. Leave the footmen here, and then have Ned ride the coachman to the next bridge. That should put the coachman close enough to Far Hope that the duke can hear of our ransom demand by tomorrow. And tell him that the duke needs to send his response to The Stag's Head in Chagford."

The woman dipped her head to indicate she understood, and then turned away. But not before giving Sandy a small sniff of disapproval.

A sniff he felt a little wounded by, honestly.

"Stand," Peregrine told Sandy, so Sandy stood, taking a moment to mourn his breeches, which now had dirt on the knees, and probably on the arse too. It was bad enough to be almost murdered and now kidnapped, but he was really, really fond of these breeches! They were sensible yet stylish, and he very much doubted the band of roving highwaymen had access to a good laundress.

There was a small sound, and Sandy looked up at the highwayman, who now had an eyebrow lifted the tiniest amount.

"Did you just sigh at me?" Sandy asked.

"We don't have time for you to inventory the state of your clothes," Peregrine said, wrapping a hand around Sandy's upper arm and dragging him up the hill. It was a very big hand, with long fingers and a wide palm. The kind of hand that would splay easily across Sandy's chest or between his shoulder blades while Sandy was being bent over a bed. "We can't risk staying here."

Sandy didn't bother to point out that *he* could risk staying here and encountering another rider or coach who might help him, because he didn't think Peregrine would appreciate the observation. In any event, they were already to Peregrine's horse, where the highwayman was pulling a coil of rope free.

He didn't object as his wrists were bound and the other end of the rope tied to the saddle, or when Peregrine slid his hands inside Sandy's jacket and up his thighs to make sure Sandy was completely unarmed. In fact, Sandy even shivered a little as Peregrine's fingers ran an efficient search along the rims of his shoes, probing the tops of his stocking-clad feet and the knobs of his ankles.

"You missed a spot," Sandy said.

"I don't think so," said the highwayman.

"But you didn't even check the most interesting places," pouted Sandy. "If you untie me, I can show you what they are."

Peregrine Hind's mouth didn't change from its humorless line, but Sandy saw the drop of his eyes, the way his gaze burned from Sandy's mouth to his chest and down to his hips. Peregrine's hand flexed at his side, and for a moment, Sandy thought his captor was about to touch him again.

But he merely shook his head and mounted his horse. Sandy's rope remained tied to the saddle; he'd have to walk alongside the horse as they went.

"I'll go slowly," Peregrine said as he took the reins. "So long as you behave."

"You'd be the first to make me," said Sandy, but he flashed a big smile to show that he'd be cooperative. He had no wish to fight the highwayman on this, because he was fairly certain he'd lose.

As Peregrine clucked at the horse and they began moving, Sandy could see every flex and press of the expert rider's legs as he rode. He could see the highwayman's strong hands on the reins, casual and powerful all at once.

And with the excellent scenery and the sedate pace, with his hands bound and his body still thrumming with the shaky glee of having just escaped death for a time, Sandy found he didn't mind the walk to the highwayman's lair very much at all.

3

Peregrine

IT WAS ONLY AN HOUR TO THE PRIORY, BUT IT FELT MUCH LONGER TO Peregrine. And that had less to do with his thwarted revenge than it did with the comely captive he had tied to his saddle.

Alexander Dartham's hair spilled everywhere in shimmering waves as he moved, and the moving continually revealed his breeches' superlative tailoring as the fabric clung to his thighs and buttocks when he walked. And whenever he would lag behind the horse and whine that he was tired of walking—which was often—Peregrine would turn around and see a lush pout designed to drive any red-blooded person wild.

By the time they'd gone through a scatter of lonely hills to the narrow seam where the priory sat hidden, Peregrine was at his wit's end. His palms itched to slide over the Dartham heir's sleek thighs; his fingers twitched to tangle themselves in all that soft hair. The scent he'd noticed in the coach was all around him now, spicy and sweet at the same time.

Peregrine's entire body was in riot just from being *near* Alexander Dartham for the length of a ride. How would he bear it when he had Alexander locked away in his hideout for days on end?

But it couldn't be that he was *really* attracted to a scion of the family he loathed, Peregrine reassured himself. It had simply been too long, that was all. During the war, there had been plenty of opportunities to satisfy himself, but being an outlaw in rural Devonshire was a different situation, and he hadn't had the time or luxury to find new lovers. He'd been living more or less like a monk for the last four years—all the more ironic, given his current home.

"I don't want to submit a complaint so early in my captivity," Alexander said as they came to a stop in front of the hideout. "But this is a little déclassé for even my deteriorated taste."

Peregrine looked at the crumbling monastery and imagined how it must look to the brother of a duke. The overgrown entrance was partially blocked by broken beams and piles of roof slates, and wild blackthorn crawled up the walls and bushed out into impenetrable, unkempt thickets. The few windows there were had long been robbed of their glass, and birdshit was everywhere, piled especially high in the doorway. It was as far away from a ducal manor as someone could get.

"I'm planning to kill you, and you're worried about your accommodations?" Peregrine asked, dismounting the horse. Now at the same level, Peregrine could see that Alexander's neckcloth had come loose at some point, exposing the long, lovely column of Alexander's throat. It was the kind of throat a man could spend hours licking, nuzzling.

Biting.

Peregrine had to remind his starved body that Alexander was the brother of his mortal enemy, and also the heir of the family he was determined to ruin. And also his captive.

Alexander tossed a curtain of dark hair over his shoulder and gave Peregrine a little moue of displeasure. "I expected death. I expected torture. But I'm too beautiful and innocent for the indignity of sleeping in a building where the threshold is literally a mound of turds. Your vengeance against my family must know no bounds."

With the pout and the rumpled clothes, Alexander looked anything but innocent. He looked downright sinful. But Peregrine didn't bother to say so.

"How do you know I want revenge?" he asked instead, leading the horse—and Alexander, too, by the other end of the rope that bound him —to the low-slung stables at the side of the priory.

"I deduced it," Alexander said, sounding a little smug. Then he added, "Also, Reginald is an unholy pile of shit, so I'm not surprised someone wants to kill him. If I'm being honest, I thought this would've happened sooner."

Peregrine tied Alexander's rope to a post and then began tending to his horse, removing the bridle and replacing it with a halter to tether his mount in place. "You're not upset I plan to kill your brother?"

Alexander tilted his head, his full mouth bunched to the side. "No. I mean, I oppose the use of murder, in general, and I have no wish to be the duke, ever, ever, so I'd *rather* he not be dead. But as I've mentioned previously, he's about as wonderful as the French pox, and half as merciful."

Peregrine was used to people loathing the Duke of Jarrell around these parts, but they were all farmers, shepherds . . . *thieves*. For a lord like Alexander to admit his brother's despicable nature to someone lowborn like Peregrine was more than a breach of familial loyalty, it was a betrayal of class as well, and that was enough to make Peregrine's curiosity—and suspicion—flare.

"And," Alexander added, "you don't seem the type to do anything for any reason that's less than entirely serious, which makes me think that whatever the motive is for your revenge, I'll have some empathy for it."

Peregrine searched the finely sculpted face in front of him. The honesty he saw in those dark eyes unsettled him. Peregrine didn't want Alexander to be honest. Or empathetic.

It would . . . complicate things.

He could feel Alexander's gaze on him as he turned to hang up the saddle and then began grooming the horse, checking his mount's legs and shoes as he worked.

"I would, you know," his captive said after a minute. Softly. "Have empathy."

Peregrine didn't look up from his work.

"And if you wanted to tell me, I would listen. I would believe you."

A strange thing happened then. Peregrine's lips parted, almost as if they were ready to speak, almost as if he were ready to talk about what Reginald had done to his family after years of holding the bitter knowledge inside himself—but that couldn't be right, could it? Peregrine had been careful to never speak of his losses, even to Lyd, because if the memories cut so deeply merely in his *thoughts*, what would they do to him as words spoken aloud?

So why was he tempted to talk to this spoiled aristocrat? Why was the brother of his enemy eliciting this urge in him when his friends and fellow thieves never had?

"I don't need your belief," Peregrine said.

"Everyone needs belief."

"Not the dead," he replied, and put away the brush and pick. Then he took the horse by the halter to walk him up and down the stable aisle. He could still feel his captive's eyes burning against him as he walked.

"Are you referring to yourself?" Alexander asked. "Or to someone you lost?"

It was too close to the truth—too perceptive. Again, Peregrine felt the strange urge to speak, to explain. And along with it came a feeling that wasn't quite fear and wasn't quite resentment, but a serrated alloy of both, sharpened by the genuine honesty he heard in his prisoner's voice.

Peregrine reminded himself that Alexander was his captive right now and would likely say anything to get Peregrine to trust him, to get Peregrine to let him go.

And that, Peregrine would not do.

He didn't answer Alexander's question. And then Alexander didn't say anything else, even after Peregrine put the horse in its stall with fresh hay and water, and then unhooked his captive's rope and led him into the priory itself.

———

"I'm gracious enough to concede I was wrong about the ignoble lodgings."

Peregrine ignored Alexander as he led him out of the small cloister and into what used to be the priory's church. When he'd first found the priory, untouched since the Dissolution, it had been in a terrifying state. Peregrine—with the help of a few local shepherds, whom he'd paid handsomely for their future silence on the matter—had restored the back half of the building to soundness while leaving the front half alone. Which meant if someone did stumble down the narrow cart-track to the abandoned monastery, it would look even worse than unsafe—it would look worthless.

The result was a warm, dry, and bird-free space that was disguised by its ruinous frontage, an ideal hideout for Peregrine and his friends. And though they'd never bothered to take a captive before, there was plenty of room to keep one. Peregrine had the perfect place in mind: the old sacristy at the back of the church. Lyd had slept there until she started sharing one of the monk's cells with Ned, so there was already a bed and a few other amenities inside.

More importantly, there was only one high, narrow window and only one door. So long as the door was guarded, escape would be impossible.

Peregrine took Alexander there now, walking through the choir and past the uncovered altar to the sacristy. Alexander's head swiveled as they went, peering through the shadows at the piles of stolen things they hadn't had a chance to sell—bolts of cloth, bundles of leather, a basket overflowing with jewelry—and the furniture, tapestries, carpets, and candlesticks which transformed the forgotten church into a medieval hall worthy of a king.

"I'm impressed, Peregrine," the younger man said as they reached the sacristy door, and Peregrine opened it to reveal a snug, furnished room. "This is a better thieves' den than I could have imagined. Complete with piles of loot and everything. Are the stories true then? That you even have escape tunnels beneath—"

"It's not going to work," Peregrine interrupted, reaching for the lamp to light it.

Alexander gave him an innocent look. "What?"

"Manipulating me, charming me, befriending me—even trying to learn more about the priory. I know you plan to escape. And you should know that it won't work."

His captive gave him a dazzling grin. "Well, you can't blame a man for trying."

Peregrine's pulse gave an unwanted kick at the sight of Alexander's smile, and he had to look away before he did something ludicrous. Like smile back at him.

He lit the lamp and then walked over to the small fireplace.

"Get on the bed," Peregrine said gruffly.

"Oh, Peregrine, I thought you'd never ask."

Alexander's coy purr sent Peregrine's pulse jumping again, and he had to tell himself that he was a villainous highwayman who wasn't affected by the charms of a rake, no matter how lissome. No matter how pretty his throat or how long his eyelashes. Peregrine also told himself that this rake's brother had both directly and indirectly killed Peregrine's entire family.

Peregrine hated the Darthams. He hated them so much that he would happily kill all of them, even Alexander.

Right?

His mind instinctively pushed away from the idea of killing Alexander, and he decided he wasn't going to think about it right now. It wouldn't be a problem until after the ransom anyway, and so he'd think about it then. He would instead focus on the present moment, which involved somehow keeping Alexander here without his escaping.

Peregrine lit the fire, then walked over to where his captive sat perched on the edge of the bed and deftly untied his wrists. There was dirt on Alexander's knees, and his hair was in windblown tangles. Peregrine sighed and stepped back.

"There's a privy through that door. It opens over a rather perilous drop, so I don't recommend using it as a means of escape. I'll bring you water and fresh clothes."

Alexander blinked up at him. "That's very thoughtful. Are you this considerate of all your captives?"

"I've never had one before," Peregrine said. "I'll return briefly. Please don't make life difficult for yourself by trying to run."

"Never." Alexander swore with such earnestness that Peregrine knew he was lying. But Peregrine also remembered too vividly how it felt to go without changing clothes or washing his body when he was on a long and bitter campaign, and he wouldn't subject Alexander to that. Maybe he'd abducted him, maybe he'd kill him, but at the very least, his prisoner could be clean and comfortable.

For the time being.

Peregrine waited until Alexander went into the privy, and then he went out into the church and past the open cloister to the small, stark cell he kept for himself. He'd furnished the hideout to a high degree of comfort, but nowadays, he gave away most of the spoils to families who'd lost their livelihoods while living on Dartham lands.

After finding a clean shirt and breeches, he filled a large ewer with water from their cistern and brought it back to the sacristy. Perhaps not surprisingly, the room was empty of pouting, long-haired rakes.

With a sigh, Peregrine deposited everything on a table and then strode out of the church to the covered walkway that led to the old scriptorium and ultimately to the front of the building. The priory wasn't massive, but it had been prosperous enough to warrant several small additions over its years, which meant a labyrinthine layout. An escaping captive would have a difficult time assessing the quickest way to the front door.

Sure enough, there was a flash of red wool through the arches of the cloister, just on the other side of the garth. Peregrine hopped over the low ledge, moved through the overgrown grass in a few long bounds, and jumped into the covered walkway on the other side in time to snag Alexander by the coat.

Alexander twisted and fought, but the game was up; Peregrine had him up and over his shoulder in a moment's work. Peregrine immediately had to ignore how warm Alexander was. How firm.

How that lovely backside was currently calling for Peregrine's palm . . . or his teeth.

Alexander stopped struggling the minute Peregrine hoisted him up, and slumped. "I thought the front door was closer," he admitted.

"It's not," Peregrine said, turning and carrying him back to the church.

"Apparently," said Alexander in a forlorn tone.

"What happened to being the best captive?"

Alexander shifted a little on Peregrine's shoulder. "I think we could debate the meaning of the word *best*, don't you? After all, from my vantage, the *best* captive would be the captive who doesn't miss an opportunity to run."

Peregrine's voice was wry when he spoke. "And from my vantage?"

Alexander paused. "Well, obviously the best captive for you would be someone lively and interesting. Entertaining. To relieve you of boredom, of course."

"Of course."

Peregrine walked through the doorway and then dropped Alexander on the bed, where the young man lay with his limbs spread like a starfish, blinking up at the ceiling.

"Is this what my captivity is going to be?" Alexander asked. "You hauling me around like a sack of grain?"

Peregrine didn't answer and instead gestured to the clothes and ewer. "I will be standing outside the door. I recommend you wash and change as I do. You'll be more comfortable."

Alexander hoisted himself up on an elbow, eyebrow curved in provocative suggestion. "More comfortable for what? Because I have some ideas."

Alexander was too playful like this, too *bright*. Just looking at him on the bed, with his eyes glittering and his mouth quirked, made Peregrine's blood feel like it was made of fire. It made Peregrine feel, period.

That was a problem, since Peregrine preferred only one feeling, and that was hatred of the Darthams. That hatred had been his only purpose, his single cold solace these last four years, and it was going to stay that way, no matter how playful or pretty this Dartham heir was.

With a shake of his head, Peregrine left the room, leaving the heavy shape of his own silence behind him.

4

Sandy

SANDY RATHER WISHED HE'D BEEN ABLE TO ESCAPE, BUT HE HAD TO ADMIT to himself that the last three hours of his life had been livelier and more interesting than the last three years put together, which probably also meant that he should admit to himself that the last few years of his life had been rather unsatisfying. Decadent, certainly, but in a way that increased his restlessness rather than soothing it.

Maybe he'd needed a good adventure to shake things up a little.

And while there was the small, pesky matter of Peregrine planning to kill him, Sandy still felt certain he could either escape or seduce his way free. Which ... given the way it felt to be slung over the brawny highwayman's shoulder earlier, Sandy wouldn't mind in the least having to do some seduction. He'd seen Peregrine's body fighting its response to his own the whole ride here, and he'd caught Peregrine staring at his mouth once or twice—or thirty times. The idea of unraveling that cold, grim mystery ... well.

It wasn't without its own appeal.

After all, if he lived to tell the tale, what was a bigger coup for a rake than being in a highwayman's bed? Even the hedonistic denizens of the Second Kingdom couldn't boast something that wild.

Sandy washed with a linen towel and some very chilly water and then changed into the clothes the highwayman had brought him. They were clean, but soft with wear and too big for his frame, which was shorter and more slender than Peregrine Hind's. The breeches settled low around his hips, and the shirt opened nearly to his sternum.

He should have felt ridiculous like this, but he didn't at all. He felt rather snug, actually—cared for. Which was an absurd thought to have about wearing a captor's clothes. But they even smelled like the highwayman, like rain and like leather. Sandy found himself breathing deep to take the scent into his lungs, and then he wanted to shake himself. Very hard.

Because it was one thing for seduction not to be a chore, but it was another thing entirely to swoon over his jailer, *even if* that jailer was unfairly worthy of swoons. Even if that jailer had eyes like moonlight itself.

Which was funny. Sandy couldn't remember ever caring about a lover's eyes before.

Not a lover! he reminded himself. *Captor.* Future *murderer.* It wouldn't do to forget that part!

Sandy was combing his hair when Peregrine knocked—a silly but almost endearing gesture, given the circumstances—and Sandy called for him to enter. Peregrine stepped in and then stilled.

"You may finish," the highwayman said, his voice devoid of inflection. But Sandy saw the swallow of the thief's throat as he watched Sandy pull the comb through his dark locks. "I don't mind."

"So generous," Sandy murmured, finishing up and then tossing his hair over his shoulder as he regarded the impassive man standing before him. "However, I have to ask about what you plan on doing with me next. Am I to be kept in this room combing my hair forever? Like a mortal woman trapped in a fairy castle?"

"Not quite," Peregrine said. "On the bed. Again."

Sandy was about to make another sly remark when he saw what Peregrine had been hiding behind his back. Not coils of rough rope like he'd used to tie Sandy's wrists earlier, but several lengths of what appeared to be silk.

Delicious images sloshed around Sandy's mind like wine in a glass. "Oh," he said.

"On the bed, Alexander."

Sandy felt strange as he obeyed—full of dread and excitement and a heady mixture of both—and then he realized, as Peregrine stepped to the edge of the bed and took hold of his wrist, that he was trembling.

Peregrine met his gaze. "I won't leave you tied up forever," he said, misunderstanding the reason for Sandy's shivers. "The others are returning, and I need to speak with them, which means we won't have a guard at the door. And obviously you can't be trusted, even for an hour or two."

"Obviously," Sandy said weakly, his heart thumping against his ribs as Peregrine cinched the silk around his wrist and then around the nearest poster of the bed. Then Peregrine moved to the other wrist, and then to a bare ankle, tying his knots firmly but not so tightly that Sandy lost feeling in his fingers or toes.

Sandy knew there was no hiding his fast-heaving chest, his hot cheeks, and above all, the insistent erection pushing against the front of his borrowed breeches, but it wasn't until the highwayman was tying Sandy's last ankle to the bed that he looked up from his work and saw what it had done to his captive.

Peregrine's lips parted, and then his silver eyes shot to Sandy's face— in confusion or in accusation, Sandy couldn't tell.

"I told you I liked being tied up," Sandy said as he twisted against his bonds, testing them. Every twist pulled at the fabric of the too-loose shirt, and so, as Peregrine watched, Sandy's stomach above the waistband of the breeches was exposed inch by quivering inch. Along with the swollen head of his cock, which peeked rudely above the waistband and leaked onto Sandy's belly.

"You like being tied up," Peregrine repeated tonelessly.

Sandy wanted so dearly to make a face at him but was too aroused to pull it off. The tightness of the restraints, the spread position of his limbs, the sheer *helplessness*—it created a tide so deep and so urgent inside him that it was pointless to resist. It would be like fighting off the pleasure in a dream, or a release inside a lover's mouth.

He would lose—and it was more fun to lose, anyway.

Peregrine's face expressed nothing as he tied the final knot, but as he straightened, Sandy could see a new tightness to the way he moved. His face remained unreadable, but his hands were curling into slow fists, and his eyes had gone more black than silver.

He looked like—well, for an instant, he looked like he wanted to eat Sandy alive.

He left without another word.

SANDY DIDN'T MAKE it long. With his bindings, the intoxicating smell of the highwayman wrapping around him, and the waistband of the breeches rubbing lightly against the underside of his prick, it was a foregone conclusion that he would spend all over his stomach, and he did. Sandy spent with long, jerking spills as he thought of the highwayman's pale eyes and big hands.

He stared up at the ceiling in a daze, wondering how long Peregrine would leave him like this and how long he could stand it. *Not forever* wasn't a very precise amount of time, and from what he could hear through the door, the other thieves had only just now made it to the sanctuary. He heard the clanking of cups and smelled the aroma of hot food, and then heard the low din of conversation.

What are they talking about? What to do with him while they waited to be paid his ransom? How to kill him once they had?

He wouldn't be there to be killed, of course, having weaseled or fucked his way free, but he did wonder how Peregrine felt about killing him.

Would he feel reluctant, maybe? Remorseful but resigned?

It was a shame they'd met like this because Sandy would've very much enjoyed being tied to a bed by Peregrine Hind on a regular basis. But after Sandy escaped, it would probably be best if he never ran into Peregrine or his eerie eyes again, for the obvious not-being-murdered-for-revenge reasons.

A tragic thought.

Sandy tried to make himself focus on possible avenues of escape while he waited for the thieves to finish talking. He'd peered through the privy hole earlier, and it had indeed led to a steep drop, and the sacristy window was too narrow to be of any use. His only way out was through the door, which was possibly guarded, and he already knew he'd be no good at fighting off a guard.

No, he'd need to stick to his strengths. Seduction, lying . . . bravado and charm.

The woman thief might be the ripest possibility. If only he could remember where he knew her from. Was she a former lover? A friend of a lover? Someone connected to the Second Kingdom?

But Sandy's mind didn't stay on escape for very long. It was impossible to think clearly while tied up like this, smelling rain and leather and knowing Peregrine would walk in eventually and see that Sandy had spilled all over himself. What would Peregrine do when he did? Would he fix Sandy with that look, that hot, hungry look? Would he get hard? Would he reach out and touch Sandy with one of those big, rough hands . . . ?

Lost in his imaginings, Sandy didn't notice the door opening until it was shutting again and Peregrine was inside. Peregrine's legs were long enough and the room was small enough that it only took him three good strides to make it to the side of the bed, and even in his lust-induced haze, Sandy noticed how quick and silent those strides were. Peregrine could move like a ghost when he wanted.

The highwayman seemed to take in Sandy's half-lidded eyes, his quivering limbs, the spatter of semen on his belly. His eyes dropped to Sandy's renewed erection, which surged happily at the attention.

"You've already spent," Peregrine said after a moment. "And you're still like this?"

"I *told* you," Sandy said, meaning to sound indignant but sounding breathless instead. "I *like* being tied up."

Peregrine's hand stretched out, and then they both watched as he dropped his fingertips to the top of Sandy's knee, right above the hem of the breeches. His fingertips rested there, over the woolen broadcloth, pressing lightly against the place where the muscles of Sandy's thigh anchored to his femur. And then, agonizingly, Peregrine trailed his fingers up, up, up to Sandy's hip.

Peregrine looked as if even he didn't know what he was doing, like he was encountering a treasure he had no idea how to steal, and Sandy was too drunk with desire to tell him this wasn't stealing. This wasn't even seduction, if he was being honest.

It was desperation.

"Please," Sandy whispered. "*Please.*"

Peregrine gave him a sharp look, and Sandy realized that he must sound like he had earlier, in the middle of the road, when he was pleading for his life.

But this was something much, much more important.

Sandy lifted his hips as much as the restraints would allow, trying to twist into Peregrine's hand, which stayed resolutely unmoving against Sandy's hip. "Please."

Peregrine's mouth was a straight line. But his eyes—he couldn't hide those hungry, blown-pupil eyes. He couldn't hide the way he swallowed over and over, as if searching for control.

"Why should I?" the highwayman finally asked.

Good question. Why should he pleasure a captive—a captive he planned on killing, and who was the brother of someone he clearly hated? Sandy blurted the first thing he could think of.

"Revenge?"

Peregrine's fingers lifted and then ghosted lightly over the inseam of the breeches, running over the place where Sandy's testicles had drawn up tight to his body. "How is this revenge for *me*?"

"Umm," Sandy said, and then added an "*Ohhhhh*" when Peregrine's fingers moved up to wander around the base of his cock. Sandy's erection bobbed, the crown dripping clear seed and burning like hot iron in the cool air.

"Well, it's humiliating," Sandy mumbled. "I'm so humiliated right now. Please, Peregrine. Please."

Peregrine's eyes flashed with some indecipherable emotion, but whatever it was had him bracing one knee on the bed as he tore at the buttons holding the breeches closed. In an instant, Sandy's prick was completely naked and then there was the hand of his abductor wrapping tight around him and stroking hard.

Sandy's back nearly bowed off the bed, even with his limbs tied, and never had he felt so helpless, so depraved, as when the man who was going to kill him was pumping his prick with a hard and vicious fist. When the release came, it felt like it was pulled right from his spine, right from the very marrow of his bones. He spurted seed all over the highwayman's fingers, all over his stomach again, and the highwayman didn't seem to mind at all, seemed to like it, in fact, because by the time Sandy's body was drained totally dry, Peregrine's cheeks were flushed and his shaft was very visibly thickened in his breeches.

His eyes met Sandy's, and Sandy saw shock there, and lust, and several other things besides. Peregrine staggered back from the bed, his hand still covered in the milky proof of Sandy's release, and he stared at that hand as if he wasn't sure how he'd ended up like this.

"I can return the favor," Sandy murmured. "You don't even have to untie me. You could use my mouth."

Peregrine shuddered, the flush deepening on his cheeks, and Sandy knew he'd found a weakness. Peregrine wanted inside his mouth. Badly.

Maybe even other places . . .

But a huge crash resounded from outside the sacristy door, followed by roars of laughter, and Peregrine seemed to snap out of whatever spell had overtaken him. With a sharp shake of his head, the highwayman walked over to the table and, using the ewer and a fresh towel, cleaned his hand. Then he came over to Sandy and wiped Sandy's messy stomach clean.

The thickness in the thief's breeches was unabated, but Peregrine didn't unbutton them to relieve his desire, and he didn't—as Sandy secretly hoped—climb onto the bed next to Sandy and make use of him. Instead, the thief began untying him, loosening the knots and then checking to make sure Sandy could still move his fingers and toes.

When he was completely untied, Sandy sat up and stared at him. "Let me make you feel better with my mouth," he said. "I'm very good at it."

Peregrine bundled the lengths of silk into neat coils as the silence after Sandy's offer filled the room. The highwayman's eyes glittered behind his lowered lashes—glittered with something less than vengeance and something more than lust. Secret things that made Sandy's pulse speed up. Finally Peregrine said brusquely, "I'm your captor."

"I thought we went over this," Sandy said impatiently. "It's revenge. You're getting revenge and stuff."

"Maybe. Or maybe you're trying to seduce your way free."

"Well, that sounds like a winning scenario for both of us!"

Peregrine leveled a look at him.

Sandy did his best to look innocent, but the effect was doubtful since he'd just done very *not* innocent things all over his stomach. "Did I mention that I'm so very good at it and also how vengeful you'll feel while it's happening?"

"Good night, Alexander," the highwayman said. "There will be a guard outside your door tonight. I'll make sure they bring in some food and wine for you too."

A sharp displeasure sliced through Sandy at the thought of Peregrine leaving. He wanted more bed-play, yes, but he also just wanted his captor *here*, with him. He wasn't sure why, exactly. Maybe it had something to do with those secrets shimmering in the highwayman's silver eyes.

"Peregrine!" Sandy called, but there was no reply. His captor had gone.

5

Peregrine

FOR AS LONG AS HE LIVED, PEREGRINE WOULD NEVER FORGET THE WAY Alexander looked while tied to a bed, hair tousled and gleaming in the lamplight, his stomach pearled with his orgasm. And for as long as he lived, he'd never forget the way Alexander's cock felt as he stroked it. Hotter than a brand, harder than steel. Yet soft and velvety too, like pure heaven in his hand.

For the sake of his own sanity, Peregrine didn't take a shift guarding Alexander's door that night or the next morning. He didn't think he could listen to Alexander rustling around in bed or sighing his put-upon sighs, and he didn't know how he'd respond if Alexander came to the door and tried to talk to him.

No. He *did* know how he'd respond. He'd push his way through that door and shove Alexander back onto the bed. And this time he wouldn't leave Alexander's cell with a cockstand still straining his pants.

Let me make you feel better.

I'm so very good at it.

Instead, Peregrine went to his cell and slept a little, waking with the sun to begin working his way through a list of things needing to be fenced soon. He'd been marking the papers for less than an hour when he heard a knock at the door.

"Yes?" he called.

Will, the youngest of their band and the person guarding Alexander today, pushed his head into the room. "Lord Alexander says he can't fall back asleep because his bed linens are too scratchy."

Peregrine stared. "Too scratchy?"

Will shrugged.

"I suppose," Peregrine said slowly, "he could have some other bed linens if we have them."

"Thanks," Will said, and then left the room and closed the door behind him. Peregrine shook his head and then went back to the inventory sheets, unsure if captives were supposed to complain about their bed linens, but also certain that it probably didn't matter, since Alexander had already proved himself to be a deeply vexing captive.

Let me make you feel better.

Well, perhaps not entirely vexing.

A few hours later, Peregrine was eating lunch in his room and finishing his tallies when he heard another knock. It was Will again.

"Yes?" Peregrine asked as the thief stepped into his room.

"Alexander says he doesn't like the beer we've served with his lunch and wants wine instead. Is that permissible?"

"Yes," Peregrine said, his patience fraying a little. "That's *permissible.*"

Not ten minutes later, Will was back. "Alexander says his wine is too sweet and he wants to know if we have a more mature vintage."

Peregrine tossed his quill on the table in exasperation. "No. You may tell Lord Alexander that he'll be drinking water from the trough if he has any more complaints about his beverages."

Will looked at little surprised at Peregrine's flare of temper—and Peregrine was surprised too. He never let his emotions creep toward the surface, even with his closest friends. Lyd, who still only knew the scantest details of why he wanted to kill Reginald Dartham, who had never seen him seethe in anger or weep in the dark—or even laugh.

It was safer that way, and better for all involved.

But with Alexander Dartham, Peregrine's curated restraint unglued itself. His lapse in control last night, his irritation today . . .

The spoiled rake was taking Peregrine apart bit by bit. If only he'd stop being so *here*, so *present*, so impossible to ignore—but there was no ignoring Lord Alexander Dartham. There were those dark eyes and that full mouth, there was his unabashed vulnerability, the way he asked for things and tried for things.

There was his earnestness, equally unabashed, as if it had never occurred to him to lie, even about something as gravely important as escaping.

With a cautious nod, Will left to give Alexander his answer, and Peregrine scrubbed his hands over his face. He had to find more control when it came to Alexander Dartham. Otherwise, he'd be entirely undone by the time he received the ransom from the duke, and he didn't know how he'd be able to do what he needed to do after—

No. He wouldn't think about that right now.

A hundred things could happen between now and then, and he needed to keep his focus on the duke instead.

Speaking of, he stood and left his cell in search of Lyd to see if there'd been any messages from Chagford. He found her in the sanctuary, her head bent over a note.

"News from Far Hope?" he asked, suddenly anxious about the answer. If it was news from Far Hope, if the duke was going to pay the ransom, then that meant Peregrine would have no more use for Alexander. It meant Alexander would become a liability rather than an asset and his death would become Peregrine's best weapon for hurting the duke—

His mind reared away from those thoughts like a shying horse, and he drew in a relieved breath when Lyd said, "Nothing from the duke yet. But our friend in Exeter sent this." She waved the note, an avid glitter to her blue eyes. "The duchess is leaving for Far Hope. She hadn't felt well enough to travel yesterday and that's why she didn't go with her husband or Sandy."

"You want to intercept her," Peregrine guessed.

"Yes," Lyd said.

"To rob her?" Peregrine asked. There was no judgment in his tone, only curiosity. He was keeping a captive, after all, and planning that captive's murder, so he hardly had a moral high ground here.

Nor did he want one.

Lyd's jaw tightened. "I don't know," she admitted after a moment. "After everything she's done to me, robbing doesn't feel like enough."

When he'd first met Lydia, she'd been pickpocketing in London, one in a thousand thieves struggling to survive. But when she'd made the mistake of pickpocketing *him*, she'd done it so adroitly and with so much fearlessness that Peregrine had been more impressed than annoyed. He'd offered her a job as a fellow knight of the road, and she'd accepted, with the caveat that any Dartham they came across would be hers.

He'd been astounded that someone else could hate that family as much as he, but after hearing Lyd's story, he'd recognized a kindred spirit. A distant cousin of the duchess, she'd been shipped off to live with the duke and duchess after her parents had died of smallpox, and they'd attempted to marry her off at sixteen to a cruel man. When she'd refused, the duchess had locked Lyd in her room for weeks, keeping her a prisoner until Lyd managed to escape through a window. Lyd maintained that scraping out an existence as a thief—even as a woman alone, and in the rough crowds of London—had been infinitely preferable to marrying the person the duchess had chosen for her.

The duchess had been adamant about the match because the suitor in question would take Lyd without a dowry, which meant the dowry and the family property Lyd was supposed to bring to a future marriage would stay in the hands of the duke and duchess. That property included Lyd's family home and her family land—the very place she'd grown up. A place she would never see again while it belonged to the Darthams.

"What she's taken from you is something impossible to replace," Peregrine said to Lyd now. "I understand why robbing her of some clothes or jewelry wouldn't feel like enough."

Lyd swore, looking out over their piles of fabric and silver goods. "Sometimes I want so much to hurt her," she said after a minute. "But other times I don't know what I'd do if I saw her again. If I'd have it in me to hurt her after all."

"I understand," Peregrine said. Lord Alexander Dartham was the still-living proof of that. "Do you know if she's leaving today or tomorrow?"

Lyd shook her head.

"You may want to plan on watching the road for a day or two, then.

Pack food and take Ned and the others. I'll stay here with our prisoner."

She looked at him. "You'd rather stay with the brother of your enemy than go out to *rob* your enemy's wife? Are you sure you're still Peregrine Hind, infamous highwayman?"

Will trotted up before Peregrine could answer, looking a little sheepish for interrupting. "Sandy wants to know if you have any books here."

"*Sandy?*" Peregrine repeated. "He's Sandy to you now?"

"*Books?*" Lyd asked at the same time.

Will held up his hands, as if indicating helplessness in the face of the circumstances. "He says he needs to occupy his mind, and we did play All Fours for a bit, but he kept winning and said it wasn't challenging enough to be any fun."

"Are you sure he was winning and not cheating?" Lyd asked, the doubt clear in her voice.

Peregrine sighed, his irritation flaring all over again. "I'll assume care of our prisoner for now. Lyd, take the others. And ride safe."

A FEW MINUTES LATER, Peregrine knocked on the door of Alexander's sacristy.

"Enter," came the magnanimous reply, and Peregrine pushed open the door to see his prisoner on the bed, lounging on one elbow. The borrowed shirt exposed a sculpted shoulder and the curve of his collarbone, both illuminated by the window high on the wall. His hair was still sleep-tousled, and his feet were bare; his shirt was rucked up enough that Peregrine could see the dark line of hair leading down from his navel.

He looked like someone had spent the night fucking him into the mattress.

"You want books," Peregrine said.

"I'm bored," whined Alexander.

You're trouble. But Peregrine didn't say it. Instead, he said, "The others are leaving, but I'm staying here. I think you'll find that I'm less amenable to requests for things."

Alexander dropped his head back with a fractious noise. "But it's so *dull* in here. What else am I to do?"

"You're a captive," Peregrine said impatiently. "Your entire existence is to wait until something happens."

Alexander sat up. "Play cards with me."

"No."

"Why not?"

"You'll cheat."

"If I did," Alexander said, giving him a mischievous grin, "you could always punish me."

A slow bloom of heat unfurled inside Peregrine. His voice was graveled with it when he spoke. "And how would I do that?"

"You could tie me up again," Alexander said, coming to a sitting position and then to his knees. He kept his eyes on Peregrine's the entire time. "You could tie me up all sorts of ways, you know, not just on my back. On my stomach, or bent over the bed, or . . . "

Peregrine had to swallow to keep himself from agreeing. Or tackling Alexander to the bed and finally putting his lips to the full curves of Alexander's mouth.

It would be so much easier if Alexander weren't so playful, so goddamn *happy*. When was the last time Peregrine himself had felt playful?

Happy?

"I will be tying you up again," he said, deciding then and there what he'd do with his captive today. He told himself it was for practical, preventing-escape reasons, and not at all for reasons of seeing Alexander bound in silk. "But not to the bed. Come with me."

FOUR HOURS LATER, they were alone in the sanctuary as the light slowly died outside and the shadows began to gather in the corners. Peregrine had bound Alexander's hands and then had dragged him along while he attended to the day's tasks—caring for the horses and fixing the wheel on one of the carts they used to haul goods to Chagford or Buckfast, and then finally making a simple dinner of roasted pheasant, apples, and bread for them to eat.

The playfulness hadn't left Peregrine's captive as Peregrine had

worked, and Lord Alexander had spent most of the afternoon perched
on a barrel, kicking his bare feet against the wood while he pestered
Peregrine with an unceasing number of questions about everything from
hay to types of hammers to when Peregrine would take pity on him and
at least let Alexander bring himself to satisfaction.

Each time Alexander asked that last question, Peregrine couldn't
keep himself from looking over at his captive—all sparkling eyes and
breeches obscenely tented from the effects of having his wrists bound—
and it would nearly stop his heart. It was like having a spoiled princeling
about, and Peregrine should hate it, should hate the pretty pouts and the
coy demands, but the honesty shining in those impish glances and
scrawled inside those flirtatious questions made hate impossible.

In fact, Peregrine felt lighter and lighter as the afternoon went on,
like Alexander was a glow of lamplight in a room he hadn't realized had
grown dim. And seeing Alexander aroused from being tied up, with
those half-lidded eyes and flush-stained cheeks . . .

Repeatedly, Peregrine had to remind himself that Alexander was a
Dartham, and moreover, his captive. He shouldn't feel anything but
grimly determined while he was around. He shouldn't have to catch his
breath whenever he saw his captive lord staring at his silk-trussed wrists
with fascination and undisguised arousal.

When it was time for dinner, Peregrine tied the free end of Alexander's rope to the arm of his chair and then watched as, despite his bindings and his visible erection, his captive ate as prettily as if he were in
front of the Queen herself. In contrast, Peregrine himself ate quickly and
efficiently, an inevitable consequence of war and four years on the run
from the law.

"You eat like a soldier," said Alexander after a moment.

"I was a soldier," Peregrine said somewhat automatically, and then
immediately wanted to unspeak the words. He knew Alexander was
trying to learn anything useful that would help him escape while also
ingratiating himself through any means possible, including friendship.
Peregrine probably shouldn't even be eating with him now, if he was
honest, but it was nicer than eating alone, and Alexander was so very
lovely to look at, and sometimes he said the funniest things.

Sometimes he almost made Peregrine smile.

"Of course you were," Alexander said. "And now you're a knight of the road. Isn't that how all the stories start? A valiant soldier returns home after the war and finds his home taken away from him, and so the only recourse he has is to steal from the very men who robbed him in the first place?"

It was too close to the truth, and Peregrine struggled not to react. "You're thinking of Robin Hood, or maybe the Royalists after the Civil War," he said carefully. "Times long past."

Alexander didn't seem to miss how Peregrine sidestepped his remark, however. "So what then makes a modern-day soldier take to the road?"

"What makes the son of a duke spend his days carousing and cheating at cards?"

"I never cheat, I only *strategize*," Alexander said, taking a dainty sip of wine. "And it's more nights than days, you know."

"But there's no other work your brother would rather put you to? No responsibilities waiting for you at Far Hope?"

Alexander's expression shuttered, and it was as if a light had gone out. He didn't like this line of questioning any more than Peregrine had liked Alexander's.

"There's plenty waiting for me at Far Hope," Alexander said cryptically.

He set down his cup and turned to face Peregrine. On the far side of the room, the fire burned in its improvised fireplace and cast Alexander's elegant features in a reddish glow.

"What?" Peregrine asked his captive, who was now staring at him with an unsettling expression.

"I was just thinking," Alexander said in a velvet voice, "that I should show you why it's worthwhile to keep a rake nearby."

A dark heat crawled up Peregrine's thighs and down his belly. He should ignore it; he knew he should. But it burned so very hot inside him. It had been kindled and stoked by seeing Alexander so coquettish all day, and Peregrine couldn't remember the last time he'd felt like this. Maybe he never had.

"Is that so?" Peregrine asked in a gruff voice.

Alexander gave him a secretive smile. He slid easily from his bench to his knees, graceful as a dancer. Within a few sinuous crawls, he was in front of Peregrine's chair.

Peregrine knew he should tell Alexander to stop, to go back to his bench. But he didn't. He couldn't.

Instead, he angled his chair and spread his legs, feeling his control slip and slip and slip as his captive moved between his feet.

Alexander brought his bound hands up between them. Peregrine had tied them so that they were separated by a few inches of silk—so he could still eat and use the privy without help—but now his captive held them folded together, like he was praying. Like he was supplicating Peregrine for a favor.

"Let me taste you," Alexander said, his voice a low, wonderful purr that no doubt had wooed many men and women to his bed over the years. "How long has it been since you've had your cock sucked, Peregrine?"

Too long, Peregrine thought, but he didn't answer out loud. He did another thing that he absolutely should not have and untucked Alexander's shirt, so he could lift it and see underneath. So he could see if Alexander's organ was pushing against his breeches like it had been last night.

It was.

"If you're wondering if I am inflamed," Alexander said, somewhat dryly, "the answer is yes."

"Is it because your hands are bound, or because you sincerely wish to do this?"

Alexander peered up at him through dark lashes. "Why can't it be both? If it comforts you, I'd want to do it even if I wasn't your captive," he added. "Please, Peregrine. Just a little. Just a taste. Let me taste you."

Peregrine didn't know how to say no to this. He needed to say no—Alexander's family had *killed* the only people he'd ever loved—and aside from that very large consideration, he wasn't the kind of man to use someone else for pleasure when that someone else was a prisoner.

But Alexander's hands were so warm through the fabric of his shirt as they pressed against his stomach, as they slowly plucked at the linen until it was completely untucked and the buttons of his breeches were exposed. And Alexander's eyes were so pretty like this, glittering under their dark fringe of lashes, and his mouth looked so soft, and knowing that he was hard as he knelt between Peregrine's feet . . .

And then Peregrine's breeches were unbuttoned and his cock was free, heavy and tumescent and pointing at the ceiling. Alexander's exhales shivered over the sensitive skin of Peregrine's shaft, sending bolts of sensation right through his body and making him swell even more. The skin stretched over his crown was so tight that it shone in the firelight.

His captive gave him a wicked grin. "I think you might need this."

Peregrine grunted. He did, but this was the last person whom he should take it from, and—*oh God.* Alexander's tongue ran a wet stripe up his cock and Peregrine nearly fainted. With another wicked grin, Alexander bent over him and took him into his hot, slick mouth.

Peregrine had forgotten. Fuck, he'd forgotten. How it felt to be inside a lover's mouth, and how much better it was than his own perfunctory hand. He'd forgotten everything else that came with a moment like this —Alexander's gorgeous hair spilling over Peregrine's lap, and the soft noises he made as he sucked, and the flirtatious flicks of his gaze up at Peregrine, as if to say, *See? See? Aren't I so good at this?*

He couldn't be sure if it was his hatred of the Darthams or concern for Alexander that made him press his fingers under Alexander's chin and force Alexander to pull away from his work, but whatever it was, it twisted inside Peregrine like smoke off a bonfire, billowing and thick. "This doesn't change anything," he told the younger man. "This *won't* change anything."

"It won't?" Alexander asked innocently. His lips were wet and slightly swollen from pleasuring Peregrine, and Peregrine couldn't take it anymore.

He leaned forward to kiss his kidnapped rake.

Alexander's mouth tasted of wine and sex, and it was so sweet on Peregrine's tongue, so silky and inviting. Alexander's tongue fluttered gently against Peregrine's, almost like he was surprised, and then he whimpered as Peregrine deepened the kiss, plundering Alexander's mouth like it was a chest of valuables stashed under a carriage seat. He stroked his tongue against Alexander's and then bit gently at his lower lip before pulling back.

"I'm not going to set you free, no matter how good you suck me."

"Hmm," Alexander said, a sly curve to his mouth. "Maybe not. Maybe you'll decide to keep me instead."

Before Peregrine could figure out how he felt about that idea,

Alexander's hair was spilling all over Peregrine's lap once more, and his tongue was doing something incredible around his slit, and then Peregrine was inside Alexander's mouth again, feeling pressure and suction and wet, wet heat.

The peak that gathered inside Peregrine's belly was ferocious and frightening—the kind of peak that would tear through him like a musket ball if he let it. And he was going to let it, because Alexander had been right: he was very, *very* good at this.

Just as his thighs tensed, Alexander looked up and met Peregrine's eyes. In the dim room, the dark sapphire of the rake's gaze was nearly impossible to make out, but Peregrine still had the strange feeling that he was seeing the color of something very important.

Something like the color of happiness itself.

His cock swelled against Alexander's tongue and began pulsing seed deep into his throat—which Alexander seemed to relish swallowing, because he didn't stop until Peregrine's cock was completely sated, and Peregrine was drained of every last drop.

Peregrine's head dropped back, his heart beating fast, his body trembling. Never, not even in a soldier's tent on the Continent, had he been so expertly and enthusiastically pleasured.

Alexander knew it too, because when Peregrine finally looked back down at his captive, there was a smug expression on his lovely face.

"Told you," Alexander said.

"You did tell me," Peregrine agreed, turning to the knot that held Alexander's bindings to his chair. Alexander watched him with the smugness fading into confusion, and then he laughed as Peregrine stood up and swung him over his shoulder.

"I didn't even have to escape this time to get carried off by my big, bad highwayman," he teased as Peregrine grabbed a candlestick with his free hand and then strode into the sacristy.

He dropped Alexander unceremoniously onto the bed, then set the candlestick down. "Clothes off," Peregrine said. "If you'd like."

"Oh, I'd always *like*," Alexander purred. "I only have one request."

Peregrine slanted him a look. "Softer sheets? Better wine? *Books?*"

"No," Alexander said with another grin the devil himself wouldn't have been able to match for its mischief. "I want your clothes off too."

6

Sandy

To Sandy's great disappointment, Peregrine didn't fulfill his most delicious wish of being fucked while still trussed up, but he did crawl over Sandy with those broad shoulders and those muscle-swollen thighs and push Sandy's bound hands above his head. And then he'd proceeded to kiss Sandy so thoroughly that Sandy was certain he was now ruined for all other kisses for the rest of his life.

Sandy knew what his best friend Juliana would say—that he'd made similar claims in the past, and they'd all fallen equally flat. Sandy had a great weakness for other rakes and rakesses, and often found himself the seduc-*ee* rather than the seduc-*er*. He usually knew when he was being seduced for someone else's amusement—being a rake himself made him quite clear-eyed when it came to such things—but he frequently surrendered himself to the melodrama of a love affair anyway, simply because it was fun and because he was bored.

But this was different somehow.

This wasn't a seduction, and there was nothing jaded or amused about the way Peregrine Hind kissed him. There was a solidity to Peregrine's touches, a gravity, and Sandy craved the weight of them. He loved the way those touches pulled on his heart and on his breath.

Sandy came with Peregrine's mouth hot and sucking on his neck and their erections trapped between their stomachs. Peregrine followed him soon after.

After Peregrine had untied him and cleaned them both, he laid back down on the bed next to Sandy. Sandy's heart stuttered as the highwayman ran his fingertips over Sandy's mouth, his pale eyes burning into Sandy's. What was Peregrine thinking right now? What was he feeling and wanting? More touching? More sex?

Did he want to tell Sandy—again—that this didn't change anything?

The idea of that was unbearable. "The best part of being in bed with a rake is that I don't expect you to croon sweet nothings to me after," Sandy informed Peregrine.

The highwayman just gave him a bland look.

"Do I seem like the type to croon sweet nothings?" Peregrine asked after a pause.

"Well. No," Sandy admitted. Peregrine seemed like the type to be found taming a wild horse up in the hills, or perhaps completing some quest that involved trudging through a barren wasteland and killing a dragon or something. There was nothing sweet about him. He was all flint and chill, with only rare glimpses of the deeply banked fire within.

But Sandy liked that about Peregrine Hind—perhaps more than was good for him—and instead of pleasuring Peregrine into a sleep deep enough for an escape attempt, Sandy propped himself up on an elbow so he could watch Peregrine's face. "Then why are you in here still?"

A pause. "I don't know."

"You don't know?"

The highwayman frowned. "I suppose I don't want to leave."

"A common reaction to my company," Sandy replied with a grin. He slid his hand down to Peregrine's cock to play it with it, thinking that was the real reason Peregrine hadn't wanted to leave, but Peregrine caught his wrist and stopped him.

Sandy froze. That was a first, and it couldn't be because Peregrine *wasn't* interested in more bed-play—his cock was already stirring for more. But Peregrine seemed to ignore it, his eyes on Sandy's face.

"Why didn't you want to talk about Far Hope?" he asked. "Before, when I'd asked about it?"

Far Hope.

The question was so surprising that Sandy couldn't even think of a way to deflect. He looked up into a veiled expression belied by an avid, searching gaze. That gaze betrayed something haunted and yet miserably alive, locked deep under the surface like living fire beneath the earth. But there was more than pain in the highwayman's eyes. There was something that spoke of surviving, of prevailing.

Of strength, maybe.

Suddenly Sandy found that he didn't *want* to deflect.

"Your voice is pure Devonshire," Sandy said after a minute. "Did you grow up near Far Hope?"

Peregrine's expression remained unreadable. "Close enough."

"I don't suppose you've heard any of the rumors about it? About what happens there?"

"My mother once said that they keep their own ways at Far Hope," Peregrine said. "I'd always assumed it meant the Dartham selfishness was congenital."

Sandy wanted to be wounded by that, but the truth was that his father had been a selfish and cruel man, and Reginald had inherited every drop of that selfishness and cruelty right along with the title.

At least Sandy wasn't willfully cruel. Or so he hoped.

"It means there are secrets at Far Hope," Sandy said, "and they all branch out from this one: there is a hidden kingdom inside the one we live in. It has many of the same citizens, but it's invisible and it's never spoken of to outsiders."

Peregrine regarded him. "Then why are you speaking of it to me?"

"Because I want to, and because—this feels ridiculous to say, given that you're planning to kill me—I trust you. Besides, I can always claim you tortured it out of me, if I survive this."

"If you survive this," Peregrine echoed, his voice betraying nothing, no confirmation . . . or refutation either.

Sandy planned on escaping before the matter of his survival became a pressing issue, but a small arrow of hurt—a lover's hurt—burrowed between his ribs at the realization that Peregrine still intended to kill him. Silly, since his eventual death had been the bargain struck from the very beginning. But Sandy had grown so fascinated by this bleak force of a man, become so strangely affectionate toward him, and he childishly wanted Peregrine to feel the same way. Less for reasons of survival than for reasons that were perilously rooted in the organ beating in his chest.

"Anyway," Sandy said, pushing all that away and down, down where he wouldn't have to feel it right then, "this hidden kingdom is centuries old. Maybe older. And though its citizens are all over the island, Far Hope is its seat, its ancestral home."

"What's the purpose of this kingdom?" Peregrine asked.

Sandy scoffed. "What's the purpose of any kingdom? To continue to exist, of course."

Peregrine tucked his arm behind his head, the better to look at Sandy, and the gesture was so casual, so familiar and *cozy*, that Sandy's chest gave an unexpected squeeze.

"I know what you're really asking, though," Sandy continued, "and the Second Kingdom has no political ambitions, no designs for more wealth or power—or at least, it's not supposed to. It's supposed to be a place where people associate freely for pleasure alone. That is our raison d'être, in fact. No law but pleasure. No limit but acquiescence. No rule but secrecy."

"This sounds like a world tailored for you."

"Or I for it," Sandy murmured, recalling not the opulent parties in the star-chambered ballroom, but instead, the fickle attentions of his parents, his father's cold smile.

"You were raised for it, then?" Peregrine asked. "To live in this secret world?"

"In a manner of speaking." Sandy had barely existed to his parents—even Reginald the heir had barely existed to them—because their mother lived for the Second Kingdom and its delights, and their father cared only for his manipulations and schemes. But Sandy had existed more than enough to his godparents, the gentle Foscourts, who'd practically adopted him. He'd spent every moment he could at Kelstone with them and their daughter Juliana, and when he was old enough, it was from them that he learned how the Second Kingdom should be. How it used to be before his father took over.

And then Reginald after him.

"There's more than living in the Second Kingdom for a Dartham, you see. The Duke of Jarrell is the head. The ruler."

"Reginald," Peregrine said. It wasn't a question.

"Yes, Reginald. He is the duke, and so the Second Kingdom is his. Fortunately, the Kingdom's members are all over the island, and there are plenty of revels held where he's not present. And so, I spend my time in London whenever I can help it, only returning when it would cause a scandal for me not to."

Sandy didn't mention that he'd all but fled to London once his education had been finished, desperate to leave behind the messy, poisonous atmosphere his parents had created and which Reginald had perpetuated. Sandy had thought that in London—and at court, no less— he'd find more people like the Foscourts, who were unbound from convention, but friendly and steady too. He could almost laugh at the absurdity of that younger Sandy if it didn't make him so depressed to remember it.

"But . . . ?" Peregrine prompted.

"How do you know there's a but?"

Peregrine just looked at him, and Sandy gave a sigh. "Yes, fine. There is a *but*. I stay away and partake mainly of the Kingdom's pleasures outside of my brother's purview, *but* sometimes I feel so restless and unhappy that I can't stand it. And sometimes that restlessness feels like homesickness."

"You miss Far Hope."

"I don't miss Far Hope as it is," Sandy clarified. "It's almost like I'm homesick for a Far Hope that doesn't exist. For the Far Hope that lives only in my mind."

"Why doesn't it exist?" Peregrine asked, sounding genuinely curious. "What's the difference between the kingdom where there's no law but pleasure and the kingdom in your mind?"

"What else?" Sandy responded. "*Who* else? Reginald. He is a shadow that covers everything."

Peregrine seemed to think about how he wanted to phrase his next question. "You say there's no limit in the Second Kingdom but acquiescence. Has he violated that limit?"

"Among the members? No, not that I know of. But with Reginald, anyone who isn't a member of the Second Kingdom, or fantastically wealthy, isn't a person to him and doesn't merit a limit."

There had been a relation of Reginald's wife who'd come to stay after her father's death, a girl who came with a profitable mill and water rights

—so long as she was married off to someone willing to cede those rights to Reginald in exchange for a well-connected bride. The relation, Lydia, hadn't wanted the marriage, had fought against it until the duchess had locked her in her room to keep her from running. She'd run anyway. Sandy had been at Oxford at the time, and so he'd only heard the tale from the servants once he'd returned for that year's Michaelmas.

No, there'd been no limit of acquiescence for Lydia. Nor concern after she'd fled. Only spittle-flecked tirades about what Reginald would do if he ever caught her, and the occasional gloating over the mill, which had stayed in Reginald and Judith's ownership after the girl's disappearance.

Then there were the enclosures, which he'd only learned of last year —again from the servants. Sandy very much doubted the farmers and cottagers around Far Hope had acquiesced to having their livelihoods taken away.

"The Kingdom is supposed to be about pleasure above all—a place where vice is celebrated. But *good* vice, do you understand? Openness instead of narrowness. Liberality instead of restriction. But Reginald only sees the Kingdom as another way to increase his wealth and his power. He can't be as ruthless with the members as he is with everyone else, but it doesn't stop him from finding other ways to achieve his end of getting ever and ever richer. His machinations taint everything in the Kingdom."

"And the other people in the Kingdom? Do they feel the same as you? Is there no way to . . . remove him from his role?"

Sandy cocked an eyebrow. "What are you, a Leveller? No, he is the duke, and the duke is the head of the kingdom. It's always been that way."

"Perhaps it could be a new way." Peregrine studied him. "Except you mentioned earlier that you didn't want to be the duke. I take that to mean you don't want to be the ruler of the Second Kingdom either?"

Sandy didn't answer at first, his mind flashing through the responsibilities, the burdens, the poisoned wells big and small that Reginald left everywhere he went. And as Sandy cataloged the work Reginald's successor would have to do, he idly ran his palm over his captor's lightly furred chest and stomach. Peregrine had a tall, broad frame, but despite his powerful shoulders and thighs, there was a spareness to him to spoke of a life without rest or luxury, and Sandy wondered again what had set him on this path, why he'd chosen this desperate vocation.

And for the first time that he could ever remember in his petted and pampered life, Sandy itched to take care of someone else. He felt it like a catch in his breath, like an ache in his bones. He wanted to feed this man until his lean frame filled and thickened. He wanted to make Peregrine sleep enough and eat enough—and fuck until all the tension was bled from his limbs.

He wanted Peregrine's grim heart in his hands, and he wanted to treasure it forever.

A stupid wish.

"I don't," Sandy said after a long a time. "I'm—I think I'm—"

He drew in a breath. Even after thinking about how he wanted to answer, he found the words hard to say. "I'm scared. Of it."

Peregrine didn't give him a look of disgust or of disbelief; he didn't prompt Sandy to say more. Instead, he waited patiently while Sandy pressed his face into the highwayman's warm shoulder and spoke the words against his skin.

"I don't have many virtues, but I do have these: I've never forced anyone into a decision they didn't want to make, and I've never defrauded someone who couldn't afford it. I've wheedled and whined and coaxed and flirted, but I've never locked someone in a room until they married whom I wanted them to marry. I've never used my position and influence to coerce someone poor and scared into my bed."

Peregrine stiffened under Sandy, but before Sandy could think too much of it, Peregrine was shifting so that he could wrap his arms around him. The warmth that tickled through Sandy's chest at this gesture was ridiculous. Who felt flattered by being held by a lover? And how could this small thing outweigh the fact that Peregrine was going to kill him?

But for the moment, it did. He relaxed into Peregrine's arms, rooting against the older man's muscled shoulder until he was totally comfortable.

Once he'd finally settled in, Peregrine asked, "Are you worried that if you'd become like Reginald if you were the duke?"

Like Reginald . . . like his father and mother . . .

Sandy had gone to London thinking he would finally be done with all the noisome games and fleeting affairs which filled the days of Reginald's denizens, and instead, he'd been drawn into just as many games, just as many affairs, all of them as noisome and fleeting. Perhaps he wasn't a villain like Reginald yet, but he'd hardly acquitted himself as a saint at court. Who knows what he'd be like with enough power, enough vipers whispering in his ear?

"Yes, of course I'm worried about that," Sandy said with a sigh. "Wouldn't you be? If your own natural virtues were so few to begin with?"

"I'm a highwayman," Peregrine reminded him. "My natural virtues are very few."

"I don't believe it," Sandy said, running a hand over Peregrine's stomach again. "I think you have some tragic, noble reason for taking to the road."

Peregrine didn't answer, but Sandy felt a new tension beneath his hand, something like stillness. Indecision, maybe.

He tilted his head up to look at the man holding him. This close, Sandy could see the dark grains of stubble on Peregrine's jaw and the tiny white starburst of a scar near his temple. His lips were parted, revealing the blunt edges of the teeth which had scored Sandy's neck and chest just an hour ago.

He could also see a faint, barely perceptible struggle in the thief's eyes. It was almost invisible—one blink too many, one blink too long— but Sandy had watched enough card players weigh whether to keep playing to recognize it.

Sandy was too impatient, too *eager* for anything of Peregrine's, for anything of this man's history or heart. "You can tell me," he said quickly, knowing he was playing his own hand too fast even as he played it. "I want to hear all about that tragic, noble reason. I want to know what my brother did to you. I want to know everything about you."

For an instant, it looked like Peregrine was going to tell him. Like he was going to trust him. His lips parted, and his throat worked, and his brow furrowed as if with effort, and—

The instant passed. Peregrine's face slid into its usual stony chill, and he efficiently disentangled himself from Sandy.

"Peregrine," Sandy said as the highwayman stood and walked to where his clothes were draped over a chair. "Stay at least. You don't have to talk. But stay."

"No."

Sandy's hands fisted on the bed. He hated being dismissed like this, and more than that, he hated that he'd told Peregrine things he'd only ever told Juliana, and now Peregrine wouldn't even *look* at him.

And—and—he didn't want Peregrine to leave. Sandy was already cold without him, and the highwayman was better than warm; he was solid. Steady.

He made Sandy feel steadier just by being nearby.

Peregrine stepped into his breeches, not looking at Sandy. "You should sleep."

"*You* should sleep. Here. With me."

"I'll be outside," he replied. "In case you were thinking of escaping."

"I'm always thinking of escaping," Sandy said, annoyed now.

Peregrine didn't bother to respond. He left Sandy the candle, and Sandy stared at the dancing flame for a long time after his captor left, acutely aware of how ridiculous it was to cry over a lover's abrupt exit when the lover was his future murderer.

Sandy did it anyway.

7

Peregrine

"Is there a reason I'm not tied up?" Alexander demanded from the doorway of the sacristy.

It was late morning, and Peregrine was tired, having spent a sleepless night on the hard stone floor outside Alexander's cell, wishing viciously that he was back inside it with a sleeping Alexander clinging to him like a limpet. But he'd had no choice. He'd come so perilously close to telling Alexander things that he'd told no one, not even Lyd, and that wasn't right, that couldn't be right, could it? That this man he was supposed to kill—or at the very least, hate—was the only person he wanted to trust with memories so painful he barely trusted *himself* with them?

No, he'd been right to leave.

Except he'd been restless all night and was miserable today, and seeing Sandy barefoot and looking like some kind of fairy-tale prince somehow made everything better and worse at the same time.

"I must be the luckiest kidnapper ever," Peregrine said. "My captive *reminds* me to keep him bound."

"It's a favor to me, really," Alexander said. "And you owe me so many favors by now."

Peregrine grunted in response.

Alexander padded across the stone floor to the table where Peregrine sat. But he didn't take a chair for himself; instead, he hopped onto the table in front of Peregrine, sitting on his papers.

Peregrine wanted to be irritated, but it was difficult when Alexander's legs were spread so wide, and when his loose shirt had pulled to the side, exposing a bronze-pink nipple . . .

"Where are the others?" Alexander asked, reaching out to run his fingertips along the edge of Peregrine's jaw. It felt so good, so comforting, that Peregrine found himself allowing the touch, even though he shouldn't.

"They went to wait for the duchess on the road."

"Judith," Alexander said, sighing. "There's no love lost between us, but you don't suppose they'll hurt her, do you?"

Peregrine shook his head that he didn't know, his eyelids beginning to close as Alexander kept petting him. He couldn't remember ever being touched like this, with such affection. With no further purpose other than to touch.

"I'm not sure how far Lyd will go, but if I had my guess, I'd say she won't hurt the duchess. Not badly, at least. I did think they'd be back by now, though."

Alexander made a thinking noise. "Judith was feeling poorly when I left two days ago. Maybe she'd planned to leave but then hadn't felt up to it."

Peregrine nodded, eyes fully closed now. This was ludicrous, foolish beyond all reason, being stroked into submission like a lazy lion by clever prey. But neither could he bring himself to stop it. Last night with Alexander had been the most sharply exhilarating pleasure he'd ever known, but this moment, with his captive perched insouciantly on the table and his caresses sweet on Peregrine's face . . .

This was the kind of moment men fought wars for.

———

PEREGRINE SPENT the rest of the morning readying baths for each of them, and then after they washed, Peregrine bound Alexander's wrists as he had yesterday. Alexander's cock was thickly visible in his breeches before Peregrine finished wrapping even a single wrist with silk, and

Peregrine's pulse sped as he thought about what might happen later, after several hours of keeping Alexander so thoroughly teased.

But despite the pleasant, if petulant, scenery of his day, Peregrine began to feel the slightest curl of concern for Lyd and the others as the sun moved across the sky. It wasn't a true worry, because Lyd was very good at her chosen vocation, and Ned and the rest were the perfect companions for highway robbery, but it was the seed of a worry. They had left witnesses to Alexander's abduction, after all, which meant there was a chance that there would be a reward already posted for their band's capture.

Which meant people would be scouring the road for traces of Peregrine and his fellow thieves even more than they usually were.

Peregrine decided to check the old alms box at the front of the priory, which was where the band left each other notes, and where any messengers from Chagford or beyond left their messages as well. Peregrine was careful only to hire people he knew he could trust, but even so, the messengers believed the priory was a waypoint for Peregrine and his thieves, a convenient place to stable horses or wait out some rain, and not their true hideout. He trusted those he hired, but even good men could be tempted by the thought of unprotected loot.

Or a handsome reward.

"I'm going outside for a few moments," he told Alexander, who was currently lying on his stomach, reading one of the books Peregrine had found for him. "Do I need to tie you down so you don't leave your bed?"

"Only my bed has this edition of the Earl of Rochester's poetry, so no," Alexander said, not taking his eyes off the book, kicking his feet in the air like a schoolboy as he read. "But leave my wrists tied, if you please."

"As you say," Peregrine said and left his pretty captive on the bed.

Peregrine quickly checked on the horses and then scouted the front of the priory to make sure there was no one about. Assured that it was only him, Alexander, and the horses nearby, he went to the box, which indeed had a small note tucked under the lid.

He replaced the note with a few shillings for the next person delivering a message, and then he ducked under the crumbling beams of the priory's entry and strode back inside, unfolding the note and reading it as he went.

He stopped.

It wasn't an update about constables or magistrates or rewards. It wasn't even a message from Lyd and the others.

It was a message from the duke.

He'd agreed to pay the ransom.

Peregrine stared at the note for another moment longer, stared until the words blurred into the shadows gathering in the creases of the paper.

I wanted this.

This is what I wanted.

It had seemed so genius when Alexander had suggested it—not only revenge, but revenge unfolded, layered over itself, plague on top of famine on top of fire. Loss, then grief, then death.

Peregrine could make the duke suffer as Peregrine himself suffered, and then when the opportunity arose again, he would kill the duke, and, at long last, the emptiness inside Peregrine would be filled. At long last, his heart would stop its seething, aching *lack*, and his world would feel right again, as it hadn't since the day he'd kissed his mother and siblings goodbye and left to join the army.

So why didn't he feel victorious right now? Why didn't he rush to pen a reply, to strategize how much more of a ransom he could negotiate the duke into paying?

Because you know it's the beginning of the end for Alexander.

The Darthams were selfish, cruel, rapacious, *evil*—the thought of them made Peregrine sick. But though he'd once hated the idea of Alexander Dartham, he didn't hate the reality of Alexander at all.

Not in the slightest.

And the thought of any kind of harm coming to the barefoot rake currently lounging on his bed and reading—the rake who was half courage, half insolence, all spoiled—made Peregrine feel like he couldn't breathe.

He'd been tying Alexander's wrists with silk because it bothered him to think of Alexander's skin being scratched by proper rope—did he really think he could kill Alexander? *Truly?* But then what did that mean about Peregrine, about his pledge to destroy the Dartham family, either through ruin or death?

What if . . . what if he could have both? Revenge without hurting Alexander?

I'm not going to set you free.

Maybe you'll decide to keep me instead, Alexander had teased.

Peregrine folded the note, his thoughts racing, his mind turning over every possible solution. It would still be a blow for the duke if Peregrine took the ransom but didn't return the ransomed heir. Perhaps Peregrine could even spread the word that he *had* killed Alexander, and all the while, Alexander would be tucked away in the priory, reading books and complaining about the wine.

The image of Alexander remaining here, staying a petulant and handsome thorn in Peregrine's side, eased the tension in his chest. His pulse slowed.

Yes, yes, that was what he would do. He'd demand the ransom but keep Alexander alive. He'd have revenge *and* his rake.

His rake. He liked how those words felt in his mind . . . like a soft breeze on a summer's night. Like a kiss in the dark.

Alexander could be his. Revenge could be his.

All of it could be his.

When he finally reached the sanctuary, he barely stopped. He dropped the note on top of his papers as he passed by the table, took something else off the dinner table nearby, and strode straight to the sacristy, where Alexander had rolled onto his back and had the book propped against his raised knees as he read. Peregrine set down the small bottle he'd brought from the sanctuary and stalked over to the bed, taking the book off Alexander's stomach and tossing it onto the mattress. He untied the rake's wrists quickly, easily, letting the silk unravel into soft coils next to Alexander's ribs.

Alexander blinked up at him, his dark eyes catching the light of the candles burning nearby.

Black and blue and gold, glittering and glittering.

"Have you come to see if I can do it?" Alexander asked softly.

Peregrine pulled off his shirt and started on his breeches. "Do what?"

"Seduce my way to freedom."

Peregrine stared at the young man on his bed. He couldn't know about the note Peregrine had just received, could he? No. No, he wouldn't have known where to look for it in the alms box to begin with, and Peregrine knew he'd betrayed nothing when he'd walked in. Nothing other than grim lust, of course.

When Peregrine didn't answer, Alexander's full mouth curled in a smile so devious that Peregrine was certain half of London had lost their hearts or purses or both to it. What a highwayman Alexander Dartham would have made—he would've ridden up to a carriage and smiled that smile and the occupants would have showered him with jewels just for being so beautiful and captivating.

Just for being so very, very wonderful.

"I seem to remember telling you that I'm always willing to try the seduction route of escape," Alexander murmured. He didn't sit up, but rather stretched like a spoiled cat in the sun, and then his hands went to his waist, where he began playing idly with the fabric of his shirt, drawing it up higher and higher until Peregrine could see the delectable well of his navel.

"What if it doesn't work?" Peregrine asked, his voice gone a little rough as he finished undressing and mounted the bed again, this time with both knees so he could crawl over Alexander, who was still smiling to himself like he was about to swindle an entire table of courtiers playing cards.

"Then I suppose," Alexander said sweetly, sliding his hands up and around Peregrine's neck, "I shall have to keep trying. You wouldn't mind that, would you? If I had to practice a few times in order to get the seduction just right?"

"It's already just right," Peregrine heard himself say.

The truth tasted sharp and sweet on his tongue as he added hoarsely, "*You're* just right."

Alexander's smile faded, and his eyebrows drew together. He looked confused, like Peregrine wasn't playing the game which Alexander had been planning to cheat at.

"Peregrine," he said, hesitantly, but Peregrine didn't think he'd be able to answer any question that came next, and so he kissed Alexander before Alexander could say anything more.

Alexander's grasp tightened on Peregrine's neck, and then his fingers were sliding into Peregrine's hair, rumpling it, tugging at it, until he finally found the ribbon tying Peregrine's queue and pulled it free. His hair tumbled around their faces like a curtain, shutting out the light from the candles and from the fire, and in that private darkness, Peregrine licked past Alexander's mouth until he could feel the sweet silk of Alexander's tongue against his.

As Peregrine kissed him, he braced on one arm and used his free hand to find the jut of Alexander's hip, then the curve of his backside. He gripped and squeezed there and then pressed them together where it mattered most. The broadcloth of Alexander's breeches was a little rough against Peregrine's cock, but the roughness felt good as he moved his hips against the other man; it had him panting after only a few thrusts.

He couldn't remember being this wound up, not even as a lad sneaking into the barn with a shepherd for the first time. He couldn't remember ever having his body pressed against someone's like this, kissing and simply *feeling*. As a soldier, any encounter had been necessarily brief and efficient. Impersonal.

But with Alexander, everything was languorous, lingering, indulgent —not merely relieving a physical need, but savoring something wonderful.

"How would you seduce me?" Peregrine breathed between kisses.

"So you admit now it's a possibility that I can?" Alexander murmured.

Peregrine could feel Alexander's mouth curving against his, and then he smiled himself. "You're awfully smug for a captive."

"Obviously, I'm smug." Alexander reached between them, and his fingertips ghosted across the corners of Peregrine's mouth. "I made the terror of the Queen's roads *smile*. And I haven't even touched his cock yet."

You've only touched everything else. His thoughts, his heart, even the faint wisps of what could be called a soul—Alexander's fingertips had brushed over them all. And Peregrine didn't know how he felt about it . . .

Only that he wasn't ready for it to stop.

"But a smile is still a long way from seduction," Alexander continued. "*Hmm*. What shall I do to win my freedom? How should I seduce such a stern"—his fingers dropped to Peregrine's bare chest, and then skated down his sides, making him shiver—"ferocious"—then his fingers tickled over Peregrine's hips and Peregrine huffed out a laugh that made the rake's evil grin spread even wider—"stoic man?"

"If you keep insulting my dignity like this, I may have to return you to your bindings," Peregrine threatened, nuzzling against Alexander's neck and inhaling the scent there. It smelled like soap and somehow still like *Alexander*—citrus and spice.

"Oh dear," said Alexander. "Oh no. Whatever shall I do."

"You could get back to seducing me properly," Peregrine suggested. He kissed Alexander's neck and then levered himself up to look down at the younger man spread underneath him. Alexander's near-black hair was in a halo of dark silk, and his already full mouth was swollen with kissing. Without breaking their gaze, Alexander slowly, carefully stripped himself out of his clothes. Peregrine eased up so his captive could pull them all the way off, and then he lowered his hips to Alexander's once he was finished undressing so that naked flesh could touch naked flesh.

Peregrine grunted in pleasure, and Alexander's gaze grew flirtatious.

"Would you like me like this?" Alexander murmured coyly, spreading his thighs even wider under Peregrine and putting his hands against Peregrine's chest. "Like a virgin? Like I don't know how good it will feel? Like I can only tremble underneath you while you show me?"

Peregrine's cock surged against Alexander's stomach, answering for him.

"Or . . . ," Alexander said, seeming to have an idea. His eyes moved past Peregrine to the closed door, and there was an icy stab of fear that his prisoner would bolt for the door while Peregrine was hazed over with lust. But then he realized that even Alexander wasn't reckless enough to plunge into the chilly moors completely naked, and also that Alexander was looking at the edge of the table instead, where Peregrine had set a small bottle of oil.

With surprising strength, Alexander flipped Peregrine onto his back. He tossed his hair over his shoulder and gave him a triumphant grin before sliding off the bed, sauntering over to the table, and getting the bottle.

Peregrine's blood was already hot enough to simmer, but watching the Dartham heir move around utterly naked with that fluid grace of his made Peregrine feel like his very skin was about to catch fire. Alexander's mussed hair waved over his shoulders, his nipples were pulled into tight points, and the small nip in his waist was so very visible like this, just waiting for Peregrine's hands. And Alexander's cock—pointed to by a narrow, elegant trail of dark hair—was beyond tempting. Straight and veined and as lovely as something carved from marble by a deeply skilled hand.

Peregrine wanted to put it in his mouth.

"Or you could be the virgin," Alexander said as he came back to the bed and climbed gracefully onto the mattress. "Would you like that? If you trembled beneath me instead?"

"What would *you* like?"

Alexander's expression shuttered and he looked away for a moment, ostensibly down to the bottle to open it. When he looked back up, his expression was the same blithe one as earlier. "I like whatever will seduce you the best, of course," he said smoothly. "Now give me your hand, please."

Peregrine hesitated. He wanted to know what Alexander had been thinking—what Alexander *wanted*—but even wondering felt ridiculous because what else would Alexander want? To be free of Peregrine and safely back to his life, of course.

Peregrine nearly opened his mouth to reassure Alexander that he wasn't planning to hurt him any longer . . . but then he couldn't bring himself to utter anything at all. Not because he didn't want Alexander to know that he was safe, but because he didn't want to bring up the subject in the first place. He was ashamed, maybe, of having ever wanted to kill Alexander at all.

Ashamed that he still didn't plan on setting Alexander free.

In any case, Alexander distracted Peregrine beyond all thought. He took Peregrine's hand in his own and then gently, carefully, drizzled oil over the first two fingers, giving Peregrine a smoldering look as he did. Peregrine's pulse kicked.

"Work me open," Alexander said, his own racing pulse obvious in the thrumming at the side of his throat. In the erratic bob and swell of the pretty cock between his thighs. "Make me ready."

And then he turned and presented himself to Peregrine.

Peregrine couldn't stop the groan that tore out of his chest at the sight. Alexander was beautiful everywhere, even in the secret places where his body opened to take a lover, and the sight of that beauty nearly undid Peregrine. His hand shaking, he reached up and grazed a single fingertip over the sensitive flesh on offer.

Alexander let out a puff of air that was almost a sigh, as if he were both relieved and excited by the touch.

Peregrine knew neither of them were virgins or seducers; he could push them to any pace, and Alexander would be right there with him. But he didn't want to push. He didn't want this to be fast, mechanical.

Forgettable.

He suddenly wanted to be all over Alexander in the same way Alexander was all over him—to touch Alexander's thoughts and his heart and his soul. Peregrine didn't know if he could do that merely from making love—he'd never tried and no one had ever tried with him—but that was what he wanted, and so that was what he would do.

He grazed over the pleated skin again as his other hand slid up Alexander's lean thigh and caressed the smooth cheek of his backside. He kept stroking that firm curve as he swirled his fingertip against Alexander's entrance and made everything sweet and slick in the process. It wasn't long before there were goose bumps all over the rake's skin, along his back and thighs and arse.

Peregrine loved feeling those goose bumps, this proof that he, who'd done nothing but the briskest and most transactional kinds of lovemaking, had the power to affect a seasoned libertine like Lord Alexander Dartham. He sanded his free hand over Alexander's skin and whispered, "Breathe."

Alexander breathed. Peregrine pushed.

There was enough oil to make passage easy, if something as searing and squeezing as this could be called *easy*. Peregrine's mind filled with images of him surging to his knees behind Alexander and taking him in one rough thrust—pushing Alexander to his stomach and mounting him—yanking him off the bed and bending him over and—

But Peregrine wanted this instead. This slow, stroking invasion that made Alexander shiver and shiver and shiver until he seemed to be nothing but panting and goose bumps, until Peregrine could see between his legs the wet spot Alexander's cock was leaving on the coverlet as clear seed leaked from the tip.

"Stroke yourself," Peregrine said, gently working his finger until he could find that swollen spot inside. Alexander let out a gasp, and then his hand flew to his organ, which he rubbed furiously, almost clumsily, his libertine's grace leaving him as Peregrine continued to caress the gland inside his body.

Peregrine found the bottle propped against a nearby pillow and added more oil, and then slid a second finger inside Alexander, which earned him a noise so guttural and yet so heavenly that Peregrine couldn't wait to hear it again. He stroked inside with two fingers now, until Alexander began moving against him, shamelessly fucking himself against the highwayman's touch.

And then Peregrine knew what he wanted, how he wanted to be seduced.

He wanted to be seduced purely by watching Alexander like this, with Alexander urgent and near helpless with how good he felt.

Peregrine slid his hand free and then pulled at Alexander's hips until the rake turned to blink at him. His cheeks and chest were flushed; his cock stuck straight out like a blunt sword. His lips were parted, and his brows were pulled together in an expression of utter bewilderment, as if he couldn't imagine *why* Peregrine would do something so awful as to stop.

"I want you on top," Peregrine murmured, already pulling Alexander over him. "I want you to make yourself come on me."

Alexander gave a little shudder, his ribs jerking with fast, tattered breaths. "Are you sure—I'm not the one being—seduced?"

Peregrine's only answer was a smile; he relished how Alexander's usual coquettish demeanor was falling apart right now—the way his eyes roved hungrily over Peregrine's body as he positioned himself to fuck—the way his tongue darted out to his lower lip in concentration as he guided Peregrine past that first slick barrier into the searing forge beyond. The way he unselfconsciously shook his hair out of his face and then gave a soft whine as he impaled himself.

Peregrine gentled his hands up and down Alexander's thighs, making soothing noises as Alexander pushed down, even as he himself had to lock every muscle in his stomach and thighs to keep from surging up into the snug velvet of Alexander's body.

His patience was rewarded, however, as Alexander fully seated himself and then gave a tentative rock forward. Another one of those heavenly noises left him, and he gave Peregrine a look of dazed help-lessness.

"Good?" Peregrine asked. His voice was rough, hoarse, and his entire body was shaking with the restraint it took to let Alexander squirm and writhe on top of him, to let the Dartham lord find the right angle, the right movements.

"Yes," Alexander breathed, his eyelids fluttering. "More than good. I've never—it's never been like this before."

"You on top?" Peregrine asked.

"No," Alexander said, his mouth hooking ruefully to the side. "Never with someone patient on the bottom. One moment—oh. *Oh.*" He seemed to have found just the right way to move, and he did it again, his erection dragging along Peregrine's abdomen and making him release another puff of air. Another *oh.*

Peregrine tried to focus on one thing, any one thing, to keep his building climax at bay, but it was impossible. Even aside from Alexander's body gripping him like a hot glove, from the sweet sensation of Alexander's cock rubbing against Peregrine's stomach, there was the *sight* of him. The slender hips, the dark hair tumbling everywhere, his face in an expression of surprised ecstasy, as if he hadn't expected it to feel as good as it did.

It made Peregrine wonder how selfish Alexander's past lovers had been, that it was a revelation for him to be able to take his time, to put his own pleasure first.

"Spend for me," Peregrine said, sliding his hands up to Alexander's hips and then up to his waist. "I want to see you."

"I think that's—normally—the seducer's line—" Alexander panted, but he braced his hands and Peregrine's chest and began riding Peregrine for all he was worth, choosing the speed and the angle and the depth. Each rock of his hips tightened the grip his body had on Peregrine's cock; each rock meant that his secret place stroked Peregrine with a slippery, viselike heat. It drew his orgasm closer; it pulled his bollocks tight to his body; it had his hips restless underneath Alexander's.

"Oh, Peregrine," Alexander said, his breaths all sounding like gasps now, all of them desperate. "I'm—it's—"

He didn't have to announce it. His prick swelled even more on top of Peregrine's stomach, and with a low cry, his hips gave a series of quick, arrhythmic thrusts. Peregrine was entranced by the sight of that beautiful organ swelling and then throbbing out jet after jet of white seed, loving the visible proof of the rake's satisfaction spilled all over his skin.

Alexander's hips stilled and his head dropped between his shoulders as he panted and quivered his way through the aftershocks. Peregrine somehow managed to hold on, to fight back the tide of his own need to spend, until Alexander was finished.

After he'd settled, the younger man peeped up through a glossy lock of hair that had tumbled over one eye and said, "Some highwayman you are. Aren't you supposed to be all about plunder and theft? What have you taken for yourself right now? Nothing. You're more rector than robber, I think."

Peregrine laughed. "I can plunder more, if you'd like."

Alexander gave him a coy look from behind his hair. "Will you show me how the soldiers do it?"

"Maybe another time," Peregrine said. "The soldier's way is hardly a seduction."

"I'll confess a secret to you, Peregrine Hind. You don't have to seduce me. If you'd like to take me like a soldier would . . . " Alexander shivered again, his sated cock stirring against Peregrine's stomach. "I have no objections."

Neither did Peregrine. If he somehow managed to steal more time with this man, he would want all kinds of lovemaking. Slow and fast, rough and whatever this had been too—not gentle maybe, and certainly not sweet, but the kind of sex where selfishness was transformed into something fantastic. Where one lover's pleasure spun a silken web around them both, where taking was also giving.

"For now," Peregrine said, "I'll take you like a highwayman." He was already pulling out, moving. Pushing the rake onto his back, and then onto his stomach, which meant his firm backside was there for Peregrine to spread and penetrate once more.

He came into Alexander with a deliberate but inexorable thrust, and then once he'd fully mounted his captive, he started fucking in earnest, with quick, rough strokes that had them both groaning together. As he rutted, he watched Alexander's slender fingers twisting in the covers; he watched as Alexander reached underneath himself and desperately handled his cock.

The orgasm wasn't only in Peregrine's prick, but in his stomach and chest and thighs too, and it thudded through his blood like the drums of war. With a ragged grunt and a surge of his hips, Peregrine's climax roiled its way up his shaft and then released torrent after torrent into Alexander's pliant, waiting heat.

Peregrine kept riding his wonderful flirt of prisoner through it all, determined to pump everything into the man in front of him. Sinuous shudders racked Alexander's body as he came for a second time, and Peregrine caught the quick movements of the rake's hand as he finished milking his orgasm free.

There was no bliss like this, no satisfaction that matched pulling out and seeing his seed dripping free of this beautiful man's body, and then rolling his lover over to see the slick mess he'd made while he'd been receiving Peregrine's pleasure.

Peregrine suddenly wanted never to leave the priory again. He only wanted this, day after day. Alexander Dartham, frolicsome and spoiled and safe.

With him.

It would be worth giving up the road for, it could even be worth giving up revenge for, but for the first time in years, Peregrine didn't want to think about revenge at all.

Stunned by that realization, and a little panicked by it too, he tidied up the mess they made and then pulled the rake tightly into his arms, trying to breathe past the sudden swell of emotion.

How could it be that this libertine, this *Dartham*, had become more important to him than the need for vengeance and justice for innocent lives? How could the mere thought of Alexander being hurt by him make Peregrine feel like he'd been torn open by cannon fire?

After only a few short days?

Peregrine didn't know the answer. He'd walked into this room so certain of his future, so confident in his solution, but perversely, he felt like he knew himself less after losing himself inside Alexander. Like he was slowly dissolving, and the only thing keeping him whole was the warm lover lying dozily in his arms.

8

Sandy

Peregrine Hind, ex-soldier, present-day kidnapper, and Terror of the Queen's Roads, snored. Rather adorably.

Sandy looked up at the man whose chest he was currently using as a pillow and couldn't help the grin on his face. He'd never fucked like that, not once. Oh sure, he'd tried every position and sex act under the sun, but never had a partner allowed the use of their body for *Sandy's* pleasure. Never had a partner waited patiently while Sandy learned what felt good, what he wanted, and then waited even more patiently as Sandy chased down a cataclysm that was more potent for the time it took to seek it out. Pleasure at Oxford—and then in the Second Kingdom once Sandy had been initiated at the age of twenty-one—had been a game, and the rules of the game were simple: if one cared too much, then one lost.

So he'd pretended not to care. He'd pretended that he was as jaded as the rest, because the alternative was either to abstain altogether or to take the way other people took—not without consent necessarily, but without concern—and he couldn't make himself do that. Perhaps it was the influence of the Foscourts, or maybe the memories of his own parents' selfishness, but he found he couldn't use someone for pleasure unless he knew the using was at least mutual. Not that he hadn't enjoyed the mutual using; he'd enjoyed it plenty! But tonight had been like discovering a new room in a house he'd always known, or a new chapter in his favorite book.

It had been a gift.

And wonder of wonders, he'd also somehow made this highwayman smile—and *laugh*. He'd seen the heat and the affection sparkling in Peregrine's silver eyes, and it had been an epiphany, a vision. He doubted Peregrine Hind would ever be a joyful man—or even an easy one—but seeing the gradual thawing of the highwayman for *him*, for Sandy Dartham, was powerfully alluring, to say the least.

Sandy watched Peregrine sleep for a few more minutes, enjoying the way those stern features softened in repose—enjoying how, even in sleep, Peregrine's arm clasped Sandy tightly to him. It was a possessive gesture, dominant and greedy, and Sandy loved how it felt so much that he could have stayed nestled there for the rest of the month. But when his stomach started growling with hunger, he slipped from the bed to hunt down something to eat.

The others still hadn't returned from their attempt to rob the duchess, and so Sandy padded out in his breeches and nothing else, shivering a little at the cool air of the sanctuary after being curled against a warm thief for so long. He poked around the table, tearing off a piece of bread and chewing on it as he wondered how the other robbers were getting on with Judith and how Judith was faring. She was a cruel woman—she and Reginald were very well matched in that respect—but she had been doing poorly when they'd stayed over in Exeter during their trip from London, and Sandy had felt bad for her. There was nothing worse than traveling while sick, and no cure for it except to get home as fast as possible; he'd even arranged for an extra coach so that she and her maid could ride in more comfort without him crowding the seat.

Still eating his bread, Sandy wandered over to the table where Peregrine sometimes sat to do his work. Funny that robbery had the same endless stacks of paper running a dukedom had. Some of it must have been correspondences, Sandy supposed, with fences and innkeepers like the one in Exeter who'd informed the band about the duchess. He unfolded the paper on top, more out of idle curiosity than anything else.

And then.

And then he saw.

> *duke to pay one thousand in coin.*
> *arrange place for payment and handing over the lord alexander?*
> *post response by dawn tomorrow.*
>
> *-x*

Sandy sat in the chair, stunned. Not *surprised*, certainly, he'd known that Reginald would ransom him—although one thousand pounds was so far beneath what Sandy had estimated his own worth to be that he was a little offended—but he supposed he hadn't considered the ransoming would happen this quickly. He'd thought that he'd have more time to escape, or to woo his freedom from his captor, or . . .

Or more time to stare into your captor's exquisite silver eyes while he fucks you into a bone-shaking climax.

Sandy stared at the note, his mind twisted up around his thoughts, his chest feeling all twisted up too. He'd somehow forgotten what it had felt like to be on his knees, watching Peregrine's finger curl over the trigger of a pistol. He'd forgotten that he *had* to escape, and escape quickly, because Peregrine was planning to kill him the moment Reginald handed over the ransom.

He'd forgotten because Peregrine made it impossible to remember.

Sandy swore at himself as he got to his feet. He knew better than to let a pretty face distract him—he knew because ordinarily, *he* was the pretty face doing the distracting. And that Peregrine's face wasn't pretty was beyond the point. He was lovely the same way the moors and hills around Far Hope were lovely, with a kind of lonely, elemental beauty. He fucked Sandy like Sandy had never been fucked before—not as a convenient playmate or as the means to an end, but like Sandy was the end itself. Like Sandy *mattered*.

And maybe it wasn't the beauty or the pleasure that had so arrested Sandy, but Peregrine's unflinching wholeness. Peregrine was, simply, honestly, *grimly* himself.

That, too, reminded Sandy of the hills around his childhood home. But that unflinching wholeness was the same reason Sandy needed to leave. Because Peregrine had never hidden that he was after revenge and revenge alone, and if Sandy had secretly hoped that his dimples and bed-play would endear the highwayman to him—at least enough to buy him his life—then it was time he admitted the enterprise had been a failure. Peregrine had said nothing about keeping him alive after the ransom, hadn't betrayed even a sliver of willingness to do so. His wordlessness in the face of this note, which he'd so obviously seen, proved it to Sandy.

His death was still part of the plan.

Sandy looked at the note again, suddenly feeling like an invisible hourglass had been turned over. Reginald could be mustering the money for the ransom right now; in fact, Sandy couldn't even be sure of when the highwayman had received the note. For all he knew, Peregrine had already arranged the ransom exchange, and Sandy was going to die tomorrow or the day after.

The reverie of being tied up and ravished into boneless pleasure was over. The cold truth had come to burn it away.

He had to run.

Now.

He set the note back where he found it, and he then went to the door of the sacristy to see if Peregrine was still soundly asleep.

He was, flat on his back and snoring softly, the sheets caught around his hips and one muscled thigh partially exposed. His lips were parted ever so slightly, his long eyelashes on his cheeks, his hair everywhere on the pillow. One arm rested exactly as it had been when Sandy had been snuggled next to him—as if, even while asleep, Peregrine was waiting for Sandy to return to bed.

Walking away from the man who was going to kill him was like being pressed with stones. Sandy could barely breathe as he did it, and each breath hurt something deep inside his chest as he dragged it in and then released it. He struggled to keep his inhales and exhales quiet as he crept to the corridor that led to the former monks' cells. Peregrine's was easy to find—it had only the essential things inside it, while the others were piled with finery and spoils. Sandy slipped inside.

He had grown up in this corner of Devonshire and knew quite well how forbidding any flight through it would be, which is why he didn't feel too guilty for taking Peregrine's extra pair of boots and a thick coat. From the sanctuary, he also took a small satchel with a flagon of water and some bread, a tinderbox, and then a wide-brimmed hat which looked like a relic from the Civil War.

Sandy considered stealing a horse, but the moment he approached the stables, there was a good deal of snorting and stomping and neighing, and he had the sudden terror the noise would wake Peregrine and scuttle his escape before he'd gotten to the lane leading out from the priory.

After taking an unlit torch from just inside the stable entrance, he backed away from the stables and then walked as quietly as he could through the dark yard to the lane. The moon was close to full, but clouds drifted over it now and again, and the world was reduced to rivers and pools of shadow. But Sandy wouldn't light the torch until he was very far from the priory, not if he could help it.

He kept looking over his shoulder, expecting Peregrine to be charging behind him on one of those noisy horses Sandy had been too timid to steal, but he never was. No one else was on the lane either, and when the lane joined to a slightly wider road, Sandy still had the route to himself—along with the occasional wild pony grazing nearby, which shuffled off whenever he got close.

Sandy breathed with relief as he turned onto the main thoroughfare, which was unoccupied but perhaps riskier, given its more exposed vantages. But it had the important benefit of being somewhat familiar. If that was the bridge he thought it was . . . and yes, if that was his favorite stone circle poking its teeth up into the moonlit sky . . . then he knew where he was. More importantly, he was perhaps only a few hours' hard walking from Far Hope. From safety.

So why didn't he feel relieved?

Because you're not there yet, Sandy told himself firmly. It couldn't be because he was regretting his flight away from Peregrine. It couldn't be because he *missed* Peregrine and being Peregrine's captive plaything. Sandy had grown up at Far Hope; he was a fully initiated citizen of the Second Kingdom, and he *knew* the difference between playing and real life.

He and Peregrine hadn't been playing a game of captivity. It had been real.

Unfortunately, everything else had been real too.

Ignoring the unhappiness that built and built inside him like a wave refusing to crest, Sandy marched on, trotting as fast as he could through the more visible areas of the road, going carefully through the hills and shadowy combes. By his reckoning, Peregrine's friends would be hunting Judith's coach some miles east of here, but he still couldn't take the chance of being found. And it was hardly like Peregrine Hind and his gang were the only thieves in Devonshire. While these moors were too remote and poorly traveled to attract the notice of most robbers, who could ever be sure? There was no point in escaping Peregrine only to die at the hands of someone else—someone who wouldn't even have moonlight eyes to soothe the unpleasantness of being murdered.

Ignoring the ache in his feet and the chill in his fingers, Sandy pressed on as fast as he could.

HE THOUGHT he might only be an hour away from Far Hope when he heard it.

Thunder. Thunder when he could look up and see the moon through the thin clouds, and the stars between them.

Someone was on the road and traveling fast.

Sandy reacted as quickly as he could, darting past a boulder and ducking, praying that the shadows would hide him, praying that it was only an ordinary traveler cantering down the road.

But of course, it was no ordinary traveler. When Sandy dared a peep over the edge of the boulder, he saw the huge black horse and the tall frame of Peregrine Hind. He had dropped down as quickly as he could, but when he heard the horse slowing as it approached, he knew he'd been sighted.

Peregrine had found him.

With a bolt of panic, Sandy surged to his feet and attempted to plunge into the murky cut of a nearby brook, but it was no use. A cold hand clamped around his wrist and yanked him back, and then Sandy was pulled into a hard body, a hand coming tight on his jaw to tilt

Sandy's face up to his pursuer's. The hat toppled off his head and fell behind him and was immediately forgotten.

"You can get on the horse willingly," Peregrine said, his voice shaking a little. "Or I can throw you over the saddle and walk you back. Which do you prefer?"

The moonlight was coming from behind Peregrine, and so Sandy couldn't read his expression, or even his eyes, which were no more than glimmers in the dark. But he could sense an implacable fury rolling off the highwayman in waves; he could hear the dangerous tremble in Peregrine's voice.

Sandy tried to think like he was playing a game of cards, like he was examining his own hand and reading the tells of the other players at the table. Except in this case, he couldn't bow out of a game gracefully if his cards were too poor to play. He could only keep betting and bluffing.

Or he could cheat.

Yes. He could cheat.

Sandy pulled away and started walking toward the horse, waiting by the saddle as Peregrine followed and gave him a look full of things Sandy couldn't properly parse. It was too dark. Peregrine mounted the horse easily, and then just as easily helped Sandy up behind him, settling Sandy onto the horse's back behind the saddle.

Peregrine turned his head and commanded, "Hold on," and then after Sandy slid his hands around Peregrine's waist, Peregrine urged the horse into a careful walk.

Sandy was already trying to decide how he'd cheat his way to freedom. Would he act contrite and attempt to elicit arousal or pity? Was he strong enough to hurt Peregrine or push him off the horse? Could he find a way to send word to Reginald once he got back to the priory—or maybe make sure the messenger got a forged note, telling Reginald that the exchange was no longer happening?

He was so wrapped up in his thoughts that he didn't notice the clapper bridge until they were clattering over it. A bridge that was very decidedly not on the way to the hideout.

"Wait," Sandy said after a moment. "We're not going back to the priory."

"Not tonight," Peregrine said. "A storm is moving in. It'll catch us before we make it back."

"So you're taking us deeper into the moors?" Sandy asked in a doubtful voice.

"No," came the low response. "There's shelter nearby."

Sandy sincerely doubted it, since they were still along the main road, and he knew there was nothing for another few miles until they reached the little parish village belonging to Far Hope. But Peregrine surprised him, and, after a mile or so, they turned onto a narrow lane bordered by low stone fences.

Though the light was still faint, Sandy could see the humps of white dotting the fields as they passed.

Sheep. Many of them.

Peregrine led them not to a shepherd's hut but to what appeared to be an abandoned longhouse—a thatched stone-built farmhouse joined to a barn at the far end. Shutters hung at crooked angles from the small windows, and the front door had a greenish film growing on the wood.

Peregrine helped Sandy dismount and then alighted from the horse himself, striding up to the door with no hesitation at all and pushing it open like he'd been there a thousand times before. Since it was the perfect kind of hiding place for a highwayman, maybe he had.

Sandy watched Peregrine's dark form disappear into the even darker house and weighed his chances of taking the horse and running, but Peregrine came back out before he could act.

"Come," the highwayman said. "Now."

Sandy followed him in, finding the highwayman already walking to the fireplace and getting to his knees as if to strike a fire. There was a stack of slender logs next to the hearth along with a small cauldron and a neat row of dried peat bricks; in front of the fireplace were two chairs and the frame for a cot.

It was rustic to be sure, but it looked like it was in regular use, and there were a few domestic touches deeper in the recesses of the house—a heavy Bible on a table, a spinning wheel, a small chair clearly built for a child. Sandy found it interesting that none of it had been burned. It would've certainly been more convenient to burn a chair or a spinning wheel than gather the scanty amounts of wood from around these parts, and it was hardly worth cutting and drying peat for a mere hideout.

The fire lit, Peregrine ducked out of the house again, and Sandy realized too late that he was walking the horse into the barn, because by the time Sandy decided this was his chance, Peregrine was rounding the corner and on his way back in. Even in the dark, Sandy could tell that the look Peregrine gave him was not an amused one, and Sandy slunk back inside.

Before he got to the fire, though, he felt that hand on his wrist again. He didn't know what he expected as he turned—anger, perhaps, or more unfeeling chill—but what he didn't expect was the unfiltered agony scrawled all over the highwayman's face, now visible in the dancing light of the fire.

Peregrine hauled Sandy against his chest, his arms tight around him and his hands roving everywhere—in Sandy's hair and along his back and even his backside—and then he pressed his face into Sandy's damp hair.

"Stay," the highwayman breathed. "Stay with me. Stay here."

"Obviously I have to stay here," Sandy muttered. "You dragged me here on your horse, remember?"

Peregrine ignored him, pulling back to cradle Sandy's face in his hands. "I was so worried," he said, his hands shaking against Sandy's cheek and jaw. "When I woke up and realized you'd gone . . . "

In the red-gold light of the fire, Sandy saw something he'd never seen on anyone's face before when looking at him, not even his parents.

Peregrine looked at Sandy like he was everything in the entire world.

No. Sandy refused to melt for that. He was indeed everything to Peregrine, because he was the key to Peregrine's revenge, and that was the only reason.

"Seems a little unproductive to worry when you plan on killing me anyway," Sandy pointed out, annoyed and hopeless and hurt and suddenly so very tired. He wanted to be in a warm bed, in a warm room, with a warm lover petting him until he fell asleep—and damn it all to hell, he wasn't picturing his townhome in London when he thought this, but the priory and his captive's cell within it. And Peregrine Hind cradling him as he drifted into sweet, satisfied dreams.

"Alexander," Peregrine said, his voice frayed.

"Don't *Alexander* me, everyone calls me Sandy anyway, and you're going to *kill* me, and—"

"I'm not going to kill you," the highwayman said softly. "Alexander. You're safe. I'm not going to hurt you."

It took a moment for the words to sink in. Sandy tucked his lower lip between his teeth and then released it. "Explain yourself."

Peregrine, against all odds, gave a short little laugh. "There's nothing to explain," he said, looking down at Sandy. "I won't kill you. I don't think I'm capable of it at this point. Maybe I could have done it in that very first moment, when I knew nothing of you except your relationship to the duke, but then again, maybe not. I haven't killed since the war, and I—" He sighed. "I can't kill our chickens or pheasants at the priory. I can't even hunt. I don't . . . I don't like it, how it feels. I don't like how the nightmares still come to me sometimes, full of the voices of the dead. So I don't know if I could have done it that night anyhow, but it hardly matters, does it, because now I *do* know you. I know how you smile and how you sigh, and the thought of you being hurt is like a bayonet through the throat."

Sandy's heart tilted and slid against his ribs, a thudding, foolish pulp of an organ. Because it wanted so badly to *hope*, and how asinine was that, that it only took a man saying he wasn't going to kill him to make Sandy all doe-eyed?

"You really don't want to kill me?" Sandy asked. "But what about Reginald? The ransom?"

"I don't know," Peregrine confessed, dropping his face closer to Sandy. "But a couple days ago, you said I might decide to keep you. What if I did?"

Sandy didn't have an answer to that. He knew of lovers in the Second Kingdom who chose to have masters or mistresses in private—to be a captive of sorts to their lover's commands. But it was always chosen in the normal circumstances when it came to sex and love and play.

These were not the normal circumstances.

"You truly won't kill me?" Sandy whispered.

"I won't."

"And you won't allow one of your band to kill me?"

"I won't," Peregrine repeated firmly. "You are safe with me. With us. I'm sorry that I didn't tell you this sooner—that I didn't see it sooner. When I think of being apart from you . . . " Peregrine didn't finish his sentence.

Instead, he brushed his mouth over Sandy's with a kiss that felt as vulnerable as it was brief. The highwayman was still trembling, Sandy realized, still shaking with relief and maybe other emotions too raw to name.

Sandy was shaking too. It felt too good to be true, and he didn't know if it was hope or doubt that made him shiver so.

And then Peregrine's mouth was back on Sandy's again, hungrier this time, the relief tasting so much like urgent, clawing need, and Sandy felt the same need rising in his blood. There was so much he didn't know, so much he didn't trust and so much he hoped for anyway, but this—*this* —he knew. He knew flesh, he knew groans and throbs and seed.

He pressed himself tighter to the highwayman, sliding his hands up to Peregrine's neck as Peregrine kissed him again and again, his hot tongue slashing into Sandy's mouth with desperate strokes, and then they were stumbling back, back until Sandy was against the wall. Below, their hips met and pressed and rubbed, and Peregrine braced his hands on either side of Sandy's head so he could push in harder, grind his hips against Sandy's even more. Their clothed cocks slipped rigid and thick against each other's, and Peregrine's kisses were so, so hot, and Sandy couldn't stand another moment without Peregrine inside him, he simply couldn't.

He struggled out of the coat and then unbuttoned his breeches, turning as he did.

"Alexander," Peregrine groaned, and Sandy decided right then and there that he liked when Peregrine called him that. He hardly ever heard *Alexander*; he'd been *Sandy* since he was a child. The irrelevant spare, the pet. But Peregrine used his full name like he was a king or an emperor.

A ruler in his own right.

It used to scare him, that possibility, whenever he thought of what might happen if he was still Reginald's heir when Reginald died and had to take over the Second Kingdom. It still did terrify him, but for the first time in his life, it electrified him a little too. Like maybe he could be a ruler if Peregrine thought he could be.

"Don't make me wait," Sandy said breathlessly, bracing his hands next to Peregrine's on the wall. "*Please.*"

The highwayman uttered a soft oath, but his hands dropped to his own breeches, and then Alexander heard him spitting into his palm.

"You wanted it like a soldier?" Peregrine asked, the wet, blunt head of his cock entreating entrance to Sandy's body. "This is much the same."

Then a thrust which felt like a sword of fire.

Sandy had done this before—a rake didn't fuck his way through London without the occasional impromptu swive with no oil on hand—so the initial discomfort wasn't a surprise. What was a surprise was the man behind him, who wasn't trying to hammer in and out right away, who added more slickness when it was needed, who was already reaching around to take Sandy's erection in his calloused palm and giving it rough, satisfying pumps as he let Sandy adjust to him.

Maybe it was the hand pleasuring him, or maybe it was the time Peregrine gave Sandy to relax into the invasion—or maybe it was just that it was Peregrine Hind, and with him, Sandy felt a deeply arousing combination of imperiled and safe.

Whatever it was, he was soon panting and moaning into the wall, rocking his prick into Peregrine's hand, fucking himself back on the thief. Which had Peregrine rubbing oh so wonderfully against the essential spot inside him. Sandy's testicles drew up tighter to his body, and astonishingly fast, he felt himself ready to surge in Peregrine's grip.

"Soldiers," Sandy gasped, "can't have been this considerate."

"Consideration is a rare thing in the tents," Peregrine admitted.

"Show me."

"As you wish," Peregrine grunted, drawing back to give Sandy a series of rough strokes that had his knees threatening to buckle.

The grunting behind him continued, each grunt matched with an arrow of pleasure right through Sandy's core, stabbing up into his belly, and he watched the big shadow on the wall behind him, all male, all brutal, all hellbent on this raw, primal act.

With Peregrine's cock hot and stroking, with the sound of the high-wayman's pleased grunts and the crackle of the fire, Sandy's climax tore through him, tore him right in half. He let out a long cry that was nearly a wail, his organ seizing hard in Peregrine's fist and then striping the wall in front of him with seed.

All of him must have been clenching and contracting, even the hole Peregrine was fucking, because Peregrine gave an animal noise and followed Sandy over the edge, his hips working to keep himself deep as he emptied himself into the man he had pinned against the wall.

They both panted there for a moment, breathing hard, slumping forward until Sandy's head was against the roughly plastered wall and Peregrine's was against the back of Sandy's neck.

"What do you think of the soldier's way of doing things?" Peregrine asked, and Sandy just laughed.

"I think I'm ready to enlist tomorrow."

9

Peregrine

"I'm plenty warm," Alexander fussed as Peregrine tried to layer his coat over the one Alexander was already wearing. "You've built a fire big enough for a Viking hall."

That demonstrably wasn't true, but Peregrine didn't argue, only settled back against the wall. There were chairs here, but he'd chosen the floor because then he could sit with Alexander between his legs and have him recline on his chest while they waited out the storm. It had begun raining outside, a thick, drenching deluge, and the coming of dawn did little to lighten the world. Peregrine was grateful to his past self for having the patience and foresight to keep this place well stocked with things for a fire.

"This isn't a Viking hall," Alexander said after a moment, squirming to get comfortable against Peregrine's chest. "But it's no shepherd's hut either. Clearly, it was a farmhouse."

"There was a whole hamlet here once. You'll see the empty houses in the daylight when we leave."

"An entire hamlet? Empty? Why do you think they left?"

Peregrine had refused to talk about his past for so long that he was surprised to hear the words fall from his lips. "Most of them couldn't make a living here anymore and had to move. But the people in this particular house died."

"Died?" Alexander said, clearly horrified. "Recently?"

"Six years ago now."

"*How?*"

Peregrine looked over at the fireplace, crackling with a fire just as it had in his earliest memories. "The short answer is a fever."

"And the long answer?"

Peregrine watched the flames dance behind the old firedogs, thinking of the day he'd gone to enlist, of his mother setting his coat and boots by the fire so they'd be warm when he left. It was strange how such a vast tree of catastrophes could come from a single seed. "The eldest son left them. Their father had been dead a while, and so he was the head of the family for a time. But he knew he would never marry, never sire children, and so he thought it best to leave the farm to his younger brother. He would go off and earn good wages to send home instead. But it's nearly impossible to send letters to infantry when they're at war, and so he didn't know that the Duke of Jarrell had decided to enclose the common land shared by everyone in the hamlet. The land they used for farming, for grazing, for their living, was gone. They'll hang a lowborn man for stealing more than twelve pence, but if a lord steals the income and sustenance from an entire village, he is given an Act of Parliament to do so and then he's heralded as a reformer and a modern man."

Peregrine took a long breath, the injustice of it burning him all over again. He had to make himself go back to the story, back to the house and the family who'd lived in it, otherwise he'd jump to his feet in a seething rage and go find the duke right then and there. "Half-starving, the sister found a way to approach the duke and plead their case. He offered her some small assistance in exchange for time spent in his bed. She agreed, because what other choice did she have?"

Alexander had gone still against his chest. "And then?" he asked quietly.

"And then the fever came," Peregrine told him. "It took the mother and the brother quickly. The sister hung on, but by this point she was swollen with the duke's child, and she never truly recovered. The duke, of course, wasn't interested in a mistress who was pregnant *or* sickly, and so refused to help or even see her. It was beyond foolish to go to

Far Hope the night she died, but she must have felt it was the only place she could go. Perhaps she thought if the duke could see her, he would take pity on her for the unborn child's sake? Perhaps she thought a servant would help? No one can say. But whatever she thought, it didn't happen. Even though the night was bitterly cold and she was very ill, no one admitted her into the house. The next morning, they found her with frost on her eyelashes and no breath left in her at all."

Alexander's voice was both sad and careful when he asked, "And the eldest son? The one who went to war?"

Peregrine took his eyes from the fire and occupied himself with Alexander's hair instead, curling the silken ends around his fingers as he spoke. "He came home a year after the sister had died and learned the story from a neighboring vicar. He found his childhood home empty, his childhood village empty, and his family in their new graves. He learned that it was the duke who had enclosed the land, starved his family, coerced his sister into his bed and then left her to die. Everything the son had become a soldier for was gone, and all the blood and death and disease he'd endured because it earned money for his family was for nothing in the end. Nothing at all."

Alexander moved so Peregrine could more easily stroke his hair. "But how did you decide to become a highwayman then?" he asked, pushing past the pretense that the story had been about anyone else. "The revenge—I see that well enough now. But why become *the* Peregrine Hind to achieve it?"

"It was an accident the first time," Peregrine said, remembering a long-ago summer evening. He'd been staying in his vacant family home after learning what had happened, lost to his grief. "There was a riding party, out quite late. Your brother wanted to show his guests the enclosed fields, boast about how much his new flock had already earned for him, and so they were riding down my lane outside."

Peregrine had stood inside his doorway like a ghost, watching as the duke had proudly told this fine, mounted party how much he'd improved the land, how he'd turned the commons from inefficient wastes into wool and then into money. And as Peregrine listened, the fathomless pain which had gnawed at him for days—which had stolen his thoughts, his sensations, even his ability to sleep and to feed himself

—had forged itself into a blade, and that blade cut through his grief. That blade gave him purpose.

And that was when Peregrine had known he was going to kill the duke.

"Fine people are so careless," Peregrine continued. "I watched as they milled around the shell of my dead hamlet, paying as much mind to me as they would one of the duke's new sheep. They had servants behind them with a cart in case they'd like to stop and have a drink or something to eat, and the cart was loaded with silver and dishes. The silver alone would have fed the village for a year or more." He paused, thinking of how it had felt to see the Duke of Jarrell call for an alfresco celebration of his successful wool venture, to see the servants open the lid of the chest on the cart and reveal gleaming silver and glass. To watch these people toast the destruction and the hunger and the death that had made the rich duke so much richer still.

It had felt like standing in front of his family's graves all over again.

"I thought, here is my chance to kill the duke," Peregrine said. "He was right there, standing like a lazy pheasant in front of my family's house, ignoring my presence and swilling wine. I'd newly come from the war, and I still had my pistols. I wouldn't even have had to leave the house . . ."

"But you didn't succeed," Alexander surmised.

"I missed. Not by much, but enough to warn him. The entire party fled down the lane in terror, thinking they were all being hunted, and the servants ran on foot after them."

"Leaving the silver," Alexander concluded.

"Leaving the silver," Peregrine said in confirmation. After staring at the booty for several minutes, Peregrine had decided he had no need of it. He'd found the other families who'd fled the hamlet and gave the silver to them in its entirety. "At first, I thought I'd stalk the road to find the duke again, get on with my revenge, and then I would—well, I wasn't sure what I would do after. But it didn't matter at first, because I couldn't find him. Only other dawdling lords and ladies, slowly rolling through the hills with jewels and coins and anything else you could think of. All on their way to Far Hope, for one party or another. It was too easy, and out on the moors, it's even easier not to get caught after, not if you grew up here and know where to hide. Not if you made friends in every town and village by giving away so much of what you've stolen."

"And so you became a fearsome highwayman entirely incidentally."

Peregrine leaned his head back against the wall, watching the rain sluice down the small window's warped panes. "It was the only thing that felt right," he admitted. "I had no farm left, no family, and I couldn't make myself go back to the army. And I liked how it felt, taking from these people who had so much and giving it to the people who had so little. Soon others joined me, Lyd—your relation by marriage, you know —joined me too."

"*Lydia*," Alexander breathed, shaking his head against Peregrine's chest in disbelief. "I hadn't seen her since she was a girl, but I should have known it was her. No wonder she was so excited to rob Judith."

Peregrine made a noise of assent.

"I know it means very little in the face of what you've lost, but I couldn't be sorrier for what Reginald has done to you and those you loved," Alexander said. "And thank you for telling me what happened, even though I'm probably the last person you want to share your past with."

The rain was so loud, so insistent, but it was almost soothing now, like it was washing away everything that wasn't this moment, that wasn't Alexander cuddled sweetly against Peregrine's chest.

"You're the only one I've ever told the entire story to," Peregrine said. "I don't know why I've never told anyone else—I suppose because it hurt so much to think about. It hurt to think that I sailed off and left my family at the mercy of the world. I never even had the chance to apologize for how I failed them. Their graves were already sprouting grass by the time I'd returned."

"Oh, Peregrine," Alexander said softly. "It wasn't your fault. If you'd been here, you wouldn't have been able to stop Reginald either. In fact, you might be dead of that same fever too."

Peregrine had to concede that this was true.

"And," Alexander added, "perhaps it hurts precisely because you haven't told anyone. You've been carrying it alone, when no one should carry something like that inside their own minds and nowhere else."

"That's very wise."

"Well," Alexander murmured, tucking his hands inside Peregrine's coat, "people have always said that wisdom is my greatest virtue."

"They have not."

"You're right," Alexander said, clearly fighting a yawn. "You've already had my greatest virtue spending all over the wall of your family home."

Peregrine snorted, and together they subsided into a gentle silence, which was all the gentler for the harsh rememberings which had come before it.

Peregrine was used to the past feeling like a broken mirror inside him, like what had happened existed only in shards and splinters in his memory, glinting and ready to cut. But this was the first time he'd ever told the entire story aloud, with all its crimes and abuses, and in the order that they'd happened. It slotted all his memories into their proper places, and now that he'd fitted the pieces of the mirror together, he could finally see what it reflected. Still horror, still pain—but it no longer felt like it was slicing him with every step he took.

He was still angry, yes, but now the anger was inside him, and not the other way around.

After four years, it was like a gift and being unmade at the same time. He felt picked apart at the seams; he felt like an unstitched doll, or the pieces of a coat laid out on a tailor's table. He didn't know what to do with himself. The only thing he did know was that the unstitching was all to do with the man in his arms, the man who'd made him smile and laugh and—and *hope*—after these many years of living in his broken-mirror world.

He held his lover, who'd now drifted all the way off to sleep, tighter and tried not to think about what would happen if Alexander left him. If he couldn't keep this sweet, spoiled rake for his own.

THE RAIN DIED down a few hours later, and Alexander stirred as Peregrine carefully extracted himself from their embrace and went to ready the horse. The younger man was yawning in the doorway as Peregrine approached with his saddled mount.

"We should go back to the priory," said Peregrine.

Alexander blinked at him. His cheeks were flushed from sleep, his hair tousled, and his eyes pupil-blown from the dim interior of the long-house. "Am I still your prisoner?" he asked quietly.

"I don't know," Peregrine said, just as quietly. "Will you try to escape again if you are?"

"Yes," replied Alexander. "Will you try to catch me again?"

Peregrine looked at him. "Do you want me to?"

Alexander looked at the ground, his lashes long against his cheeks and his breathing deep as if he were confronting some uncomfortable truth. Finally, he answered. "Yes."

Peregrine's own breath stuttered and then filled his lungs, as if Alexander's answer were the only air he needed to breathe. Whatever was between them wouldn't end now, thank every god and spirit who'd ever been worshipped in these lonely hills.

With heady relief and an even headier greed coursing through his veins, Peregrine held out his hand to take Alexander's, and with hands linked, they began to walk down the lane, Peregrine leading the horse behind them.

10

Peregrine

THE TRIP BACK TO THE PRIORY DIDN'T FEEL NEARLY LONG ENOUGH TO
Peregrine. He supposed it was because once they returned, they'd have
to decide what happened next and whether he would release Alexander
for real. Whether he would still attempt to claim a ransom from the
duke . . . whether he would build new plans for killing Reginald and
fulfilling his revenge.

As they walked through the newly washed world, with its trees and
shrubs bleeding into the jewel tones of autumn—and as he held Alexander's hand tighter than was necessary, pulling him close, savoring his
rake's eternal Christmas scent—Peregrine wondered if his appetite for
revenge had dulled somewhat. If the blade which had once cut through
his grief and pain had finally blunted itself. Or had been blunted by the
mere existence of Lord Alexander Dartham.

Alexander, who was everything he should hate and somehow, everything he needed instead.

They arrived at the priory, and as they entered the stables, they saw
the horses belonging to the other thieves already munching hay inside
their stalls. They took care of the animal and then went inside the
church, where the gang was gathered with a hearty meal and a few open

bottles of wine. They were clearly a few cups in, most of them sitting with their boots propped on the table and roaring with laughter at each other's stories.

"I take it the robbery went well?" Peregrine asked Lyd as they approached the table.

"There was no robbery," Lyd said. "And where *were* you two?"

"I tried to escape," Alexander volunteered. "It was a very good escape, if you must know."

"Why was there no robbery?" Peregrine asked, ignoring Alexander. "Did the duchess take another road to Far Hope?"

"And why didn't you just tell me you were Judith's cousin!" Alexander burst out. "I would have begged you to help me escape!"

Lyd had made grown men piss themselves for taking such a tone with her, so Peregrine was genuinely shocked when she answered, almost kindly, "Because I didn't trust you to be any different than your brother or sister-in-law, Lord Alexander, and I wasn't interested in helping a Dartham with anything. But things have changed."

"They have?" Alexander asked, confused.

Lyd gave them both a look and sighed. "I think you deserve some privacy for this. Follow me."

They went into the sacristy. Lyd didn't bother closing the door, but her voice was quiet as she told them, "The duchess is dead."

Next to him, Alexander went still in a way that Peregrine had learned meant he was upset. Without thinking about it, Peregrine drew him close, wrapping an arm around his lover's slender waist.

Lyd's eyebrow raised at the familiar gesture, but she didn't remark on it. Their crowd was rather free with lovers, men and women alike, although it had to be said that Peregrine would be the first in their group to consort with someone he'd halted on the road.

"How did she die?" Alexander asked, his voice small.

"Whatever illness she had was worse than anyone thought, at least according to the innkeeper. She died there at the inn, and her body is being taken to Far Hope now."

Lyd's voice was level, factual, but her shoulders were loose and her eyes clear. Peregrine met her gaze, and she gave him a short nod. They had years of silent communication between them, and he knew what she was saying. She would never have her moment of justice with

Judith, but the relief of Judith never being able to hurt her again was enough.

"Her husband is ill now too," Lyd added. "The same malady, most likely."

Fear flashed through Peregrine, hot and bright. If Reginald was also sick, and they'd all been traveling together . . .

"Alexander, you haven't been—you're not feeling ill?"

"We didn't see each other before we set out, and then we took separate coaches after Basingstoke so she could be more comfortable," Alexander replied faintly "I don't feel sick in the least."

The relief that flooded through Peregrine then nearly knocked him over. If Alexander took ill—if Alexander *died*—no. He couldn't bear it. The very thought made Peregrine feel like he was being drawn and quartered.

Lyd had paused, as if considering how to phrase what she was going to say next. "His doctor is saying he might only have a few days left."

Alexander was like a statue in Peregrine's hold, unmoving, maybe unbreathing, and Peregrine pulled him closer, wrapped him in both arms. And instead of burrowing into him, instead of pouting or whining or rattling off a hundred different thoughts, Alexander was completely still. When Peregrine moved back and lifted Alexander's face to his, his chest hurt at the sight.

He'd seen more life in a child's doll than in Alexander's face right now.

Peregrine should have welcomed the news about the duke with pleasure, exultation even, but now he felt . . . nothing. No pleasure, no relief.

His enemy was dying, and the only thing he felt was worry for Alexander. All he wanted to do was make everything better, *fix* this or ease this for him somehow. His sweet rake hadn't wanted to be the duke or the leader of the Second Kingdom, and now the possibility was bearing down on him like a runaway coach—it would run him over whether he was ready or not.

And that Alexander's worst fear would come on the heels of his brother's death . . .

Peregrine felt something shift inside him, as if some final, vital seam had been ripped open. As if the Peregrine Hind of four hours ago really had been nothing more than those unstitched pieces on a table.

He would have to be made into something new. And whatever it would be, he wanted that something to put Alexander first, always.

"I'll take you to him," Peregrine said.

"What?" Alexander asked.

"*What?*" demanded Lyd.

Peregrine turned so he could see Alexander's face, cupping his jaw so he could look into Alexander's dark eyes. Even though there was a table of carousing thieves in the next room over, even though Lyd was watching them with a curious, perceptive stare, it almost felt like they were alone. "I didn't get to say goodbye to my mother or my siblings before they died, and I don't want that for you. You should be with him. You should be home."

"But you hate Reginald," Alexander whispered.

"I do. But what I feel for you," Peregrine whispered back, pressing his forehead against Alexander's, "is stronger than any hatred. It's fiercer than any revenge."

"Oh," Alexander said, his breath catching a little. "Oh."

"Yes," Peregrine said, affirming the unspoken questions in those *ohs*. Whatever the questions were, Peregrine knew the answer was *yes*.

"But I never wanted to see him before now," Alexander said after a moment. "What if he doesn't deserve a goodbye?"

"I know with certainty that he doesn't," replied Peregrine. "But you do."

Alexander met the highwayman's gaze with raw blue eyes. "I thought you'd be happier about this. About him dying."

"I would have been," Peregrine admitted. "Up until this very week. But telling you about what happened has made it easier to bear. And not only speaking of it, but speaking of it to you. You are so much to me, so much more than . . . " He trailed off, uncertain of how to frame what he meant. Alexander had shown him the way to something other than grief and anger; Alexander was a future filled with hope and possibility when before there'd only been an agony-laden past.

"I thought his death would kill my grief," Peregrine started again, still trying to explain. "I thought his suffering would ease my own. But suffering cannot be bought or sold like that, and neither can grief. I am so—"

Here he stopped, aware of Lyd watching them, of the other thieves nearby. Aware that the words he was about to utter were in no way adequate in the face of what he'd done.

"I'm so ashamed, Alexander. I was so ready to spill Dartham blood that it stopped mattering who carried it in their veins. I'm ashamed that I scared you, threatened you, and made you bargain for your life. And I'm ashamed that I ever once entertained the idea of killing you."

Peregrine took Alexander's hand and laced his fingers through his, bringing the younger man's knuckles to his mouth to kiss. "But more than being ashamed, I am sorry. Sorry past what my words can describe. I won't ask forgiveness for it. But I want you to know that you're safe from me."

"I think," Alexander said, his eyes searching Peregrine's face, "I must have known that, deep down. I think I knew I was safe from the beginning. After all," he said, the corner of his mouth lifting, "not many captors take the trouble to find silk for their captive's wrists instead of rope."

Peregrine smiled back. "If I'd known how much you would enjoy the silk, I would have bound your entire body in it."

Despite everything, Alexander's pupils dilated with interest. "There will be time," he murmured.

Peregrine didn't think so, but he didn't say that out loud. Getting Alexander to Far Hope was the main thing, and if he cast any doubt on their being together in the future, Alexander might react like . . . well, like Alexander.

Perhaps not. Perhaps Alexander would understand. Perhaps he'd even be relieved that Peregrine saw the future so sensibly. But speed was of the essence, and Peregrine couldn't risk this conversation now. It would have to happen later, if it ever did.

"I'll ready a fresh horse," Peregrine said. "Gather what you need and then meet me outside."

THE SUN WAS SINKING as they rode, but at least the wind was mild and the skies newly free of clouds. Alexander chattered the entire way about how much the Second Kingdom would love Peregrine, even though he'd openly robbed a fair number of them by now, and about where Peregrine could sleep, and about how Alexander would make sure Peregrine didn't have to see the duke while he was at Far Hope.

Peregrine recognized the chatter as Alexander's way of deflecting worry about his brother—and likely also the possibility of becoming the duke—and let him continue. It seemed to make him feel better, and if he had the notion that Peregrine would be staying with him at Far Hope, then Peregrine still didn't have the heart to disabuse him of it. Especially after hearing Alexander's nervous prattle, after observing his rigid but trembling form as they rode.

Alexander would find out soon enough when they got there, and in the future, he would thank Peregrine for his levelheadedness. After all, it was absurdity to think that the duke could openly parade a male lover around London, and even more absurdity when the lover in question was a notorious criminal.

And even if the Second Kingdom wouldn't mind, Alexander would be a duke. He'd have a responsibility to marry and sire heirs, and Peregrine didn't think he could survive watching Alexander marry someone else. He didn't want to be a mistress, tucked away somewhere, contributing to yet another unhappy aristocratic marriage. It sounded like a way for three people to be miserable—but if he left, he could lower that number to one.

Himself.

Highwaymen didn't get happy endings. They didn't die old and gray in a lover's arms. They died young and they died alone.

But it was no use trying to explain this to Alexander. He wouldn't accept that some things were out of even a rake's reach.

Or a duke's.

It was fully dark by the time they reached the narrow vale of the Hope Valley and passed through the crooked standing stones at its entrance. A shallow river wound beside the road as they rode through the small village, and then, after a mile or so, the stern edifice of Far Hope revealed itself, its many windows glowing against the dark.

Somehow, that didn't make it seem any more welcoming to Peregrine. It rather reminded him of lights along a rampart or behind a defensive ditch, like Far Hope was a fortress enduring on from a grimmer time. Hardly where he would have expected a hidden society of hedonism and pleasure—but then again, perhaps that was why the

Second Kingdom was there. Far Hope did feel like a castle of its own remote kingdom, set in a land even emperors and kings had struggled to properly conquer.

"It used to be an abbey," Alexander said, talking in that quick, overly bright way. "A Saxon one, and then a Norman one, which was converted and partially swallowed up by the medieval manor house. That's why it's so irregular—they say the tower there was originally a bell tower for the abbey church, but that may just be a story. I'll take you up there, though, so you can see the views in daylight, because it's fantastic, a vista like nothing else."

Peregrine made noises of acknowledgment as they rode through the open gate to the house. He came to a stop in front of the large wooden door at the front and then he held the reins for Alexander's horse as Alexander dismounted.

His former captive looked up at him. With the light coming from the manor house, half his face was cast in gold and the other in pure shadow.

"You're not getting off with me?" Alexander asked. "Oh," he went on, still with that brittle, fast tone, "of course, you're going to go to the stables first. I can come with you if you'd like. Or wait here, and then we can go in together."

"Go see your brother," Peregrine said, as gently as a man like him was capable. "He'll be grateful to see you alive and well and free."

Alexander made a face. "If that's true, it'll only be because he will savor not paying a ransom, even on his deathbed."

"Perhaps. But there's only one way to know."

Alexander hesitated. "You are coming too, right? You don't have to see him, but you can stay here, and . . . " He stopped. Maybe he was realizing, as Peregrine already had, that in sickness, death, funeral arrangements, and becoming a peer, there wouldn't be much room for a kept lover. Especially one that was officially wanted for crimes punishable by death.

"I think we both know the answer to that, Alexander," Peregrine said.

In the gold-hued light, Peregrine could see the quiver in Alexander's beautiful mouth.

He knew exactly how Alexander felt right now because Peregrine felt the same. Like his heart was being torn out.

"Stay well," Peregrine said quietly. "You aren't allowed to take ill, do you understand? Say your goodbyes at a distance and listen to everything the physician tells you."

"If I take ill, will you come here right away?" the rake said, mouth continuing to tremble, but with petulance now as well as hurt.

Peregrine gave him his sternest look. "*Alexander.*"

Alexander swallowed, stepping back in time for Peregrine to see a tear glittering its way down his high-boned cheek. It took everything Peregrine had not to haul the rake back in his arms where he belonged, but somehow, he managed. Somehow, he kept his tears to himself. Even though he'd just surrendered everything he'd held on to for the last four years.

He'd given up revenge. He'd given up Alexander.

What did he have left now?

11

Sandy

"WILL YOU NOT AT LEAST KISS ME GOODBYE THEN?" SANDY ASKED, HIS voice thick and his eyes burning. He was panicked and he was numb; he was furious and he was frozen with hurt.

He was everything and nothing all at once, and it was this horrible highwayman's fault.

"You will cheat and pull me off my horse if I lean down to kiss you," said Peregrine with a fond smile.

"Of course I will," Sandy managed to huff. His throat ached so much he couldn't stand it. "You can't mean to leave me here, can you? You can't mean to ride off in the dark and not stay?"

"Think of it as your escape," Peregrine told him. His voice was gentle. "You've escaped me now. You're free."

"Goddammit, Peregrine, you cannot just *leave* me like this!" Sandy said furiously, another tear tracking down his cheek. He realized, distantly, that it was the first time he'd cried all week. Even being kidnapped, threatened with death, and used as a pawn against his brother hadn't made him cry. But this—Peregrine just *leaving* him here when he needed him most—

When Peregrine didn't answer, Sandy asked desperately, "But I will see you again, right? Soon? When everything is settled?"

He took a step toward Peregrine's horse right as a shadow passed behind a nearby window. They'd been heard, and soon someone would be at the door to investigate. Peregrine sighed as Sandy reached out to put a hand on the highwayman's thigh. It was firm and unyielding, like the man it belonged to. Sandy wished he had the strength to drag Peregrine from his horse. He wished he were strong enough to abduct Peregrine as Peregrine had abducted him.

It couldn't be that he'd spent years chasing the hope of something solid and real, only to find it and then lose it within a matter of days. It made no sense, practically or cosmically. Sandy was Lord Alexander Dartham, and he could do almost anything he wanted. And if the worst happened and he was made the duke, the *only* consolation to such a horror would be the power to have the lover he wanted in his bed.

No, he wouldn't stand for this. He couldn't. If he didn't have this highwayman with him, then he wouldn't survive whatever came next, and he wouldn't want to, and—

Peregrine's hand came over his. It was cold, since he'd ridden without gloves, but it was so big and so strong. It completely covered Sandy's hand and pinned it hard to the warm thigh underneath.

"Yes, Alexander." Peregrine's voice was low and rough, but steady as stone. "You'll see me again once everything is settled."

Sandy looked up into the thief's eyes, which glittered with the light from Far Hope. "You swear?" Sandy whispered.

Peregrine gave Sandy's hand a hard, long squeeze. "I swear. Now go, fast. Your brother needs you."

Sandy drank him in with one last glance and then left with an abrupt motion, tearing himself away with all the willpower he had. He had to go to his brother; he had to face whatever fate awaited him.

All he could do was hope that this was not the last he'd seen of Peregrine Hind.

12

Sandy

Six Months Later

ALEXANDER DARTHAM, THE NEW DUKE OF JARRELL, WAS ABSOLUTELY fucking miserable.

As if it wasn't bad enough on its own to learn how to run the ducal estate with all its dealings and enterprises, Sandy also had to confront the sheer scale of Reginald's sins. Peregrine's hamlet hadn't been the only village gutted by Reginald's enclosures, and searching for the villagers and cottagers who'd migrated away so Sandy could offer some kind of restitution was long, difficult work. Some had gone to towns where they had relations; some had tried to eke out a new living elsewhere in the countryside. Some had gone all the way to London, and one family had even emigrated to America. But with the help of the Foscourts, he managed to find a way. Sandy liked to think that he would have tried to ameliorate the wounds Reginald had left behind even if he'd never met Peregrine Hind, but he couldn't deny that it was Peregrine's face he saw in his thoughts when he directed his lawyers to issue payments, Peregrine's voice he heard in his mind when he read the letters of thanks some of villagers sent in return.

And while Sandy didn't miss Reginald and Judith in the usual ways of grief, he had to accept that their deaths still affected him—perhaps more so for the complicated relationships he'd had with them before they died. Figuring out how to mourn while figuring out how to duke was already unpleasant. Added to his new responsibilities with the Second Kingdom and the continual ache in his chest from Peregrine's absence, it was torment.

And after months had passed and his highwayman still hadn't returned, Sandy didn't even bother trying the things that he used to do in order numb his unhappiness. There was no amount of bed-play or gambling or wine that would erase the truth.

Peregrine Hind, the first person Sandy had ever fallen in love with, had lied. He wasn't coming back.

Sandy was alone, and there was a beautiful irony to that.

He had placed his bloody, trusting heart in Peregrine's hands the night the highwayman had ridden away from him, having no idea that the thief would trample it underneath his steed's hooves the minute he turned and left. Sandy had hoped and longed and *cared* like he never had before, and it was thrown back in his face every day that Peregrine didn't come back.

He was haunted and bereft, and so, in a perverse way, Peregrine had his revenge against the Dartham family at long last.

Because the Duke of Jarrell was as miserable as a living person could be.

ONE OF THE first things he'd done as the duke was return Lyd's family property to her, which had been a fucking *headache*, since thieves were not generally reachable by mail or courier. He'd had to personally loiter on the road to Exeter for several nights in a row, having his driver roll an unmarked but expensive carriage back and forth for hours until he'd finally baited Lyd out of hiding. The first thing he'd done when he'd been hauled out of his carriage by Ned was to search for Peregrine's grim face and broad shoulders. When he couldn't find his highwayman among the band, his shoulders had slumped and his heart had slowly slid into his stomach, where it sat there like a dead, disappointed weight.

"Here," Sandy had said, handing Lyd a sheaf of paper when she'd grumpily lowered her pistol after realizing who she was aiming it at. "The property is yours again. Free and clear. Along with the ransom my brother would have paid you."

She'd stared at him, not taking the papers. "Why?"

Sandy had flapped the papers at her. "Because it should have been yours to begin with. And I'm trying to be better than Reginald. And— and—" He made a face, screwing up the courage to say what he needed to say. "And because I'm sorry that I didn't do more to help you when I could have. I could have searched for you after I found out what happened, or tried to get your family land back to you earlier, or at least made better sure that Reginald and Judith would stop searching for you. And I didn't. I'm sorry."

He looked up to see Lyd's mouth twisting to the side—but in thought, not in disgust.

Finally, with a short nod, she took the papers from him. "Very well, then."

"All the rights to the water and the mill have been restored to you," Sandy said. "With that and your share of the ransom, you could live very comfortably without taking to the road ever again."

"Hmm."

Sandy asked, with all the casual charm he could muster, "So, are you still going to rob people?"

Lyd cocked a grin, tossing a look over her shoulder to the other thieves, who were grinning back at her like Sandy had just told an incredible joke. "Maybe," she said with mock-coyness.

"Will you at least stop robbing my guests?"

"Is that a condition of this?" Lyd asked, holding up the papers.

"No," Sandy said honestly. "But it never hurts to ask." He gave her his biggest smile, the one that usually got him whatever he wanted.

She didn't look impressed, but she did say, "I'll think on it."

"You really still prefer this life?" Sandy asked, gesturing to the cold night around them. "Waiting in the cold and in the dark? Robbing people? Fleeing from them?"

Lyd had grinned again. "People flee from *me*, Sandy. Should I go back to embroidery by the window? Sitting quietly in church and thinking of what repairs the dairy will need next year? After I've gone wherever I've liked, done whatever I've liked, and chosen who shares my bed and when? Do you really think I would want to go back to a quiet gentry life after that?"

"Well, when you put it that way," Sandy said. "But there's always the Second Kingdom. I could invite you, you know."

Her smile turned into a baring of teeth. "I don't want your kingdom of rich hypocrites, Sandy."

"I'm trying to make the Kingdom better," Sandy said, a little wearily.

"Is it working?"

Sandy could only be honest. "I don't know," he'd said. "But I have to try, don't I?"

Who else would, if he didn't? He was the duke, and the Kingdom was his. It was his duty to end the petty infighting and favoritism that Reginald had fostered, and he hoped that things were already changing. He only wished he didn't have to do it alone. He had Juliana and her family as staunch allies, and a few other friends in the Kingdom, but he wanted someone at his side, nearby always, holding him at night while he worked through the never-ending list of problems that came with the Kingdom.

He wanted Peregrine.

He finally asked Lyd what he'd been dying to from the moment they'd stopped his carriage. "Is Peregrine with you?"

Lyd gave Sandy a pitying look.

"Please," Sandy said quietly, not above begging, not above demanding they take him captive again just so they could bring him back to Peregrine. "Please, Lydia."

"He isn't with us, Sandy," Lyd said. "I'm sorry."

"No—" he started as she moved back toward the others and their horses. "Lyd, wait—"

But it was too late. They were on their horses and riding away, leaving Sandy only with his driver in the dark. He'd climbed numbly back in the carriage, signaled for the return to Far Hope, and tried not to cry the entire way back. He'd believed Lyd when she said that Peregrine wasn't with them, but then where was he?

Had he retired? Rusticated? Left the country altogether?

God. Was that really so preferable to a life with Sandy?

"SO YOU'RE NOT PLANNING on marrying? At all?"

Sandy and Juliana Durrington née Foscourt, the daughter of the Earl of Kellow and Sandy's lifelong friend, were walking through the ballroom with stars on the ceiling after a heavy lunch. She'd come to stay for the latest Second Kingdom revel—only the third that Sandy had presided over in the last half year—and he'd shamelessly made her plan the entire thing. It was enough to adjudicate the membership disputes and manage the tangle of internecine politics Reginald had left behind. He couldn't be bothered to plan the menus for the orgies too.

Luckily for him, Juliana lived for such things, and even luckier for him, she was more than happy to seed little rumors on his behalf here and there. Mainly that his current abstention from the pleasures of the Kingdom was due to the loss of his beloved brother and sister-in-law, and for no other more scandalous reason.

Like that he was pining for a lover who didn't want him back—and who was also currently wanted by the Crown.

It was raining buckets and buckets outside, making a dull roar everywhere in the manor house, a roar which echoed the noise inside Sandy's head these days.

He took a minute to answer Juliana's question. "I have a passel of first cousins already, and all of them are breeding like rabbits. There are plenty of heirs with the Dartham name."

Juliana looked over at him. "Are you sure, though?" she asked softly. "A marriage doesn't have to be about heirs alone. A wife could help shoulder the burden of the dukedom and the Second Kingdom. She could make life easier for you—and be a friend and companion."

Sandy cut her a look. "Are you volunteering, Juliana?"

She let out a laugh. "No, no, I'm quite enjoying my new life as a widow. But it's something to consider. You've bedded women before, after all, and you might also find someone who is happy to seek their pleasure outside your bed, if you'd rather not have a sexual relationship."

"I've bedded *everyone* before," Sandy said impatiently. "But that doesn't mean I'm willing to marry someone so I can have help answering letters."

Juliana seemed to think about that, the silk of her mantua hissing on the ballroom floor and mingling with the sound of the rain as they walked. "It's about him, isn't it?" she asked. "The highwayman?"

Sandy had told Juliana everything once the dust had settled after Reginald and Judith's deaths, and so she knew exactly how much it had gutted Sandy when Peregrine had ridden off into the night.

How much more it had gutted him when Peregrine never came back.

"I'm a goddamn fool," Sandy said bitterly. "I'm here with a broken heart, pathetic and moping, and he's probably off kidnapping some other future duke and tying him to a bed."

"Didn't you tell me that he'd been living like a monk before you?" Juliana asked. "And at any rate, he's not kidnapping anyone, *or* even robbing travelers anymore. He's disappeared."

"He's *what*?" asked Sandy.

"I'm shocked you haven't heard. I thought you'd searched for him?"

"I went to the priory two months or so after Reginald died, but it had been abandoned. I'd thought they must have moved their hideout because of me . . . I hadn't realized they'd stopped altogether."

Maybe Lyd had listened to his advice after he'd given her the rights to her property back. Maybe she'd settled down with her house and her money and taken up a nice, quiet hobby that didn't involve pistols.

"*Peregrine Hind* hasn't been seen on the road," Juliana said. "But his former band has. Led by a woman, they say."

Ah. Well, that was Lyd for you.

"Sandy," Juliana said in the careful voice of a friend about to point out the obvious. "Have you given any thought as to why he'd stay away?"

"Of course I have," snapped Sandy. "Because I'm a Dartham, and I'm everything he hates and because I complained too much about the wine when I was his captive."

Juliana stopped walking, turning to face Sandy with a look that was both impatient and pitying. "No, you fopdoodle. He's staying away because he thinks there's no place in your life for him."

Sandy nearly sputtered. "That's ridiculous. I told him all about the Second Kingdom. He should know that in our world—"

Juliana waved a hand. "You don't live your entire life in the Second Kingdom, Sandy. He would know that you'd be expected to marry and that you'd have duties in London to fulfill. And he would know even inside the Second Kingdom that there'd be plenty of people whom he'd robbed and who wouldn't exactly be happy to see him at your right hand. If I were him, I would assume that staying in your life would not only compromise you as the duke, but as the leader of Second Kingdom as well, and that he could love you best by giving you the very thing you wanted most when you were his captive: freedom from him."

Alexander frowned. "But then why not just *say* all that to me? I could have told him immediately how wrong he was!"

"Is he wrong?" Juliana asked quietly. "Would it not make your life harder and his less safe to have him at your side?"

Alexander hated that she was right, but he couldn't deny it. "A wanted criminal does have some inconveniences as a lover," he finally admitted. "But I—"

He stopped, clarity coming like the rain outside, cold and drenching.

"I am a duke now," he said, realizing slowly. "I could fix this."

"You could," Juliana agreed.

"A pardon," said Alexander, getting excited. "James Clavell was issued one, wasn't he? And so many others too! If Peregrine's issued a pardon, then even if a disgruntled member of the Second Kingdom wanted to turn him in, it wouldn't matter."

He paced once and then stopped. "But if I do this, how will I find him to tell him?"

Juliana shrugged. "Think like a highwayman. Where would a highwayman go to hide?"

13

Peregrine

A FULL MOON HUNG OVER THE MOORS AS PEREGRINE WALKED ALONG THE road. He'd gone up to Lyd's new hideout near her old family home to see how the band was getting on, but they'd been out riding, it seemed, because their new lair was empty. Strange, because it had been Lyd herself to invite him to visit, but Peregrine was made of time now, so what was one wasted day? It wasn't as if he had anything to occupy him other than scratching out a garden in the tiny plots that had been left adjacent to the houses in his village when the fields had been enclosed. It hadn't been enough for the hamlet or even for a family, but for a single person who had the money to buy his own grain rather than grow it, it was serviceable.

He couldn't live like this forever, he knew. Rattling around like a ghost in his childhood home, eating beets and drinking wine while he brooded at the fire. But he also didn't know what else to do. His career as a thief had been so bundled up in the idea of revenge that once he let the revenge go, the idea of stealing no longer held much appeal. He had more than enough to live on, and he'd given so much away to those who needed it most that it no longer felt necessary or interesting to punish the fine people in their fine coaches.

Maybe he was tired.

Or maybe some fights weren't meant to be fought for entire lifetimes. One could only pass their fingers through a flame so many times before they got burned.

Truthfully, though, he knew why he stayed. Why he brooded alone with ghosts instead of finding a new place to live or seeking out some other occupation. The idea of leaving Far Hope's demesne hurt more than he could describe. At least here, he could walk to Alexander's house and watch it from the hills surrounding the valley. At least here, he could sometimes go to the now-empty priory and wander through its abandoned spaces, remembering how it felt that week to have Alexander as his very own.

Peregrine was thinking about all this as he walked through a little valley choked with trees, and that's when he heard a suspicious rustling.

And then a *shh*, and then a horse sprang out in front of him.

"Stand and deliver!" a voice cried out, loud enough to send an owl flapping away in irritation. Peregrine's heart stopped and then skidded back into action with several fast, hungry beats. But not from fear.

He knew that voice. He knew that voice from every dream he'd dreamed in the last six months.

And then the voice said, "Did I say that right? Is that how it goes?"

Lyd—of all fucking people—and Ned and the others stepped out of the shadows to the mounted figure.

"You could have been louder," Lyd said dryly, and then turned to him. "Hello, Peregrine. This is a robbery."

"I thought it was an abduction," said Ned, and Lyd put her palm to her forehead.

"That's right," she said, "this is an abduction. You're being abducted right now."

Peregrine was ignoring them, already walking up to the horse where the mounted rider sat. The rider's hair tumbled over his shoulder in gleaming waves, and his full lips were curled into a secretive little smile.

Just looking at him made Peregrine's chest ache with longing.

"Are you my kidnapper?" asked Peregrine, his heart tumbling all over itself inside his chest, like a newborn foal that couldn't find its legs. He'd tried to stay away from Alexander, tried to do the right thing after so many years of doing the wrong thing, but he couldn't deny that he'd hoped—yearned—for something like this. A moment when he could see Alexander's sparkling eyes again.

"I am your kidnapper," agreed Alexander with great dignity. "I'm here to whisk you away."

Peregrine was very close to Alexander now. He put a possessive hand on the man's thigh, squeezing gently. The feeling of Alexander's warm, lithe muscles under his grip made blood surge to his cock.

"How did you find me?" Peregrine asked.

"Unfortunately, Sandy and I are friends now," Lyd said with a heavy sigh. "And then this week, he popped around my hideout with some sad story about missing you and wanting to see you again."

Peregrine looked to Alexander. "You missed me."

"Yes, you awful, criminal fool, I missed you," replied Alexander impatiently. "I missed you so much that I got a pardon for you from the Crown so that you can come live with me without worrying that someone will inform the local magistrate about a highwayman in my bed."

Peregrine's heart thudded. "You did?"

"I did." Alexander's gaze softened. "You will be safe with me, Peregrine. I swear it."

Peregrine forced himself to think rationally, to think unselfishly. He'd had plenty of time to mull over his decisions, after all, and as much as they hurt—and they really fucking hurt—he still couldn't see that he'd chosen wrongly.

"You'll need to marry," he said softly, his hand lingering possessively on Alexander's thigh. "Have children. I know some married couples are willing to—"

"Ugh, *stop*," Alexander huffed. "I'm not getting married."

"But the dukedom—"

"There are plenty of little ones in line, don't worry about the dukedom and heirs," Alexander said. He reached out to touch Peregrine's jaw with leather-gloved fingertips. "Can't you see, Peregrine Hind?" he whispered. "I only want you. Let me kidnap you, and I swear that I'll make the rest of your life worth it."

"The rest of my life?" Peregrine asked. There was a buzz in his lips, on his tongue, inside his veins.

It felt like hope.

"That's what people do with the ones they love, right?" asked Alexander. "They grow old with them?"

The ones they love.

Yes, somehow, despite everything, those words felt right. As right as a strong horse underneath him, as right as a bright moon on a clear night. As good having a rake tied to his bed.

"If that's the case," Peregrine said, the hope swallowing what was left of his doubts and worries, "then you must know that I want to grow old with you too."

Alexander gave him a big grin—one of those spoiled but bewitching ones Peregrine loved so much—and gestured to an empty cart waiting farther down the road. "Then you must allow to me to get on with my abduction," he said, and Peregrine smiled.

He looked to Lyd, who gave him a mock-salute back. "Thank you for assisting in my kidnapping," he told her as Alexander dismounted with an easy grace and took Peregrine's hand.

"Wouldn't have missed it for all the gold in the kingdom," she said, and then, with a whistle, she and the band moved back toward the trees, where they'd presumably tethered their horses. They waved goodbye, and Peregrine and his captor went to the cart, hitched the horse to the front, and climbed inside.

Alexander at first sat so that he and Peregrine were side by side, but Peregrine had no patience for this, instead pulling Alexander onto his lap and wrapping his arms firmly around Alexander's waist.

Giving a quiet cluck, Alexander took the reins and urged the horse forward to start off for Far Hope.

"I'm nervous your friends in the Second Kingdom won't like me," Peregrine said, his hands beginning to wander all over Alexander's body. It had been so long, so painfully long, and Peregrine's body responded ferociously to the supple duke pressed against him. He also couldn't drag in enough of Alexander's spicy, citrus scent, burying his face in Alexander's hair and breathing it in over and over again.

"You are pardoned now, and you are mine, so they can fuck right off," Alexander said pleasantly. "Besides, they'll eventually see it as a grand story. Anything rare or unusual is like a shiny object to them, I promise you."

"Mm," Peregrine said. He was relieved to hear it, although he knew it might take time for Alexander's world to accept him. Luckily, time was something he was not short on.

"And what role will I be expected to play in this kingdom?" Peregrine asked, still nosing all that soft, wonderful hair. "I have to warn you that I don't want to be with anyone else."

"There's no rule in the kingdom about having to fuck every person you meet." Alexander laughed. "You can be as devoted to me as you like."

"And you?" Peregrine asked, suddenly confronted with the reality that he might have to share his rake. "Will you be . . . partaking in your kingdom?"

Alexander turned, seeming amused. "Why, Peregrine, is that possessiveness I hear in your voice?"

Peregrine growled. Yes, dammit, he was possessive. But he would also give Alexander the world and everything in it, and if Alexander wanted to share his body with people other than Peregrine, then Peregrine would endure—so long it was him Alexander came back to at the end of the night.

Alexander gave Peregrine a soft kiss, then turned and settled against Peregrine's chest. "No," the rake said after a minute, "I don't think I'll be partaking anymore. I may change my mind, of course, I'm flighty like that, but right now all I want is this grim thief I've fallen in love with."

"Truly?"

"I've had the affairs and the games and the pleasures, Peregrine; I've drank fully from every cup I ever found, either at the Kingdom or at court. I want something different now. You."

"I don't want to make you a captive again," Peregrine said. "Please know that. So if you change your mind . . . "

"You'll be the first to know," Alexander promised. "In the meantime, I plan on quenching my insatiate lusts with a certain former solider."

Peregrine growled again, this time in satisfaction, pulling Alexander closer and dropping his hands to Alexander's lap.

"Now, about your captivity," Alexander said, giving a long shudder as Peregrine's fingers began picking open the buttons of his breeches, brushing over the swell of Alexander's erection as they did. "I have some rather—oh, that feels good—"

Peregrine had found Alexander's prick and drawn it out of his clothes, and while the cart pulled them up the road, Peregrine slowly shuttled his grip up and down the stiff flesh. "You were saying?" he murmured into the duke's ear.

"I was saying that I have some rather unusual requests," Alexander said breathlessly, wriggling on Peregrine's lap as Peregrine stroked Alexander's rigidity. It was hot velvet against his palm.

"And what are those?"

"Well, I may b-be the captor this time, but I think you should tie me up. A lot."

Peregrine laughed a little. "I think we can manage that. Anything else?"

"Yes. I know you're no longer filling your nights with crimes on the road. But I won't mind in the least if you're fill your nights being a criminal with *me*."

"And what does a criminal do with you?" Peregrine murmured, loving the feel of Alexander shivering against his chest, the way he rocked against Peregrine's ferocious cockstand.

"Well, I mentioned the tying up," Alexander said, gasping a little. "You could tease me mercilessly. You could deny me until I'm begging for it. You could use me like you did in the farmhouse."

Peregrine's cock jerked against the duke, ready to get started on all those things, but it was his heart which swelled and throbbed the most as he buried his face in Alexander's neck again and inhaled the Christmas scent of his rake-turned-duke-turned-captor. He didn't deserve this—not after the war, not after stalking the roads and raining hellfire upon the travelers he'd found. Not after what he did to Sandy when they first met. But perhaps he could earn it. Earn it like he'd earned peace from his grief over the last six months, earn it like he'd earned the tender, emerald shoots in his new garden behind his family farmhouse. With care and love.

And he knew exactly who he'd care for first.

"In that case, Your Grace," Peregrine said, coaxing Alexander to into a jerking, quivering spend all over his fist, "I shall save all my crimes for you."

"Truly?"

"Every last one."

"Thank God."

And with kisses to his duke's neck, Peregrine took the reins and guided them over the purple moors to Far Hope, and to home.

The end.

Want more dangerous historical romance from Sierra Simone?

Check out *The Awakening of Ivy Leavold*—scorching hot guardian/ward romance with plenty of gothic and forbidden vibes— for completely free!

ALSO BY SIERRA SIMONE

The Priest Series:

Priest

Midnight Mass: A Priest Novella

Sinner

Saint

Thornchapel:

A Lesson in Thorns

Feast of Sparks

Harvest of Sighs

Door of Bruises

Misadventures:

Misadventures with a Professor

Misadventures of a Curvy Girl

Misadventures in Blue

The New Camelot Trilogy:

American Queen

American Prince

American King

The Moon (Merlin's Novella)

American Squire (A Thornchapel and New Camelot Crossover)

Co-Written with Laurelin Paige

Porn Star

Hot Cop

The Markham Hall Series:

The Awakening of Ivy Leavold
The Education of Ivy Leavold
The Punishment of Ivy Leavold

The London Lovers:
The Seduction of Molly O'Flaherty
The Wedding of Molly O'Flaherty

ABOUT THE AUTHOR

Sierra Simone is a USA Today bestselling former librarian who spent too much time reading romance novels at the information desk. She lives with her husband and family in Kansas City.

Sign up for her newsletter to be notified of releases, books going on sale, events, and other news!

www.thesierrasimone.com
thesierrasimone@gmail.com

TWO RAKES FOR MRS. SPARKWELL

EVA LEIGH

1

THIS WAS SURELY HOW HELL SOUNDED.

Vivian Sparkwell nervously crossed the threshold into the gambling den and stumbled backward from the oppressive heat and noise that met her. For a full year, she'd been surrounded by silence, enclosed in a protective cocoon of gentle voices confined to the same rooms. The largest demand to her attention had been following the progress of a mote of dust falling to the floor in leisurely circles.

Even in the past month since she'd left mourning, she'd only dined with no more than four people at a given time, and everyone had comported themselves with genteel decorum. No raised voices, no harsh, braying laughter, and no foul language.

"Out of the way," someone said in a deep, uncompromising voice.

She pressed herself against the wall as a very large blond man marched past her, holding a florid, wriggling gentleman by the nape of his neck. In his efforts to break free, the struggling man's wig tilted over his eyes. He lashed out with flailing fists, but was held far enough away that none of his blows struck.

"'Tis ungentlemanly," the captive yelled, "to be treated in such an appalling fashion."

"'Tis ungentlemanly to try to steal from the house," the big man said calmly, his words lightly musical with a Welsh accent.

"Did no such thing!"

"Management says otherwise. Out you go."

Vivian stared as the big fair-haired man carried the combative gentleman toward the door as easily as if his prisoner weighed merely a stone. As a footman held the door open, the Welshman bodily threw the other man out onto the street. Before the accused cheater even hit the pavement, the door closed and the blond man strode past her as calmly as if he'd just gone out to the garden to pick daffodils.

As he walked, he glanced in her direction, and she quickly averted her gaze. Yet not before she noticed the bright azure of his eyes, and the sharp awareness within them. Then he was gone and it was as though nothing had happened.

Except Vivian had seen it. Was it a sign of what was to come? Would the next few minutes be as terrifying?

Perhaps she ought to turn around. Go home, back to her still and silent rooms, take off this immodest gown, and pretend she'd never come to this infernal place.

She dragged in an uneven breath, though the air was hot and thick in her lungs, and stepped farther into the gaming hell. Never in the whole of her twenty-nine years had she ever done anything this daring, this scandalous, but that was precisely the point. She *had* to be daring and scandalous if she was to have any control over the rest of her life.

The entryway immediately opened up into a large room paneled with dark wood. Smoke clung to the ceiling like a ghost, and the hazy atmosphere swirled around dozens of figures gathered around tables playing games of chance such as hazard and faro. Dice rattled, sounding too much like bones and chattering teeth, but that noise was dim beneath hard, raucous voices. A few women dotted the throng, though largely the crowd was comprised of men. Men with red faces, men sweating in their long waistcoats and full-skirted frock coats, men with wig powder and sweat on their hairlines, men yelling and laughing in ways that Vivian had never heard before.

Despite the heat, a chill worked its way through her body. She suppressed a shiver as she made herself take a step and then another and another, deeper into the gaming hell.

She surveyed the crowd. To her astonishment, she knew a handful of people, including two gentlemen who had been frequent guests at her dining table when William had been alive. If the men recognized her, they gave no sign. In fact, their gazes moved right past her—which was hardly a surprise. This was not the sort of establishment one might find the respectable, unassuming Mrs. Sparkwell.

"Not going to catch many toms in that dowdy fur, my love," a woman said as she swayed close. She wore a bright yellow satin gown, the neckline cut so low that the very top edges of her nipples were visible.

The woman fingered the lace of Vivian's bodice. "This needs to be two inches lower to show your little bubbies," she said critically. "And for God's sake, leave off this grim color."

"'Tis red..." Vivian protested, her voice faint.

The woman snorted. "'Tis the shade of muddy wine, and no one wants to drink that. You must be new to the trade."

"Oh, I, no—" No one had ever mistaken Vivian for a courtesan before.

"No shame, my love." The woman patted Vivian's cheek. "We've all got to earn our coin however we can. With that wholesome face of yours, your arse will get well familiar with the feel of a mattress. Get you to Madame Lisette's in Piccadilly, and she'll set you up with a good gown, mayhap in a shade of soft blue with lots of fluffy white lace so you look even more of an innocent. Aye, that'll set you up nice. Tell Lisette that Buttercup sent you."

"Th-thank you," Vivian stammered. It was one thing to see a few expensive courtesans at the theater, but it was a far different experience to watch these women boldly drape themselves on the gamesters and talk and laugh in voices just as loud as their male companions. And to get *advice* from one.

"Back to it," Buttercup said after grabbing a goblet of wine and downing it in one gulp. "Those cocks aren't going to fuck themselves."

After patting Vivian's cheek one more time, Buttercup sauntered toward a tall, gaunt-faced gentleman and wound her arms around him. The man chuckled as Buttercup's fingers toyed with the buttons of his waistcoat and sometimes dipped between them to stroke his chest and stomach.

Tonight was the first time she'd ever been mistaken for a whore. Yet perhaps it wouldn't be the last time. Not if her plan succeeded.

She couldn't lose sight of her objective, no matter how many shocking distractions presented themselves. Hopefully, the man she sought was here. Through her maid's network of gossip, she'd learned that Rushton Cantley appeared at this gaming hell thrice weekly, and tonight was supposed to be one of those nights.

Where *was* the man? She ought to have asked Buttercup, but being taken for a prostitute had a way of mixing up one's thoughts.

A burst of laughter rose up above the din, and she turned toward it. A group of five bucks and three women gathered around one man, all of them smiling adoringly at him—which was no wonder, given his looks.

She hadn't known men could be beautiful. Yet this man was. He eschewed a wig, and wore his ink-dark hair in a simple queue, tied with a black satin ribbon that matched the hue of his eyes. The scar at the corner of his lush mouth only accentuated his masculinity, emphasized by the stubble that shaded his jaw. Other men were taller, yet his dark indigo frock coat and white silk waistcoat molded to his long, lean form. White satin breeches clung to his taut thighs, and were tucked into tall, shining black boots that rose over his knee.

Whoever he was, this man was the most attractive person Vivian had ever beheld. The urge to turn and run rose up her legs and coiled in her belly.

"A song, Cantley," one of the man's admirers demanded jovially. "Let us hear that dulcet voice of yours."

Vivian's heart pitched into her stomach.

"If I sang," Rushton Cantley answered, his voice low and velvet, "then you'd have precisely what you wanted. I shall be bereft when you desert me entirely afterward."

"We'd never abandon you," someone else asserted.

"All the same," Rushton Cantley replied with a flash of white teeth, "I shall save my songs for those I wish to bless. Come, friends, the game play is high and so is my good fortune."

He turned to the hazard table and cast the dice. The crowd cheered —he must have won, which was further evident when two women draped themselves on him.

Vivian swallowed around the dry lump in her throat. What was the best way to approach him? On the way here tonight, she'd rehearsed many versions of her speech, but as she walked toward him now, those words scattered like vermin fleeing a burning building.

She stared at the expanse of his back as she drew closer. For all his slimness of build, he possessed intimidatingly wide shoulders. How did he come by such shoulders? Did he take exercise like other gentlemen of his station? Perhaps he fenced, or visited a pugilism academy, or—

"What are you gaping at, rabbit?" one of the women festooning him snapped. "Can't you see this one's been claimed?"

"Stand down, Cora." Rushton Cantley barely spared Vivian a glance as he chided Cora with amusement. "Such a gentle little creature hardly constitutes a threat."

Heat flared in Vivian's cheeks and her chest tightened. To make such assertions about her, with hardly a peek in her direction!

"Mr. Cantley." Her voice was too soft to be heard, so she tried again. "Excuse me, Mr. Cantley. I must speak with you."

He *did* look at her then, a flick of his gaze that quickly touched on her face and her body. More heat rose up in her, but whatever he saw didn't hold his interest for long. He returned his attention to the gaming table, and she was presented with his back once again.

"Go home, little creature," he said over his shoulder. "I don't deal with foolish men's wives seeking clemency for their spouses' gaming debts."

"I—" She cleared her throat. "I'm no one's wife—I *was*—but that's not why I'm here. Well, it *is* why I'm here. I—oh, curse it."

This *did* get his attention, and he slowly turned to face Vivian. Yet she didn't feel any better having the full measure of his regard fixed to her. Because while she'd mentally prepared herself to be in the company of London's most notorious rake, the sharp and incisive intelligence in his gaze was unexpected, and not especially welcome.

"A morass of words is falling from your lips," he drawled, "yet they are worth far less than the sum of their parts. Begin again, little creature, and be certain to pause for both inhalations *and* exhalations."

She fought to keep from frowning at his continued use of the sobriquet *little creature*, yet to him, she surely appeared to be no more than a vole, blinking in the glare of a chandelier's artificial sun.

"I need to speak with you, Mr. Cantley." There, that didn't sound *too* flustered.

"We're speaking at this present moment," he said with a wave of his broad hand. Rings glittered upon several of his long fingers, drawing her attention and lulling her mind.

This was how tiny furry animals met their end—entranced by a serpent's display, until the snake struck and there was nothing to do but accept the poison flowing into their blood.

The women draped over him snickered, snapping Vivian from her momentary stupor.

"In private, Mr. Cantley," she said tightly. "Please."

"Privacy is scarce at places such as this." One of his thick dark brows arched up. "Particularly the variety that will protect your reputation."

"Imagine *having* a reputation," Cora said with a smirk.

"Never saw the value in 'em," the other woman tittered.

Cantley held up his hand, and the courtesans silenced themselves, though the two women continued to look at her with amused disdain.

"'Tis my reputation that brings me here to you tonight," Vivian pressed on. "In truth, 'tis *both* our reputations that are my concern. In plain words, Mr. Cantley, I've sought you out tonight for a very specific purpose."

"What *is* that purpose, madam?" He sounded on the verge of boredom. But if she failed to engage his interest, if he dismissed her, she truly had no alternative. Either she captured his attention, or a miserable fate awaited her.

If ever she possessed a fleck of courage, she called on it now. She took a deep, scorching breath.

In a whisper that only he could hear, she said, "I need you to ruin me."

2

RUSH WATCHED WITH GROWING INTEREST AS PINK BLOOMED ACROSS THE plain woman's cheeks. It didn't make her beautiful, but beauty was easily found in the city, much like the paste diamonds that choked every London pawn dealer's shop. What her blush *did* do, however, was brighten her eyes and straighten her spine. She was no longer unremarkable, becoming almost as intriguing as the words she'd just uttered.

I need you to ruin me.

"I've been approached many times by many people," he said, examining her, "all of them demanding certain things of me—predominantly a place in my bed. Yet what they're after is pleasure, not ruination."

"A pox on you!" a man shouted at the faro table. "Cheats and thieves!"

The woman in the unfortunate burgundy gown turned to gawk at the burly man, who pushed the faro dealer to the ground. In an instant, Jack appeared, wearing an even-tempered expression.

"Be at ease, friend," Jack said in his musical Welsh tones. "Else you'll be escorted to the doors."

"The hell I will," the man spat. He pointed a finger at the dealer, who had scrambled to his feet. "'Tis a crooked house that's run here and I'll shout the walls down like Jericho if you don't give me back my blunt."

"I saw the whole thing," Jack replied with remarkable calm. "You lost fairly, sir."

"The devil I did. I ain't leaving without my blunt." The burly man took a single threatening step toward the dealer before Jack clapped a hand on his shoulder. Though from the outside it didn't appear to be a particularly tight grip, the stocky man grimaced in pain and nearly went to his knees.

Rush had seen Jack crush oranges with those paws of his, until juice and pulp had run between his fingers.

"You'll apologize to Ned," Jack said mildly, "and then, sir, you'll be on your way."

"S-sorry," the burly chap stammered as he continued to wince. "'Twas my error in judgment."

"Very good, sir." His hand still on the man's shoulder, Jack steered him toward the front entrance before finally relinquishing his hold. "Have a fine evening."

One of Wexham's staff held the door open as the man lurched out without a backward glance. Once the door closed behind him, the din started up again, and Jack accepted pats on the back from Ned and Wexham himself. He nodded when he caught sight of Rush watching him, and Rush tilted his head in response.

Turning back to the plain woman, Rush saw that her gray eyes were round and the intriguing pink had fled her cheeks. She truly was a terrified and helpless little creature, clearly so far away from anything she'd ever known.

But where *had* she come from, and why in the name of Christ would she ask him to ruin her?

He stepped away from the game. Cora and Ruby hovered nearby, murmuring to each other, though they kept casting wary glances at the woman.

"How long has it been since your husband died?" he asked her.

"A year," she answered at once. Though it was difficult to hear her voice above the racket, what he could catch of it was soft and surprisingly husky. "And a month. But how do you know I'm a widow?"

"You mentioned that you had been married," he noted. "'Tis nearly impossible for anyone to legally divorce, and you wear no wedding band."

"Perhaps I've abandoned my husband."

"Were you any other woman, I might presume so. However..." He gestured to her, standing so meek and uncertain in the middle of a gaming hell.

She nodded sadly, as if she understood that she did not present like the sort of woman who might walk away from a husband. But whoever this demure widow was, she *had* just asked him to ruin her.

"Cora, Ruby," he said to the two harlots who continued to linger close to him. "With my compliments." He placed coins into each of their hands and waved them away.

As a matter of practice, Rush only paid whores for their company and not for use of their cunts. He found enough people to fuck without having to part with any blunt. Yet the little widow watched this exchange with silent amazement. There were whores all over London, and it was a measure of this lady's sheltered existence that she was even the slightest bit shocked.

"The wisest thing," he said to her, "would be to pat you on your head and send you home, little creature."

"I beg you, Mr. Cantley," she pled. "I need a moment, only a moment of your time. Perhaps if I..." She fumbled in her pockets and produced a small purse.

"Madam," Rush said coldly, drawing back. "My allowance as a viscount's second son keeps me very comfortable. I'd scare be able to stomach myself were I to take pennies from widows."

"I'm so sorry." What looked suspiciously like tears glistened in her storm-colored eyes. "This was a horrible mistake. I was so desperate, and you were truly my one hope, but—"

She moved to flee, and Rush watched with amazement as his hand came up to clasp her wrist. Her skin was warm and lightly dampened with perspiration, which, he noted, dewed her throat and gathered in tiny droplets across her cheeks. It *was* appallingly hot in the gaming room, yet evidence of her fear and uncertainty was written everywhere on her face and along her body. Likely beneath her gown, her shift clung to her torso and thighs.

"A quieter venue might be obtainable," he said as she stared down at where his fingers wrapped around her wrist. "They know me well enough here."

He walked toward Jack, who had taken up his usual place in the northwest corner of the chamber. Jack lifted a brow as he neared, and glanced behind him, reminding Rush that he hadn't let go of the little widow. She trailed after him without a word of protest. So, she was used to being told what to do and where to go.

Had someone put her up to approaching him tonight? Was she acting under someone else's orders, or was this scheme entirely her own design? The way she stared up at him with a stunned expression made him think the former. She couldn't possibly possess enough spine to venture out to Wexham's of her own volition, especially not with such an outrageous proposition.

"I've need of a place with some quiet," he said to Jack.

"Not your usual variety," Jack replied, glancing at the widow, who gaped back.

"The lady says she's desperate, thus..." Rush had no intention of fucking the meek creature beneath Wexham's roof. In truth, she *wasn't* to his taste, but at the least he wanted to satisfy his curiosity about her purpose in searching him out this evening.

A corner of Jack's mouth lifted. "The payroll clerk's office is free, third door down the corridor, but mind you don't go scattering papers and ledgers everywhere."

"'Twill be a most tidy assignation." With a salute, Rush headed toward the clerk's office. He was careful to keep his hold on the widow loose so she could free herself if she chose, yet she didn't pull away, and he gently tugged her behind him.

Rush rapped on the office door before entering. He released the woman so he might light a candle and, once he did, shut the door to block out the ongoing din that continued to pour out of the gaming room.

He faced the widow, who stood in the middle of the cramped room that was, as Jack had promised, crammed full of the many documents and ledgers that comprised the tedious business of running a prospering London gaming hell. The woman looked around the room with a panicked expression.

"Whatever you might have heard," he said on a sigh, "ravishing unwilling women is an endeavor that holds little interest for me. The door is just there, madam, and you are welcome to walk through it, unhindered, at any time."

She let out a shuddering exhale and offered a smile that seemed, at best, tenuous. "My thanks. Especially after what you said to that rather enormous person, 'tis gentlemanly of you."

"For not forcing myself on a terrified woman? Madam, you have a low threshold for what constitutes polite behavior." He crossed his arms over his chest and sat on the edge of a desk. "You desired to speak with me in a private place, and here we are. Speak your piece, madam."

"Yes. Yes, of course." She took a breath, smoothing her hands down her stomacher in a motion that seemed designed to soothe. "As you ascertained, Mr. Cantley, I am a widow. My husband died a year ago, and I have been out of mourning for a month."

"A young man, your deceased spouse?" The woman herself couldn't have been above thirty.

"Indeed, no. I was William's second wife, and he has an adult son from that first union. In truth, it is because of that son that I am here tonight. Or rather, what John has told me that brought me to this establishment." She held up her hands. "Forgive me, my thoughts are all a-scatter and I'm doing my best to net them like butterflies."

He smiled at that picture, the widow chasing winged ideas and notions through a field like a natural philosopher in search of specimens. "Let them alight at their will rather than attempting to ensnare them."

"I must speak quickly and to my purpose," she said tremulously, "lest I lose what little courage I possess." She ran her hand down the ruffles of her stomacher again. Clearly, she found touch reassuring, but how much touch had she received in the past year? Or over the course of her whole life?

"I await your pleasure, madam." In life, as in seduction, forbearance was met with greater rewards than impatience.

"John came to see me this morning," she said after a moment, "and revealed to me something that I had hitherto no knowledge of. My marriage contract. It was negotiated by my father with the late Mr. Sparkwell. Apparently, 'twas a matter of concern to both gentlemen that, should Mr. Sparkwell go the Lord in advance of my own passing, I would have no man to see to my welfare. Left to my own devices, my father and my late husband feared I would founder." She said this last part with a bitter twist of her mouth.

"They made a proviso," Rush said.

"To ensure that I *do* remarry after Mr. Sparkwell's death," she continued grimly, "I cannot refuse any reasonable offer of marriage. If I decline a marriage proposal, my jointure is forfeit."

Rush sat up straighter. "*Any* offer of marriage?"

"Provided it isn't made by a bedlamite or a boy who has not reached his majority," she added.

"What a relief *that* stipulation must be," he said dryly.

She shot him an equally arid look, which was a surprise. He hadn't anticipated that the widow—Mrs. Sparkwell, apparently—had such spine.

"To add to my astonishment," she continued, "John has already selected my next husband."

"You've no desire to wed this prospective bridegroom?"

"I've no desire to wed *anyone*," she said vehemently. "'Tis intolerable to contemplate that I have no say in determining which man I must be chained to for the rest of my life, and who has control over my person."

"Reasonable," he said with a nod. "Yet you've no wish to remarry at all? Whyever not?" A woman such as she, who seemed conventional in almost every way, surely yearned for the soporific companionship of a husband, and the ensuing brats smearing snot across her skirts.

"'Tis little concern of yours," she answered quickly. "I am unable to refuse any man seeking my hand, else I shan't receive a farthing. After John left my parlor this morning, I realized there was but one way to ensure remaining unmarried in perpetuity."

"Thus, your request that I ruin you."

She nodded, her expression relieved that he guessed her intention. "Any suitor would cry off if my reputation was sufficiently damaged."

"And for such a task," he said with a wave of his hand, "you come to me."

"Do you feign ignorance of your reputation as London's most notorious rake?"

He smirked. "To the contrary, madam. I cultivate it as surely as anyone tends an orchid in a glasshouse. Rather flattering, my reputation.

Anyone who fucks as often and with such dedicated abandon as I do ought to be recognized for their efforts."

"I—ah." Her face went rosy, and the stain spread down her neck and across her bosom. A rather fine bosom it was, too. Not abundant, but well-shaped. Her breasts would fit nicely in his hands.

He looked at her, truly looked at her, for the first time. The common aesthetic might find her face to be unremarkable, but common aesthetics were often modeled on the most facile definitions of beauty. Mrs. Sparkwell wouldn't adorn an enameled miniature, but her gray eyes reminded him of the mists off the coast of an enchanted isle, and she did have a slight uncanny look about her, like one of the fey folk who walked the shore of that mystical island. Her straight eyebrows were the same walnut shade of her hair, and there was an intriguing curve to her pink lips, the faintest hint of sensuality that she might not identify in herself.

Rush recognized it, though. Something hot and erotic hovered just beneath her mild exterior, a gleam of fire glimpsed through ice, evidenced in the way she kept touching herself. She craved the feel of hands on her.

Twelvemonths of mourning. Had Mr. Sparkwell been ill before his demise? And before that, did they fuck regularly, and if so, was it the sort of dutiful, dry coupling that so often caused dissatisfaction—which sent frustrated women to *his* bed? Or perhaps the late Mr. Sparkwell had discovered a second springtime in himself with his young bride, and it was *that* his widow missed?

She continued to stare at him now. His coarse language had shocked her, but perhaps some of her blush came from the barest hint of arousal.

Bedding her would be quite different from his usual trysts. She might remain reserved and meek throughout the whole encounter or—and this he suspected even more—she might have untapped reserves of passion even *she* was unaware of. But he saw it, glimpses of something fiery and passionate beneath her demure façade.

It *would* be a fascinating experience to have her in his bed. And he actually wanted her there.

"The details of your situation are indeed compelling," he continued, musing on her enthralling rosiness, "yet what I fail to see is the reason *why* I ought to assist you in your ruination. My character ought to have convinced you that I seldom do anything for anyone's benefit. An incentive is needed."

Her brows climbed. "Surely if you are named as the agent of my ruin, it should benefit your reputation as a rake."

"I already *have* such a reputation. The conquest of one demure widow hardly adds to it."

A pleat of anger creased her forehead. Good. The woman had some backbone. "When I offered you financial compensation, that offer was rebuffed."

"Blunt isn't required for me to fuck someone—"

"I wish you wouldn't use such words," she said sullenly.

"Madam," he answered, straightening, "if you cannot hear me *say* it, how do you expect me to *do* it?"

"Do it?" She backed away, but collided with a bureau and halted her retreat. "My request was only for you to give the *impression* of ruining me."

Rush planted his hands on his hips. With enforced patience, he said, "A man of honor I am not, but I've a smattering of dictums by which I lead my life. One is that I do not engage in the revolting practice of intimidation, particularly that of women. The other is that I do not *pretend* to do anything. Either I genuinely engage in something, or not at all. You grasp my meaning?"

"We shall not feign being lovers," she said faintly. "We *will* be lovers."

"Just so."

He waited for her immediate refusal. Surely it would be coming presently. Yet she absently rubbed her thumb back and forth across her lower lip as she actually considered his stipulation. He couldn't stop watching that slow, hypnotic movement, back and forth across soft, petal-hued skin.

"Would you be willing?" she asked, her voice soft but her eyes wondering. "To bed me?"

"I fail to see why it should surprise you that I would."

"'Twas not a task..." She swallowed. "Mr. Sparkwell did not show much enthusiasm for participating in the activity with me."

"Perhaps," Rush suggested, dropping his voice, "the fault was with Mr. Sparkwell and not with you. For I find myself much intrigued by the possibility."

How could he not be intrigued, given the way her gaze trailed up and down his body, alighting on his chest, his thighs, and briefly—but definitely—on his groin? She was considering it, contemplating what it would be like if they did go to bed together. Whatever she imagined, it tinted her cheeks a deep pink and made her breath come faster.

And there went her thumb again, stroking over her lip.

"In this life," he murmured, "I make few vows. Few adhere to them, and words are transitory. Yet," he continued, drawing closer and gratified to see that she did not recoil, "I vow this: if we *are* to become lovers, I will make it very, very good for you."

"I..." Her words were barely a whisper, but her gaze locked to his. "I believe you."

"I wager no man has ever eaten your cunt," he mused.

She sucked in a breath. "I'm unfamiliar with that practice."

"That shall be remedied." His cock stirred with increased interest. What would she look like when she came? What sounds would she make? Soft, suppressed gasps, or would she cry out loudly in abandon? "We're getting ahead of ourselves. What are the terms of our arrangement? How long shall this period of debauchery last?"

She blinked, clearing the haze from her eyes. "Until I am declared completely ruined and utterly unmarriageable."

"Understood. We're agreed?" He held out his hand, and she stared at it for a long time. Doubt flitted across her face, and fear, but then she jutted her chin forward as if daring herself to take this final step.

At last, her hand slid into his, pressing palm to palm. She did not have especially small hands, but his dwarfed hers, and an unwelcome sense of protectiveness surged at the feel of her against him. She was so unlike his usual lovers—which should have sent him running into the shadows. And yet he shook her hand, sealing their compact.

"We're agreed," she said with more strength than he anticipated.

"When would you like to begin?"

Again, she surprised him. "Immediately."

3

THE SLOW, WICKED SMILE ON RUSHTON CANTLEY'S FACE ECHOED IN A HOT current through Vivian's body.

Immediately.

She couldn't take the words back. They had been spoken, committing her to what was the most outrageous, daring, and deliberately reckless act of her whole life.

She was going to have an affair with an infamous rake. In so doing, she herself would become infamous. If everything went according to her hopes, her name would only be spoken in scandalized whispers, and then as a cautionary tale to other women who would stray from the path of respectability. And in the aftermath, she'd retreat to the quiet life she had long desired.

But before that, she would go to bed with him, and have the pleasure that he promised, doing the wicked things he described... Her heart slammed against her ribs.

The best thing to do was to get it over with at once. That way, she wouldn't be afraid and she could have done with this whole process as quickly as possible.

Yet instead of pouncing on her like the large black wolf he appeared to be, he bent over her hand in his and pressed the lightest of kisses to her knuckles.

"Rushton Cantley, your servant." His breath was warm across her skin and it drifted over her like smoke. "My friends call me Cantley, and my lovers call me Rush."

"Rush," she repeated. His gaze darkened as she spoke his name, so she added, "I'm Vivian."

Straightening, he nodded as if this made perfect sense. "Like the enchantress who entombed the sorcerer Merlin."

A startled laugh burst from her. "I'm hardly an enchantress."

"You may astonish yourself," he said enigmatically. "You've astonished me."

She could hardly fathom why, but it would be unwise to press him on this point, lest he suddenly decide to rescind his agreement. Which was entirely possible, given how much he asserted that he was not a particularly honorable man.

But he *had* agreed to ruin her. Facing the alternative was a disaster and fear jumped down her spine to consider it. Walking down the aisle of the church, marrying someone she could not refuse, once again being a man's possession...

She repressed a shudder. Rush promising pleasure was a benefit, but truly, she'd endure graceless pawing or mechanical rutting rather than wed a stranger.

"Is your home far from here?" she asked. The sooner this process began, the sooner it would be over, with blissful solitude and blessed retreat back into obscurity as her reward.

"Hieing immediately to the bedchamber shan't facilitate your ruination." He smiled, and her stomach leapt. "We are going to be *seen*."

⸻

"This is a novel experience for me," Rush said, leading Vivian back down the corridor toward the main gaming room. The noise emanating from the chamber was still terrific, but now she expected it and didn't wince or cower in response.

"'Tis difficult to believe that *anything* is novel for you," she answered.

He shot her a grin, and her belly fluttered. She'd never met anyone with such a potent smile, one that made her think of things she'd been cautioned to avoid. Yet, for all her education in being a proper and demure lady, she leaned toward his forbidden promise the way one might steal deeper into the shadows, to discover what creatures lurked there.

"Never before have I ruined anyone," he said. "For which I must thank you. Here I'd believed that I *had* experienced all that life had to offer, and here you come, proving that there is yet more in the world to taste."

They came to a stop on the threshold of the gaming room, and it had grown even more crowded and hot in the intervening minutes. And more boisterous, too. Yet, overseeing everything was the blond giant whom she had witnessed throw out two unruly patrons.

Rush walked to him now. "My thanks for the use of the room. Nothing was disturbed."

"Hartley will be pleased to know that no one fucked on his desk," the blond man answered.

"Not *tonight*," Rush answered, "yet I make no promises."

The blond man smirked. His plain brown coat stretched across the widest shoulders Vivian had ever seen, accentuated by thick arms crossed over his broad chest, and he stood half a head taller than any of the other fellows in the room. She tried not to gape at the size of his hands, though he'd already demonstrated just how strong those hands were. Standing near him, she felt as small as a poppet taken from the nursery floor.

It was his face that held the most fascination. It was rugged and weathered, with fans of lines at the corners of his blue eyes and creases around his mouth. His substantial nose was slightly crooked, with a bump on the bridge that suggested a prior break. His expression was even and steady, almost impassive, yet his gaze moved alertly back and forth across the room. He looked like a brute, but there was a keen intelligence at work.

In Rush and the man's conversation, there was a note of affability, almost warmth between them. A rake and a gaming hell's enforcer weren't friends—were they?

"Time to demonstrate your newfound impropriety," Rush said, and she started when his hand wrapped around her waist to guide her away from the blond man. Even through her many layers of silk, stays, and linen, the warmth of him permeated her skin. Her panniers kept him at a slight distance, yet she'd never been closer to a man who wasn't her spouse or relative.

"Be at ease, little creature." His eyes glittered as he looked down into her startled face. "If Society's to believe that you are well and truly ruined, we cannot stand as strangers. Yet," he added softly, "I can remove my hand if you so desire."

"Let it remain." It *did* make sense that he ought to touch her in public. Despite the fact that the feel of him made her heart beat as quickly as if she'd run up a flight of stairs, the sensation of his broad, hot hand on her was...pleasant.

If she was to complete the picture of a debauched woman, she should act like one.

Tentatively, she slid her own hand to his waist. His firm, taut body contracted as he sucked in a breath. Surely the rake had experienced touches far more daring than hers, yet the column of his throat worked beneath his stock.

He caught her gazing at him, and gave a self-deprecating chuckle. "I commend your initiative, madam. Let us into the fray so that many eyes may behold your debauching." In a voice that could surely be heard across the room, he declared, "Shall we, Mrs. Sparkwell?"

They moved into the gaming room and, as promised, dozens of faces followed their progress around the chamber. She shrank against Rush's side.

"Hardly the time for diffidence." Amusement tinged his voice.

"'Tis the result of a year away from such gazes." That wasn't entirely true. For most of her life, she'd felt others' gazes glide across her in search of someone more significant, more important and worthwhile. Which had been entirely the point, in her father's house, and later, after her marriage to William. She had been merely the conduit to direct people's attention to men, and men's ambitions, and when anyone paid her more regard, she did her utmost to divert it away.

"Surely no one here in Wexham's would give me a moment's consideration," she said as he led her toward a servant carrying refreshments, "were it not for the fact that *you* are the one holding me closely."

"Such an ungenerous thought." Rush plucked one cup of wine from the tray and handed it to her, before taking one for himself. He drank, his arm still around her waist.

She also sipped from her glass, and the wine slid down her throat, spreading warmth. Tilting her head back, she drained her cup before reaching for another.

"No drunkenness," he said warningly. "I never take anyone to bed who isn't in full command of their faculties."

She set her empty cup on the tray, and when he also dispensed with his vessel, he nodded in dismissal at the servant.

"Being a rake has far more regulations than I'd believed," she mused.

"Novice rakes adhere to no code of conduct." His hand slid to the small of her back, drawing her closer. For all the garments providing barriers between them, none of the fabric seemed to exist. He was searingly hot, and, this close, she caught his scent of woodsmoke and slick male skin. In a low purr, he said, "I am no novice."

Gazing up at him, she could not remember the rudiments of breathing. He *was* a phenomenal specimen of masculine beauty, and at that moment, his gaze was fixed entirely on her. The gaming hell was as rowdy as ever, yet nothing seemed to hold his attention more than she did. As if he found her fascinating. As if he desired her.

'Twas nothing more than performance for an audience. Though if it *was* a pretense, it was a remarkably convincing one, especially the way his eyes darkened and his nostrils flared.

"Are you going to kiss me?" Her words were breathless.

"In good time. For now..." He bent close, his face mere inches from hers. His breath was warm and rich with the fragrance of spiced wine, and she fought to keep her eyes open as he dipped lower to lightly drag his lips along her throat.

They were soft, his lips, and yet they left a scorched trail across her flesh. She hadn't known until that moment that her neck was this responsive, this attuned to sensation, yet pleasure drifted through her to collect in the tips of her breasts and nestle between her legs.

If this was what he could do in public, by simply touching his mouth to her throat, what could she expect from him in the privacy of his bed?

"Do you like what I'm doing?" he murmured against her skin. When she made a dazed noise of assent, he said, "Then show me. Show *them*."

She did not move—she'd never done anything like this before. But that was why she was here tonight.

A moment later, she gripped his shoulders. They were startlingly wide and solid, barely yielding as she dug her fingers into them to pull him closer.

"A splendid effort," he whispered approvingly. As he spoke lowly, his lips traced blazing shapes along her neck and jaw. "There's so much pleasure to be had in the smallest of touches. A feast in sips and bites. And you taste so very good, Mrs. Sparkwell."

"How...how do I taste?"

"Sweet with a hint of brine." He lightly stroked the tip of his tongue behind her ear. "I find myself impatient to sample all your flavors."

She shivered. He'd said the most outrageous thing to her earlier, that he would put his mouth between her legs. His mouth and tongue already worked magic merely on her neck, but to do such things on her most hidden part...oh, God. How would she survive it?

He chuckled, the sound moving over her flesh. To her disappointment, he straightened and looked down at her through lowered lids. His eyes gleamed beneath the thick fringe of his lashes.

"You don't need to stop," she said throatily.

"Delicious as this is," he replied, "our audience at Wexham's has seen enough."

This man *was* otherworldly, to make her forget that they stood in the middle of a chaotic, crowded gaming hell as he touched her with far more intimacy than her husband ever had.

Lord knew, she'd never blushed as much as she had this evening. And it was barely after midnight.

"To your rooms?" There was eagerness in her voice, a variety that was almost entirely unknown to her.

"I am a thorough man," he answered, guiding her toward the front door. "And there's more work to be done before we can retreat to blessed privacy."

As they moved closer to the exit, Rush gave the enormous blond man a nod. The giant's gaze flicked to her—*how* was it possible for her to grow even warmer?—before he returned Rush's nod.

"How unexpected," she said softly. "Camaraderie between a rake and a gaming hell enforcer."

"I'd be a fool not to count Jack Morgan as a friend," Rush answered with far more vehemence than she would have thought him capable of. How had two such different men become the unlikeliest of friends?

The thought fled once she and Rush were outside the gaming hell. He flagged a hackney and helped her into the somewhat dilapidated vehicle.

"Dare I ask where we're going?" she asked once he'd given the driver an address.

His grin was wicked. "To sow more scandal."

4

"THERE'S A GREAT DEAL OF DISTANCE BETWEEN US." RUSH EYED THE SPAN between himself and the unexpected Mrs. Vivian Sparkwell as she sat opposite him in the carriage. He patted the seat beside him. "Let's not be strangers."

Intermittent lamps cast light across her skeptical face.

"We're alone," she said, puzzled.

"'Tis indeed a small coach," he noted with a smile, "and hardly able to accommodate a crowd."

"There seems little point in me sitting beside you," she replied, "if no one witnesses it."

"Not everything this night is for an audience's benefit." Though the interior of the vehicle was small, he did his best to stretch out his legs. The calf of his boot disappeared beneath Vivian's rustling skirts. Later, he intended to follow the same path beneath her gown.

His body tightened in anticipation. It *had* been calculated, how he'd held and touched her when they had been at Wexham's. His reaction hadn't been nearly as intentional. When her slow-blooming response to him had finally come, it whetted his appetite for more. Mrs. Sparkwell brimmed with erotic potential—she didn't quite understand it yet.

He understood, and wanted more. When he finally brought her to his bed, it would be explosive, and he would be the fortunate bastard to behold her awakening.

"I'd hardly merit the title of *rake*," he continued, watching her gaze move up his body, "if I couldn't make my lover want more. If I couldn't make her want *me*."

"I admit astonishment that it should matter to you at all what my experience is," she said uncertainly.

"*My* pleasure lies in giving *you* pleasure." He placed his hands on his knees and leaned forward. "Let me bestow it upon you."

It was no surprise that she deliberated. Everything Mrs. Vivian Sparkwell did was in careful, thought-out measures. It would be wondrous to see her when she lost all ability to think, and released herself entirely.

Her skirts made a delectable swishing sound as she moved to sit beside him. Though she was a small thing, the cramped carriage meant that their thighs pressed snug against each other. He'd experienced far more salacious touch in the course of his life, yet heat streaked through him at the feel of her just like it had back at the gaming hell.

He suppressed a chuckle when she turned to him, closed her eyes, and tilted her face up, clearly expecting a kiss.

Instead, he laced his fingers with hers, and pressed their palms together. Merely that, and nothing more. Even so, she opened her eyes and her breath went ragged.

Rush stroked his thumb along her wrist, feeling the flutter of her pulse, the softness of her skin. He turned her hand over to cradle it in his own, and traced his finger over her skin.

"At Bartholomew Fair," he said lowly, "it costs a penny to have your palm read. I'm no believer in divination—this is a rational age—yet there are things to learn about a person from observing their hands."

"Their profession," she guessed, though the breathlessness in her voice belied her sensible words. "If they are a regular correspondent, evidenced by ink or calluses on their fingers."

"You are perspicacious." He smiled down at their joined hands. "Aye, there are many clues to be seen. But I've always been of a mind that the mouth is more sensitive than either one's fingers or eyes."

He lowered his lips to her palm. A soft noise of wonderment escaped her as he moved his mouth back and forth over her hand, which trembled like a tiny beast of the field beneath him. Moving to her fingers, he kissed each of them in turn, then pulled her index finger between his lips and gently sucked.

A moan slipped from her, shooting straight to his cock.

The urge to lay her back against the squabs and fuck her surged through him. Yet she was practically an innocent, so he *must* take his time, and give her all the pleasure that he'd vowed he would.

He drew her finger out of his mouth to trail kisses across her palm, and then to her tender wrist where her pulse continued to throb. Then he went higher, stroking the softness of her forearm with his lips. The lace of her engageantes brushed against his face, and he let the sensations of her skin and the delicate fabric swirl around him.

"God, the *feel* of you," he said huskily. "Soft everywhere. And the sounds you make. Those little moans, so exquisite."

She whimpered yet did not pull away.

"Do you know what I think?" he asked between kisses.

"I...cannot begin...to fathom how...your...mind works."

His lips curved at that. "'Tis my belief that when I do finally get you into my bed, *you* will devastate *me.*"

"Doubtful," she said shakily. Yet her breath came fast and she wet her lips.

"I cannot resist a challenge." His own arousal gleamed within him, to see how she responded, and to anticipate what was to come. "Have faith in me, madam, and faith in yourself."

The hackney halted with a lurch, and the cabman called down that they'd reached their destination. Reluctantly, Rush sat up and released Vivian, ruefully pleased to see the disappointment on her face.

"There's yet more to tonight's performance," he said before climbing out of the carriage. He flipped a coin to the driver, then handed Vivian down from the creaking vehicle.

"What is this place?" she asked as they stood outside the narrow but elegant brick facade of the home on Albemarle Street.

"A friend's home. She's a generous host, if you've any concern at not having a formal invitation. Very little about Adelaide is formal. But her salons are attended by the biggest gossips in London, so word will surely spread if we are seen together here." He held out his arm, and Vivian took it.

A liveried footman opened the door for them, but Rush didn't need instruction to know that Adelaide's gatherings always happened in her upstairs parlor. Vivian was quiet and wide-eyed beside him as they climbed the stairs towards the sounds of voices and laughter. At the top of the steps, he made certain to draw Vivian close, his arm yet again coming to press against the small of her back. She followed his lead, her own hand clasping his waist.

It felt far too good to hold her and be held like this. As though they truly meant something to each other.

He shook his head, scattering the surprising thought. For his protection, and for hers, there was no place for such notions.

In the dimly lit parlor, men and women gathered with cups of wine and flirtatious looks. The hostess herself reclined on one of many chaises, yet she pulled a long-stemmed tobacco pipe from her lips to cry out in greeting, "The evening is a success! We are joined by my dearest Rush."

"Lady Adelaide Dyner," he said, stepping forward to kiss her hand. He gazed down at Vivian, letting his desire for her show in his eyes. "Mrs. Vivian Sparkwell."

"My lady, thank you for your hospitality." Vivian curtsied as she spoke.

The lady's brows rose. Glancing around the room, he noticed many of the other guests contemplating Vivian as though she was a humble dove that had wound up in a tree full of vivid parrots.

"What's Cantley doing with *her*?" one fop whispered loudly. His female companion tittered into her fan.

Vivian shifted beside him, and her gaze dropped to the floor.

Tight heat snaked up Rush's neck and down his arms. He drew Vivian closer to his side before escorting her to one of the unoccupied chaises that were scattered throughout the room, and then reclining upon it. She was stiff and awkward at first when he eased her down to lie back against him, her attention still fixed upon the parquet.

"Missed a splendid recitation earlier, Cantley," a dandy said, approaching. Rush recognized him as Burton. Burton eyed Vivian, a gleam of mockery in his gaze. "An erotic poem I penned. You would have found it entirely too shocking, madam."

Vivian was silent, and Rush held her closer.

"Mrs. Sparkwell would have been shocked by the triteness of your verses," Rush drawled. "They titillate only the most uninspired of palates."

"I shan't waste your time with a repeat performance," Burton sniffed, then swanned away.

"How dull I am," she whispered once the dandy had retreated to the opposite end of the parlor.

"None of them know," Rush whispered against the shell of Vivian's ear, "what you're truly capable of. Shall we prove them wrong?"

She gave a small nod, but added, "I don't know what to do."

"Whatever you desire," he murmured. "Surely in the depths of the night, you've put your hands on yourself and wished for a lover you could touch in any way you please. Ah, that naughty little smile tells me you've done precisely that." He leaned back farther and turned her so that her hands pressed against his chest, and he had a delectable view of her small breasts.

His palm spread at the base of her spine, and he brought his other hand to cradle her cheek. Their faces were close enough that he could see how her pupils threatened to engulf the cloud gray of her irises. He stifled a groan when her gaze drifted to his mouth. Yet she didn't speak.

"Have you ever kissed a man?" he asked.

"William kissed me many times," she answered.

"Did *you* ever kiss him?"

"Pecks on the cheek," she admitted. "I tried once to kiss him upon the mouth, and he said it wasn't seemly for a woman to assert herself in that fashion."

"Assert yourself," Rush said.

A crease appeared between her brows, and she looked captivatingly studious as she contemplated his mouth. She adjusted her position, her palms spread over his thudding heart, before closing her eyes. Then, slowly, she brought her lips to his.

At the first touch of her mouth, desire roared through him. *Go slowly, oaf*, he reminded himself, forcing his body to hold still and not plunder as he needed. Her kiss verged on chaste, yet as her exploration continued, it lingered and deepened. She parted her lips to lightly touch her tongue to him, and he opened immediately. When he slicked his tongue against hers, she shivered yet pressed herself snugly against him.

"More?" he asked on a rasp.

"More," she answered, her own voice husky.

He stroked his hand up her back in wordless encouragement, and she kissed him again with growing boldness. Gripping tightly to his shoulders, she angled her head to draw deeply from his mouth. Her body shifted, nestling closer, and she made a small, frustrated sound when her skirts bunched between them. With a practiced movement, Rush collected armfuls of silk and petticoats and arranged them so she could straddle him. She made a different noise this time, one of gratification, as she pressed her hips into his. He growled his approval.

She seemed lost to her pursuit of pleasure, her lips needy and demanding, her hands roaming over his body, sharpening his arousal with each stroke and caress. He let her lead them where she wanted and needed them to go. Normally, Rush was the one to take command, yet this journey was hers. She would find her way, and he was fortune's favored son to be the man accompanying her on this voyage.

The need to claim her, mark her, roared through him.

"Pax, madam, pax." His hands gentled her as her movements became more frenzied. For all his hopes of what she would be like when she finally untethered herself, she'd surpassed those hopes and would burn *him* to cinders.

She drew back, her eyes hazed with desire.

"I want nothing more than to see where this leads," he said throatily, "yet in your need of ruination, 'tis doubtful you want *all* of our endeavors to be public."

"Oh, God." Her body stiffened as awareness of her surroundings seemed to come in an instant. She glanced down at herself straddling him, and her eyes closed as an expression of mortification flitted across her face. "I've made a fool of myself."

"Hardly that." He helped her to ease off of him, though his throbbing cock protested her absence. She started to cover her face with her hands, but he gently tugged them down. "Not a soul here believes you a fool. Look at them, the envy and desire in their eyes. You've made them want something they didn't realize they wanted."

She cast a quick, wary glance around the room. Men and women watched her with avid interest.

"Nary a one of them are laughing or sneering," Rush said softly.

"They understand now that their knowledge of you was faulty and incomplete. And they envy me."

Her embarrassment gave way to wonder, and then, to his delight, a smile touched her kiss-swollen lips, at once shy and wicked.

"I *was* rather wild," she whispered, half to herself. "And they saw it all."

That was unexpected.

It took many moments for his cockstand to flag, and when he felt reasonably certain it had, he stood and held out his hand to her. "The time's come, Mrs. Sparkwell, for us to seek more secluded arrangements. If you so desire."

"I do desire," she answered, and to his bafflement, he exhaled in relief. As if he'd been afraid she would say no.

Lust had been his daily companion from his earliest memories. Sensual experience was as vital to him as the open sky was to a falcon, and yet, as he escorted Mrs. Vivian Sparkwell from the parlor and out of Adelaide's home, he could not recall such a sharp, ravenous need for someone. Not the way he ached with desire for a woman who, hours before, he'd been too blind to see properly.

Caution, he warned himself. He'd wanted too much in the past, then learned that his desires were incompatible with the truths of this world. But he'd matured since then, and knew better now.

He had to hold tightly to that hard-won wisdom, for Vivian's sake, and for his own.

5

WHATEVER VIVIAN EXPECTED WHEN ENVISIONING AN INFAMOUS RAKE'S home, it did not include tastefully simple furniture, porcelain vases of wildflowers, or shelves groaning under the weight of what had to be the largest number of books she'd ever encountered outside of a circulating library.

"Where are the erotic paintings?" She turned in a slow circle, taking in all the details of Rush's rooms. "The billet-doux stuffed with desperate pleas and locks of hair? The scattering of ladies' undergarments upon the floor?"

"I sent word to my charwoman to clean all of them out in advance of your arrival." Rush stood at a small table and poured them both glasses of wine, before striding over and handing her one goblet. "You've read a great many novels, if that's what you anticipated. I think I've a copy of *Clarissa* somewhere around here, though Richardson's moralizing is the height of tedium. At least in church, you can imagine ways to defile the altar."

"And how many editions do you have of *Fanny Hill*?" Hopefully, he couldn't see how her hand shook as she lifted her wine to her lips. It was far easier to talk about decor and books rather than face what was to come.

She *had* enjoyed his touches and his kisses, so much so she'd almost forgotten that she was in public—yet something about the fact that many eyes had watched her give way to sensual abandon had made her desire burn hotter and higher.

Good Lord, what did it say about her that she actually wanted to be seen as she'd behaved so wantonly? And that she ached to experience it again?

Yet the carriage ride here had given her far too much time to consider that she was about to be intimate with a man she'd only met that night. Granted, he didn't treat her like a stranger, and had been unexpectedly kind and encouraging, but all her life she'd been told that sexual intercourse was the exclusive province of married people. The only man who was permitted access to her body was supposed to be her husband.

There was nothing husbandly about Rushton Cantley. Husbands didn't kiss with such devastating sensuality, and there had been no mistaking the thick ridge of his erection when she'd straddled him so wantonly. Even now, as she trembled, heat lingered on her lips, in her breasts, and between her thighs.

"Such varied reading tastes for such a decorous widow." He smiled at her over the rim of his glass.

"I found a copy in William's bedside table," she confessed. "Embarrassment got the better of me, and I never read it."

"You *were* curious." He tilted his head as she sipped at her wine. "Tell me what you like."

"I...don't know." There was no pretending that she didn't understand what he meant. Her cheeks warmed as she admitted, "When William exerted his marital rights, we simply did it the way he preferred." That entailed him fondling her breasts for a minute before he lifted her nightgown and heaved himself between her legs, which usually took five minutes—he'd keep saying he wasn't a young man anymore—and then he'd shudder, kiss her cheek, and leave.

"Did you ever come?"

"Perhaps?" More heat flushed her cheeks, both at his candid question, and her anemic response.

He scowled, but when she shrank back, he said, "My anger's for that buffoon you were yoked to. The fact that you don't know if you came is a searing indictment against not just his ability to fuck, but his intolerable selfishness. Not ensuring your lover's pleasure is a serious, unforgivable crime. At the least, tell me you've achieved a climax at your own hand."

It was simply *too* mortifying to admit aloud, but she managed a quick nod. She dared not tell him that she'd been diddling herself for a very long time, and once, when she was fourteen, had been caught by her nanny, who had spanked her ruthlessly and told her that only sluts did such things.

Nanny's warnings had prevented her from touching herself again—for a week. And then she'd been back to her practice of self-pleasuring twice daily. If anything, her year of mourning, without even William's unsatisfying rutting, had increased the number of times she frigged herself.

"Then you know a little of what to expect," Rush said after finishing his wine and setting it aside.

"It will be much the same." She set her goblet aside. "I assume it will be very nice."

His brows climbed. "*Very nice* is a pale candle flame compared to the bonfire of a good orgasm. Fear not, madam," he added in a purr, "'twill be as bright as Guy Fawkes Night this evening. 'Tis time we began our festivities."

She strode away from him, anxiety nipping at her like a terrier. Distracting herself with the many books on the shelves, she stared at their spines. In addition to novels and treatises on natural philosophy, there were volumes in French, Spanish, Latin, and Greek.

"This is a gentleman's library," she noted, pulling *Species Plantarum* from the shelf.

"I am a gentleman by birth." She started to hear his deep voice directly behind her. He plucked the book from her hands and slid it back into place. "Yet neither my pedigree nor my books are why I am sought out. 'Tis pleasure I can provide. Many moments of pleasure."

"And what happens after those moments are over?" She faced him, in time to see a brief frown pleat between his brows.

"I move on to the next," he answered, "as they do."

"It seems...lonely."

His frown deepened. "'Tis what I want. What they want. When you approached me at Wexham's, 'twas with the understanding that I was to provide a service—and some pleasure—but nothing more. If you're in search of something with greater permanence or meaning, you sought out the wrong rake."

"You're fearful," she said in wonderment.

"Ridiculous," he muttered, scowling. "My intent is to protect *you*, madam."

She tilted her head, contemplating him. There *was* fear behind his determined sybaritic stance, lurking in the shades of his eyes and in the taut line of his jaw. Not merely fear, but hurt, and contained behind his polished, sophisticated shell throbbed a fragile, needy heart.

Something had happened to him in his past, something that made him fashion this rakish, debauched persona. And it made her own soul ache.

With a determined expression, he placed his hands on either side of her, surrounding her as he leaned close. His warmth was all around her, and it permeated all the way to her bones. It engulfed and drugged her with his nearness and potency.

"Tonight is for you, little creature," he said, his voice deep and velvety. "All your fantasies shall become reality."

"I haven't any fantasies." Her skin tingled with embarrassment.

"Everyone does." As he had at the gaming hell, he glided his lips along her throat, turning her mortification to arousal.

"My role was to help William find his release," she explained. "'Twas for him, never for me. Everything in my life," she went on with growing understanding, "has been for others. Not myself. Never myself."

He made a noise of disapproval. "You've lived in the shadows, but you need to be out in the sun."

The thought brought another flare of heat to her face and through her limbs. It was too outlandish to think that she might in some way become the focus, and yet, the way the people at the salon had watched her abandon herself to Rush's attentions, to have him attend only to her needs, her ecstasy... Molten desire pooled between her legs.

He brought his lips to hers. They kissed hungrily, exploring each other's depths. He tasted of wine and smoke and all the fantasies she'd never permitted for herself. The way he devoured her, as though she truly was worth desiring, turned her fluid and restless. Needing support for her liquid body, she leaned against the bookshelves, and he grew more demanding, more intent, his tongue lapping against hers.

His hands pressed her hips against the shelves. He held her steady as his kisses glided from her mouth, down her neck, and into the dips behind her clavicle. With hot slicks of his lips, he tasted the hollow of her throat. She moaned as he kissed the tops of her breasts, and she wanted the many layers of clothing between them gone.

She made an unhappy sound when he took his mouth from her skin, but the noise died in her throat as he lowered his lean body to kneel before her. Astonished, excited, she watched as he gathered up her skirts in his broad hands, the silk bunching over his forearms. He stroked up her legs, each caress making her tremble, and when he massaged the bare skin of her thighs, she gasped.

His dark head bent as he kissed his way up her soft flesh, his lips nimble and attentive.

"You're not going to..." she whispered, mortified and marveling.

"I am." He bared her quim and a feral noise escaped him.

As his breath fanned over her, she lifted her hands to cover her face.

"Look at me," he commanded. "I want you to watch as I eat your cunt."

Her shaking hands dropped away, and he angled her hips to bring her quim closer to his mouth. His gaze held hers as he leaned nearer, and nearer, and then—

He swiped his tongue between her lips.

"Oh, God," she cried.

Rush growled lowly as he continued to lick her. He possessed a *most* adept tongue, and it slicked over her tender, sensitive flesh, tracing her inner lips before swirling around her clitoris. Fastening his mouth over the bud, he sucked, watching her the whole time. His eyes were hazed with arousal, and if the sensation of his lips on her quim wasn't devastating enough, the fact that *he* enjoyed giving her pleasure made her own soar.

He kept one hand on her hip, pinning her to the shelves before pausing in his ministrations to lick the fingers of his free hand. His gaze was hot as he circled her passage with one finger, then slowly sank it into her.

She clapped her palm over her mouth to silence her scream.

"Let me hear you," he rasped. "Every noise you make shoots straight to my cock."

Dragging her hand away, she mewled as he thrust in and out. All the while, he licked her clitoris, circling it with his tongue and sucking upon it like a boiled sweet. The beginnings of a climax gathered in her. He added a second finger to the first to stroke over a swollen spot deep in her passage, and her release hit with the force of a storm.

She bucked and shuddered as tides of pleasure surged, engulfing her. Yet no sooner had one torrent ebbed, another began, urged on by his unrelenting mouth and fingers. Never before had she been so thoroughly *fucked* as she was by his lips, his hands.

Yet there was an ache within her, a demand she didn't fully understand.

"Please," she moaned. "Rush, please."

"Need more, little creature?" His words flowed over her quim, hot and wicked. "Is it my cock you crave?"

"Aye." She was too lost in her desire to care that she sounded like the veriest lightskirt. Nothing mattered but getting his cock into her.

He didn't tease and he didn't make her wait. Instead, he stood and swept her up into his arms. With long, impatient strides, he carried her into his bedchamber—she had a quick glimpse of a room filled with more books—and set her down beside an enormous bed.

His movements were quick and fierce as he shucked his coat and tore the stock from around his neck. Yet he didn't bother undressing any further, only undid the placket of his breeches to free his thick, upright cock.

Her eyes went wide to see his hand wrap around himself and give two hard, almost brutal strokes. His face contorted in pleasure, but he stilled his movements. Then he sat on the edge of the bed and drew her toward him.

"The way you rode me at the salon," he said, his voice rough. "Do it now. Take command."

"Is that—" She swallowed. "Is that what *you* want?"

He looked at her blankly, as if he could not quite understand the question. "What *I*...?"

"As much pleasure as you've promised me," she said, "I want you to have the same pleasure."

His confusion lasted a moment longer, and then he looked almost touched that she'd considered him. But why shouldn't she? Didn't his experience matter?

"What *you* want, love," he finally rumbled, "*I* want. And if that means you riding me hard, that's precisely what I desire."

Her legs shook beneath her, yet with his help, she straddled him and he guided her hips into place. She gripped his shoulders in an attempt to steady herself. He took his cock in hand once again to fit the slick head to her entrance. A cry of pleasure tore from her at the feel of his bare flesh against hers.

Yet, potent as the moment was, she had to gasp, "We must be cautious. I cannot get with child."

"I'll keep you safe," he vowed huskily. "Now, fuck me."

His coarse words traveled in a hot current through her. She sank onto him, filling herself with his cock. Vivian bit her lip at how he stretched her, and could only lower down an inch. A whimper escaped her.

"Breathe, love," he urged, his eyes mere slits. "Breathe, and take all of me."

She did as he commanded, letting out a long, ragged exhale as she brought her hips lower. His thickness slid deeper and deeper still in an alchemy of pleasure and pain, until, at last, he was seated to the hilt. She paused, breath after breath sawing through her, yet in slow, gradual waves the pain disappeared and only ecstasy remained.

"Brave lady," he crooned in approval. "Delicious creature. You set the pace. I'm yours to use."

Tentatively, she rose up slightly before sinking down again. With each movement of her hips, pleasure blossomed brightly. She discovered that if she angled herself just so, she could grind her clitoris against him, and she moaned at the double sensation of friction at precisely the right place whilst being completely filled.

She moved faster, caught up in sensation. Flushed color spread across his cheeks and his mouth opened as he panted. She loved how lost he was to their sex, his own hips drumming up into her.

She glanced down to see how his tall boots gleamed in the candle-light, and the leather creaked with each flex of his legs. Desperate—they were desperate for each other, evidenced by the fact that they were both almost completely clothed. She sweated into her gown and didn't care. All that mattered was this, them fucking each other hard and fierce.

Movement in the corner of her eye caught her attention. She turned and gasped as Jack Morgan—the enforcer from the gaming hell—leaned against the door. His arms were crossed over his massive chest, and, jaw tight, eyes gleaming, he watched Vivian ride Rush's cock.

Her gaze moved lower and she gasped again. Jack's breeches were snug against his erect length. He unfolded his arms and rubbed the heel of his palm up his shaft.

She ducked her head, tucking it against Rush's neck as she closed her eyes. A quake of shame shook her, even as she ground down on Rush's cock and her breasts ached behind her stomacher.

"We aren't there yet, Jack," Rush said. Another tremor racked her. A moment later, Rush murmured, "Alone again, love."

She lifted her head slightly and cracked open her eyes. The doorway to the bedchamber was indeed empty.

Questions flew through her mind, yet Rush was still inside her, still moving his hips so that pleasure continued to reverberate hotly.

"Did you like that, little creature?" His voice was a husky torment as his hands gripped her waist. "Having Jack see us? See *you* fuck me like all you care about is cock?"

A moan escaped her as she pushed down hard onto him. She kept picturing the raw lust in Jack Morgan's eyes, and how he had to touch himself while watching her.

"Ah, you did like that," Rush rumbled. "What if he joined us, love? What if Jack and I fucked you at the same time?"

"People don't...do that," she panted.

"They assuredly do." In the midst of his pleasure, he smirked. "We share women, Jack and I. You would enjoy it exceedingly. Can you picture it, little creature? My cock in your cunt whilst Jack fucks your mouth?"

Images of outrageous lewdness saturated her, images so unbearably depraved she moaned. She rode Rush hard until her thighs ached, but she didn't care, all that mattered was filling herself with him as she pictured taking Jack Morgan's cock between her lips. If the shape in his breeches was any indicator, he would be enormous, so large that she likely couldn't fit all of him in her mouth. She'd choke on him and not care, abandoning herself to erotic frenzy.

"There would be only you," Rush continued to rasp, his words coming in gasps as he continued to stroke up into her. "The center of our universe as both of us fucked you."

Her climax struck hard, pleasure flooding her. A cry ripped from her throat, and she gripped her inner muscles around his cock as she clutched his shoulders. He brought his thumb against her clitoris and stroked it, until, incredibly, she came once more.

He was unrelenting as his hips pounded against hers, the guttural noises he made verging on animalistic. Then he pulled from her and seed shot from his cock, spattering across his waistcoat.

Rush collapsed back to the bed, and she went with him, sprawling over his steaming, heaving body. His hand splayed in the small of her back to move in gentle circles, and the movement soothed her in the aftermath of what had been the most stunning experience in the whole of her life.

The outrageous things she'd done tonight with him...how absolutely unbridled she'd become in the throes of her desire...and then, when Jack Morgan had watched, and the scenario Rush had painted for her of the *both* of them making love to her... She trembled again as an echo of her climax quaked through her.

"Do you..." Her throat was raw from her cries of ecstasy. "Do you *truly* share women with him?"

"When the lady is amenable," Rush said, his voice lightly slurred with well-earned exhaustion. "I assure you, everyone leaves the bed satisfied. On the occasions that we make it to the bed."

"I'd no idea." She pressed her heated cheek against Rush's chest.

And she'd not the faintest inkling that she would ever desire such a thing for herself.

"'Tis a marvelous place, this world," he assured her. His other hand stroked the back of her head, smoothing her hair with a touch so gentle, she barely believed he was the same lover who had been so gloriously unrelenting in his pursuit of her ecstasy. He pressed a kiss to the crown of her head. "You did well, love. In everything—your bravery is extraordinary."

It would be so easy to crave this. To yearn for both his passion and his tender care. Yet he'd been quite purposeful in articulating that there would never be anything more between them than this physical act. She wasn't looking for another man to bind herself to, in any event. They'd both gotten what they wanted, for surely after the spectacle she'd made of herself at the gaming hell and then at Lady Adelaide's, she was now a ruined woman.

Slowly, she peeled her limp body off him and struggled to stand. He lifted up onto his elbows and watched her futile efforts before helping her onto her feet. Even though he'd pulled from her before spilling, the insides of her thighs were slick with her arousal. He cleaned himself with a corner of the blanket and tucked his partially hard length back into his breeches.

"I should go," she said before he could tell her to leave.

He frowned as if he didn't quite understand the words she spoke.

"'Tis late," she continued, shaking out her skirts and patting her hair before backing toward the door. This was what worldly women with lovers did. They made their exit with cool sophistication, never telling their paramours that they had been shaken to their very core by the intensity of the experience, or by revelations of their own wickedness. "And I find myself much fatigued."

Slowly, he stood, and she retreated to keep their bodies from touching. His hair had slid from its queue and hung loosely about his face—she forced her hands to remain at her sides rather than tuck some of the black locks behind his ears.

"I'll call for a carriage and see you home." His voice was impossibly deep, yet she made herself turn away.

"Such attention is unnecessary," she answered. "There were sedan bearers just outside. 'Twill be easy enough to summon a chair to take me home."

"Vivian—"

She hurried out of his bedchamber and toward the front door, barely taking note of the front room. Behind her, his solid but light footsteps sounded, and she said over her shoulder, "My thanks for agreeing to this scheme of mine."

"The pleasure was both of ours."

She tried to laugh like one of the women at Lady Adelaide's home, but the sound was slightly panicked. This was supposed to be about ruining her reputation, and though the pleasure had been a wonderful addition, she'd never intended to feel anything for him. Which she didn't. She most certainly did not.

6

LEGS STILL UNSTEADY FROM WHAT HAD BEEN ONE OF THE MOST POWERFUL climaxes of his life, Rush watched the door close behind Vivian. He frowned at the space she'd just occupied as if by staring intently at the air, he could conjure her back into existence.

"Never seen a woman bolt like a horse fleeing a burning barn," Jack said behind him.

Rush made himself shrug, though he'd half an urge to race down the stairs in pursuit of the little widow and beg her to return to his bed. This time, he'd promise, they would actually strip and take their time, learning more about what made her smile, what made her gasp, what could make her scream his name and plead for more.

This was about his usefulness to her—nothing beyond that. He'd wanted to experience her unleashed passion, and he'd done so. Each of them had their roles to play, which they'd accomplished admirably. He knew the limits of his value. Craving anything further was foolish.

"Lurking in shadows is a waste of your talents." Rush began pulling off his clothing and dropping the items to the floor. His valet appeared at noon to repair the damages from the previous evening and prepare him for the day and night ahead.

Turning, he faced Jack, who lounged in one of the few chairs sizable enough to contain him.

"As my services weren't particularly wanted," Jack answered, "I took my ease until you were finished with the lady."

"By *took your ease* you mean frigged yourself," Rush said dryly as he strode back into his bedchamber.

"An inspiring performance." The chair creaking beneath him, Jack rose and followed Rush.

After removing the rest of his garments and tugging off his boots—it *had* been delightful to fuck Vivian while still wearing them—Rush walked to his washstand and poured water into the basin. He scrubbed a damp cloth over his nude body, though it was a shame to rinse away any of her lingering vanilla scent. There wouldn't be much of her on his skin, unfortunately, since they'd both been almost fully dressed when they'd fucked. They hadn't even made it into bed, so she wouldn't fragrance his sheets or pillows.

Once he'd cleaned himself, he threw on a banyan and stood by the fire, warming himself in the chill that followed Vivian's hurried departure.

"Not your usual variety of hothouse orchids." Jack leaned against the escritoire, crossing one booted ankle over the other. "More like one of the springtime bluebells I'd find growing in the woodlands."

"The pugilist is also a poet," Rush said. When Jack only shrugged his wide shoulders, Rush added, "Her circumstances are somewhat extraordinary."

Concisely, he explained Mrs. Vivian Sparkwell's dire situation, noting with surprise how the usually impassive Jack's expression shifted from surprise to anger.

"'Twas a vile thing her father and husband did," Jack growled, "taking any choice away from her."

"The lady has devised a winning strategy." Rush grinned, propping his elbow on the mantel. "Certainly, I shan't complain about it. I'll own that I *had* hoped she would reveal hidden passion, but what she gave me went far beyond those hopes. Vivian is..." He rubbed his jaw. "Unexpected."

"Getting steak and kidney pie when you've ordered fried oysters is unexpected," Jack answered.

Rush exhaled a laugh. "Vivian is no pie, nor a plate of fried oysters. She's..." He mulled over precisely the right words. "Courageous. Intelligent. Passionate. All hidden beneath an unobtrusive facade. Yet 'tis no wonder she learned to disguise her truer self."

His ribs tightened. It was reprehensible, the way she'd been treated by her father and the disagreeable Mr. Sparkwell, as if she didn't matter.

"Hm," Jack said, narrowing his gaze.

"What the devil does that lone syllable mean?" Rush demanded.

"So many words to describe her character," Jack answered, "and none to describe her cunt. And you're rubbing your chest."

"Dyspepsia, and nothing more." Rush picked up the fire poker and jabbed it into the smoldering logs, causing flames to rise up like curses.

"I'll summon a sawbones to administer a purgative." Jack chuckled.

Rush returned the poker to its place and faced his friend with purposeful calm. Yet his insides did twist, and it had nothing to do with the meal he'd taken earlier at a chophouse.

"Neglected wives are frequent visitors to my bed," he said offhandedly, purposefully consigning Vivian to an established category—when there was nothing typical about her.

"Yet here you are," Jack pointed out, "the disinterested rake on the verge of chasing after the Widow Sparkwell when she fled from his embrace."

"Piss off," Rush threw back without anger.

"Surely her pussy possesses no sorcery to thus enchant you. Though from the looks and sounds of things," Jack continued, "there *was* magic."

"Never came harder in my life," Rush admitted. He'd known many lovers in the course of his seven and thirty years, and yet the experience with Vivian had truly leveled him in a way he'd not foreseen.

He shook his head. "We are means to an end for each other. If we played our parts well enough tonight, she'll have no need to return."

Rush rubbed his chest again, but the tightness remained. Even though he did his utmost to keep in prime condition, perhaps he did need to see a physician. Whatever ailed him, it was merely corporeal. It had nothing at all to do with the fact that he prayed Vivian wasn't yet ruined, and the rise of hope within him that he'd see her once more.

"MORE TEA, MADAM?" the maid asked as Vivian's head drooped. "Something to give you a bit of liveliness?"

Seated at her escritoire, Vivian blinked, trying to rouse herself. The few hours of sleep she'd managed when she had finally returned home last night—or rather, early this morning—did little to sustain her through the afternoon. Yet the prospect of attempting a nap was impossible, not when she awaited the day's mail. Hopefully, it would be minimal, if not nonexistent.

"That won't be necessary, Sue." She rubbed her face. "Have you my correspondence?"

"Yes, madam."

Vivian's stomach churned as her maid handed her a substantial packet of letters. When Sue curtseyed and left her private parlor, Vivian anxiously reviewed her correspondence. In addition to a few letters from relatives, there were an alarming number of invitations. But perhaps all was not lost. Everything had likely been mailed yesterday, long before Vivian had been seen with Rush, and gossip traveled far faster than the post.

She tightly gripped the edge of an invitation requesting the honor of her company at a private assembly given in four days at Lord Jarnett's Mayfair home. The earl was known for the number of guests he hosted at sundry balls. Perhaps Rush would be there. After all, even though he was an infamous rake, he was a viscount's son.

Heat flooded her cheeks as she set Lord Jarnett's invitation aside. The things she'd done last night with Rush...in the light of day, it hardly seemed real. Yet the soreness between her legs proved otherwise. Behaving outrageously in public had been a mere tile in the mosaic of her wantonness. She'd made love—no, she'd *fucked* Rush, but not before he licked and sucked her quim with single-minded vigor, as though her pleasure was all that signified to him, as though she herself mattered.

When Jack Morgan had briefly appeared, she'd been so aroused by him watching her, and then Rush had made the shocking declaration that the two men *shared* women...and painted a picture of *her* being that woman...

She squeezed her thighs together as her quim grew slick. Was something wrong with her? How could she desire anything so lustful, so utterly forbidden?

Last night was a temporary erotic madness, yet Rush's words to her continued to reverberate. He'd said that he was sought out only for physical pleasure, insisting there'd be no deeper emotional connections with his lovers. His eyes had shone with loneliness, however. She saw them now, dark and deep. They lingered in her mind as her body continued to throb in the aftermath of last night.

Her very well-serviced body. Gracious, could that man fuck.

A tap sounded at the door to her parlor.

Pressing her hands to her cheeks to hide their telltale rosiness, she saw that her stepson John had poked his head in. He did look so like his father, especially now, smiling as though pleased with himself.

"Good afternoon, madam," he said cheerfully. "I beg a moment of your time."

Even as he asked permission—though it didn't quite sound like a request—he stepped into the chamber. He was suitably dressed as a landed gentleman, with his neat wig freshly powdered, and his clothes tasteful but not excessively French. Such a marked contrast to Rush's fashionable but effortless style.

"You look overheated, madam." He peered at her. "I can summon my private physician to bleed you, should you require."

"A kind offer," she replied, reaching for her fan and cooling her face. "'Tis merely the repercussions of taking my tea too hot."

"I trust I am not interrupting you," John said as he seated himself on the divan.

What if I said he was? "Not a bit. Merely reviewing my correspondence. There's an abundance of it," she said, trying to hide her disquiet. "My presence is requested at numerous events."

"Do save room on your schedule for a week from Thursday," he said, sounding very gratified both for her and with himself. "We are invited to dine with Lord and Lady Grenham, and someone will be in attendance who is most keen to make your acquaintance. In truth," he added, chuckling, "Mr. Colville desires more than an acquaintanceship with you. We're both members of the same club, and he has confided in me that 'tis his intention to court you."

Her stomach pitched, and she stared at John in disbelief.

"I am out of mourning but a month," she protested. "And I've never met the man."

"What is time in comparison to an eager bridegroom?" When she failed to laugh at John's jest, he continued, "'Tis not unusual for widows to remarry soon after reentering society, and as for meeting Mr. Colville, you have already at Mrs. Vane's assembly two Seasons ago."

A vague impression flitted into her mind of a tallish man, approximating handsomeness, some fifteen years her senior. But as to the content of their conversation, and the sort of man he might be, she couldn't recollect.

"His residence in town is quite fine," John went on, "and I'm told that his estate in Lancashire has some of the best fishing in the county."

"I do not fish, John," she replied in a remarkably calm voice despite the pounding of her heart.

"Of course you don't." He smiled at her munificently. "All this is to say that he will keep you very well, and that you needn't fear the awful insecurity of widowhood."

"I feel perfectly secure," she answered.

"For how long?" Her stepson regarded her with concern. "Managing your own affairs must be dreadfully daunting, and not a little exhausting. With a husband to oversee everything, you can rest easy and know that you are being taken care of."

Vivian drew a breath, battling for calm when all she wanted to do was scream. "Such benevolence is not required."

"Oh, I don't mind," he answered, either unaware or ignoring the edge in her words. "Your father and my father, God rest both their souls, made certain that you would never want for safekeeping. 'Tis my honor to shoulder that responsibility."

She *could* take care of herself quite well, and had been the one responsible for the overseeing of both her father's household, and William's, as well. All debts were settled, the servants were managed and also paid promptly, and, to the best of her knowledge, she never left the house with her petticoat over her head.

Yet if Mr. Colville made a formal offer for her hand, she had to accept, else she would lose everything. She had no living male relative to whom she might apply for assistance. Even genteel poverty seemed beyond her reach.

"John," she said flatly. "I do *not* wish to marry."

He blinked at her for a moment, then smiled. "'Tis very becoming in a widow to insist that no man will ever take the place of her late husband. However," he added indulgently, "all women require a man's protection. This is an unkind world, madam, especially to women without husbands, and I'd be remiss in my duties if I did not find someone to take my father's place."

"I could remain unmarried," she pointed out.

"Dependent on your widow's portion?" He looked alarmed by the thought. "That can hardly be enough to keep you. And, I ought to remind you, that there will come a time when I marry, and my wife will shoulder the position as mistress of this house. Our children will take precedence, and you deserve better than begging for crumbs from our table."

"I don't require much." Frustration climbed up Vivian's throat. "Even crumbs will suffice."

"No, no, madam. I have sworn to do my duty by you, and I shall." He rose. "Much as I'd delight in discussing this exciting matrimonial prospect, I've a meeting at the Crown Coffee House in half an hour. Don't expect me home for supper."

He strode to her and kissed her cheek. "Are you certain you don't want to be bled? Your face is exceedingly hot."

"Sue will bring me some soothing lavender oil to rub on my temples," she answered.

"Ah, a female's nervous complaint." He nodded sagely, although he was unmarried and had no sisters, before heading out the door. "A pleasant afternoon and evening, madam."

Alone, she stood from her escritoire and walked to the window. The master's bedroom had a better view of the back garden, hers being obscured by an elm with spreading branches, but she stared at the tidy walkways of crushed shells that wended their way around the hedges and plants. All the paths lead to the same wall at the back of the garden. From there, you had to simply turn around and head back the way you'd come. There was no going forward and no true destination.

Anxiety turned to excitement as she moved from her window to tug on the bell pull. She fought for calm but it had been in short supply since yesterday. Still, she took a steadying breath as she donned her cloak and tied the ribbons of a flat-crowned chip hat beneath her chin.

"I'm going out," she said when Sue appeared, "and require a chair."

"Yes, madam. Shall we expect you for supper?"

"A cold collation will suffice for whenever I do come home."

Vivian headed down the stairs and waited in the entryway while her footman called for a sedan chair. She examined herself in the mirror, nervously fussing with the ribbons of her hat. Her cheeks still carried hectic color, and her eyes were bright with a mixture of apprehension and eagerness.

"The chair is here, madam," the footman informed her. "Where shall I tell them to take you? Oxford Street?"

"I'm not shopping today, Tom," she answered. "Tell the chairmen that I'm going to Dean and Queen streets."

If the footman thought it unusual that she intended to go to Soho, he said nothing. Instead, he bowed, and left to give instructions to the men carrying the sedan chair as to where the mistress of the house intended to go.

The entryway loomed around her, with its paintings of prized horses, the vases of Staffordshire porcelain, the three-branched silver candelabra that stood ready to light the way when the master of the house returned after dark.

This had never been *her* home. It belonged to William, and now it was John's. Just as she had been one of William's possessions, she was being treated by her stepson as something he'd inherited, like a cracked ewer he wanted to foist on someone else.

She would do whatever was necessary to ensure that she no longer was any man's asset to be implemented or discarded as he determined.

Straightening her shoulders, she crossed the threshold of the house.

JACK WOVE JUST IN TIME TO AVOID A FIST STRAIGHT TO HIS JAW, BUT HOB'S knuckles still grazed his cheek. It was a greenhorn mistake, not keeping his eyes on his sparring partner, but the flash of bluebell satin hovering near the ring had distracted him. Most of the men who visited Hob Dugan's pugilism academy didn't favor clothing the color of wildflowers.

Dancing around Hob, Jack took the chance to see who had come into this citadel of belligerent masculinity wearing such a hue. His footing faltered when he saw that a woman lingered at the ropes, and not just any woman, but Mrs. Vivian Sparkwell.

Difficult to remain focused on sparring when the last time he'd seen the widow, she'd been wildly fucking Rush to a fare-thee-well. Flushed cheeks, open mouth, eyes lustrous with desire. She'd been the picture of raw sexuality, and Jack had been forced to go into the other room to frig himself as he listened to her and Rush rutting like beasts.

Hob's fist connected with his shoulder and Jack grunted.

"Where's your head at, jackass?" Hob growled. His trainer's attention moved toward Mrs. Sparkwell, and he snorted. "Distracted by a bit of mutton. No use going on if you're thinking with your cock and not your fists."

Hob lumbered from the ring, leaving Jack to stare at the wide-eyed widow. Her gaze moved from his face to his bare chest, which was slick with sweat, and then lower, along his stomach and to the line of hair that trailed from under his navel to beneath the waistband of his low-slung breeches.

Her eyes widened even more, and Jack swallowed a groan when she licked her lips.

Needing a moment to collect himself, he went to the bucket of water in one corner of the ring and dipped a rag into it, which he wrung over his head. The water did little to cool him, and Mrs. Sparkwell seemed fascinated by the path it took as it ran in rivulets over his body.

He padded over and looked down at her. She clung to the lowest rope, her grip tight, yet she didn't back away.

"I...I was looking for Rush," she said when he remained silent. He wasn't very good with words when it came to women he fancied. "They said at his rooms that I might find him here."

"Found me, instead," he answered. He almost asked if she was disappointed by this, but the stain of pink in her cheeks and avid gaze said otherwise.

Her lashes lowered, and she spoke softly. So softly that he crouched down to hear her better.

"What's that?" he asked, bending toward her.

"'Twas a rather new experience," she whispered. "Having someone see me whilst I'm..." Her lips formed a rosebud of embarrassment, then she added, "Yet for you, 'twas not so novel."

Your turn to speak, he reminded himself when he found himself merely staring at her. "Rush told you, then. That—we share women."

More color flooded her cheeks but her gaze locked on his. "Is it a common occurrence?"

"'Tisn't—" He cleared his throat. "For everyone."

Amazing that she stood here, talking to him about how he and Rush fucked the same woman, and even though the idea clearly shocked her, she wasn't running away. If anything, she looked fascinated.

His cock twitched.

She was so unlike the women Rush shared with him, this soft little petal of a woman, with her big gray eyes and gentle voice. When she'd come into the gaming hell last night, it had been clear that she trod in entirely unfamiliar territory. Then, later, Rush had explained her situation, and the miserable conditions of her jointure.

All Jack wanted to do was sweep her up in his arms and carry her somewhere hidden so he could keep her safe. Yet the way she'd taken command of her circumstance by making such an outlandish proposition to Rush, perhaps she didn't need Jack's protection. Perhaps she was much stronger than anyone gave her credit for.

"Do *you* enjoy it?" she asked lowly.

"I'd never done...such things," he said, struggling to speak, getting more tongue-tied by the fact that she seemed to care what *he* felt. "Before I met Rush. I like it, though."

The arrangement had begun almost by happenstance, years ago. Rush had needed someone to keep watch while he'd fucked a married lady, and had asked Jack to perform as lookout. But the lady had taken one look at Jack and suggested that he join them.

The woman had been so delighted by the results, word had spread about Jack and Rush's skill in pleasuring a woman together. In short order, he and Rush were in great demand.

It *was* gratifying, watching a woman come apart as he and Rush simultaneously pleasured her. To see her lose herself to frenzy, and to know that he made that happen for her.

If, in the aftermath, when the woman left and he returned to his solitary bed, he wished for someone to hold all night long, to kiss her awake in the morning, to watch as she brushed out her hair and made ready for the day...if he craved that, he pushed such wants away. Men like him had nothing to offer but big muscles and fragile hearts, and that wasn't enough to keep anyone.

Certainly not someone like Mrs. Sparkwell, who deserved more than a brute with barely any coin in his pocket, who could hardly hammer two words together in her presence.

Besides, she was here for Rush, not him.

"Oi, Morgan!" Hob shouted. "Got a match tomorrow. You going to train or get your cock sucked?"

Jack's gaze met Mrs. Sparkwell's, and even though her eyes were round as dinner plates, she murmured, "I don't believe that gentleman will provide both services."

A stunned bark of laughter leapt from Jack. "Everyone says Hob uses too much teeth, anyway."

She pressed her fingertips to her lips, and something bright and shiny gleamed in the center of his chest.

But, like the bastard Hob said, he *did* have a match in a day, and needed extra time in the ring if he was to have any chance at winning the purse. Reluctantly, he stood and headed back toward where his trainer waited impatiently. Yet Jack couldn't resist a glance over his shoulder, only to find Mrs. Sparkwell ogling the span of his back as well as the shape of his arse.

She might never be his, the little widow, but at least he knew she thought about having him in her bed. It would have to be enough.

Rush stepped out of the chamber set aside for men to change from their street clothing and into a state of dress more appropriate for taking exercise. Shirtless, barefoot, and with his hands wrapped in preparation for sparring, he entered the large open space where Hob Dugan had three boxing rings set up. At present, all three of them were occupied.

Jack sparred with Dugan in the center ring, which was no surprise, as tomorrow night Jack was slated to fight in a match at the Summerville Pleasure Gardens. Yet Rush's steps slowed when he saw Vivian watching Jack train. Her attention never left Jack's massive, gleaming body, so she clearly enjoyed the sight.

Rush's breath came quickly, and there was a peculiar sensation in his belly that reminded him of waking up on his birthday.

Well, he was only taken off guard by seeing her here at the pugilism academy. After the way she'd bolted last night, he hadn't expected to see her again, so it made sense that he'd be a bit thrown by her sudden reappearance.

If his steps sped to bring him closer to her, that was merely the effect of drinking a cup of strong coffee shortly before coming to the academy.

"Dugan's the best pugilism trainer in London," he said with admirable sangfroid as he neared, "so if you're looking for instruction, you've come to the right place. Jack's his star protege."

Vivian spun to face him, looking delightfully flustered and entirely edible. However, she managed to collect herself enough to say, "'Tis fortunate, then, as my left hook needs improvement."

"There *are* women who fight, though the practice is to fight completely nude above the waist." He drew closer. "That would certainly ruin you, or make your fortune."

In their haste last night, they hadn't undressed, which was a shame because she promised to be soft and round and luscious. He, however, was partially naked, and he smiled to himself as she barely hid her fascination with his body. In particular, she seemed riveted by the ridges of his abdomen. Her hand curled into itself as if to prevent her from reaching out and touching his flesh.

His muscles quivered as if she truly had run her fingers over his stomach.

"Further ruination is necessary, I take it." He didn't anticipate the expectancy in his voice.

She pulled her attention back to his face. "John has found a suitor for me, a man I barely know." She cleared her throat. "Forgive me—I shouldn't have tracked you here, only, 'tis almost certain this suitor will soon make an offer for me."

"And we cannot have that," Rush drawled.

"We *did* agree to continue on with our...arrangement...until I was declared unmarriageable."

"Faith, love," he said, coming closer so she had to tilt her head back to look at him, "you will not find me unwilling to honor our bargain." He toyed with the bow tied beneath her chin. "You're a present I'm eager to unwrap."

"I would very much like you to unwrap me," she said breathlessly.

The sound of fist connecting with flesh sounded from the ring, and both Rush and Vivian turned to see Jack had landed a solid uppercut to Dugan's belly. The trainer stumbled and fell onto his back, but when Jack loomed over him, Dugan let out a wheezing laugh.

"That's the way, my boy!" the trainer croaked.

Jack cracked a smile and helped Dugan to his feet, but as he did so, his gaze strayed to Vivian, and his smile faltered. After using his body like a well-honed weapon to lay out another man, Jack looked *shy* to have Vivian's attention.

Oh, the poor blighter. Jack was massive, yet tenderhearted as a lamb.

"Finally made your introduction to Jack, I see," Rush said affably.

"A, um, charming fellow."

Rush tipped his head back and laughed. "Charm's never been part of Jack's armory."

"I like him," she answered, raising her chin in defiance.

"I like him, too." Rush planted his hands on his hips.

"You must," she replied, "if you..." She made a vague gesture with her hand. "He said you did."

A smile quirked Rush's lips. "The idea appealed to you last night. As I recall, the mere mention of the prospect had you coming like a madwoman."

What a glorious sight it had been, and he'd been the lucky man who'd had his cock in her at the time. That same organ thickened at the recollection.

Rush clasped his hands in front of his groin. Much as he appreciated his cockstands in other circumstances, they could result in injury at Dugan's.

"I..." She swallowed. "The notion might have its appeal."

"God, you're delightful," he said huskily.

"Before we can consider *those* matters," she plowed on, "'twould benefit me to be seen in your company once more. Perhaps somewhere more public than a gaming hell or a private salon."

"Summerville Pleasure Gardens ought to suffice," he said. "Are you familiar with it?"

"Once, early in our marriage, William took me to Ranelagh, but we never made it to Vauxhall or Summerville."

"An excellent place," Rush confirmed. "Pavilions and follies and music. All manner of delights, but the most appealing feature is that there will be a large number of people in attendance tomorrow night to see Jack Morgan face off against Davy 'Slaughter' Smith."

"Fighting a man called *Slaughter* sounds highly unpleasant." Color drained from her face, and she glanced at Jack, who shadowboxed as Dugan continued to catch his breath.

"A solid bet, that Jack," Rush said. "I trust you're amenable to a very public and scandalous night at the pleasure garden."

"For many reasons," she said distractedly as she continued to stare at Jack.

There was little purpose in jealousy. The arrangement with Vivian was merely to ensure that she'd be ruined and achieve her freedom.

Feeling the bite of envy as she seemed rather smitten by Jack was ludicrous—and contrary to his every instinct.

All the same, he touched his fingertips to her chin and guided her
attention back to him. "A kiss to seal our plans."

Her eyes widened, yet she nodded.

He stepped even nearer, catching that warm scent of vanilla that
clung to her skin. As he bent his head, her lashes fluttered shut and she
offered her lips to him. He kissed her, lightly at first, but at her sound of
pleasure, he drank deeply from her. When her hands clutched at his
bare biceps, fingers digging into his skin, he growled into her mouth.

She gave herself so fully to each experience, as if she burned with a
ravenous need.

A jolt of fear coursed through him, and he broke the kiss.

Heavy-lidded, she gazed back at him.

"Only last night," he said, his voice raspier than he expected, "you
were uneasy to kiss me in Adelaide's salon. Yet here we're kissing in
Dugan's pugilism academy, and where are your blushes?"

"I assure you," she answered, her words equally husky, "I am
blushing in places that you cannot see."

He tightened his jaw against a tide of desire. In the course of his long
existence as a rake, he'd known many lovers, people who deployed
suggestive words with calculation. It was a game of strategy, seduction.
Everyone striving to get ahead, to come out the winner, and the prize was
remaining unscathed. There was pleasure to be sure, but almost nothing
was done without purposeful intent.

Not so with Vivian. She'd no concealed motivation, no aim to emerge
the victor. What she said and did was genuine, just as *she* was genuine.

He ought to call an end to their arrangement—she could damage
him in ways he didn't want to consider.

And yet he said, "Tomorrow night. I shall meet you at the entrance to
the pleasure garden. Ten o' the clock. Wear something conspicuous."

"Tomorrow night." She took several steps, before turning to look
back at him. Her gaze moved to the boxing ring, where Jack punched
small padded bags in each of Dugan's hands. As if aware that he was
being watched, Jack's blows slowed, and he straightened to stare at
Vivian.

Jack blinked when Vivian spun on her heels and hurried out of the pugilism academy. He murmured something to Dugan, who muttered in response before climbing down from the ring.

Rush hoisted himself up onto the platform and dipped between the ropes. His feet slapped against the canvas as he approached Jack, his friend fussing with the wrappings around his hands, and occasionally shooting glances in Rush's direction.

"How charming," Rush said with a smirk, "properly meeting the delightful widow."

"Don't know if you'd call it a proper meeting." Jack grunted when he fumbled with the wrappings and the cloth strip on his right hand dangled loose. "Unless you count me stammering and bleating like a goat."

"I was unaware that you were ever concerned with *talking* to my latest lover." Rush stepped closer and began to wind the cloth back around Jack's hand. "For fuck's sake, you could knock ships out of the ocean with these Brobdingnagian paws of yours."

Jack frowned at him, and a measure of shame tightened Rush's muscles. He'd deliberately chosen a word that a man of limited education might not know. Jack was a miner's son who knew his letters but the cost of books was beyond his means, and he surely hadn't read Swift.

Tugging his hand free from Rush's ministrations, Jack's scowl deepened. "*Your* lover. That sounds oddly exclusive for a slut like you."

"You've seldom complained when I fail to share a woman with you," Rush replied. There was no use in protesting against being called a slut —he certainly was one, and there was no shame in such an appellation.

"She's special." Jack finished wrapping his hand and began to shadowbox.

"Do you know," Rush said, "she was more concerned about your welfare against Slaughter Smith than she was about besmirching her reputation?"

Jack's movements slowed, but didn't stop. With feigned indifference, he said, "Foolish of her, when only one should matter."

"Not *foolish*," Rush returned. "She's kindhearted. Like you."

"And she kisses and fucks *you* as if she was born for it."

The longing palpable in Jack's voice, Rush contemplated his friend. If Rush was a good man, he'd find some way to bring Jack and Vivian together and step aside. After all, an affair with a boxer who was also a gaming hell enforcer would surely cause enough scandal to ruin her.

But Rush wasn't a good man. He was selfish and avaricious and part of Vivian was *his*.

Was it wrong to deny her and Jack when they both clearly were captivated by each other?

"I'm bringing her to Summerville tomorrow night," he said, and that made Jack halt.

"She'll watch me fight?" His friend sounded both pleased and terrified by the notion.

"Better make a good show of it." Rush sent an experimental jab in Jack's direction, and his friend dodged the blow easily—which was a little insulting, but he ought to take comfort in the fact that Jack was a paid and trained pugilist, whilst Rush boxed merely to ensure that he could fuck with greater stamina.

There had been naked hunger in Vivian's eyes as she'd ogled him. His efforts at maintaining himself were well rewarded. Yesterday, she'd been a timid widow, and today, she had evolved into a woman who let herself feel the fullness of her desire.

If Rush succeeded at nothing, he needed to help Vivian on her path of discovering who she truly was. For how much longer he would be part of that journey, he didn't know.

And somewhere, hovering at the periphery, was Jack. Rush wasn't certain what part his friend would play in all of this, but there was a way for everyone to get what they wanted. For a little longer.

8

HEART POUNDING, VIVIAN STEPPED DOWN FROM THE SEDAN CHAIR AND shook out her skirts. She'd taken extra care with her appearance before heading out tonight, and congratulated her past self for making the impulsive acquisition of a cherry-red silk robe a la française. The gown was slightly out of date, having been purchased two years ago, but hopefully the guests at the pleasure garden wouldn't notice the minuscule details that said it wasn't the very latest in fashion.

She'd pinned up her hair and tied a black velvet ribbon around her neck, and even wore a daring patch just beside her mouth. Would she blend in tonight amongst the festively-dressed revelers, or would she stand out? What would Rush think of her ensemble?

It didn't matter—he'd proven himself willing to bed her, and agreed to more time in public to ensure her ruining. Yet it *did* matter.

"I've a mind to skip Summerville entirely and hie you straight to my bedchamber," he growled in her ear, startling her with his sudden appearance.

"Yet," he continued in a low murmur, "I'm supposedly a gentleman, and must honor my obligations."

She closed her eyes as he stepped behind her and stroked his hands up and down her arms. Even this small touch lit flames of awareness and arousal in her.

Her eyes opened when she heard someone nearby giggle. A quartet
of people passed her and Rush, eyeing their public display with expressions ranging from scandalized to titillated. She quashed the instinct to
shy away from attracting attention—that's what this was about. Everything had to be done publicly.

Even without that motivation to permit Rush's attentions, being this
near felt too good to break away from him.

Continuing to stand close to her, he handed a coin to one of the chair
bearers, who collected another fare before trundling off into the night.

"Even so," Rush said on a sigh, "I must enjoy tormenting myself for I
want you to turn around so I may look my fill of you."

"I'm nothing if not obliging," Vivian said, turning in his arms.

His wolfish gaze moved from the crown of her head to where the
jeweled buckles of her shoes peeked out from beneath the ruffled hem of
her gown. His attention lingered on her face, the length of her throat,
and the expanse of skin bared by her low-cut neckline.

His nostrils flared. Could he catch the perfume she'd dabbed
between her breasts?

"Minx," he chided silkily. "If you were obliging you would not taunt
me thus by looking so ravishing, and us so far from an available bed."

She opened her mouth to tell him that she was not and never would
be ravishing, before pressing her lips together. Tonight, at the least, she
was as beautiful as she was in his eyes, and equally desirable.

"I trust this gown is suitably conspicuous," she said, glancing down at
herself.

"No one will be able to tear their eyes from you. Observe." Rush
nodded toward more guests entering the garden, many of them staring
openly at them. He took her hand in his and placed it on his forearm,
before leading her toward the iron gates that marked the entrance to the
pleasure garden. "But only *I* am the lucky one who has you on his arm."

"Together, we make the handsomest couple in attendance." At the
very least, *he* was magnificent in his coat, waistcoat, and breeches of
ebony satin, with scarlet and gold embroidery dancing along the lapels
and cuffs. To her delight, he wore his thigh-high leather boots, making
him resemble a wicked elven creature ready to spirit her away.

He gave the attendant at the gate another coin, and they entered
what had to be an enchanted kingdom. Though Summerville was

smaller than Ranelagh, it still made her breath catch in her throat. Torches and colored lanterns lined the paths, and more lanterns danced from tree branches. There were night-blooming plants filling the air with scent, and vines snaking around cunning pavilions that resembled giant jewel boxes. Strolling musicians dressed like commedia characters enjoined guests to spontaneously dance upon the lawn.

Rush paused by a woman wearing a Columbina costume who was selling ices for a ha'penny. Whatever additional sum he paid for their refreshments must have been extraordinary, because Columbina's eyes widened behind her mask when he dropped money into the open box that served as the till.

"Thank you, my lord," the vendor said in amazement.

Rush merely nodded before taking two silver cups full of pink ice and handing one to Vivian. She brought a spoonful of ice to her lips, tasted it, and laughed at the flavor.

"Rose, strawberry, and champagne," she said when he looked at her with amused curiosity. "Unexpected—like you."

"If either of us is unexpected," he answered as they strolled through the garden, "'tis you, my dear Mrs. Sparkwell."

Ah—he'd been careful to use her name in public, and many people around them seemed to take note. Very considerate of him, to ensure scandal.

They paused to watch a woman holding ribbons dance to a fiddler's tune before moving on. Rush seemed to purposefully guide her towards the most crowded places, particularly once he'd finished his ice and kept his warm hand nestled in the small of her back.

"'Tis understandable," he said in an offhand manner, "that the idea of marrying a man not of your choosing would be objectionable. Yet I was under the impression that ladies on the whole desired the institution of marriage."

"I was one of them." Her spoon scraped the bottom of the cup, and she handed them to a servant walking by with a tray. "William was a neighbor of ours in Durham. He was nearly the same age as my father, and I attended his first wife's funeral when childbed fever took her and her babe. John was a little boy then, and I often took care of him when Mr. Sparkwell and my father adjourned for manly business in the study.

"Truly," she went on, watching a man juggle crystal glasses, "I hadn't anticipated marrying William, but…" She cleared her throat, yet there was no hiding the next embarrassing fact. "My first Season was disastrous. No suitors, and no one asked for my hand. Except for William. I didn't *want* a husband so much older than me, but my father insisted his was the best offer I would receive, and so we wed."

"Hardly the sort of scenario a girl might dream of," Rush noted, but his eyes were kind.

"He wasn't a *bad* husband," she felt obliged to say. "Treated me with decency, and wasn't particularly angry when I failed to get with child. He had John already, so an heir wasn't necessary."

She wouldn't tell Rush that William's visits to her bed were infrequent, especially after it became evident that no pregnancy ever resulted from their efforts. If he had a mistress, William had been courteous enough to be discreet about it. That, in itself, was a modest blessing.

"And yet…" Rush said. They stopped and stood on the bank of an artificial lake, where miniature boats floated. "He did not treat you in the manner you deserved."

"My own notions of what I deserved were minimal, and I soon learned what he expected of me." She exhaled as memories assailed her, dimming the enchantment of the garden. "William was an ambitious man, in many ways. Socially, politically. My role was to facilitate his goals, and so I did, hosting dinners and levees with important people. In all of these gatherings, the focus always had to be William."

"Never you," Rush said darkly.

She couldn't stop her bitter laugh. "Gracious, no. He'd get rather cross, in fact, if I spoke too much or did anything that diverted attention away from him."

"Did he hurt you?" Rush asked, his voice edged and tight.

"Not physically," she allowed. "But once he was holding forth at the dinner table, and someone asked me my opinion of a novel—God, I forget which one now—and I made the unforgivable mistake of speaking my thoughts for no fewer than five whole minutes, distracting the company *away* from him and *to* me." Her lips twisted. "He wouldn't speak to me for a week after that."

The silence from Rush stretched on, and, puzzled, she glanced at him. His lips were pressed into a thin line, and a muscle in his jaw twitched.

"'Twas not so terrible," she said hurriedly.

"You've no obligation to defend indefensible behavior," Rush answered, sharpness in his words. "What's especially unconscionable is that fool Sparkwell convinced you that you don't merit anyone's attention, when the opposite is true."

She exhaled—the city's most renowned rake defended her. *Her.*

"Mayhap you're right," she conceded. "I'd not given it much consideration."

"You ought to."

"After William died," she said pensively as two miniature ships sailed by, "my intention had been to live quietly. There's a tidy little dower cottage on the country estate's property with its own garden, and I saw myself sitting on a bench in the sun, reading novels with an orange tabby cat at my feet."

"*Had* been," Rush noted. "And now?"

"Now..." She laughed ruefully. "Now, I'm attracting infamy. Which seems the furthest thing from a garden and books and cats."

"I trust you're enjoying your time as one of the scandalous."

She tapped her finger against her chin. "*Am* I scandalous?"

"We'll make damned certain you are," he said, stepping close so that their bodies almost touched, "Come, love."

He wove their fingers together and led her back toward where many guests congregated. In truth, he could have guided her toward the mouth of Hell and she would've gone willingly. Yet he was *not* the Devil, and instead of the entrance to Hades, he took her to a large octagonal stone and marble floor. Musicians stood in a nearby pavilion, and as they struck up a tune, revelers gathered.

"When was the last time you danced, Mrs. Sparkwell?" Rush took both of her hands in his and drew her onto the floor.

She didn't recognize everyone in attendance, though a few faces looked familiar, and with nervous anticipation, she noted how they watched her take the floor with a rake.

"Long enough ago to fear that I shan't recall the steps," she confessed. Her heart thudded—she'd hoped to be scandalous, but would she instead look like the veriest ninny stumbling through a country dance?

"Surprising, what the body remembers." He bowed to her, and she apprehensively curtsied.

The fiddle began to play, followed by the drum, and as the dance began, she did indeed shuffle through the first steps. Then Rush took her hand, murmuring, "Don't concern yourself with anyone else. The music is yours to enjoy—just as *I* am yours to enjoy."

She fixed her awareness on him and his glittering onyx eyes. Lilting, joyous music flowed over and around her. She watched his feet glide nimbly through the dance, and she mirrored his movements until she moved easily, turning and swaying in time with Rush. Her heart spun and she was borne upward like a whirligig upon the breeze.

And the way he looked at her...his focus never strayed from her face, despite all the beautiful distractions around them. There came a point in the dance when they changed partners, yet even then, he did not look at the beautiful new woman he was paired with. Instead, his gaze remained on Vivian, as though he could not wait to return to her.

'Tis all part of the scheme. He's supposed to show the world that we are lovers.

Yet her foolhardy heart refused to listen, and when the figures of the dance required her to return to him, she was light and giddy and gleaming.

The tune ended, too soon. Everyone applauded, and she prepared herself for Rush to lead her off the dance floor. Yet when the musicians played a slower tune, Rush bowed to her again—he did make such a lovely leg—and they danced once more.

These figures were slower, her palm pressed to Rush's, as they circled each other in time with the melody.

"My history, such as it is, has been laid before you," she said as they danced. "And yet my knowledge of you remains paltry."

"Little to tell," he answered. "'London's as abundant with men such as me as rats are abundant with fleas. A second son with too much money and time, caring only for pleasure."

"That remains your sole object?" She regarded him as they moved. "Surely you require more." It seemed such a thin existence, reduced to all but the most transitory experiences.

"I don't make demands on myself that I cannot meet," he replied blandly, as if he hadn't just admitted himself incapable of deep feeling.

"You give yourself too little credit."

His smile was rueful. "I've seven and thirty years' knowledge of myself. And there's abundant proof that, between my heart and my cock, the latter is the only organ that anyone desires."

"I cannot believe it." The dance's figures required her to turn around him as he stood still, and she circled him like a satellite fearful for the planet's soul.

"Belinda was her name," he said, his voice flat. "A sophisticated woman married to an equally sophisticated viscount."

"I see." She oughtn't dislike a woman she didn't know, and sourness curled in her stomach.

"Belinda was beautiful and witty and worldly, and you couldn't help but adore her." Rush took her hand again and they promenaded up the dance floor. "*I* couldn't help but adore her."

It wasn't fair to feel this sting of jealousy, and yet it bit her anyway. "You were lovers."

Rush's lips formed a cold shadow of a smile. "A fiery affair that consumed us both."

Vivian and Rush fell silent for a moment as the dance's figures required them to separate and make a turn alone around the floor. The steps were measured and deliberate, in time with the music, but her heart was not.

"I see by your face that you are prepared to pity me," he said wryly when Vivian returned to him. "That effort is unnecessary. The buffoon of the piece dances with you now, Mrs. Sparkwell. Because when I confessed to Belinda that I loved her, and we should run away together..." His expression turned grim. "I learned that I had vastly overestimated my significance to her."

"The witch," Vivian said hotly.

"I don't blame her," he said dispassionately, "and neither should you. From the beginning, she had been candid in her intentions. All she desired was a young lover with a hard cock, and I provided that. Certainly, it wasn't enough to destroy her marriage, her life. What she and I shared was a brief collection of trysts, not an affair, which can ruin the foundation of a life. 'Twas *I* who violated the rules by falling in love."

The dance ended, and Vivian stared at him as he bowed. Her chest ached to see the wintry resignation on his face, yet when she tried to hold his gaze, he looked away. Like polite strangers, he led her from the dance floor.

"You cannot help loving someone," she said softly as they walked side by side down a path.

"I *can* be wise, and know my place." He guided her around him as they continued to perform the dance. "I *am* an excellent fuck, and so Belinda recommended me as a lover to her friends."

Vivian stopped and faced him. "She *handed* you to others, like loaning a parasol?"

"It was most gracious of her," he replied with a tight smile. "For since that time, I've never been without company in my bed, and I am always careful to keep myself from making the same mistake with others that I made with Belinda."

"And you keep your affairs transitory. But, Rush," she went on, looking into his beautiful, cool face, "that doesn't mean you should never love *anyone*."

"When someone wants only pleasure, they seek me out. That is the summation of my usefulness. I'd be a fool to believe myself good for anything else."

Her ribs were tight, and her eyes grew hot. She took his hands in hers, stroking her thumbs over his wrists as he'd once done to her. His intention had been to enflame, and hers was to comfort.

"There exists another possibility," she said softly. "Someone might come to love you."

He looked hopeful, then stricken, and then, finally, a charming smile slid into place, obscuring anything that might hint at the wounded man beneath.

"Have I told you about the time I challenged a friend of mine to see who could earn the most money here at Summerville?" His grin flashed in the pale peach light from a lantern. "Poor Oxley tried his hand at acrobatics and wound up with only a tuppence and a thrown back."

"How did you best him?" It was clear what Rush's intention was, yet she wouldn't press him here for more. She'd no right to, in any case. The plan was to have her ruined, and then for her to move into her dower's cottage with her books and cat and solitude. He would go on with his rakehell life as he always did. Nowhere in their agreement had they mentioned anything deeper or more lasting.

That pain between her ribs spread through her, however, so that even as they stood together in this magical pleasure garden with laughter and music all around, loss whispered in her ears.

"Went home with one pound ten," Rush said proudly. "All earned from my singing. My voice won me prizes at Eton."

He tilted his head, waiting for a nearby flute and fiddle to quiet, and then he sang.

"It is not that I love you less/ Than when before your feet I lay:/ But to prevent the sad increase/ Of hopeless love, I keep away."

Her lips formed a wry smile. His message had been received. Yet the purity and beauty of his tenor voice still arrowed through her. As declarations of *keep away* went, it had been gorgeously rendered.

People had gathered as he'd sung, and clapped at the conclusion of his song. A few of them tossed coins in his direction, and he bowed.

"Had I a pianoforte to play in accompaniment," he said, sweeping up the coins, "I would've earned three pounds at least."

"Is there no end to your talents?" she asked, at once dazzled and dispirited.

Heavy-lidded, he drew her close. Awareness sparkled through her as she lifted her face to his. She had been warned, and yet it was no use. She wanted Rush, yes, and she knew with a sinking heart that she was already half in love with him.

"'Tis the barest hint of my capabilities that I've shown you," he said in a velvety caress. "*Viz*, I've revealed barely half the things I can do with my tongue. Allow me to demonstrate."

One hand cradling her jaw, he angled her face up. Her breath came quickly as he lowered his lips to hers, and took her mouth in a slow, deep kiss. She opened at once to him, and his tongue swept into her mouth, savoring her as if she were an exquisite delicacy. Molten heat gathered in her breasts and in her quim. She clutched at the hard muscles of his forearms, craving the feel of him and needing his steadiness when her legs were jelly beneath her. A dark growl vibrated from his chest.

"Mrs. Sparkwell!" a sharp female voice cried. "Have you no decency, madam?"

Vivian surfaced from the sensual haze Rush had cast, opening her eyes to see Augustine, Lady Bowles glaring at her. The baronet's wife was only a few years older than Vivian, but pinched lines formed around Lady Bowles's mouth as she looked at Vivian with outrage.

"From him, I expect as much," Lady Bowles snapped, gesturing at Rush with her fan, who merely gazed back at the woman with a disinterested smirk. "But you are an esteemed gentleman's widow, madam. And the spectacle you are making of yourself rivals any lurid pyrotechnic display."

"I should hope so." Vivian made no move to pull out of Rush's embrace.

When it became evident that Vivian had no intention of apologizing or appearing in any way ashamed or contrite, Lady Bowles made a huffing sound and marched away.

"Hopefully," Vivian said, watching the woman head toward a group of lords and ladies, "she's as free with her gossip as she is with her opinions on how other people conduct themselves."

Rush chuckled. "Such a vixen you've become."

"Lady Bowles is certainly a bitch."

That earned Vivian a full laugh from him.

A blare of horns sounded, and he wrapped an arm around her waist. He guided her away from the lake and toward a brightly lit pavilion. "Do you sicken at the sight of blood?"

"You aren't planning on *murdering* Lady Bowles?" Vivian asked in alarm. When he shook his head, she said, "I used to help bandage the workers on our estate when they were injured."

"I should have known that you'd be durable." As they walked, the crowds grew thicker and thicker, until they reached the large pavilion. Risers had been erected, and guests stood on them to get a view of the central attraction: a boxing ring, surrounded by torches. Rush led her to a riser that gave them a perfect view of the ring. One man, a hulking brute with a shaved head, stood shirtless in one corner, shaking out his arms.

Vivian gasped when she saw Jack in the opposite corner. He, too, had taken off his shirt, and bounced on the balls of his feet, making himself limber and ready for the brawl that was to come.

"Gentlemen, ladies," a man shouted from the center of the ring, "may I present for your enjoyment, Slaughter Smith versus Jack Morgan!"

The crowd shouted as the boxers gave quick bows. Someone rang a bell and the two fighters approached each other in the middle of the ring. Her stomach leapt to see the determined, focused expressions on their faces.

Jack might be prepared for the battle to come, but Vivian wasn't certain *she* was.

9

THIS WASN'T THE FIRST TIME RUSH HAD SEEN JACK FIGHT, YET IT WAS always riveting to witness his friend unleash the warrior within him.

"You could use his opponent as a bulwark," Vivian said anxiously. She clutched his forearm as they watched Jack and Slaughter Smith touch fists in the center of the ring whilst the judge looked on.

Her grip on Rush's arm was strong, but any excuse to have her hand upon him was a good one, so he'd no objections.

It *was* concerning that, big as Jack was, Slaughter Smith was even bigger. Smith also had an impressive record, and had killed three men in the ring, while five others had emerged so damaged that they hadn't been able to box again.

"Jack's no half-witted bruiser," Rush assured Vivian. "If Slaughter Smith has weaknesses, he'll find them."

She nodded, but didn't look much convinced by his assurances.

The bell rang and, the crowd cheering, Jack and Smith circled each other. Each man took exploratory jabs, none of the punches connecting as they continued to move around the canvas.

"Ten pounds on Smith," the robust gent standing next to Rush said.

"Done." Rush shook his hand before they both turned their attention to the fight.

Yet Smith and Jack continued to circle and jab, maintaining an arm's length between each other, and the spectators grew restless. They muttered and grumbled, until someone booed. More boos went up as Jack dodged Smith's left hook and danced back.

"Admittedly, I know little about pugilism," Vivian said, glancing around worriedly. "Yet I thought you were supposed to actually *hit* your opponent."

"They're testing the waters," Rush explained above the jeers. "Figuring out how their opponent fights. Smith's pushing but Jack won't exhaust himself in the first round by unleashing a barrage of punches. And he knows that Slaughter Smith is bigger, which means he'll tire faster, so if Jack can last longer, Smith'll wear himself out. A strategist, that Jack."

Vivian appeared impressed by the depth of Rush's knowledge, and he smirked at himself even as he preened.

Easier to focus on the fight, rather than the way she'd listened and looked at him with caring. It had stirred something deep within him, something it was better not to examine.

The bell rang, and the two fighters retreated to their corners. Dugan and Jack conferred seriously, while Slaughter Smith's trainer bellowed something in his boxer's face.

"Your man ain't got no bollocks," the gent next to Rush said smugly. "Thinks he's at a public assembly, not a boxing match."

"No need to hire a fiddle player just yet," Rush replied.

"He's calling the steps," Vivian added defiantly, "not following them."

Rush winked at her and she beamed up at him, but then her smile fell away when the bell rang once more. The crowd restively cheered as Jack and Smith approached each other.

Smith came out swinging. Jack was agile on his feet, and turned in time to avoid a hard hit, but Smith's wrapped knuckles grazed across Jack's cheek. Spectators roared in approval as blood dripped down Jack's face.

Vivian's hold on Rush tightened. "He's hurt!"

"Scrapes like that bleed abundantly," Rush assured her, "but they're negligible. If anything, our man's been inspired."

Rush well knew that determined look on Jack's face. Jack launched into a series of jabs aimed at Smith's head. The bigger man lifted his fists to guard himself. Jack inched his blows higher, causing Smith to raise his guard in an effort to protect his face.

"He can't break through his opponent's defenses," Vivian said unhappily.

"'Tisn't his intention," Rush answered. Louder, he yelled, "That's a lad, Jack!"

If Jack heard him, he didn't show it, but kept at his strategy. He took a few body blows, hits that would have laid Rush out for a good fortnight, but Jack was made of tougher stuff.

The bell rang once more. The sweat slicking Jack's body gleamed in the torchlight as he stalked back to his corner. Rush shot a glance at Vivian, and smiled as he noted the keen female interest in her gaze as she stared at Jack's shining torso, his every muscle clearly defined as his breeches hung low on his hips.

Jack and Dugan conferred once more as one of Dugan's assistants offered Jack a skin of water. Taking the skin, Jack rinsed out his mouth, spat the water on the ground, and dragged his brawny forearm across his lips.

It was primal and raw, and Vivian's chest rose and fell rapidly as she watched him.

No, Rush wasn't jealous. If anything, seeing her appreciation for Jack only whetted the edge of his own expectancy. Rush was a strategist, too, planning out in his mind how the rest of the night would unfold. His body went hot and tight in anticipation.

Once more, the bell rang, and again, Jack and Smith strode to the center of the ring to face each other. Smith seemed to be impatient for a bloodier brawl, and his punches were wild as he launched an attack that sent Jack shuffling backward until he was up against the ropes. The onlookers bellowed excitedly.

"He's done for," Vivian cried mournfully.

"Far from it." Rush turned to the gent beside him. "Make it fifteen pounds that Morgan takes Smith out with a body blow in the next minute."

The man pulled a timepiece out from his waistcoat pocket. "Done."

"Take note," Rush murmured in Vivian's ear. "Observe Jack."

"He's—" Her eyes went wide as Jack aimed more jabs at Smith's face.

Rush winked and placed his finger against his lips.

As Jack continued to direct short, quick blows toward Smith's head, Smith raised his guard. Higher and higher. Until Jack delivered a hard punch into his foe's right side. Into his liver.

Rush and Vivian cheered.

Agony twisted Smith's expression as he crumpled, and though he struggled to stand, it was clear that the hit had robbed Smith of his fight.

Jack raised his fists as the man gasped and groaned.

Cries of "Finish him!" rose up from the crowd. Thirsting for blood.

Vivian shot Rush a concerned look. It would be exceptionally easy for Jack to slam his fist into Smith's head and deal him a devastating hit. One Smith might not wake up from.

As the spectators shrieked, Jack loomed closer, and closer still. Smith fell to his knees, looking up at Jack with a weary, accepting expression.

Jack pushed his fist into Smith's shoulder. The boxer swayed and then toppled to the canvas. He was conscious, but motionless, and lay there as a judge counted to ten. Then the judge grabbed Jack's hand and raised it high.

Jack was the winner.

The crowd remained silent for a moment, then erupted into deafening cheers. If anyone grumbled that Jack Morgan hadn't spattered his opponent's blood and teeth across the canvas, those complaints couldn't be heard above the applause.

Rush added his voice to the acclaim, and beside him, Vivian jumped up and down as she shouted her praise.

Looking grim but victorious, Jack faced the spectators, giving small nods of thanks for their accolades. A moment later, he tugged his hand free from the judge's grip and went to help Smith's trainer get the other boxer to his feet. Together, they aided Smith as he staggered out of the ring before they, and Dugan, disappeared behind a curtain.

Turning to the man beside him, Rush yelled above the din, "That's fifteen pounds."

"Stuff it down your gullet," the gent answered angrily, shoving a wad of notes into Rush's hand before stalking off. The pavilion began to empty out as revelers went in search of other entertainments on the Summerville grounds.

"You knew," Vivian said as Rush tucked the money into a pocket, "what Jack's strategy would be. The high jabs ensured Slaughter Smith left his guard open on his body, so Jack could come in with the hit to his ribs."

"As I said," Rush noted, guiding Vivian out of the risers, "Jack's a technical fighter. All careful consideration and meticulously executed plans."

"Here I'd believed pugilism was nothing but brute force," she admitted.

"Brute force is only occasionally warranted. Strategy is by far the better option."

Instead of joining the throngs leaving the pavilion, Rush led her behind the curtain through which Jack, Dugan, and the others had exited. They found themselves facing a low building where members of the staff of Summerville milled. There were dancers and acrobats lounging on crates, and through an open door, Rush observed several musicians crammed into a room where they smoked pipes and passed a wineskin. In one of the small rooms, Smith lay upon a mat on the floor, eyes closed, while the fighter's trainer and a sawbones attended to his injuries.

Rush and Vivian peered into the next open door. Sure enough, Jack was there, tiredly leaning against a table as Dugan excitedly discussed the fight.

"A born scholar, you are," the trainer exclaimed. "Always knew you'd outthink Smith. A'course, 'twas my training that made certain you had the skills to back up the theory."

Jack said nothing, though he listened with a wry smile.

Rush tapped on the open door. "We're here to laud the champion."

He glanced down at Vivian, who shyly stood beside him. Her gaze kept flitting to Jack, still bare chested and shining with sweat, before skittering to the floor, and then back to Jack.

Jack himself straightened at the sight of Vivian. For a man who'd just beaten another man into near insensibility, he seemed awfully bashful.

Rush stepped into the room, with Vivian still sticking close to his side.

"Refresh yourself, Dugan," Rush said, handing the trainer a crown.

Dugan chattered his thanks before ducking out of the room. Once he'd gone, Rush closed the door, blocking out the prattle from outside. The small chamber felt even smaller, barely able to contain a table, a cane-back chair, and various pieces of detritus that a pleasure garden might generate.

Both Vivian and Jack seemed adorably uncertain, but Rush had no such hesitancy. He dropped into the chair—it creaked threateningly beneath him—and sprawled indolently.

"Vivian, love," he drawled, and gestured toward Jack. "Perhaps 'tis time to reward the victor."

10

VIVIAN GLANCED BACK AND FORTH BETWEEN JACK MORGAN, WHO WATCHED her with cautious but hopeful eyes, and Rush, lounging like a large black cat. Surely, Rush couldn't mean...?

Her heart, which had been pounding ever since Jack had entered the boxing ring, now set up a fierce beat beneath her ribs.

Swallowing, she took a step closer to Jack. There was an ewer and basin on the floor, along with a towel of marginal cleanliness, and she wet the towel before cautiously approaching Jack.

"The cut on your face," she murmured.

Absently, as if he'd forgotten about it, he dragged the back of his hand across the scrape, spreading blood over his broad cheekbone.

"Let me," she said softly, and raised up on her feet to dab the cloth over his cut. Obligingly, he leaned down so she might have better access to his injury. He didn't wince or flinch as she cleaned him, only watched her carefully. The space between them was barely a few inches, and his body held a clean tang of sweat. There was no denying the yearning in his crystal-blue eyes—it made hot need curl in her belly and thicken her blood.

"You'd the opportunity to deal a killing blow to Smith," she said, her words low in the narrow span that separated them. "Yet you didn't."

"He was done," Jack answered. His voice was rough as gravel yet gentle. "I don't hurt men who can't defend themselves."

"Not many have your ethic." The cut was clean now. She rinsed the cloth before returning to him and stroking it down his neck and over his torso's wide, hard planes, and the thick bunching muscles of his arms. This was how a gladiator's woman felt, tending to her warrior after brutal combat.

Jack Morgan wasn't *hers*, still the thought made her heart squeeze and a jolt of arousal shoot between her legs.

He merely shrugged one vast shoulder. Though a ruddy blush stained his cheeks, he continued to regard her closely as she went on cleaning him. With each stroke of the cloth over his body, his breath came faster, just as hers did.

"Did you like it," he rasped. "Seeing me fight?"

"I didn't think I would," she admitted. "Yet I couldn't take my eyes off of you. I was worried for you."

"For *me*?" His blush deepened.

"He was so big, your opponent. Terrifying. I didn't want you to get hurt. When you got that awful cut on your face, and there was so much blood..." She pressed a hand to her heart. "I wanted to jump into the ring and get you to safety."

He stared at her as if he couldn't quite understand what she was saying. "People usually like it when I bleed. Makes for a good show."

"The show doesn't matter," she murmured. "*You* do."

"Rush said you'd be in the crowd," he said gruffly. "I kept thinking about that, about you watching me. I wanted—" He cleared his throat. "I wanted you to like what you saw. I fought hard." He dragged in a breath. Hard for you."

She closed her eyes as a wave of need pulsed through her. How could she be so touched and so enflamed at the same time? To have this powerful fighter admit that he wanted to please her, however, nearly made her swoon.

At her silence, he said grimly, "Suppose you think I'm a brute."

Her heart ached. There was so much longing in his voice, so much gentleness, in contrast to the warrior he'd been in the ring.

"I think," she said, opening her eyes and setting the cloth on the table, "that I very much want to kiss you. May I?"

His nostrils flared. He gave a short nod, as if he didn't trust himself to speak.

Carefully, slowly, she cupped her hands around his hard jaw. Stubble prickled her palms, and she stroked her thumbs over the rasp of his incipient beard, loving the contrast of texture against her tender skin.

She touched her mouth to his. He was surprisingly soft against her, and, even though he made a low noise of pleasure, held himself almost motionless as she kissed him. Yet when her tongue came out to lick at the seam between his lips, the pleasured sound became a groan, and he opened to her.

He kissed her hungrily, as if he was a man finally given his first taste of sustenance after a long famine. One of his massive hands cupped her head, and the other folded around her waist, and she'd never felt so small yet so protected.

His breath heaved in and out jaggedly as their kiss grew more ravenous. He dragged his hand from her waist to cup her breast, kneading and stroking her through her gown. She sucked in air as his wide fingers dipped beneath her dress's neckline to find her tight nipple. He pinched it gently and she moaned into his mouth.

Between her legs, her clitoris pulsed, slick need glossing her folds.

There was a creaking noise behind her. She opened her eyes to look into the mirror, perched atop the table. Reflected back at her was Rush, leaning forward with avid interest as he watched her and Jack kiss.

His dark eyes burned with arousal, and he made no attempt to hide the thick shape of his erect cock that jutted against the front of his black satin breeches.

"That's right, love," Rush growled. "Let Jack pleasure you the way you both deserve."

She was *supposed* to feel embarrassed. She *ought* to be ashamed to kiss and caress a man while another watched. Such activities were only for brazen harlots, women who had abandoned themselves to licentiousness.

Her breasts grew heavier and tighter, and her juices ran in rivulets down the inside of her thighs. Through her lashes, she watched Rush watch her and Jack. Another moan slipped from her when Rush ran a hand down the length of his cock.

"Ah, you like that," Rush rumbled. "That seeing you and Jack makes me hard."

She gasped into Jack's mouth, and he deepened the kiss. Stepping between his open legs, she held on as tightly as she could to his slick back, his muscles shifting and knotting beneath her hands. He continued to play with her breasts, one then the other, and each stroke of his fingers over her taut nipples resounded hotly in her quim.

He hissed in a breath, and she watched with fascination as he adjusted the thick column of his cock wedged tightly in his breeches.

"Are you in pain?" she asked lowly.

He exhaled ruefully. "Aye."

"Mayhap I can help."

He swallowed audibly, then nodded. Jack leaned back slightly, his legs falling open, and she stared at the size of him. Even through fabric, he was astonishing.

Slowly, she reached for him. His gaze was slitted, burning, and when she tentatively cupped his cock through his breeches, he cursed.

"I'm sorry," she said, snatching her hand away though she ached to feel more of him.

"No apologies," he gritted. "You feel—so fucking good." He took hold of her hand and guided her back to him. When she circled his shaft, he swore again, reverently.

She grew bolder, and stroked him, his hand guiding her. He was wondrous beneath her hand, yet—

"These blasted breeches," she muttered.

Jack released her long enough to tear open his fall. She gasped as his length rose up unencumbered, and stared at his thick cock, veined and red, with a broad, smooth head slipping free of his foreskin. Her mouth watered at the bead of moisture glistening at the slit.

"Let me tend you," she whispered. At his nod, she rinsed the rag once more and then stroked it over his cock. She cleaned him with lustful worship, loving how his muscles quivered and his breath came quickly as she massaged him. After several more swipes of the damp cloth, she set it aside and wrapped her bare hand around him.

Good God, her fingers couldn't meet around his girth. More wetness saturated her quim as she pumped her hand up and down. As she did, he leaned forward and claimed her mouth in a hot, ferocious kiss.

"Such pretty lips," he rasped into her mouth. "Will you...put them on me?"

She jolted at the request.

"Damn," he muttered. "I shouldn't have—I'd no right to ask."

"I want to," she whispered. She'd never done such a thing before, and only a few times had she even heard of the act. Now it was her turn to try it. Her pulse was frantic between her legs, and she glanced down at the floor in preparation for kneeling.

"Madam, your servant," Rush said smoothly, coming forward to lay his folded coat upon the ground. He gestured to it courteously, and she couldn't stop herself from smiling as she knelt on the expensive garment.

Then he backed away, leaving her presented with a very aroused Jack and his sizable cock. Breathing quickly, she wrapped her hand around it before wetting her lips. Uncertainly, she licked the head, and tasted salt.

"Fuck," Jack snarled. Yet his expression was blissful.

Growing more emboldened, she licked the crown once more, swirling her tongue around it before fitting it into her mouth. He was hot and satiny, and, following instinct, she sucked on him. More swears and oaths poured from him as his hips involuntarily bucked up, pushing him deeper between her lips.

She did her best to take more of him into her mouth, widening her jaw to accommodate his size, but there was simply too much of him. She wrapped her hand around the remainder of his length. Finding her rhythm, she bobbed her head up and down, stroking him as she did so. One of his hands clutched the edge of the table, while the other rested lightly on the back of her head, holding her gently in place as she sucked him.

"Fuck—you're so—you're so perfect," he said hoarsely. "So beautiful."

Never had she *felt* so beautiful, or powerful, than she did at that moment with Jack's throbbing cock in her mouth and his praise falling like raindrops all around her. She might not be the most experienced with this act, but by God, she loved doing it.

She glanced at the mirror behind Jack, and while his body blocked Vivian's view of herself, she *could* see Rush. He'd also opened his breeches, and pumped his fist up and down his cock as he watched her.

The look on his face was both euphoric and ferocious, his eyes heavy-lidded, his mouth open as he gasped with each stroke.

A shudder of pure lust racked her. To have Jack's cock in her mouth, and to witness how the sight aroused Rush, turned her own desire monstrous. It would devour her whole, yet she wouldn't mind, not if it meant feeling this sharp pleasure.

"Stop, stop," Jack snarled.

She pulled back, his cock sliding from her mouth. Panicked, she asked, "Am I doing something wrong?"

"Don't want to—shoot my seed—too soon." He carefully pulled her to stand, and kissed her with hard, hungry desperation. "I want to—want to fuck you."

"Yes," she said on a moan.

He picked her up as easily as one might move a handful of leaves, reversing their positions so that she sat at the edge of the table and he stood between her legs. Panting with eagerness, she helped him gather up her skirts. He swore when she bared her quim, and when he covered her mound with one large hand and slipped a thick finger between her swollen lips, it was her turn to curse.

"Jesus God," he growled. "So wet."

"Yes," she gasped.

He gripped her hips, securing her, and placed the head of his cock at her waiting entrance. Despite her eagerness, he didn't plow into her right away. Instead, his piercing gaze held hers. Dizzy, she disappeared into the bright blue of his eyes, and the heartfelt need blazing there.

"You want me?" he said gruffly.

"I do." Her answer was little more than a gasp of desire.

"Say my name," he urged, throaty. "Say, *Jack, I want you.*"

"Jack," she said on a long moan, "I want you."

He thrust into her. She cried out—though she was soaking wet, she had to breathe through a slight haze of discomfort as she stretched to fit his incredible size. He wasn't even fully sheathed in her but seemed to sense that she needed a moment, and held himself still, though his breath came hot and hard as a steam engine.

In a gradual wave, her body became liquid, accepting him into her, and he slid all the way in to the root. She'd never been so completely filled, yet when he began to move, she clung to him, whispering *more* and *harder*.

He did as she asked, fucking her with relentless demand. The table beneath her shook and shuddered, but she didn't care. She didn't care if the building collapsed and London burned and the world ended. All that mattered was Jack and his cock and the ecstasy that built and built within her.

Jack slid one hand from her hip, bringing his fingers to her clitoris. As he stroked into her, he circled and pinched her bud, and pleasure arced through her, fiery and fierce. Through her lashes, she looked over Jack's shoulder and moaned at what she saw.

Rush continued to watch them, his hand gripping his cock so tightly it surely pained him. Yet his expression was one of rapture as he pumped himself in time with Jack's thrusts in her cunt.

Release shattered her. She cried out, so hard her throat went raw. Jack did not slacken his pace, though, and went on fucking her and stroking her clitoris. His face had gone tight and focused, small grunts of pleasure escaping him as he drove into her. When she cried out with another orgasm, he made a low, animal growl as if pleased that he could give her one more climax.

Then he pulled from her. He fisted his cock, gave it two vicious strokes, and seed shot from him in a thick, hot arc that spilled across her stomach.

They panted together, and she pulled her gaze up to look into his eyes. The adoration that glowed back at her made her already fluttering pulse speed even faster. She cupped her hand to his jaw, and he leaned into her palm, rubbing his cheek against her skin.

Their reverie was broken by a rough, pained sound from Rush. He continued to stroke himself, but his expression was agonized, as if the release he sought eluded him.

In the whole of her time upon this earth, she'd never done anything remotely as filthy. Though she'd just had two devastating orgasms, the idea of what she contemplated made her ache for more, even with Jack's seed splattered on her belly.

Jack must have sensed what she was about to propose. He smiled, and gave her a small nod.

"Rush," she said, still hoarse from crying out at her release. "Come here. Come to me and get what you need."

If she was being honest, this was not completely for Rush's benefit.

He did not need convincing. As Jack moved aside, tugging up his breeches, Rush advanced. His expression was feral, and when he reached her, still perched on the edge of the table, he grabbed the back of her neck and kissed her greedily.

She held tight to him, overwhelmed by the onslaught of his desire. As his tongue danced with hers, a hot longing resounded in her quim, and she whimpered from its insistent demand.

She had enough presence of mind to reach for the nearby rag to clean Jack's seed from her stomach. Rush's hand stilled hers.

"Leave it," he said roughly. "I like seeing you well used. Well loved."

Fire coursed through her body. Then Rush lifted her off the table, and set her on her feet. He spun her around so that she faced the table and her own reflection—wild hair sliding free of its pins, cheeks flushed, lips swollen from kisses, eyes glassy from her climaxes. She *did* look well used and well loved, and her heart lifted even as her stomach clenched with arousal.

Rush guided her down, so that her chest pressed against the tabletop. With her skirts still bunched around her waist, she was bared lewdly to him, and he gazed avariciously at her behind and quim.

"Are you a good girl or a bad girl?" he rumbled.

She could only stare at him. How was she to answer?

"I think you're bad," he said on a growl. "Taunting me with your beautiful arse and wet cunt. Making me watch you fuck like a demoness."

"I..."

"Maybe I ought to punish you, minx." He stroked the flesh just above her buttocks. "Perhaps that's what you need."

Heat poured through her, a heady mixture of shame and desire. "Perhaps I do."

His hand came down with a stinging slap on one of her cheeks.

She jolted, and moaned. Did people *do* this? What did it matter what anyone else did? This felt far too wicked, too good, to stop.

She writhed against the table, her hard nipples rubbing against the inside of her stays.

"Do you need to be fucked again, minx?" he demanded. "You need my cock?"

"Yes," she panted.

She could hardly believe the words that tumbled from her lips, but she was past the point of caring now. When he gripped her hip, she arched back, offering herself.

"This is what you want," he crooned, using his other hand to trace her soaking lips with the head of his cock.

"Please," she pled.

"I don't know if I should," he said, almost idly. "You're so very wicked. Do you deserve my cock?"

She made a keening noise of complaint.

"Fuck her, Rush," Jack urged, leaning against the wall as he watched them. "And make it hard, the way she likes."

A tremor of blazing arousal coursed through her limbs, her body, and centered in her quim. She watched Rush's reflection in the mirror as he bared his teeth. Then, he thrust into her so powerfully, her feet briefly left the ground.

"*This*," he growled. "*This* is how you want it."

She made a wild sound devoid of all meaning except: *more.*

Rush slammed into her, again and again, the small room filled with the sounds of flesh meeting flesh. Through his powerful thrusts, she gazed at him in the mirror, seeing how his face contorted with pleasure.

"Watch yourself," he commanded. "See yourself as I fuck you."

Embarrassed, aroused, she did as he ordered. Each of his strokes registered on her face—she looked like a woman who lived solely to be fucked. Shameless. Wanton. Free.

He brought his fingers to her clitoris, tapping it firmly as he thrust. Sparks exploded behind her eyes. Hands splayed on the rough wooden table, she could no longer hold back, and came with a loud cry. He did not slacken his pace, continuing to plunge into her as he lavished attention on her clitoris. Another climax detonated, scouring her, robbing her body of strength even as she was filled with glimmering brilliance.

She managed to open her eyes to see Jack's reflection in the mirror, his focus entirely on her, blissfully watching as she came apart.

Rush's speed increased—he was close. Despite his directive, she watched him in the mirror, how he took in great gulps of air with each surge of his hips, and the glassiness of his eyes as they glazed with plea-sure. She loved watching him in the throes of his ecstasy, and she exulted that *she* was the one to make him feel this.

He pulled from her in time to come with a roar. His seed coated the hollow directly above her buttocks, and she adored the mess. Two men had lavished all their attention on her, and two men now helped her to stand when her body was boneless in the aftermath.

Both Rush and Jack carefully cleaned her as though she was some-thing precious and valuable. They straightened her clothing and smoothed her hair into a semblance of order with gentle care.

"Magnificent, magnificent creature," Rush murmured against her lips.

"Beautiful woman." Jack kissed her sweetly. "You humble me."

Her heart lodged in her throat to see how tenderly they treated her, to have them pet and praise her, and look at her as if she was truly the center of the universe. She glanced back and forth between them—Rush, dark and sleek like an onyx blade, and Jack, big and tawny as a lion—and sudden understanding made her belly leap.

She had lost her heart. Not just to one man, but to two. Yet there would come a time that they would have to part, with twice the heartbreak.

11

THE SHOPGIRL WRAPPED UP THE RED SATIN GARTERS, HER GAZE DARTING back and forth between Vivian and the bright hue of the items in question. One only wore such provocatively colored garters if they were going to be seen. A smile curved Vivian's mouth to think of Rush and Jack's expressions when they saw her clad in stockings, red garters, and nothing else.

Good Lord—she was imagining *both* of them in the room with her when she revealed herself. Truly, she had become someone else from the quiet helpmeet she'd been for most of her adult life.

"Will that be all, madam?" the shopgirl asked uncertainly.

"For now," Vivian answered. She had her eye on the most salacious black stays, which would complement the garters quite nicely. But she'd limit her purchases for today.

She paid the shopgirl and tucked the paper-wrapped parcel under her arm. As she turned from the counter, three women stopped whispering but stared at her with scandalized expressions, even as she left the shop.

Once she was back on the street, more fashionable men and women whispered and gawked at her progress down the pavement. Their shocked regard continued in the next shop, where she purchased a pretty hat pin, and once more on the street.

There would have been a time that to have so much attention directed at her would have made her scurry for cover. Now, she strolled down Oxford Street with her chin high, nodding and murmuring greetings to the stunned people she passed. There was no fear or discomfort from being noticed, only mildly amusement, and cautious hope.

She took a sedan chair back home, and when she alit, several of her neighbors—out for a promenade—stopped in their tracks and gaped, their gazes following Vivian all the way to her front door. While she did not quite mind being the object of their regard, her body sagged in relief when the door closed behind her, shutting everyone out.

"Good afternoon, madam," Sue said as she approached cautiously.

"Any correspondence?" Vivian asked, handing her hat and purchases to her maid.

Sue looked at the marble-inlaid floor. "No, madam."

A bubble of excited laughter broke from Vivian's lips. Her maid stared, clearly expecting that this news would be met with sadness or anger

"Oh, I'd forgotten, madam." Sue produced two small letters from a pocket in her apron. "These are the only ones that came."

It wasn't complete silence, but it was better than the deluge of missives Vivian typically received. She took the letters from her maid and studied them. Both had unfamiliar handwriting, so she'd no idea who had sent them.

"Begging your pardon, madam," Sue said. "You wanted me to remind you that you're expected at a dinner at Lord and Lady Grenham's tonight, and I'm to help you change."

Perhaps it had been too much to hope for that her ostracism would be complete. There was still this dreadful dinner, and the expectant Mr. Colville, who was so eager to make her Mrs. Colville. Apprehension formed icicles in her stomach—would Mr. Colville leap right into courtship and then a proposal of marriage? How much time left did she have before her fate was sealed, a fate without Rush and Jack?

"Very well," she said. There would be time later to read her two slim letters from unknown persons.

She climbed the stairs to her rooms, with Sue trailing behind, discussing her gown options for the night.

"Pick whatever you like," Vivian said. "It matters not at all to me."

Sue nodded, although from the uncertainty in her face, Vivian's lack of interest caught her off guard. Evidently, word had gotten out amongst the servants that the master of the house meant to foist her off on some prospective bridegroom who would be in attendance at the dinner this evening.

Reaching the landing, Vivian decided not to discuss the matter with Sue. Surely her maid had already told the other servants that her mistress had been coming home in the small hours of the morning, disheveled and reeking of sex. That could only help Vivian's cause, since servants were the best source of information outside of a newspaper, and with better circulation.

Vivian stopped short in the doorway to her parlor. John sat on the sofa, jogging his leg, but when he saw her, he jumped to his feet.

"I don't recall us having an appointment," Vivian said, coming into the chamber. She set the two letters on her escritoire before facing her unhappy stepson. "You seem unwell, John. Perhaps a bloodletting might set you to rights."

"Dismiss your maid," he said tightly.

Vivian nodded at Sue, who slid from the chamber. Still, it was certain that her maid hovered near the door to catch every word.

"I *will* need her, though," Vivian said crisply, "if I'm to make myself ready for dinner with Lord and Lady Grenham."

"Dinner will be at home tonight," John answered, grim. "Tonight, and every night."

Her heart pounded in her throat. The small flickers of hope that burned within her began to grow and brighten.

"Before Mr. Colville even made a formal offer, he has cried off," John went on, crestfallen. "And Lord and Lady Grenham say if I'm to come to dinner tonight, 'tis to be without you. They cannot taint their house with your scandal."

It was all she could do to keep from clapping her hands and jumping with exultation. Yet she wasn't certain if she was in the clear.

"In plain language, madam," he continued, looking at her balefully, "'tis impossible for me to find you a husband. You are..." His jaw clenched. "Completely unsuitable to be anyone's wife."

"I see," she answered, fighting the impulse to laugh in triumph.

"Is that all you can say?" John took a step forward, his expression anguished. "Madam, the way you have been carrying on has been utterly disgraceful. I'd hoped that perhaps, after whispers reached me from one incident, it was a momentary madness brought about by grief. Yet when Lady Bowles saw you at Summerville, *kissing* Rushton Cantley in full view of everyone there, 'twas clear you were beyond hope."

"I suppose that I am." She pressed her fingertips to her mouth to smother a grin.

"In the name of all that's holy," John said miserably, "why would you do such a thing?"

Her smile falling away, she faced him. "I did what I thought was best for myself."

"Carrying on publicly with an infamous rake?" He looked at her in disbelief. "That is *not* what's best for you, madam. Do you not see, this is *precisely* what my father, your father, and I wanted to protect you from? But we acted too late for you to see your own folly."

"'Twas not a rash imprudence. I acted deliberately." Words clear and steady, she said, "No one gave me any choice. I have been robbed of my voice, no one listening when I said what *I* wanted for *myself*. Your disappointment is your own to bear, but now my life belongs to me. Fear not," she added, when he continued to look wretched, "your own reputation will emerge unscathed."

His shoulders sagged, and for a moment, she truly pitied him, yet she couldn't support his insistence in carrying out his father's callous directive.

"'Twould be best," he said heavily, as if handing her a prisoner's sentence, "if you quit London as soon as possible. The dowager cottage will have to suffice."

"As you see fit." She dared not tell him that was precisely her intended goal, lest he revoke it as punishment.

"I'll just...I'll..." His bewildered words trailed off as he left her parlor.

Alone at last, she indulged herself by clapping her hands together. It was done. She was free. She was a ruined woman, in disgrace, and no one from Society would ever trouble her again.

She spun in a circle, then stopped when she spotted the two letters on her escritoire.

After breaking the wafer on the first letter, she read.

My dear Mrs. S.,

*I don't write letters and this isn't my handwriting on account that my penman-
ship's rubbish.*

*What do people say in letters? I don't know. There's a girl outside selling
flowers but they're roses and I think you'd like daisies better but that's not what
she has so I couldn't send this with flowers. But if she <u>did</u> have daisies I would
have sent them. I hope this is a good letter.*

Yrs, &c.
Jack Morgan

The signature had been done by another hand from the body of the
text, and it was a large, heavy scrawl. He'd signed it himself.

She pressed the letter to her bosom, and the feel of the paper against
her skin spread warmth through her.

Her gaze fell on the second letter. She promised herself that she
would reread Jack's as soon as she attended to this other missive.
Opening it, she noted that the paper was exceedingly fine. As she read,
desire and anticipation uncoiled in her belly.

Vivian,

Tonight. Wexham's.

-R.

Post scriptum, I cannot wait to see you.

Her heart capered in her chest. She was free now, free to continue
with Jack and Rush, with no threat of an unwanted marriage looming
over her. The world opened up to her like an atlas, showing her all the
wondrous places she could go.

12

VIVIAN APPROACHED THE GAMING HELL, JUST AS SHE'D DONE A LITTLE OVER a week ago. This time, she eagerly climbed the steps. Past Vivian had been frightened of what unknown things she might face within Wexham's walls, and the daunting task of asking London's most scandalous rake to ruin her.

He'd done what she'd asked of him, and it was for that reason that Present Vivian hurried to the door, eager to tell him of their success.

She knocked, and a footman opened the door. The servant looked at her with recognition, then waved her toward the main gaming room. She hurried toward it.

Something fizzy sparkled within her when she saw Jack standing in his usual place in the corner, his attention never stopping in one place as he made certain that no one got too unruly. The fizziness turned to effervescence—she would have so much more time to see his rough-hewn face again, and feel his calloused, gentle hands on her, and witness the depths of his heart reflected in his blue eyes.

As he made a visual sweep of the room, his gaze landed on her, and stopped. She smiled and him, and creases formed in his cheeks as he smiled back. He nodded toward where Rush stood at a hazard table.

Eagerly, she approached him. Her smile faltered, though, when he turned to face her, his expression grim.

"We need to talk," he said before she could, then headed out of the gaming room. Vivian followed him, tiny shards of uncertainty piercing her.

Rush motioned for Jack to join them, who made a hand signal at one of the other enforcers before following.

Moments later, she was alone with Rush and Jack in that same narrow office where they'd had their first meeting.

"Your stepson visited Jack and me early this evening," Rush said without preamble. "It seems your scheme accomplished its intention."

She stepped close and pressed her hands to his chest. "No possible offers of marriage, no threats for me to lose my widow's portion. Wonderful, isn't it?"

"*Is* it?" Rush asked, his voice tight.

"Of course it is," she answered, fighting to hold on to her happiness. "This is what we sought, and we accomplished it. This is the *best* news."

Jack's face fell, and he stared down at the floor as if it was a mire that threatened to drag him beneath its surface.

"Again," Rush said, his words strangely clipped, "*is* it?"

Vivian recoiled to see the bleakness in Rush's eyes. "This *is* good, Rush. We have what we want. You, and me, and Jack."

"And what you want is a peaceful, undisturbed existence. Which you cannot have if there is a *we*." When she looked at him with a frown, he went on. "Should we continue being lovers, all of that will be taken away from you. I'm a man with a wicked reputation, Vivian, and what made me the ideal person to harm your reputation can destroy the rest of your life. Especially if Jack and I are *both* your lovers. There's such a thing as being *too* ruined, love, which means you'll get nothing."

"That can't be," she said, but he spoke over her.

"Your stepson was quite clear this afternoon. He said England could never contain such a horrendous scandal, and that if I ever saw you again, he'd turn you out of your dowager's cottage. I'm certain that if he knew about Jack, his repercussions would be even more dire."

"I—" She went still as the truth of the situation became clear.

"Sparkwell said he'd find a way to terminate your widow's portion, too," Rush went on grimly. "He knows powerful men who could manipulate the situation to deny you your bequest. You'd be out of a home, with no means of supporting yourself."

"No," she insisted.

"Yes." Rush's throat worked beneath his stock. "And I won't destroy your chances at having what you want."

"Is it true, Jack?" Her eyes burned, and she dragged her hand across them.

The hope she'd had that Jack would deny Rush's assertion died when she saw his grim expression. "It is true. I heard every bloody word from Sparkwell's lips."

"No," she said again. She looked back and forth between them as more and more cracks threaded through her heart. The whole thing would shatter into tiny pieces in a moment. She'd only learned how wonderful the world could be with Rush and Jack in it, and now she had to lose them both.

"We'll miss you." Jack cupped his hand against her cheek. "*I'll* miss you."

"I loved your letter." She leaned into Jack's touch, savoring it.

"Did you?" Jack's smile was bittersweet. "Takes me forever to read something, but if you write me, I promise I'll read your letters."

"I *will* write," she vowed. "It won't be enough—nothing is going to be enough—but the smallest remnant of our connection is welcome once I'm gone."

"You'll leave London?" Jack asked.

"I should. If what Rush says is true, the longer I remain, the worse it will be."

"How..." Rush's voice was a rasp. "How long until you go?"

"It will take me a week to attend to everything before I can leave for the country. I'm certain John will want me gone sooner." She turned to Rush. "Can I see you one last time before I depart?"

His eyes were dark agony. "That isn't wise. Tonight was enough of a risk."

"Yes. Yes, of course." She kissed Jack's hand before going to Rush. Lifting up on her toes, she pressed her lips to his cheek. He didn't move or try to touch her. "Not even a farewell kiss?"

"If I give you more, love," he said, bleak, "I'll never want to stop. And I *must* stop. We're strangers now, you and I. That's how it has to be."

As if to prove his point, he stepped away from her, leaving a void of space between them.

Something broke apart inside her, and she pressed her hand against her chest as if she could keep all the pieces together. It was a hopeless effort, though. If she had any sense of self-preservation, she would leave this place before she was reduced to a heap of china shards that someone would have to sweep up and dispose of.

"Goodbye, Jack." She took his hands between hers, gave them one last squeeze, then turned back to Rush. "Good evening, Mr. Cantley."

She pulled open the office door and fled down the corridor, Jack's voice calling after her. But she didn't slow and she didn't stop, not until she was back on the street and running into the welcome shelter of darkness.

13

RUSH GLARED AT THE BOTTOM OF HIS TANKARD, THEN SCOWLED AT THE tapster hurrying to fill other customers' mugs.

"What the deuce is the matter with these things?" Rush bellowed, waving his tankard. It was early evening. Most of the Painted Strumpet's usual combative clientele was still bestirring in their straw pallets, so in the quiet, Rush's irate outburst echoed off the tavern's low ceiling. "They're too small to begin with, and they can't hold a drop of ale for barely a minute before it all runs out."

"See here," the tapster said angrily, "that's the fifth time you've made that complaint and I keep telling you, the fault lies in yourself, not the mug."

"How Shakespearean," Rush sneered. He threw the drinking vessel to the floor and it clattered noisily across the grimy flagstones.

"Awright, Sir Bluster," the tapster snapped. Pointing to the front door, he announced, "Time to get your pampered arse out of here. Can't nothing in this place make you happy, anyhow."

"'Tis unnecessary to throw me out," Rush said, staggering to his feet. "I'm leaving this reeking piss hole."

He lurched out the door and down the uneven street. The ground hadn't been steady for days, not since that day at Wexham's. The last time he had seen and would see Vivian.

Despite the fact that he'd done the right thing, no amount of whisky, ale, and gin he'd imbibed in the intervening days erased him waking up, aching for the feel of her, or spending his conscious hours praying their paths would cross, or falling into a fitful sleep abundant with tormenting dreams where she slipped from his fingers like so much morning mist.

His usual remedy for melancholia was a fine night out spent in the company of dice and eager women. Yet a rancid taste filled his mouth to think of putting his arms around another female, let alone other parts of his anatomy, and he spat upon the cobbles to rid himself of the acrid flavor.

He hailed a sedan, and though the chairmen looked at him warily as he stumbled toward them, they nodded when he fell into the seat and called out, "Wexham's." Revelry and games of chance held little appeal, but he needed to do something with himself rather than find out where Vivian lived and stand outside her window, praying for a glimpse of her.

The journey to the gaming hell was agonizingly slow and nauseating as the sedan chair swayed from side to side, and made Rush's already spinning head even more unsteady.

He pictured Vivian's hands stroking his forehead, and heard her low, sweet voice murmuring comfort. She would be good at tending to someone who wasn't feeling well. But no, she deserved someone looking after *her*, making certain that her every need was met, and that she felt cherished.

He'd done his best to look after her, telling her painful truths to keep her safe. But Belinda had been right all along. He was the man someone only turned to for transitory pleasure. He could never be meant for more.

His stomach roiled. It was only through sheer willpower that he managed not to be sick, but the illness within him didn't go away.

Finally, the chair reached Wexham's, and he was able to get out and pay the bearers without too much harm to his body or dignity. Well, his body seemed marginally decent. His dignity, however, was questionable.

Especially when he reached the front door of the gaming hell, and before he could even knock, Jack emerged. His friend stood forbiddingly, arms crossed over his chest, and he stared at Rush grimly.

"Management said you're not welcome here," Jack answered. "Not after the last few nights. Half the patrons insist they won't come back until you've formally apologized for attempting to start fights."

Rush said nothing, recalling those encounters only vaguely. It made sense, however. His humor had been black as Hades ever since he'd last seen Vivian.

"You should go home," Jack answered, his voice surprisingly gentle. "Drinking and brawling yourself into a stupor isn't going to bring her back."

The floor pitched beneath Rush, and, in search of stability, he leaned against Jack. "She's gone."

"She hasn't left yet," Jack continued, softly. "Go and see her. Say goodbye."

"If I do that," Rush said with his eyes screwed closed, "I'll throw myself at her feet and beg her to take me back. Take *us* back," he added, cracking open one eye to look at Jack's sympathetic expression. "But that's not possible."

Jack's chest rose and fell, and Rush had to cling tightly to his friend's waistcoat to keep from sliding to the ground.

He struggled to stand on his own, swaying on his feet. Jack reached out and steadied Rush, who looked away from the pity on his friend's face.

"I miss her, too," Jack said lowly. "So bad I don't sleep and I don't eat. And she *will* go on with her life, without you and without me. But I can face her one final time, and let her know that I won't ever forget her. Maybe you should do the same."

"I've been through goodbyes, and I couldn't survive another." Seeing her, only to lose her again, would destroy him.

"Then," Jack said, turning Rush around like a toy soldier, "go home, my friend. There's nothing here for you."

He walked Rush to the curb and hailed a hackney. When the vehicle stopped, Jack helped Rush inside. As the hackney rolled away, Rush peered out the window to watch his friend walk slowly back to the gaming hell, like a man facing the world's most protracted execution.

14

"Servants' entrance is in the back," the footman said haughtily, eyeing Jack like he was a bull that had broken free of its tether and wound up on the front step this James Street home.

It would be quite easy for Jack to push the bloke to the ground and simply walk inside. Even though the footman had probably been hired because he was tall and hale, Jack easily outweighed the lad by two stone, and surely this stripling in livery didn't train with Hob Dugan.

"I'm not a tradesman," Jack answered. "I'm here to see the mistress of the house. Mrs. Sparkwell." Merely saying Vivian's name made something flutter in his belly, but he had to quash any nerves or else he'd turn and run for Hampstead Heath.

The footman's eyebrows rose. "No one's been to see the mistress in nearly a week. She's set to leave tomorrow."

Jack's gut *did* squeeze then. He hadn't much time.

"Tell her Jack Morgan's at her door," he said, taking off his tricorn and holding it as respectfully as possible. He wouldn't storm her house, not if she didn't want to see him. Respecting her wishes was his prime concern.

When the footman hesitated, Jack urged with more firmness, "Go tell her." For good measure, he slipped a coin into the servant's hand. Losing that money meant Jack wouldn't be able to pay for his supper, but he'd go hungry if it meant seeing her once more.

"Wait here." The footman pocketed the coin before closing the door in Jack's face.

As he bided his time, Jack shifted from foot to foot, studying the elegant marble urns that flanked the front door. The glass in the windows was abundant, and remarkably clear. Craning his neck, he looked at the two stories above him, with their neatly painted shutters and even more glass.

It wasn't as though he hadn't seen or been in fine homes before. Many of the women whom he shared with Rush had been genteel, and they seemed to take great delight in having a common-born bruiser like him lumbering up to and within their damask-filled bedchambers. That practice was over now.

The door swung open, revealing the footman. "Follow me."

Jack did as he was instructed, trailing after the servant as he was led through the house. For a moment, it seemed like the footman was going to guide him all the way to the back exit, and there kick him out into the mews. But then they stepped out into a spacious garden and toward a glasshouse.

The servant paused at the door to the glasshouse and waved him inside. "Mr. Jack Morgan," he announced before bowing and disappearing.

Jack's heart slammed into his throat when he saw Vivian, in a soft green dress, standing amidst some foliage. Most of the shelves and tables were bare, however, and there was dirt scattered on the floor.

Looking directly at her, when everything in him longed to drink up the sight of her, was simply too much, and he approached slowly rather than run up and pull her to him.

"Never been in a glasshouse before," he mumbled. "I always thought there'd be—more."

"This was William's exotic plant collection," she explained softly. "The direction of their care fell to me in his illness and death. John said I could sell nearly everything off, as I won't be in London any longer."

"When do you leave?"

"Tomorrow."

He did look at her, then, and bit back a curse to see how pale and shadowed she'd become in the course of a week. He took a step toward her, then stopped. It wasn't his place to offer her support.

Even so, he blurted, "I'll—I'll miss you. When you go." He winced. As poetic declarations went, his had been merely a handful of babbled words.

"And I, you." Her eyes brimmed, and he closed the distance between them, drawn to her because he couldn't stay away.

Even so, he left several feet between them, as his body and heart ached. He'd do nothing without her permission.

She looked desolately at the distance between them, then stepped into his arms.

He cradled her to him, and she pressed her face against his chest as tears coursed down her cheeks.

"I'm getting you rather wet," she sniffled.

"I don't give a fuck." He growled at himself. "I shouldn't use that kind of language around a lady."

"You weren't so inhibited when you had me on that table."

He jolted with arousal—and sorrow. "How beautiful you were. *Are*," he amended.

"I never have been," she said softly. "Less so now."

Tipping her face up, he looked at her ashen cheeks, slightly blotchy now and streaked with tears, her red nose, and pallid lips.

"Always beautiful," he answered firmly. "I'll remember your lovely face for the rest of my days. I've come," he exhaled roughly, "to say goodbye."

She pressed her trembling lips together. "I wish you could come and visit me."

"We both know that can't happen. The scandal would rob you of everything you've desired for yourself."

Looking up at him, she asked, "And what do *you* desire for yourself?"

"I don't understand," he said, puzzled.

"You're part of this, too," she said gently. "What you want and what you feel matter. They matter to me, and they matter to Rush."

"I—" He had to step back and put distance between them. What was he supposed to do with her kindness? A measure of him wanted to pick up one of these tables and use it like a thick wooden shield, protecting himself from things that were too big, too painful. He also ached to enfold her in his arms and never let her go.

"Doesn't matter what I desire," he said gruffly.

"Of course it does," she insisted. "It has always mattered."

"But what I desire, I can't ever have. 'Twas never meant to be mine."

He used to be satisfied with the way his life played out, the transitory lovers, his existence on the edges of society. Having known what it was to be seen and accepted—having *her* see and accept him—gave him a glimpse of happiness, made all the more bitter by the fact that it was over before it had truly begun.

"It could be." She stepped to him and stroked a finger along his cheek. "Tell me, Jack."

He clenched his jaw, but the words tumbled from him anyway. "Someone of my own. Not just for an evening or a fortnight, but forever. Doesn't have to be vows in a church. Only—I want to wake up with somebody beside me, and go to sleep with that same person next to me. And they never want me to be something, someone I'm not. They take me as I am."

He shook his head, trying to dispel the dream that he resented. "Fancies. Stupid fancies."

"You deserve all of that, Jack," she whispered.

"Just as you deserve the life you've always wanted to lead." He turned his hat around in his hands. "I'm sorry Rush isn't here to say his goodbyes."

A flash of pain crossed her face, and she looked away.

"I've broken my nose three times," Jack said, tapping the crooked bridge. He held up his fist. "Split the skin here so much I've lost count, but the scars remind me how many punches I've thrown. And there's a gouge on my back where a devious trainer stabbed me when I was in the ring. There's more, too, from working at Wexham's."

"It pains me to think of you being hurt," she said, her gaze tender.

A burning web contracted around his heart. Yet he said, "'Tis part of the work I do. It's left visible marks on me. But the scars that Rush carries...they can't be seen. And I don't think they ever truly healed. 'Tis why he's stayed away."

"To protect himself," she said lowly.

"And you." He held her gaze for many moments. "Do you know how we met? I'd just come to London. Didn't have but a coin in my pocket, so I was in a rough part of the city for lodgings and work. I came across some blokes trying to rob the prettiest chap I'd ever seen. He gave 'em a good fight, but it was three against one and he couldn't win. So, I stepped in to lend my fists, and between us, we pummeled those bastards to the ground. When it was over, Rush slung his arm around my shoulder, said, 'That deserves a pint, don't you think? That deserves *several* pints.'"

Jack and Vivian chuckled together.

"Over our ales, he asked about me and learned that I was some Welshman without a friend or a farthing. Then he marched me to Wexham's and told them to hire me immediately. The money he gave me to find lodging was strictly a loan, he said, as he was uncommonly annoyed by charity." Jack smiled ruefully. "He knew I wouldn't just take his blunt."

"And from then to now," she murmured, "you've been friends."

"In all the time I've known him," Jack said, "he's let women go without a thought. They got what they needed, and he moved on, a quip and a grin. But with you..." Jack smiled sadly. "With you, 'tis different. His scar from you isn't visible, but it cleaves him right down the middle."

She wiped at her eyes. "Is that why you're here, Jack? To explain why Rush hasn't come?"

"I only wanted to see you one more time." He moved to her and stroked his fingers down her cheek.

"I wish..." She squeezed his hand, and even though she was so much smaller than him, there was strength in her grip. "I wish things were different. I wish the world was different."

"It won't change for the likes of you or me. But I'll be glad knowing that you're happy out in the country. That'll be enough." He kissed her cheek before stepping away. "Goodbye, Vivian."

"Goodbye, Jack," she said thickly. "I hope you find *your* happiness."

He wouldn't tell her that was impossible now, because he wasn't cruel. "Wish me luck on my voyage."

For both of their sakes, he turned to leave the glasshouse without a backward glance.

"Jack," she said, "wait."

"WHERE ARE YOU GOING?" Vivian asked, trying to smother her alarm.

"The Americas." His expression seemed determinedly blank as he faced her.

"So far away," she exclaimed.

"Not much to keep me in England," he said with a shrug, "let alone London."

"Your friendship with Rush?"

"There's naught I can do for him," Jack said heavily.

Her heart clenched. But as he'd turned to go, she'd had to act. This could not, *would not*, be the last time she'd see him. Now was the time for her to draw on every ounce of mettle she possessed—and as her time with Jack and Rush had shown her, she had far more courage than she'd ever believed.

"I'd hoped," she said, drawing on that bravery, "that *I* could keep you here."

"We've talked of this." His brow lowered. "'Tisn't possible."

She went to him and stared up at his face, aching to touch his cheek, though she could not. Not until she'd laid everything out. "'Tis something I need to say to you *and* Rush. Come with me."

He shifted slightly as though impelled to follow her, while holding himself back.

"Please," she said, intent, "come with me to Rush's."

She watched the shift of emotions on his face, fighting the impulse to throw her arms around him and beg for this chance. It wouldn't be fair, however, to employ such a tactic.

Finally, when she thought she might toss away her principles and truly implore him to come with her, he said, grudgingly, "Alright."

Weeks ago, she would never have taken such a risk as this. Yet she'd changed since then, and now she had to gamble everything for a chance at happiness. For Jack, for Rush, and for herself.

15

Knocking on Rush's door only produced the thud of something being thrown against the wood, followed by inarticulate yelling.

Vivian shared a concerned look with Jack. The carriage ride from Cheapside to Soho had been mostly silent, though as they'd driven westward, Jack had owned that Rush had been barred from nearly every one of his usual haunts. Sobriety had also made itself scarce from Rush's routine. And while Rush had the privilege of wealth and birth to shield him from possible legal action, Jack possessed neither—forcing Jack to stay away from his friend.

Would Rush be in his cups now? What she had to say to him couldn't be done if he was intoxicated—but she'd wait as long as necessary for him to become clearheaded.

Jack shot her a questioning look.

"I won't be scared away," she said, holding firm to her resolve.

From his waistcoat pocket, he produced a key and fitted it to the lock. Of course, he could let himself in—it was impossible to forget that first night with Rush, and the exquisite astonishment of finding Jack as he watched her and Rush fuck.

She shook her head, trying to dispel the rush of arousal. It would level her to be rejected whilst in the throes of desire.

Jack opened the door, and thick, stale air poured out. He led her inside to find Rush's rooms saturated in shadows, even at this hour of the afternoon.

"Begone, Mrs. Davies," Rush's voice said from somewhere amidst the gloom. "Save your lamb pies and beef tea for someone who wants them. Don't bother straightening things, either," he added grimly. "The chaos suits me."

He didn't *sound* inebriated, which was some comfort, and, squinting in the darkness, Vivian made out his form slouched in a chair by the cold fireplace. She wove her way around shapes that vaguely resembled furniture, until she reached the window.

She sharply tugged open the drapes and pushed the window open. Air and light poured into the chamber, illuminating Rush in the wing-back seat. Cursing, he shielded his eyes from the glare.

"The chaos doesn't suit *me*." She faced him.

"Vivian?" Dark circles ringed Rush's eyes, his beard had almost completely come in, his hair was free of a queue, and yet she silently exhaled to see the clarity in his gaze.

Joy bloomed across his angular face, but before that seed of happiness could take root in her, his expression shuttered.

"No questions as to why I'm here?" she asked.

"Our paths have diverged, love," he answered. "Coming here only reminds us of what we cannot have."

"At the least," Jack said from the other side of the room, "you ought to bathe."

Rush grumbled, but to Vivian's surprise, he got to his feet. He was clad in a banyan, which he shucked heedlessly so it fell in a heap to the floor. He stood in only a pair of breeches, which hung on his hips, and nothing else. He was a lean man, and in the span of just a week, his body had become almost spare.

Turning away, he went into his bedchamber, and a moment later came the sound of water being poured into a basin.

The parlor was a disaster, with books and papers and clothes everywhere—no dirty plates, so he hadn't been eating—but she resisted the impulse to tidy.

Jack, however, couldn't seem to stop himself, gathering up an armful of books and gingerly setting them atop a table. Creases of worry formed around his mouth and between his eyes as he tried to set things to rights.

She went to stand in the doorway of Rush's bedchamber, fully intending to speak, but her mouth went dry at the sight of Rush, nude, cleaning himself. He impassively scrubbed a cloth behind his ears, across his chest, and even over his penis, which hung thick and long amidst a nest of dark hair.

As he washed, he said, "The temple has fallen into ruin. Not much to see." Yet his cock firmed slightly as she stared.

"This is a novel sight for me," she admitted. "Other than seeing you without a shirt at Dugan's, you've been almost fully clothed."

"'Tis not a charming sight."

"You're..." She took a step into the bedchamber. "Beautiful."

Once more, a bright look of happiness crossed his face before his expression shuttered.

"If you've any kindness, love," he said, bleak, "you'll leave now and not come back. There's no sense in tormenting us with what isn't possible."

"I've learned that many things are possible," she answered, "if one has the strength and courage to pursue them. 'Tis something I've learned from you, Rush. And you, Jack," she added as the larger man eased around her to stand at the periphery of the bedchamber. "My education with you both has been extensive, and extraordinary."

Moving deeper into the room, she said, "I thought I knew what it was I sought for myself. What would bring be happiness. I believed it was a life of solitude and quiet. And you did what you thought was necessary ensure that I had that life. Yet after Jack came to see me, I had to ask myself, was that *truly* what my heart desired? And the answer was *no*."

Their gazes were fixed on her now, and she let her heart show in her eyes, in her face, and in her voice. "You've revealed to me I've the strength to pursue what I want. It was because of you. Rush, bold, enthralling, but gentle. And Jack," she said, turning to the other man, "a giant with a heart as big as the sky. How could I not love you? *Both* of you."

Poets and painters only depicted love between two people, not three. Yet that reflected their own narrow ideas of what a human could feel. She had enough love in her to adore Jack *and* Rush.

Jack sucked in a breath. "You *love* us? Me?"

"I do love you, Jack." She went to him and took his massive hand between her smaller ones. "So much I could fly with its power."

A shudder ran through him, and a lone tear tracked down his cheek. She stroked it away, though it left a shining streak on his face. Body shaking, he enfolded her in his arms and pressed her close.

"I've waited for you forever," he said with his lips against her forehead, "and 'twas worth it. Because I love you, Vivian."

Half of her heart brimmed with joy. He'd given to her his love, so openly.

Yet there was another...

Within the shelter of Jack's embrace, she looked at Rush. Yearning was writ across his features, but he held himself still.

"I love you, Rush," she said, as exposed as she'd ever been.

He jolted as if struck, and closed his eyes. "I'm not the sort of man someone loves."

She pressed a kiss to Jack's lips, shared an understanding look with him, and then eased from his hold before walking to Rush.

"You are," she said intently, reaching for him, "and I do. You are worthy of being loved."

Uncertainty filled Rush's face. She pressed one hand to her aching, longing heart, while she kept her other hand stretched out to him. Inviting him. Daring him. Accepting him.

Rush did not move. There was fear in his dark eyes, fear mirrored in her own soul that she might give him everything, but it wouldn't be enough.

"If you take this leap," she said softly, "I shall be there to catch you."

"We'll both catch you," Jack said, warm and reassuring as stood behind her and cupped one hand over her shoulder.

His chest heaving, Rush gazed at them both. Then, slowly, he smiled. Not a rake's raffish grin, or a brittle baring of teeth, but a genuine smile full of happiness. Something did take flight within her then, winging high as he approached her.

"I'm not a religious man." His voice was a throbbing, velvet caress. "I never pray, and haven't been in a church in over a decade. Yet what I feel is a miracle. Because," he said as he curved his hand around the back of her head, "I love you, little creature. Surpassing all measure, and filling me to excess, I love you."

Joy consumed her when he brought his lips to hers. It was a kiss of surpassing sweetness, lingering and tender.

Yet she wanted more. She wanted all of him, and parted her lips. He devoured her, and it was all the better having Jack there, stroking between her shoulder blades, and holding her securely when she felt certain that elation would indeed cause her to fly into the heavens.

As Rush kissed her, Jack trailed his lips along her neck. Reverence turned carnal, Jack stroking up from her waist to cup her breasts through the stiff material of her bodice. She gasped into Rush's mouth. Her head spun with having both of them focused on her, and she clutched at Rush's shoulders in an attempt to regain balance.

"Do we overwhelm you, love?" he asked huskily.

Jack stilled, as did Rush. This was her moment, her choice.

There was no fear. They would do nothing without her permission. All judgments, all thoughts of what *should* be or how she *ought* to feel love, they didn't signify. The only thing that did matter was what her own heart yearned for, and that these two men would give that to her.

"I need this." She looked back and forth between them, her dark and light lovers, who gazed at her as though she was indeed the center of the universe. "I want you. Both."

Rush caressed her throat. "But, love, you cannot have us. Not if you're to have peace and solitude. So your stepson threatened."

"Nothing matters to me more than you and Jack," she answered vehemently. "To hell with anyone or anything that keeps us apart."

"Fierce creature," Jack said, kissing the place beneath her ear. "England will never tolerate such an arrangement."

Her heart sank, but Rush said, "We'll speak of that later. Now, one thing must happen before we can go any further."

He purred as he brushed his lips over Vivian's ear. She tried to keep her eyes open, tried to focus on what he said, but with Jack's hands stroking her sensitive flesh cresting above her bodice, and Rush's warm breath fanning across her face, it was all she could do not to fall into a sensual haze.

"What—what might that be?" she managed to say.

He pulled back slightly and gave her a molten look. "We must strip you bare."

The two men eased away from her, just enough space to start removing her clothing. She helped as best she could, though it was a morass of hands and turning her this way and that to divest her of her many layers of clothing. Rush was unsurprisingly adept at unpinning her stomacher and undoing her petticoat's tapes, but Jack was quite skillful, too, easing her gown up and away from her body.

"You've greatly undersold yourself," she teased Jack, "to undress me like a man well familiar with the workings of a woman's complex garments. I'm getting two rakes instead of one."

Jack flashed her a grin, thigh-clenching in its wickedness, but continued to wordlessly disrobe her.

At last, she stood in nothing but her shift, stockings, and garters. When she pulled her shift off, Rush and Jack both cursed as they stared at her legs.

She glanced down, and smiled. Deliberately, she'd chosen the red satin garters, and they flashed indecently just above her knees.

"Who is this minx?" Rush growled, his gaze transfixed by the garters. "Certainly not the fearful mouse that first sought me out at Wexham's."

"Grown into a tiger," Jack said, also entranced. He fingered a strip of crimson satin, stroking across her flesh as he did so. He grazed the skin just beside her mound, yet did not touch where she already ached. "Leave these on."

She shivered, her nipples tightening into points. Had she stood nude before Jack and Rush only weeks ago, she would have instinctively covered herself, shy beneath their avid gazes. Now, she let them look their fill, loving how they devoured her with their gazes. Everywhere their regard touched— her small breasts, her soft belly, the plush expanse of her thighs, the damp curls above her quim—she grew liquid and supple, blazing with need.

More powerful than ever, she looked back at them. Rush was gloriously naked, though slightly leaner than he'd been a week ago, and his cock was full and upright, as it twitched with eagerness to earn her attention.

"I don't know about you, Jack," he said, keeping his attention fixed on her, "but I've taken my cock in hand many a time, imagining our lovely widow clad in only her blush. Though, the garters are a welcome addition."

"Frigged myself raw, thinking about seeing her dainty tits, her silken thighs," Jack said throatily. "Her sweet little cunt."

Heat roared through her to hear not just their words, but to imagine both Rush and Jack pleasuring themselves to thoughts of her.

"Now 'tis your turn to take off your clothes," she said, turning to Jack. "Off with it. Every stitch."

He made short work of his garments, tossing everything aside as if the mere touch of fabric and buckskin against his flesh burned him. Then he was naked, too. She gasped at the sight. Though she'd seen him bare to the waist before, seeing the sum total of his nakedness made her heart pound. He was so large, so thickly muscled, from the broad slabs of his pectorals to the corrugation of his abdomen to the brawn of his massive thighs. And his huge cock...

How had she taken him into her body before? Yet, merely looking at him, and how he panted with eagerness to be with her now, her cunt grew soaked in readiness.

In silent agreement, they all came together beside Rush's substantial bed. Rush stood behind her, tipping her head back so he could kiss her mouth. In front of her, Jack dragged his lips along her collarbone.

Their hands...their hands were everywhere. Jack cupped her breasts, lightly pinching her nipples as Rush skimmed his fingers over her belly, then lower, to dip into her quim.

She was surrounded by desire, afloat on lust and pleasure. It became impossible to know where she ended and they began. They were on all sides of her, enfolding her in heat. And both men were in tune with each other, moving in synchronicity as they faultlessly played her body.

When Jack fastened his lips around her nipple and sucked, Rush stroked two fingers up her passage. He circled her clitoris as Jack drew on the tip of her breast, making her gasp and shake.

They both moved her so that she lay upon the bed. Then Jack was between her legs, a thick finger inside her as he licked her cunt. He thrust again and again, finding that place within her that made light gleam behind her eyelids.

The bed dipped as Rush climbed on to kneel beside her head, his eyes fever bright, his cock ruddy and curved upright—so close to her lips.

"Suck me, love," he rumbled.

"Yes," she gasped.

Rush carefully cupped her head, guiding her mouth to his cock. She licked the round, full head, tasting musk, and then took him all the way in. Grasping the base, she bobbed up and down, licking and sucking, adoring this crude, divine act.

Jack growled as wetness flooded her cunt, and he added another finger within her. He fucked her intently as he lapped at her clitoris, while her own tongue eagerly swirled around Rush's cock.

She cried out, a climax shattering her.

"That right, love," Rush said, hoarse, "scream with my cock in your throat."

Her release was overwhelming, brought about by both men devoting themselves to her.

She made a noise of distress when Jack's fingers and mouth disappeared, but that sound became a cry of ecstasy when he knelt between her legs, clasped her hips, and thrust his cock into her. Her orgasm had prepared her for him, yet even so, he filled her so fully it robbed her of all thought.

As Rush continued to fuck her mouth, Jack stroked in and out of her cunt. The two men wore taut, aroused expressions, seemingly lost in pleasure.

"Such a good lass," Jack rasped as he plunged into her. "Beautiful woman. Taking us both."

Some wild sound escaped her. She wanted to have them within her as much as she could, and drew hard on Rush's cock as she pushed her hips to meet Jack's strokes. Sweat glazed her, and them, the air ripe with the scent of sex and the sounds of flesh slapping against flesh.

Fingers strummed against her clitoris, and she saw that it was Rush who touched the sensitive nub while Jack continued to fuck her.

She came again, the force so great she arched up from the bed.

Jack grunted, slamming into her, before he pulled out. He grasped his cock and gave it a single, brutal stroke, then seed shot from him, viscously painting her skin.

Rush slid from her mouth. As she panted, Jack turned her onto her stomach and lifted up so she was on her hands and knees. Rush moved to kneel behind her, hands tight at her waist, the crown of his cock circling her entrance.

"Do you want me, love?" he growled. "To fuck you after Jack has fucked you? Because you're a greedy minx who loves being filled with our cocks?"

"Please," she moaned.

"Good girl." Rush snarled as he thrust into her, and her own gasp was swallowed as Jack kissed her.

Jack's hand tenderly but firmly held her throat as Rush hammered into her. Her eyes rolled back to be so magnificently used. While Rush continued to fuck her, he brought his fingers to her clitoris, lightly slapping against it.

"Come for me, love," he urged gutturally.

She did, bones melting with the heat of her release. A moment later, Rush pulled out and growled with his climax.

The room dissolved around her, and when she surfaced, Rush and Jack had cleaned her and removed her garters and stockings before tucking her between them. Jack cradled her from behind, his big body snug against hers, while Rush faced her as he stroked over her arms and legs. Both men murmured praise as they kissed her.

She, Rush, and Jack were a tangle of sweaty limbs and pounding hearts and slowing breaths, and she was important and cherished, surrounded by them.

"Extraordinary woman," Rush murmured, kissing along her collarbone as she traced her fingers through the dark hair curing across his chest. "Only with you...only with you is it like this."

"'Tis true," Jack added when she looked to him for confirmation.

Rush caressed the side of her face, his expression tender. "You sharing with us not just your body but your heart...that changes everything. I love you both, you know," he added, sharing a warm look with Jack. "It frightens me a little, but I'm certain that we can fuck that fear out of me."

"And you called *me* greedy." She chuckled.

"I am utterly brazen," Rush agreed.

"He is indeed a slut," Jack said with a smile.

"I refuse to let you both go," she said, rising up slightly so she could look both of them in the eyes. "'Tis as John said, England could never tolerate such scandal."

"Italy," Rush murmured, "can be a remarkably permissive place."

Her heart pounded. "A snug but sunny Tuscan villa."

"For three," Jack added.

She nodded eagerly, but regarded them with caution, uncertain what they would think of this plan. "'Tis a rather substantial change in all of our lives, I own, but I'd rather dwell in some faraway land than part with either of you. And as for my widow's portion, if John decides to take it from me, I've been longing to write some wicked tales. I could earn some coin penning tales of forbidden love. There's always readers eager for scandal."

"A wonderful idea," Jack said, a smile filling his weathered face. He leaned forward and kissed her. "I'm half packed already so I can leave in a trice."

Brimming with affection, she nuzzled him. "Wherever we are, Jack, I'll always be yours, as you will be mine."

"'Tis all I've ever wanted." His eyes were shining azure as he gazed at her.

She gave him one more kiss before turning to Rush, and let all the love she felt for him show in her face and in the warm timbre of her voice. "And you, Mr. Cantley? Will you join me and Jack in Tuscany? I love you both so desperately, I cannot part with either of you."

She caressed both their chests, reveling in the differences between these two men, though they did share one trait: they looked at her with unrestrained love. Never would she have believed that she could find one man to love her, let alone two, and the fact that she loved them back was even more extraordinary.

Rush stroked his thumb across her lip, so much devotion in his expression she could scarce catch her breath. Yet he did not speak, making her slightly uneasy.

"Granted," she added, "'tis a rather domestic arrangement for a rake."

"My dearest Mrs. Sparkwell," he murmured, "where my twin hearts, go, I readily follow. Besides," he added as he kissed her hungrily, "between two rakes and one widow, I warrant we've enough imagination to give our lives and your tales just the right amount of scandal."

The End.

Craving more rake-infused romance from Eva Leigh?

Check out The Good Girl's Guide to Rakes, a delicious tale about a notorious rake and an innocent debutante who together strike a very scandalous bargain...

ALSO BY EVA LEIGH

Last Chance Scoundrels:

The Good Girl's Guide to Rakes

The Union of the Rakes:

My Fake Rake

Would I Lie to the Duke

Waiting For a Scot Like You

The London Underground:

From Duke Till Dawn

Counting on a Countess

Dare to Love a Duke

The Wicked Quills of London:

Forever Your Earl

Scandal Takes the Stage

Temptations of a Wallflower

Standalones:

An Education in Pleasure

ABOUT THE AUTHOR

Eva Leigh is a USA Today bestselling romance author who has always loved romance. She writes novels chock-full of determined women and men who are here for it. She enjoys baking, spending too much time on the Internet, and listening to music from the '80s. Eva and her husband live in Central California.

Eva also writes in multiple romance genres as Zoë Archer and Alexis Stanton.

You can sign up for Eva's newsletter here!

evaleighauthor.com

A RAKE, HIS PATRON, & THEIR MUSE

NICOLA DAVIDSON

1

London, April 1815

THE SITUATION WAS OFFICIALLY ALARMING: HIS WRITING MALADY COULD not be fixed by an orgy.

Lennox Townsend scowled as he sat up in bed and gazed around the luxurious chamber of his rented Golden Square house. There were eight other equally naked people, and while last night's private gathering of hot-blooded women and men had been delightful, somehow...he'd expected more. That the dark restlessness in his soul would ease long enough for a cornucopia of words to unleash from his mind onto paper.

But he had nothing. He was a playwright without a script. No, far worse than that, a playwright without a single idea, a hellish dilemma for the most celebrated writer in London.

For five years he had packed Drury Lane with plays so overflowing in melodrama that audiences were wrenched through the full gauntlet of human emotion and back again. He had a standing invitation to Carlton House. His latest patron was the youngest brother of a powerful duke. Tailors and bootmakers and jewelers battled to offer complimentary items, because Lennox Townsend wearing something they'd created always resulted in a flurry of sales. Yet if the public discovered the imagination well had run dry, he would be discarded like the contents of a chamber pot. Without a new script he was just another jaded, thirty-year-old rake, and the city had an abundance of those.

Trying to quell his clawing tension, Lennox carefully climbed out of bed so he didn't disturb the Almack's patroness, House of Commons politician, and young countess who had joined him. Except now he had to tip-toe past the duke, duchess, and foreign ambassador slumbering in a velvet cushion nest on the floor, and the grizzled army brigadier cradling a silver-haired magistrate on a chaise. Negotiating the aftermath of an orgy was a vastly underrated feat of skill and athleticism; fortunately, he had years of experience.

After donning a quilted satin robe, Lennox padded over to the chamber door and out into the thankfully deserted hallway. The last thing he wanted right now were probing questions, or worse, more bedsport. Indeed, this damned writing malady had stolen not just words, but also his other great joy: pleasure. In the past, a banquet of mouths and cunts and arses had sated his rampant sexual appetite, but his contentment with this group had fled alongside his imagination. Sure, they met his need for multiple lovers at once; however they weren't interested in darker arts like dominance and pain play. None wanted to be disciplined or restrained or made to beg, especially by a social inferior. But how much longer could he suppress a critical part of himself? Hell, last night he had actually *feigned* enjoyment.

Shuddering, Lennox hurried downstairs to the dining room where freshly brewed tea would be waiting. But he wasn't alone: a blond-haired, blue-eyed, six-foot-four-inch mountain of a man sat at the table reading a newspaper.

"Morning, Jon," he greeted.

"Good morning, Lennox," replied Lord Jonathan Grant, as he set aside the newspaper and beamed.

Lennox paused to bask in the warmth of that smile, then turned to the sideboard and selected breakfast: a steaming cup of tea, and buttered toast with a dollop of orange marmalade.

While writers usually viewed early morning patron visits as a frightening event involving lectures, threats, or toe-breakage depending on how late the pages were, for him it was a treat. Jon might be nicknamed the Notorious Norseman due to his height, build, and coloring, but he was an absolute kitten; twenty-eight years old, awkwardly shy, and the sweetest man who had ever walked the earth. Most days Lennox fought the urge to smooth Jon's hair or feed him sweets. Most nights he dreamed of disciplining Jon's naked, bound form, while the young lord begged his master and mistress—some special woman who would make their trio complete—to be allowed to come.

But no. He would never corrupt his very own ray of sunshine. Although Jon occasionally asked halting, scarlet-cheeked questions about orgies or bedding another man, he never participated. Nor had he spoken of pain play, even in jest. In any event, it wasn't a good idea to mix business and pleasure. Patrons were lavished with time and attention for their money; one did not order them to suck cock.

Lennox cleared his throat. "I greatly appreciate you staying over to assist with tidying up."

"I greatly appreciate that you call the removal of blue-bloods who linger too long after an orgy as tidying up," Jon replied, his smile widening until it displayed the dimples in his cheeks. "But I have to earn my keep somehow."

Damn it, why did Jon have to be so adorable? It only provoked even darker, lustier thoughts within him.

"As the playwright, I believe that is my line," said Lennox gruffly.

"Speaking of lines," said Jon, his expression easing to concern, "did the party, er...assist?"

Lennox sighed. "I'd love to say yes, that I now have an entire play demanding to be unleashed onto paper, but I don't. I'm at a complete loss. Pressed against the wall in a putrid alley with a dagger at my neck. Clinging to the jagged cliff face with my last fingernail. Staring into the endless bleak chasm of my future as an accounts clerk. Or a politician."

The other man shook his head. "You don't have a mathematical bone in your body. Nor would I watch you tumble into the festering cesspit of politics. If I might be so bold, though, I do have an idea that could help."

How very Jon. The world's best patron, who never barked or demanded. He coaxed and encouraged, sent baked goods and velvet slippers, and organized household staff. The man was an angel; disappointing him made Lennox's gut hurt in a peculiar way.

"Thank God," Lennox replied, taking a restorative gulp of tea. "Tell me. I'm fresh out of ideas. In fact, if the kitchens didn't provide a pot of marmalade, I might have lost the last vestiges of sanity deciding what to slather on my toast."

"I thought perhaps...a complete change of scenery," said Jon, sitting forward in his chair and hunching his shoulders; a man trying to appear much smaller than he was. Thanks to the wretched Grant family's mockery, Jon remained sensitive about his body.

"Go on."

"How would you feel about a brief sojourn to the country? My brother's friend owns a quiet, well-appointed boarding house south of St. Albans. If we stayed there for a week, dosed ourselves with fresh air and hearty food, never know what might happen."

Lennox raised an eyebrow. "You'd be willing to accompany me to the middle of nowhere? That goes well beyond the bounds of duty."

His patron blushed and looked away. Then coughed. "I would do anything for...ah...I must protect my investment."

That blush.

So obvious with Jon's fair coloring, and the exact dusky pink of a well-disciplined arse.

As his unsatisfied cock throbbed, Lennox took several bites of toast to distract himself. It didn't help. His fingers itched to tangle in Jon's hair as he came in the younger man's mouth.

Christ.

A country sojourn was probably a terrible mistake with his imagination a dried-up husk and his lust at fever point, yet the thought of leaving the gray city made him feel better. Lighter even. While his dreams had come true in London—where else could an orphaned Whitechapel lad fight, charm, and lie his way to the heart of high society—perhaps he did require a change of scenery.

Lennox nodded slowly. "Then we must go. When?"

His patron's face lit up. "As soon as you like. I need to pack a satchel, but could return this afternoon with my traveling carriage, or tomorrow morning if that is more agreeable."

"Today," he replied decisively, his spirits lifting further at Jon's joy. "Let's steal away for a dull retreat so I might find my misplaced imagination. But before you go, can I ask one tiny favor..."

"Escort the crowd from your chamber?"

"Precisely. Yours is the only face I wish to gaze upon."

Jon stood, his cheeks now ruby red. "Consider it done."

Taking another bite of toast, Lennox sighed in anticipation. A week in Hertfordshire might just turn his fortunes around, and he couldn't wait to begin.

Glutton for punishment, thy name is Lord Jonathan Grant.

Jon paused in his packing and sank onto the edge of his oversized bed with a full-body shudder.

In his entire life he'd staged just one rebellion against his powerful ducal family, and that had been to snatch up Lennox Townsend after the playwright's previous patron died in early January. Lennox was everything the family loathed: confident and brilliant without title or Etonian education. But perhaps worse, a hedonist who followed few rules in his pursuit of pleasure.

He'd been intrigued, yet within hours of meeting Lennox he'd fallen helplessly in love, and the subsequent months had been an exquisite torment of closeness and distance: unpeeling the layers of a complicated genius who never spoke of his past but was so frank about the ebb and flow of writing or the different facets of lust. That openness had provoked him to privately explore his own desires, namely visiting London's most respected pain play madam, Theresa Berkley, at her establishment in Soho Square. Dearest Theresa had introduced him to a startling new world: spanking, then birches and nettle straps. But he loved the flogger best—in the tranquil, blissful aftermath of a dozen cruel kisses from those thin leather strips, it seemed like all things were possible. Even telling Lennox how he truly felt.

And now they were retreating to the country for a week. Together.

Perhaps this time he could at last gather the courage to say I love you.

Bah. Lennox Townsend has the world at his feet. He possesses a face so handsome it would make the angels weep. That he permits you to be his patron, even occasionally sleep nearby, is a miracle in itself. But he will never be your master. Never cradle you in his arms after a session of discipline and fucking so rough you won't be able to sit down for days. He'll never love you in return. And you know why; your family have explained it often enough. No one wants an awkward oaf.

Jon rubbed his arms, cold despite the lavish surroundings and fire-heated warmth of the bedchamber. While his brother's imposing Grosvenor Square townhouse had plenty of rooms, he didn't belong here. Not when he wasn't the previous duke's son, but the result of his mother's affair with a foreign diplomat. She had only confessed after her husband's death, when it became increasingly apparent that his height and coloring were vastly different to his older brothers and sisters. Society thought him a throwback to some all-conquering ancestor; they called him the Notorious Norseman, although not to his face. But the Grants knew the truth. And no matter what Jon did to make himself more like them, leaner and shorter and smarter and elegant...so did he.

"Going somewhere, Jonathan?"

Glancing over to the chamber door where his brown-haired and icily beautiful sister-in-law, the Duchess of Falston, waited, he immediately stood and bowed. "Good afternoon, Henrietta. Yes. I'm off to stay at the Prescott's boarding house for a week with Lennox Townsend."

Her lip curled. "The sooner this city gets past their ridiculous obsession with that walking, talking scandal, the better. It is a source of endless embarrassment to the family that you are his patron. Why can't you waste funds on something respectable, like horses?"

Because I'm the one who wishes to feel the riding crop.

"Lennox has a gift. It is my honor to help him share it," Jon replied softly, to keep his natural baritone in check.

"Your money, I suppose. But Falston and I shall be most displeased if that man causes trouble in Hertfordshire and we are forced to ride to the rescue. You are only a half-brother, after all. Hardly worth the effort."

"I understand..."

His voice trailed off, for Henrietta had already turned on her heel and departed. Sighing, he added a pile of linen shirts, waistcoats, buckskins, and warm woolen stockings to his satchel. Not only would he and Lennox enjoy fresh air and hearty food, but they could dress informally if they wished. There. Packing complete.

Except for your accessories.

Jon bit his lip as he stared at the drawstring canvas bag resting next to his pillow. The bag accompanied him everywhere and contained a collection of toys: a flogger, nipple clamps, Florentine leather dildo, and a bottle of oil. Twice now he had secretly watched Lennox during his orgies, stumbled back to the guest bedchamber, and punished himself.

He shouldn't take the bag to Hertfordshire. Or even think of being a voyeur, let alone actually do so. But the way Lennox fucked, so skilled and dominant, was a sight to behold. Passionate kisses. Teasing laps and tender bites to their nipples. Carefully preparing a lover to receive his thick cock; feasting until a cunt dripped with honey, or easing his way into a tight arse with oil-slick fingers. Then last of all, the sheer brutal power as he forced them to several orgasms before he withdrew and lashed their bellies or lower back with seed. It was difficult to decide who he envied more; the men and women who received that rampant cock, or Lennox, a true cunt connoisseur.

Jon sighed despondently. He adored the musky taste of a woman, but bedding ladies had often been a lackluster affair. They expected him to take control and dominate with his size; he yearned for orders and discipline, all while terrified he might accidentally hurt their slender, petite figures. He'd almost given up hope of finding the tall, plump mistress of his dreams, one who would ride his cock or face, ruthlessly using him for her pleasure before Lennox did the same...

Good God. Stop torturing yourself with the unobtainable.

Straightening his shoulders, Jon fastened his satchel. Then he seized the canvas bag of toys and shoved it into the buckled side pocket.

A quarter hour later, he was on his way to Golden Square. It was about 15 miles to the boarding house, so he'd packed a basket with meat pasties, fresh bread, apple tarts, and flagons of wine for the journey. But when the carriage pulled up in front of Lennox's home, Jon's stomach churned, forcing him to take several deep breaths.

Why are you doing this to yourself? Several hours confined together in a carriage followed by a full week in Lennox's company, to pine and yearn and generally behave like a complete lovesick twit?

Jon fought the urge to tap the roof and turn around. However, he couldn't change his mind now, for Lennox was strolling toward the carriage with a bulging satchel slung over his shoulder.

God. The way he *moved*. Sensual as a tiger on the hunt, loose-limbed yet purposeful. Every article of clothing artfully arranged: his usual jewel-tone jacket utterly contemptuous of Brummell's grays, with tight black breeches that drew the eye to an impressive bulge, and a shirt with enough lace at the cuffs to stir a breeze. Lennox Townsend was a rake. No, king of the rakes. Forever may he reign.

"Jon," he said cheerfully, as he tossed in his satchel then climbed into the spacious carriage and sprawled on the opposite seat. "Punctual as usual. And you've brought food! Capital. I'd be lost without you."

It was one thing to observe from a distance, but in close proximity, that roguish grin and long-lashed brown gaze could be classified as deadly weapons. Combined with skin far too swarthy for April and hair as black as night, he looked like a pirate.

A mouthwatering, sinfully splendid pirate.

Jon gripped his thighs, discreetly pinching himself, and the welcome bite of pain jolted him out of his lustful stupor. Well, enough to hold back words like 'I love you' or 'please may I kneel and suck your cock,' in any event.

"Better to travel with food," Jon said instead, smiling. "Otherwise, if you got hungry, you might start feasting on me. Enough for several meals at least."

GAH. He'd meant it as a jest, but as per usual it had come out wrong and now Lennox was tilting his head and studying him as one might something very, very curious. Did he suspect something? Or far worse, had he discovered his patron's wickedest secrets and wanted no part of them?

Jon desperately wanted to know. And yet at the same time remain completely oblivious.

This would officially be the longest carriage ride in history.

Prescott Boarding House, south of St. Albans, Hertfordshire

I can't do this anymore.

Mrs. Viola Prescott barely suppressed a banshee wail as she paused in unpegging a freshly laundered sheet from the rope strung between two stately oak trees.

A decade of abject misery was surely enough penance for any sins. Five years of marriage to Ned Prescott, a feckless gentry arse who had destroyed her stage career with his gambling then died while fleeing a high-stakes card game he'd been caught cheating at. After that, left with nothing in her widowhood, five years of managing the fashionable boarding house belonging to Ned's disapproving brother Oswald and his wife Pauline; a relentlessly bleak existence of gray gowns, endless chores, and definitely no dancing.

Only in her dreams did she perform now; swaying and whirling to music, her plump curves not confined by stays and modest necklines but on show for all to admire in a sheer tunic. Only in her dreams did she hear the fervent cheers and applause of a lust-struck audience, see their yearning faces and restless hands as she seduced each one with nary a touch. Yet every morning she awoke in this genteel prison without money or prospects, knowing that at the age of thirty-five, the opportunity for love and passion and a home of her own slipped further and further away.

"Viola! Viola, where are you, petal?"

She frowned at the frantic hail, and peered around the sheet to see four elderly boarding house residents hurrying toward her. Captain Timothy Talbot, Mrs. Gillian Talbot, Mr. Reuben Calder, and Mr. Piers Vincent. Most called them stalwarts of St. Albans society; Viola called them the Brigands, for they were absolute rascals who required constant supervision. Not that she would ever tell them, they were bold enough already, but the Brigands made life bearable.

"What have you done now?" asked Viola sternly. "Broken the hammock? I've told you time and time again it cannot support the weight of two people fucking like barn cats."

The captain, a retired Navy man, sniffed. "You said that about the lawn furniture, and it still stands."

Viola groaned. "And what if either Prescott sees? You know the rules."

Gillian rolled her eyes. "Those two icicles are far too busy making social calls. And if anyone did see our moonlight escapades, we'd simply say it was an opium-induced dream. Timmy has a few old pills which could be used for evidence; they're kept in my blue hatbox. Not to be confused with my pink hatbox, which holds gunpowder in the event a distraction is needed for our escape."

"I did not hear that."

"Yes, you did," said Reuben, a retired tailor. "Definitely an accomplice now."

"Oh, stop teasing the gel," said Piers, a retired clerk and Reuben's longtime lover. "We come bearing exciting news. Important guests have arrived!"

Huzzah. Even more work.

"How is that exciting?" said Viola. "Guests come and go every day."

"Not ones like Lord Jonathan Grant and Mr. Lennox Townsend."

She actually gasped. The celebrated playwright and his Notorious Norseman?

No. Surely it must be a trick. This boarding house was patronized by well-to-do elderly couples, lawyers and clerks who regularly traveled to London, and scholars studying the ancient St. Albans church or Roman ruins. Certainly not a young, handsome, and scandalous rake, let alone *two*.

"Are you sure?" Viola asked dubiously. "Their names weren't in the register."

"Of course, we're sure," said Reuben. "It's an impromptu visit. Which means Almighty God hath seen your sorrow and guided premium London cock to the doorstep; it is your holy duty to ride both."

She laughed. "So, I just saunter up and inquire if they would enjoy some well-seasoned redhead for supper I suppose?"

All four Brigands stared at her solemnly, nodding.

Oh God. They were serious.

It was an exceedingly risky idea. Oswald and Pauline forbade any intimate activity with guests. Besides, men like them could have anyone they wanted. A salty, too-tall, mature woman would hardly be their first choice for bedsport.

But what if they said yes?

Viola almost moaned at the thought. Back in her wild dancing days, she'd traveled with a troupe and enjoyed many lovers. Pleasure had not been a sin, but a necessity, a way to relax after a performance. If there was one thing she knew about London rakes, they weren't stuffy about bold offers, and as a widow, there would be no impediment to bedding if she remained discreet...

"Very well," she blurted. "I'll ask."

Her friends cheered.

"Go on, petal," said the captain encouragingly. "Give those city cocks a taste of country hospitality."

"But don't forget to dust away the cobwebs down there," said Gillian, her eyes glinting. "Unlike us, it really has been a while."

Irredeemable reprobates.

Viola poked out her tongue, gathered the rest of the laundry, and walked inside. Only to be immediately accosted by her petite blond sister-in-law in the kitchens.

"Where have you been?" snapped Pauline. "I called for you thrice. You are needed upstairs at once!"

"What is the matter?"

"I'm sure you know of our dear friend, the Duke of Falston."

Viola sighed. As Oswald and Pauline wove the fact into every conversation they had, it would be impossible not to know. "Yes."

"Well, his younger brother Lord Jonathan and the renowned playwright Lennox Townsend have come to stay. But there is a problem, and it's entirely your fault. Their suites are not ready and the maids are all busy. You must make up the beds in rooms five and six at once!"

She nodded then hurried upstairs and down the hallway. The rooms were the most expensive in the boarding house, reserved for honored guests. Each was large and elegantly furnished with a four-poster bed, oak desk, leather chairs, and private supper table. There was also an adjoining door between the rooms that could be propped open or locked depending on preference.

Starting with room five, Viola took the linen sitting on a chair and made the bed, ensuring the sheet corners were neatly tucked and the embroidered quilt pulled high. Next, she continued on to room six, her ears straining for the sound of footsteps in the hallway. It was true. Lennox Townsend and Lord Jonathan Grant were actually here. Anticipation made her usually nimble fingers clumsy, and Viola cursed as she banged her elbow on the wooden bedpost closest to the wall. Nearly done. Nearly...

ARGH.

Her too-enthusiastic flick of the sheet had hit the candelabra and knocked one of the unlit beeswax candles onto the floor. Naturally, it rolled under the bed.

Dropping to her knees, she stretched her arm under the wooden frame to fetch it. Beeswax candles cost significantly more than tallow, and Pauline would turn purple if she requested a fresh one when the stubs had just been replaced.

Where was the wretched thing?

Conceding defeat, Viola bent right down so she could peer under the frame; rump high in the air, breasts squashed against the floor, leaning on one forearm while the other darted about trying to locate the candle. There. There it was.

"Got you, you festering weasel turd," she crowed, snatching it up and brandishing it about.

"Congratulations. A job well done."

Viola froze. Smooth as satin and rich with amusement, that masculine voice invited her to laugh with him before agreeing to every sexual act ever discovered. Only one man could possibly speak like that: Lennox Townsend. But his first impression was a large gray-gowned arse swaying about and an unhinged screech about weasel turds. Something guaranteed to put him in the mood for fucking.

Cheeks hot with mortification, Viola hauled herself upright and bobbed a curtsy.

"Beg pardon, sir," she said, returning the candle to its rightful place. "I apologize that your room wasn't quite ready. And for my...er...colorful language. Do excuse me."

"Wait."

The word wasn't harsh or even loud. But the command was unmistakable, and Viola shivered as she turned and drank in the perfection of London's premier playwright. Lennox Townsend stood just a few inches taller than her, his body leanly muscled and expensively, vibrantly dressed. And his face...no man had the right to be this handsome. Yet it wasn't just his fathomless brown eyes, sculpted jaw, and crooked grin. It was his intent expression.

Like he recognized her.

Viola gulped. "I...ah...yes?"

"Have we met?" Lennox asked, taking her hand and rubbing his thumb across her knuckles until they tingled. "You look so familiar."

She trembled, resisting the urge to twine around his body like ivy on a trellis. "No. But how does one go about bedding you? Is it invitation only? Would it help if I begged?"

His eyes widened.

Oh no. She'd actually said that out loud. To Lennox Townsend.

"Miss—"

"Excuse me," Viola mumbled, yanking her hand from his and fleeing the chamber.

It seemed the cobwebs were doomed to remain.

2

NOT EVEN A SHAPELESS GRAY GOWN COULD DIM THE VIVID RED-HAIRED beauty—or lush curves—of Mrs. Viola Prescott.

Jon tried not to stare as he finished his breakfast of coddled eggs, ham, and toasted bread with butter in the boarding house dining room, but she was just...*stunning*. Even attending to tasks as mundane as pouring tea and conversing with guests, she strolled about like a goddess bestowing favor on fortunate mortals.

Although Viola was a tall woman, she wasn't awkward or clumsy like him. There was a rhythm and lightness to her step, yet also a barely leashed sensuality to the sway of her wide hips and rounded arse that drew the gaze and insisted it linger and appreciate. As for her ample breasts, well. He couldn't think of a more heavenly place for a lover to rest their weary head and be petted after pleasing her. No doubt in the next week he'd be punishing himself with several frigid sponge baths; the dream of being disciplined and fucked by Lennox had been joined by another equally alluring fantasy: pleasuring Mrs. Prescott with his tongue until she drenched him in sweet cunt honey...

"More tea?"

Jon almost fell off his chair at the husky feminine voice, and as he scrambled to right himself, the back of his hand knocked over his half-full cup. "Damnation! Forgive me, Mrs. Prescott. Crockery is never safe when I'm about."

"You do have exceptionally large paws, my lord."

He barely suppressed a moan at her tone, a heady blend of censure and amusement. It was easy to imagine Mrs. Prescott working at Theresa's establishment as a wicked governess; one who stroked hair and offered treats if her body was worshipped appropriately, but who never spared a flogging for misbehavior.

For God's sake man, you're wearing buckskins in a dining room. Do not think of worshipping Mrs. Prescott. Or how she might flog your arse until it burns.

Too late.

Jon snatched up a linen napkin and dabbed at the spilled liquid. "Large all over, alas."

Mrs. Prescott laughed. "Of that I have no doubt whatsoever."

Horrified heat exploded across his cheekbones, and he scrubbed harder at the stained tablecloth. "I didn't mean my co...er...that is... forgive me. I never say the right thing."

"My lord—"

"Jon. Just Jon," he blurted. "I don't stand on ceremony like my brother."

"Very well, Jon. Let me take care of that tea mishap," Mrs. Prescott replied, as she gently but firmly removed the napkin from his hand. The brush of cool, smooth fingertips against his skin sent a jolt of fierce arousal through him, and he shuddered.

"Yes, ma'am."

He tried to sit still as she deftly removed his plate, cutlery, and cup, replaced the stained tablecloth and reset the table. Yet her nearness, a faint scent of citrus, and her brisk competence had his heart racing. Did she know? Was Mrs. Prescott aware that an aristocratic guest—one with supposedly good manners—sat in her dining room with a monstrous erection just because she'd laughed and touched his hand?

Don't be a fool.

Then she did it once more. A featherlight caress, trailing around his wrist.

Oh God. It was deliberate.

A beautiful, statuesque woman discreetly teasing him, with other guests sitting just fifteen feet away.

Jon gasped, almost quivering with need. "Again, Mrs. Prescott. *Please.*"

"You may call me Viola," she whispered, draping a new napkin across his lap then adjusting it so the crisp linen rubbed against the straining fall of his buckskins in an agonizingly good way. "Our families are so close, after all."

"Yes, Viola."

"Now, was there anything else you required, Jon? I am here to ensure your stay is thoroughly enjoyable."

He swallowed hard as a tiny smile played about her rose-pink lips, one that promised all manner of carnal delights. This woman would be a jewel of knowledge and bold in her desires, he was sure of it.

Force me to my knees. Use me for your pleasure. Do whatever you desire, mistress.

The words were right there and Jon willed them to spill forth. For once in his life to say, without shame or dissembling, what he truly wished for.

"Viola—"

"Morning," drawled an achingly familiar voice from the other side of the dining room. "Wretched time of the day, it should be illegal to do anything before noon. Jon, have you eaten? Mrs. Prescott, will you join us for tea?"

Jon sucked in a breath, trying desperately to regain his composure. Lennox Townsend *and* Viola Prescott at his table? What if they both touched him, even inadvertently? He would be the spectacle that proved a cock could indeed burst through buckskins and spurt seed a hundred feet in the air like a damned volcano.

Gripping the napkin in his lap so firmly his knuckles turned white, Jon smiled at Lennox. "Morning."

But Viola bobbed a curtsy and shook her head, her cheeks pink. "Unfortunately, I cannot, Mr. Townsend. I have duties to attend to. Excuse me."

With a hip sway like that it was a pleasure to watch her leave, yet at the same time regret crashed through him. Had he once more missed his chance due to a lack of courage?

Yes, you fool.

"How did you make it downstairs so early, Jon?" grumbled Lennox as he thumped down a full plate of coddled eggs, ham, sautéed potato, toasted bread and orange marmalade. "I thought this was supposed to be a holiday of sorts. Refreshment of the mind."

Jon stifled a fond smile. Bears woken from hibernation possessed more charm than Lennox before noon and unfed; however, even with his eyes shooting daggers at the bright sunlight and his sensual mouth curled in a scowl, he remained the most attractive man in England. The cleverest, too. Looking even more pirate-like than usual in an emerald-green waistcoat, old-fashioned black breeches, and a billowing white shirt with lace cuffs.

"My stomach awakens me," he confessed. "If I do not eat at least five or six meals a day, it rumbles loud enough to wake the dead. I did not wish to rattle the boarding house foundations and disturb the other guests."

"I'd wager you just wished to admire Mrs. Prescott, which is completely understandable. What a fascinating woman. Tell me everything you know."

With anyone else it might have been horribly embarrassing to be so obvious, but Lennox didn't comment slyly or to cause hurt. He merely stated facts.

Jon leaned back in his chair and tapped his chin. "As you are aware, Oswald went to Eton with my brother; they are great friends and visit each other at least several times a year. But I never met Viola because she doesn't accompany the Prescotts to London, nor is she invited to social functions when Falston and Henrietta travel here. They all hiss about her, though. Frequently. Her hair, her manners, her figure..."

Lennox snorted. "I am thoroughly unsurprised that quartet of stuffed shirts feels that way about her most delightful qualities. But why does Mrs. Prescott work here rather than enjoy her widowhood?"

"Because of her late husband. Ned Prescott was a spoiled, self-absorbed weasel. He took whatever he wanted; thought living within his means something only others had to do. Oswald always paid his debts but once Ned married Viola, deemed far below his station, they cut him off. So, he turned to gambling to fund his habits, but he was terrible at it. Got caught cheating quite often. The day Ned died...he tried to fleece the wrong people and was pursued by both smugglers and the local constable. The fool tried to jump a gate, fell off his horse, and broke his neck. That left poor Viola with nothing, so Oswald and Pauline took her in. Not as family, though. As a servant."

Lennox actually paused in eating a forkful of ham, his eyes wide. "Hell."

"Indeed."

"But why was Viola deemed below Ned?"

"He met her at a show," said Jon, trying to remember the story he'd overheard. "She was a dancer, part of a very popular traveling troupe with a risqué reputation. They performed at inns and private clubs rather than theaters. Her own family disowned her for that."

"I see."

Lennox grew strangely quiet, and envy curled around Jon's heart. He knew that look; lusty rake pondering the best way to invite a beautiful woman to bed. Lennox was always successful. *Always.* Sure as the sun rose each day, Viola would be coming so many times she'd forget her own name tonight.

Perhaps even sooner than that.

And he...well, he'd have naught but a small bag of accessories for company; the punishment for his cowardice in not speaking up to either Lennox or Viola.

Yet another evening alone.

WHEN HIS BRAWNY ray of sunshine's smile dipped, even for a moment, it affected him in ways that were difficult to describe.

Lennox took a few more bites of food, and a gulp of hot tea, just for time to gather his thoughts. And remind himself that the dining room of a stuffy boarding house was not the place to kiss another man. Or discipline him.

No matter how much he might want to.

It would be entirely Jon's fault if he got kissed or disciplined, though. Sitting there in that chair, all adorably pink-cheeked and flustered and pouting. What had Mrs. Prescott said to him? Or should the question be, what had she done? He'd caught a glimpse of Jon's buckskins after bringing his plate to the table; his patron had been sporting a rather sizeable erection. But if those two thought to play without him, they would find themselves in all sorts of trouble.

"So," said Lennox. "What are your plans for the day?"

Jon blinked. "I'm not sure. Might explore the grounds a bit while the sun is out. I'm as bad as a pup if I don't get my daily walk; I may start destroying the furniture. No, wait, I've already destroyed a tablecloth. Poor Viola…Mrs. Prescott, I mean, had to put a fresh one on and reset the table after I knocked over my cup of tea."

He says her name so warmly. Yet with such reverence, too. Interesting.

"Bah, it is entirely the teacup's fault for being too delicate. Which reminds me, we should find a shop that sells large, sturdy mugs. If not, we'll have some made. The cup must suit you, not the other way around."

The younger man relaxed. "I shall remember that next time I have a mishap. Are you going to write today? Perhaps make some notes about characters or a setting?"

"Careful," warned Lennox. "You almost sounded like a patron. You'll get pages, I swear…ah, now I know why you brought up the tablecloth story, you devilish fiend. A veiled threat to my person. Pages or I get dragged away and given the lye soap treatment."

"Mwa hahaha," said Jon, the attempt at a villainous laugh quite ruined by his cherubic grin. The man really was a complete kitten.

"I will try to write, though, while you are doing revoltingly robust activities like strolling outside. Directly after I find Mrs. Prescott. I failed to answer a question of hers yesterday, for which I must make amends. By the by, did I interrupt a conversation between the two of you earlier? Any message you wish to pass on?"

His patron hesitated for a long moment, then shook his head. "No. You go."

Lennox pushed back his chair and stood. "Very well. I'll see you later. Behave, now. The only acceptable furniture destruction is caused by too many people in a bed."

Jon nodded, his gaze oddly wistful. "Words to live by."

Damnation. Now he really wanted to kiss the man. And not a brief peck to the cheek, but a long punishing kiss where he gripped the back of Jon's neck and crushed his lips until the young lord fully surrendered to his master.

Instead, he restricted himself to clapping Jon's shoulder as he moved past him toward the dining room door. It was time to find Viola Prescott and continue the conversation she'd started about his bedding preferences, before she'd lost confidence and fled his chamber.

"Psst! Mr. Townsend!"

Lennox halted and glanced to his left to see a table with four elderly guests, three men and one woman. All were dressed conservatively; the men in elegantly tailored jackets and trousers, the woman in a purple gown and matching turban, but the expression on each face could only be described as...conspiratorial.

Curious indeed.

He inclined his head. "Madam. Gentlemen. How may I be of service?"

The woman smiled. "My name is Mrs. Gillian Talbot. This is my husband Captain Timothy Talbot, and our friends Mr. Piers Vincent and Mr. Reuben Calder. We are all great, great admirers of your plays, although they could do with a lot more lust."

"I'm gratified to hear that, and I agree," Lennox replied in amusement. "However, you must take the matter up with my arch-enemy: the Examiner of Plays, Mr. John Larpent. He reports to the Lord Chamberlain and decides whether licenses are granted. Alas, he is very strict."

"Wretched censorship," said Mrs. Talbot with a dramatic harrumph. "The government insisting that if we don't hear cursing or see bare bottoms and bedsport, we'll all behave. Ha!"

He grinned. "Sounds like you were a marvelously wild lass, madam."

"Still is, m'boy," said Captain Talbot with a wink. "But see here. We four look out for Viola. Nothing as soft and cuddly as grandparents, more like...bloodthirsty hawks protecting a chick or ships armed to the gills and ready to fire at will."

"I see," said Lennox gravely, unsure whether to laugh or go directly to St. Albans for a suit of armor. "Is this a warning? A request to discover my intentions?"

Mr. Vincent snorted. "Seeing as you're a playwright, the Talbots thought you would appreciate a theatrical touch. I'm far more sensible. We overheard you saying you need to find our gel and ask her a question. It is our sincere hope that your intentions are to tend a sadly neglected garden. Needs a vigorous rake, that's for certain."

Christ. He'd had some unusual conversations in his life, but never had he thought some gentry boarding house guests would actively *encourage* his pursuit of a woman. Although according to Jon, Viola had been treated terribly by the Prescotts. In truth he was glad she had people in her life who genuinely cared for her, even if they were eccentric as hell.

"Mrs. Prescott is fortunate in her friends," Lennox replied.

Mr. Calder laughed and took a sip of tea. "Viola calls us the Brigands. We cannot be tamed...well, apart from breaking a hip or something. Limbs aren't quite as flexible as they used to be, the perils of old age. Still having more fun than her, though. So be a good chap and attend to the matter, will you? When Viola's avoiding her in-laws, she can be found in the small antechamber next to the music room. Third door down from the kitchens."

He bowed. "My thanks. Madam. Gentlemen. Good day."

Next stop: the antechamber next to the music room.

To avoid attracting attention, Lennox sauntered rather than hurried out of the dining room and down the hallway, nodding pleasantly to maids and footmen who were scurrying about attending to tasks. Then, with a glance left and right to ensure no one observed him, he ducked into the music room. There was an expensive pianoforte in one corner with a well-thumbed book atop it, and in another corner sat a harp covered in a linen sheet. He continued past both, turning left when he spotted a small doorway next to the fireplace.

Not wanting to startle her if she was in the antechamber, Lennox coughed. "Mrs. Prescott?"

A moment later she appeared, a wary expression on her face. "Mr. Townsend. How did you find me?"

"I hate to reveal a source, but somehow I don't imagine you'll be surprised. The Brigands were generous with their information."

Mrs. Prescott groaned. "The only surprise is that they restrained themselves to information rather than something more direct like a key to my chamber."

Lennox tilted his head. She kept stepping side to side, but it wasn't a nervous, jerky movement. No, it was the unconscious act of a supremely skilled dancer who had once ruled the stage. When he'd first set eyes on Viola Prescott in his room, he'd been struck by the sense of familiarity, but only after Jon mentioned she'd been part of a troupe had he pieced the puzzle together. Years ago, he'd seen her perform at an inn and been utterly ruined for redheads, for who could possibly compare?

"I wouldn't have used a key. I prefer to make my own arrangements," he began. "But yesterday after making up the bed in my chamber, you asked me three questions, which I failed to answer with sufficient haste. How one goes about bedding me, is it invitation only, and would it help if you begged. I should be delighted to reply in great detail, on the proviso you answer a question of mine first: what the hell is the legendary Madam Viola doing working as a servant in the backwaters of St. Albans?"

VIOLA OFTEN CAME to this tiny, cluttered antechamber when she needed a retreat from the boarding house, for it reminded her of a troupe dressing room. Today she'd needed a quiet space to ponder her fierce attraction to two very different men: bold and lusty Lennox Townsend, and sweet, shy Jon Grant.

But Mr. Townsend had found her. And now he'd asked the question she had waited a lifetime to hear.

For five endless years she'd suppressed her true self just to keep a roof over her head. Oswald and Pauline insisted on so many rules; the modest gray gowns of half-mourning, for her to behave like a cloistered nun, and receive next to no wages. All as punishment for the crimes they blamed her for: Ned marrying far below his station, her lack of children, and him subsequently dying.

But she couldn't do it anymore. Couldn't live as a shadow of herself.

Viola took a deep breath. "You recognized me. I wondered if you did."

Mr. Townsend shrugged. "Must have been a good ten years ago now, I think I'd just turned twenty. When I saw the posted notice, I hoarded all my funds and purchased a ticket to watch you perform at the Thorny Rose Inn. It seared into my mind. Never have I seen such grace. Such wicked sensuality. Such luscious curves and vibrant red hair. The way you seduced an entire audience and held them in the palm of your hand, made them cheer and clap and stomp their feet...I wanted that power.

Not with dance, but with dialogue. You inspired me to start writing my first play, you know. Madam Viola, my one and only muse."

Her jaw dropped at his gruff words and she stared at him, searching his face for signs of trickery or jest. But there were none.

The emperor of the theatrical world was serious.

"I wish we'd met then, Mr. Townsend," Viola whispered. "My life might have turned out so very differently if I'd declined Ned Prescott's proposal."

"Call me Lennox. And yes, life certainly would've been better had you told that bilious barnacle on the arse of the world to go fuck a tree trunk."

She almost laughed. "Ned was the worst, but don't tell Oswald or Pauline I said that; they still think him a perfect soul lured into a Jezebel's clutches and I am to blame for everything that happened. Ha. All I know is that my husband pursued me relentlessly as my star rose, told me that he was proud of my career and would support it always. However..."

"Let me guess," said Lennox with a dark scowl. "Your success didn't glorify Ned sufficiently. I've seen it many times in the theater world. Husbands with no talent whatsoever clipping a woman's wings if she flies too high. As a fledgling playwright I even had a few fame-hungry patrons myself, although these days I am very, very fortunate in Jon. He is an angel. I adore him."

Viola briefly closed her eyes in a futile attempt at composure. It shouldn't be such a momentous thing to have someone understand —*truly* understand—her plight, but it damned well was. And now all that rage, that hurt and frustration she'd carried so long after her inglorious fall from grace, was bubbling up inside.

"Ned didn't just clip my wings," she spat. "He burned them off. His jealous petulance ruined every business relationship I had, for he insisted on accompanying me to rehearsals, only to interrupt them constantly with instructions and demands. After that he stole from the troupe to fund his drinking and gambling. They unceremoniously dismissed me two days later. Naturally, once other troupes heard the tale, I was less appealing than rotten vegetables. No one wants to hire a dancer dragging that kind of poisoned shackle behind her."

"*Christ.*"

"I h-hate him for what he d-did."

Tears burned her eyes, and Viola dashed a hand across her face in an attempt to stop them, but it was too late. They were already trickling down her cheeks and dripping onto her gown. Wonderful.

Yet Lennox didn't flee. Instead, he hauled her against his firm chest and held her tightly in his strong arms while one hand rubbed her back.

"Cry it out," he said. "There's a good girl."

Freed by the command, Viola sagged against him and proceeded to sob on his shoulder for a full five minutes. But when the tears ran dry and her mind eventually unscrambled, all she could think about was the man holding her so securely.

No. Not just a man, a gloriously handsome rake who had pleasured most of London and left every single one blissfully satisfied. But would he even be interested now after witnessing such an emotional display?

She cleared her throat and pulled back a little. "I must look a fright. I wish I was a delicate crier, but I'm just not, and blotchy cheeks and pink nose do not match well with red hair."

"Whereas I see beauty in its rawest form," said Lennox, his dark eyes fixed on her. Piercing her armor all the way to her soul. "Far more alluring than a cold mask."

Viola tentatively placed her hand on his chest. "You...promised to answer my questions."

His lips curled into the most sinful smile in England. "Ah, yes. Hmmm. To be invited to my bed, one must first express a fervent desire. And yes, I do rather like it when a lover begs. In fact...the more they surrender to me, the more I feel compelled to make them come until they see stars. Repeatedly."

Oh God.

"That's quite a claim," she managed. "You have a degree in providing orgasms from Came-bridge, I suppose?"

"Hardly," he replied, looking mildly affronted. "Coxford. Now, about that begging..."

Viola swallowed a moan as her nipples hardened painfully and scraped against the bodice of her hideous gray gown. Rather like she had scraped the napkin over Jon's erection earlier. "Ah..."

"Something the matter?"

"I know I'm doing everything possible to turn you away, but I must confess that I teased your patron earlier. When I put a fresh napkin over Jon's lap in the dining room, I touched his cock. He is a very attractive man. And so sweet."

"I am aware."

Well. Three short words with a wealth of emotion behind them. Viola almost asked a too-personal question about the true relationship between playwright and patron, yet when Lennox's hand moved to cup her backside, she whimpered instead. "You don't mind I'm also attracted to him?"

"Darling," he chided. "I often take part in orgies. Wanting to fuck more than one person is as natural to me as breathing."

Pure relief flooded her. "Then would you fuck me? I am quite prepared to beg, although I'll only kneel on cushions. Thirty-five-year-old knees do not like wooden floors."

Lennox nodded, and for a moment she thought he might kiss her. Instead, he did something infinitely better: he leaned forward and gently bit her neck, sending a shocking jolt of pleasure directly to her needy cunt. "It would be my great honor to do so. I believe after what you have endured at the hands of various Prescotts, you deserve numerous orgasms. I shall enjoy making you scream."

Viola trembled, pressing her thighs together to ease the unbearable ache. There was only one more question left to ask. "When?"

"I've ordered a bath to be brought to my room after supper tonight. Ten o'clock. Perhaps you'd like to scrub my back."

"Yes. Oh God, yes."

3

SOON HE WOULD BE FUCKING THE REDHEAD OF HIS DREAMS.

Lennox surveyed his chamber with a stern eye, needing to ensure everything in the room was just so. For the past ten years, he'd kept an eye out in all buildings, on all streets, hoping to see Madam Viola once again. But she'd first been trapped with a manure pile masquerading as a husband, then here with her frightful in-laws, and their wretched treatment had actually reduced a daring, spirited woman to tears. One night of pleasure couldn't begin to make up for that, but he would do his best, for Viola intrigued him.

A lover who enjoyed submitting to another, yet also liked to take the lead as she'd done with Jon in the dining room? Now that was rare and utterly delicious. And he already felt such ease in her presence, for they had a surprising amount in common. With Viola's dancing history, she knew the elation of owning an audience, but she'd also experienced the lows of the theatrical world, and understood how much work went into something that appeared so effortless. Much like with Jon, he wouldn't have to pretend with her.

In truth, the only fly in his ointment right now was Jon retreating to his room after supper with a nasty headache. Poor kitten. He'd checked on his patron to see if he needed a tonic or cold compress, but the younger man had blushed and waved him away, imploring him to go and do what a rake was supposed to.

Lennox grinned. He needed no further encouragement. Not with a woman possessing his absolute favorite combination of attributes: flaming red hair, plump curves, a dusting of freckles across her pert nose, emerald-green eyes, and a saucy mouth. In about a quarter hour or so, he would know the sounds Viola made when she came, the taste of her sweet honey, and the hot clasp of her cunt. Perhaps she might even share a little more of her history. Oddly enough, he wanted to hear her hopes and dreams and most intimate desires, and it wasn't just because playwrights were curious bastards who liked hearing a story. It went far beyond that, something he'd not really felt for a woman he wished to bed before.

And he certainly wished to bed Viola.

How would she like to fuck?

It was a question he always pondered with a new lover. Whether to slowly tease or roughly take; which parts of their body were especially sensitive or receptive to touch. If they wanted to hear nothing but a symphony of flesh slapping and ragged moans, or be told in explicit terms exactly what would happen next...

A knock at the door interrupted his musings. Ah. Quarter to ten. This would be the tub and hot water he'd ordered for his bath.

"Enter!" Lennox called.

"Here you are, sir," said a footman as he and another walked in carrying a large copper tub, trailed by several maids carrying buckets of steaming hot water. They set up his bath behind an embroidered screen along with towels and scented soap; their faces brightening when he fetched his money purse and handed them a sixpence each for the trouble. Equally as quickly he was alone again, and unwilling to sit still, he discarded his shoes and stockings and began to pace.

Just when he feared the clock would never chime ten, there came a soft tap at the door.

Lennox marched over and yanked it open. Viola stood there, snugly wrapped in a dressing gown and her red hair in a braid, yet even after their frank conversation in the antechamber she looked a trifle uncertain. He offered a warm smile and ushered her into the chamber. "Good evening."

"Good evening," she said, folding her arms over her breasts.

"Viola," he said seriously, "if you're having second thoughts for any reason, just say so. No hard feelings whatsoever. I only bed those who are willing and eager."

"I am very, very willing and eager," Viola replied, her cheeks turning pink in a way that reminded him of Jon. How strange he'd think of that. "Only...it has, ah, been a while. I'm not sure how to behave. No, how you wish me to behave."

"How long is a while? A month? A year?"

"Longer."

"Then I think, madam," he replied gruffly as he securely latched the door, "you should behave as a castle chatelaine of old and start by bathing your guest. Feel free to discard whatever clothing you feel comfortable discarding. But grant me a boon and unbraid those luscious locks. Red hair should live in its natural state: untamed."

She tugged the ribbon from her hair, finger combing the unruly curls that fell past her shoulders. Next, she removed her dressing gown, slippers, and nightgown, but kept on her chemise. The garment was old and rather threadbare, the fabric so transparent in the firelight that it revealed far more than it concealed. Christ, what a bounty. Viola's breasts were even fuller than he'd first thought, tipped with large pale brown nipples. Her stomach was fleshy, her hips wide, and her thighs sturdy. A thick bush of auburn hair covered her mound, and his mouth watered to lick her sweet cunt until she drenched his mouth and chin.

The woman was irresistible.

Lennox drew Viola to him and captured her lips with his. He tried to be slow and gentle, but she melted against him with a carnal whimper, opening her mouth for his tongue and rubbing her already hard nipples against his chest in an unmistakable plea. A hot-blooded Venus indeed.

"Mr. Townsend—"

"I told you to call me Lennox."

"*Lennox*. Please. I need to come so badly. I've been waiting forever..."

He smiled and nipped the silken skin of her neck, reveling in her choked moan. "Not long now, darling. I said I would make you scream, and I am a man of my word."

Viola closed her eyes and let her head fall back, fully permitting him access to her body. Intending to taste every inch, he explored the expanse of her shoulders and the gentle curve of her collarbone. Then he kissed the satiny skin, scraping with his teeth and lapping with his tongue until her hands gripped his arms, her breath coming in short, panting gasps.

"Shall I touch your nipples?" he asked lazily, untying the ribbon of her chemise bodice at a speed an ancient snail would be ashamed of.

Viola mewled in frustration as she arched her back, thrusting her breasts against his hand. Anticipation roared through him; no prim and proper maiden here, but a passionate, experienced woman too long denied what she needed. He would, however, make her beg for pleasure. Just like she hadn't hidden her tears or desire to orgasm from him, he would not conceal his true dominant nature from her.

Lennox tsked as he ran his fingertip down below her collarbone, tracing a pattern that grazed the swell of her upper breasts but not venturing near her nipples. "I asked you a question, madam."

"I'm not sure how long I can play this game," she whispered raggedly. "Pleasure is not a wish or even a desire anymore. It's something critical like breathing or eating. I need you to touch my nipples. To pinch them hard. To suck them until I cannot bear how sensitive they are. I love that. It will make me so wet, wet enough to take that thick cock of yours."

"Darling, I solemnly swear you'll be soaked before you're stuffed full," Lennox replied, gently plucking each nipple between his thumb and forefinger. Then he halted. "But to gain your reward you must first attend to my bath."

Viola shuddered, the need she'd just spoken of clear on her face. Seconds later, she sank to her knees on a cushion beside the copper tub. "Very well. Let me please you."

AFTER BEING STARVED of lustful touch for years, the wait was unbearable.

Yet for Viola, this feeling was achingly, wonderfully familiar. As a dancer she'd rehearsed nearly every day for the reward of a late-night performance, those heady moments on stage when a thousand eyes fixed upon her, envious, admiring, worshipping. Lennox understood the power of delayed gratification, and it only made her arousal burn hotter.

Eager to begin, Viola rocked on her knees as he removed his clothing to reveal a swarthy, leanly muscled form and a cock so thick her cunt clenched in desperation. Once Lennox had settled in the copper tub, Viola soaped a washcloth to scrub his shoulders and arms, but when she leaned over the hot water, the steam dampened her chemise until it clung to her breasts. He made a growling sound, his fingers tracing her nipples through the fabric before pinching the taut peaks, and she gasped at the corresponding throb that arrowed directly to her core.

"Sensitive," said Lennox, his smile knowing.

"Do that again," Viola demanded.

"Wash my chest and we'll see."

Trembling with desire now, she dutifully ran the washcloth back and forth over his hair-roughened skin. Soon his mouth fastened around her left nipple and sucked hard, the sinfully good play of lips and teeth and tongue making her moan as the rest of her needy body wailed for the same expert attention. For the longest time she'd been alone in the darkest, coldest abyss. But now there was light. Intense heat.

"Please," Viola whispered, so close to orgasm she dropped the cloth and gripped the side of the tub.

"Poor darling. You really need to come, don't you? Would you prefer fingers, tongue or cock to start?"

That was like being asked to choose her favorite sweet. But she craved the burn of that thick shaft stretching her wide.

"Cock," she said decisively. "You promised to stuff me full."

Lennox nodded and hauled himself upright to swiftly wash his belly, groin, and legs with the cloth. After stepping out of the tub he dried off with a towel, then led her over to an armchair in front of the crackling fireplace. "Before we begin, do you have a sponge? Or are you happy for me to withdraw and spill outside?"

"Withdrawing is acceptable," said Viola, warmed at the matter-of-fact conversation. Lennox made no assumptions or judgments and clearly valued her preferences. While he had nothing to worry about in regard to fatherhood—her barrenness was long established and had kept her in favor with troupe leaders until Ned ruined everything—she certainly appreciated the care in the question.

"Anything you don't enjoy?"

"Tongue in my ear. Ugh."

He chuckled. "Duly noted. But let me know if there is anything else."

Once in the armchair, Lennox guided her onto his lap so she strad-dled him, her thighs spread wide. A decadent pose; it allowed him full access while leaving her slightly helpless.

Perfect.

Momentarily, he halted. "Would you remove your chemise? Not even thin linen should impede such a magnificent view."

"That sounds like you aren't opposed to plump figures."

"Are you jesting? My one prayer is not to disgrace myself by coming too soon. Ample curves like yours, all soft and lush, call to me like a Siren."

Viola giggled as she discarded the garment. "I swear there are no rocks to ruin you."

"No," Lennox replied, cupping her mound and pressing the heel of his hand directly against her swollen clitoris. "A smooth ride ahead."

She came.

The sudden burst of pulsing waves between her legs and the low scream that tore from her throat were shocking; it had been far too long between man-led orgasms. Ned's actions had ensured any desire for him died; marital relations became her most hated chore and she'd always feigned a response so he wouldn't linger. But Lennox didn't destroy, he created. Nor did she have to worry whether he knew what he was doing or if he might tattle to her in-laws.

With Lennox, for this small window in time, she could be free.

Grateful beyond measure, Viola caressed his cheek before reaching for his engorged cock.

"Wait," he said.

She stilled at the order, and the way Lennox stared over her shoulder. He had the strangest expression on his face, pensive and yet...even more aroused? "Is something wrong?"

"I don't want to alarm you, darling," he said in her ear. "But we have an audience."

An audience?

Someone was watching them fuck?

Impossible. The door to the hallway was in the other direction and Lennox had securely latched it. The only other door adjoined...Jon's room?

That sweet, shy man-mountain was a *voyeur*?

The thought made her whimper. An evening with Lennox was the rarest of treats, but an experienced rake to pleasure her senseless *and* a handsome lord to perform for?

Heavenly.

"Jon likes to watch?" she murmured, unable to conceal her excitement as she moved restlessly on Lennox's lap.

A slow smile curled his lips. "Apparently so. I was going to ask if we should shoo him away with a scolding for such impertinence, but your greedy cunt is drenching my hand at the prospect of an audience. You want to tease him again, don't you?"

Viola nodded, moaning as Lennox knit three fingers together and plunged them inside her. Caressing. Twisting. In. Out. In. Out. The blissfully rough penetration had her bucking, her fingernails digging into his shoulders at the storm of intense sensation. But knowing that Jon was watching...yearning...

A wild ecstatic cry unleashed from the depths of her soul, the powerful orgasm lasting and lasting as it washed over her like a spring tide.

"Oh God," she stammered, clinging to Lennox as the world eventually righted itself.

He withdrew his hand and gently rubbed her back. "Splendid, beautiful darling. But I'm going to expose Jon now. My patron must be punished for spying without permission."

"Yes. He must."

"Jon! Cease skulking about and get in here immediately!"

The door opened fully, and one oversized blond lord stumbled into the chamber. His arms were clamped to his sides, his head bowed, but the enormous bulge straining against his buckskins, even bigger than in the dining room, was a sight to behold.

"Lennox. Viola," Jon mumbled. "I don't know what to say. I cannot explain my actions. Please accept my apologies—"

"Sit down on the end of my bed," said Lennox, calm yet stern. "I take it no headache?"

"No," said Jon as he perched awkwardly and gripped his thighs, still not meeting their gaze.

Viola considered him. Back in the troupe there had been several men who enjoyed sexual submission. After misbehaving in the express hope of punishment, they had all behaved much like Jon: a chastened pet. Was it possible the brawny lord craved the same? From what she'd observed, it certainly seemed likely. But despite Jon's eagerness to be teased in the dining room, there was a connection between him and Lennox that appeared much stronger than patron and playwright. What did he truly want?

"I wonder, Jon," said Viola. "Who were you admiring when that huge cock of yours got so hard? Were you envious of me or Lennox?"

"I...ah..."

"Answer the question, please," she replied in her best governess-like tone.

Jon quivered. "Both, ma'am. I am very attracted to you both. I like men and women, you see."

"You never told me," said Lennox sharply.

"It's not an easy thing to confess," said Jon, his cheeks scarlet.

Her lust rising again, Viola stroked Lennox's chest. "Scold him later. I want to perform some more."

Lennox nodded. "Turn around, darling. Show him the most perfect breasts and hottest cunt in England."

At Jon's gasp they exchanged a wicked grin, and Viola maneuvered herself so she faced outward, her back to Lennox's chest. Then she slowly sank onto his stone-hard cock.

All three moaned.

God. Lennox's fingers were magical, but nothing compared to the fullness of his thick length inside her. Scorching heat. An ache that danced on the fine line between pleasure and pain. Needing more, Viola pinched her nipples. At the resulting burn, her hips jerked and she took Lennox's cock even deeper.

All three moaned again.

"Well, Jon?" she managed as she rocked back and forth. "Are you enjoying the show?"

The young lord was the very portrait of agonized desire. "Have mercy."

"What do you think, Lennox? Should we be merciful?"

"Open the fall of your buckskins, Jon," growled Lennox as he bit her neck and sparked another internal inferno. "But don't you dare touch your cock. You may only watch us fuck."

Viola smiled in true joy. One man to master her and another she could instruct.

This was indeed the best sexual experience of her life.

IN THE PAST QUARTER HOUR, Jon had run a full gauntlet of emotions: envy at the easy rapport between Lennox and Viola, lust as she'd bathed him and been touched in return, shame at being caught watching, contrition and a little fear as he waited for judgment.

Not for a second had he considered such a dastardly punishment; permitted to stay but not take part, to free his painfully hard erection but not gain relief.

Fingers almost clumsy with need, Jon finally managed to unbutton the fall of his buckskins so his cock sprang out. Yet he couldn't do anything but sit with one hand each side of his body and grip the embroidered quilt, as just ten feet away Lennox fucked Viola the way of a true master. Powerfully. Expertly.

They were a well-matched pair. He so bronzed and darkly hand-some, she the living embodiment of Botticelli's Venus; a vision of pale curves and flaming red hair. Viola might be on top but Lennox was in full control as he used his strong thighs to bounce her up and down on his cock, his right hand gripping her hip while the other curved tenderly around her neck like a collar. And Viola loved it; the bedchamber echoed with her ragged moans and breathless cries of delight, her whole body trembling with each ruthless foray into the wet, eager center nearly hidden by her bush.

"Are you watching carefully, Jon?"

At Lennox's brusque tone, Jon bit his lip against another fierce surge of arousal. "Yes," he whispered, completely captivated by the spectacle of raw, unabashed, unfeigned pleasure.

"Do you think I should let her come?"

Viola nodded frantically as she fondled her swollen, dusky nipples.

"Soon," said Jon; for it seemed even during punishment, that contrary part of him could not be wholly suppressed.

Lennox chuckled and slid the hand at Viola's hip down to rub her clitoris, eliciting a heartfelt wail. "Not soon. Now, because my Siren has pleased me. Come again for me, darling. I'll muffle you."

As though she'd been waiting for permission, Viola orgasmed.

Jon stared, spellbound as she writhed in a violent dance of ecstasy while her screams were mostly contained by Lennox's left hand. Then he choked back an envious whimper.

Fuck me. Own me. Love me.

Let me please you both.

Moments later, Viola balanced her feet on the floor and rose up from Lennox's lap. Lennox withdrew and vigorously handled his cock until he snarled in release, his seed spurting with great force across her lower belly and mound. When they kissed, Lennox smeared the pearly mess across Viola's skin. Marking her.

Jon groaned, the need to come all-consuming. His cock was so hard it bobbed against his abdomen, but his hands remained on the quilt, chained by Lennox's earlier command.

When Viola had fully recovered, she stood and strolled toward the bed. The heady scents of wet cunt and spent seed surrounded Jon, and he inhaled so deeply it made his head spin.

"Now," she said crisply, putting her hands on her hips and staring at him with a narrowed green gaze. "What are we to do with a very naughty lord who spies without permission?"

Shame engulfed him once more. He had far overstepped his bounds to do so. As Theresa had instructed him so often in Soho Square, consent was critical. She always asked first. Always ensured his comfort with her actions. At no point was it acceptable to watch someone when they weren't aware.

"I know that was wrong," he said contritely. "I hope you can forgive me. I won't...I won't do it again. Ever."

Abruptly his chin was grasped with quill-callused fingers and jerked upward.

Jon shuddered as moisture trickled from the head of his cock.

Yes. Rough. Please. Please.

"Have you ever watched me previously?" asked Lennox. "Be truthful."

"Twice," he confessed. "At your orgies. The door always remained open a little way so I stood in the hallway then returned to the guest room afterward."

"To do what?"

Punish myself.

The words hovered on his tongue, yearning to burst forth. To speak of his darkest desires and most urgent needs: the sensual helplessness of restraints, the possessive stretch of a dildo buried in his arse, the joyous burn from the nipple clamps and flogger that renewed his soul and brought him peace. Yet he couldn't do it. He was already on thin ice after being caught spying without permission. If the man he loved so ardently and the woman who had already captured his imagination both were to turn away from him in disgust or scorn, he might never recover.

"I would make myself come," Jon said at last, for he couldn't outright lie either, and this was relatively truthful.

"Did you watch because you are a voyeur," asked Viola, her expression curious rather than annoyed, "or because you wanted something you thought you couldn't have?"

Startled, his jaw dropped. How had she seen through him so easily? Then again, Viola did spend every day managing staff and guests, and had been part of a risqué troupe. No doubt she'd seen the best and worst of humanity and knew all their quirks and foibles. "Er..."

"Answer her," said Lennox sternly.

Jon's fingers clenched the quilt once more. That tone would be the death of him. Or at least the reason he ruined his buckskins. "I'm not a voyeur. Well, not in general. I like to be...involved."

"Go on."

He stared at the floor, his wretched cheeks hot enough to boil water. Why couldn't he just ask for what he craved? Viola and Lennox had made a bargain within a day of meeting, and she'd been skillfully guided to several orgasms. He'd known Lennox for months and hadn't gathered the courage to do any damned thing. "Well...ah..."

"Jon," said Viola, sinking onto the bed beside him. "Correct me if I'm wrong, but this morning in the dining room I gained the impression that you are a man who prefers to be instructed in lusty play. Now I wonder if you watched us for the sole reason of being caught and punished. So, if I told you to get on your knees and lick my cunt clean right this minute, what would you do?"

Obey you, mistress.

Even the thought of Viola owning him in such a way made his hips thrust involuntarily, and he sucked in an uneven breath. "I would do so."

"Glad to hear it," said Lennox. "Such an act might return you to my good graces. A man who resides there could discover a great many new pleasures."

Almost speechless with excitement, Jon moved from the bed and dropped to his knees in front of Viola. "May I?"

She nodded and spread her thighs. Just for a moment, he stared reverently at the abundance in front of him: the glistening rosy petals of her labia, the swollen, darker pink nub of her clitoris, the damp auburn bush. But apparently that was too slow, for Viola tangled her fingers in his hair and tugged him forward until her bush brushed his chin. Desperate to please and knowing she would be sensitive, he parted the hair and learned those silken petals with just the tip of his tongue, before carefully lapping up the delectable mix of musky cunt juices and earthy seed while she moaned and demanded more.

When Lennox caressed the nape of his neck in the way of an affectionate master, Jon nearly faltered. But he quickly remembered himself and licked Viola a little harder, fluttering his tongue against her clitoris until she ground her mound against him and sobbed out her release.

"Good. Very good," murmured Lennox in his ear. "You may touch yourself."

Relieved and grateful, Jon braced one hand on the bed and closed the other around his engorged length. It wouldn't take much to come, a few strokes at most...

Without warning his hand was covered by Lennox's, forcing his cock into a vise-like grip. They moved together in a harsh, primitive rhythm, the roughness he'd always dreamed of from the man he loved. With a low blissful roar, Jon surrendered to the exhilarating rush of orgasm and covered their fingers with seed.

God.

The taste of Viola's sweet cunt in his mouth. Lennox's hand wrapped around his cock. It wasn't nearly all he needed on this earth...

But it was a grand start.

4

THE TROUBLE WITH ORGASMS: ONE NIGHT OF PLENTY, AND YOU NEVER wanted to leave the oasis.

Viola sighed as she added a tiny vase of spring blooms to the tea trolley, ready to serve in the parlor. The Brigands insisted it arrive at precisely eleven o'clock; if she was even a minute late, those already rambunctious elders would turn feral, storm the kitchens, and hold Cook for ransom until their demands were met.

This lesson had been learned the hard way.

Today, though, it was even more difficult to concentrate than usual. Her inner thighs still ached from being spread so wide, her nipples, cunt and clitoris were tender from the surfeit of attention. Lennox had mastered her body. Jon had worshipped it. And even the thought of that being a one-night-only affair made her innards shrivel.

"Better hurry, Mrs. P. Those who shall not be named are getting restless in there."

Grimacing at the parlor maid's words, Viola quickly added some sugar cubes to the bowl and fresh lemon slices to a plate. Then she pushed the trolley out of the kitchens and down the hallway to the parlor where the captain, Gillian, Reuben, and Piers waited.

"Tea!" trilled Viola as she entered the room.

All four Brigands stared at her.

"Just as well, petal," said Piers, as per usual sitting next to Reuben on an overstuffed chaise. "Only one minute to spare according to my pocket watch."

"Your pocket watch has been unreliable since the turn of the century, everyone knows that," she retorted.

"Ooooh, feisty today," said the captain in his broad northern accent. "Who puffed wind in your sails?"

"I can guess what happened," said Gillian happily, today resplendent in a blue turban and matching velvet gown. "Praise be to Almighty God; Viola has the tired yet smug air of a woman who had all the cobwebs blown out. I wager we have Mr. Townsend to thank."

"Or Lord Jonathan," said Reuben, polishing his signet ring against his trousers. "So, who was it, gel?"

Four pairs of eyes peered at her over their spectacles and Viola giggled, almost spilling the tea as she poured. "I beg your pardon?"

"Don't be missish," said Piers. The breaking of your lust drought is a momentous occasion. A dozen more interludes and you might catch up to our weekly total."

"Nobody likes a braggart."

"Bah," said Gillian, waving a hand. "You need all the advice you can get after years of wasting away in your tower like some sort of gothic heroine. But we salute the seizing of a grand opportunity. Is he as good as the rumors declare?"

"A lady never tells," Viola replied in her best obnoxious dowager voice.

Reuben winced. "Don't use that tone even in jest. It's horrifying. Reminds me of the matrons who used to come into the shop. I still wake up with nightmares sometimes, Piers has to hold me until I calm down."

"There, there," said Piers, stroking Reuben's hand. "But you may as well confess, Viola. You did walk in with the well-bedded duck waddle."

Viola rolled her eyes. "Drink your tea and I may consider it."

They obediently picked up their cups and saucers, added sugar or lemon, and drank. The brief silence was a welcome respite from the magisterial interrogation, although the four of them were only their true naughty selves with her. When Pauline or Oswald were about, each behaved like stuffy gentry. Hell, her in-laws actually believed Piers and Reuben were *cousins*.

If her sole task was minding the Brigands, this job might even be tolerable. The captain's stories of his time in the navy were both enthralling and gut-churning, full of blockades and battles and rum rations. Gillian had first been a nurse, then a tireless fundraiser for hospitals and injured sailors, and both had traveled extensively. Reuben and Piers seemed to know everyone in Hertfordshire and sniffed out gossip better than the most dedicated of church ladies, so always returned from outings to St. Albans with juicy tales. But no. Like anything good, she got an hour a day at most.

Today, though, for the first time in forever, she actually had a story of her own to tell.

"Well, dear?" asked Gillian encouragingly.

Viola sat down in the spare parlor chair, all while keeping one eye on the door. Pauline and Oswald sent her the dirtiest of looks if she stopped her duties even for the shortest time; it was always better if they weren't aware. "I may have had companionship last night."

"I knew it!" exclaimed Reuben. "Good for you. So, Townsend or Lord Jonathan? Each is scrumptious in his own way."

All eyes bored into her once again, and her cheeks grew warm.

"Saints alive," said the captain with a low whistle. "Never say it was both! Gilly and I had some grand three-in-a-bed adventures in Paris. Nothing like adding an extra body for some filthy fun, eh?"

Viola shook her head as she succumbed to a grin. "Rascals, the lot of you."

Piers winked. "No idea what you're speaking of, petal. We are each respectable, upstanding members of society, as everyone knows. But we're dashed proud of you. When will you take your stallions for another ride?"

She hesitated. "I don't know. I mean...it wasn't really discussed."

The shoulders of each Brigand drooped in disappointment, and Viola grimaced. When you were the poor relation reliant on someone else's charity for a roof overhead and employment, even arranging one rendezvous was difficult. More than that, nigh-on impossible. Besides, these four had found true love early on and had fifty years of bliss behind them. Half a century of laughter and care and sinfully good bedsport, rather than the fears and doubts of a plump thirty-five-year-old widow. None of the Brigands had been forced to start all over again, confidence shattered, after a disastrous marriage which had crushed their dreams to powder.

Gillian adjusted her turban and offered a sympathetic smile. "I know it is hard, but the best thing you can do is march up those stairs right now and find out. They are here for a week, after all. Why waste time fretting when you could be planning another interlude?"

Viola nodded reluctantly and rose to her feet. "Very well. I'll take them a tea tray. If you hear a heart-wrenching wail, it was a one-night only affair."

"Godspeed," said Reuben, and the others offered equally supportive murmurs.

In the kitchens she prepared a fresh tray and added two apple tarts sprinkled with sugar and nutmeg; it was quite possible that wrangling a manuscript had destroyed Lennox and Jon's will to live and they needed a restorative sweet. Then she hesitated. Did they even like apple tarts? Should she offer slices of fruit cake instead? Perhaps two raisin buns?

Viola cursed under her breath. Now she was just being foolish, acting like a green girl in the first blush of love rather than a mature woman. Even if they didn't wish to pleasure her a second time, she could cherish the memory of last night forever. It was time to take those two bulls by the horns and have a frank conversation.

Please God, let them want me again.

THE CREATIVE PROCESS was both awe-inspiring and utterly disturbing.

From the safety of his chair across the room, Jon silently watched Lennox at work. After months of observation he had reached the conclusion that writing a play was twenty percent pacing, thirty percent staring into space, ten percent rearranging furniture, twenty percent downing brandy, five percent trying to come up with a title, ten percent cursing, and the remaining five percent actually dipping a quill in ink and adding words to paper.

Lennox hadn't yet got to the part about words on paper, but Jon had unwavering faith that step would begin very soon. One only had to look at the man's history of enormous success to know a play would get written, and a splendid play at that.

"I can't write when you are staring at me, my lord patron."

Jon blinked at the disgruntled tone. "Humblest apologies. Should I turn around and face the wall?"

The playwright's gaze narrowed. "Saucy."

His cheeks heated and he bowed his head. Most unhelpful, for it only reminded him of the previous evening when he'd been ordered to lick Viola's delicious cunt. And the way Lennox had caressed his neck and made him roughly handle his own cock until he'd spurted seed all over their hands. Oddly, Lennox hadn't mentioned their lusty play when they'd met for breakfast, nor afterward in this chamber. It was like having a large, slumbering beast in the corner of the room, ready to awaken and cause havoc at any moment.

Had it been unexceptional for a man who regularly indulged in orgies? A chore? Did Lennox regret his actions in the cold light of day? Or worst of all, had he and Viola talked and decided they wished to continue their affair without him?

Jon winced. God. To think he'd actually believed that being honest and admitting the tamest of his desires would be freeing somehow. No. It had just wound him up in more knots than ever.

"Then I'll offer my humblest apologies again," he said eventually, daring to peek up at Lennox. The other man didn't look angry, though. More...exasperated. "Is there some way I might help? I'll do anything."

Lennox sighed and sat back in his chair, drumming his fingers on the desk. "I don't know. Maybe. The problem is, for the first time in my career I'm not sure what to write. I don't even have a setting or main characters yet. You are the best patron a playwright could wish for, and the thought of letting you down is gut-wrenching, but my mind is emptier than Prinny's purse."

Jon nodded, bashful at the *best patron* praise. "What do you want to write?"

The older man looked startled. "I've only ever written melodrama. Love, virtue and vice, social issues and struggles, villains in top hats, all with a score to hum along to. It's hard to imagine a city that encapsulates good and evil more than London; always been plenty of fodder for plots. Although in fairness, I have been increasingly constrained by devil-spawned Larpent."

"But if you could write anything without penalty or censoring from the dreaded Examiner of Plays, what would it be?"

"That is an excellent question," said Lennox. "Don't laugh, but as a lad I enjoyed otherworldly tales. Fairies and trolls. Angels and demons. Werewolves howling and mermaids frolicking in the waves. Nowadays I'd want them to be wicked. Think *A Midsummer Night's Dream* but far lustier, more fantastical and no tiresome marital plots whatsoever."

Jon gasped. *A Midsummer Night's Dream* was his favorite Shakespearean play. The whimsy of fairies and sprites getting up to mischief in an enchanted forest, where anything was possible, even love. "So why don't you? Weave a lusty otherworldly fantasy, I mean."

"I must warn you, Jon, that sounded like my patron giving imagination free reign. An exceptionally dangerous exercise—"

A soft knock at the door interrupted him, and Jon immediately got to his feet and crossed the bedchamber to open it. If a maid had come to tidy, he would request she come back later, especially as he and Lennox might finally be breaking through the stubborn wall of his writer's malady.

But when he opened the door, a smile broke across his face to see the most beautiful redhead in the world carrying a tray of food and drink. "Viola!"

She inclined her head tentatively and lifted the tray. "I brought tea. But also, apple tarts, fruit cake, and raisin buns. Wasn't quite sure what you each preferred for a light repast."

"That is so thoughtful," said Jon, wanting to hug her. While Viola's forthright manner and naughty teasing aroused him unmercifully, she possessed an underlying kindness that was so damned comforting. "Come in."

"Yes, come in, darling," called Lennox. "Anyone who brings sweets is clearly a friend."

"I'd hate to disturb your work," she said, her cheeks a little pink.

Jon frowned. Not her too. Why were they all so hesitant today?

"Do come in," he repeated. "It is a treat to see you."

Viola smiled at that and strolled into the room to place the tray down on the supper table in front of the fire. Even dressed in her usual gray calico gown with her unruly hair in a neat chignon she looked lovely, although his first choice would forever be her naked. Preferably sitting on his face or taking him to task with a flogger.

"I'm not sure how to ask this graciously," she said, clasping her hands together. "But after last night..."

"If you're asking if it could be repeated," said Lennox, "my answer is a resounding yes. And, as any playwright worth his salt would say, less tell, more show. Come and give me a kiss, Viola."

She relaxed and her whole face lit up, turning lovely into goddess. With an impish grin, Viola walked over to Lennox, hips swaying and breasts bouncing, before settling herself on his lap and winding her arms about his shoulders. He slid one hand around her waist while the other cupped the back of her neck, kissing her with such passion that Jon gripped his thighs at the sheer eroticism.

Unexpectedly, she turned her head and beckoned him over. "I want a kiss from you as well, Jon. You might have to kneel, though."

Heart stuttering in his chest, Jon continued forward until he stood beside Viola and Lennox. Then he sank to his knees, his face almost directly across from hers.

When she winked and leaned forward, one hand tangling in his cravat and the other mimicking Lennox's neck hold, Jon gasped. But soon his world improved even further, as she captured his lips in a demanding kiss that jolted him to the tips of his toes.

"That's the way," said Lennox. "Now open your mouth for Viola's tongue, Jon."

A sound of need rumbled in his chest; he obeyed until their tongues twined together and her hand tugged on his cravat like it was a leash, making him moan.

If only. If only. If only.

All too soon it ended and Jon sank back on his heels, a trifle light-headed. But how did Lennox feel about this? Was he unbothered that Viola had called another man over for a kiss, or annoyed?

Uncertain of his place, or if indeed he even had a future as part of a trio, Jon peered up at Lennox, searching for some sort of sign. Really, it would be completely understandable if the playwright did not wish his business life and personal life to intertwine.

But Lennox's face remained uncomfortably inscrutable.

Oh hell.

HE SAT RIGHT at the heart of a cozy domestic scene, comfortable armchair, fresh tea tray, and roaring fireplace. Well, a cozy domestic scene for a dominant man who preferred multiple lovers; one plump Siren curled up in his lap, and one brawny patron kneeling beside his chair, his pale blue gaze all trusting and hopeful.

It was decidedly unnerving.

Lennox Townsend did not do cozy domestic scenes. He fucked his lovers into exhaustion then bid them a cheery farewell. No cuddling, no intimate meals, certainly no promises for the future. And yet here he was...not hating it?

It took all his will to remain relaxed and not by so much as a twitch reveal any discomfort to his two companions. After making Viola come several times and dominating Jon, his appetite had been fully whetted and he wanted to push even more sexual boundaries with both. The issue was, he liked them. Far more than was wise for a dedicated rake with an exceedingly bleak past. And yet in the early hours, once Jon and Viola departed his chamber so they were in their own beds when servants brought firewood and fresh water at dawn...he'd actually *missed* them.

Lennox clenched his jaw so he didn't scowl. The only rational solution was to bed each repeatedly during his week in Hertfordshire, get over the novelty of an obedient pet and a fiery Siren, then return to London with pages of sparkling prose. He'd have to find a new patron; it certainly wouldn't be fair to lead Jon on with thoughts of a future together, or Viola for that matter. Lennox Townsend was a loner. A product of the streets. Experience had demonstrated that daring to love only led to agonizing loss.

He patted Jon's shoulder and swatted Viola on the arse, making her giggle. "You are both very naughty, distracting me like this. I have words to write."

She scrambled to her feet. "Would you like a cup of tea? Something to eat?"

Well, perhaps a little more companionship wouldn't hurt. His solitary existence did get lonely sometimes.

"Tea with lemon," Lennox replied. "And one of those apple tarts."

Viola nodded. "And you, Jon?"

"I can get it—"

"You stay right there and behave, young man."

Jon blushed. "I'm only a few years younger. Can't be much more than five or so."

"Beside the point. How do you like your tea? And which sweet?"

"Two sugar cubes, a slice of fruit cake. Are you sure I can't—"

"Sit," growled Lennox, and the other man quivered before awkwardly settling his huge frame on the rug.

"So," said Viola, as she bustled about with the tea tray. "May I ask what you are writing this time, Lennox?"

He glared at the blank paper and unused quill on the desk in front of him. "It was supposed to be another melodrama. However, my intrepid patron was in the process of convincing me to forgo all logic and financial sense to write the story of my heart instead."

"Which is?" she asked, as she brought him a steaming cup of tea and an apple tart, then fetched Jon's cup and the fruit cake.

Jon beamed as he took them from her. "Oh, it will be marvelous, Viola. An otherworldly tale of fairies and trolls, angels and demons, and werewolves and mermaids. But not chaste or coy. *Lusty*."

Viola gasped and pressed a hand to her breast. "You mean the actors would be near-naked on stage? An otherworldly orgy?"

Yes.

In the depths of Lennox's gut, something stirred. A sizzle of pure excitement that only occurred when a spark lit fully within his imagination.

"Indeed," he said slowly, turning the idea over in his head and letting it gain in strength and clarity. "It is summer solstice in the otherworld, and everyone is coming together for a magnificent ball. The Flame of Passion keeps the kingdom mighty...but lately it has been dimming, for there is not enough bedsport."

"Oh no!" said Viola, her green eyes wide. "Tell me more."

"Write it down, write it down," said Jon, briefly falling into the role of patron who actually demanded.

Lennox picked up his quill and started making notes. "It has been chaotic in the kingdom," he muttered, annoyed at his hand for not keeping pace with the ideas feverishly swirling within his mind. "The werewolves kept burying the pleasure toys belonging to the fairies; now they have feathers instead of fur. The mermaids adore bedding demons, but demons don't swim so well. Trolls care only for the upkeep of bridges they fuck under, so the rest of the otherworld is getting neglected. And the angels are so exasperated that they refuse to participate in the threesomes that create rainbows. This ball is the last chance for everyone to come together and make merry. To laugh, drink, fuck their cares away and renew the Flame of Passion. Otherwise..."

"Otherwise what?" breathed Viola. "The puritan humans will invade and turn the whole kingdom gray?"

Jon sat forward. "Yes! Gray. No sunshine or happiness or orgasms... just London in the middle of winter. Cold, damp and dreary. Er...I mean...whatever you think is best, Lennox."

A grin tugged at his lips and he leaped to his feet so he could pace away the lightning now fizzing in his veins. "I like that. A monstrous evil forever threatening the kingdom: the color gray. Eat shit, Brummell. And the Prescotts, for that matter."

His two fledgling assistants burst out laughing and applauded. Lennox was about to bow, when a fist pounded on the door. Viola immediately went still, all joy leaving her face, and Jon retreated to sit beside the fireplace.

Now allowing that scowl to unleash, Lennox marched over to the door and yanked it open. Ugh. Bloody Oswald Prescott.

"Yes?" Lennox snapped. "Was there something you needed? I am writing and do not appreciate interruptions."

"I do beg your pardon, sir, but Viola is neglecting her duties downstairs."

"Mrs. Prescott just delivered a tea tray," he retorted. "I fail to see how that is a dereliction of duty."

The man puffed up like some sort of exotic fish. "Well...there is a leak in the kitchen roof. One of the maids spilled coal. And there may be insufficient buttered asparagus for the supper table."

"Goodness," said Viola stiffly. "Emergencies all. Do excuse me, Mr. Townsend. Lord Jonathan."

"Wait one moment, Mrs. Prescott," said Jon. "You will be free tomorrow to escort us to St. Albans? We have our hearts set on that research trip you offered to guide."

Lennox stifled a snort at the pained expression that crossed Oswald's face. Utter reluctance to let Viola loose even for a minute, against the strong desire to please his ducal friend's brother and a socially feted playwright.

"I can arrange another suitable escort," said Oswald.

"Is your sister-in-law a prisoner here?" asked Lennox in his silkiest voice. "Dear me, his lordship and I simply cannot condone oppression of women."

"No, no," said the stuffed shirt quickly. "Viola may accompany you for the afternoon as long as she completes all her morning tasks. And takes footmen for propriety's sake."

"I have my own staff," said Jon. "On my honor, Mrs. Prescott will be well looked after."

Viola clapped her hands together. "It is decided. I shall scurry about with my duties tomorrow morning, then escort these gentlemen to town. Shall we say two o'clock?"

"Perfect," said Lennox, giving her a subtle wink. "I am most grateful for your kindness, Mr. Prescott, and shall certainly consider recommending this boarding house when we return to London."

Oswald gaped at them, his brow furrowed.

Lennox merely smiled. Tomorrow would be interesting indeed.

5

HE'D BEEN ON TENTERHOOKS ALL DAY WAITING FOR HIS TREAT: AN OUTING with Lennox and Viola. It felt like forever since he and Lennox had seen her, after the confrontation with Oswald in the bedchamber, each had agreed that remaining apart overnight would be best to avoid any suspicion.

Jon glanced once more into his carriage, casting his eye over the immaculate squabs and fittings, and the basket he'd requested from the kitchens containing freshly baked bread with butter, a dish of berries, meat pasties, ginger cake, and bottles of wine and lemonade.

Everything needed to be perfect for such a special occasion. He already knew it would be thoroughly enjoyable; yesterday they'd had a wonderful time discussing ideas for Lennox's next script. As always when he served the playwright, he just felt so *useful*. So necessary. Like he actually belonged somewhere. The fictitious research trip had been a desperate, unformed suggestion, but the others had played along beautifully, and now they had something better than a stolen night in a bedchamber; time to be together away from the confining air of the boarding house.

"Ready, Jon?"

He smiled as Lennox strolled up and hauled himself into the carriage to sprawl across the seat. Today Lennox wore fawn buckskins, white linen shirt with lace cuffs, and a ruby-red jacket. As usual that word fluttered through his mind: pirate. But not one who hurt or maimed, a pirate who plundered with his cock. "Ready. Just waiting for Viola—"

"I'm here!" she called, hurrying toward the carriage, and Jon took a moment to admire the way her breasts and backside bounced underneath her gray gown. Unlike most, though, he knew what those curves looked like naked. Absolute perfection.

"Ma'am," he said, bowing and offering a hand to help her up into the carriage, before climbing in himself and shutting the door behind him. One tap on the roof later, and they were on their way.

"So," said Lennox. "Where are we to go, madam guide?"

Viola bit her lip. "I know it might sound a bit strange, but I thought perhaps the Roman ruins southwest of the abbey. It's my favorite escape; rather like a stage where I can imagine different times and different people. Ancient lives and loves. Plus, there is the River Ver nearby if we get overwarm and need to dip our feet. Lots of trees and shrubs, so quite private. Lush and green and otherworldly."

"Sounds superb."

She grinned. "You have no idea how happy I am to have a few hours away from the boarding house. It is as good as a holiday, except no long lectures on sin or vice to endure."

Jon tapped his cheek as he looked at her. It was shameful how large a burden Viola was expected to carry on behalf of her in-laws. The couple traveled frequently to London and other parts of the country, but naturally insisted that Viola remain and oversee the boarding house. Not even Falston and Henrietta treated their servants so shabbily, and they were the coldest people he knew.

"Why do you stay when the Prescotts are so awful?" he asked abruptly.

Lennox groaned. "That is a very personal question for our happy journey, Jon."

He flushed, bracing one hand on the carriage wall to lessen the sway along the uneven road. "Forgive me. I did not mean to make you uncomfortable, Viola."

Viola sighed. "The answer isn't complex or a secret. Money. People with coin always have choices; where they go, what they do. As a widow of the gentry, I should lead a comfortable life with relative freedom. But I can't, because of my late husband's gambling. I don't have a home or even a widow's portion, and it suits Oswald and Pauline far too much that I live at the boarding house and work for them to provide a sum or even a loan."

His blood boiling at the injustice, Jon stared at his feet. This was a sharp reminder that even if society discovered the truth of his parentage and shunned him, he would still have ample funds due to a substantial inheritance from his maternal grandparents. Viola was a prime example of how few rights women had when it came to marriage, and how sour it could go in the event of their husband's death. Not all families or lawyers were honest and fair in their dealings. In fact, some, like the bloody Prescotts, were downright appalling.

What choices did Viola have, really?

"I asked Lennox what he would write if he faced no penalty," said Jon, forcing himself to look at Viola. "What would you do or where would you go?"

She laughed, a terribly brittle sound, and his heart broke for her. "Where would I go? That is easy. My one true home: the stage. I'd give anything to perform in front of an audience again, to bask in their appreciation, feel their envy and lust caress my soul and give me life. That is what I miss most..."

"I saw Viola dance once, many years ago," said Lennox. "She is magnificent. And let me tell you, there is nothing like the arousal when you're in a room with several hundred other people all equally lust-struck, desperate to rip their clothes off and pleasure themselves because they've been so skillfully provoked."

Jon swallowed hard as his cock began to throb. "Could they have you, Viola? The audience, I mean."

"No," she whispered. "The public may only watch. For I belong to those I love and who love me in return. Not ties of duty, but bonds of affection."

God. Such yearning on her face. He knew that feeling well; an aching need to belong somewhere and to someone, not as a curiosity or a charity or an annoyance, but fully accepted. No, more than that. To be *cherished*. Viola wished to be near-naked on stage. He wished to serve and be disciplined by a caring owner. But they were both difficult dreams in a world of oppressive society and family expectations. Uncon-ditional love was a lot to ask for when you broke rules, did not conform to religious dictates, and had specific sexual needs.

Lennox cleared his throat. "Looks like we are here; I can see the abbey tower just ahead. Is it a long walk to the ruins?"

Viola shook her head, her smile determinedly bright. "Not at all. A half mile, if that. It's a beautiful afternoon, we could have a picnic beside the river."

"Sounds like an excellent idea," said Jon, eager to soothe the air of awkwardness in the carriage that he'd started with his intemperate ques-tion. He could see in Viola's face that she already regretted being so frank about her dreams, and he wasn't quite sure how to make her feel better. Lennox, of course, hadn't shared anything personal, but he couldn't bring himself to criticize the man he loved. Not when his own situation remained such a mess. In truth, Viola Prescott had shown more courage in the past few days than Lord Jonathan Grant ever had.

Gah. To think he'd craved love. No one had warned him it would be this hard. Or complicated.

And it wouldn't be improving any time soon.

VIOLA BRACED herself as the luxurious carriage came to a shuddering halt near the ancient abbey at St. Albans. These days she tried to avoid the once-magnificent Norman structure famed as a pilgrimage site, a place of learning, and where the first draft of the Magna Carta had been drawn up over six hundred years ago. The abbey had been starved of love and become...well...*shabby*, with cracks in the walls, a rotting roof, and equally unstable timber. Starved of love and shabby struck entirely too close to the bone with her own existence.

At least the abbey held its secrets, though. No babbling about dancing on stage and belonging to a lover. That had been complete fool-ishness. What kind of twit blurted her deepest desires to men she'd known three days? To men she very much hoped to bed again? A London rake and his lordly patron wanted a cheerful, no-obligation affair, not a miserable widow baring her soul. Bah. Gillian's comment about her being locked in a tower like some sort of gothic heroine was uncomfortably true. She certainly had the social graces of one.

Wincing, Viola waited as the two men climbed out of the carriage. Lennox was unusually quiet and brooding, while Jon tried to be jovial as he turned and assisted her onto the grass verge. It really was a beautiful day; to feel the sun on her face and know that Pauline and Oswald were miles away was worth every single freckle she would add to her collection.

Firmly suppressing her disquiet and embarrassment at being so candid about her dreams, Viola smiled brightly. "Shall we go to the ruins?"

Jon lifted a full basket. "I have the food and drink."

"Lead on, madam guide," said Lennox, offering his arm.

Seemingly unable to be silent, Viola kept up a constant flow of chatter as they walked along the tree-lined lane that trailed southwest from the abbey down to the ruins. She pointed out arguably the oldest tavern in England called The Round House on their right, and the narrow River Ver, almost completely hidden by thick shrubbery.

Lennox snorted. "River? Ha. The Thames and Severn and Trent are rivers. How can this possibly warrant such a grand title when I could spurt seed from one bank to the other?"

She laughed. "You do have an especially gifted cock, though."

"Why thank you," he replied, his shoulders relaxing and his lazy grin thankfully appearing at last.

"Is that the Roman wall up ahead?" asked Jon. "It's much higher that I thought it would be."

"Come and take a closer look," said Viola eagerly. "Let me amaze and bore you rigid with my knowledge. The wall was originally about sixteen feet high and two miles long. It had a huge earthen bank behind it and a defensive ditch in front. Way, way back in time this area was a Roman town called Verulamium, and over there stood the London gate, part of the route from Dover to Chester."

Lennox let out a low whistle as they approached the ruins of the wall, constructed of rubble with layers of brick bonding. It was, like most Roman ruins, evidence of jaw-droppingly clever design.

"Right now," he said slowly, "we're standing where the Romans did a thousand years ago. It is hard to wrap my mind around that."

"I know," said Viola, almost twirling in the face of their genuine interest. "But it's more like fifteen hundred years. And the evidence is all over the country. The roads we travel on. The baths and aqueducts. Each built to last."

"Fascinating. If my parish school had employed Madam Viola to teach history, I would've been an excellent student and actually learned something," said Lennox.

Parish school?

She almost faltered at the words. He spoke like a blue-blood; if asked, she would have assumed governess and tutors followed by Eton or Harrow, and Cambridge or Oxford. But Lennox had humble beginnings like herself? How very interesting.

"Behave, young Master Townsend," Viola replied quickly, pretending to peer over spectacles at him.

"In the carriage you said you imagine different times and different people here," said Jon as he set down the picnic basket then ran his fingertips over the wall's roughly hewn rubble. "Any people in particular?"

She blushed. "I pretend I am a Roman noblewoman, being carried about town in a curtained litter. Or attending a bustling market with friends by day, and a lavish party with my lover at night. Not doing laundry, beating rugs, or listening to Oswald and Pauline, but a woman in charge of her own household. People bring *me* wine and sweets."

Lennox tilted his head and stared at her. "That is one of the reasons I like writing plays. I can be many different people in one story. A respite from...myself."

Now she was actually astonished. He wanted respite from himself? But how could that be? Lennox Townsend was feted from coast to coast, his talent unrivalled since the time of Shakespeare and Marlowe. He lived as he pleased with enough money to fund whatever whim he had, and enjoyed a devoted patron to boot.

Could he still be lonely? A rake who wanted something more?

Viola reached out, thinking to squeeze Lennox's hand, but in the blink of an eye he stepped back and moved over to where Jon stood beside the wall.

Jon's glance was thoroughly sympathetic, and somehow that made her feel worse. She'd already scolded herself in the carriage for blurting out far too much, and now she had gone and attempted a wifely gesture of support. Ugh. She needed to pull herself together before she started crooning the two men lullabies and feeding them stewed fruit.

You are supposed to be a Siren, damn it. Act like you are on stage once more!

Viola paused to calm her chaotic thoughts, then discarded her shoes and stockings. "Well, I don't know about you two, but I am terribly over-warm and the only cure is a quick splash in the non-river Ver. I dare you to join me!"

Hitching up her calico skirts, she began to run. Undoubtably the most foolish act in the world for someone of ample size and thirty-five-year-old joints, and she soon slowed to an ungainly half-walk, half-trot. However, seconds later, one brawny Jon-arm curled around her waist and for the first time in her life she was tossed over a man's shoulder as though she were petite and slender.

Oh my.

"I must protest, sir!" Viola said breathlessly, trying not to squeak in delight. "How dare you accost a respectable noblewoman like myself!"

"Beg pardon, ma'am," said Jon. "But my orders were to secure the runaway redhead, find a secluded spot beside the Ver, and await further instructions."

She peeked over his shoulder to see Lennox trailing behind them, picnic basket and her shoes and stockings in hand, his face frustratingly expressionless once more.

Exactly what did the wicked man have in mind?

Viola Prescott and Jonathan Grant were *dangerous.*

Lennox gritted his teeth as he walked toward the river—a stream at best—and pondered how the hell he'd been lulled into confessing two very personal facts.

No one knew he'd sometimes attended a wretched and near-derelict parish school in Whitechapel. He wanted to forget that boy, the cold and starving orphan who had slept rough, eaten what he could find, and worn whatever fit best from the church charity box. But one thing had always stood him in good stead: his imagination. On countless occasions, he'd been able to weave a tale in exchange for supper, a spot in front of a fireplace, or to avoid trouble. Only in the past five years had his writing taken him to the heights he'd once dreamed of, but it was both a blessing and a curse. While he could conjure thoughts of the good and great, he could just as easily remember the dark and bleak, which led to bouts of melancholia.

On those days, his enduring fear of being exposed as a fraud was strongest. That society or Jon would discover he wasn't a well-bred gentleman rake, but someone who had named himself from a haberdashery sign, and the end of town. Someone who had been taught letters, numbers, and how to enunciate like a blue-blood by Theresa Berkley, the fiercely intelligent and no-nonsense madam of a pain play club in Soho Square.

There was only one thing to do. Wrest back control with his other great skill: pleasure. Those who were befuddled by orgasmic bliss couldn't ask probing questions or lull him into revealing more secrets.

"Jon," said Lennox abruptly, "Have you found us somewhere to sit?"

His patron, still with Viola draped over his shoulder, nodded. "There," he said, pointing to a reasonably flat and grassy section of the bank with trees to shade them from the afternoon sun.

Taking a folded rug from the basket, Lennox spread it across the grass while ensuring there were no stones or thistle patches to hurt unwary backsides. Then he unpacked the food. "Take a seat. Drink, anyone?"

Jon carefully set Viola down, then knelt beside her. "Roman noble-women before gentlemen."

She grinned. "Some wine perhaps?"

"Of course, madam," said Lennox, uncorking a bottle. "And how will you pay for that?"

"Hmmm. A kiss?"

He shook his head. "This is quality wine."

Viola shivered, her nipples visibly hardening against the bodice of her ghastly gray gown. Christ, he hated that color. "I have a fine outdoor stage here. Perhaps...a little entertainment?"

"Excellent idea. Here on this rug, you shall dance for us the way you did in all those inns and clubs. Poor Jon never had the good fortune to witness that."

"Sounds fair."

"Alas, I'm not finished. As I said, this is quality wine. Keeping in mind that our time here is limited...when we return to the carriage, you'll remove that gray shroud and your delectable body shall be a toy for us to play with the entire journey back. To lick and suck and finger and fuck. We might take turns. Or we might take you together. Have you ever been filled with two cocks at the same time?"

She gasped, her cheeks pink and eyes heavy-lidded. "N-no. Not yet. But I should like to try that very much. I've always wanted to."

Lennox smiled and poured Viola a goblet of wine, then handed her a chunk of buttered bread, some berries, and a large slice of ginger cake. "Eat up. You'll need your strength. As will you, Jon. Now, what would you like?"

"Wine," said the other man hoarsely, his fingers gripping his thighs. "And some of everything."

Frowning, Lennox leaned forward and rested a hand on his arm. "Are you unwell?"

"No! I just...ah...I've also not been with two people. Only watched. I won't know what to do. Don't want to hurt anyone, especially Viola. I'm so very...awkward. Lumbering."

"You are marvelous, just as you are," said Viola indignantly. "Do you know how long I've waited to be tossed over a man's shoulder? Forever."

"And what you'll do," Lennox added, once again silently cursing anyone who had ever made Jon feel bad about himself, "is obey my commands. I'll guide you. Understand?"

Jon exhaled, a smile lighting up his face as he nodded. "Yes, ma...of course."

Had he almost said master?

Don't be a fool. It was a slip of the tongue. Jon is a shy aristocratic kitten who got caught watching. That's all. Not someone to be disciplined with restraints, clamps, a collar, or a damned good flogging.

"Good," he said brusquely, trying to ignore the way his cock throbbed at the thought of doing such things to Jon, before fucking his mouth and coming deep in that firm arse.

Annoyed at himself, Lennox snatched up a meat pastie and ate it in three bites. Then he downed a handful of berries, two slices of bread, and about a quarter of the ginger cake. But not even that, or two goblets of wine, could free his mind of those darkly erotic thoughts.

Fortunately, with exquisite timing, Viola chose that moment to move to the center of the rug and bob a curtsy. "Gentlemen. May I introduce... me. Madam Viola, performing one of my most popular dances."

He and Jon applauded enthusiastically, but soon they were both transfixed as Viola began to hum a tune while her hips swayed and she raised her arms toward the clear blue sky, her head falling back a little as a dreamy smile curled her lips.

Lennox nodded in satisfaction. The woman was born to perform.

Next, she lowered her hands to cup her breasts, thumbing her taut nipples. Ghastly gray calico soon became a tool of sensual torment as it lovingly clung to her ample curves yet provided nary a glimpse of creamy breast or dusky brown nipple. After that she provoked them further still, as with a mischievous smile, she grasped her skirts and slid them upward. First revealing her calves and knees. Then her thighs.

Transfixed, Lennox willed her to reveal all. "Higher," he growled, adjusting his painfully hard cock. "You know we are great admirers of your splendid cunt."

Viola mock-gasped, her eyes sparkling. "Sir! I am a virtuous noblewoman!"

"Please," Jon whispered, his hands clasped in entreaty. "Please, Madam Viola."

She danced quadrille steps around the rug, before turning away and lifting her skirts high enough to briefly show her dimpled bare arse.

"Naughty," scolded Lennox.

Viola laughed, a bewitching, sultry sound. "What are you going to do? Fuck me senseless in a carriage? Oh dear, how *terrible*."

He sprang to his feet, moving swiftly to curl one arm about her waist and secure her wrists in front of her. Next, he kissed a slow path to the sensitive spot where her neck met her shoulder, making her whimper. "You have a saucy tongue, madam. Jon, lift this wayward noblewoman's skirts and tell me what you see."

Jon shuffled forward on his knees, his cock a blatant and mouthwatering bulge against his buckskins, and carefully lifted Viola's gown to her waist. Then he licked his lips. "She is wet. Very wet. Greedy to be filled, I believe."

Viola began to pant, her hips circling as she tried to get closer to Jon's mouth.

In retribution, Lennox bit her neck. "We enjoyed the first act. But now it is time for the second. Are you ready to take two cocks inside you, darling?"

Her soft moan floated away on the breeze. "Yes. Oh yes."

6

AT THE AGE OF THIRTY-FIVE, FINALLY, *FINALLY* A LONG-HELD SEXUAL DREAM was about to come true: to be with two men at the same time.

Viola wriggled impatiently, eager to begin. In this spacious, well-sprung traveling carriage with smooth, sun-warmed leather squabs and large windows with the blinds rolled up, she had a glorious stage. But even better than that, she had two glorious lovers to pleasure her.

With deft fingers, Lennox unfastened the buttons at the nape of her gown and lifted it over her head. He swiftly removed her petticoat but lingered on her stays, teasing her with the rasping sound of laces being loosened. When her heavy breasts were free at last, clad only in her thin chemise, she arched her back and sighed in relief.

"Jon," said Lennox, his tone the embodiment of sin. "Remove Viola's chemise and attend to those lovely big nipples."

A wildness overcame her, and rather than waiting for the young lord to lean forward from where he sat on the opposite side, she scrambled onto his lap, tore off her thigh-length chemise, and shoved her breasts in his face.

"Suck," she demanded, nudging his lips with one taut nipple.

Jon groaned, the depth of yearning in his eyes almost shocking. Then she couldn't think at all as his mouth fastened around the rigid peak and sucked voraciously. He was neither smooth nor practiced, yet somehow the heat of his mouth, flick of his tongue, and rough tugging on her nipple was all the better for it. This was pure want, and Viola gripped the nape of his neck to force more of her breast into his mouth. When that nipple was almost unbearably sensitive and carmine in color, she guided his head to the other. But soon she had more delicious sensations competing for her attention, as Lennox's hand slid between her legs from behind to caress her soaking wet center.

Oh God.

His fingers performed their own skillful dance; stroking her inner thighs and circling her swollen clitoris. Two repeatedly delved into her sheath to bring forth even more wetness, before he added a third finger and thrust hard.

Viola cried out, her blood pulsing in time with the swaying carriage. "Please. Yes. That."

"Is this what you need, darling?" asked Lennox, as he knit those three together and started fucking her with merciless precision while Jon toyed with her aching nipples.

"More. I need more," she begged, almost incoherent now at the intoxicating contrast of power and restraint. The few hours she'd enjoyed with these men back in Lennox's bedchamber wasn't nearly enough to quench her thirst, not when she had years of drought and oppression to make up for. "I can't be a shadow any longer. I want everyone who looks in the windows as they drive past to see me full to the brim with cock. No...*two* cocks."

"I understand. Let's turn you around. Jon will fill that sweet cunt and I'll take your mouth."

Trembling in feverish anticipation, Viola went up on her knees while Jon unfastened the fall of his buckskins and freed his straining cock. Both men helped her into position, with her back to Jon's chest and her feet braced on the carriage floor.

"Ma'am, wait," panted Jon in her ear as he gripped his cock and swirled the near-purple head in her copious wetness. "Forgive me. I'm afraid I won't withdraw in time. I'm...er...not nearly as experienced as Lennox. Perhaps he should—"

"Don't fret, precious," she said, turning her head to kiss his cheek before taking his hands and placing them each side of her waist. "I have an eager cunt and barren womb. Fill me."

Both Jon and Lennox halted, and Viola cursed inwardly. Why hadn't she said something earlier? Gah. They probably assumed her crushed by the fact rather than accepting of it. Ned had not believed her when she'd told him she was barren, insisting that his seed could cure any such problem. When it didn't, he returned to his mistress and sired two children, something he'd greatly enjoyed taunting her about at every opportunity. Truth be told, it was far more upsetting to live without love, pleasure, and dancing. Her lack of children did not contribute in any way to her general feeling of frustration and unmet needs.

"Viola darling..." said Lennox as he cupped her cheek. "I—"

"Don't say it," she replied, pressing one finger against his lips. "I know being barren makes some women tremendously sad and my heart aches for them, but I do not feel that way myself. So please, let's have no more discussion about it. This carriage is a place of freedom and respite. My stage. Let me have that."

He nodded, and a wicked smile curled his lips. "Brace your hand on my shoulder to steady yourself while you take Jon's cock. Slowly now, he is very large."

Even slowly, the fit was so tight Viola whimpered as she took the swollen tip inside her throbbing center. But Jon remained perfectly still and allowed her to set the pace, his choked gasps in her ear an indication of his noble sacrifice, and she gradually sank further down.

"Good," said Lennox as he tweaked her nipples, both distracting her and heightening her desire. "That's the way. Well done, darling. You too, Jon."

When her backside at last met the fabric of Jon's buckskins, Viola allowed herself a moment to savor the way his smooth length pulsed and jerked inside her. But now she needed the second promised treat.

"Your cock please, Lennox," she said politely, as though asking for more tea.

He laughed and freed the fall of his own buckskins, before standing with his calves braced against the seat, one hand delving into her hair and the other pressed against the roof. "It's all yours, madam."

Languidly to start, Viola took the head of Lennox's cock into her mouth and learned his girth and texture. It was exhilarating to lave and flick and suck, and she inwardly rejoiced as a little seed trickled onto her tongue, the earthy taste etching itself in her memory forever. At the same time, she allowed Jon to move her up and down on his cock, and the men's raw sounds of pleasure made her blood fizz. How strange that Lennox and Jon had her completely at their mercy with their firm holds and thick cocks, yet she felt such a heady sense of power. Perhaps she truly could be the sensual goddess, the sexual Siren like they claimed. Perhaps it was possible to be wild and free once more.

Viola moaned as a violent orgasm beckoned, riding Jon with greater determination while she took Lennox's cock deeper in her mouth. Then one of Jon's hands moved just an inch, enough so his fingertips pressed on her aching clitoris, and Lennox withdrew his cock, met her gaze and said one word: *come.*

Staggering bliss rushed through her body. It started at her core and radiated out like a sunburst, the release forcing a scream of ecstasy from her throat. One lover providing carnal pleasure was a luscious experience. But there was woefully insufficient talk on how much better two lovers were at the task. Not even in her most elaborate fantasies had she imagined an orgasm like that.

"Thank you," she said, unable to string together anything more articulate when her mind still drifted somewhere amongst the stars. "That... oh God..."

Lennox smiled. "Darling Viola. That was just the beginning."

***

HIS NEED TO come had reached clawing urgency, but he couldn't. Not without permission from Lennox.

Jon took quick, shallow breaths as he concentrated on remaining still inside Viola while she recovered from her orgasm. A part of him wanted to shout in triumph at the way she'd screamed when her tight channel gripped and released his cock, bathing him in even more honey. Another part wanted to kneel and lick her clean so he could once again have that heavenly musky taste in his mouth. But the remaining contrary part craved the impossible: to be disciplined and utterly dominated by owners who loved him.

It had become a torment now; the brief occasions where Lennox or

Viola inadvertently gave him a sample of what he needed. Like the other night when his cock had been wrapped in Lennox's harsh grip. Or earlier, when Viola had straddled him, ordered the sucking of her nipples, and held him by the scruff of the neck. But he had no right to ask for more. Not when the strong risk remained that his baser desires might cause them to turn away forever. Sure, Lennox made risqué jests or indulged in orgies, but he'd never spoken of whips or restraints. And poor Viola had only this week returned to bedding lovers, after a most unsatisfactory marriage and years trapped with the Prescotts without the coin to leave. He could hardly pass her a flogger and assume the position.

No, he just had to accept that a lover couldn't meet all his needs. That was why establishments in London like Theresa's existed.

"Jon!"

He jerked at the sound of his name on Lennox's lips. Viola gasped, her inner walls rippling around him, and Jon groaned as the throbbing of his cock reached unbearable heights, only made worse by the constant movement of the carriage.

"Yes?" he replied hoarsely.

"I asked you a question, and you were woolgathering," growled Lennox as he handled his own cock, damp and glistening from Viola's mouth.

Heat scorched across his cheeks, but he couldn't look away from the delectable sight. "Beg pardon."

Viola giggled. "If you want an answer, Lennox, you cannot distract him by waving that pole of yours about."

"Once again with the saucy tongue, madam. I should gag you with this *pole*, but that would hardly be fair to Jon when he's been so good and obedient."

His breath catching, Jon could only stare at Lennox. Did that mean what he hoped it did? Would he also be permitted to take that magnificent column of flesh in his mouth? "Are you saying...er..."

"I'm offering you a choice. Would you like to suck my cock down your throat as Viola did, or no?"

Jon clenched his jaw as his own cock jerked inside Viola once again, making her cry out. He wasn't the only one excited beyond measure; even after her orgasm, her heartbeat remained fast and honey dripped from her center onto his inner thighs. But one thing was certain, he wanted what she had just experienced. Except rather than a slow and careful thrust into his mouth, rough and forceful. "I want it. Yes. Right now," he blurted, far too needy for niceties.

"Let him come," said Viola. "I want to feel that rush inside me... ooooh, he's so close. And I need another orgasm."

"Listen to the pair of you, giving me orders," said Lennox, shaking his head and lightly stroking his cock. "I should just attend to myself."

Jon whimpered, almost distraught at the thought of being denied a reward he could practically taste on his tongue. If Viola rode him and Lennox took his mouth, he could pretend, just for a short time, that they owned him. That he was a toy for their pleasure. "Please may I suck your cock down my throat?"

The playwright tilted his head. "The thing is, I'm so damned hard after Viola's teasing, I'm not sure I can be gentle."

"I don't want gentle," he replied, need loosening his tongue. "Fuck my mouth. Make me take it all while madam uses my cock."

The air in the carriage seemed to disappear. For an endless moment Lennox stared at him, his fathomless gaze darker and hotter than it had ever been, about as opposite from the devil-may-care rake the world knew as it was possible to be.

Who was Lennox Townsend, really?

But he had no time to give serious consideration to the question. Lennox kissed Viola and stepped around her to move closer, before resting his hand on Jon's head and smoothing his hair. Such unexpected tenderness was startling enough, then that nimble, strong hand continued down his face, callused fingertips stroking his cheek, thumb rubbing back and forth along his lower lip.

Jon moaned at the affectionate touch, but when Lennox's hand dropped further to lightly cup his throat like a collar, agonizing hope flooded his senses.

"Open your mouth, Jon," said Lennox softly. "And Viola darling, ride him like he's a colt that needs to be broken in."

Soon Jon gasped in bliss as she began lifting up and sinking down, the tight clasp of her cunt massaging his cock so exquisitely he could barely think. Then Lennox's hard length shoved past his lips, neither slow nor gentle, but perfectly rough and forceful. Tears of joy seeped from Jon's eyes as he swallowed the warm, satin-smooth cock further down his throat; choking a little in his eagerness to please as he sucked with his lips and fluttered his tongue against the underside, before hollowing his cheeks for greater pressure.

But it was too much, far, far too much goodness for one man to be ridden by a lusty beauty like Viola, *and* have Lennox's hand at his throat and cock in his mouth. With a feral snarl he didn't even know himself capable of making, Jon came. His back arched, his cock surged, and seed gushed into Viola's welcoming heat. Yet still she rode him like the goddess she was, hips circling, thighs straining, fingernails digging into his hands at her waist until her head fell back and she screamed his name.

When Jon finally regained his wits, he was slumped against the seat, Viola curled up beside him, their fingers interlaced. However, Lennox still stood, his engorged cock in hand, his face strained and damp with perspiration.

Jon bolted upright. "You didn't...oh no. I failed. Forgive me."

A faint smile lifted the other man's lips. "A powerful orgasm in a swaying carriage makes a mouth harder to control. I chose to withdraw in the knowledge you would make it up to me. And you will, won't you?"

I love you, master.

The words almost escaped, and Jon coughed to suppress them. Instead, he opened his mouth once more.

"Please. Let me try again."

LENNOX HAD PLAYED THE CHARMING, carefree rake for so long it had become second nature now. But Jon and Viola called to a part of him that he'd kept buried, knowing it was too carnal and primitive for his society orgies. With these two, sexual mastery came naturally.

They wanted it as much as he did, and it just felt so *right*.

Taking a deep breath, Lennox tried to regain some semblance of control. But his cock was painfully hard and this carriage was a respite from society for each of them; a stage for pleasure-dazed Viola who sat with one bare breast pressed to the window for all to see; a collar for Jon who had made it clear in both words and deeds that he craved stern instruction and rough fucking; and for himself, a place to both indulge his dominant side and free his mind from the bleak thoughts that sometimes encroached. Here, for these short, blissful hours, they could each be their true selves.

"Take off your clothes, Jon," he ordered. "I want to see you as naked as Viola."

His patron was clumsy as he complied, managing to lose a button from the fall of his buckskins and tear the hem of his linen shirt. Yet the eagerness was endearing rather than any sort of annoyance, and when Jon looked up at him with such trust, waiting for his next instruction, Lennox couldn't help caressing that smooth, bare chest.

Jon's back arched, encouraging Lennox's fingertips to brush one flat nipple.

Oh, that is what you want, is it?

He grasped Jon's chin, rubbing his thumb across the other man's lower lip as he'd done earlier. "You like to have your nipples played with? Pinched perhaps?"

"Y-yes. Please."

"Earn it," he replied harshly, guiding his engorged length into Jon's mouth once more and sighing in pure pleasure as his patron swallowed him to the hilt. Lovers genuinely enthusiastic to suck cock were precious indeed, and he had *two*.

A soft moan to his right temporarily distracted him, and Lennox turned his head to see Viola's hand resting on her thigh, mere inches away from her seed-and-honey-slick mound.

No. That simply wouldn't do.

"Madam. You weren't going to touch yourself without permission, were you?" he asked in an equally harsh tone, smiling inwardly when Jon quivered and faltered in his task. The young lord certainly enjoyed submissive play; even after coming inside Viola, he was already getting hard again.

She moved restlessly on the leather squab. "Please may I rub my clitoris? Watching Jon attend to your cock is so...so arousing."

"You may. We are in agreement that Jon has a talented tongue. You certainly loved it licking your cunt, didn't you?"

"Yes," Viola gasped as she parted the auburn curls between her legs and caressed the tender pink flesh.

Soon, all Lennox could hear was a sensual symphony of desire: fingers working feverishly in wet cunt, hard cock brutally taking open mouth, the ragged pants and low moans of three people striving to reach their pinnacle once more. The sheer hedonism of the occasion was only enhanced by the scents of fucking; the musky honey, spilled seed, and light sweat. Combined with sun-warmed leather, a faint hint of herbal soap and clean linen, it was the most perfect perfume ever made.

His control gone, Lennox moved his hand to Jon's chest. He teased the smooth flesh with a too-light caress, before trapping Jon's left nipple between his forefinger and thumb and squeezing hard. "You're going take my seed. Every fucking drop."

Jon moaned as he came and the vibration hurled Lennox over the edge, forcing an untamed roar from the depths of his chest as he spurted seed again and again into the other man's mouth. Almost simultaneously, Viola orgasmed with a low cry, her whole body writhing on the seat as she too succumbed to her erotic play.

After Jon had licked him clean and he'd gently disengaged, Lennox fell back onto the opposite seat, his legs no longer able to support him.

Christ.

If anyone asked his name or occupation or the color of grass right now, he probably wouldn't be able to tell them. Orgasms were always delicious, but never in his life, not in all the swift interludes and prolonged nights, not with one person, two, or any orgy he'd participated in, had he come like that. How was it even possible?

Because Jon and Viola submitted so sweetly.

Yes, perhaps. Occasions where he could be as dominant as he wished were rare.

Because you prefer to fuck multiple people at a time.

Also true.

Because you trust Jon and Viola in a way you've never allowed yourself previously. You've revealed more about your past this week than you ever have. Some might even say you cared. That you were...falling in love.

Lennox froze.

No. Impossible. Love was something he wrote about based on observing other people, reading books or poetry, and raw imagination. He'd certainly never experienced it in a romantic sense. Besides, wasn't love something that grew over time? That required months or years to be sure?

Ha! Lennox Townsend, he of the made-up name and the hidden past is falling in love. But Jon and Viola will soon grow tired of you. Of your strange writerly quirks and melancholic mind. Cock and quill only get you so far, m'boy...

"Lennox? Is something wrong?"

He blinked at Jon who had looked so joyful and now just appeared... lost. Uncertain. He was hunching his shoulders the way he did when trying to make himself smaller. Viola had actually picked up her chemise and draped it over herself.

Damn it. What the hell is wrong with you? Neglecting lovers after rough fucking is nothing short of cruelty. The least you can do is hold them for a few minutes.

If I hold them, I might never let them go...

Lennox cleared his throat and offered a smile. "Everything is splendid, thanks to my two magnificent lovers. However, I recognized an old oak tree out the window and believe we are fast approaching the boarding house. Time to get dressed before we put on another show— the bold and laughable pretense that we did nothing more in this carriage than admire the countryside or the weather like stuffy gentry would."

Viola peered out the window and sighed. "It's true, we are quite close now. Back to real life. Will you assist me with my stays and gown? I must look as fresh as a daisy when we arrive, then at least I have a chance of denying all when the gossips pull up later."

His heart clenched at the false cheer, no doubt something she did several times a day in her employment. But they really did need to right themselves lest the puritan Prescott pair suspect anything and punish her for it.

Lennox offered his handkerchief around to assist with clean up, and attended to Viola's stays and gown buttons. After that he secured Jon's torn buckskin fall with one of Viola's hair pins.

When the traveling carriage pulled up in front of the boarding house, Lennox climbed out first to help Viola down, and made a show of bowing. "Madam. It is been my honor and pleasure. A research outing has never been so educational or enjoyable."

She curtsied. "No trouble whatsoever, Mr. Townsend. But I must return to my duties. Farewell, Lord Jonathan."

"Farewell," said Jon quietly as they both watched her hurry into the house. "Back to real life for all of us."

Lennox scowled.

Never had anything sounded so bloody miserable.

7

AFTER A SLEEPLESS NIGHT STARING AT THE BED CANOPY WHILE HIS STOMACH churned with uncertainty, breakfast was the last thing Jon wanted. However, his huge frame needed sustenance, and swooning down a staircase would only create more problems, so he had to eat. Fortunately, his room had a private supper table, so he didn't have to face the dining room and other guests.

Jon forced himself to finish the last slice of toasted bread smothered in butter and blackberry preserve, a large gulp of tea assisting with the effort. But much like Falston House back in London, this boarding house bedchamber now felt like a prison.

Yet another place he didn't really belong.

Not in a thousand years had he thought a *carriage* would be where he finally found freedom. True joy. The greatest pleasure he'd ever known. He'd relived those short hours over and over in his mind; that first shockingly good orgasm deep inside Viola, and the second as Lennox fucked his mouth and pinched his nipples. But just like darkest night followed brightest day, he also relived the disappointment and confusion when Lennox had withdrawn, not just physically, but emotionally as well.

Don't be a twit. He had an excellent reason; thinking of Viola and her precarious place with the Prescotts. Your need to be cossetted is not Lennox's problem. He is not your master, no matter how much you wish him to be.

Jon grimaced and ambled over to the window overlooking the large garden below. Perhaps gazing at some dark green shrubs would soothe his delicate sensibilities. Instead, all he saw was Viola toiling in the mid-morning sun, valiantly attempting to move a heavy wrought-iron table across the grass.

Before he'd even thought about it, Jon left his bedchamber and hurried down the stairs, trying not to wince at the harsh clomp of his oversized shoes on the wood. After two failed efforts, he eventually found the door to get to the enclosed garden, and burst outside to blink owlishly in the sunlight.

"Viola," he called, waving.

She froze, then near-sprinted over. "Shhhh! They'll hear you."

"The Prescotts?"

"No, the Brigands."

Jon grinned, his spirits lifting a little. "Lennox met them the other day. They scolded him because his plays aren't lusty enough."

"That sounds about right. Imagine four rascal residents in their seventies with too much time on their hands, no shame whatsoever, and the kind of skill and cunning a London magistrate would envy. Now imagine them cornering you in a garden. I think the longest anyone has held out on one of their relentless and exceedingly personal interrogations is two minutes. And that was me."

"Good God."

"Precisely. I'm hoping if I stay out here moving furniture for the garden party this afternoon, someone else will take them their tea at eleven o'clock. I'm really not in the mood today. Certain things are too precious to share, like my first carriage threesome," Viola finished, a faint blush spreading across her cheekbones as she swatted a bug from her arm.

He nodded. "I feel the same way, really. I wish we'd had more time. Afterward, I mean. It felt...abrupt to part ways like that. Is it too pathetic to say I enjoy affectionate touch as much as fucking?"

"On the contrary. It would have been lovely to curl up with you and Lennox in the sunshine, all naked and lazy. I think rough fucking and tender cuddling is the very best combination, although I enjoy being watched far more than is sensible."

"Sensible has nothing to do with it. You like what you like. I admire the fact you make no apology for your desires and wish I had your courage."

Viola studied him, her soft smile far too understanding. "Being sweet and shy is not a flaw. The world needs balance for the bold and gruff. But...oh God, this is probably going to sound so foolish..."

"Just say it."

"I wonder if all your needs are being met. You really seemed to love it when," her voice lowered to a whisper, "Lennox grasped your throat and pinched your nipples. Have you ever worn a collar? Not a cravat but an actual leather collar. Back in my troupe, there were several men who enjoyed accessories like that."

Jon stared at her, consumed by such longing he couldn't even speak. He had his own set of clamps in the canvas bag back in his room, and of course he'd seen people wearing collars; several of Theresa's other clients sported them. It always filled him with the most painful envy, for those gentlemen had owners. A stern wife, bold mistress, or dominant lover. And while some were shy like him, others were very powerful men in society who just happened to appreciate a good flogging or caning in private.

"I've never worn a collar," Jon replied hesitantly. He needed to change the subject before he started getting an erection. "Talking about parties though, I saw you out the window trying to move ridiculously heavy furniture. So I ventured down to help. Unless there are footmen or maids coming?"

Viola looked briefly disappointed at his evasion, then snorted. "Pauline hired some girls from church to assist later, but as per usual, the bulk of the work must be done by me. Oh, by the by, you and Lennox are invited this afternoon."

"We are?"

"Yes indeed, as guests of honor. Half the county is coming to admire the two prize bulls at the fair. I'm sure you're aware how often my in-laws brag about their friendship with Falston; surely you didn't think you and such a renowned playwright would escape a dreadful imposition on your time?"

Jon shuddered. "I would like it known that I do this for you alone, Madam Viola."

"How kind," she purred. "You shall forever remain in my good graces. Now, if you wish to assist, let's get to it, my fine workhorse."

He blinked, overcome by the memory of this lush beauty riding his cock and screaming her pleasure. But not only that, holding his hand afterward, as though she'd known he needed an anchor.

Perhaps she'd needed one as well.

"As you like," Jon replied.

For the next half hour, he lugged tables and chairs, draped heavy satin ribbon about a tall wooden bower, folded linen napkins, and checked countless forks and glasses to ensure they were smudge-free. At one point, he could have sworn he felt Lennox's eyes upon him, but when he glanced up to the bedchamber window, there was no one there.

When at last they were finished, Viola stood with her hands on her hips, smiling in satisfaction. "A job well done. I had no idea grand lords could be so helpful."

Jon bowed. "I sometimes stay at Lennox's townhouse when he hosts a party. I've dismantled many a display the following morning, and escorted lingering guests away. So, if one of the Brigands tries your patience too sorely, or perhaps the mayor gets intoxicated and starts fondling backsides, I know what to do."

Viola laughed, her eyes sparkling. "Not only marvelous but a most useful gentleman! You have no idea how much I want to kiss you right now."

"I would adore that," Jon said quietly. "But perhaps later, without the risk of Prescotts or Brigands interrupting us."

"I look forward to it, and the rest. There are so many things I'd like to do. Perhaps I'll make you beg for treats. Or, for being so helpful, just strip you bare and suck your cock."

He swallowed hard, ready to lay down his cape for this queen. "You are so beautiful—"

"Mrs. P!"

At the hail from a maid standing at the kitchen door, they both sighed.

"Yes?" she asked impatiently.

"Apparently there is an issue in Mr. Townsend's chamber. Mr. Prescott requested you attend to it at once."

Viola looked at Jon. "Come along then. Let's see what our favorite playwright requires."

He nodded.

The sexual compatibility of their threesome was the most intense imaginable. But an honest discussion regarding tender feelings lurking underneath was well overdue.

HIS BACK ACHED. His fingers were cramped and ink stained. His eyes were so bleary he could barely see, and there was probably a small tree's worth of paper screwed up on the floor. But he had no further completed pages of his otherworldly play to show for it. Not even one, thanks to a raging internal battle between hard-won control and wayward emotions.

The emotions were winning.

Furious at himself, Lennox continued his frenzied pacing of the bedchamber. But it didn't help. The angels and demons, fairies and werewolves, and mermaids and trolls remained on the periphery of his mind, enjoying their soiree on the other side of a curtain he couldn't quite see through.

Why couldn't he bloody well create?

You know why. Your muse and patron are downstairs without you. They slept in their own beds last night when they should have been in here, kissed and held and cossetted after that magnificent carriage threesome. But you let them down. Now, they'll probably let you go.

Fuck.

Lennox ran his hands through his disheveled hair. The only way to make amends was to take a risk and tell Jon and Viola the truth: that he needed them. Not just in bed, but as life companions. He couldn't be a lone wolf anymore, not when his soul insisted they were his pack. Only with Jon and Viola did he feel like bone-deep happiness was possible, for they each satisfied needs in him that no one else could. Darling Viola, his bold red-haired exhibitionist. And Jon, his sweet and caring submissive pet. Not to mention they both understood the theatrical world and respected a complicated, critical part of him: writing. It was Jon and Viola who had enthusiastically encouraged him to write the story of his heart, and inspired all the ideas he had thus far. Hell, even now he could imagine handing out scripts while Jon dashed about managing their theater and Viola twirled around the stage wearing next to nothing.

The future started today.

Lennox's stomach rumbled and he absently patted it. Hopefully the tea and toast he'd ordered would arrive soon; when he was writing, or at least trying to, tasks like eating and shaving and brushing his hair fell by the wayside. But he needed to clean himself up before Jon and Viola saw him; not even Jon knew how a playwright really looked when mired in creative purgatory. No one needed such a terrifying image lodged in their mind, not the general public, and certainly not his lovers.

A knock sounded at the door, and he hurried across the room to answer it. Christ, he really needed food or his stomach would start consuming his liver or other vital organ.

"Morning," Lennox said as he yanked open the door. "I—"

It wasn't a maid or footman or Oswald Prescott, but Viola and Jon. Who were now staring at him like he'd sprouted a second head.

"Good grief," said Viola, her eyes wide. "Did you sleep at all?"

Lennox attempted a laugh; it sounded more like ancient chains being dragged across rubble. "Are you implying I look less than glorious, madam?"

Jon's brow furrowed. "You never look less than glorious, but..."

"Well. Now you know the truth," he grumbled, embarrassed to be caught in such a shameful state. "There is a very good reason why writing is a solitary pursuit. We turn feral. Running away from me would be quite sensible."

Viola folded her arms. "What twaddle. I shall fetch some breakfast from the kitchens, and Jon is going to act as your valet. You'll feel much better fed and shaved."

Lennox opened his mouth to argue, but she had already spun on her heel and hurried down the hallway, leaving him alone with his patron.

"I'll just stoke that fire and warm some water," said Jon, his lips twitching.

He scowled. "Let it be known I tolerate coddling under great sufferance."

"Duly noted."

Huffing out a breath, Lennox returned to his bed and perched on the end while Jon bustled about. The other man was looking more cheerful by the moment as he arranged warm water, soap and flannel, fresh clothing and shaving kit.

After a swift sponge bath, Lennox dressed in clean breeches, linen shirt, and a sapphire-blue jacket, then sat in the chair ready to be shaved. However, Jon didn't pick up the razor, instead he placed his big hands upon Lennox's shoulders and began to knead them.

It felt good. Very, very good.

"Bloody coddling," Lennox repeated, even as he leaned further into his patron's touch.

"Mmm hmmm," said Jon, pressing harder around his neck and under his shoulder blades with divine precision.

He groaned softly as his abused muscles eased. Previously he'd always avoided affectionate touch so no one thought a liaison more than it was, or worse, assumed they had some sort of control over him. But this was Jon, a man he trusted implicitly. A ray of sunshine who merely wished to serve and soothe.

"You have a gift," Lennox said gruffly. "I feel less like a tavern floor at dawn, now."

His patron beamed. "Glad to hear it."

Shortly afterward, Viola marched back into the room holding a tray crammed with dishes.

"Breakfast!" she sang out, placing the tray on the dressing table in front of him, momentarily not a Siren but a red-haired angel of mercy.

The toasted bread and cheese melted in his mouth, the bacon was crisped to perfection, and the tea piping hot, just the way he liked it. "My compliments to the kitchens," Lennox said once he'd eaten. "Excellent breakfast. All my favorites."

"Of course," Viola said simply, leaning down and kissing the top of his head.

Overwhelmed at the tenderness that demonstrated such *knowing*, he cursed and they both went very still.

"Lennox?" asked Jon as he wrapped his arms around himself.

"I don't deserve this," Lennox said irritably. "Not after the way I behaved yesterday. We should have spent the night together in my bed. I'm aware it's too small for three, and Jon might have sprawled on the floor if he tried to roll over, but an attempt at least. I did you both a grave disservice and here you are caring for me. You're both far better than I."

Now Jon and Viola just looked baffled, and he thumped down his teacup. Yes, he could write the words, but could he make a goddamned romantic declaration when it mattered? Not in a thousand years. Perhaps it would be better if he just remained a rake who strolled from conquest to conquest with no ties, no promises, and no questions. Certainly no coddling.

"I mean..." Lennox gritted out. "I—"

"Making a mistake or unwise decision never means you're unworthy of care," said Viola crisply, as she picked up the shaving kit and began preparing his jaw. "It just offers an opportunity to be better. Everyone can be better. Everyone can choose to open their hearts, allow hurt out and happiness in. Now, we have a wretched garden party to attend, but tonight I think a very frank conversation about the future is required. Jon?"

His patron nodded. "In truth, I don't mind if I end up on the floor. Even a few minutes in bed with you both would be worth it. I'm hoping for much more than that, though. Please, Lennox. Let's talk."

Lennox gazed at their earnest faces, his fierce need for them warring with that old instinctive desire to conceal anything that might be considered a weakness. Or too dark to bear. "Very well," he said eventually. "Tonight."

THE ONLY PLACE Viola wanted to be right now was Lennox's chamber with him and Jon. But for the last few hours she'd been trapped in this garden with a good portion of Hertfordshire society; managing issues, chatting about inconsequential topics, and most importantly, ensuring Oswald and Pauline appeared to be the best hosts in England.

She was so very, very tired of this particular duty.

Frustrated beyond measure, Viola swooped to steady a lemonade glass before it spilled its contents all over the trestle tablecloth. Then she straightened a drooping satin bow on the bower, and gestured to a footman to refresh a platter of buttered bread with thinly sliced ham.

"What are you even doing here, petal?"

Sighing inwardly, she turned and nodded politely at Piers and the three other Brigands. A consequence for her concentration lapse; being cornered against the manicured hedgerow for an interrogation. "My job."

Gillian shook her head. "You are making calf eyes at his lordship and Mr. Townsend. They are making calf eyes at you. Why are you working at this wretched boarding house when you could be anywhere else, falling deeper in love?"

"It's true, gel," said the captain. "The good Lord—and I mean Him Above not the strapping blond—has sent you a sign that it's time to spread your wings and fly again. So, what do you need? Money? Carriage? Gunpowder explosion to divert the Prescotts while you flee? Tell us and we'll arrange it. Been far too long since I had a decent campaign to sink my teeth into."

A tiny smile tugged at Viola's lips. "If you tell anyone I will lace your tea with a purging tonic...but there is to be a discussion this evening. A *frank* discussion."

"Huzzah!" cheered Reuben, saluting her with his lemonade glass.

"It's far too early to cheer. We are three very complicated people. And it's not an overly common situation."

Gillian snorted. "Threesomes are far more common than you think, people just don't trot around announcing it like a town crier. And if, after everything you've endured, you don't grab onto a chance at happiness with both hands...I will box your ears most severely, young lady."

"Indeed," said Piers, glaring at her over his spectacles. "You think Reuben and I haven't had our trials and nonsense from society? Of course we have. Even moved house a few times when it got unbearable. There will always be risks, especially with the wretched law as it is. Always be those meddling, judgmental sewer rats who just love to stick their snouts in the business of others. But each and every time we had a choice. And we chose love. Because, my sweet petal, it is worth it."

Viola took a shuddering breath as she glanced once more over at Lennox, currently being held captive by several church ladies next to the sweets table. Then at Jon who was discreetly smoothing tablecloths and straightening forks as he ambled from group to group. They were such different men, Lennox so brilliant and forceful and Jon so sweet and obliging. Yet one trait they shared: an unconditional acceptance of her.

Neither had ever said mind your place or forget your dreams or a woman should keep her clothing on in public.

They granted wishes. Made her feel alive inside. And had introduced her to greater pleasures than she'd ever known.

She looked back at Piers. "I know it is worth it. That *I* am worth it. So I'm positively itching for time to speed up so all the guests can leave and I can scoop up my men and declare my feelings. I cannot imagine a future without them, even though it's been less than a week."

"Bah," said Reuben, patting her hand. "I decided in a day that Piers would be my forever love."

"That long?" said Piers with a sniff. "I knew in a matter of hours."

"You both move slower than treacle," said the captain loftily. "I danced with Gilly then very politely asked her if she would accompany me to Gretna Green so we didn't have to fuss about with the reading of the banns. We were galloping north from Carlisle within thirty minutes."

Viola blinked and turned to Gillian. "Thirty *minutes*?"

The elderly woman blushed. "I was an impetuous lassie. But in all honesty, the first time I looked into Timothy's sea-weathered face, I knew. I needed a bold man. A brave one. But also...unconventional. A man who wouldn't clip my wings, but be the breeze on which I soared. I see that part of myself in you, my dear. Do not fall prey to the false or staid again. Embrace your true self. Be free."

Viola swallowed hard against a boulder in her throat as all four Brigands smiled at her with such wisdom and understanding. Each of these exceptional people had taken a risk and followed their hearts when true love came calling. In return they'd won the greatest prize possible: happily ever after. Decade after decade of the bliss only found when you lived the life you were supposed to. "I'm not sure I can wait until tonight for the discussion."

"Then don't," said the captain. "But do keep in mind that our offer of a gunpowder explosion is always on the table. It will only take me a few minutes to fetch Gilly's pink hat box."

Swiftly dashing a hand against her eyes, Viola kissed each of them on the cheek before strolling over to where Jon was feigning interest in a spirited conversation about wool prices.

"Beg pardon, my lord," she said, curtsying. "But the...er...vicar is quite desperate to make your acquaintance. Would you mind accompanying me to the parlor?"

Jon's eyes widened with relieved gratitude and he offered his arm. "Anything for the clergy, madam. Please excuse me, gentlemen."

"Do not look at anyone, do not wave, continue straight ahead," hissed Viola as they turned and walked toward the house. "I'm afraid this is an abduction."

"Excellent," said Jon, squeezing her hand. "One more minute of sheep talk and I would have curled up on the ground and started rocking. Where's Lennox?"

"The church ladies are ruthless and have him surrounded, but I am quietly confident I can distract them by cartwheeling naked across the lawn."

"Shall I join you?"

Viola halted. "You actually would, wouldn't you?"

He nodded solemnly. "If it made you happy."

A wondrous feeling of warmth spread through her, and without thinking, she went up on her toes and kissed Jon on the lips. No brief buss, but a thorough exploration of his mouth, her darting tongue a possessive stamp of ownership.

"*Viola Prescott*! What is the meaning of this!"

Still gripping Jon's hand, Viola winced as Pauline's screech echoed around the garden. Even worse...her sister-in-law wasn't alone. Standing next to her were three other people; the local vicar Reverend Lane, and the Duke and Duchess of Falston.

Oh God.

The captain had been wrong. A gunpowder explosion wouldn't be necessary; all it took for the sky to fall was a widowed poor relation completely forgetting propriety at a Hertfordshire garden party.

Oh God.

As it turned out, one hundred people could be astonishingly quiet, but it was the eye of the storm. Any second now, actual hell would unleash, and Viola and Jon would be bombarded from all sides.

A ferocious growl rumbled in Lennox's chest. Bad enough that the Prescotts treated their sister-in-law as a servant at their boarding house and the duke openly kept his youngest brother at arm's length, but now they thought to publicly scold and humiliate them? Like they were a pair of amorous sixteen-year-olds caught behind a barn rather than two unwed adults?

No. Not today. Not when they both belonged to him. He had let them down earlier in the week but would never do so again.

Lennox bowed to the group of local ladies who had surrounded him earlier to enquire about the current popular fabrics and trims in London. Or more accurately, fire questions like a hail of arrows. If the Church of England's women took over from constables, no crime would go unsolved. "Excuse me."

One of them grasped his wrist and tittered. "Surely, Mr. Townsend, you aren't thinking to get involved in that? Viola Prescott may dress as a virtuous widow in gray, but we always knew better. She is a strumpet, as brazen as her hair, and should be turned away from decent society. Dear Pauline is a saint to have housed her for so long."

He smiled coldly. "I see no evidence of *decent society* here. Now, I must insist you unhand me, lest you find yourself arse over ears in prickly shrubbery."

Every member of the group took a step back, acute alarm etched on their features. Obviously his baring of teeth came straight from the feral playwright collection. But it cleared a space for him to cross the lawn and get to Jon and Viola, who were standing almost frozen in front of Pauline, the duke and duchess, and a somberly dressed man of the cloth.

"Gracious," Lennox drawled as he came to a halt behind Jon and Viola and rested a light hand on each of their backs, so they knew he offered his full support. Propriety be damned, he'd had quite enough of gentry horseshit. "Terribly bad form to have a private party without me. My dear Pauline, do you need to sit down? Your face is an unpleasant shade of puce. Although in fairness, your high-ranking companions are sporting a similar hue. Must say, I'm surprised to see you here, Your Graces; didn't think an obscure garden party in Hertfordshire would be your sort of gathering. But you brought your own vicar? How very...righteous."

"Actually, I reside just down the road. This is my parish, sir," said the silver-haired reverend pleasantly. Then he froze and gaped at Lennox, before a huge smile lit up his face. "Oh my word. My word! Surely not... young Huw Jenkins all grown up? It's me, Mr. Lane! How many years has it been, m'boy? Nearly twenty? And you look so well! What a tremendous blessing to see you again, haven't we both progressed a long way from Whitechapel!"

No. No. Oh Christ no.

Lennox's blood chilled, and his entire body went clammy as perspiration gathered at his temples and the nape of his neck. For in the space of a moment, he'd flown back in time to the austere and joyless parish school he'd attended where a curate named Mr. Lane had come in twice a week to teach Latin. Unlike most, he'd been firm yet fair and sparing with the cane. But the man in front of him, this good-hearted vicar who meant no malice at all, was casually destroying a house of cards that had taken twenty years to construct. Because Reverend Lane knew the truth: that Lennox Townsend hadn't been born, he'd been created, just like every other tale he'd written.

Fuck.

He'd come over here to distract everyone from the fact that Viola had kissed Jon, and now his entire existence had been blown apart. Pauline was staring at him with shocked suspicion. The duke and duchess with supreme aristocratic disdain. And Jon and Viola had both gone rigid beneath his touch, no doubt remembering he'd opened his wretched fool mouth at the Roman ruins and talked about a *parish school.*

Lennox cleared his throat, relieved to be standing behind his lovers, so acute was his shame. It was indeed true; secrets eventually came to light, even the ones buried deepest. But not in a thousand years had he thought his moment of greatest vulnerability, his complete exposure, would be in the middle of a goddamned Hertfordshire garden party. "Reverend."

The vicar's face fell. "Oh dear," he said uncertainly. "Have I said something out of turn? Am I mistaken? Do forgive me, sir."

He couldn't salvage this. Everyone had heard; the whispers behind him were as loud as autumn leaves crunching under boots. In front of him, the way the Falstons were twitching, the duke swinging his jet-topped cane and the duchess practically rocking on her heeled slippers, they couldn't wait to return to London and share such a juicy morsel of gossip. Lennox Townsend's reign as the playwright with the golden quill would very abruptly end.

But worst of all, Jon and Viola would certainly discard him now. What use had a nobleman and a gentry widow for a foundling fraud?

FUCK.

He should have known this would happen and not even considered letting his guard down. Some people just weren't destined for happily ever after.

Lennox forced a rasping chuckle. "It is me who should ask forgiveness, Reverend. It was startling to be hailed by a name I left behind some years ago. Everyone knows me as Lennox Townsend. I'm a playwright. Perhaps you've heard of me."

The vicar brightened. "I have! Alas though, I've not yet seen one of your plays. Oh, well done Huw. Er, Lennox. Well done. I always knew God would reveal his gifts in you."

At the clergyman's gentle gaze, so compassionate and understanding, Lennox almost screamed in agony. Damn it, why did Reverend Lane have to be an actual good person? Why couldn't he be a walking, talking pile of shit like Oswald and Pauline Prescott or the Falstons? Then it would be easy to hate him for inadvertently revealing the truth.

Lennox inclined his head; all he could manage in his current state. "Thank you, sir. I have indeed come a long way. Now, I might retire inside, a bit too much sun I think. Never a good idea to give a writer too long outdoors, we might get ideas above our station, like we are people or something. Isn't that correct, my lord patron?"

Jon nodded, his shoulders so stiff they could have been used to hold up the side of a building. "Quite. Yes. Get thee indoors, Lennox. Where are my pages?"

"I'll fetch some tea," blurted Viola.

"I think we could all do with tea," said the duchess, a catlike smile playing at her lips. "Let us accompany Mr. Jenkins...beg pardon, Mr. *Townsend* to the parlor. Perhaps he will explain his abhorrent deceit, but as a family we must also condemn Viola's lewd behavior toward Lord Jonathan. Run along, Viola, do not let us keep you from your kitchen maid duties. Lord Jonathan, come with me. Reverend? Will you join us?"

"No, Your Grace. Unlike some, I walk a path of kindness and must attend to my flock who clearly require some remedial scripture," said the vicar with surprising curtness, before bowing and hurrying away toward the church ladies.

Grinding his teeth to halt a cry only heard on haunted moors, Lennox trudged back into the boarding house to hear the verdict of his trial by duchess.

Not even with a writer's imagination could he see recovery from this.

IT WAS gut-wrenching how fast something wonderful could turn bad.

Jon bit his lip in distress as he glanced around the comfortably furnished parlor about to be used by his family as a courtroom of sorts. A place to berate and humiliate.

A quarter hour ago, he'd actually been happy when Viola kissed him with such possessive passion. But that had led to a public scolding, and Lennox being recognized by the vicar and accidentally exposed as someone who'd risen from the humblest background and changed his name. Despite Lennox's brave face, Jon could practically feel his playwright's pain, see him withdrawing and constructing an invisible wall of solid steel and rock around himself. If he and Viola didn't pull Lennox back from his personal abyss and lavish him with love, they might lose him forever. And they needed that gloriously dominant man, that brilliant mind, that master of pleasure, to make their trio complete.

Gripping his thighs, Jon resisted the overwhelming urge to run to the man he loved and offer physical comfort. To rub his shoulders, kiss him, suck his cock, whatever his lover wished to feel better. Because for a man like Lennox who relished control, having his past unexpectedly and bluntly revealed in front of all those stuffy, gossiping strangers, would be a devastating blow. No doubt Falston and Henrietta would also take the opportunity to demand he cease his patronage of Lennox.

Ha. When there were snowstorms in purgatory.

"So," said Henrietta, now seated on an embroidered chaise and observing them with the cold superiority of a tyrannical empress, "We have ourselves quite the scandal. While I suspected that Jonathan escorting Mr. Jenkins—"

"Townsend," said Jon quietly. "My playwright's name is Lennox Townsend."

"Do not interrupt me. As I was saying, while I suspected this jaunt would prove to be a grave error, I did not fathom how grave. Pauline, you must be applauded for sending a note and alerting His Grace and I to the desperately shameful behavior that has been occurring."

Jon blinked and turned to stare at Pauline, who stood near the door. "A note?"

The woman's cheeks flushed, but Oswald had joined her and now both were huffing and puffing in righteous indignation. "Yes, a note! Surely you did not think that your carriage outing would remain a secret, my lord? No less than six people visited to inform me what they'd seen through the windows. Nakedness! Such *deviancy*—"

"Only six?" said Viola, as she wheeled a full tea trolley into the parlor. "Interesting. The gossip didn't spread very far from the carriages and carts that passed by, then. Perhaps the others decided to mind their own business or were inspired to go home and indulge in some good old-fashioned fucking themselves. I can hardly blame them. Lennox and Jon are *magnificent* lovers."

"You are vulgar," said Henrietta icily. "As vulgar as that hair."

"Viola is a harlot. A she-wolf. A Jezebel," spat Pauline. "I will cast her out on the streets where she belongs. Ned never should have wed her. The only mistake of his sainted life."

"Really?" said Viola, quirking an eyebrow. "I can think of several others, like him losing everything we owned because he couldn't stop lying and cheating at cards. So do be quiet. Your opinion is irrelevant."

Jon almost cheered as Pauline got the dressing down she so richly deserved, but before he could say anything, his brother thumped his cane on the floor.

"My opinion isn't, however," snapped Falston. "It's plain to see that Jonathan has been led astray by lowborn scum. Unsurprising though, he has always been the fool of the family. And we know why that is, don't we brother? *Because not a single drop of ducal blood runs through your veins.*"

Henrietta pretended to swoon, as though shocked beyond measure at the dramatic announcement. Oswald gasped and Pauline shrieked while fanning herself frantically. Yet Viola continued pouring tea and Lennox leaned forward in his chair, looking more impatient than anything else.

Jon waited for the gouging pain that surely followed the act of public disownment. And yet...it didn't come. Instead, the only emotion swirling through his body was a sense of utter relief. Of freedom.

Perhaps now, he could finally start to live. To be his true self.

"That is accurate," he confirmed. "I am the result of an affair, only confessed by my mother after the old duke's death. I'm glad His Grace wasn't hurt by the news, for he was a decent man who treated me kindly even if he had his own suspicions. But I'm not sure why you chose to share it here, Falston. To humiliate? This news doesn't have that power, for I am not to blame for the acts that conceived me. To deprive me of money? You cannot touch the inheritance I received from Mother's family. To remove me from your home and high society? That, I am more than willing to do. I want no further part of it."

Falston stared at him, his eyes bulging. "Clearly, you don't understand, Jonathan. You won't be invited to balls or soirees. All the clubs will slam their doors in your face. No one of note will receive you."

"I will," snarled Lennox as he rose to his feet, fists clenched, his dark gaze shooting daggers at the ducal couple.

"Me too," said Viola fiercely.

"Are you jesting?" Henrietta spluttered. "Oh, I wash my hands of this. You three may play in the gutter together. Falston, we should leave this boarding house. It certainly isn't for those of our birth and station."

"Good riddance," muttered Jon.

His brother and sister-in-law gaped at him, turning several hues of red. When he didn't immediately crumble at their feet, they stalked from the room, Oswald and Pauline chasing after them with pleading cries to stay. Now, it was just him and Lennox and Viola. There was so much to be said, yet Jon didn't know where on earth to begin.

"Tea?" said Viola hesitantly, holding up the pot.

He fought an absurd desire to laugh. "The British cure for every ill. In all honesty I think I'd rather leave this parlor."

"I think that best," she replied. "This particular room has lived a sheltered life. It might never recover from what it has learned this day. Viola Prescott, a harlot, she-wolf *and* Jezebel, luring two men into deviant acts in a carriage."

"Jonathan Grant, illegitimate child of an affair, shortly to be cast out of the *ton*," he said with a tentative smile.

"The parlor might be shocked, but the garden needs a double dose of hartshorn," said Lennox, his voice uncharacteristically hesitant. "It learned I am a fraud with a made-up name, a foundling from the worst streets of London."

Jon winced at the pain in those dark eyes. Impulsively, he stepped forward and took Lennox's hand, then Viola's as well. "Let us pray for the parlor and garden, may they find peace."

"Amen," said Viola, her lips twitching. "I am, however, assured that the carriage and bedchamber are quite well and encourage lusty, happy threesomes. I myself, am *strongly* in favor of those. So, as Oswald and Pauline are otherwise occupied begging for crumbs of ducal attention and the loose-lipped Reverend Lane is tending to his flock...perhaps we might steal some food from the kitchens, go upstairs, and latch the door? I feel there is much to be said. Necessary things. What do you think, Lennox?"

It seemed to take an eternity, but eventually Lennox nodded brusquely. "Agreed. Jon?"

He nodded. "No more secrets. I wish to start as I mean to go on: with an open heart."

Yet even as he said the words, a frisson of fear slithered down his spine. His true parentage was one thing. But would they accept his darkest desires?

That remained the question he was almost afraid to know the answer to.

———

AFTER HELPING themselves to some food from the kitchens, they enjoyed an impromptu picnic on the supper table in Lennox's chamber. But now the cakes were eaten and the lemonade gulped down, the only thing left to do was bare their souls.

Viola sat back in her chair and smiled cautiously; even after their hand-holding downstairs, nerves were twisting around her innards like uncomfortable little whirlwinds. This might well be the most important conversation of her life, when she wanted the feelings in her heart and the words on her tongue to match perfectly. To show these two men that she had fallen in love with them, that they needed her, that they belonged together as a trio.

"So," she began. "Those revelations downstairs were...well, I don't think anyone thought those particular topics were going to come up at a garden party. I hate that those people hurt you both, whether deliberate or not. But know this: your past or birth isn't who you are. It's not the whole story. I think that is true for all of us; each of our battles made us stronger. Then fate brought us together in this boarding house at just the right time."

Jon drummed his fingers on his knee. "In truth, escorting Lennox here for a retreat to help his writer malady may well be the best decision I ever make."

"I concur," said Lennox, smiling faintly. "Even after the garden and parlor debacles."

"I'm not sure I can forgive Falston or Henrietta for that bloody nonsense," continued Jon. "They were trying to hurt me, but once this gets out it will hurt my mother and the late duke's memory. It serves no purpose. And it's almost amusing that they think banishment from the *ton* is such a terrible punishment. There are a few decent people, but most are selfish and shallow. They have so much money and power to do good in the world, but will they lift a finger to help? No."

"I can think of one superb lord," said Viola warmly. "Very tall. Very kind. Extremely supportive of the arts. Other special talents include party preparation, tossing a plump woman over his shoulder, a mouth that unfailingly provides starburst orgasms, and being a rampant stallion to ride."

Jon blushed scarlet. "Why thank you, madam."

Lennox cleared his throat. "I've said it many times, but I don't think you quite understand how much you mean to me, Jon. You make me want to be better. To work harder. You remind me that there is good in the world. And then we met Viola, who is fire and passion and a reminder to be courageous, take chances, and reveal all."

"I love revealing all," she said with a mischievous wink. "I feel so free."

"I think that is what we've each been searching for. Freedom. And others who understand and accept who we truly are. It's so rare. So damned precious. Now that I have you both...I find I cannot bear to let you go. But I'm asking a lot, knowing the scandal that is about to unleash."

"Will you share your story?" asked Jon softly.

Lennox rubbed a hand across his face, then nodded. "As the vicar said, my birth name was Huw Jenkins. My parents were Welsh, they brought me and my older sister Bethan to London for a better life. They worked in a factory while I attended a parish school. Well, sometimes attended. One day a fire broke out in the factory. I saw the smoke and ran to help carry water...but the building was old and the windows were nailed shut for warmth. It just collapsed. My family was snatched from me so fast. I hate gray because it reminds me of ash. Of exhausted people crammed into derelict spaces and worked to death for greed. The bastard owner paid me a guinea for my loss. That's all three Welsh lives were worth. I've never spent that coin but I carry it with me always. It's Mam and Dad and Bethie..."

"Oh Lennox," Viola breathed as she leaned over and clasped his hand, horrified at what he'd endured.

He squeezed her fingers. "I don't want to remember what I had to do to survive those years afterward. My imagination saved me on countless occasions. But I'm here now, a thirty-year-old playwright and noted king of rakes, wanting to keep my job, discard my crown and live happily ever after with those I care about most."

Jon got to his feet, walked around to Lennox's chair, and knelt down beside it. "I love being your patron. Not for the status, but the chance to serve you. Yet if I could serve you *and* Viola...I would be the happiest man alive."

"I need you both in my life," said Lennox gruffly. "Though it's humiliating that I have so little to offer right now."

Viola winced at the shame in his voice. One thing she could not abide was Lennox thinking that he only had value when writing or fucking. That he was somehow unworthy of happiness. And dear Jon, who had grown up in an elegant but cold environment, punished for his mother's choices. They might think it their task to take care of her, but she would take care of them right back. Lavish them with all the love overflowing in her heart.

She stood and held out her hands. "Can we retire over to the bed? I am in serious need of some cuddling from my men."

Soon they were curled up on top of the quilt, Lennox lounging against the pillows, Jon to his left, and she to his right. But they were all connected, with arms around each other, and even now she felt better.

"Viola," said Lennox abruptly. "Back in the carriage when you spoke of being barren...are you certain it was you and not your husband? He would hardly be the first man to blame his wife when the issue was entirely his."

She sighed, those old feelings of frustration threatening to rear their ugly head. "Definitely me. I had several lovers during my time with the troupe, and nothing. That actually helped me rise to a more senior role. Also...Ned's mistress had two children. They live in the cottage that should have been my dower property, but I could hardly put young ones out on the street. She calls herself Mrs. Prescott, you know. And Oswald and Pauline send bank drafts. All one big happy family."

"*What?*" said Jon, his jaw dropping. "That's outrageous."

Viola sat up and took a deep breath. "Tell me truthfully. Do either of you want children? Because I well understand how the world unravels when feelings differ on the subject."

"No," said Lennox, the word unequivocal. "I have never wanted to be a father. My plays are my legacy and I am utterly content with that."

Jon shook his head. "Between my older brothers and sisters, I have ten nieces and nephews if I ever feel a pressing desire for a tea party or tin soldier battle. But for myself...I have different dreams. Different needs."

He sounded so wistful. So anxious. Viola turned on her side and rested her head on Lennox's chest so she could look directly at Jon. "You both know my dream, to perform on stage again and be near-naked in public as often as possible. I love that you indulged me so splendidly in the carriage without any judgment. It meant the world. But what about you, Jon? What do you truly desire?"

The young lord exhaled slowly. "I can show you. But I'll offer a warning; it is...different. Most people don't understand, which is hard to bear when it brings me such peace."

And with that, he left the bed and hurried through the connecting door to his room.

Viola could only exchange a puzzled glance with Lennox.

What could his secret possibly be?

9

Jon stood in his chamber, clutching the small canvas bag of accessories to his chest. Every time he'd visited Theresa, he'd dreamed of the day his flogging was delivered by a loving master or mistress who understood the exhilarating union of pain and pleasure and wished to reward his devoted service.

Had that day at last arrived?

Was he a fool to even hope?

Even the most openminded people could have an aversion to causing pain. Others might agree to use a cane or riding crop, but not a flogger. He'd tried various tools with Theresa, but the cane reminded him too much of school, and the riding crop just didn't offer the variety of sensations that a flogger did. Whether he wanted a thudding, almost massaging feel, or a whipping sting, a flogger in the hands of someone skilled felt truly magical. Yet it would be perfectly acceptable and reasonable for Lennox and Viola to refuse. Pain play needed to be satisfying for everyone involved.

Gathering all his courage, Jon straightened his shoulders and returned to Lennox's chamber. Then he silently upended the bag until the bottle of oil, leather dildo, silver nipple clamps, and flogger fell onto the quilt in front of Lennox and Viola. "These are accessories I enjoy very much, although I have mostly played alone or sought professional expertise from an establishment in London—"

"The White House?" asked Lennox, pausing his stroking of Viola's hair to sit up and look closer at the toys. "That looks like one of Theresa's floggers."

Jon froze, trying to control his shock at the matter-of-fact reply. "You've visited?"

The playwright smiled. "I lived there for a decade. Two years after the fire, I was so hungry I attempted to steal Theresa's reticule for coin. She unleashed a terrifying thunder and brimstone lecture, then offered me a job running errands, which I gladly accepted. Theresa taught me to read and write and speak like a young gentleman, and when I was older, I assisted at the pleasure club. In my mind she is the most brilliant businesswoman in London. With the White House, Theresa saw a need, met that need, and told the puritans to go bathe in the Thames. I always wanted to do the same with my plays."

"Did you ever...er...learn some of her particular skills?"

"My dear Jon," purred Lennox, as he climbed off the bed and sauntered around it to stand beside him. "If you're asking do I know how to wield a flogger, the answer is yes."

Jon gasped. "Would you...would you flog me?" he asked, so tentatively his voice was scarcely more than a whisper.

"I really think you should, Lennox," said Viola as she went up on her knees, her eyes glittering. "That is something I'd adore to watch."

"Darling, you won't just be watching. You'll be assisting."

Incredulous at his good fortune to have both lovers not only interested but involved, Jon could only stare. "What must I do?"

"Get undressed. Now, would you prefer to be bound or unbound?"

"Bound," he choked out as raw excitement flooded his senses.

Soon Jon stood naked at the foot of the four-poster bed, his left wrist tied to one post and his right wrist to the other. The cravat bindings were soft and comfortable; loose enough for him to flex his arms so they didn't seize up, but still leaving him wonderfully helpless.

"Pet is secured," Viola murmured, before kissing him and plunging her tongue into his mouth. Then, even more diabolically, she wet her fingertips and circled his nipples.

Jon moaned, quivering at the too-gentle touch. "*Viola.*"

"You dare address me so informally?" she replied, shaking her head. "Madam Viola, if you please. It is obvious immediate discipline is required to correct such behavior. Lennox, should I start with these clamps?"

"An excellent idea."

For what seemed like an eternity, his lovers sensually tormented him. Viola sucked his nipples to aching tautness before affixing the silver clamps, the initial bite making him cry out in delight. But they didn't touch his engorged cock, currently bobbing against his belly. Instead, he received countless butterfly-light kisses; to his lips and neck, his shoulders and chest and inner thighs until he wanted to howl in pure need.

"Please," Jon begged, when perspiration covered his body like a fine mist. "Flog me."

Lennox nipped his shoulder. "Madam Viola was correct. You are far too informal. How should your master be addressed?"

Tears of joy gathered in his eyes, and he blinked furiously to try and hold them back. "Sir. Please flog me, *sir.*"

"And what will you say if you wish me to stop?"

"Halt. I'll say halt. More to continue."

"Very well. Spread your legs, Jon."

At the first wispy flick of leather strips against his hair-roughened thighs, Jon shuddered in anticipation. But Lennox was in no hurry; denying him precious lashes to instead trail the flogger over his hip and down to caress his painfully hard shaft. God. Used like this the leather was deceptively benign, offering chaste kisses that brought forth copious moisture from his swollen cockhead.

Eventually, though, Lennox brought the flogger back to his thighs. Then, without warning, the leather strips whipped against the fleshy part of his arse, once, twice, three times. Jon groaned in bliss and jerked against his bonds. "More. More!"

Yet rather than administering further lashes, Lennox leaned against the bedpost, smiling wickedly. "Viola, my darling, you are trembling. Does it make your pretty cunt wet, watching Jon get disciplined?"

"Yes," she whispered. "I need to come."

"You may do so."

Jon gulped, speechless with lust as Viola lay back on the bed, rucked up her gown, and spread her thighs wide to expose her soaked center. Then she stroked her visibly swollen clitoris, the chamber echoing with her breathy little moans. He inhaled deeply, intoxicating himself with the scent of aroused woman. "I want a taste."

The flogger whipped his arse, harsher this time, and Jon strained against his linen restraints until the bedposts creaked. So good. So, so good.

"You think to make demands, pet? See what happens," drawled Lennox, moving around the bed and leaning down to kiss Viola, before plunging his fingers into her cunt and fucking her with them until she orgasmed with a low scream. Then he withdrew his fingers and nonchalantly licked them clean. "Mmmm. Delicious."

Lennox understood. He truly understood.

Sheer relief nearly buckled Jon's knees. His master would be stern and unyielding as he took him to that glorious edge and made him wait. Made him beg. Just as he'd always dreamed.

A sob caught in his throat at such a gift. "Please, sir. Please, please flog me until I come."

Lennox returned, grasped Jon's chin and tugged his head down for a bruising kiss. "You beg so sweetly."

"Reward him, Lennox," said Viola, rising up on her knees to resume watching.

Then, oh God, the leather lashed his arse and thighs over and over, harder and harder, and Jon bucked, glorying in the cleansing, healing fire. When at last he emerged and soared to the stars, a guttural roar tore from his chest as Viola sucked his cock down her throat, forcing him to give her every drop of his endless spurting release.

Jon sagged in his bonds, struggling for breath, tears pouring down his cheeks. But he wasn't alone, no, he had a master at his back and a mistress at his front, and they were holding him tenderly. Kissing him. Stroking his hair. Murmuring lavish words of praise.

"I love you both," he said hoarsely. "So much."

Indeed, the world at this moment was absolutely perfect.

"Are the guests still gossiping down there?"

Viola smiled as Lennox's arms closed around her and she leaned back against his chest with a contented sigh. She'd been watching the party out the bedchamber window, rather delighted that particular duty was now someone else's headache. "The Brigands have my in-laws and the duke and duchess cornered at the far end of the garden. I wondered why we hadn't yet been evicted. Now I know. How is Jon?"

Lennox kissed her neck, eliciting a shiver. "Our pet will be ready to play again as soon as that salve on his backside dries. Young ones recover much faster."

"Ha! Speak for yourself," she replied archly. "I am in my prime."

"An inarguable truth. Wearing far too many clothes, though."

Viola bit her lip as Lennox unfastened her gown buttons and removed the garment, before scraping his teeth over her bare shoulder. "Sir, I must p-protest."

"Oh?"

"You aren't undressing me swiftly enough."

Lennox laughed as he attended to her stays and petticoat, then grasped each side of her threadbare chemise and tore it in two. "Is that better? Now those respectable, dutiful guests down there only have to look up and they'll see your magnificent breasts. Why don't you unpin your hair and dance for your audience? After that I'm going to make you come so hard that they'll all hear you."

A soft whimper escaped. But she was already freeing her hair from the restriction of the pins, sighing in relief as the heavy mass fell to the small of her back. Ah. So much better. Lennox started humming a tune, and lost in the moment, Viola kicked away her torn chemise and began to dance.

"You move so gracefully," said Jon, from where he lay front down on the bed. "But when naked, you positively glow."

She winked and twirled at the window so both her indoor and outdoor audience could fully appreciate the view. "Why thank you."

"A much bigger stage is required though," said Lennox. "A proper theatrical one."

"I agree," said Jon, carefully maneuvering himself onto his side and stretching his limbs. "But the lusty otherworldly play will need to be performed at a private club to get around those foolish licensing laws. I'm going to purchase a property with a large ballroom and garden so the theater can be inside or out depending on season."

Viola nearly stumbled. "What?"

Lennox grinned. "Darling, I've decided you'll appear in all my plays from now on. Your first role shall be as a fairy princess in *The Flame of Passion*. Alas, though, due to...er, financial constraints, your costume will consist only of satin wings, flower crown, and a gold muslin tunic. The audience will be able to see *everything*."

She stared at him, almost afraid to believe. Thirty-five was too old for miracles, surely. "Are you jesting?"

"I never jest about casting decisions. Ever."

"Oh God."

"Lennox or master will do," he replied, his eyes glinting. "Now show me the dance of a fairy princess who must reignite the flame. Show me how you'll have the audience in transports, desperate to touch themselves in the theater of Jon's private club."

"Our private club," said Jon.

"I don't know what to s-say," she choked out, joy making her voice hoarse. "A stage and a home and two men to love sounds like paradise."

"Say yes," said Lennox. "A resounding yes to happiness."

Humming the opening bars to a new tune, Viola moved sinuously in time, swaying her hips and cupping her breasts, offering her body to be admired. Soon she would be living her own happily ever after, her own way, just like the Brigands. True love brought freedom, and it was a wondrous thing.

She turned to Lennox. "I recall a certain playwright promising to make me come so hard that everyone downstairs would hear me. I should like that to happen immediately, beloved."

"Would you indeed?" he replied, quirking one eyebrow.

"Don't make me wait. As I've already said, I don't have Jon's steely nerves."

Lennox took her in his arms and waltzed her over to the bed. Their brawny lord's cock was erect once more and she glanced between the two men, her blood heating at the thought of curling up with them each night.

"One day soon I should like to ride you, Jon, while Lennox fucks my backside," she blurted. "But I need to crawl before I walk. Perhaps you might show me how it is done properly."

Jon quivered, his expression unabashed lust. "I'd love that."

Lennox smoothed Jon's hair. "First, you'll suck Viola's nipples while I introduce her to arse play. After we've made her come a few times, I'm going to fuck you."

"Please. Yes, sir."

Moving onto the bed, Viola settled herself so she lay on her side facing Jon. Then she draped one thigh over his so her dripping cunt nudged his hard cock, and she was also fully open for Lennox's wicked touch. Jon groaned as she teased him, but inflicted a little vengeance of his own as he cupped her breasts and began to play, licking and sucking her nipples until she whimpered. However, that whimper soon turned into a guttural moan as Lennox crouched behind her to lash the tender petals of her labia with his tongue while two fingers sank into her sheath.

Oh God.

She loved having her nipples sucked and cunt licked, but at the same time? Incredible. Never mind those downstairs hearing her orgasm, more like everyone in Hertfordshire.

Closing her eyes briefly, Viola wallowed in the sensation of being worshipped. This was how a plump woman should be bedded; her body a bountiful feast for tongues and mouths to savor. Next, Lennox's honey-wet fingers trailed up to her back entrance, and when he circled it over and over, pressing a little deeper each time, she wriggled her bottom so he would stop teasing and start penetrating.

Lennox laughed. "Patience is a virtue."

"No, it bloody well isn't," she retorted, turning her head to glare at him. "I want to come."

Sweet Jon sucked harder on her nipples and Viola cried out as jolts of pleasure arrowed directly to her clitoris. Wretched Lennox continued to torment her with the circling and pressing, occasionally giving her a fingertip, but swiftly withdrawing again.

"Something to say, my darling?" he crooned.

Viola panted, clinging to Jon as her only rock in an impending pleasure storm. "You're going to make *me* beg, aren't you?"

Lennox trailed kisses along her thigh and hip. "Tell your master what you need and he'll provide it."

"Finger my backside. Let me come. *Please, sir.*"

Finally, he took pity on her. Good God. How could a man be so dexterous with both hands? Having two fingers twisting inside her soaked cunt was nearly enough to steal her wits; but when he eased two more into her tight rear passage, the resulting burn and stretch, the glorious friction of the digits rubbing through the thinnest of walls, had her sobbing his name.

Close. So close.

Without warning, Jon cupped her mound with one big hand, pressing directly against her throbbing clitoris. Then he bit her nipple.

Viola screamed in ecstasy as shocking pleasure bombarded her from all sides, lifting her up and turning her inside out and upside down in a writhing, bucking dance of sensation that seemed to last an eternity. Eventually, Lennox and Jon withdrew their hands and kissed her tenderly, then Viola closed her legs and cuddled between them, unsure if she would ever be able to move again.

This. This was the love she'd dreamed of. The exquisite pleasure. The total acceptance.

And it was absolutely worth waiting for.

IT WAS RATHER astonishing how a short sojourn to Hertfordshire had completely changed his life. He'd started writing the play of his heart. Met and fallen head over heels for his original muse: darling Viola. Had his hidden past abruptly exposed, yet somehow made peace with it. Flogged Jon, his closest friend and patron, the man who had twined around his heart and healed it with sweetness.

And now they were going to fuck for the first time.

Lennox breathed deeply in a futile attempt to calm the fierce lust swirling through his body. After penetrating Viola's cunt and arse and feeling her inner walls nearly crush his fingers as she came, he now needed Jon's full sexual submission.

"Viola, my love," he said gruffly. "I need you to move up to the pillows so I can fuck our pet's fine flogged arse."

"I hope you know you're asking the moon, wanting my limbs to work," she replied in an amused yet exhausted voice as she crawled forward and flopped onto the pile of pillows, all wanton hair, flushed and dewy skin, and sated green gaze.

Siren. There really was no other word to describe her.

"Now, up on your hands and knees, Jon," commanded Lennox. "Let me see my handiwork."

Jon hesitated and looked beseechingly at Viola. "May I kiss your cunt, madam? I need your taste in my mouth while master fucks me."

When she nodded permission, Jon crouched between her legs, bending his head to delicately lap the honey from her swollen, dark pink folds. "Mmmm. Thank you."

Lennox stifled a grin, even though the ache of his cock had reached a torturous level. It seemed the poets were correct, damn them. Bedsport was a thousand times lustier and more fulfilling when you indulged with those you loved.

As soon as Jon was positioned on the bed, Lennox knelt behind him and lovingly traced the flogger welts until Jon gasped and spread his legs in blatant invitation. Taking pity on them both, Lennox reached for the oil from the accessory bag. Uncorking the bottle, he poured a little into his palm to coat his engorged cock and help ease the way. "I'm going to take you now."

"Good," purred Viola. "I'm looking forward to the show."

Jon shuddered. "I've dreamed of this so many times, Lennox. Of being owned by you in every way. But it's even better than I imagined because madam owns me too."

"Damned right I do."

"I always wanted your submission," said Lennox as he lowered his head to kiss Jon's shoulders and down his spine, nodding in satisfaction when the other man's hips jerked. "And the right woman to make our trio complete. To have you both is...indescribable."

"Please, sir," said Jon hoarsely. "Please fuck me."

"Very well."

Lennox pushed two oiled fingers into Jon's arse, gently thrusting and withdrawing them until the young lord moaned and arched his back.

"Master is very talented at that, isn't he?" said Viola as she threaded her fingers through Jon's hair and tugged. "Those fingers are magical with more than a quill."

Jon nodded frantically. "I want more."

Lennox paused. "Demands?"

"Please, please, please may I have your cock, sir. I need this so badly."

You and me both.

With one hand gripping Jon's hip to hold him in place, Lennox took his oil-slick cock and carefully penetrated Jon's tight hole.

They both groaned.

Christ, the sensation. A heated pulsing pressure as that narrow channel both stretched to welcome his invading cock and clamped down to resist it. Yet Lennox continued on, his hips circling in a diabolically lazy movement that would keep Jon on the precipice of pleasure and pain, but not allow him to come.

"Tell me, pet," he said, withdrawing a few inches then easing back in. "How does it feel to have your arse stuffed full with my cock?"

Jon panted, his fingers nearly clawing the quilt. "I'll do anything. Anything at all, if you just fuck me roughly."

Viola giggled as she cupped his cheek. "Be more specific, Jon. You want Lennox to come in you, don't you? To mark you as his. Should I provide a temporary collar?"

"Yes," Jon said raggedly. "Yes, yes, yes. Collar me, madam, while master comes in me. Please. *Please.*"

Lennox exchanged a glance with Viola. She nodded, curved her hand around Jon's throat, and squeezed gently. At the same time, Lennox forced his cock deeper into Jon's arse, thrusting in quick, hard shoves that showed his patron no mercy. It felt extraordinary, and hearing Jon's mindless ecstasy, seeing his arms strain and shoulders flex as he rocked in time, soon brought Lennox close to orgasm.

Reaching around, he took Jon's cock in hand and pumped it firmly, using the oil from his fingers to create a smooth glide. "Come for me," he commanded. "Now."

Jon bucked with a wild cry and seed erupted all over Lennox's fingers. His patron's full surrender demanded nothing less than everything he had to give; Lennox thrust hard and came forcefully, endlessly inside Jon, the release so powerful he roared his pleasure.

It might have been minutes or hours later, but he carefully withdrew his softened cock, before taking one of the cravats from the earlier bondage session and using it to clean them both. Then, with a supremely satisfied sigh, Lennox curled around Jon and reached across to take Viola's hand. "Everyone well?"

"What day is it?" asked Jon dazedly, his cheek resting on Viola's belly. "Where am I?"

He chuckled. "In bed, pet. With your master and mistress."

"So, paradise."

"Exactly," said Viola. "And I definitely want to have my backside fucked. Very soon. That was...ooooh."

"You'll need training to take both of us, darling," said Lennox. "We'll purchase a few dildos to start...don't pout at me, Jon, I'll get more for you as well. My God, I can see you'll require regular discipline lest you turn wayward."

His patron beamed. "I cannot wait to begin our life together as a threesome."

"One thing though," said Viola, her gaze momentarily uncertain. "After my first husband, I...uh...never thought I'd have the desire to marry again. But with you two it is different. And I would adore to leave behind the name Prescott forever. That's not me. I don't want to be her anymore."

Lennox pondered the issue. No one understood better than him about leaving bad memories related to a certain name behind. "While you'll be wife to us both, if you officially wed Jon, you would outrank Pauline. And if you took my surname as well, the duke and duchess's heads would actually explode. Farewell Viola Prescott, all hail Viola Townsend-Grant. How does that sound?"

"I think it sounds perfect and would adore to wed you," said Jon shyly. "But whatever you wish, madam."

Her whole face lit up. "Viola Townsend-Grant. It will look just so on a playbill. Well, if our beloved actually finishes the otherworldly story..."

Both Jon and Viola peeped up at him, batting their lashes.

Lennox mock scowled. "Trust me to fall in love with my patron and my muse. Support and inspiration every day. Damn it. There will indeed be pages. In fact..."

Rising from the bed, he sauntered across to the chamber desk.

Already he could feel his characters clearing their throats, ready to share the rest of their lusty fantasy.

Lennox smiled fondly at his lovers as he picked up his quill. The road to this point had been long and arduous, but they had indeed found paradise.

With love, all dreams were possible.

This threesome would live happily ever after.

EPILOGUE

"THERE ARE SO MANY PEOPLE OUTSIDE. HOW ARE THERE SO MANY PEOPLE?"

Jon grinned as he trailed his wife from one end of the dressing room to the other, wooden comb in hand. Each time she paused at the window to view the endless line of carriages in the estate driveway, he managed to untangle another section of her hair. Soon he could attend to the next task on his list: checking that every flower in her crown was firmly affixed. "It is a scandalous and uncensored new play from Lennox Townsend. It features Viola Townsend-Grant, the most sensual and beautiful dancer the realm has ever seen, in her first performance for a decade. Of course the public are here."

Viola turned and kissed him, before straightening the embroidered leather collar fastened about his neck. "Are they here for the play, or to gain first-hand gossip on the most notorious household of three since the Devonshires and Elizabeth Foster? We did stir one hell of a scandal."

"It might be a little of that. Say five percent. I never thought I'd be grateful to Falston, but his exposure as a cheat at the race track was priceless in its timing to distract the *ton*. Henrietta still won't receive callers. I find my sympathy for their plight remains…negligible."

"As it should be. Wretched pair."

"Far more importantly, how are you feeling?" Jon asked, as he carefully removed the last tangle from her hair then tucked the comb back into the small satchel belted around his waist.

"I'm so excited," Viola said, twirling in place. "I cannot believe opening night has finally arrived. I'm desperate to put that tunic on and perform."

"I know," Jon said as he began massaging her robe-covered shoulders. The gold muslin tunic she would wear onstage was so fine and prone to smudges that it only went on two minutes prior to curtain call. "I'm excited too."

"Have you eaten? You mustn't forget. I worry when you start adding further tasks to that already endless list. Here, have some fruit cake," said Viola, reaching for a plate resting on a side table.

"Yes, madam." He smiled and dutifully ate the delicious cake. The way she cared for him and Lennox was quite simply glorious. In fact, Lennox almost tolerated their coddling now, although he still retained his legendary rumpled curmudgeon persona before noon.

Viola tapped her cheek. "I wonder how Master is faring. It's one thing for us to say *The Flame of Passion* is his best work ever, but he'll want to see and hear the audience to believe it."

Jon chuckled. "I am away to see him next. I think between the pair of you, you've paced to the seaside and back."

"Go on, then," she replied, laughing. "I need to have more rouge slathered on my face, anyway. But I know your preparation will be perfect. Be sure to give Lennox an abundance of kisses."

"I love you," said Jon. "You'll be incomparable."

His wife curved her hand around his arse. "And I love you, my precious pet. Just remember we three have supper plans after the performance."

A heartfelt moan escaped. Food, flogging, and fucking: the actual holy trinity. "Yes, madam."

After he'd checked her fairy princess crown, Viola sat at her dressing table and waggled her fingers in farewell. Jon then hurried from the room and down the hallway toward the cavernous ballroom. There was a lot to think about tonight, but thankfully the burden was shared, for he had a team of bold Brigands to assist. A month after he and Viola had wed by special license, and with Lennox purchased this estate, a carriage near-groaning with trunks had pulled up to reveal Timothy and Gillian Talbot, Piers Vincent, and Reuben Calder. They had informed Viola that the Prescotts were doing terribly and life at the boarding house had become insufferably dull since her departure, so they'd come to stay and assist with the new venture. Thus, alongside a small army of maids and footmen, the Talbots were minding the props, Piers the tickets and money, and Reuben the costume repairs.

Jon adored the amusing, naughty Brigands who had warmly welcomed him and Lennox into their created family, although they really did insist on tea at eleven o'clock and God help the world if it was a second late.

As soon as he rounded the corner, that small army converged on him.

"Lord Jon, the curtain cord is twisted!"

"Lord Jon, someone spilled blue paint!"

"Lord Jon, we need more benches!"

He paused, not in anxiety, but elation. It was impossible to imagine ever growing tired of this colorful and challenging theatrical world, not when he felt so useful each day, and so cherished each night. Even when they weren't in the same room he had the clasp of Lennox and Viola's love around his neck, and to be so secure had done wonders for his confidence. He'd found his voice, although crockery would never truly be safe around him.

Once he'd attended to the pressing issues, Jon made his way to the private box with a premium view of the constructed stage. Below him the string quartet began to play, signaling the start of the performance.

Lennox had already discarded his cravat and sat perched on an over-stuffed chair in black breeches and embroidered gold jacket, drumming a rolled-up copy of the script against his knee. On a chain around his neck swung the guinea representing the beloved family who would live forever in his heart. "Well, what do you think?"

"It's going to be magnificent, sir," said Jon, as he sat down on a large velvet cushion in front of the chair and kissed Lennox's hand. "From me and Viola."

"I needed that," said Lennox, affectionately stroking Jon's hair.

Minutes later, the opening scene began...one that included a certain red-haired fairy princess tempting the audience unmercifully with her voluptuous curves as she twirled and strutted about the stage.

Jon grinned as cheers and applause almost lifted the damned roof. "Our wife is having a marvelous time. And the audience is loving *The Flame of Passion*. Listen to them!"

Lennox relaxed back in his chair. "My compliments to the theater manager. All's well that ends well, as the bard would say."

Indeed. Life could not get any better than this.

The end.

Need another scorching hot MMF historical romance?

Travel to medieval Scotland with Wicked Passions.

ALSO BY NICOLA DAVIDSON

Wickedly Wed series

Duke in Darkness (#1)

The Best Marquess (#2)

The London Lords series

To Love a Hellion (#1)

Rake to Riches (#2)

Tempting the Marquess (#3)

Fallen trilogy

Surrender to Sin (#1)

The Devil's Submission (#2)

The Seduction of Viscount Vice (#3)

Surrey SFS quintet

My Lady's Lover (#1)

To Tame a Wicked Widow (#2)

My Lord, Lady, and Gentleman (#3)

At His Lady's Command (#4)

A Very Surrey SFS Christmas (#5)

Surrey SFS - The Complete Series boxset

Regency Standalones

Her Virgin Duke

Duke For Hire

Mistletoe Mistress

Joy to the Earl

Once Upon a Promise

ABOUT THE AUTHOR

USA Today bestselling author NICOLA DAVIDSON worked for many years in media and government communications, but hasn't looked back since she decided writing erotic historical romance was infinitely more fun.

When not chained to a computer she can be found ambling along one of New Zealand's beautiful beaches, cheering on the All Blacks rugby team, history geeking on the internet, or daydreaming. If this includes dessert —even better!

Nicola's books have appeared in *USA Today*, *NPR*, and *Entertainment Weekly*.

Keep up with Nicola's news on social media or her website www.nicola-davidson.com.

You can sign up for Nicola's newsletter here!

MONSIEUR X

ADRIANA HERRERA

1

Paris, 1888

TONIGHT WAS FOR PLEASURE, JOSEPH CANTOR MARSHALL REMINDED himself as he stood at the threshold of one of the most fiercely guarded secrets in Paris—Le Bureau Là-Bas. It was the enterprise of the infamous Cisse-Kelly siblings, the Irish-Senegalese proprietors of the luxurious and scandalous Parisian brothel, Le Bureau. Like its sister establishment, Là-Bas had been created to provide the most exclusive clientele in Paris with every carnal fantasy they could devise—and those they scarcely dared to voice out loud. And while Le Bureau served any client who wished to spend some time in more conventional erotic pursuits, this new locale specialized in those whose tastes were a bit more unortho-dox. There were, of course, many brothels in Paris catering to patrons craving a little pain with their pleasure, but there was none that did it quite so lavishly.

Cantor's best friend Dionisio had spent the last few months persuading him to attend Jeudi Noir, the masked soiree hosted by Là-Bas the first and third Thursday of every month. He'd been tempted, but unlike Le Bureau, Là-Bas was notorious for reasons that could cause a man like himself to gain a reputation. Cantor was fastidious when it came to his personal life. His clients and his admirers only knew a curated version of who he was. And being seen at this sort of place would surely send tongues wagging.

As the most sought-after portrait artist in Europe, he was aware of how fortunate he was to have reached his level of success, how fickle the wealthy and titled could be when it came to those they deemed as "the help." Which he most certainly was. Help to whom they paid a fortune for the privilege of having him capture their likeness, but the help nonetheless. For that reason, he had cultivated his public persona meticulously. Salacious enough to provoke curiosity, but never anything to be considered unsavory. His background—a nomad born in Florence to a Cuban opera singer and a Creole architect—was a disadvantage among people who held on to their prejudices as fiercely as they did their titles. Therefore, attending orgies, masked or not, was something he rarely indulged in. Too many things could go wrong.

And he already had plenty to worry about, like the fact that his muse had all but deserted him in the last few months. Which was how he'd even arrived at the decision to come here this evening. After hours of scarcely getting any work done, he'd decided he needed to do something drastic. All day he'd stood in front of the empty canvas which had been taunting him for months, with literally nothing to show for his work. It had taken Cantor years to build up his clientele and gain the notice of the right people in London and Paris. His efforts had yielded fruit, but his renown came with unexpected burdens. Although that wasn't exactly true. He'd anticipated that success, if it came, would have some costs. He just never imagined the price of fame and fortune to be quite so steep. The pressure to continue rendering dynamic, complex portraits when it felt like he was drawing the same subject again and again was . . . crushing.

It was uninspiring.

What was worse, he was almost out of time to turn in a piece to the Académie des Beaux Arts for his entry at the Exposition Universelle, which would be held the next year. It was a once-in-a-lifetime opportunity, but he could not settle on what to paint. The committee who requested his participation had asked for something that reflected Cantor's inspiration, which was easier said than done. He knew what *he* would like to do, but it would likely offend the sensibilities of the committee. Not that it mattered. He was already two months late. Cantor could not remember the last time something had truly captured his attention, could not even recall the last time he'd been stopped in his tracks by something so captivating, so enthralling that it demanded he bring it to life on a canvas.

Even the city had begun to feel stifling. Perhaps he needed to leave Paris. It had been almost two years since his last adventure—six months traveling through Mexico and the Caribbean. His journeys had filled him with colors and textures to paint and draw. But the vibrancy of those parts of the world was not what the committee expected from him.

A few hours of physical pleasure, of finding a willing—ideally eager —man in whom he could lose himself for a while, would put him in a more affable state of mind. Then perhaps he'd go back and face the empty canvas. A good fuck always energized Cantor. He found great pleasure in giving a lover what they needed, no matter what that was. He felt cleansed and renewed after using a body at his leisure. It wiped clean the slate of his cluttered thoughts and helped him focus.

He desperately needed that.

With that in mind, he took the steps up to the mansion located in the 11th arrondissement. To an outside observer, the building looked like any other Parisian grand home, except for the number 12 placed on top of the door. The plaque was oversized and painted in bright red, white, and yellow, a marker for the residents of the street and potential patrons of the business being done behind the stately doors. In Paris, the sex trade was not something one necessarily had to hide. The proprietors of these establishments only needed to make sure it was clear to passersby what they would find inside. Unless, of course, like Cantor, one preferred engaging in such pursuits with members of the same sex. Then one had to be far more discreet.

Which was exactly the kind of socializing Cantor craved. After he entered Le Bureau, Cantor walked down the length of the building until he arrived at the entrance of a private alcove. The room, guarded by two men, looked like a small parlor. A place one came to for a respite from the noise. The only thing that appeared out of the ordinary were the two large blokes flanking the entryway—blokes almost as large as Cantor, who stood over six feet and four inches in his stockings.

"Bon soir," Cantor said amiably to one of them, pulling out the sanguine card that served as an invitation.

After a quick inspection, the guard stepped aside and waved him into the room. Cantor reached the blood-red wall in only a few steps and knocked three times, waited a moment, then knocked another three. Not a second later, a section of the wall opened, allowing him entry into the winter garden which served as the bridge between Le Bureau and Là-Bas.

The way into the other brothel was actually the rear entrance of a mansion the Cisse-Kelly siblings purchased a couple of years earlier. The Irish-Senegalese twins had spared no expense to create an experience for their patrons that was simply unmatched. The garden was filled with tropical trees and flowers they'd personally collected from their travels. The path to the door on the other side of the garden was lined with large banana trees which made a natural canopy, enhancing the feeling of entering a new climate. *One level further down in Hades*, Cantor thought. He intended to indulge in all the glorious wickedness being offered.

It was only his second time here, but he already knew the steps. He handed his card to a woman behind a lectern who offered him a radiant smile as she plucked it from his hand. Arresting in Le Bureau burgundy, she was as visually lush as everything else in the room. The cups holding her breasts were embellished with an intricate design of peonies in silver thread and black beading, and the effect was striking against her richly brown skin. For jewelry, she wore a collar around her neck, the gold ring on it set with black diamonds. Nothing here was subtle. But one did not come to Là-Bas for innuendo. The accessories a person chose to wear communicated to other patrons what kind of activities they preferred to indulge in. Cantor, for one, appreciated being able to know where he should spend his energies.

Cantor continued to observe her as she examined his invitation. She was intriguing, a feast for the eyes. Even to one whose tastes did not gravitate in that direction. The lines of her face were exquisite. Cantor's hand itched, instinctively reaching for the small sketch pad and piece of charcoal he always carried in his pocket. Not that he would try. In a place that demanded absolute discretion, no one would appreciate him walking around, capturing their countenance. And with two mildly menacing men on either side of the woman, Cantor certainly was not going to ask if she minded. Regardless, it had been a good idea to come here. The muse was already calling to him, and he had not even gone inside.

"Bienvenu Monsieur Marshall, votre nom pour la soirée?" His card did not bear any personal information, only a number, but Cantor was certain his full name and membership details were jotted down on the ledger lying open on the lectern. For the small fortune he'd paid for entry, a personalized greeting was the least one could expect. And he supposed there were not many bearded men four inches above six feet with golden brown skin walking into this place either.

"Achilles," he told her, using Dionisio's nickname for him. *You're both oversized, arrogant, prodigious bastards who like to show off*, his friend had said. Cantor could not exactly deny it, and for an occasion like this one, it worked beautifully. The name of the Greek demigod would display his expectations and preferences for the evening well enough. He *was* big and commanding, and he liked control. He also relished taking care of those he loved. But after one too many disappointments, he'd given up on finding someone whose needs matched his.

And it wasn't only because society seemed unable to digest the idea of people of the same sex falling in love—although that was tiresome. But as the child of a Black father and a Cuban mother, Cantor never quite had the luxury of being blissfully indifferent to the prejudices of the world. There were still many places where he was not allowed entry, and it had nothing to do with whom he slept. Still, being a man with his preferences meant that he'd never be able to show affection for his beloved openly without extreme caution. But it *could* be done. Cantor had quite a few friends who were happily living in a variety of arrangements that were far from what was considered traditional. And though there were limitations, they were content. Satisfied.

He'd never thought of himself as someone who would crave that kind of domesticity—he'd always thrived on finding new things to feed his curiosity—but lately he yearned for something deeper. He would not likely find it by patronizing brothels, but he had to be pragmatic.

The real problem was that the right man for him simply didn't exist.

Cantor *had* tried. Over the years, he'd attempted to bring lovers whom he'd met at clubs into his private life. Those fruitless efforts had worked as effectively as trying to settle a fish on dry land. A lot of gasping, followed by even more flailing. And then there were the other prospects. The painfully polite, fastidiously groomed high society gentlemen he'd met at salons or soirées hosted by friends, all who saw Cantor as a prized exotic bull to play with, didn't share his tastes in the bedroom, or simply left him cold. No matter how much he yearned for companionship, enlightening aristocrats on his humanity was not his idea of flirtatious banter. Even with his reputation as a man with an appetite for carnal pleasures, he was not sure he'd survive being accused of something untoward by an aristo.

It was not ideal, and it could be lonely, but recently, he'd chosen to focus on enjoying the things he did have: a wildly successful and extremely lucrative career as a portrait artist. Money to buy him an invitation to places like Le Bureau. Good friends and a few family members who loved him and accepted him for who he was.

For any man, this made for not merely a good life, but a life to treasure. He would not be greedy, even if he still felt like something essential was missing.

"Monsieur Achilles." The hostess's melodious voice cut through his reverie. He lowered his gaze to the tray on the table she was pointing to and saw an array of neatly laid out masks in black and gold. Gold, the hostess reminded him, was for those who preferred a more submissive role in their erotic play. Black was for those who favored dominance. Cantor plucked the simplest of the lot in the black and turned so the woman could secure it on his head. After a few tugs, she announced with a succinct "bon" that he was ready, and Cantor was ushered through a set of glass doors.

The room he stepped into gave him the impression of an unfinished silo. It was a perfect semicircle with a tall ceiling, from which dangled a very long and sumptuous bronze chandelier dripping with black and red crystals. The only thing in the room besides the candelabrum was a curved black marble staircase leading to a mezzanine. As Cantor ascended, he was distracted briefly by the glittering red fleurs-de-lis on the slate wallpaper, all shimmering like jewels. They were a reminder that with each step he took, he was leaving Paris behind and entering a place where those within made the rules.

When he reached the landing, he found a woman and a man in blood-red masks on either side of a threshold painted in black. Without a word, one of them pushed open the massive black door and stepped aside, welcoming Cantor. Frissons of excitement crawled up his spine as he made his way inside. As much as he wanted that special connection to someone who only belonged to him, he also enjoyed a good fuck.

People didn't realize the discipline and the physical labor that went into his work. Cantor strived to become a master at what he did, doggedly honing his craft. It meant hours, days, standing on his feet, straining his eyesight, holding his arms at awkward angles until they felt like they would fall out of their sockets. His art was vigorous, mentally draining work. He loved and excelled at it, but when the day was done, he needed something . . . restorative.

A gritty, breathless, frenzied copulation worked wonders.

Cantor was in the mood for unmitigated debauchery this evening, and he set about finding someone in the room on whom he could unleash all his pent-up energy. He took in the space, spotting lovers in corners, smiling faces, dark stares, and even a particularly enthusiastic coupling in plain view of the attendants. He observed it all with a trained eye. It was second nature now to take things in as a frame, just as he did when he was mulling over a scene for a painting. He'd block the shadow, the light, identify all the interesting bits, the elements that would transform a painting into something unforgettable.

Cantor picked up a coupe of champagne from one of the masked servers and did a circuit of the periphery of the room. He'd heard from Dionisio that the space had formerly served as a ballroom. Which made sense, given its size. It was large enough to easily accommodate a hundred people, but tonight, there were only a few dozen. The ceiling was spectacularly high, with smaller versions of the grand chandelier lined up across its expanse. The lighting was sufficiently bright for one to make out faces, but not quite enough to see what was occurring in the darker corners. The furnishings were upholstered in a sumptuous velvet of that same deep red that was Le Bureau's signature color. In the low light, the dark blue flecked wallpaper with gold leaf gave one the feeling you'd stepped into the starry night sky.

Along the walls were banquettes with tables and additional chairs for sitting—and any other uses those invited to Jeudi Noir devised. It all looked entirely conventional. But if one happened to look at the ceiling, they'd see that each table could easily be hidden from view. If one found a willing partner and things became heated enough to need some privacy—not that it was necessary, public sex was very much on the menu here—it was as simple as closing the thick red velvet curtains hanging from the golden circular rods over every table. Leather restraints, if they were needed, were accessible under the chairs. And every table had convenient compartments equipped with all the implements required for indulging in a bit of depravity, for those who liked to be more creative in their play. It was truly a place where a man felt free to explore his darkest desires.

As it usually went at this kind of gathering, the term "formal wear" was interpreted loosely. He'd donned his evening dress, but some of the patrons opted for less constricting attire, partial nudity being commonplace. His attention was drawn to a beautiful dark-skinned woman in a black mask on the far side of the room. She was wearing a frothy silver skirt with a matching corset that did not quite cover her breasts. Her nipples were pierced with what looked like gold hoops. At that moment, one of them was caught between the teeth of a lovely young blonde in a gold mask. The dominant had the blonde's hair fisted in her hand as she used a flogger on her lover's exposed bottom. Their enthusiastic play was gathering a small circle of onlookers, which only seemed to spur the blonde on. Despite women not being what Cantor was after, he could not deny they were incendiary together.

"Dear God, Joseph Cantor, you couldn't wear something that revealed the slightest bit of personality?"

Cantor smirked, shaking his head at Dionisio's rebuke. With his face still turned in the direction of the two women, he gave a sideways look to his friend who, like he, had opted for evening dress. Except Dionisio's was all black. Tie, shirt, waistcoat, all of it the color of pitch. Likewise, his face was half covered in a black mask with small horns that made him look positively demonic—his long sable hair was tied in a queue at the base of his neck. The finishing touch to his ensemble was a pair of gold loops in his ears.

"I don't need to dress like Beelzebub to attract attention, Dionisio,"

Cantor said pointedly, to which his friend responded with a booming laugh.

"But if I don't, how will all the docile young ladies looking for a dominant know who to approach?" he inquired, and Cantor could only smile and shake his head as they continued to watch the crowd. They made quite the pair of wallflowers—*walltrees*, more like.

Like Cantor, Dionisio's father was from the United States, while his mother was Brazilian. They'd met as adolescents at one of the salons their parents attended and became fast friends. Both their families had socialized within a set of expatriates in Florence. While Cantor's family was merely financially comfortable, Dionisio's parents came from lavish wealth. His father had been the youngest son of a well-established Bostonian family, and his mother was a Brazilian heiress. As far as temperaments went, they were opposites. Cantor was observant, not prone to taking risks, while Dionisio jumped into things fearlessly. Despite this, their friendship had now lasted over half their lives. They balanced each other, Cantor thought. Cantor pulled Dionisio back when necessary, while his friend gave him a nudge occasionally . . . like tonight.

"Truly, Cantor, these evenings are supposed to be about exploring fantasies. You're dressed like you've just come from dinner at some boring banker's house. And you're supposed to be the premier portrait artist in Europe."

"I am not that tonight. Tonight, I am Achilles, looking to find an amenable Patroclus."

"Oh, God," Dionisio drawled in a teasing tone. "You do lay it on thick."

"I am not trying to be coy. I am trying to find a man who is willing and able to engage in extreme depravity with me. The clearer that is, the easier things will proceed. I just prefer not to dress in the equivalent of a visual foghorn, like some people." Dionisio choked and Cantor grinned. "What name are you using?"

"Mephistopheles." This time it was Cantor's laughter that roared around them.

"Then what are you giving me grief for?" he asked after taking another sip from his glass. Dionisio's lascivious grin was his only answer. Cantor was about to ask his friend if he had a spiked tail somewhere in his trousers when he spotted a half-hidden lone figure across the room from where they stood. His naked back was muscular—not heavily so, more like the muscles one developed from swimming or fencing—and he had a tattoo that ran across his spine. Also not unusual. The practice of adding art to the body was becoming a fashion among the aristocrats. He couldn't quite read the tattooed words from this far, though.

"Mm . . . let the games begin." Dionisio's suggestive tone barely registered. Cantor could not take his eyes off the stranger. His pulse throbbed, a fluttery anticipation fizzing under his skin.

Let me see you, he urged silently. Then the man finally turned, and Cantor saw the golden mask. His entire body stiffened as though electricity coursed through it. It was a simple mask from what Cantor could see at a distance, and it covered most of his face but for his mouth and jaw.

"That is very much your cup of tea, Achilles," Dionisio intoned, and Cantor grunted in agreement. He quickly drained his glass and placed it on the small table behind him, eyes still on the mysterious man. He noticed that in addition to the tattoo, the man wore a leather band around his neck, about two inches thick, with a metal—possibly gold— circle in front. Cantor's mouth went dry at the thought of all the ways he could use that. He let his gaze roam down to the hairless, sculpted chest. Two little gold hoops glinted in the dark from his pierced nipples, a small gold chain suspended between them. He had to bite back a moan when he imagined pulling on the thin metal while he fucked that sweet mouth with his cock.

Come on, Cantor thought. *Let me see those pretty eyes.* And as if he willed it, the boy's gaze landed on Cantor. His body jolted to attention as the gaze turned piercing, seeking him out from across the room. They locked eyes for just a second before the smaller man cast his demurely down. He thought then that whatever he'd felt earlier had not been electricity. *This* was. Cantor's blood heated, lust burning in his gut. Oh yes, this was going to be very good indeed.

"Are you all right?" Dionisio teased. "You're practically vibrating."

"I'm going to . . . ," Cantor said distractedly, his fingers already moving as if attempting to capture what his eyes were taking in.

"Go," Dionisio urged. "I see a promising situation I could probably insinuate myself into," he said, pointing at the blonde and the corseted

Black woman from earlier. Cantor barely nodded, his feet propelling him across the room, eyes fixed on the shirtless man.

As he took the final step toward his quarry, he drew in a silent, long breath. As he got close enough to really see the details, he observed that the man's skin was bronzed and not the typical sickly pallor that high society seemed to prefer. This was either his natural complexion, or he spent a lot of time in the outdoors. His hair was longer than Cantor had initially thought, and it was free of any product to tame it. Wild curls whirled around his head like a fluffy halo.

Cantor was enthralled . . . eager. He wanted to touch, but those were not the rules. First, he had to be invited to do so. He opened his mouth and found that he was nervous, which wouldn't do. He was the one in charge here.

"Are you free to play?" he asked, quick and to the point.

"Perhaps." The man's voice was soft, but firm. And though the stranger's response to Cantor had not exactly been an invitation, he couldn't remember the last time a man had looked at him with such fire.

"I'll come closer so you can get a better look," Cantor teased as he took a step toward the other man and observed those plump lips part slightly. "May I?" Cantor asked as he lifted a hand.

A single nod. A step forward. Cantor traced the man's top lip with his thumb. His hands were not soft. They were roughened from handling turpentine and harsh chemicals and had gained calluses from holding paintbrushes and pencils for hours at a time.

But he didn't think this boy wanted soft.

"Are you free to play now?" he asked again, trying very hard not to sound overeager. Heavy-lidded dark eyes, adorned with kohl, focused on him. Cantor's cock stiffened painfully in his trousers. He didn't mind a good chase as long as he got what he wanted in the end. But when the focus of his attention finally spoke, there was no playfulness in his voice.

"First, I need to know a few things." His voice was very soft, almost a whisper, and though he was trying to sound stern, Cantor could hear the nervousness. If he dismissed him or mocked this man's attempt to set some ground rules, he'd lose him.

"All right." Cantor nodded.

"I won't be made to feel ashamed for what I desire." Cantor dipped his head in understanding. "I will submit to you, and I will take what you give me, as long as we both know we're doing this together." Cantor's spine straightened at the sharpness in the man's words. Someone had misused this man.

"Nothing happens unless you want it. Everything about this will be a joint effort." Cantor saw those bronzed shoulders relax. "*But* if we're doing this, I will take the reins," Cantor warned, using his finger to tug softly on the chain—which elicited a lusty gasp.

"I'd like that," the man said, licking his lips, and Cantor gritted his teeth to keep from bringing him in for a kiss.

"I'd like that, what?"

"Sir," he said with an adorable gulp. Cantor wanted hear him hoarse and wrung out. Voice raspy from taking his cock.

"You can call me Achilles." A shiver ran through the man at Cantor's request. Interesting. "What do I call you, other than boy?"

"X," the man said succinctly.

"Only X." A nod. "And not what's written on your back? I couldn't see from where I was standing."

X's lips lifted into a tiny smile and he shook his head. "The tattoo, that's the . . ." Another nervous gulp. Oh, he was sweet. It would be delicious to utterly ravish him. "The psyche," he finally explained, now truly capturing Cantor's attention.

What was inked on the man's back amounted to life, the breath, the soul. Now Cantor truly needed to see what the tattoo said. Before he could ask, X turned, and soon Cantor was the one shivering.

Agapitos.

The letters were done in a heavy Gothic style. It was no wonder that saying the name Achilles got the reaction it did. For men who preferred men, that word could have many meanings, but it all boiled down to the fact that the Agapitos was the beloved. The one to cherish and care for. And that was something that called to Cantor's very soul, a primal urge always prickling right under his skin. He would never be brave enough to etch it *into* his skin. To let the world see what he yearned for. But X had been, and that made Cantor want him all the more.

"Why did you choose to get this?" Cantor knew one of the rules was not to ask personal questions. These were supposed to be anonymous encounters. But he was curious. It was one thing to reveal your desires in this place, but quite another to emblazon them across your back. The other man's shoulder rose in answer at first, but after a moment, he offered a quiet but firm answer.

"I wanted to do something that would speak for me even when I was not feeling brave enough to do so for myself. I am not ashamed of who I am, and whatever words the moralists wield at men like me to remind us of our aberrant desires, I know who I am. Men like us already spend too much time hiding from the world. I refuse to hide from myself."

A long, shuddering breath escaped Cantor's lips at that impassioned declaration.

"Strong are those who are not afraid to show their vulnerabilities," he said, running the pad of his fingers over the black letters on X's back.

"I don't see my desire to submit to another as a weakness," X said sharply. "And if that's your opinion, then—"

"That's not what I said," Cantor said, frustrated with himself for dampening the mood. He was usually better at this, but the man's boldness, strength, and smoky eyes had turned Cantor's mind. He searched for words to fix this. "I said vulnerabilities, not weakness. It takes a strong man to expose his secrets to another." Much more than strength —it took conviction and defiance. "I respect that."

The smaller man sniffed, his masked countenance still hidden from view, but those golden, bare shoulders softened infinitesimally. Cantor clenched and unclenched his hands at his sides to keep from touching. If this was going to happen between them, X would need to take the next step.

At length he turned to Cantor, the tension around his mouth smoothed somewhat.

"You're not going to regale me with a list of reasons why you are granting me a favor by indulging me? How fortunate I am that you are willing to lower yourself to this kind of play?" The resigned bitterness in the other man took him aback, and fury rose in him. There were men that did this. That hated themselves for who they were and took it out on the very people they desired.

"I don't make a habit of parroting those who revile me," he told X, and he saw those eyes widen in surprise. That paired with a small smile, told Cantor he'd said the right thing. "I also don't much care to hear about who will be saved or who will be damned from the same people who for centuries benefited from atrocities that can never be atoned for."

That won him a real smile that made a flame settle right behind his sternum, warm and flickery.

X looked up at him for a long moment, as if reconsidering him, then moved closer. Cantor was much taller, almost half a foot. Standing this close X had to turn his head up to look at him. When Cantor leaned down, he finally got a better look at that mouth. His own went dry at the sight.

"Are you going to make me beg, Sir?" he asked. That dark, challenging gaze lifted to Cantor's. "Will you use me, ruin me, and then put me back together?"

Harsh breaths sawed in and out of Cantor's lungs as the other man spun a web around him. He was the dominant here, he reminded himself, then clapped a hand around the back of X's neck. A sweet little sound of pleasure escaped his lips, and Cantor tightened his grip. They were close enough that he felt X harden against him.

"I'm going to leave you soaked in my seed, boy."

X's Adam's apple bobbed, lips falling open.

Yes, sweet boy, melt for me. "I'll use this mouth until I spend, and then if I feel like it, I'll let you come. Is that what you want?" Cantor tugged on the ring on the man's collar and received another shiver in response. This was going to be a delight.

"Yes, please." Cantor felt a tremor pass through X, but instead of pulling away, he leaned into Cantor's touch.

"Please what?" Cantor asked sternly, leaning in so their faces were only inches away.

"Please, sir," X said through a shuddering breath. Cantor wished he could strip them both down so that they were skin to skin. But when one had voracious appetites, it served to pace oneself. He had a feast in his hands, and he would not let amateur greediness ruin it.

"Are you comfortable with playing here?"

"Yes." The hunger in that one word slithered up Cantor's spine.

"What do you say if you do not want to continue?"

"Stop," X answered in that firm tone he'd used earlier, making Cantor smile. This man was the best kind of surprise. He turned X around, wanting to see the tattoo one more time—and uttered a sound he hoped conveyed his approval as he ran his fingers over it. Then he leaned down to kiss the spot at the nape of X's neck where his spine began. Cantor

lapped at the skin with his tongue, and X moaned, pressing his pert bottom to Cantor's groin. With a hand wrapped around X, he quickly assessed their surroundings. There were a few empty tables just beyond where they stood. He pointed to one a short distance away.

"There. I want you on my lap." With X's back still pressed to his chest, Cantor walked X to the table, letting his hand roam down to the smaller man's nipples along the way, pinching until a groan of pleasure escaped his playmate's lips.

"They're very sensitive," X explained, arching his back to give Cantor more access.

"I see that," he said, worrying one of the nubs between his fingers as X writhed against him. "Have you ever climaxed just from this?" The other man shook his head, his silky curls brushing against Cantor's lapels.

"Perhaps we should investigate how far we can get you," he mused as he flicked the tight tip with a fingernail, eliciting a hiss. "I wonder if I were to suck on these pretty pink nipples—"

"They're brown," X gasped, and it took Cantor a moment to understand what he'd said. "In the light, you would see."

Interesting point to make, but Cantor was much too aroused to stop for a question.

"They will be red when I'm done with you, pet," Cantor promised. "I'll bite and suck and perhaps once you're on the cusp, I'll use my hands here." He brought the hand to the other man's hard cock over his pants. "I'll take this pretty cock out and stroke it until you're begging."

"Ungh," X moaned, back arching further.

"You like to be manhandled? Rough hands and filthy words?"

"Yes." It usually didn't happen this fast. There was a dance to these things, an adjustment period when one had to find the alignment. Discover how the proclivities of each person were compatible. But with X, the spark was instant.

It was heady, and Cantor, knowing all too well that perfection was a matter of perspective a trick of the light, did not stop to question it. Playground diversions being what they were, he'd throw himself into the moment and walk away when it was over.

"Mm, I like the sounds you make, so sweet. I am looking forward to hearing what you sound like when I've stuffed your mouth full of cock."

Cantor gripped the man's hardened staff over his trousers, eliciting a cry. "I want to see my spend dribbling down to your chin. Watch you try and swallow everything I give you." X was breathing hard now, chest rising and falling, arse rubbing against Cantor's hard cock. "You are aching for it, aren't you?"

There was something thrilling about knowing that a man like X, who had the spine to voice out loud who he was, could turn over his body to Cantor's care. It was intoxicating, and already he had a sense that this time, walking away would not be as easy.

X was practically mewling. Cantor brushed the edge of his teeth on a soft earlobe, then pressed two fingers into the man's mouth.

"Suck," he ordered, and the smaller man applied himself to the job as if he'd been waiting his entire life for the chance. "Such a talented mouth. I wonder how it'll feel around my cock." X bucked against him and sucked harder.

"Let me have it, please, Daddy."

Lightning crackled down Cantor's spine. "What did you call me?" he demanded.

"Daddy," X stuttered, a little uncertain, as though he just realized what he'd said. A possessive groan escaped Cantor's lips as the nature of X's fantasy revealed itself. Cantor responded to that call viscerally.

Daddy.

The caretaker, the disciplinarian, the one to take control. He wanted to be all those things for X tonight.

"Is that what you want, a daddy to give you what you need?" There was a frantic nod from the other man as he swirled his tongue around Cantor's fingers. "I might be of a mind to test just how good a boy you are." Still standing behind X, Cantor pinched the tight rump and was rewarded with a delicious squeal and a wiggle.

"Yes, Daddy." X sounded so eager, and Cantor's blood boiled in response. He was already imagining how the man would look kneeling at the foot of his bed, arms tied behind his back while Cantor took him from behind in rough, shallow thrusts.

This was the trouble with him—he always wanted more than he could have. He could ruin this by turning into something it couldn't possibly be or he could enjoy this delicious, pliable gift that had been handed to him. The answer came easily this time.

"Go, Daddy wants to see that pretty cock." He prompted X with a swat on that delicious posterior. Without the slightest hesitation, X took the few steps to the chair and knelt by it, eyes downcast, waiting patiently for Cantor. He took a moment to appreciate the sight, then adjusted his throbbing prick and went to him.

Now the games would truly begin.

2

As soon as Cantor sat, he tapped his thigh and the man promptly climbed on his lap. His naked back pressed against Cantor's chest. He fit there perfectly, as if made to be nestled against Cantor's frame. X smelled like bay rum and cloves. His skin glowed in the red-tinted glimmer of the room. Other than the tattoo on his back and the small gold rings on his nipples, his skin was completely unblemished. Smooth and bronzed all over. He looked like one of those Roman youths Michelangelo sculpted out of marble. Except X was a furnace of energy and heat who could not sit still.

"Are you trying to torture me with all this wiggling?" Cantor muttered as he nipped, then licked along the X's shoulders.

"I'm not," came the breathless reply, even as that round bottom tortured Cantor's erection relentlessly. "It's just that you . . . agitate me."

"Agitate." Cantor laughed as a barrage of perverse thoughts assaulted his mind. The things he wanted to do to X. He moved a hand from where he had it at the base of X's throat to the delicate gold chain between his nipples. "This is very convenient." He tugged on the chain, and X gasped, his hips rolling against Cantor. He brought his other hand back to X's crotch and pressed his thumb to the head of the man's cock. "Take it out for me," he ordered as he continued to tweak his playmate's nipples.

"Oh God," X gasped, his head thrown back until it rested on Cantor's shoulders. For a second, he wished he could take the mask off. See X's ecstatic, needy countenance in all its glory. But this was too good to interrupt . . . or to complicate. X undid the placket of his trousers with shaking hands, and within seconds, Cantor had the man's staff in his hand. He grazed a nail over the head, which had a stream of clear liquid spilling from it.

"So wet for me, sweetheart." Cantor swiped a pearl from the tip with his thumb and brought it to X's lips. The man opened for him instantly. "Show me how you're going to take it." X did not need to be asked twice. He threw himself into the task with enough gusto that Cantor worried he'd spill in his undergarments. He eagerly suckled on Cantor's digit and widened his mouth as if asking for more. Cantor obliged, giving him three fingers.

"Is your arse as greedy as that mouth of yours?" he asked hotly as X twirled his tongue around his index and ring finger, and then greedily lapped them with rough swipes. All while emitting sweet little mewls of pleasure, like Cantor's hand was the most delectable thing to ever pass his lips. "I'd love to take you hard, prepare you for my cock with my tongue and fingers and then pound into you until you're screaming." X's breaths became harsher and the steady suction on Cantor's fingers faltered.

"You love a good fucking, don't you? To choke on a fat cock, then have your ass pounded." A cry escaped X's lips, and he spurted a little more liquid. "Doesn't matter as long you're stuffed." X was vibrating on his lap so intensely, Cantor wondered if the man would spend with nothing more than a few strokes. And that would be a shame because he was nowhere near done. "I think I'll fuck your mouth now," he said in the same tone he'd use to ask for another dram of rum. "Perhaps I'll have you lick my balls too." X's jolt almost toppled him off Cantor's lap.

"I want it, Daddy," X pleaded as Cantor stroked him roughly, then gripped the sack of his balls.

"You like to make a spectacle. For everyone to see you on your knees while I use your throat." Cantor could barely recognize his own voice, gravelly and frantic as he worked X to a frenzy. He ripped his fingers out the man's mouth and went back to pinching his nipples.

"Mm," X groaned as shivers racked him. He was fucking into Cantor's hand in earnest now, lost in chasing his climax. Cantor heard a sharp intake of breath coming from his left and looked up to find they'd drawn a few onlookers. He wasn't particularly interested in being observed, but one learned to let go of those inhibitions on occasions like this.

"Looks like we have an audience." Another trickle of liquid dripped out of X's hard prick. "You *do* like this, all these people watching you splayed out with your cock in Daddy's hand, moaning like his slut. Tell me," Cantor demanded viciously, his blood on fire now.

"I love it, ah God, please . . . ," X begged, widening his stance even further until his thighs were over Cantor's. His mouth was slack and he ground his head into Cantor's shoulder, utterly mindless in his pleasure.

"After you spend, I'm going to feed you every drop so everyone will see what a hungry little whore you are."

"Ah," X shouted, his body going rigid as ropes of seed spurted out of his cock, the muscles in his neck taut as he climaxed. Cantor had to grit his teeth and clench every muscle in his lower body to keep his own orgasm at bay. He soothed and petted, whispering nonsensical words as the other man practically purred. As promised, Cantor fastidiously gathered up the semen coating his hand and fed it to X, who licked it up eagerly. The spectators standing close stayed to watch the scene, and for a moment, Cantor thought of telling them to go, of closing the curtain around them. He wanted this moment just for himself. He wanted to turn X around so they were face to face, to take his mouth and get a taste. But that was another level of intimacy, one he had not yet asked for.

"Thank you, Daddy," he X gasped. The sound dragged Cantor from his thoughts.

The warmth of the smaller man's skin seeped into Cantor's bones. Even as painfully hard as he was, he could've stayed like this for hours, with X's limp, prone body resting on him. But this was not that kind of place, and it was best not to fool himself. X was here to play a role and so was Cantor. He brought his hand to the back of the man's head, low enough to avoid disturbing the mask, and fisted a handful of curls. "On your knees."

X let out a sound of pained ecstasy and, with his softening cock still lolling out of his trousers. Cantor couldn't see X's eye color in the dimly lit room, but he was certain his pupils were dilated. His mouth hung open, a pink tongue darting out to wet his lips. He looked so eager.

Needy. Perfect. He seemed aflame with desire. An answering fire roared to life inside Cantor.

"Open my trousers, " Cantor grunted, without taking his eyes off that plump mouth.

X flew to his task. He unbuttoned the placket with nimble, elegant fingers. When he was done, he briskly moved Cantor's shirt and under-clothes aside until his cock and balls were on display. X leaned in and pressed his nose to the crease of Cantor's groin, inhaling deeply, humming. X's tongue swiped over his bottom lip as if he could already taste Cantor. The man looked like a child in front his favorite sweets.

The air in the room was thick with the smell of sex. Cantor couldn't remember when he'd been this painfully aroused. When he'd felt this unraveled. He palmed his erection with one hand and with the other, reached for the back of X's neck.

"Open," Cantor growled, and he saw a shiver pass through the other man's body. X bowed his head, gripping the chair on either side of Cantor's legs for balance. His lips parted just enough that Cantor could see his tongue peeking out. "Is this what you want?"

Curls bounced around X's dark head as he nodded. "Yes, Daddy."

Carajo. That word. It obliterated his senses.

Cantor tapped the head of his cock against the kneeling man's cheek and pressed into that hot, receiving mouth. In a heartbeat, he was engulfed in a tight, wet, velvet heat. Cantor was no novice. He'd had more men suck his cock than he could count, but he'd never seen anyone revel in it the way X did. He feasted on Cantor, eyes shut in apparent ecstasy.

How could a mouth be that sweet and indecent all at once?

The smaller man hummed with pleasure as he took Cantor to the root, and the vibrations of it were their own exquisite agony. X ran his tongue over every inch of Cantor, lapped at the veins along the shaft, suckled on the head with little cat licks, and then in one gulp took him to the back of his throat. He was a man utterly lost to what he was doing.

What a sight it was—Cantor's wet, slick cock disappearing into X's willing mouth again and again. The way his eyelashes fluttered when he took him deep. It had been seconds and he was already close to combusting. When he looked down he saw that X's prick was hard again, bobbing in the air as he sucked Cantor.

"Take yourself in hand, but don't come until I tell you," he commanded, through gritted teeth. "So good, sweetheart. Take my balls in your mouth again." X did so with fervor. One, then the other. "God, you suck like you were born for it. Such a greedy mouth." Cantor tugged X off his sack and fed him his cock again. "Take it," he coaxed as he slid back into that perfect heat. Cantor gripped X's hair hard enough to make it hurt, and that only made the man work to take him deeper.

God, he was perfect.

Cantor leaned against lush velvet cushions, one arm braced on the back of the chair, and fucked in earnest. X kept his eyes closed as if in prayer. His hand gripped Cantor's hip almost painfully. Again he wanted to take their masks off, see if there were tears running down the other man's face from taking Cantor so deeply. The sucking intensified. His vision had begun to blur when he heard the frantic, wet strokes of X's hand on his own cock. The little devil was distracting him so he could make himself come.

"Stop," Cantor roared as he squeezed every muscle in his lower body in an effort to pull the imp off him without spending. "You'll spend when I say so," Cantor grunted, even as he felt the swirling heat in his groin and up his spine. X reluctantly placed his hands demurely on his lap, his thin, long cock—it was almost dainty—lolling in the air, the tip glistening in the low light. The boy's lips were bruised and swollen, and Cantor ached to kiss him.

"Are you going to behave?" Cantor asked, pressing his cock against those willing lips.

"Yes, Daddy" was the only answer X could give before he pushed in again. Cantor took the man's mouth again and again, giving him no quarter until his orgasm slammed into him like a tidal wave. Cantor sank into it, feeling as though his limbs were melting wax. That sweet mouth worked every drop out of him until he was dry.

"Make yourself come," he ordered the boy, and heard a squeal of relief, followed by rapid strokes. X never took his mouth off him. It was startlingly intimate to have the man suckle on him so sweetly while chasing his own climax. Seconds later, he came with a muffled shout.

"Thank you, Daddy" fell from his lips once he sat back.

X was a marvel.

For the first time ever, Cantor wanted an encore. He wanted to lift X off his knees, wrap his arms around X's waist, and walk him home to his flat by Parc Monceau. But since that would be utterly absurd, he decided to go with a reasonable alternative: Ask to meet him here again the next Jeudi Noir. He was working himself up to it when X began moving.

Cantor watched the other man felt for his mask, and for a giddy moment, he thought the man would take it off. But he only reached behind himself to tighten it. Then he righted himself and, after placing a ridiculously demure kiss on the head of Cantor's cock, he tucked Cantor away as well.

"Thank you, sir." Cantor hesitated at the detached tone of the man's voice. All the heat and playfulness were gone, replaced with an aloofness that almost made him recoil. He was surprised by how unnerving it was to lose the intimacy he'd shared with X.

"I'd like to see you again," Cantor said, irritated by the uncertainty in his voice. Especially when he wasn't bold enough to ask for what he truly wanted.

A rendezvous outside Là-Bas, to see X with no mask, in Cantor's bedchamber. But he knew the score. The experiences soured beyond these walls. In the harsh light of the real world, no one ever looked quite as appealing, himself included.

Ants crawled on his skin as he awaited X's answer. The man's dark gaze considered him for what felt like an eternity. At length, he got to his feet as gracefully as he'd lowered to the floor and leaned to kiss Cantor on what was exposed of his cheek.

"I am flattered, and tempted, but I don't do repeat performances." He sounded almost regretful, but not less firm. "If that's what you're looking for, I'm not who you want." With that, X walked away from Cantor and out of the ballroom without a backward glance.

3

First Sitting

It had been a week since that night at Là-Bas and X still plagued Cantor's thoughts. It was madness to crave the man like this when their interlude could not have lasted more than a quarter of an hour. Yet Cantor could not rid himself of the feeling that he'd allowed something vital to slip from his fingers.

Not that he hadn't tried. Once he realized X was not coming back, he'd attempted to make some inquiries. He didn't get very far. The Cisse-Kelly siblings had not earned their reputation as the most discreet brothel owners in Paris by revealing their clients' secrets. The only thing he was able to extract from the hostess who'd attended him was that it had been X's first time at Là-Bas, which would get Cantor absolutely nowhere when it came to finding the man. All he had was a memory of alluring, sensual lips and dark eyes. The only chance he had of seeing him again was returning to the next Jeudi Noir. It meant another seven days of waiting. Until then, he had to apply himself to his work, and at least, in that sense, things *were* improving.

The night with X had rekindled his muse.

He was still desperately stuck on what to send for the exposition, but on a canvas in his solarium, he'd begun rendering a kneeling, shadowy figure. It had started as a way to purge from his mind the incessant images of X, but now it was taking shape.

A fallen angel on his knees, bare back with black ink etched on his wide shoulders. That golden skin, shining as if lit from within. He'd come back to the piece again and again since he'd started it the morning after Là-Bas. He'd worked on it between sitters. He'd get lost in thought, considering where to add shading or which forms needed more work. He hadn't felt like this in months—energized, filled with ideas. It was an enormous relief to finally feel that pull to the canvas again, and he couldn't even thank the man who had inspired it.

The clock chimed eleven, and Cantor cursed.

Lord Maximus Gregorio Bretton was now a full hour late. Cantor fumed as he moved around his space again, ensuring everything was to his liking. His signature fresh-cut white lilies were in their vase, sitting on a round table laden with lemonade and chilled champagne, as well as delicacies from the kitchen. Cantor had learned that the aristocracy was easy to please once you made yourself a rare commodity. And there was nothing more coveted among the rich and powerful than a Joseph Cantor Marshall portrait. The great and the good happily forked over a thousand guineas for the opportunity to have their likeness done by Cantor, and so he made sure to provide an experience.

He offered them exquisitely made chocolates from a Haitian choco-latier with whom he'd had a short but very energetic tryst a few summers ago. He poured them chilled champagne from his private cellar. He presented them with Persian pomegranates, Valencia oranges, black cherries from Portugal, thinly sliced Pata Negra ham and fresh St. Marcelin cheese brought from his farm in the Loire Valley—in short, a feast. That, in addition to the sonatas and danzas he played on the piano between strokes on the canvas made for quite the afternoon for his clients. The aristocracy loved a performance, and Cantor was more than happy to oblige . . . for his asking price. What he could not abide was anyone wasting his extremely valuable time.

"Is he not here yet?" he bellowed, grudgingly leaving his solarium for his studio. He sighed when his secretary Dilania popped her head in the doorway. She shook her head no. "Can you send a message to my aunt?" he asked through gritted teeth.

"And tell her what, Cantor?" In addition to being his secretary,

Dilania was his dear friend. They'd known each other since they were children. She was the most sensible and even-keeled person he knew. She was also irritating to the extreme.

"Inform her that this is the last morning I will squander waiting for Lord Maximus. My time is in great demand." Dilania only rolled her eyes. "I have highly important people who have been waiting months to sit for me and this man has now missed his appointment three times." His indignation, as usual, left her unaffected. "Just this week I declined to do portraits for two heads of state and one of the most popular sopranos in Italy." He realized he sounded like a pompous ass, but this was ridiculous. It was the last time that he'd let his aunt Violet talk him into taking one of her many acquaintances as clients. "Well," he said, moving his hand in a gesture that indicated writing.

"You do realize I manage your schedule? I know who you had to turn down and who has not come to their sittings," Dilania told him, completely uncowed. "Both our lives would be much more pleasant if you learned to accept that when it comes to people you care about, you are unable to employ the word 'no.'"

"Three days, Dilania!" he cried, close to pulling his hair out. She turned and left the room, leaving him to fume on his own.

Cantor suppressed yet another sigh and applied himself to arranging his paints again. Dilania *was* right. He could never deny his aunt anything. What's more, she rarely took advantage of that fact. When he'd lost his parents at fourteen, she'd taken Cantor in and raised him with fierce protectiveness and unconditional love. She'd nurtured his interest in the arts, and instead of taking him back to Philadelphia to the bosom of the Marshall family, she'd moved her residence to Florence so Cantor would not have to leave his home. When he was old enough to enter art school, she'd brought him to Paris and had moved heaven and earth to find him an apprenticeship with one of the most well-known portrait artists in Europe. She even made sure he received the training necessary to pass the rigorous entry exams for the Académie des Beaux Arts, which he did. In fact, he was the youngest person to ever pass them. What he owed his aunt Violet could never be repaid. Not with a thousand portraits to her friends.

"Margarita has been such a good friend to me, Joseph dear, and she desperately wants a portrait from you," his aunt had cajoled him the last time he'd visited her, as though portraiture were a matter of life and death. "Her youngest has never sat for one and he's here in Paris for a few months. Please, querido, for me? It will give you a chance to meet with Maximus again. He was so taken with your work when he was younger."

He had liked the Brettons on the couple of occasions his aunt brought him along for a visit to their estate in Essex. Margarita Caceres Bretton, his aunt's old friend, was known to London's high society as the Marchioness of Harwood, the woman who, over thirty years ago, had married the Marquess of Harwood after a fast and passionate courtship during his visit to Hispaniola as an envoy of Queen Victoria. It had been the scandal of the decade for a highborn man like the young and very eligible marquess to attach himself to the daughter of a candlemaker from the tropics. But the gossips soon lost their interest when it turned out that the man was madly in love with his wife, and it seemed she felt the same way.

Happy people rarely made for interesting drawing room gossip.

The last time he'd seen Lord Maximus Gregorio Bretton, he'd been a gangly adolescent of fourteen with a remarkable curiosity. That had been twelve years ago, on a week-long visit to which Aunt Violet had insisted he accompany her. Cantor couldn't recall much of the stay other than the stunning views of the sea, which he'd sketched furiously, and of the happy, warm people that were the Brettons. But he did remember Maximus being quieter than the rest of his boisterous family. His older siblings Rex and Regina—the Brettons were not subtle when it came to naming their children—were a pair of twins who had been closer to Cantor's age. Max was the baby and they treated him as such, ribbing him for his smaller frame and shy nature. But with Cantor, Maximus had been talkative, not exactly outgoing, but affable. He'd come to the edge of the cliffs where Cantor set his canvas to paint, and he'd watch Cantor for hours, all while commenting on the history of the place and telling stories of pirates who'd hidden treasures along the coastline.

That had been a long time ago, and from what Cantor had heard, the baby of the family had evolved into quite the rake. At least until he married his best friend four years ago, only to have the woman die tragically in a carriage accident a year later while traveling with her older brother. According to some of the rumors Cantor had heard, Lord

Maximus had gone half mad with grief and had only emerged from his mourning in the last year. That reminder did temper Cantor's annoyance somewhat, but he really would put his foot down if the man stood him up again today.

"He's here." Cantor turned from fiddling with his brushes and easel to find Dilania grinning from ear to ear.

"Why are you smiling?" Her sense of humor usually only appeared when there was something that would potentially infuriate him, so Cantor could only brace himself.

"He's darling," she said, leaving a pregnant silence, which Cantor presumed was meant to be filled with a request to elaborate.

"Puppies are darling. He's a grown man." Dilania rolled her eyes. "Besides, I've met the man before and *I* am running out of patience," he snapped peevishly.

"You've been advised." Dilania's grin was so exuberant that the corners of her mouth neared her eyes.

"Dilania, I have four more clients today," Cantor groused, pinching the bridge of his nose.

"Because you are obsessed with work," she retorted. This was her favorite point to make whenever his busy schedule came up. That he never stopped, that he was uninspired because he rarely gave his mind, his eyes, his *muse* a rest. They weren't exactly the same jabs his critics took at him, claiming he was selling his talents to the highest bidder like a whore. He knew she said it out of concern for his health. She'd seen how frustrated he'd been in the past few months. She also knew what drove him.

Because I want the prized possession of every aristocrat in Europe to be a portrait done by a Black man whose grandmother was bought and sold by people like them.

He knew Dilania worried about him overexerting himself. And perhaps he did, but one thing Cantor knew above all else was that for people like him, nothing was promised. That those who today begged for one of his portraits would relish nothing more than scorning him if they got the chance. He worked like this, relentlessly, because he didn't know how long this boon would last. Because if the day ever came when everything was lost, he wanted security. He wanted to leave something for posterity. Something that would outlive him. His work was his pantheon, and perhaps it made him vain, but he wanted his place in history to be undeniable, indelible.

"You have nothing to prove," she insisted.

"I also highly enjoy money," he admitted with a sly grin. This time, she only shook her head at him and sighed.

"Half of which you use to sponsor African and Latin American art students at the Académie Fabian. Please spare me your mercenary delusions. You're a softhearted, brilliant man, addicted to his work." Cantor opened his mouth to remind her that those students were identified, procured, and brought in large part thanks to her, but the words never left his mouth. Because in the next instant, the whirlwind known as Lord Maximus swept into his studio.

"I do apologize for my tardiness, or tardinesses." Two big, brown eyes stared up at Cantor from behind wire-rimmed spectacles, which were perched on a frankly angelic face.

"Three missed appointments, Lord Maximus. An hour late today," Cantor said without heat.

It didn't seem to matter anymore as the annoyance from seconds ago was replaced with a jolt of something completely different. He was instantly pulled in by Lord Maximus, almost too intensely. Examining a sitter was part of the process, he reminded himself as his eyes studied every inch of the young lord's face. The lines and angles of Lord Maximus's countenance were a painter's dream. Cantor resisted the urge to get closer and walk around him to see how the light from different areas of the room caught the planes of his face.

Even his ears were perfect.

But the place Cantor's gaze kept returning to were those dark eyes, fringed with thick lashes. His hair was finer than Cantor's and very dark. The younger man kept it just a little longer than what was strictly fashionable. Cantor approved. It would be crime to shear off those sable curls. His skin would look like brushed bronze on the canvas. It was that tone between sand and caramel that was common in children of mixed parentage. Maximus could likely pass in the winter, but by July he'd start getting questions like "Are you Italian?"

"Did my secretary not let you know?" Lord Maximus asked, owlish eyes canted up, and damn it all, he really was darling. He was also anxious. His voice was tight, not with annoyance, but with . . . nerves?

That's when Cantor realized he'd been gawking at the man without saying a word.

It was hard to stop. He would be a pleasure to paint. And that mouth —lush and broad, with pink lips. It made Cantor think of biting into a ripe mamey. His eyes kept snagging on the shape of it. The perfect bow of the upper lip, the shades of pink and brown. Suddenly, his heart began to race as it dawned on him.

He *knew* that plump bottom lip.

Not only did he know it, but he was also almost certain he'd had it between his teeth a week ago. The memory assaulted him: that ripe mouth, bruised and glistening from taking his cock.

Daddy.

There was a crash on the floor, and Cantor realized he'd dropped the brushes he'd been holding. It couldn't be. He had to be imagining things. His obsession with X was making him see what wasn't there. It wasn't as if he was naïve enough to believe that a marquess's son wouldn't frequent clubs like Là-Bas. The establishment thrived precisely because of people of his class, but the man was a widower. A widower who, as far as Cantor knew, had been devastated by his wife's passing. With great effort, Cantor willed his traitorous prick to behave and redirected his focus to Lord Maximus, his client, he forcefully reminded himself.

"Your secretary," Cantor stated neutrally, even as he tried to puzzle out anything in Lord Maximus that gave away any indication of recognition. But the man seemed oblivious. It had to be Cantor's mind toying with him. He *was* rather sleep deprived.

"Yes. That I might be late." Maximus was not precisely apologetic, but it was still surprising to Cantor that he was being offered any kind of explanation. In his experience, aristocrats did not tend to admit their shortcomings. It was one of the more cumbersome aspects of dealing with customers who expected the world to accommodate their every whim. "I'm an engineer, you see."

"I don't think I see, no," Cantor responded, genuinely curious to hear how the man's work as an engineer had prevented him from appearing for his sitting appointment. This was the kind of thing that would typically send him into a fit of bad temper. That would reinforce his reputation as rigid and cantankerous, particularities his clients found amusing.

Leave it to the wealthy and spoiled to interpret his request that they not waste his time as an eccentricity.

"I am working with Monsieur Eiffel, from the tower," Maximus explained, and Cantor had to bite the inside of his cheeks to keep from laughing. He was rather charming too. Whether it was intentional or not was another question.

There was not a single resident of Paris who was not aware of the steel monstrosity going up in the 7th arrondissement, which would be the showpiece of next year's exposition commemorating the centennial of the revolution. Gustave Eiffel and his tower were all Parisians seemed to be talking about. And this young lord was part of the team? He had to be good. Eiffel was known for his demanding and rigorous work ethic.

Interesting.

Cantor opened his mouth to ask something but was distracted by the curve of Lord Maximus's neck. Cantor recognized it, too, was almost certain he'd hungrily sucked on the skin right at the place where the slope of the neck dipped into the shoulder. It was madness that this bespectacled engineer, with his nervous hands and rumpled appearance, could the incubus haunting his dreams for the past week.

"What kind of engineer?" he asked, voice roughened by the maelstrom of conflicting feelings.

"Mechanical, hydraulics mostly." Cantor could only stare. This was not the kind of profession one expected of the ton's offspring. The man spoke in a measured tone, every word delivered with precision. He remembered this about the fourteen-year-old Maximus. It also made him recall the direct manner in which X had spoken to him at Là-Bas.

"Do you enjoy your work?" he heard himself ask as he labored to veer his gaze off the younger man's throat.

"I do. It's far more interesting than lounging around at White's until the card tables open." There was a hint of self-mockery in his tone, and Cantor liked the man even more.

"You don't approve of a life of leisure, then?" Cantor asked before he could stop himself. He usually conversed with his sitters, inquired about their likes and dislikes. It was an effective way of getting them comfortable while also studying their reactions. The thing was that with Maximus, Cantor was too eager to hear the answers, and *that* was treacherous territory.

He watched as the man mused over the question, his hands behind his back. When he began gnawing at his bottom lip, Cantor's entire body was hit by a bolt of something that had no place in the room where he did his work.

"It's not that I don't approve of it. It's just not the way *I* like to spend my time," Maximus confessed, his liquid brown eyes earnest. Open and bright as a summer sky. "If I don't occupy my mind, I get melancholy. And that's ... it's not good." They stood in silence for a moment with that vulnerable truth suspended between them. It had been merely minutes since Lord Maximus had entered his studio, and just as with X, he was instantly and powerfully drawn in.

The difference was that X was a masked, anonymous man at a sex club. This was the son of a marquess. The legacy Cantor had just been yammering about to Dilania could be gone in a second if he made a faulty step here. He cleared his throat, determined to regain the appearance of a professional and not a besotted fool. "I . . . I'm glad you've found something that satisfies you."

Maximus's back straightened, his gaze suddenly glowing with something very different from before.

"I wouldn't say satisfied, but it's challenging and occasionally gratifying." Heat surged through Cantor in response to the other man's words. It was remarkable how much he could communicate, even behind the spectacles. Just as X had from behind the mask. "Do *you* like your work, Monsieur Marshall? Dealing with the capriciousness of the aristocracy."

Cantor didn't think anyone had ever asked him if he enjoyed his work. People made all manner of remarks about his paintings, his style, his technique. There had even been pieces written about his peculiar way of working. His sitters found how he rushed back and forth between them and the canvas and his aggressive brushstrokes peculiar, and soon people wanted to know what exactly happened at a sitting with Joseph Cantor Marshall.

That was all for show, of course. Still he did enjoy the challenge of capturing an expression, a thought, or a mood that spoke to the observer. He'd labored for his skills, and he felt pride and satisfaction in seeing the fruits of it on the canvas. It was somewhat discomfiting to realize he'd never been asked to articulate any of it.

"I do find pleasure in my work," he said, opting for the safe answer.

Then without thinking, he spoke again. "As for capriciousness, I comfort myself with the knowledge that I have something *they* want. And I can also exercise my whims by denying certain people portraits."

"Did you think of denying *me*?" There appeared a glint in Maximus's dark regard. Was it recognition? Playfulness, perhaps? And why did Cantor suddenly feel like the prey in this tableau?

"Was the portrait your idea?" Cantor said, redirecting. He was curious to know if the man was here out of his own volition, or if it was just a way to appease his mother.

Maximus proffered another one of those pained smiles. Almost a grimace. "No, my mother asked," he said. "But I wanted to do it. One would be a fool to turn down a chance to sit for the great Joseph Cantor Marshall." The smiled faded, and Cantor felt himself shiver under that direct, almost intrusive gaze. "I like your work, not only your portraits. I saw your piece at the salon last year."

"What did you like about it?" Cantor had practically been laughed out of Paris when he'd shown a portrait of an old fisherman he'd encountered on a beach in Veracruz. He'd been captivated by the grizzled man with his toothless smile and clear, twinkling eyes, sitting under a coconut palm. The Paris salon didn't find it quite as compelling. After that, he'd gone to London and bought a studio space in Chelsea. He'd told everyone it was because he could see his clients from America there, but in truth, the scorn he'd felt at that salon had been unsettling. He'd considered leaving Paris altogether.

"I loved the textures," Lord Maximus responded, and Cantor raised an eyebrow, intrigued despite himself. The other man smiled and lifted a shoulder. "The waves in the background and the roughness of the bark of the tree. They were so rich." Cantor didn't speak a word, wanting to hear everything else Lord Maximus had to say. "I was taken by the sheer size of it," Maximus said, turning his gaze to something in the distance, as if attempting to recall the details. "But particularly, I was taken by the joy of it." Maximus directed his gaze to Cantor then, and something inside his chest tightened. "One rarely sees such movement in paintings, the energy of being alive, the happy, unguarded moments."

Cantor almost wished the piece hadn't sold so he could revisit it with Lord Maximus's words still fresh in his mind. Because, indeed, despite the cold reception of the piece, it had sold to an anonymous buyer for almost twice what he'd expected.

"I am glad it was to your liking," he finally said, a bit hoarsely.

"I see things are progressing nicely," Dilania said, interrupting their conversation. He didn't have to turn around to know there was a smug expression on his secretary's face. "Do you require anything else, Monsieur Marshall?"

You mean, other than Lord Maximo Gregorio Bretton splendidly naked on my bed, screaming for mercy?

"No." Cantor couldn't be certain this was X. Except he'd caught the looks the young aristocrat had directed his way. There was interest, and quite possibly, recognition. "Lord Maximus and I were about to get started."

"Max," the lordling said, then turned those chocolate brown eyes on Cantor. "Please." A finger of fire slithered up his back at that word. *Please.* Cantor suddenly had an image of Max on his knees, whispering it in a raspy, desperate voice, pleading for Cantor to take him, fuck him, kiss him . . . enough.

Enough.

"We should get on with it," he said in a clipped tone, and extended a hand toward the dais he'd placed for the best use of the midday light. "Take a seat."

Max seemed completely unaware of Cantor's peevishness and applied himself to examining the room with undisguised curiosity. His gaze roamed over the covered canvases scattered around the room and paused on the offerings of the table. Cantor repressed a groan when Max licked his lips, looking at the Pata Negra ham with something akin to lust. The way the man ran his tongue over that lush bottom lip was indecent.

"Is this food for me?" he asked with a lopsided grin that crinkled his eyes.

"It's for all my sitters," Cantor explained. Was everything between him and this man going to turn into a battle for control?

"That's how you tempt us to arrive on time, then?" Another one of those self-mocking smiles, but this time, Cantor thought Max was attempting to share the joke.

"Most sitters consider a chance to have me do their likeness a precious opportunity." Was he flirting with the man?

"It is typical of me to squander precious opportunities." There was that tone again, that harsh speech about himself. It made Cantor's skin prickle with unease. Saying anything to the man about it would be gauche. It would be offensive. But he was still considering it when Max completely changed the topic of conversation.

"Your mother was from the Caribbean," Maximus observed offhandedly, but Cantor sensed the comment was not remotely casual.

"Like yours," Cantor answered.

"Yes." The young lord seemed to warm at the establishment of that kinship, his smile deepening as he continued to look around the room. Once he was finished with his inspection, he calmly walked to his seat.

In an attempt to shake loose the tendrils of desire gripping his body, Cantor busied himself by packing globs of paint on his palette, a task he usually did while glancing at the sitter. He did that a lot in the beginning —stealing glances, trying to capture in his mind images of his subjects when they were distracted. However, with Lord Maximus, the practice seemed a risky proposition. The more he looked, the more he wanted.

"Don't you have to sketch me first?" The question made Cantor jump, which only managed to disorder him further. "You're standing so far away. Your sight must be like an eagle's."

"I will sketch on the canvas with a brush," he explained waspishly. He was utterly scattered. What in the world was the matter with him? This was not the first time a beautiful man sat for him. They came through this studio regularly.

But none of them have been the debauched angel you can't stop thinking about.

Cantor picked up one of his thicker brushes and focused on the white expanse of the fresh canvas. He breathed in through his nose and attempted, once again, to focus. When he felt more in control, he shifted, putting Max in his line of sight.

"I like to take in the picture from a distance and then get closer as I gather a better sense of the shadow and light," he explained while selecting the brushes and paints he needed, placing them on the wooden box he'd had nailed to the easel for that purpose.

"My mother said you could only receive me three times." Cantor's head snapped up, and he encountered Max's inquisitive regard. There was something almost taunting in the way he looked at Cantor. "Since I've already missed two sessions, I suppose this will have to do."

Absolutely not. The words practically rang in his ears.

"No, that won't be enough." Cantor grimaced at the force in his tone. Max looked surprised—and pleased. Cantor was beginning to feel like he'd been knocked on the head by an anvil. "I meant," he corrected, "that it may take more than three sittings I can manage with three if the sitter is only here temporarily, but if you're able, ideally it should be close to ten sittings."

He'd finished portraits with two.

A few good sketches in solid light and the aid of a photograph could do the trick when necessary. And given that, ten minutes into the first sitting, Cantor was already lying and contemplating breaking his very sensible rules of etiquette, it was precisely what he *should* do with this man. "Three times a week over the next fortnight. At the same time, so that we have the same light." This was purely for his own indulgence. Professionalism, it seemed, had flown out the door with common sense the moment Lord Maximus arrived.

"Six times, then." The shy, yet knowing smirk on Max's lips made Cantor stumble.

"Let's make it eight," he said pathetically, unable to rein himself in.

"You'll have me at eleven in the morning," the brat said as he pulled out his pocket watch, then glanced at Cantor with guileless eyes.

"*Ten* in the morning," Cantor countered, closing the distance between them. "You were an hour late, Lord Maximus." This he said for his own benefit, as they both likely knew he would receive the young lord whenever he deigned to arrive.

"Max," he corrected sweetly. "and I offered my apologies." Those big brown puppy eyes were lethal.

"I need you to . . . ," he began, lifting a hand to Max's face, but then thought better of it and dropped it.

"You need me to," Max repeated with a slight hitch in his breath that made Cantor's blood boil. He *needed* to get closer, to press his lips to the man in front of him and confirm that it was indeed the mouth he'd bruised and bitten at Là-Bas a week ago. He wished he could ask, but the rules were what they were. No one could reveal their attendance to Jeudi

Noir. Especially not him as a dominant, and certainly not to a sitter, and an aristocrat at that.

"I need to instruct you on how you must hold your head." Under the scorching gaze of Lord Maximus, Cantor shook out his hand and gingerly placed two fingers under a clean-shaven chin. What should've been a cursory touch—a necessary step to show the young lord how to hold his head for the portrait—stunned, burned, and chilled him at once.

"Did you procure three identical sets of clothes to the one you're wearing?" He was scrambling to stay on course.

"I . . . ," Max said with hesitation, and for the first time, Cantor saw the teasing glint in his eyes disappear. "I forgot to send for them." Something that Cantor hadn't seen yet crossed the man's face. "I can get distracted with work or too focused on something. I'm forgetful." His eyes dimmed, and Cantor felt as though all the lights had been snuffed out in the room.

The sudden change in Max was about more than being forgetful. Someone had made this man feel like this was an unforgivable flaw. That there was something wrong with him. Had his family done this to him? Cantor had only stayed with them once, and it had been more than a decade ago, but his impression then had been the contrary.

"You don't need to remember everything. That's what a good staff is for," Cantor declared, perfectly aware that merely moments earlier, he'd been berating Max for his tardiness. He fought the urge to send his own footman for the garments and offer to keep them at his own house.

"I have a cook and a maid who do the upkeep, but I . . ." Now Max's gaze was fixed on the ground. Discomfort radiated off him. "I prefer my privacy." Big brown eyes looked at Cantor from under long lashes. "I don't like people in my rooms all the time. I have my secretary who takes care of things like shopping, but part of my coming to Paris was an experiment in living a bit more independently."

That was interesting. Perhaps his family's affection was not as welcome as Cantor thought.

"You weren't independent in London?" he asked as tactfully as he could.

Max shook his head, eyes on the stained-glass window on the far wall. "After my—" His Adam's apple bobbed as he attempted to speak, and the urge to reach for him was overpowering. "After my beloved died, I went back home," Max explained, his eyes faraway and unbearably sad. "I was not . . . well." Cantor didn't know what it was to lose a spouse, one's beloved. But he understood loss that changed the world around you forever. That muted the colors, that blunted every ounce of joy. It was a fog one had to fight tooth and nail to escape.

"I am sorry for your loss," Cantor said, surprised at the emotion in his own voice. "I'd heard about your wife." Max's mouth twisted bitterly at the word, confusing Cantor. "From my aunt Violet. She's friends with your mother," he added, and then inexplicably said, "I visited your family with my aunt once. You were fourteen, perhaps."

"I remember you too," Maximus said.

The simple words crested and crashed like waves inside him. Cantor wanted to open his mouth and name it. *You're X and I haven't stopped thinking about you since last Thursday. That night has me aching, wanting, and I don't know where to go with all this need.* But neither of them said a word.

Cantor angled his head to look at Max. What he saw there made him hurt. In the next second, his hands reached for his sketchpad and charcoal. It was either that or pull the man's face to his chest.

"I thought you said you didn't sketch," Max asked, surprised. Cantor made a frustrated sound, eyes on the paper. This was not for the portrait. It was for him. There were emotions and feelings that certain things, certain *people* evoked in Cantor, and the only way to make sense of it was to render it.

When he was fifteen, about a year after his parents died, there had been a puddle of water in front of his family's home in Florence during a summer with heavy rains. Every time he walked past, Cantor would feel unsettled and overwhelmed with sadness for hours. Finally, one day, he came out with a little sketchpad and drew the shallow pool of water. After he was done, he realized the water reflected the roses his mother had planted on the terrace in her bedroom. Cantor, who had not been able to enter his parents' room since their deaths, was confronted with what was lost every time he walked by that puddle. But he had not seen it until he put it on paper.

Now he began by drawing the curve of Max's upper lip, his hands flying, eyes darting back and forth. With every line pressed onto the creamy surface of the pad, Cantor revealed what he'd known from the moment Max walked into his studio. Blood rushed through his temples, his hands tingling as he moved the charcoal, but he did not stop.

"Just," he told Max, holding a hand up, palm out, "stay like that for me, just a minute."

"All right." Max held his head in place, his countenance still holding that raw, naked stare. The mouth and the eyes, that was all Cantor drew. When he finished, he could see it clearly. The parted lips, the curled lashes.

X.

With his heart hammering, Cantor turned on his heel, picked up his brush, and launched himself at the canvas. If he stopped, he'd open his mouth and say things that would likely cause some trouble. They both knew what was happening here, but he would not be the one to name it.

"You're very tall," Max observed as Cantor circled the dais, cataloging the shapes of Lord Maximus. So many details to pick up on—a dipped eyebrow, lines at the corner of wide eyes that connected to a slightly upturned mouth. Chin tipped toward the window just so. He was the very picture of open curiosity. If the portrait were one of his own pieces, he'd title it something silly, like "The Searching Sitter."

"My father was taller. He boxed," Cantor told him as he labored to capture the angles of Max's cheekbones. From where he stood, he heard the other man's appreciative sound, as if he were picturing Cantor's oversized forebears.

"Do you engage in pugilism, Monsieur Marshall?"

Cantor dragged his gaze off the shadow work he was doing to glance at Max.

"I spar every morning." Another one of those appreciative sounds came out of Lord Maximus.

"Are you as hard on your opponents as you are on your . . . paintings?" The brat. He was provoking him.

"Harder." Cantor didn't take his eyes off the canvas. "I don't rush my strikes, so they land precisely where they're most effective. I take my time." It was anyone's guess what he was referring to at this point. But when Cantor finally looked at Max, he had that knowing smirk on his lips that seemed to burrow under Cantor's skin.

"You're very . . . forceful."

"And you're very curious."

Max smiled at the comment, and Cantor's lip quirked up out of its own volition.

"I like looking at you work," Max mused, and Cantor's brush skidded on the canvas. He bit back a curse and stepped back to see how bad the damage was.

Did he want Cantor to ask him?

What did it matter? It wasn't as if they could engage in the games they'd played at Là-Bas here at the studio. The brothel existed for a reason. Some things were not meant to be brought home. Yet the words were still burning in his mouth. He let his gaze drop from Max's like a coward and focused on the work. For the next hour, Cantor painted with his nerves on edge. The more he added to the canvas, the more unavoidable the truth was.

"Tomorrow is Thursday," Cantor heard himself say in a detached voice as he applied some black paint to a corner of the canvas, careful not to meet Max's eyes.

A noise of something like surprise came from where X, *Max*, sat.

"Indeed," the younger man said. "Shall I make myself available to you?"

Every muscle in Cantor's body locked at once. This was the outside of enough.

"I suggest you reconsider what games you're playing, Lord Maximus," he told the man, brush suspended in the air. He knew if he even tried to paint in the state he was, he'd ruin the portrait. After a long moment, when he forced air in and out of his lungs, he turned to look at Max, but he didn't find the teasing, saucy expression he'd imagined. The man looked unsure. Scared. Cantor closed the space between them in a few steps.

"I know you," he said quietly, needing to keep the words between them, even if no one would come in here without him calling for them. "You're—"

Max lifted a finger to Cantor's mouth before he could say. They stared at each other for what felt like hours, while Cantor agonized with the need to touch. Finally, he dared, and brushed a thumb to the other man's chest, encountering two small metal rings under his shirt. Max's eyes shone with things Cantor could not quite deduce. Their ragged breaths echoed through the room.

"I can't be *him* here," Max said, chest rising and falling as he stared up at Cantor. *Him.*

"I—" Cantor's words left him.

"He can't exist outside the club." The younger man's eyes were pleading, but there was something there that Cantor could not quite figure out.

But I want you too. I want you both.

At best, this would be complicated. At worst, it could be bloody catastrophic. He was perilously close to undoing years of an impeccable, untainted reputation with his clientele. He'd worked too hard for far too long to throw it all away like this. It only took one rumor, *even in Paris.* And yet, instead of retreating, he pushed forward until he was only centimeters from Maximus. The younger man listed toward him, pupils dilated, nostrils flaring. Then it was a matter of millimeters. If he canted his head just so, their lips would collide. Cantor's mouth watered at the thought. Especially when he saw a hint of that pink tongue he'd tasted at Là-Bas. Reputation and career be damned, he was going to do it.

He never got to.

"I must go," Max declared, standing abruptly and forcing Cantor to step out of his way.

"But," he sputtered as Maximus scrambled off the dais and rushed toward the door of the studio.

"Thank you, I shall return!" Max called over his shoulder before disappearing down the hallway. By the time Cantor made himself follow him, he'd already run out like the hounds of hell were behind him.

4

___

Fourth Sitting

"He's back, and he's got something for you." Dilania's strong voice brought Cantor out of his thoughts. The mention of "he" could only mean one thing. Immediately, his heart squeezed in his chest, then began that frantic stammer that seemed to go hand-in-hand with Max's presence.

A week had passed since Lord Maximus's first visit. He *did* return the day after running off on Cantor. But there had been no more suggestive looks, no more innuendo. Despite his disappointment, Cantor heeded the other man's unspoken request. If the man wasn't interested in Cantor that way, his pride was not so fragile that he could not keep things cordial while he did the man's portrait. And he had been painstakingly cordial, even when Lord Maximus came and went as he pleased.

Today, for instance, he arrived unannounced at 10:00 a.m., as if that hour of the day belonged to him, after three days of silence. On a Thursday morning, nonetheless. On a Jeudi Noir Thursday morning, at that. But would Cantor turn him away or berate him for not respecting the guidelines he scrupulously observed with other sitters?

He would not.

He was still swallowing that bitter pill when he heard what sounded like someone dragging a piece of furniture through his studio. He quickly put the palette and brush down and had grabbed a cloth to wipe his hands when Max made an appearance at the doorway, pushing a contraption which looked very much like a decapitated wooden horse. He labored with the thing until it was a few feet from Cantor.

"I made you a chair," he announced proudly, gesturing toward the apparatus. Cantor angled his head and squinted, hoping the design would make sense to him. Max was a shambles, his suit rumpled, eyes bleary, spectacles askew, his mass of curls wild as always. He looked like he hadn't slept in days. Everything in Cantor wanted to swoop him up in his arms, feed him, lay him down and cover him with kisses until he fell asleep. But given Cantor reminded himself once again that it was not his place.

"A chair?" Cantor finally asked, genuinely bemused.

"Yes, I've been working on it for a few days. That's why I missed my sitting."

"Sittings," Cantor corrected, eliciting an apologetic smile.

"Yes, my apologies," he answered a bit unsteadily, and Cantor felt like an utter heel. "You have to sit on it," Maximus urged, tapping on the seat, which was curiously similar to the ones Cantor had seen on bicycles. "Try it."

He beckoned Cantor over and ran a hand over two padded squares. "Your legs rest here. It distributes the weight better, and you can use it to paint so you don't have to stand all the time. You get tired being on your feet so much."

Cantor could only stare.

This was probably the most considerate, yet somewhat presumptuous gift he'd ever gotten. He did get tired. He was a big man, and he sometimes was on his feet fourteen hours a day. He'd had probably a hundred people come and sit for him. If one of them had noticed how long he stood, they never said.

"When you say a few days . . . ?" Cantor watched Max tinker with the contraption.

"Two." Max lifted a shoulder as he adjusted levers on the chair. "I noticed on my second visit that you rub your thigh a lot, and I heard from a friend that sciatic pain can be relieved by taking stress off the legs and hips. So, I went home, designed this, and then made it."

"Have you eaten today?" Cantor asked, heart racing. Max canted his head to the side as if trying to recall what the word meant.

"That's pretty," Max said, pointing at the canvas instead of answering the question. "What is it?"

"I'll tell you in a minute." Cantor fought back a smile. The man was like a hummingbird. "*Did you eat?*"

"You know, I don't remember," he answered through a jaw-cracking yawn. Cantor fought the urge to take Max in hand. He'd never met a person more in need of a keeper than Maximus Gregorio Bretton. He almost berated him for not taking care of himself, but then Cantor saw the smile on his face as he fiddled with the chair. It was sweet, thoughtful, and a little absurd, just like the man who had brought it for him.

The pre-Maximus Cantor would've been disgruntled at having his day disrupted. His mornings had been monopolized in such a manner that he no longer booked clients until the afternoon. Max had his schedule in tatters. And yet, every morning since the first sitting, Cantor had woken with a smile on his face, looking forward to seeing the young lord walk into his studio in his perennially disheveled state. Maximus was such a contradiction. In the world where he belonged to a class that implicitly granted him power and position, he was shy and reserved, and in the one where he willingly submitted, he was unapologetically proud and bold.

Cantor had never wanted anyone more.

"Did you go home last night?" he asked, knowing very well this was not the appropriate way to address a client, much less one who happened to be the son of a marquess. But Cantor was done pretending this was the just another sitter.

"Not exactly." The rueful smile on Max's face, coupled with him running a hand over his wrinkled jacket and tie, seemed to make the ground under Cantor's feet turn to quicksand. "It's been a madhouse at the fairgrounds. We are getting ready to begin the next stage of the build and it's all hands on deck."

"Which seemed like a good time to design and manufacture a chair?" Max's laugh was a little embarrassed.

"Once I get an idea in my head, it's hard to let it go." He stuck a hand behind his neck and offered Cantor a sheepish look from behind his gold-framed spectacles. Those pinked cheeks and fluttering eyelashes had a devastating effect. "After I left you the last time, I went straight to the work site and didn't leave for twenty-four hours." He slid his hands into his trouser pockets and shook his head like wet dog, almost making his spectacles fly off his head. "Then I went home and remembered I wanted to make you a chair and before I knew it, it was morning."

"Your suit for the sitting is there," Cantor said, tipping his chin toward the screen. Cantor had broken after the second time Max showed up to the sitting in the wrong clothes and sent his footman to procure it. It was now pressed, cleaned, and hanging from a hook on the wall. "Go change and Dilania will bring you some breakfast."

"I am too much trouble," Max said, cheeks flushed with red, and Cantor bit the inside of his mouth so hard he was sure he'd drawn blood. "Whyever do you put up with me?"

"I'm doing your portrait," Cantor stated, as if this was any sort of normal arrangement with a client. "And your mother is my mother's dear friend." That seemed to take a bit of the wind out of Max's sails. Cantor turned his attention to the canvas. There had to be a screw that needed to be tightened on the easel or a brush that needed to be cleaned. "Magdalena made torrejas with the brioche this morning." Max gasped at the mention of the sliced bread dipped in egg custard, which was then pan-fried and soaked in spiced syrup.

"With cinnamon?" he asked, coming to stand next to Cantor. A toothy grin was now firmly in place. Damn it all, the radiance of that smile. "I thought you didn't like them." Now Cantor was the one feeling sheepish.

The last time Max had come for a sitting, he'd asked Dilania where the delicious smell was coming from. When she said it was the torrejas from her breakfast, his eyes had gone wide, and he'd proceeded to lick his lips so obscenely that Cantor had to leave the room. Since then, he'd been asking for the bloody things every morning in case Lord Maximus turned up.

"I like torrejas," Cantor lied. He'd never had a taste for sweets.

"He absolutely hates them," Dilania, that traitor, declared as she walked by them with a platter loaded with torrejas topped with fresh strawberries and powdered sugar. Cantor locked his jaw and pretended to inspect the contraption Max had brought him.

"Vaya a vestirse, Señorito Maximo, aqui le dejo su desayuno." Among the many amazing feats Maximus Gregorio had accomplished, the most astounding of these was completely enchanting Cantor's cantankerous secretary. Dilania, who as far as he knew had absolutely no use whatsoever for men, doted on Maximus in a manner that bordered on coddling. He would say something, but it was a lost cause: his household and his own existence would likely remain tangled around Max's little finger.

"You said they were your favorites. I aim to please my clients," Cantor demurred, and Dilania scoffed at him from the small table she was setting. After a moment, she excused herself, and it was just Max and him in the studio.

"Go on," he told the younger man.

"Try the seat first, please," Max begged. It looked quite awkward, and Cantor wasn't certain he could fold himself into it or unfold himself *out* of it for that matter.

"It's like a stool with pads for kneeling," Max encouraged.

Cantor would probably rip his trousers and look like a complete dolt in the process, but he did it anyway. He obediently dropped himself onto the thing and slid his legs in until they were against the pads.

To his surprise, it was very comfortable. The kneeling position allowed for his feet to rest and took the pressure off his lower back.

"You can adjust your easel so that it's low enough to reach from there," Max informed him as he circled the chair. Max was a good six inches shorter than he and, with as many meals as he missed, was much leaner too. There was no question who could overpower who. Yet Cantor shivered under the smaller man's inspection. He almost jumped out of his skin when strong hands clasped his shoulders.

"Does it feel supportive?"

"Yes." His voice was barely audible as his entire body reacted to Max's hands. "It's good," he said, clearing his throat. "Thank you." Cantor turned his gaze up just in time to see a satisfied smile settle on Max's lips.

"I'm pleased that it fits you."

"It does. I look forward to trying to work from it," Cantor said sincerely. "How did you come up with this design?"

Max had mentioned he liked playing with designs. But this was a very different skill than whatever was required to erect ten thousand tons of iron on the banks of the Seine.

"Oh." Max paused in front of Cantor, his brown eyes never quite meeting his. "It's just." More evasive looks, combined with fidgeting. "I've been toying with devices that allow for a person to kneel for long periods of time." His voice lowered to a scrape, and the sound went straight to Cantor's cock.

"Kneeling." The mere thought of Max making this chair to play with anyone else sent the blood rushing hot in his veins. "What exactly would require something like that?" He stood, because face to face, it would be harder for Max to avoid his gaze, and when he asked the next question, Cantor wanted a full view of his client's face. But Max didn't answer, a pink blush all over his countenance.

Blushing Max was the most dangerous Max.

"You're not going to tell me, then?"

Max looked up at him, brown eyes big and round behind his spectacles, and shook his head. "Tell you what?"

"Max," Cantor growled, pressing closer until the other man was flush against him.

"Not yet. I can't yet," Max said stubbornly. Cantor resisted the urge to cajole, to push until Max let them have what they both wanted.

"We were perfect at Là—"

Max frantically covered Cantor's mouth, as if keeping him from voicing the words would somehow make what they knew less true. "Don't say it," he begged, almost frantically.

"But why do you—" his words were muffled under Max's hand, and the other man only shook his head.

"You'll tire of me." Cantor could see Max truly believed that. His eyes seemed so bleak, resigned. "Once you know how I truly am, you will. Once my oddities and my neediness wears on you. It will happen. It's best to keep things separate. That I slake my needs separately from my life."

"Did your wife ask for that?"

Max cast down his eyes at the mention of his deceased wife.

"Arabella was my friend." Oh. Now Cantor was beginning to understand. "We married because she desperately needed to escape the betrothal her father had arranged for her with an older, cruel man. I had . . . someone."

That wasn't rare, not among men like them. Especially men with the means to make a desirable husband.

"Did she resent you taking a lover?"

Max laughed bitterly, but he kept his head tightly pressed to Cantor's chest.

"I made her acquaintance through my lover." He shuddered out a heavy sigh. Cantor could feel the tremors racking his slim form. "Arnie. He was her brother." The brother who had died in the accident with his wife.

"Oh, sweetheart," Cantor soothed as the other man sniffled. He could scarcely imagine living through that. Losing the love of your life, then having to pretend you were mourning a friend.

"When he died," he said through what sounded like sobs, "we'd had an argument and he and Arabella left for London that afternoon." There was that tinge of shame, of self-loathing again.

"An argument?" Cantor prodded.

"I was jealous," Max said, in explanation. "Arnie didn't like it when I displayed 'my ugly possessive side,' or when I became 'unreasonable.' You won't like it either."

What were you possessive about?" Max only shook his head.

Cantor tipped Max's head up. He encountered eyes brimming with tears and a hollowness that tore his heart in two.

"Tell me, darling." Shivers ran through Max at the request, his body softening against Cantor's. This was what this boy needed, someone to belong to. Cantor would gladly assume that role, as long as Max let him.

Max opened his mouth, clearly struggling with what to say. Then he shook his head. "I can't."

Cantor let him go. After all, it was Thursday.

5

THREE KNOCKS ON THE DOOR, THEN THREE MORE KNOCKS, AND HE WAS IN.

"Bonsoir, Monsieur Achilles," the hostess greeted him smoothly. Cantor only nodded. No need to show an invitation this time. He felt restless, his body full of nervous energy. The whole day had been a wash. From the moment Max walked out of his house, Cantor had bided his time until he could come to the club. Max was not as bold as X was. What's more, Cantor suspected the man truly believed that the only side of him worth keeping was the one that came out at Là-Bas. The way he'd held on to Cantor that morning, the need in him, the yearning to be cherished, all was palpable. But the moment they got close, Max ran. Cantor knew why—he'd been tossed aside before. He'd been made to feel that what he needed was too much to ask.

For this to work, he would have to make it very clear that as addictive as X had been from the first taste, Cantor was equally drawn to the shy aristocrat who labored as an engineer. The widower who, years after his lover's passing, still carried such raw, naked grief for his beloved. The man who wanted, no, deserved someone who could treasure every part of him.

"Monsieur," the hostess called to him, and he realized he'd been standing there without saying a word.

"Pardon," he answered, bringing himself back to the moment.

"Is this good for you?" The woman asked, and now he was certain he'd entirely missed what she'd said.

"Sorry, what?" Cantor asked, embarrassed.

The hostess smiled. Perhaps his gobsmacked state was more obvious than he thought.

"Monsieur X has requested your company this evening." Cantor's heart leaped. His skin thrumming with excitement, the nervous energy now of a completely different kind, a sun hot and bright and pulsing in his chest.

"Is he in the main room?" Cantor was impressed by how unaffected he sounded when there were tremors coursing through his body. How could Cantor, infamous bachelor, feel this much, this deeply for a man he'd only met weeks ago. How could he desire a lover who he'd had merely minutes with his intensely? He could scarcely understand what was happening to him. But it didn't make his feelings any less real.

"He's reserved a private room," she explained. "Would you like to join him?" He could only nod.

"Very well," the hostess said, and scribbled something on the ledger in front of her. "He's asked you remain masked, and he will do the same."

More games, then.

They both knew who they were outside of here, and yet Max, X, wanted to maintain the pretense that they were strangers. He remembered his words from earlier that day, the certainty that Cantor would tire of Max, his belief that only X was desirable.

You need to earn his trust, and pushing for what you want when he's not ready will destroy any chance of that.

"What room?" he asked, picking up a mask from the tray before handing it to the hostess and turning around. A niggle of doubt edged into his mind. One well aimed comment to the right person and Max could do away with everything Cantor had built. Why was he taking such a big chance on a man he barely knew?

Because he already feels like he's yours.

"Once you get to the main floor, one of the ushers there will guide you." Cantor stopped himself from running up the stairs, reminding himself how much control he'd already conceded by allowing Max to summon him like this.

As promised, one of the men guarding the main room promptly

guided him up two more flights of stairs, and within seconds he was at a red door with a brass number eight on it. He used the key he'd been given to open it, his hands shaking. As he stepped inside, he swore he could almost hear his own heartbeat echoing from the walls.

The room was empty, but someone had been here. The electric light fixture by the bed was on, and there were two glasses of champagne on a little table in the front of the room. The four-poster bed was turned down, and a few objects had been laid on a sideboard next to a door he assumed led to a washroom. He took a couple of steps toward it to look more closely at the display. The moment he saw what they were, his cock hardened painfully in his trousers.

One was a large glass phallus with a small jar by it. Cantor picked up the jar and opened the lid, placing it close to his nose. Petroleum jelly. His gut tightened with anticipation. There was also a length of thin, soft rope that had Cantor groaning in agony. The last thing on the table was a paddle. He was testing the grip of the wooden implement when the other door in the room opened, and X stepped out.

His mask was firmly in place, but other than the collar he'd had on that first night a couple of weeks ago, he was completely naked. And watching him now, taking in that stance, left foot tilted out just so, shoulders level, the curve of his lips that both could challenge and beg, and that halo of sable curls—how hadn't he seen it instantly? His mouth watered at the sight of those pierced nipples and lush, inviting lips.

On his way to the club, he'd wondered if, when he saw the man, he'd want to treat him differently from that first night. If he'd be compelled to be gentler. If the urge to soothe and protect that he'd felt with Max would be present now. Need was certainly present, but whereas with Max, Cantor wanted to cocoon and to shelter. With X, he wanted to own.

He wanted to use X and leave him soaked in sweat and semen. Cantor's skin buzzed with the need for it, with conflicting waves of relief and gratitude roiling right underneath. Relief that he still wanted X like this, that his feelings for Max, as confusing as they were, had not suffused his appetite. Gratitude that the darkest and gentlest of his fantasies could be embodied in the same person.

He'd finally found him. His perfect person.

Desperate to have this out, to claim this man completely, Cantor opened his mouth to ask that they both take their masks off and do this openly. Then he observed that same hollowness he'd seen in Max's eyes that morning. Max would run from him if pushed, and Cantor was too weak with need to risk it. This had to be about what they both came looking for in this place. After that need had been slaked, after those flames had become ashes, then they would talk.

Now he was ready to fuck.

Silently and without acknowledging X's presence, he undid the placket of his trousers and pulled out his rigid cock. He kept his gaze on the other man and watched as X's mouth went slack at the sight of Cantor's hardness. X licked his bottom lip, throat moving as if he could already feel Cantor's cock choking him. Fishing for more lustful reactions, Cantor rudely tugged on his balls, then ran a thumb over the head, where a bead of liquid had escaped. X whimpered, body listing forward, his own stand bobbing in front of him.

"Where do you belong, boy?" Cantor growled, and X sank to the ground without a moment's hesitation, head bowed in supplication. Cantor thought his heart would burst out of his chest with the beauty of his lover's submission. X crawled on his knees to him, that round posterior in the air, eyes lifted to Cantor's. Still on all fours, he pressed his nose to the juncture of Cantor's thighs, inhaling deeply as if he'd been dying to take that musk in. He mouthed Cantor's cock, the wetness making an urgent frisson crawl up Cantor's spine. He was testing him, pushing boundaries, and Cantor would be happy to play along. Without warning, he gripped the younger man's hair and tore him away. "Did I say you could have my cock?"

"No, Daddy," the other man said with a shudder. Cantor hated the mask in that moment. He wanted to tear it off X's face.

"You can't help yourself," he growled. "Bloody cock whore." X's body jolted, small breaths puffing out of his mouth. Cantor fed him the head and X's hot tongue lapped and laved it like it was the only thing the man had to eat in an age. "You love a hard piece in your mouth, don't you?" he asked through clenched teeth as he pushed in farther. X took him in eagerly. "Maybe I should ram it in all at once. Make you gag with it." X's nostrils flared, little moans of ecstasy escaping him as Cantor kept up a litany of filthy promises.

"Mm," Cantor encouraged. "Take it all." He thrust in a couple of times and felt X's tongue swirling around him, watched X's hollowed cheeks as he sucked with gusto. He gripped the back of Cantor's thighs as if he wanted to drown in him. Before he spilled down the smaller man's throat, Cantor roughly tugged him off by his collar. X moaned in frustration, his tongue sliding against the underside of Cantor's cock as he was pulled away from it.

"Beg for it." Cantor sounded like his throat was raw from smoke. And he did feel on fire. His entire body could combust from the desire coursing through him. He tightened the hand on the other man's collar.

"May I have more, please?" X swiped his pink tongue over his bottom lip, which was glistening. Then he closed his eyes as if savoring traces on Cantor on his tongue.

"Later." A pout and slump of the shoulders. But X stayed put, waiting. "Take off my trousers," Cantor commanded. X worked efficiently, his chest heaving. His gaze locked on to Cantor's face, hunger shining in those liquid brown depths.

"You are magnificent," X breathed as he ran his hands appreciatively over Cantor's thighs and flanks. "So big."

Cantor knew what he looked like. He was tall, brown-skinned, with a thick pelt of coarse black hair on his chest. He swam, boxed, and rode to keep his body strong. His thick muscles were not like X's lithe form, and with the mask, he looked menacing.

"I'm not what the ton would consider beautiful, as I lack the pallor and perennially hungry air that's fashionable." He didn't care what society thought about his appearance. But he could be vain, and he wanted to hear compliments from the man who appealed to him more than any other ever had.

"You are everything I've dreamed of." X's voice was reverent.

"I'm not going to go easy on you," Cantor warned as he lifted X to his feet and carried him to the bed. The other man sat at the edge, cock so hard it had to be painful, but he didn't seem to notice, riveted as he was by Cantor's prick. "What word do you use if you don't want to continue?"

"Stop." X let himself fall onto the bed, pulling his knees up until he was completely on display. Hard prick. Tight balls. That pulsing, furrowed entrance, which Cantor wanted to push into with relentless thrusts. Without a word, he leaned over X and took one nipple into his mouth, sucking hard. Then he did the same to the other, eliciting grateful mewls from his lover. He made his way down the man's torso, sucking and biting as X encouraged him. Once he got to his groin, he took him into his mouth in one gulp. X cried out as Cantor engulfed him. He pleasured the man for a few fevered seconds, his fingers looking for X's tight bud. Once he found it, he rubbed circles there, and X pushed into the touch.

"I'm going to spend, sir, oh, please." Cantor sucked hard for a few moments, then let X's prick go with a popping sound. Cantor loved a prick, but he was captivated by the other man's ass. A shudder ran through him at the idea of being inside him, of that tight, velvet grip.

"I'm going to mark you," Cantor warned as he grazed his teeth along the other man's neck. "So you'll remember how I owned you tonight." X whimpered. It was the only word that did the pained and aroused sound justice.

He pushed X up and, without a word, took his mouth. X kissed like the world was crumbling under his feet. Urgent nips and bites that spurred Cantor on in a way nothing and no one ever had before. Again, he wished he could take the mask off, but focused instead on what he did have: lips to suck on, a velvety tongue to tangle with his, and hands gripping him like he was harbor in a storm.

"Yes," X begged. By now he was thrusting into Cantor's stomach, his weeping cock leaving streaks on Cantor's shirt. "More, more." The way he submitted to Cantor undid him. Every moan, every pliant gesture rushed through his blood like liquid fire.

"More what?" Cantor demanded before breaching X's entrance with the tip of a dry finger.

"You," X said in a rush of breath, and Cantor stumbled. "Fuck me, please." He reached for Cantor's cock.

"Not yet," Cantor bit out, moving away. "Kneel on the edge of the bed." The other man moved so quickly that he almost lost his balance. Within seconds he was in the position Cantor had ordered—on his knees at the end of the four-poster bed. Cantor moved around the room, gathering what he needed. He reached for the small bottle of oil, the glass dildo, and the rope. Then he removed his jacket, waistcoat, and shirt, and with the implements in his hand, he approached the bed where X was waiting for him. There was a bench at the foot of it. Cantor moved it out of the way so he could stand behind X, who despite his kneeling position had his back ramrod straight with that round delicious rump on full display. Cantor's mouth watered at the thought of bending him over and burying his face in it.

"I'll use the rope to spread you for me," Cantor said briskly, and his lover nodded. He stroked the swell of X' backside, the expanse of his shoulders where "Agapitos" was tattooed on his skin. *Beloved.* The duality of it made X perfection. He was sweet, shy Maximus during his days, and carnal, sensual, submissive X at night.

One man to care for and spoil, the other to fuck and possess.

Cantor put a hand on his warm back over the tattoo and slid it down to the crease of his rum, then spread him for his view. He kissed one cheek, then the other, and ran his tongue over the exposed pucker, making his lover jump. He tasted like soap and skin. Cantor blew a bit of air into that bud, eliciting a shiver and a groan from his lover.

"Daddy, please," X begged, and Cantor laughed viciously.

"So polite when you want my mouth on you. Ask again," he demanded as he swatted a heated cheek.

"Please, I want your fingers pressing inside, taking me. Your tongue licking into me. I need you."

Cantor closed his hands into fists to keep the trembling at bay. He palmed a cheek in each hand to pull them even wider. He massaged the rim with oiled fingers, the floral scent of orange blossom tickling his nose. Then he licked, the hard tip of his tongue circling the puckered opening as his fingers pressed inside. All the while, X whined under him, pushing himself into Cantor's ministrations.

"I could do this for hours," he said in between licks, pushing in a second finger. X was propped on both hands now and fucking himself into Cantor's mouth and fingers. Cantor couldn't help running his palms over that delicious, round arse. "But I have lofty plans for this sweet little hole." Without warning he plunged three fingers inside, the stretch making the other man writhe under Cantor's hands.

"Ah," X moaned, spine arching like a large cat looking for scratch.

"I'm of a mind to take you right now," Cantor mused as he pumped in and out of his lover's ass.

"Take me." X's voice was stripped raw. Cantor kept one hand working that tight hole, and used the other to torture his nipples. First the left, then the right, causing X's torso to twist in agony.

"I'll give you what I want, boy," he said roughly, feeling the tremors racking X's body. He removed his fingers from X, who cried out in displeasure. Cantor's chest tightened at the reaction. He already found it extremely difficult to deny the man anything. He grabbed the small bottle of oil, bit off the topper, and poured some onto X. He watched a trickle of the viscous liquid slide down the crack. Cantor reached for X's balls, playing with the sensitive sacs as he pushed three fingers back inside. The smaller man bucked into his hand as if he'd been struck by lightning, and let himself fall flat on to the sheet, his cheek pressed to the sheets.

"Oh God." X was shaking like a leaf, undulating his hips in a circle as Cantor fondled that place inside that obliterated men's minds with pleasure. "Let me come, please, sir," X pleaded as he mindlessly ground his ass into Cantor's fingers.

"You'll come after I've spilled inside you, boy." Cantor grunted, roughly squeezing X's balls to fend off the impending orgasm.

"I need it. I need you, please. I'll be so good for you." Cantor's heart was in his throat, lust coursing through him like a storm. Cantor moved to cover X's back until their heads were pressed together.

"Do I need to gag you, boy?" he barked, mouth pressed to the man under him, dangerously close to unmasking them both. He let a litany of dark, dirty promises escape his lips. "Maybe I need to turn you around and ram my stand into your mouth while I fill this greedy hole with that glass cock you left for me." X's entrance contracted around Cantor's fingers in a viselike grip. He was close. Cantor could hear it in the way X's breath was coming in short bursts.

"Please," X begged, completely beyond shame.

"No." Cantor smiled cruelly. "Not until I say so." Cantor used his knees to spread X's thighs even wider until the smaller man was plastered to the mattress.

"One more sound that isn't 'thank you Daddy,'" Cantor warned as his open palm connected with the swell of X's plump ass, "and I won't let you come at all." He bit down on the place where his hand had connected, and X gave another one of those jolts, except this time his breath got shallower and Cantor noticed that his hands were under him, and he was bringing himself off . . . again.

"Since you can't be trusted to obey, I'm going to bind your arms." Roughly, he grabbed X's forearms and reached for the rope. "Then I'll lift this ass up in the air and fuck it until I tire of it." More panting as the smaller man's ass wiggled against Cantor's cock. He gritted his teeth as he wrapped X's forearms in a binding, leaving enough give in it for him to hold on. Once he was satisfied, he stuffed a couple of pillows under X until his ass and glistening, soft hole were on display. Cantor coated his turgid prick in oil and let the head kiss X's entrance.

"You're lucky I'm in a giving mood," he growled in a voice he could hardly recognize before pushing in.

"More," cried X as he attempted to press against Cantor.

"Did I give you permission to take more of my cock, boy?" Cantor asked, roughly gripping the other man's nape, eliciting a purr from him. "You love to be handled roughly, don't you?"

"By you," X confessed as Cantor tightened his hold. He then let out a shout of exquisite agony when Cantor sheathed himself to the hilt.

God, he was perfect.

"You'll be feeling me for days," he said, pulling almost completely out, only to slam back into that velvet heat. "So tight and sweet. Who owns this?" Cantor growled as he planted another swat on X's rump.

"You," X said through a ragged gasp. "Only you, Cantor."

For a moment his lungs stopped working and he had to gasp for air. Hearing his name in that desperate, reedy voice knocked the wind out of him. He quickly undid the ropes on Max's arms and, with something close to desperation, pulled out so that he could lay the man on his back. Max's mask was askew, his mouth swollen. Without hesitation, Cantor took his own off and entered Max again. They both gasped from the joining.

Cantor waited as Max raised a hand to lift his own mask off. One heartbeat, then two, and then there it was, that face, that mouth, those eyes that had finally come to claim him.

"There you are," he said, helpless to hide the reverence in his voice. "Say my name." Flames roared through Cantor as he swiveled his hips, targeting that perfect spot that made X's ragged cries of pleasure echo in the room.

"Cantor."

"You're both mine now," he promised as Max's gaze roamed over his face. "Tell me."

He needed to hear it. They both did.

"All yours," Max said, and arched his spine upward, hips seeking, always greedy, demanding what Cantor ached to give him. Cantor planted a foot on the mattress to steady himself, and with a hand on X's throat, he started moving again.

He entered X with desperate intensity, thrusting into him without quarter as the other man cried and begged for more. After a few powerful thrusts, he heard a grunt and felt his lover stiffen under him. Cantor bit back a curse as his climax churned in his groin, hot and urgent. X's tear-streaked cheeks were the last thing he saw before his vision whited out and lighting tore through him with such intensity it was almost painful. He let himself sink into it, limbs liquid, emptying his soul into the supine form under him.

He gathered Max in his arms and found his mouth. Max kissed him in that frenzied way he had, sucked on Cantor's tongue, digging his fingers into Cantor's shoulders. Like he wanted to meld them together. It was a long moment before either of them spoke.

They both knew everything had changed, and though Cantor had told himself he was ready for this, now he felt unsure. Would he be enough for this man? Could he care for him like he deserved? Would he be strong enough to give him what he needed?

"Will you come back . . . ," he began, but Max shook his head.

"Not just yet," he begged before luring Cantor in with a long and languid kiss. They tasted each other while Cantor ran his hands over that tight, lithe body that shouldn't have felt as familiar as it did. He'd only had Max twice, but it already seemed like he belonged to Cantor. "I'd like to continue seeing you, after the portrait," Cantor whispered against Max's ear, breaking the last of the rules.

"You won't want more than this." Max laughed, but it was broken, brittle. X was gone, replaced by Max, who was certain Cantor would not want him.

He tipped Max's face up, and the pain he saw there undid him.

"Everything I see in you, I desire. What's more, I want to know you better. I want to understand how that mind of yours works."

Max rubbed his face against Cantor's chest like a cat, avoiding his eyes when he spoke again. "I am scattered," he explained, as it was an undeniable fact. "I'm selfish." The way he those things made the hair on

Cantor's neck stand up. As though he was parroting something he'd heard again and again. "I don't sleep. Too much trouble."

"I don't see what the trouble is. You are sweet and utterly beddable. Brilliant and kind. Everything I want."

Against his chest, Max murmured something that sounded to Cantor a lot like, "You say that now."

What had happened between him and Arnie? Not that Cantor wanted to disparage a dead man, but something was not right here. It was on the tip of his tongue to push, but he didn't want to give Max a reason to pull away, not when Cantor finally had him.

"Will you come for the rest of your sittings?" he asked instead.

Max tipped his head up then, smiling.

"I might be able to manage that. If you have some of that Pata Negra ham waiting for me."

"Brat. Maybe I'll have you kneel on that chair you made for me, next time." Cantor swatted that lush posterior.

Max's eye widened for a second, and Cantor held his breath, suddenly nervous he'd pushed the man too far. But after a moment, Max slid his arms around Cantor's neck and pushed up to kiss him.

"That is not much of a threat . . . Daddy."

6

Eighth (and last) Sitting

BY NOW THEY HAD A ROUTINE, OF SORTS. MAX CAME AND WENT, WITH DAYS of silence in between—three this time. After that night at Là-Bas, Max had not returned to the studio for a couple of days, and once he did, there had not been any semblance of X outside of the club. They'd begun what Cantor could only consider a chaste kind of courting, a very careful friendship. Maximus was an intelligent man, with a sharp wit and deliciously insightful mind, but so far, in the light of day, there had been nothing of that lusty, insatiable man from Jeudi Noir. It was disorienting to converse with the mild-mannered aristocrat during the day, knowing and at night, he might encounter the wickedly lusty X. Though Lord Maximus, like X, kept Cantor on his toes . . . in a completely different manner. The last two weeks would've tested the patience of a saint, and he was not a saintly man on his best days.

Lord Maximus Gregorio Bretton was . . .unpredictable. He was almost always late to his sittings. He'd send notes announcing the time he'd arrive the next day and then appear hours earlier or later, or not at all, as though Cantor's mornings belonged exclusively to him. To Dilania's utter delight, he was yet to put the imp to get on a proper schedule.

The result was that Cantor's fastidious daily routine had been in tatters for the better part of a month. Which was all his own doing, of course.

What was worse, he found himself anticipating whatever mishap or disaster Max would arrive with each time.

There was *always* something amiss. He'd arrive wearing the wrong set of clothing or walk out in the middle of the sitting because he remembered he was supposed to be elsewhere. One day, he'd turned up at eight in the morning, right as Cantor was returning from his daily swim and bout at the gymnasium, claiming he'd worked all night and figured that he'd just come straight to the sitting. This had resulted in Dilania feeding the man while Cantor bathed and dressed.

Pandemonium.

Cantor's perfectly organized life was in utter chaos, and he was . . . smitten. Smite marks all over his heart. And at a loss. Because as delectably wicked as X could be, Lord Maximus had erected an impenetrable wall regarding that side of himself. There had been no allusion, not even a slip of the tongue, to their nights together at Jeudi Noir. He could never have more than one side of the man, and what Cantor wanted was absolutely everything. For Max to let Cantor see all parts of him.

He suspected there was a difficult history there. From the things Max had said about his dead lover, Cantor knew there was more to Max's dogged belief that no man could love him fully than the moralistic hogwash they were all fed from birth.

He clearly found pleasure in submitting to Cantor, in being cared for, in being appreciated. And it was not only Cantor doing the giving. Maximus, in that inquisitive, quiet way of his, had managed to tap into parts of Cantor that few had noticed. It had begun on the day he'd come with the chair and seen the painting Cantor had been working on. Since then, he'd been more and more curious about his work beyond portraiture, asking Cantor all manner of questions about what he loved to paint, what he would render if he were able to choose freely. The questions had reminded Cantor of the pieces he'd started years before and abandoned when the demand for his portraits increased. Pieces like the one he was working on now.

He took a step back to take in some of his brushwork. The composition was good, and so were the colors. At the center of the canvas was a dancer in mid-movement, her bright yellow skirt swirling around her. She had a red rose in her hair and braids coiled around her head like an onyx crown. Peeking out of her skirt was a foot, lifted in the air. Behind her, to the right, stood a dance partner dressed in black trousers fringed with gold and a short jacket like those used by the charros. On the floor between them was the man's wide-brimmed black felt hat. The man was in profile with one foot pointed forward, the other leg bent as if he was leaning back to give her space to move. His golden-brown hand was extended to her. Their eyes locked in a heated gaze. There were others in the background, looking at the pair. Other women in equally colorful costumes were poised to join the dance. Cantor had painted the sky in purples, oranges, and pinks to evoke that evening in Guadalajara when he'd happened upon the dancers at the plaza in front of a cathedral. The type of dance, he'd been told, was the Jarabe Tapatio, and it had been mesmerizing to watch. He hoped the piece evoked some of the movement and vibrance of what he'd witnessed that day. It was certainly bolder than anything he'd ever dared show in a Paris salon. It also one of the best things he'd done.

His best painting, which no one would ever see.

"You're working on it," Max said with delight, surprising Cantor. "Dilania said I'd find you here in the solarium."

The clock struck ten, surprising Cantor further. Max was on time. Cantor shook his head at the irony of Max arriving on time for the last sitting. It was true that he could make excuses to extend their time, but he was eager to end these forced visits and begin to court the man properly.

"Lord Maximus," he said, placing the brush and palette down and coming closer. Not to kiss or embrace. He had not been granted freedom to do that beyond the walls of Là-Bas. To his surprise, it was Max who placed his arms around his neck and rose to kiss him. It was deep, languorous thing. Cantor froze in surprise, but soon found himself grunting in pleasure at Max's eagerness. He pulled back to look at his lover. "What was that for?"

"Nothing." Max shrugged, his smile a little subdued. "It had been a few days, that's all."

"Work?" Cantor asked, even though he already knew the answer. Max only sighed and nodded in response.

"Shall I have Dilania bring your breakfast?"

Max turned from him before he answered. "No, I've already eaten." That gave Cantor pause, but before he could ask, Max spoke. "Shall we get on with it? My last sitting with the great Joseph Cantor Marshall," he said a little too brightly.

"All right." That was all he managed as he led the way to the studio. The moment he picked up the brush and turned to look at Max, he knew something was wrong. It was like a completely different man was sitting for him. As usual, once he made himself take things in with his artist's eyes, everything seemed clearer. Max was unhappy. Sadness and melancholy enveloped Max like a blanket. Cantor made himself work, to apply paint to the canvas and make small talk as he thought of what to say.

"Is that the painting you plan to send for the exposition?" Max asked after what felt like hours of silence. Cantor was so surprised at the question that he had to step away from the canvas to face the other man.

"The dancers?" He was guessing, since it was what he'd been working on when Max arrived.

"Yes."

"No," Cantor confessed, uncomfortable with the look of disappointment he received from Max.

"You should, it's brilliant." He stood then, and seemed so unsteady on his feet that Cantor almost went to hold him up.

"I must go," Max informed him as he walked to the easel and stood next to Cantor. "That man looks very at ease," Max muttered, inspecting his likeness. "I can't say I recognize that particular expression."

"It's the one I see whenever you're here. It's the expression of someone who after only one sitting could see exactly what I needed to do my work more comfortably. The eyes of the man who has charmed everyone in my home with his kindness and grace." That elicited a pained expression from Max. He looked horrified by Cantor's effusiveness, so much so he almost didn't say the next thing. But Cantor suspected that if he didn't do it now, he'd never get the chance. "It's the image of the man I'm beginning to love." The other man's face crumpled, horror etched in its beautiful lines.

"Please, don't. You don't mean that. You don't. I must go." He backed away from Cantor as though he'd been scalded by the words. Max was slipping from his fingers and Cantor was helpless to stop him. He wouldn't keep Max here if he didn't want to stay. So when his lover pushed up and kissed him on the cheek, he kept him there for a second, but then, he let him go.

7

"ARE YOU TRULY SENDING HIM THE PORTRAIT?" DILANIA ASKED IN A TONE heavy with disapproval. The question was superfluous since Cantor had been clear about his intentions. Two days ago, after more than a week without a word, he'd received a note from Max saying he wanted to come and see Cantor the next morning. Max never came, which was a strong enough message. Cantor would send Max the finished portrait and a note letting him know their business was done.

Without responding to Dilania, he continued what he was doing, which was laying Max's portrait on a large piece of waxed paper that he'd special-ordered from a stationery at the Rue de La Paix. The royal-blue paper had on it his signature embossed in gold so that everyone could recognize what it was when it was delivered. He rarely packed his portraits himself, but he had to do something to keep himself occupied.

"What am I supposed to do? Go chasing after him?"

"Obviously."

Cantor only shook his head. After Max walked out of the studio the day of his last sitting, Cantor had not gone after him, had not hounded him with messages. Had refrained from going to the man's house and demanded Max tell him how he could walk away from what they'd found in each other's arms. Instead, he'd waited until Thursday and gone to Là-Bas, looking for X. But when he'd approached the hostess, she'd given a discreet shake of her head. After almost an hour walking around aimlessly in the ballroom, he gave up and went home.

It hurt that Max didn't seem to value what they'd shared, but Cantor didn't want to harass the man. He knew things were different in Max's world. That he had familial expectations that Cantor, because of his own family tragedy, never had to grapple with. Still, he really believed there was something worth pursuing.

Perhaps he'd made more of what had happened than what actually did. Maybe he had been seeing what he wanted to see and not what was really there. But the way that X, that Maximus, had given himself to Cantor was undeniable. The intensity between them, the way they could instinctually anticipate what the other needed, was unlike anything Cantor had ever experienced. It had been so easy to have him in his home, to talk to Max about his art, his plans. No, he hadn't imagined their connection.

"I can't go chasing after a man who has not given me any indication he's interested in anything beyond anonymous encounters."

"He made you a *chair*," Dilania said, as if the gift of furniture was the highest evidence of affection. After a second, she let out a sad laugh. "Well, something chairlike, in any case."

"That doesn't mean anything." Cantor prevaricated as if his life depended on it, but even he could hear the desperate hope in his voice.

"Joseph Cantor Marshall, I really thought you were smarter than that."

"My behavior of the last few weeks should've have disabused you of that notion," he answered petulantly.

Dilania pursed her lips and shook her head. "You also know that's not true. Even if it didn't mean anything for your young lord, which I seriously doubt. It meant something to *you,* and you reached for it. Your happiness is worth taking a few chances on."

"Dilania, you know the risks involved. Men like us cannot take leaps like that. It's too dangerous. And he's still grieving."

"I am aware that there are things to consider." She came to stand by him and ran her finger over the edge of the canvas. "It's one of the best things you've done," she told him, looking at the portrait.

Cantor was proud of this one. He'd captured Max's curious, incisive stare. The sparkling brown, sparkling eyes that shone with quiet intensity. The curve of his lips that tilted up ever so slightly when he was looking at something for the first time and was about to ask a question. The proud nose and perennially sun-kissed complexion. Cantor ached just looking at it, thinking of how Max fit with him, in his life, in ways Cantor had never thought possible. Fate had brought them together. One of them had to be brave enough to take the gift.

"You deserve some happiness, Cantor."

"I am happy," he assured her as he wrapped the parcel. He loved his work, relished that he could use his talent and be so handsomely, lavishly compensated for it. He was satisfied with what he'd made of his life, but he *was* lonely. These last few weeks during which Max had swept into his days, and the nights he'd had with X, had been the happiest in a very long time.

"I don't want to make a fool out of myself."

"Maybe he's thinking the same thing. This is why there will always be wars while men remain in charge," she fumed. "Would it kill you to just tell him how you feel?"

"It might," he told her, to which she responded with a very rude sound.

"He could be waiting for you to take the next step." Maybe Max was unsure too. Maybe he thought Cantor didn't go after him because he wasn't interested.

Maybe, maybe, maybe.

Max's silence was all the answer he needed. Maximus Gregorio Bretton had come for a portrait and that was what he would receive. Cantor's battered heart would learn to heal in time. . .or maybe it wouldn't.

"Call Jean-Luc, please. I'd like for him to deliver this to Mr. Bretton directly."

"I don't know why I insist on reasoning with you." Dilania heaved an annoyed sigh and took the painting from his hands. When she left the room, he went to his bedchamber and sat on his bed, looking at his other portrait of Max. The image was of a shirtless man on his knees, arms tied above his head, his face in profile. Sweat dripped down a tattooed back. His mouth was open, his eyes closed in an expression exquisite agony as he pressed his face into his lover's hand. That one had come to him in a gust of inspiration in the middle of the night after Max's first sitting. It was the only reminder he'd have of what he'd found with the elusive Lord Maximus.

HE STARTED at the portrait for what felt like hours until a knock on his door startled him out of his reverie.

"It's me," called Dilania, and the tightness in her voice made him rush to the door. As soon as he saw her face, he knew something was amiss.

"What is it?" For a split second she looked mildly apologetic, but then that stubborn jut of her jaw reappeared, and she opened her mouth.

"I asked Jean-Luc to request Lord Maximus send a reply that the portrait was received in good condition."

"Dilania," Cantor said reproachfully, but his concern about what she wasn't saying won over. "Is he all right? Did he respond?"

"That's just it. He's been convalescent."

"He's been what?" he shouted, a sick feeling instantly settling in his gut. Max was ill, hurting, and he'd been here sulking.

"Apparently, he only goes to work at night. He took a bad fall at the site days ago and broke his arm. And his foot was badly cut. That's why he didn't come."

"But he could've sent word."

"The maid who opened the door said he's been holed up in his room and has sent away most of the staff."

"I'm going to him," he said, already moving.

"This is the only intelligent thing you've said since the last time he was here." She was grinning while she said it, so Cantor let her get away with the insult. "Jean-Luc is waiting for you."

Cantor didn't stop to chastise her for making assumptions of what he would do. What would be the point? She'd been absolutely right.

"Tell Magdalena to make a caldo and some torrejas for when I bring him home." Dilania nodded. If she thought him presumptuous, she did not say. "As terrible as he is taking care of himself, my assumption is he has not been eating properly. Do we still have the candied pineapple the Duchess of Linley sent last week?"

"Yes, I'll get everything ready. It's about time you found something other than your work to pour your heart into."

Cantor grabbed his cane and hat and within minutes, he was in his carriage. On the way to Max's home, the adrenaline began to wear off, and doubt crept in. Had he made the right decision, or would he just be intruding?

Before he could decide, Jean-Luc pulled up to one of the new buildings in the eleventh designed by a young and innovative architect named Grimard. The thing looked like something out of a Brothers Grimm fairytale, but it was clearly an upscale residence. Cantor stepped out of the carriage and walked in through a small gate. The house had a rose garden in front, which one could not see from the street as tall walls completely concealed it. Before he could lift the doorknocker, a man dressed in livery opened the door.

He looked harried and nervous. Cantor scanned the room and took in the sumptuous furniture and ostentatious décor that didn't seem very much like Max's style. It was too stuffy, too much like it was there to impress. Cantor would've imagined Max surrounded by furnishings that would give him comfort.

"I'm Joseph Cantor Marshall," he told the man. "I'm here to see Lord Maximus Bretton."

The man looked at Cantor with open curiosity, clearly unsure what to make of this visit. Cantor *had* just sent the painting. He didn't blame the man for being confused.

"Lord Maximus has been indisposed due to a work injury," the man explained as he continued to scrutinize Cantor, presumably for some clue as to why he was here.

"Where's his bedroom?" Cantor asked impatiently. He needed to see with his own eyes if X—if Max was all right.

"Sir, I—" The servant hesitated when an older woman walked into the living room, dressed in a maid uniform. Her skin was a deep brown, her hair coiled into a long braid that wrapped around her head. He couldn't quite read her expression, but as soon as she appeared, the male servant stepped back as if ceding her the floor.

"I'm a friend of Lord Maximus and I'd like to go up and see him," he told the woman. His determination to see the master of the house must've been sufficiently clear. Without a word, the older woman turned on her heel and waved for him to follow. When they reached the door at the end of the hallway, she looked at Cantor.

"He hasn't let anyone come tend to him. It's been two days. He doesn't use a valet, doesn't like people fussing over him. But with his arm as it is, he can't be faring well," she explained, concern etched on her face. She knocked twice on the door, and a muffled groan came from the other side. Cantor's heart clenched in his chest at the pitiful sound. Still he hesitated, unsure of his welcome. But when he heard a thump, then a crash in the room, he decided he could apologize after he'd confirmed that Max had not maimed himself further. He turned the knob, stepped into the bedchamber, and found a bare-chested and extremely disheveled Max trying to sit upright on the bed.

"Cantor," he said with a gasp. "I'm. . . perfectly fine," Max claimed weakly.

"You most certainly do not look perfectly fine." Cantor scoffed and kept walking forward.

Max was a right mess. His arm was in a sling, and there were books scattered all over the floor. His hair was standing on end, and he had an angry scrape on the side of his face. There was also a black-and-blue bruise on his ribcage, just below one of the little gold rings on his nipples, and despite the situation, Cantor's cock jerked eagerly at the sight. Max was tempting, even in this sorry state. But Cantor was feeling much more than lust. Just being in Max's presence soothed something in Cantor that had been restless for days. After so many years of wondering what he was looking for, he'd finally found him. The one who filled every corner of his heart.

"You're hurt." Now only a few feet from the bed, Cantor could see the bruises were more severe than he initially thought.

"It looks a lot worse than it is," Max told him, then winced when he tried to move.

"I seriously doubt that." He stopped at the bedside and noticed Max was wearing trousers. "Are you still wearing the clothes you went to work with days ago?"

"Well . . . yes." Max grinned sheepishly.

Cantor pursed his lips. "Max, for God's sake!"

"I did see a doctor, he's a friend. Like us," he explained, then dropped his head on a pillow.

He looked exhausted. Cantor would do and say whatever he had to in order to convince Max to let him take care of him.

"I don't use a valet because of"—he waved a hand at his chest and back, wincing when his arm went up—"and a certain Greek demigod left so many bite marks on me that I feared anyone who saw might think I got attacked by a vampire."

A sound very close to a growl escaped Cantor's lips at the reminder of just how painstakingly he'd marked that delectable body the last time he'd been granted access to it. But this was not Là-Bas, where he could touch as he wanted. This was Max's home. And the truth was he had no idea if the man he was falling for felt the same way he did.

"Are you in pain?" he asked.

"Come closer," Max coaxed, and Cantor went, the resentment of the past couple of days replaced with relief that he was wanted.

"What should I call you?" It still was disorienting for him to have the two men he wanted in one endlessly, enticing body.

"You tell me," Max challenged.

Mine. It was on the tip of his tongue.

"Maximus," he said instead.

Max made a face, and Cantor laughed. "That's what my mother calls me." It was a challenge to concentrate when Max was within touching distance and the bruises Cantor had left on Max's chest were in view.

"I like 'sweetheart,'" Max groused, and Cantor's own chest filled with bone melting warmth.

"You are sweet and maddening," He told his lover without heat, and inched closer. He could see the smudges under Max's eyes. "When was the last time you slept?"

"I don't know," Max said, eyes lowering. "I want you to kiss me."

"You're convalescent."

"My arm is sprained, but my mouth is in perfect working order. So are most of my other parts." With his eyes leveled on Cantor, Max slid his hand down to his crotch and cupped his visibly hard cock. "Would you like to hear which ones?" Cantor had to dig his heels into the plush carpet under his feet to keep from pouncing.

"Don't provoke me. And take your hand off that." Unable to keep himself back, he stepped up and briskly pulled Max's hand off. "Eso es mio."

Max angled his head, his rumpled curls flopping about as he moved. His eyes dug into Cantor as if looking for something. He suspected it had to do with all the warnings that he would eventually tire of Max's needs. Cantor had to put all of that to rest. He made quick work of placing Max on his lap. The other man didn't protest, molding himself against him, cradling his injured arm and his face against Cantor's chest.

"What am I going to do with you?" Max only sniffed and shook his head. The soft caress of his hair against Cantor's sternum was like cool breeze after a day in the scorching sun. "Before you, I thought I was content with spending the rest of my life alone."

"I make everything complicated," Max said in that self-deprecating, defeated voice that Cantor had come to despise. "I can never make up my mind, and I keep letting down the people who care for me."

Cantor almost laughed, but he saw the bleakness in Max's eyes. Max truly believed that. "You've made my life infinitely more wonderful in the short time you've been a part of it. You are loving to the people in my home, you give me infinite pleasure." Max's breath caught, and he had to press a kiss to that lush mouth. "And not just with your body, but your mind is a marvel. Your curiosity, your bravery. In merely weeks you've filled me up." He gently tipped Max's face up and kissed. "It's not unreasonable to need time after all you've lost. If things are moving too fast for you if you don't want more—"

Max shook his head, curling his hand around Cantor's neck. "It's the opposite problem," he said, hiding his eyes from Cantor again. "I want to be in your house every morning. I wish that Là-Bas could happen every night. I just want to be with you, but—" He stopped talking then, eyes downcast.

"What is it?" Cantor coaxed, attempting to bring the other man's chin up. But Max stubbornly kept his head down.

"I just want to give you enough time."

Time to pull away, Cantor thought. Time to decide Max wasn't worth the trouble. He smothered the words of frustration attempting to crawl up his throat. "I don't need time. I know what I want. The moment I realized Max and X where one in the same, I knew I'd found the perfect man." Max frowned a little, but his eyes looked hopeful. "Every side of you is exactly right for me." A sound of disbelief escaped Max's lips, but Cantor knew that his boy didn't believe yet. Max needed time to trust that Cantor would not change his mind. "Promise me, please, that you won't do this again. That you won't climb ladders and roam around that massive hole in the ground alone, in the dark." Max lowered his eyes, his bottom lip caught in his teeth.

"I can't sleep at night. I go to the site and get work done. I come home exhausted and that way, I can get some rest." Which was why he always arrived late, and looked rumpled for the sittings. His poor darling.

"That night at Là-Bas, I had to wake you up." That night they'd met in the private room, he'd watched X—Max—sleep for hours, his face angelic in his slumber.

"I feel safe with you," Max said.

"Good, I will make it my mission to always be that for you." He whispered the words into the space between them. A promise as much for himself as for the man in his arms. "You are fucking miracle. A perfectly dirty, sweet, glorious miracle." Cantor sounded winded, and he felt it. A life he had never dared to imagine was within reach if he only let himself take it. If he convinced Max they could have it. "Come home with me."

It was not a demand. They both knew who was in control here.

"I'm jealous," Max told him, brown eyes blazing like he was daring Cantor to utter a single word of praise to him. "I am inconsiderate and selfish."

"And yet you hide your pain from your family so as not to worry them. You've been suffering alone because you don't want to be a burden. You saw my discomfort from standing once and didn't sleep for days making me something to help. You are anything but selfish." Cantor's heart constricted at the desolation on Max's face.

"I ran off to punish Arnie." Max's voice broke, the boundless agony in those few words shattering Cantor. "He'd been . . ." His Adam's apple bobbed as he clearly struggled with what he had to say. "He'd been seeing someone without my knowledge—an officer of the Royal Navy." His eyes welled with tears. "I found them in our bed. I'd been visiting my family and came home early. He was coming after me when the carriage turned over . . ." He couldn't go on, and hid his desperate sobs in Cantor's chest.

"God, that's terrible. I am so sorry, sweetheart." Cantor soothed Max as he cried. No wonder he was twisted in knots. What a mess. "It was not your fault. Not the accident and not his betrayal."

"If I hadn't run off," Max said in a small, broken voice.

"You were hurt. It's understandable." Cantor lifted that sweet mouth and pressed his own to it. Max opened to him on a soft, grateful sigh and slid his tongue against Cantor's in that strong, purposeful way he kissed. Unexpectedly forceful and possessive when their mouths were joined. In true form, Max was soon writhing on Cantor's lap. Needy, toe-curling sounds escaped his lips as they kissed. Gingerly, Cantor arranged Max so he was astride his hips. He also placed an arm around his lover's waist to support the side with the sling.

They probably shouldn't have been doing this. Max was hurt, and what Cantor wanted was to keep him swaddled in a nest of blankets and feed him caldo de pollo until that haunted, gaunt look left his eyes. But he also needed this, to touch, kiss, and taste in the light of day. Where he could finally see that beautiful face twisted in pleasure. Max moved against him in that now familiar rhythm that made Cantor's blood boil. But he didn't want to do this here. He wanted Max safe in his house, in his bed. *His.*

"Let me bring you to my flat."

"Yes." Max nodded as he pressed kisses to Cantor's chest. "Take me home."

8

"Is that . . . me?"

Max's stunned voice, still laced with sleepiness, pulled Cantor's focus from the canvas in front of him.

It was late, almost midnight, according to the clock. After getting themselves in order, Cantor helped Max dress, gather some personal things, and brought him home. Under Dilania's approving gaze, he'd put Max in bed after helping him take a warm bath. He looked cozy and delicious with his black mop of curls all around his head, his body swimming in Cantor's dressing gown.

"It is," Cantor said as he put down his palette and brush.

Cantor moved so that Max could see the portrait better. His heart thumped in his chest as he watched the man he loved gaze upon the other portrait he'd done of him. Max didn't answer as he moved further into the room, still focused on the canvas. There would be no use in explaining what Max could see with his own eyes: Himself. On his knees, head thrown back, lips parted, face lifted to the figure in front of him. There was adoration and absolute submission in his expression. It was not subtle or ambiguous in any way. This was the image of a man lost in his lover.

The very picture of Cantor's fantasies.

"You're still recovering. We should take you back to bed," Cantor said, little quakes of nervousness moving up and down his limbs. He'd been less agitated when he'd presented his commission to the queen. Max didn't answer for what seemed like a very long time. He studied the canvas, angling his head to this side and that, face impassive. Then he let out a long, shuddering sigh. Cantor observed him, unsure of what to do or say. But then his lover turned his attention to the other painting, the portrait that Cantor had brought back from Max's house with the intention of framing it. Max's attention flitted between the two for a few heartbeats. Then he turned to Cantor. His face split into a beatific smile, his caramel-colored cheeks dusky with a pink flush.

"Is that how you see me?"

"I don't think I could ever do you justice. Capture how beautiful you are when you give yourself to me." The flush on Max's cheeks deepened, and Cantor moved closer so he could wrap him in his arms.

"I think you are the only one that sees me as gloriously."

"Most people don't possess my ability to identify true beauty." Max's big brown eyes looked at him from under thick eyelashes, and Cantor felt himself hardening.

Would there ever be a time that Max's mere presence didn't set his blood on fire?

"Where are the dancers?" The change in subject surprised Cantor, but the canny tone in Max's voice told him he was asking a different question: whether Cantor had gotten past his insecurities and sent the work he wanted to show at the exhibit and not the one he thought people would approve of.

"I sent it to the committee at the exposition," he admitted.

"You took my advice, then." The younger man preened, and Cantor's heart thumped wildly.

"Don't get cheeky with me, boy," Cantor rebuked softly, even as he leaned to suck on Max's bottom lip. That quickly turned into a slide of tongues and then a deeper, hotter kiss. "But it was good advice. Thank you."

"Everyone will be talking about that piece. It's stunning."

Cantor warmed at the praise and believed it. "The opening isn't until next summer." He made himself say the next sentence. "I'd like you there with me."

"How are we going to do this?" Max asked, but Cantor could see the fire in his eyes. His boy wanted this as much as he did.

"Simple. You stay here in Paris with me, or I go to London. We stay together."

"People will talk. You don't like gossip."

"I don't, but I love you, which makes for more than a fair exchange."

"You love me," Max stated, not a question, but more of a declaration. Cantor watched his face, observing the flutter in his jaw, the trembling lip.

"Yes, and I'm not going anywhere. I won't leave you like he did."

"I don't want to be a burden," he said in that bleak, detached way he used to speak about himself. Cantor would not rest until every trace of self-loathing, of feeling like his needs were an imposition was fully gone from Max's voice.

"You are mine," Cantor growled, and bent to take Max's mouth. He sucked Max's tongue and felt himself sink into his lover. The way he always did. After a long and hungry kiss, Cantor felt the blanket on Max's shoulder fall on the floor, and without much effort, he lifted Max from the floor. The smaller man instinctively wrapped his legs around Cantor's waist. "I'm taking you to bed, and once we're there, we're talking this through, mi amor."

"Say it again," Max urged, pressing kisses to his neck.

"Mi amor," Cantor repeated, and felt that purrlike noise his lover made when he was pleased. "Mi vida," he intoned, carrying Max to the bedchamber. "Mi corazon, mi cielo. Is that sufficient, or shall I commence to expound my devotion in Italian? Caro mio," he said before kissing him deeply.

"In French now," Max demanded, making Cantor smile helplessly.

"Mon amour." A kiss on the nose. "Mon trésor." A lick of the lips. "Mon chou." A pinch on the bum. "I love you," he finally said, eyes wide open and locked with the man in his arms. "You were who I was looking for. The someone I yearned for and never imagined could exist, perfectly made for me." A tear rolled down Max's cheek as Cantor confessed everything that was in his heart.

"I will almost certainly forget to come home sometimes when I get distracted from work," he said in an apparent attempt to temper Cantor's passions.

"I will come to where you are and bring you here," Cantor answered, and Max's chin wobbled.

"There are days that I'm too melancholy to do anything but lie in bed and stare into space."

"I'll love you through it," Cantor said, and the truth of it felt like newly chartered territory in his heart that Max had discovered and promptly conquered.

"And I'll try my best to let you," Max said, beaming up at him as he pulled Cantor down for more kisses. "And," his lover promised against his lips, in a voice so soft it sounded to Cantor like a vow, "I'll devotedly, thoroughly, love you back." And in the darkness of the Paris night, they made love with exquisite tenderness as the first day of their forever began.

The End.

Want more high heat historical romance from Adriana Herrera?

Check out A Caribbean Heiress in Paris, a brand new romance about a rum heiress who tumbles into a marriage of convenience with an earl bent on revenge...

ALSO BY ADRIANA HERRERA

Las Léonas:

A Caribbean Heiress in Paris

(Coming May 2022!)

Sambrano Studios:

One Week to Claim It All

Just For the Holidays...

The Dreamer Series

American Dreamer

American Fairytale

American Love Story

American Sweethearts

American Christmas

Standalones

Mangos and Mistletoe

Her Night with Santa (a F/F Romance)

Finding Joy

Here to Stay

Anthologies

Caught Looking (He's Come Undone)

The Duke Makes Me Feel... (from the Duke I'd Like to F... Anthology)

ABOUT THE AUTHOR

Adriana was born and raised in the Caribbean, but for the last fifteen years has let her job (and her spouse) take her all over the world. She loves writing stories about people who look and sound like her people, getting unapologetic happy endings.

Her *Dreamers* series has received starred reviews from Publisher's Weekly and Booklist and has been featured in The TODAY Show on NBC, Entertainment Weekly, OPRAH Magazine, NPR, Library Journal, The New York Times, and The Washington Post. She's a trauma therapist in New York City, working with survivors of domestic and sexual violence.

You can sign up for Adriana's newsletter here!

SOLD TO THE DUKE

JOANNA SHUPE

1

The Chapel, London, 1895

A STRANGER WAS ABOUT TO BID ON HER BODY, FOR THE RIGHT TO TAKE what belonged to a husband.

But Eliza had no husband, nor did she want one. What she wanted was money—a lot of it.

Most people didn't understand desperation. Not true desperation, the kind that sat in one's belly, rotten and relentless, dragging a person down into a pit of despair. Over the last year, as her sister grew sicker, Eliza had come to know desperation well. Too well, in fact. She was drowning in it, completely out of decent options.

Which left her with only indecent options.

The Chapel auctions were legendary in certain segments of London, whispered about on the streets, with women bragging of the money to be had and the chance to find a wealthy protector. After thinking on it for two months, Eliza finally submitted her name, agreeing to auction herself off.

Please, let him be kind.

"Cor, you look bloody nervous." A woman sat next to Eliza. "Is this your first time, love? It won't be as bad as that."

Eliza swallowed and wrapped her arms around herself. They'd given all the women a simple white shift to wear, the fabric nearly transparent. "Yes, it's my first auction." *My first everything.*

The woman's brows rose slightly at hearing Eliza's accent, which still held hints of Mayfair. "What's a fancy dove like you doing here?"

"Same as everyone else. I need the money."

The woman struck out her hand. "I'm Helen."

They shook hands. "Eliza."

"Nice to meet you, Eliza. This is my third time. You'll be fine. Just do as he asks for seven nights and then you'll go home with a fat purse full of coin."

Seven nights.

A cold prickle of fear snaked down Eliza's spine. For seven nights she would be at the mercy of a stranger, one who had unlimited rights to her person.

This was your choice. You knew what you were agreeing to.

If there was any other option, she would take it. But she had a younger sister to consider, one who would die without treatment. This required money—and Eliza did not want to become a mistress, at the mercy of a man's whims. She wanted to keep her independence, which was why the auction was perfect. Seven nights, then she was free.

"Never heard of a cruel buyer," Helen was saying. "The owner's particular about who he lets attend. It's why the women are so eager to get a spot each month." She patted Eliza's knee. "Stay bricky and you'll be fine."

Eliza drew in a deep breath. No matter what happened, she would be fine, wouldn't she? She'd survive this, as she had everything else.

She'd survived the death of her parents, as well as the death of her brother, Robert.

She'd survived being cast out with only a few possessions by the new earl, their second cousin and Robert's successor.

She and her sister had survived the streets, the uncertainty. The hunger. Demeaning jobs for meager wages.

Eliza would survive this, too.

It's only your body. No one can touch your heart or your mind.

For one week, she could do anything if it helped Fanny get better.

"Thank you," she murmured to Helen gratefully.

"You're welcome. Oh, and go see the midwife for some pennyroyal at the end of the week. The kind that prevents consequences."

"My neighbor suggested cotton root tea." Martha worked in a bordello, and she'd filled Eliza in on what to expect after the auction. According to Martha, intimacies with a man were generally pleasurable, if not downright addicting. Eliza figured it must be true, considering all the babies in the world.

In the last five years, Eliza had seen and heard quite a lot. Knife fights, opium addicts, pickpockets . . .and yes, sexual favors. The alleys were full of all kinds of grunts and groans, people desperate for physical release.

Most of Eliza's education, however, came from their former neighbors, who'd been loud and enthusiastic in their intimacies, not to mention very specific about what they liked. Thanks to thin walls Eliza wasn't completely ignorant as to what would occur during these seven nights.

Truthfully, she was looking forward to ridding herself of her innocence. Eliza didn't have time for courting—those dreams died long ago, about the time she cleaned her first privy—but she would like to be held, to experience true pleasure, and to pleasure someone in return. Someone to fulfill these *urges* that haunted her at night, the physical cravings that had her reaching underneath the bedclothes to touch between her legs. . . .

Being a virgin was lonely and exhausting.

"Yes," Helen said, "cotton root tea works too, though I think the pennyroyal tastes better."

Before she could thank Helen again, the side door opened and the room fell silent. A woman holding a journal entered and began reading names. It was the same woman who'd signed Eliza up for the auction. Each auction participant answered when her name was called.

"Eliza," the woman said.

"Here," Eliza said in the loudest voice she could muster.

"Are you still a virgin, love?"

The air seemed to disappear out of the room as every head swung her way. "Yes."

The woman nodded once and closed her journal. "Ladies, we'll begin shortly."

Then she left, leaving the women alone, and Eliza's skin burned. Everyone here now knew she was innocent.

"A virgin," Helen said, her voice full of wonder, as if Eliza had declared herself a mermaid. "Bloomin' hell. You're going to fetch a fortune."

HANDS WERE EVERYWHERE.

Lucien groaned, lust heavy in his blood, like a drug weighing down his veins. The carriage had stopped ages ago and he truly didn't wish to break up this lovely party...but he'd promised.

"My darlings," he said gently, trying to gain the attention of his distracted companions. Delicate fingers slid inside his trousers to stroke his hard cock through his underclothes, and he groaned. Ginny was sliding to her knees, a devilish twinkle in her eye, while Mollie pushed her bare breast deeper into Lucien's hand. He tweaked her nipple, unable to help himself.

"Your Grace needn't attend this auction," Ginny cooed as her fingers started on the buttons of his undergarment. "We are perfectly happy seeing to your needs."

How well he knew this. Ginny and Mollie were delightful in every way, the two actresses having been his regular bed partners for three months. Their time together had been a blur of orgasms and sensual spankings, but he'd promised Jasper, his closest friend, that he'd attend tonight.

"I'm not bidding on a girl." Reluctantly, he covered Mollie's abundant tits with her dress. "Nevertheless, my presence has been requested."

While Lucien avoided the auctions, preferring to get women through natural charm, Jasper attended often. Unfortunately, Jasper had terrible taste in people—hence their friendship—and was no stranger to getting fleeced by unscrupulous women. He'd begged for Lucien's help in selecting a girl tonight, and Lucien hadn't been able to refuse.

Mollie's lips met the edge of his ear. "Wouldn't you rather fuck me up the bum instead?"

A rush of need surged inside him, his cock pulsing as if pleading for Lucien to follow through on the suggestion. *Damn it.*

Lucien closed his eyes and dug deep for control. Once he had a grip on himself, he helped Ginny up off the floor and began righting his clothing. The girls laughed as his fingers fumbled on the task, his haste and hunger making him clumsy.

He pressed a long, deep kiss to Mollie's mouth, then gave Ginny the same. "I won't be long, loves. You may wait here or the house in Cheapside. I'll find you after."

Before they could argue or tempt him further, he alighted from the carriage. The cool night air slapped his overheated skin and he willed his erection away. Aware of the rules for auction nights, he removed the domino from his coat pocket and slipped it over his face. Then he straightened his shoulders and walked toward the club, determined to get this over with as quickly as possible.

The smell of sweat and desperation hung heavy inside, the interior of the club crowded with men clad in evening suits and masks, each hoping to win a woman for seven nights. *Fools.*

"I was beginning to wonder if you were coming," said a voice behind him.

Annoyed, Lucien turned to his friend. "Have you any idea what you've interrupted? This had better not take long."

"Your mistresses, I know. Don't worry. You'll help me win a woman and then we shall all go our separate ways."

"Why do you keep bidding on these women if you can't trust them?"

"That's what I need you for. The last woman I won here stole two of my favorite paintings."

Christ, Jasper was too trusting by half. "You are hopeless."

"Yes, absolutely. But if anyone knows women, it's you. Please, you must help me, Luc." Jasper clapped him on the shoulder, pushing Lucien through the doorway. "Just sit down. I'll have you out of here shortly."

Instead of arguing, Lucien continued into the room. An empty table along the side seemed as good as any, so Lucien sat and surveyed the crowd. The masks provided appallingly little anonymity, and he could identify most everyone here, the titled gents and rich industrialists who frequented all the same clubs and theaters.

He had to hand it to the owners. These auctions were quite the rage. To participate, a man required someone respectable to vouch for him, and any hint of violence in one's past was just cause for refusal. This meant women came willingly, eager to be auctioned, and they received every quid of the auction price paid. The owners knew the real money was in the exorbitant participation fee and the liquor sold when the room was packed.

Lucien ordered drinks for them both and relaxed. Within minutes, movement from behind the curtain caught his eye. The audience quieted, anticipation thick like fog in the room.

A large barrel-chested man stepped out onto the stage. "Owner of the Chapel," Jasper whispered.

The owner, who looked like a dockside worker, gave a speech about how the auction would proceed, the rules for how the women were to be treated, and the consequences for those who disobeyed those rules. Lucien had little doubt that those consequences were doled out by the owner himself, whose hands could probably snap a smaller man in half.

The auction began. Woman after woman was paraded on the stage as men shouted their bids. Jasper settled on a cheeky-looking blond beauty somewhere along the way.

"May I leave now?" Lucien asked after Jasper was declared the winning bidder.

"No. You must meet her, just to see if she's going to give me trouble."

Though eager to bolt, Lucien sighed and forced himself to stay seated. Only for Jasper would Lucien postpone a night of glorious fucking and debauchery.

Bored by the auction proceedings, he studied the crowd. Odd, but several men here hadn't bid at all, their hawkish gazes never leaving the stage. Rathbone was one, a marquess who, according to Mollie, had sexual tastes that skewed toward the macabre. Something about cutting the insides of Mollie's friend's thighs before he fucked her—as she pretended to be a corpse. The owner was careful about the men allowed to bid; it was what ensured these auctions were safe and popular. Has word not gotten around about Rathbone?

Lucien leaned over to Jasper. "I've heard some unsavory stories about Rathbone. Surprised to see him here."

"Unsavory? Rathbone? I've never heard any hint of that."

"Mollie has a friend, said he—"

"And now," the auctioneer said, "we have our final offering for the night. Gents, I give you, Lady E."

The curtains parted and a pale young woman slowly emerged. She was lovely, with golden blond hair piled atop her head, wisps surrounding her delicate face. Bright blue eyes surveyed the crowd nervously, her body shaking in a clear case of nerves. She couldn't have been more than nineteen or twenty.

The shift she wore did little to cover her. Dusky nipples, furled into hard points thanks to the cold air and lack of undergarments, poked the thin fabric, the small swell of her breasts evident. She had long bony legs, thin arms, and he could see the hint of dark hair that covered her mound.

Something nagged in his brain at the sight of her. Why did she look vaguely familiar? The auctioneer took the girl's hand and led her around the stage, like a prized stallion at Tattersall's. Lucien couldn't tear his gaze away, knowing there was something about her. Something familiar. A puzzle he couldn't quite solve.

"Lady E is the Chapel's most special offering," the man crowed. "Genteel, mannered, and best of all . . . a virgin."

A collective gasp went through the room.

"That's right, gents. This lovely creature has never had a man between her thighs. Whoever wins her for seven nights will be her first."

Color suffused the girl's skin from head to toe, but she did not run or pull away. Was she truly here willingly? Who would do such a thing for their first time? Bad enough to let a stranger take her innocence, but then keep her for a week? That seemed cruel.

"Now, where shall we start the bidding? I think ten thousand pounds."

"Ten thousand!" someone in the crowd shouted.

Jasper edged closer. "Why do I feel as if I recognize her?"

That feeling returned, the one that told Lucien the answer was staring him right in the face, like a maths problem he couldn't solve. He scowled as the bidding progressed, now above twenty thousand pounds. "I feel as though I do, too. Who—?"

All of a sudden Lucien's body jerked. The puzzle clicked into place, the solution as plain as dirt. That golden hair and those big round eyes that used to stare at him like he was the most fascinating man on earth.

No. *No, no, no.*

Lady E. *Eliza.*

"No," he repeated. "I don't believe it."

"Who?"

"Goddamn it. Robert's sister. Lady Eliza." Her brother had been the Earl of Barnett before he died.

Sharp pain pushed under Lucien's sternum, the familiar guilt twisting him up inside. The memories rushed through him, of the three of them—Jasper, Robert and Lucien—and their steadfast friendship. Without siblings of his own, Lucien had considered the two men like brothers, and he'd spent quite a bit of time at Robert's home. That was back when everything was simpler. Back when Lucien actually gave a damn about being a duke and doing right by his responsibilities.

He remembered Eliza. She'd been a serious girl with a keen head for numbers, and Lucien used to give her maths problems to solve at the dinner table. Robert had tried to quiet her, saying it wasn't appropriate for a girl, but Lucien enjoyed the interactions with her. There had been something pure and innocent about her, a thirst for knowledge so sharp he could almost touch it.

The last time he saw her was at Robert's funeral, a sad-eyed fourteen-year-old girl gripping the hand of her younger sister. The two girls had been surrounded by family—or at least what he'd assumed to be family.

So why was she here, selling her body to a stranger?

"Fuck," Jasper said. "We have to help her, Luc—and I don't have the funds left to outbid them."

Eliza bit her lip and ducked her head, holding onto the auctioneer as if her legs wouldn't hold her without support. What had brought Robert's sister here, nothing more than skin and bones, willing to sell her innocence to the highest bidder? Where was her second cousin, the current earl? Why wasn't she married, with a husband taking care of her?

Robert wouldn't want this for her.

Rathbone called out a bid for forty thousand pounds, an outrageous sum of money.

Before Lucien could blink, the words tumbled out of his mouth. "Fifty thousand pounds."

"Sixty." Rathbone's voice cut through the room, his lifeless eyes daring Lucien to outbid him.

Undeterred, Lucien glared at the other man. "Seventy."

Rathbone's mouth flattened, frustration and determination etched in every line of his face. "Seventy-five."

The idea of Rathbone winning Eliza and subjecting her to his . . .proclivities sent a cold streak of fear through Lucien. He would not allow it to happen. He'd wager his entire estate, his fortune, his *life* to prevent it.

Tossing back the rest of his drink, he slammed the glass on the table. "We all have things to do, so I will cease wasting everyone's time. One hundred thousand pounds."

2

No one spoke. The man with the lower bid stood up and stormed out, which meant the auction was now over.

She'd been sold.

Eliza clutched the arm of the auctioneer like a safety line, her lungs sucking in air. Was this truly happening?

"One hundred thousand pounds, it is! Lady E is sold to that gentleman there for the next seven nights."

The room broke out in applause, and Eliza's mind reeled at the staggering amount as she was led off stage.

It was . . .unthinkable. With this amount of money, she could take Fanny to a sanitarium in America with fresh air and healing waters. They could buy a nice house somewhere no one knew them and start over.

Once upon a time, she'd hoped to study at one of the women's colleges at Oxford. Her brother laughed at this, saying an earl's daughter needn't be well educated. They'd fought over it many times, with Robert insisting aristocratic ladies should marry and reproduce, not attend college. Eliza held onto that dream, however, planning to prove him wrong. With this money, perhaps she could finally go to school in America.

"Good for you, dearie!" one of the women cheered in the anteroom as Eliza entered.

"I'm a virgin, too, if it could get me a hundred thousand quid," another one said.

"Cor, you ain't no virgin, Jane," came a shout. "Your cunt's been ridden more than a horse."

Eliza was shown to a separate room to wait. Within seconds, the door opened and Eliza crossed her arms over her chest in an attempt at modesty. Probably pointless, but it bolstered her courage.

Two men entered. The larger man was the club's owner—and the other was the masked man who'd bought her. He was tall and fit, and younger than she'd anticipated.

The owner closed the door. "Lady E, I'd like to present you with your buyer."

The bidder reached up and untied his domino. When it fell, Eliza gasped, her body rocking as if she'd been dealt a blow.

No, impossible. Utterly impossible.

Blackwood.

More specifically, Lucien, the Duke of Blackwood. Her late brother's best friend.

And Eliza's girlhood obsession.

Oh, God. Every bit of her skin burned as if she stood too close to a fire. Lucien had bid on her. Had paid one hundred thousand pounds to bed her and take her virginity. Was she dreaming right now?

Emotions fluttered in her chest, and any embarrassment over appearing half-naked in a room full of men was replaced with relief. It wasn't a stranger who would take her virginity.

Instead, it was a man she'd known as a girl—the serious and kind duke who gave her maths problems to solve at the dinner table, much to the chagrin of her older brother. The man who caused a buzzing sensation under her skin every time she looked at him.

Yes, Lucien was exactly the right man for her first time.

The owner spoke first. "You have any troubles, you come to me, miss," he said, jerking a thumb to his chest. "These gents know what happens if they misbehave."

"Leave us," Blackwood said to the other man, his eyes never leaving

Eliza's face. "And I'll have a word with you later about some of the *gents* you allow to participate in these proceedings."

After a frown in the duke's direction, the owner left them alone, and Eliza could feel her heart pounding in her chest as she regarded him. He was so . . .much. Still handsome, with his same windswept black hair and intense brown-green eyes, but his features had sharpened in the last five years. His shoulders had widened, too. Blimey, he was attractive.

"Thank goodness it's you," Eliza blurted. "I was worried about who would buy me."

"I'm certainly surprised, as well. Care to explain?"

He spoke to her as if she were a child who needed reprimanding, which she didn't like, nor did she understand. "What needs explaining, Your Grace? It's a fairly straightforward exchange. I have something to offer and Your Grace has purchased it."

Lucien cocked a brow. "Straightforward? Tonight was anything but, Lady Eliza."

"Please don't call me that." No one used her honorific any longer.

"Why? You are a lady."

"I *was* a lady. That was a long time ago, Your Grace."

"I'll stop calling you a lady if you stop calling me Your Grace. Now, where is your family?"

"Dead, except for my sister."

He winced. "I meant your brother's successor. The new earl."

"Haven't a clue. He turned Fanny and I out five years ago."

Lucien's jaw fell open. "He . . .turned you out? Without providing for you at all?"

This was old news, so Eliza lifted a shoulder. "Apparently Robert hadn't altered his will to include us. Everything went to William, his second cousin."

"Your cousin let it be known you'd gone to live with an aunt in Scotland."

"I have no aunt in Scotland."

"Dash it," he muttered, pinching the bridge of his nose between a thumb and forefinger. "Why not hire a solicitor to look into the matter, then?"

"With what funds, Your Grace?"

"Then why not come to me? Or to Jasper? We gladly would have helped you."

It hadn't occurred to Eliza to beg from Robert's friends, not while she was focused on finding food and shelter. Besides, no one had reached out after the funeral. Every friend and acquaintance forgot about her and Fanny, just two more young girls who were someone else's problem.

Which meant they were no one's problem.

Regardless—and Eliza didn't mind bragging—she'd done a damn decent job of providing for the two of them. If not for Fanny's illness, they would gladly have lived out their days in their rented one-room apartment in Shoreditch. The aristocracy, Eliza discovered, weren't as essential as they believed. Happiness could be found outside of Mayfair.

In fact, being common was generally a relief. The life she'd once lived, with its restrictions and excess and expectations, had been entirely at a man's whim—first her father, then her brother. And even that had all been taken away by another man, her cousin.

She and Fanny lived simpler lives now, but lives of their own choosing, with no one controlling them. Eliza would never allow a man to dictate her future ever again.

Which was why she would make good on this transaction. An even exchange: her virginity for one hundred thousand pounds. Her decision, her control.

Lucien stood, shrugged out of his coat, then came to drape it over her shoulders. The fine wool caressed her bare skin, while the smell of cigar and sandalwood filled her head. She could still feel the warmth from his body on the material, and it sank into her bones. "Thank you," she said gratefully.

"Eliza, honestly. Why didn't you come to me? You look malnourished. I fear a strong wind will blow you over."

That stung. She frowned up at him. "We're doing fine for ourselves. If not for Fanny's—" She snapped her jaw closed. Her sister's illness was not anyone's business.

"Fanny's what?"

"Nothing."

Simple transaction, even exchange. Then she and Fanny would start over in America.

She lifted her chin and gave him what she hoped was an eager smile. "So, when do our seven nights begin?"

Lucien frowned, irritated she'd even ask. "Never."

She gaped, her eyes revealing her surprise and confusion, so he held up a hand and said, "However, I will give you the hundred thousand pounds."

"Why on earth would you do that?"

"Because your brother was a friend of mine." His best friend, actually. *And I'm responsible for his death.*

The furrow between her brows deepened. "You cannot give me the money outright."

The words hung there, but he couldn't make sense of them. She was *protesting?* Why wasn't she relieved? She couldn't *want* to sleep with him; she'd sold her innocence for the coin. "Why not?"

"Because I would feel beholden to you."

Beholden? She deserved this money. Had Robert known, he would've enlisted Lucien's promise to take care of his sisters. Then she never would've ended up in this predicament—too thin and selling her body like a common streetwalker.

"You won't take my money, but it's fine to sell your virginity to the highest bidder? To a stranger? Come, Eliza. Be sensible. Let's put this ugliness behind us, and I'll ensure that you and Fanny have all the money you ever need."

"Why?"

"Because your brother was my closest friend."

"Still, that is no reason to give me a huge sum of money for nothing."

"It's what your brother would have wanted."

"I don't understand. You didn't bid on me because you wanted to sleep with me? You don't wish to take my virginity?"

Did she sound disappointed, or was he imagining it? A whisper of heat slithered along his spine and through his groin, but shame quickly followed. While he was a dissolute bastard, he hadn't ever taken advantage of a woman—and he wouldn't start with the little sister of his dead best friend. "Absolutely not. Your brother would be horrified."

"My brother is dead. I no longer have the luxury of wondering over his feelings, not when there are far more pressing matters at hand."

"Regardless, I won't f—" He stopped himself from using the crude word, which was definitely not appropriate to say in front of a lady. "I won't sleep with you."

"Why did you bid on me, then, if you didn't fancy sleeping with me?"

"To save you from the jackals out there. I know those men, and none of them are worthy of you." *Including me.*

"If you won't sleep with me, I'll just arrange for another auction."

The back of his neck grew hot. "The hell—heck—you will. You'll take my money and go live your life."

"No, I won't. I don't want to take money for nothin'. It never does a woman any good."

He could hear the East End in her speech, and his guilt doubled, sharpening his tone. "I'll not allow you to enter another auction. The owner wouldn't dare risk my ire."

"This is ridiculous. Am I so hideous, then?"

Guilt slashed his insides at her words. "That isn't it at all. You're quite lovely, if I am being honest."

An understatement, actually. Eliza was glorious, even more so up close, with lush blonde hair barely contained by pins, and blue eyes that were almost aqua, like the Mediterranean Sea in the morning. Her body was too thin, but she had womanly curves that any man would appreciate—and soon those curves would fill out.

Lucien would personally see to it. From now on, Robert's sisters would want for nothing. By next week, they'd be nibbling on tea cakes and petit fours in a drawing room somewhere, doted on by a collection of servants. Everything would be set to rights.

He couldn't bring Robert back, but he could see to Eliza's future.

Her nose wrinkled adorably as she studied him. "Then why not take my virginity? If there's a woman in your bed at the moment, I'm certain she'll understand."

"It's *women*, actually, and that hardly matters. I won't bed you."

"Even when you've paid for it?"

"When she is the little sister of my best friend, the answer remains no."

She wrapped his coat tighter around her body as she stood. "My brother is gone. You cannot continue to use him as a reason. It's illogical."

"You'll accept the money, Eliza. Save your innocence for a husband."

"No. I won't accept the money until you've had your seven nights. It's a fair exchange, and I'd rather have you than some other titled lord who won't care if he hurts me or not."

I'd rather have you.

Oh, Christ. He couldn't. It was wrong to even consider it, despite the dark thrill those words gave him.

Ready to put an end to the discussion, he stalked forward until he loomed over her. "You'll take the money, Eliza. No bedding and no seven nights. Stop being childish. Now, come. I'll see you home."

Her eyes flashed fire as she took a step back. "I'm not a child, and I'm able to see myself home."

"In this city? At this hour? Dressed like that? Absolutely not."

"I have clothes here. I'm used to doing for myself, Your Grace."

"Stop calling me that—and I will see you home if I have to tie your hands and feet and carry you out of here like a rolled-up carpet. Believe me, no one would stop me."

"Fine," she said, taking off his coat and shoving it at him. "At the very least it'll save me the fare."

Relieved, he requested her clothing, then waited outside the door while Eliza dressed. When she emerged, she was wearing a shabby brown garment hanging loose on her too-thin frame. He took her hand, not giving her a chance to escape. "My carriage is out front."

They didn't speak on the way. He could sense her unhappiness, but he didn't care. She would learn how this was going to go. He would give her the money and a house, a new life for her and Fanny, and she would accept it.

Then perhaps his guilt would ease a tiny fraction and he'd be able to sleep at night.

When he jerked open the carriage door, movement inside startled him. Oh, bollocks. How had he forgotten about Mollie and Ginny?

"Your Grace," Mollie said, wide-eyed as she took in the young girl at his side. "You said you weren't buying one tonight."

"I didn't. Move over, loves."

Mollie and Ginny slid to the far side of the carriage, sitting across from each other. From their swollen lips and disheveled clothes, it was clear his mistresses had been busy whilst he'd been away, but he was too worried about Robert's sister to regret missing the fun. He assisted Eliza inside then followed. The four of them barely fit, their knees bumping into one another, but it couldn't be helped.

"Where to, Eliza?"

"Kingsland Road in Shoreditch, please."

After he relayed the direction to his driver an awkward silence fell inside the carriage. He was about to make introductions when Eliza turned to the girls and blurted, "Hello, I'm Eliza. The duke bought my virginity tonight. We're going to spend the next seven nights together."

Before Lucien could correct that statement, Mollie dropped her hand on Lucien's thigh, close to his groin. "Is that what you want, darling? A little bit of blood and trepidation? Ginny and I can accommodate you."

"I'm not taking her virginity. Eliza is the sister of a friend of mine. We are seeing her home."

Eliza waved her hand. "He's still a bit overwhelmed at the prospect. Never fear, I'll bring him around. Actually, perhaps you ladies can help me. What are the duke's preferences in bed?"

Ginny and Mollie grinned, eyes sparkling like they'd made a new friend, while Lucien scowled. Just as Ginny opened her mouth to speak, Lucien pointed at her. "Do not answer that." Then he pinned Eliza with a hard stare, one he rarely used anymore. "Eliza, stop it this instant. We will not sleep together."

She turned to the street, ignoring him. Something told him she hadn't quite agreed, but he would convince her. He was quite in control of his cock, thank you very much, and it had no chance of meeting Eliza's quim. Ever.

Eventually they pulled up to a sad-looking East End building, and Lucien's blood turned cold. Fucking hell, it was terrible. Garbage littered the street and there was clearly a stable close by. Drunken men loitered on the stoop two houses down.

Robert's sisters lived here?

"Absolutely not," he snapped, watching a rat scurry into an alley. "Pack your things, Eliza. I'm taking you and Fanny back to Mayfair."

The girl had the audacity to reach for the handle like he hadn't spoken. "You cannot order me around, Your Grace."

"My hundred thousand pounds says I can, actually. Hurry up. We'll wait."

Her eyes narrowed as she jabbed a finger in his direction. "I *knew* it. I knew you would use that money to try to lord over my life—which is why this must remain a simple business transaction. You are not buying *me*; you are buying my body for seven nights. There is a difference."

Frustrated, he adjusted his tone to plead with her. "I cannot in good conscience leave you here in this neighborhood one second longer. My God, Eliza. You had such big plans when you were younger—you even talked of going to university. This is not the life you wanted. Go, pack your things. You're coming to stay with me in Grosvenor Square."

Mouths agape, Ginny and Mollie were following the conversation, heads swiveling as if they were at a tennis match. He remained focused on Robert's maddening sister, who was currently staring at him like he was muck under her shoe.

"No," she said, her voice brittle and angry. "I've built a life here. It may not meet with Your Grace's approval, but it's ours—and no man will ever take it away from us. I'll see you tomorrow night."

She threw open the door and slipped out of the carriage before he could stop her. Damn it.

Once on the ground, she hurried away, but Lucien unfolded from the vehicle and gave chase. Unfortunately, he lost her in the dark, crooked streets almost immediately. "Christ!" he yelled, kicking an empty jar with his boot as he trudged back to his carriage.

Tomorrow, he would find Eliza and her sister, even if he had to tear the whole city apart to do it.

3

HIS BED WAS ENORMOUS.

Eliza stood in Lucien's empty bedroom with just the silvery light of the moon to guide her. She and Fanny discussed this plan many times today. They decided the quickest way to get the money was for Eliza to show up and seduce him. Then their seven nights would commence, and he would have no choice but to see it through.

A monetary gift, even from Lucien, was too risky. As she'd seen many times, gifts from men always came with strings. Like when a former landlord agreed to give them a few more days on their rent—if Eliza showed him her quim. She'd refused and moved them out the next day.

Then there was the first doctor to see Fanny, who offered free treatment if Eliza rubbed her stocking feet on his crotch after every visit. Most recent was the marquess who owned the garment factory. He agreed to let Eliza move from an apprentice to her own sewing machine, but only if she became his mistress.

Did anyone honestly believe Lucien would give her that much money, wish her well, and disappear from her life? She snorted in the darkness. Even last night he'd tried ordering her about—using just the *promise* of the money as leverage. Eliza wouldn't let another man control her or her sister again.

This time was *her* choice. She wanted to earn this money, fair and square.

Her gaze drifted back to the bed, and her corset suddenly felt too tight, her clothes too itchy. The pulse between her legs was distracting, an insistent ache that began whenever she thought of him. Crikey, she was looking forward to this.

As a girl, she'd experienced a girlish giddiness in Lucien's presence, like her chest was full of butterflies and bees. She stared at him during his visits, obsessed with his soft smile and biting sense of humor. They both liked maths and playing croquet, and what more had a young girl needed to know other than that? He was utterly perfect to her mind.

So, where was he? Would he stay out the entire night? Pleasuring two mistresses was double the work, after all. Would he have the verve to relieve Eliza of her innocence tonight?

His exhaustion would definitely add a wrinkle to her plan, but it wouldn't dissuade her. She could wait and return tomorrow night. And the night after that. As many nights as it took to convince him to take her virginity. It had to work eventually.

Footsteps in the corridor caught her attention. She slipped into the shadows, held her breath, and waited. It could be Lucien—or a servant. And Eliza hadn't crossed the city in the dead of night, crawled through an unlocked window, and crept through his house . . .only to be thrown out by a snooty valet.

The latch turned and a large shape filled the doorway.

Lucien.

She bit her lip, her body vibrating with . . .nerves. Excitement. Fear. Excitement. Surely there were others, but she couldn't pinpoint them.

He closed the door and draped the room in darkness once more. Her eyes had already adjusted, so she could see him rip off his top coat, then toe off his shoes. "Fuck me," he growled.

Why was he angry?

Stomping to the bed, he flopped down onto his back. "Bugger it." His broad chest rose and fell with the force of his breath.

When he didn't move, she stepped out of the darkness. "May I help, Your Grace?"

Blinking, he came up on his elbows. "Eliza?"

"Hello, duke."

His brow creased, the lines too numerous to count. "They looked for you all bloody day. Turned Shoreditch upside down. I've been going out of my mind with worry ever since last night."

He'd tried to find her? She didn't know whether to be flattered or horrified. "I told you I would come tonight."

"Excellent. I'll write you a bank draft and send you back home."

"Let me undress first. How would you like to take my virginity? With me on my back, or on my hands and knees? I did see a drawing once of a woman upside down—"

"Eliza," he snapped. "None of that is happening. I cannot sleep with you."

Oh. He'd already exhausted himself, then. "Have your mistresses worn out your cock tonight?"

"Jesus, no—and do not think for one second that I have issues with stamina. I meant I cannot sleep with you and live with myself, Eliza. It isn't right."

She smothered a smile. Poor man. He had no idea who he was up against. The last five years had taught Eliza patience, of planning and waiting. She knew that with slow and steady progress, she would eventually reach any goal she set out to achieve.

Her goal at the moment was for Lucien to want her desperately enough to overlook his sense of misplaced honor toward her dead brother.

She moved closer to the bed and ran her fingers over his shin bone. "You could kiss me. That wouldn't be so terrible, would it?"

The noise that escaped his throat sounded tortured. "I know what you are doing, you clever girl. You are hoping I'll kiss you and become so overcome with lust that I end up between your thighs."

He wasn't that far off. "Actually, I was hoping you would show me what a real kiss feels like. The kisses I've experienced have—"

"Who has kissed you?" Abruptly, he sat up, his dark eyes blazing. "Were they rough with you? Did they force you? Because I swear to God . . ."

"Calm down, Lucien." She rose and moved between his legs. They were face-to-face now, her hands coming to rest on his shoulders. "They were mere boys, sloppy and inexperienced. No one forced me. I kissed them because I wanted to, just like I want to kiss you."

Seconds ticked by while he examined her face, brow wrinkled like he couldn't believe she actually wanted to kiss him. Yet she did. Badly.

She liked this serious, protective side of him, more like the Lucien she remembered, the one who had defended her intelligence to Robert and her parents. The man who made her feel valued and *seen* at a time when young girls were often ignored and dismissed. Lord, how she'd loved him once.

Finally, his mouth hitched in a way that caused her stomach to flip. "I am definitely no sloppy and inexperienced boy."

"No, you certainly are not, which is why I want to know what it's like to be kissed by you."

He leaned in, as if drawn to her, but didn't come close enough to actually kiss her. His breath ghosted over her skin as he spoke. "I would make it so good for you, Eliza. I would take my time, explore every bit of you with my lips and tongue. You would feel so safe with me, angel. I'd never let anyone hurt you again."

Was he talking about kissing . . . or something more?

Her lower body clenched at his seductive words, the area between her legs growing damp and hot. It would be so easy to believe him, so easy to let herself rely on someone else to take care of everything for her. But she would not trade her hard-fought independence for anything. Lucien could have her body for seven nights, but he would never have more.

She said none of this, however. She merely edged forward until their lips nearly touched. "Show me, Lucien. *Please.*"

LUCIEN'S HEAD SWAM—AND the dizziness had nothing to do with the scotch he'd swallowed earlier. No, his little angel had him off-balance, sneaking into his bedroom and asking him to kiss her. God, he wanted to. More than anything else, he longed to drag her beneath him and show her how good it could be between them. Teach her how to please him.

I could be her first.

Fuck. He had to stop thinking like that.

As much as he wanted to stretch her wide, watch as his cock speared her virgin flesh, he couldn't. This was Robert's sister, a proper lady, and she would hate him if she knew the truth behind her brother's death. That he was the reason for the loss of her family home, her wealth and position.

So despite his desire for her, it was dangerous to contemplate fucking her—and she deserved better.

Moonlight bathed her in a soft glow, showing off her slightly parted lips and the flush on her cheeks. She was absolutely lovely, her face free of cosmetics and lip paint. He stared at the delicate curve of her jaw, the slim column of her throat, both begging to be explored by his mouth. Was the skin there as soft as it appeared?

No, no, no. He couldn't. Could he?

Her fingers found their way into his hair, their bodies nearly flush, with her lower half appallingly close to his. He wanted to touch her so badly, his hands shook with it. Why wasn't she afraid? Weren't most virgins supposed to be terrified, wilting creatures?

Eliza appeared almost . . .aroused.

Was that possible?

"Why aren't you scared?" he whispered, their breath mingling.

"Because it's you."

Swallowing, he came to a decision right then. As long as he didn't fuck her, he could show her everything her little curious heart desired—and in the meantime convince her to stay here until he could get her into better lodgings.

He was not above using pleasure to achieve what he wanted, which was Robert's sisters safe and back where they belonged in a decent neighborhood.

"I'm going to kiss you, Eliza."

Her response was instant. "All right."

"But just kissing." He could do this. Just a few minutes exploring her mouth, rubbing her sweet little tongue with his, before he made her agree to return to Mayfair. "Do you remember when we used to do maths together?"

"Yes, of course." The words came out on a soft sigh, as if the memory was a good one. He hoped so—those were pleasant memories for him, too. Clever and eager, she'd been able to hold her own with his complex questions, and he'd been suitably impressed.

"Kissing is like solving an equation," he told her, sliding his hands onto her hips. "You have this mystery to unravel, a puzzle, and it requires careful examination and thought. Planning and patience. The answer is there, but you cannot rush it."

"And what is the answer?"

"For me, it's discovering what makes a woman purr into my mouth and rub against me like she longs to feel me everywhere. What makes her hot and eager, wet between her legs."

He paused, half-hoping he'd shocked or scared her into leaving. It was best for both of them if this never went any further.

"But I already feel that," she said, "and you haven't even kissed me yet."

His cock pulsed, a jolt of lust careening through him at her honesty, and he moved closer. "Then just relax. Let me taste you."

A willing pupil, she held perfectly still, allowing him to close the distance and cover her mouth with his own. He briefly wondered how far she'd gone with those boys, whether she'd let any of them stroke her between her thighs, but he shoved those thoughts away. Tonight was just kissing.

Her lips were soft and wet, like she'd licked them in preparation for his kiss, and he moved carefully, gently, learning the shape and feel of her, while giving her the chance to do the same. He swept back and forth lightly, brushing and teasing, enjoying the anticipation building between them. Many partners complained kissing was unnecessary, but Lucien loved it. There was something about the connection, the shared breath and slick exchange of saliva, that was both dirty and beautiful. Hedonistic and necessary.

That he was kissing this particular woman, the one who used to look at him with stars in her eyes, made it all the sweeter. He suddenly remembered how her stare made him feel twenty feet tall all those years ago, like he was the only man in the room. How had he ever forgotten?

Desperate for more, he deepened the kiss, holding her face in his palms and adding more pressure. Then he nipped her lips, and was rewarded when her mouth parted to allow him inside.

It was worth the wait.

Her tongue was wet and hot, and he suddenly couldn't get enough. She was thorough, her mouth mimicking his movements, and he lost himself in the flicks and swirls, the moans and gasps as the kiss wore on. Part of him worried this might be a mistake, because he liked it *too much*, but the other part—the selfish and depraved half—wanted to take everything she offered, ruin her for other men.

Ruin her, period.

This is Eliza, Robert's sister. Get a hold of yourself, man.

Somehow he managed to hold himself in check, not once losing the thin threads of his self control. When her hands gripped his shoulders, he fought the urge to move closer. When her fingers slid into his hair, he fought the urge to cup her breasts in his palms.

And when she shifted into the cradle of his thighs, he fought the urge to grind his cock into her mound.

It wasn't easy, especially when her eagerness and innocence beckoned him like a treat just out of reach, but this must remain a kiss, nothing more.

So when she shoved his shoulders, he wasn't ready for it. Actually, he had no idea what was happening until he was flat on his back on the bed. "Eliza, what—"

His jaw snapped shut when she crawled directly over him, her legs straddling his thighs. Oh, Christ. What was happening?

The ceiling stared down at him blankly, as if to mock him. *You fool. Your hubris knows no bounds.*

Weakly, he tried to move but it was too late. Her glorious weight came down on him and his hands clasped the back of her knees under her skirts. Before he could ask her to get up, she rocked her core over his erection, and white-hot pleasure shot through him like a bolt of electricity, obliterating everything else.

Goddamn it. Need clawed inside his belly, robbing him of all good sense. Why was fate so fucking cruel?

She pulled a small tin from her dress pocket. "I brought a shield."

He stared at her hand, his cock throbbing. The idea that she'd come prepared, that she'd turned aggressive—that she *wanted* this so desperately—nearly did him in. It would be so easy to free his erection and let her slide down, pierce her virgin cunt slowly. She would undoubtedly grip him tightly, tighter than anything he'd ever—

No. This wasn't right.

Eliza was a lady, whether she admitted it or not. Gently bred and raised to expect marriage. Lucien couldn't treat her like a mistress, no matter the fever currently burning inside him to have her. She deserved better.

Carefully, he moved her off him and onto the bed. "Let's slow down, shall we? There's no rush."

"What are you talking about? Of course, there is a bleedin' rush. This is only seven nights, Lucien."

"I've always loved the sound of my name coming out of your mouth." It was an idiotic thing to say, but absolutely true.

Her mouth curved in a way that almost made him nervous, as if he'd handed her a dangerous weapon. "Indeed, 'tis a nice name." She leaned over him, her hand firmly on his chest. "Will you kiss me again, Lucien?"

"No, because you and your shield are attempting to turn this into a deflowering, and I most definitely need you to stay flowered."

"That is not a word," she said with a chuckle.

"Perhaps, but you know what I mean. I will not bed you."

"You may use crude words with me, you know. I promise you won't offend my delicate sensibilities. I told you, I'm no longer a lady, and I've heard all manner of improper words in the last five years."

"You are a lady and you shouldn't know those words."

"Like fuck?"

"Dash it, Eliza. This has gone far enough—"

"Fine." She held the shield up where he could see it and slowly placed the tin on the small table by his bed. "There. Now we may focus on kissing and whatever else may happen."

He groaned as images of *whatever else* raced through his mind. "You don't know what you're asking for."

"Why? What are you worried might happen?"

"Any number of wicked scenarios that involve your naked body."

"Such as?"

"Things I'll never share with you."

"Because you're not attracted to me?"

"Because of *Robert*," he snapped. "Have you not been paying attention, woman?"

"Right." Her lips twitched like she was amused. "What if we focused on wicked scenarios that involved your naked body instead?"

While his cock was more than eager for this plan, Lucien wasn't fooled. She didn't know the first thing about pleasuring a man. How could she, as a virgin?

It was past time to illuminate her innocence and their incompatibility. If this was the only way to do it, so be it. Then she would see this was foolish, that she wasn't ready for seven nights of sin with a virtual stranger. That she should save herself for a husband.

Whether she wanted to admit it or not, she was a lady. No doubt she'd go running from the room the moment his cock appeared.

Indeed, this was the best way to put an end to this right now.

Stretching his arms up above his head, he spread his body out like a buffet, a feast for the taking. "If you can ask nicely for it, then maybe I'll let you."

4

———

WAS THIS A NEW GAME? IF SO, ELIZA WAS READY. IT WAS NO HARDSHIP TO explore him. Attractive and well proportioned, the duke was big, his clothes outlining a fit frame with a broad chest and flat stomach. A light dusting of whiskers coated his jaw, and she longed to test the roughness of that skin with her fingertips.

"May I touch you?"

One of his dark eyebrows lifted. "I'm no thirteen-year-old boy, Eliza. If you wish to touch me, you need to be explicit. Tell me where and what you plan to do."

She bit the inside of her cheek to keep from smiling. Was he being deliberately cruel to embarrass her? Probably. Lucien was very clever—probably the smartest man she'd ever met—and fixated on his loyalty to Robert. No doubt he was hoping she would blush and stammer, as any gently bred virgin would in this situation.

But Eliza was not gently bred, not anymore.

Drawing closer, she ran a fingertip over his stomach. "May I unfasten your trousers, Your Grace?"

"And why would you like to unfasten my trousers, angel?"

In for a penny, as the saying went.

"To see your cock. I want to lavish it with kisses and lick it all over."

Lucien's face paled, his lips parting ever so slightly. He seemed to be stuck, not breathing, his gaze fixated on her mouth. Was he imagining what it would feel like?

"How . . .?" His voice trailed off.

"Had you thought I was unfamiliar with the act? Or that I would be too embarrassed to speak about it?" She shook her head. "I'm not the sheltered girl you once knew."

"Have you ever . . .done that before?"

"No, but I'd like for you to teach me how."

His eyes slammed closed, his face twisted as if he were in pain. "Jesus, Eliza. You shouldn't say such things to a man like me."

"And what type of man are you?"

"A degenerate. A selfish wastrel. A man who will ride you so hard, you'll feel it for days to come."

Gorblimey.

An inferno ignited in her belly, followed by waves of wanting that skimmed through her veins. Was he hoping to scare her? Because honestly, the idea of his big muscled body moving over hers, giving pleasure that would haunt her long after, was more than appealing. It reinforced her sense that Lucien was the perfect man to rid her of her virginity.

He would take care with her. Provide her with seven nights of fun, then she would depart for America—and he would return to his mistresses and ducal debauchery.

She gave him her best attempt at a sultry smile. "If that was intended to deter me, dear man, I'm afraid you have failed."

He groaned, his hands scrubbing his face. "Has anyone ever told you that you are stubborn?"

"Many times." Fanny mentioned it quite often. But Eliza preferred *determined*, a trait that had helped her and her sister survive after being tossed out like trash. "Which means your resistance is futile."

He pinned her with his brownish-green stare. "Let's make a bargain."

She never agreed to anything without hearing all the details. Being cheated once in the Covent Garden market had taught her that. "Tell me the terms first."

"You let me pleasure you tonight. My trousers stay on. Then you and Fanny move in here tomorrow, and we discuss setting up a new life for you both."

"No. Here are my terms: you teach me how to pleasure you tonight, then I will return tomorrow night for more lessons."

"Damn it, Eliza."

He started to sit up—probably to throw her out or yell at her—and she panicked. Moving swiftly, she threw her leg over his hips and moved on top of him. Again. But this time her core landed on his erection, which was thick and hard under her center. They both froze.

This was his cock. Directly between her legs. Good God. It was much larger than she'd expected.

"What are you doing?" His voice sounded strangled.

She hadn't the faintest. "I'm not certain but it feels right. Should I move off you?"

"No. Yes. Wait, no."

His hesitation was promising. Because begging worked earlier for kissing, she tried it again. "Teach me, Lucien." She splayed her fingers on his chest and rocked her hips. Sakes alive, that felt delicious. "Please."

When she did it once more, they both groaned.

"Christ," he murmured as he fell back onto the bed. "I'm definitely going to Hell for even considering this."

"Is that a yes?"

"Eliza, let me lick you—"

She rolled her hips along the large ridge again and shivered as pleasure coursed through her. Leaning forward, she whispered, "You bought me, Lucien. You may do whatever you like with me tonight."

His cock jerked against her. Oh, he *liked* that.

She didn't stop, either her movements or her words. "Wouldn't you like to be my first?"

"Oh, God," he said on a rough exhale. "Why are you torturing me?"

"Do you want me to stop . . .or do you want to show me what it feels like to have your cock between my legs?"

"Jesus Christ!" He arched, every muscle pulled taut, with his expression twisted in what appeared like agony. Without warning, his hands shot out to clasp her hips. His eyes were wild, a man pushed to the edge of his sanity. "Roll your hips, darling," he rasped. "Make us both come."

"What about your trousers?"

"They remain on. Trust me, you'll like it. Rub your sex over the cloth and along my shaft." He guided her. "Just keep going. Yes, exactly like that."

Tingles raced along the back of her thighs as she dragged her body over his. Why was this so amazing? The friction had her seeing stars. The strength of her reaction surprised her, but she wasn't worried.

Lucien will take care of me.

She knew it in her bones. He'd been so kind to her all those years ago, telling Robert to mind his own business when her brother tried to belittle her. Lucien had made her feel special, and she hadn't forgotten it.

His fingertips tightened on her hips. "How badly do you want to please me, angel?"

She peeked at him through her lashes. "Very, very badly, Your Grace."

"Then we do this once. One time and no more. No seven nights, just this. Our clothes stay on. Say you understand."

He didn't ask if she agreed, only that she understood. Hiding a smile, she kept churning her hips, grinding on top of him. "I understand."

He grunted and let his eyelids fall briefly, his long eyelashes kissing his cheeks. "You will thank me someday."

Doubtful, but there was no arguing with him, not now.

"Does it feel good for you?" Her palms rested on his stomach as she moved, again and again, in a steady rhythm. "Because I think it feels incredible."

"God, yes, it feels good. I'm so hard for you."

The more she rocked, the more heat that built inside her. The pleasure made her dizzy, like she was drunk on sensation, chasing a high slightly out of reach. She dug her nails into his skin, the ache drawing tighter, her body on fire. "Oh, Lucien."

"Yes, keep going." His chest heaved and his lips parted on a ragged breath. "Lift your skirts with one hand. Let me see you drag your pussy over my cock and make yourself come. I need to see it."

Her thighs trembled as she gathered her skirts in her fingers and lifted them out of the way. "You're the first man to ever see it," she whispered. "You could also be the first man to touch it."

"Fuck, fuck, fuck," he chanted, his stare locked on the bare skin revealed by the slit in her drawers. "I want that so badly. I want to finger you and lick you and fuck you."

"I see couples doing those things in the alleys," she told him, closing her eyes and imagining her and Lucien in the open air, where anyone could walk by and watch him taking her from behind. The sparks doubled, quadrupled in her blood, and she moved faster, her hips becoming uncoordinated as the pleasure dragged her under.

White-hot heat rushed up from her toes, flooding her, and her core contracted as she quivered and shook. It was better than anything she had imagined. The waves caused her to shudder, the man beneath her the only tether to the ground.

"I can see how wet you are," he growled when she floated back to earth. "May I taste it? Please? Run your finger through your slickness and give me one small taste."

It never occurred to her to refuse. He appeared desperate for her, feverish, like he might be close to his own climax, and she wanted to drive him wild. Dipping her finger into her sex, she coated the digit in her arousal and lifted it to his mouth. "Here."

He sucked her finger past his lips and into his mouth, his tongue swirling over her skin greedily. A groan rumbled in his throat and his eyes nearly rolled back in his head. Did he truly like the taste so much as that?

She leaned in and whispered, "Have you ever tasted a virgin before?"

His hips began bucking, nearly unseating her. "Oh, fuck. I'm—" He stiffened and his back bowed, air heaving in and out of his chest, and his shout filled the room to echo off the walls. The erection beneath her pulsed, the cloth of his trousers growing warm and wet on her skin. His *seed*. Pride filled her at his completion. She'd made him do that. Her, a virgin.

He'd never be able to resist her now.

LUCIEN MAY HAVE UNDERESTIMATED HER.

His sweet little virgin had a wicked mouth and was eager to please. His new favorite qualities in bed, apparently. That this was Robert's sister was a worry for tomorrow. Right now, she was merely Eliza, the woman who caused him to come in his trousers like a schoolboy.

He hadn't expected her to be so . . . filthy. Or competent. She rode him like a thoroughbred at Ascot, and he'd loved every second of it. The proof was now cooling and sticking to his skin.

When she'd lifted her skirts to her waist, the slit in her drawers revealed her cunt and he'd nearly climaxed right then. Christ, she was gorgeous. Downy hair covered her mound, while the pink lips of her sex glistened with arousal. For him. And the taste? Ambrosia. He wanted to bury his face there, breathe her in, taste her and lick her and have her come on his tongue, over and over until they were exhausted.

Grinning, she slid off him. "That was fun. We should do that again. Tomorrow night, say ten o'clock?"

"No. Now, what time may I expect you and Fanny in the morning?"

Her expression cleared, a wariness returning to her gaze. "I beg your pardon?"

"You and Fanny. Moving in tomorrow. What time?"

She had the audacity to shake her head. "We're not moving in with you. I told you this already."

He exhaled heavily. "Eliza, you agreed."

"No, I certainly did not."

"Let me put this plainly. If you and Fanny are not here by nine o'clock tomorrow morning, baggage in hand, there will be no hundred thousand pounds."

"Stop trying to control me with money. And!" She pointed to his crotch. "At the very least you owe me fourteen thousand two-hundred and eight-five quid."

"And 71 pence." Yes, he could do maths, too. "That amount was for your virginity, Eliza, which you still possess."

"This is ridiculous."

"No, ridiculous is you insisting on living in a hovel when I have offered to put you up here."

Her lip curled in distaste, eyes turning cold, but he had no idea how he'd offended her. Every word was the truth.

He kept going, playing his only card. "You may say farewell to the hundred thousand pounds if you do not bring your sister here in the morning."

They stared at one another for a long moment. He could see her mind working, as it had all those years ago at the dinner table when she examined a problem from every side. Logically, as he would. There was no way out of this, though, because he would not bend. She would leave that rat-infested neighborhood and come stay with him, where he would look after her like a ward.

A ward who had once ridden his cock and made them both come.

His chest ached, perhaps with regret. Or perhaps with the knowledge this evening could never be repeated. It didn't matter. He would not take advantage of her whilst she was living under his roof. She needed to feel safe here, well provided for. Exactly as her brother would have expected.

When she didn't speak, he added, "I am merely looking out for you. It's what your brother would have wanted." *And what my guilt demands.*

She gestured to the bed. "Do you sincerely believe if I moved in that *this* would not happen again?"

He felt a real flash of fear in his belly. Eliza dressing and undressing under his roof. Seeing her smile every place he turned. Watching her eat and laugh over dinner. Thinking about her lying in bed, perhaps touching herself at the memories . . . .

Could he stand it?

He bolted off the bed. Damn it, his trousers were a bloody mess. "I will behave myself," he said with more certainty than he felt. "I trust you can do the same whilst here. Now, I will clean up and see you home. Wait here a few moments."

"That isn't necessary."

"Of course, it is. I'll not have you running hurdy-gurdy through the streets of London at this hour."

She studied him, then leaned back and relaxed on the bed. "If that's what Your Grace wants," she murmured with a small smile twisting the edges of her mouth.

The words nearly caused him to trip as he headed to the washroom. God almighty, he liked her compliance. Too much, actually.

You bought me, Lucien. You may do whatever you like with me tonight.

The dark thrill at that shamed him to his soul. He'd bedded his fair share of women in the last ten years, but never had he experienced such mindless lust at a couple of sentences strung together. Yes, he wanted to own her, to be her first. To teach her and ruin her for all others.

But it was dangerous—not to mention wrong.

He spent a few minutes in the washroom cleaning up as best he could, stripping out of his soiled undergarment and putting his trousers back on. The scent of her soaked the cloth, and if it were up to him the garment would never be sent to the laundry. He'd keep them dirty and stained as a reminder of their night together, of the one time his little virgin vixen teased and tormented him.

Finally, he finished putting himself to rights and returned to his bedroom, ready to see Eliza home.

Except the bed was empty. Nor could he find her anywhere inside the townhouse.

She had disappeared.

5

ELIZA LEFT HER FLAT THE NEXT MORNING AT EIGHT O'CLOCK, AS USUAL. SHE was due at Mrs. O'Toole's, where she would spend the day mending clothes. It didn't pay much, but it was easy work.

The task would keep her hands and mind occupied, which was a relief after last night. Upon returning home from Lucien's, she'd tossed and turned, both angry and relieved. Sated and frustrated. The dratted man should grant her the seven nights, claim her virginity, then let her go on her merry way. Why was he insisting on complicating everything?

Fanny agreed with Eliza that accepting the money from Lucien without services rendered was a mistake. Then her sister minimized her illness, saying they didn't need the money quite as badly as that. Eliza knew better.

They did need the money. Eliza hated hearing his sister cough and struggle to breathe at night, and Fanny couldn't work because employers and coworkers were terrified she had consumption. According to Dr. Humphries, the doctor who treated Fanny, it wasn't consumption and a lengthy stay at a sanitarium should help her completely recover. But such facilities were expensive, and their savings wouldn't begin to touch the cost.

"Eliza," a deep voice suddenly said from close behind her. Too close.

She whirled and drew to a stop. The Marquess of Rathbone stood on the walk, looming over her like a gargoyle. Taking a step back, she shivered and rubbed her arms despite the heat outside. "My lord. Good morning."

Three months ago she apprenticed in Rathbone's garment factory, where they made coats and shirts. After recognizing her, he'd made a point to talk to her each time he visited the floor. She was polite, even though the reminder of her brother and her family stung, while doing her best to deter him. Still, Rathbone lingered more and more, distracting her from the work.

When she requested a sewing machine of her own, the manager said Rathbone made those decisions—even though the marquess hadn't promoted any other apprentice. Eliza suspected his involvement was special to her, which should have sent her packing straight away.

Instead, she foolishly approached him and requested a machine. The marquess turned it into an opportunity to proposition her, during which he asked her to become his mistress. Eliza quit that very day, never even collecting her last paycheck.

"There you go, always so busy," he said. "May I offer you a ride?"

A slick black brougham waited at the curb. The idea of sitting in such a confined space with him turned her stomach. "Thank you, my lord, but I'm fine to walk. It's not far."

"Then allow me to walk with you. It would be a shame if you were set upon. These streets are not safe for a young girl like yourself."

"Your lordship is very kind, but that's unnecessary. Good day, sir."

When she started to turn away, he took her arm. He wasn't hurting her, and to a passerby it would appear he was assisting her, but he hadn't asked permission to touch her. If he had, she certainly would not have granted it.

He began leading her along the walk. "See, isn't that better?"

"Please, my lord. Let me go."

"Nonsense. I'm happy to help." He leaned in, his hot breath hitting her skin. "In fact, I know just the sort of help you need. Do not be too proud to accept it from me, girl."

"Rathbone." The word cut through the noise on the street like the crack of a whip.

Lucien was there, the brim of his bowler doing little to hide the absolute fury in his gaze. "I believe the lady asked you to let her go."

Rathbone frowned, but otherwise didn't move. "This doesn't concern you, Blackwood."

"It does, actually. The lady is due with me this morning."

Eliza couldn't believe this. What was Lucien doing here at this hour? How had he found her?

Lucien stared at Rathbone, as if daring him to argue. Tension strung between the two men like a wire, taut and dangerous, and she wondered if they would come to blows.

Using the distraction to her advantage, she pulled free of Rathbone and shifted closer to Lucien. "It's true. His Grace requested my presence today."

A flash of something dark, something terrifying, crossed Rathbone's face before he cleared it. "We will speak later, then." He tipped his bowler and walked in the direction of his carriage.

Lucien took Eliza's arm and began leading her in the opposite direction. She didn't fight him, but she had questions. "What are you doing here? How did you find—"

"Quiet," he snapped.

"Oh, you think to order me about, too?"

"He's watching. Follow me and I'll explain in my carriage."

Glancing over her shoulder, she saw that Rathbone was, in fact, lingering near the street, his hollow eyes tracking her and Lucien as they walked away. A cold prickle slithered over her skin. Unnerved, she pressed her lips together and remained silent.

A block over, a closed black carriage awaited. The conveyance looked totally out of place here, with its shiny lacquered sides and matching horses, and Eliza remembered rides in carriages such as this. She hadn't thought twice about it then, and hadn't realized her privilege until it was taken away by a system and society governed by men.

The reminder annoyed her, so she dug in her heels before Lucien could drag her any closer. "While I'm grateful for your assistance with Rathbone, I'm perilously close to being late for work. So, if you'll excuse me." She tried to tug out of his grasp, but he didn't let go.

"Get in my carriage, Eliza," he growled. "Right now."

Her jaw fell open. "You're angry with me? The bloody nerve! I've done nothing wrong."

He stepped closer and lowered his voice. "Other than sneaking out of my home last night after I told you to wait? Did it ever occur to you that I might be worried sick? That I might have stayed up half the night picturing you eviscerated in some alley?"

She bit the inside of her cheek and shoved aside the guilt. "And I told you I was perfectly fine seeing myself home. As you can see, I was right."

Closing his eyelids tightly like he was struggling for patience, he bit out, "Get in the carriage. You are embarrassing us both, arguing with me like a fishwife on the street."

Anger suffused her entire body. Embarrassing him? This was her neighborhood, not his, and she wouldn't be put back in that restrictive, proper aristocratic box ever again.

She would show him true embarrassment.

Angling back, she shouted, "Corblimey, guv! That's one right big tallywag you 'ave for a toff. Let me get me muff ready and you can roger it proper."

A passerby snickered, and Lucien turned an alarming shade of red. He spoke through clenched teeth. "If you want to see my solicitor, then I suggest you get moving."

She blinked. "Your solicitor? Why?"

"Because I asked him to look into the situation with Robert's estate. Now, do you want to get in on your own, or would you rather I throw you over my shoulder and toss you in myself?"

His solicitor? Hope flared in her chest and she considered whether to go with him. Mrs. O'Toole would understand Eliza's absence, but it meant Eliza wouldn't earn her sixpence for the day.

Perhaps I could earn another fourteen thousand two-hundred and eighty-five quid instead.

Yes, that sounded like a more reasonable financial decision.

Patting Lucien's chest, she smiled. "Whatever Your Grace wishes."

Suspicion crossed his features and his eyes narrowed, yet he said nothing as she climbed inside the fancy carriage. The inside smelled of him—leather and fancy spices—which was a far cry from the ripe horse and refuse odor on the street. She settled into the plush seat and decided to enjoy the day with him.

Soon they set off, the wheels clattering along the uneven Shoreditch streets. They hadn't even gone a block when Lucien growled, "How do you know Rathbone?"

She glanced over at him, wondering at his sharp tone. Was Lucien jealous? No, that was ridiculous. "I worked at his factory for four months."

"He owns a factory?"

"Yes, a garment factory. They make coats and shirts."

"What did you do there?"

"I was an apprentice. Fetched bobbins and learned how to cut and make clothing. I tried to get my own machine, but Rathbone wouldn't allow it unless I granted him certain privileges."

Lucien tensed next to her, his muscles stiff. "That bastard."

"It's not an original story, I'm afraid. Though his offer was better than most. It included a townhouse and a staff of my own."

"I hope you punched him in the jaw."

She lifted a shoulder. "It's not much different from what you offered."

He swung to glare at her, a tinge of red on his high cheekbones. "It's hardly the same. I want to give you a hundred thousand pounds and your own home."

"I don't want it, not until the end of our agreement. We have a simple business transaction, Lucien. Nothing more. You cannot order me about or use that money to control me. I am not your ward or your mistress. I am the woman you bought for seven nights."

"My God!" He tossed his bowler onto the opposite seat. "I have never seen such foolishness in all my life. You're wearing threadbare clothing and are clearly in need of a hot meal. You could be wearing diamonds and Worth gowns, woman. Drinking champagne and eating the finest foods, while being waited on by a bevy of servants. Why are you so insistent on clinging to your poverty?"

The words slashed through her, cutting deep. Did he really think so little of her, judging her because she was no longer a spoiled Mayfair princess? Couldn't he see she was something better? She'd been cast out with a sister to take care of, no money, no one to turn to, and had carved out a life for them with her bare hands. With her blood, sweat and tears, and no help from anyone, thank you very much.

And while they might not have a lot, Eliza was proud of every bit of it.

"Nothing comes for free in this life, Your Grace. Not for women. If the past five years have taught me a single thing, it's precisely that."

"You're wrong. I only want to help you as repayment for Robert."

"Repayment? For what?"

He shifted toward the window and fiddled with his cuff. "For ignoring you all this time. For believing that story about Scotland and your aunt and not checking on you myself."

Something about his words didn't ring true. He was lying, but why?

Before she could contemplate what Lucien might be hiding, he lifted her arm and held it. "Did Rathbone hurt you?" he asked quietly, then pressed his warm lips to the sensitive skin inside her wrist.

The shifts in his mood were boggling. Has she ever met a more confusing man? His touch distracted her, though, with his gentle kisses sending goosebumps up and down her arm. "No," she whispered.

"Are you certain?" He lingered there, his warm breath and wet mouth worshipping her skin, and her muscles grew heavy, limbs sinking into the leather. He murmured, "Because I will destroy him and everything he cares about if he ever hurts you."

"Why?"

"Because you're mine, Eliza."

He hadn't meant to say it.

But once the words were out, Lucien wouldn't take them back. She was his. She'd belonged to him ever since those dinners when they discussed maths and her studies, and when she'd asked him questions about university and his classes. When her insatiable thirst for knowledge had her hanging on his every word, making him feel like the smartest man in the room.

The thought of truly claiming this woman, of being the first to slide inside her body and spill his seed there, had tortured him all night. It had been so long since he felt worthy of such a gift—not after Robert's death, certainly—and he didn't deserve it, especially from Eliza.

She'd hate him if she knew what happened. Only Jasper knew the truth, that Lucien's selfishness had caused Robert's death, and that if Lucien had been there instead . . .

In the end Lucien lost a friend and gained a mountain of guilt.

So, no. He wouldn't fuck her, and he certainly couldn't keep her.

But he could kiss her.

Removing his gloves, he unbuttoned the cuff of her shirtwaist and slid the fabric out of his way. Her skin was soft and supple, and he lavished kisses all the way up her forearm, loving the way she trembled in his grasp. He could still hear her moans in his ears from last night, the sounds of pleasure when she rode his body.

He wanted to hear them again.

She's only allowing this because you bought her.

The lust roaring in his blood cooled. What was he doing? Eliza wasn't his lover or his mistress. Both of them grew carried away last night, lost in the moment, but said moment had passed.

He lowered her arm, rebuttoned her cuff, then set her hand on her lap.

"You are the most confusing man," she said. "For a reprobate, you are surprisingly hard to seduce."

"Is that what you are doing? Trying to seduce me?"

"Yes, you daft man. I still have nearly eighty-six thousand quid to earn."

He scoffed. "Rounding numbers? For shame, Eliza."

"Eighty-five thousand seven hundred and fifteen."

"Always forgetting the pence. Do you need a piece of paper? An abacus, perhaps?"

She shoved at his shoulder. "Stop—or I'll climb in your lap right here and repeat last night's payment."

Jesus. His groin tightened at the idea, cock thickening in his trousers. He shifted, hoping to ease the sudden ache, and tried to sound stern. "You'll do nothing of the sort, young lady."

He heard her breath hitch a second before she moved even closer, dash her. "Or what? Will you punish me, Lucien? I've heard about what teachers do to naughty young boys." Her fingers danced along his thigh, toward his groin. "Will you make me stand in the corner or paddle my bottom with a ruler?"

"Fuck, Eliza." He snatched her wrist before she could go higher. "Stop it."

"I can see you're hard. You want me."

"I want you, yes, but I won't act on it. Perhaps I'll visit Mollie and Ginny today instead." Even saying the words caused his cock to deflate, but Eliza needn't know that. Better she believed him a worthless degenerate than to hold out hope that he would take her virginity.

"No, I don't think you will," she said. "I think you want someone more innocent. More . . .inexperienced. A young girl who needs you to teach her what to do—"

Fire licked through his veins, and he snapped, "Cease speaking this instant."

Eliza laughed, a musical sound that felt like a caress over his bollocks, and crossed her arms. Thankfully, they rode the rest of the way in silence, Lucien holding onto his sanity by a thread.

By the time they arrived at his solicitor's place of business, he'd regained his equilibrium. He held her hand politely and helped her down to the walk. And if his touch lingered a shade too long as he assisted her inside, she didn't comment on it.

The secretary looked up as they entered. "May I help you?"

"The Duke of Blackwood and Lady Eliza Hawthorne to see Mr. Turner."

"Your Grace, my lady," the secretary said. "Good morning. Please, have a seat and I shall see if Mr. Turner is ready."

"Look," Eliza whispered when they were alone. "Is that a *ruler* on the desk? Shall we save it for later?"

God, he wanted that, but he couldn't. He *couldn't*. He was responsible for what happened to Robert, for what happened to her. She would hate him if she knew.

No matter her words, no matter how tempting the package, Lucien had to resist her. "Behave."

She chuckled and walked around the room, examining the art on the walls. "These look expensive. How much are you paying this solicitor?"

"I haven't the foggiest, actually." He had a business manager and secretary for those sorts of things.

Lucien hadn't troubled himself with the estate and businesses since Robert's death, more than happy to let others shoulder the burdens for a while. He'd failed at his responsibilities, had proven unworthy of anyone depending on him for anything, so it seemed best to step aside and let others do it.

"Your Grace," an older man said from the office doorway. "My lady. Won't you both come in?"

"Hello, Mr. Turner," Lucien said. "Thank you for seeing us."

"Of course, of course. Have a seat, if you please."

Lucien helped Eliza into a chair, then took his own. "Have you an answer for her ladyship on the late earl's estate?"

"I'm afraid there's not much good news. The will left by your ladyship's brother transferred all the assets to the next earl. No portion or entailment was set aside for you or your sister."

"Well, this was a waste of time." Slapping her hands on the armrests, Eliza started to get up out of the chair.

Lucien put his arm out to stay her. "Turner, there's nothing through her mother's family or distant relatives? Her mother's or father's will? Nothing at all?"

"No, I'm afraid not, Your Grace."

"Is there anything to be done about the current earl? Undoubtedly, Lady Eliza had possessions in the house at the time of her brother's death. Is she not entitled to get those possessions out?"

"I suppose, if we could prove they belonged to her and not the estate."

"He's likely thrown it all out," Eliza said with a frown. "Why would he keep anything five years later?"

"We won't know until we try," Lucien said. "And I'd like to have a little chat with his lordship anyway."

Turner cleared his throat to gain their attention. "Your Grace, I did learn that the current earl is having some financial difficulties. Perhaps if you offered him the right price . . . ."

"Good work, Turner."

Lucien started to rise as Turner reached for a stack of papers on his desk. "Wait, if you please. Whilst Your Grace is here, may I return the final paperwork for the land sale?"

He dropped back into his seat. "Land sale?"

"Yes, it came through Your Grace's secretary. It's the property in Hampstead." When Lucien didn't say anything, the solicitor cleared his throat. "I . . .That is, I assumed you knew. It has the ducal signature on it."

Lucien held out his hand. Turner placed the papers in Lucien's grasp, then withdrew a handkerchief to blot his forehead. Looking down, Lucien quickly read the legalese, authorizing a sale of some land his grandfather had purchased up in Hampstead. If he recalled correctly, it was mainly used for sheep grazing.

He flipped to the last page and saw his signature and seal.

What in the bloody hell?

"I didn't authorize this. Is it too late to stop it?"

"Of course, Your Grace. The papers come to me to finalize and file. I can misplace that one."

"Papers?" Lucien snapped. "Plural?"

Turner pulled at his collar. "I thought you knew. That is, there have been more of them as of late, but I assumed Your Grace was offloading some assets. Paring down the estate."

Lucien couldn't speak. He was stunned. Paring down the estate?

"Mr. Turner," Eliza spoke up. "May we see all the papers to which you are referring? I believe His Grace would like to review any business you've conducted on his behalf for the last few years."

"Yes," Lucien said, numbly. "Quite."

6

ELIZA ALMOST COULDN'T BELIEVE HER EYES. "LUCIEN, YOUR ACCOUNTS ARE a mess."

After they left his solicitor, they went straight to his business manager's office. Then, after taking every book, ledger, and piece of paper associated with the Blackwood estate, he fired both his business manager and his secretary, telling them legal proceedings were to follow if he found anything amiss.

Now back at his townhouse, they were inside his study, reviewing his ledgers.

"This is unbelievable," he shouted, throwing one of the thick books against the wall. "Those miserable parasites! Selling off my land and assets to put the money in their own pockets. I'll have them strung up!"

"You most definitely should press charges," she said, reviewing the lines again. "Because they've stolen quite a bit of money from you."

"Damn it!" he yelled, tearing at his hair as if trying to rip the strands out of his head. "I should have paid better attention."

"Why didn't you?"

When he didn't immediately answer, she looked up. He was staring at the fire, his chin set at a stubborn angle. She frowned at him. "Well? Why not?"

"Because I was busy elsewhere, Eliza. I didn't want to review boring reports and add up numbers all day."

That wasn't like the Lucien she remembered. What had caused such a drastic change in him? "Busy with parties and women and such? That sort of busy?"

"You try being a reasonably attractive, wealthy duke under the age of thirty and see how easy it is to resist temptation."

His words rang false. Something else happened all those years ago. But if he wanted to lie, then she couldn't stop him. They weren't friends, and he owed her nothing more than six nights of mindless pleasure.

She returned to the ledger, staying quiet as he continued to brood. After a bit, he stood and went to the sideboard. "Drink?" he called.

"Yes, please. Whisky, if you have it."

A crystal tumbler containing a splash of amber liquid appeared before her eyes. "I wouldn't have taken you for a whisky girl," he said.

"No? What type of girl do I seem like?"

He dropped into the seat next to her. "I don't know. I never imagined you drinking spirits."

"I like almost everything except gin."

He shuddered. "Can't stand the stuff. Tastes like perfume."

"Exactly."

They drank in silence, while the fire crackled. It was cozy, a scene her thirteen-year-old self would've killed to experience. But so much has changed since then. She was no longer that wide-eyed girl, and this was not a romance. He'd bought her virginity, that was all.

She hoped Fanny was faring all right at home alone. Eliza didn't feel good about leaving her sister for too long. Nights, when Fanny slept, were different. But during the day, when Eliza returned from work, there were meals to prepare, clothes to launder. The apartment needed tidying, too. Fanny did what she could, but Dr. Humphries said her sister shouldn't tax herself, and Eliza didn't mind looking after them both.

"What are you thinking about?" he asked, shifting toward her slightly.

"My sister. She'll soon wonder where I am."

"My driver can take you home. Thank you for trying to help me untangle this mess." He gestured toward the desk and the mound of paperwork, his expression angry and dejected.

She didn't like seeing him hurt. She wanted to ease those worry lines on his brow and kiss away the frown he wore. Wanted to make him smile and laugh, hear him growl into her ear and call her angel, and feel the rough press of his fingertips in her skin.

Eliza didn't want to leave him.

She finished the rest of her drink, disgusted with herself. No matter what else, she couldn't allow herself to become attached to him. This was mindless pleasure, the end. It would never be anything more, and their second night needed to get underway.

Setting the empty glass on the desk, she stood up. Then she began slipping the tiny buttons of her shirtwaist through the holes, undoing them. She'd managed five before Lucien realized what was happening.

He jerked in his seat. "Eliza, what are you playing at?"

Moving swiftly, she worked her way down her sternum, revealing more and more skin and undergarments along the way. It helped to serve as one's own lady's maid—she'd dressed and undressed herself every day for five years.

Lucien's gaze bounced around the room nervously, as if he were searching for an escape. The hand holding his drink trembled slightly. "There are servants in the house. It's not yet nighttime. What about your sister?" He swallowed hard. "This is wrong. You needn't do this. I will give you the money. Christ, Eliza. Please, I'm begging you. Fasten all those buttons at once."

Never had he said he didn't desire her.

Which meant she kept going, of course.

Her body felt feverish, her heart racing as she disrobed in front of him. With every garment that hit the floor, her blood ran hotter, her breath turning shallow. Her sex grew embarrassingly damp. Was he able to tell?

His expression darkened as she popped open her corset and let it fall. The bulge behind his trousers made her mouth water, and she wondered if he would finally let her see his cock.

"This is wrong," he rasped through harsh breaths as she lifted her chemise over her head. Then he reclined in his armchair, limbs loose and sprawled, like he'd given up the fight. "But oh, fuck. Keep going. God help me, don't stop."

After untying her drawers, she removed everything below her waist in one go, leaving her bare. Lucien studied her with a hot hooded gaze, removing any hint of shyness she might've felt.

"Bloody hell, you're beautiful." He downed the rest of his whisky and plunked his glass down, hard. "Get on the sofa, angel."

Excitement raced through her as she went to the long sofa against the wall. Lucien stood slowly and removed his coat, then his waistcoat and cravat. Now in shirtsleeves and trousers, he approached her, a devious glint in his eye. "Spread your legs."

Her thighs parted at his command, her body ready to do whatever he said. She felt giddy and drunk, though it wasn't from whisky. It was from this gorgeous and charming man she'd adored when she was a girl.

Instead of mounting her, as she expected, he knelt on the carpet and grasped her hips. "You keep trying to seduce me. I think you need to be punished."

"Are you going to paddle me with a ruler?"

His lips twitched but he shook his head. "No, not yet. Right now I plan to lick your pussy until you cry, begging me to stop because you cannot possibly come again."

Without giving her a chance to respond, he lowered his head and ran his tongue through her slit. She sucked in a breath, while Lucien let out a long groan. "You are so wet. You truly want me, don't you, little virgin?"

"Yes," she whispered. "Please, Lucien."

Humming in his throat, he licked her again, the flat of his tongue scraping across her most sensitive area. He lapped at her, exploring, never touching the place she craved him most, that little button atop her sex that throbbed with wanting. She rocked her hips, seeking, but he held her down.

"You tortured me last night," he said, flicking the tip of his tongue around her entrance. "It's my turn to torture you. Be still."

There was no more air for talking because Lucien began using his lips and tongue on her, swirling and caressing her clitoris, and everything else disappeared. There was just his mouth and the incessant tingles racing down her spine, along her legs. Corblimey, this felt good.

The tension built inside her, her insides pulling tighter, as he drove her higher, those warm licks and kisses like nothing she'd imagined. When he sucked the bud into his mouth, scraping it with his teeth, she exploded, the bliss overcoming her in a rush. "Oh, my God," she gasped as her walls pulsed in sheer happiness.

When it ebbed, Lucien gentled but didn't stop. Even when she grew sensitive and squirmed, he held her down and continued to lave at her. She considered protesting, but then she felt his finger probing at her entrance.

"You're soaking," he murmured. "Absolutely drenched. It's like heaven."

"Lucien," she panted. "Please."

She wasn't altogether certain what she was begging for, only that she needed more. Her body felt empty, needy, even in the aftermath of the best orgasm of her life. Was he planning to take her virginity here?

Suddenly, she wanted that more than anything else in the world.

"I'll take care of you, angel," he said, the tip of his finger sliding inside her pussy. His tongue painted her clitoris, which was swollen from earlier, and her back arched from the sensations battering her system.

"Yes, Lucien. It's so good."

The stretch of her inner tissues was strange and forbidden, a wicked touch that had her panting and rocking, trying to get him deeper. He was gentle, so very gentle, however, slowly filling her for the first time. When his finger was finally seated inside her, he rubbed a spot that made her see stars. "Hellfire and damnation!" she cried. "What was that?"

"Magic. Do you like it?"

He repeated the motion, and she reacted instantly, grabbing his hair and rocking her hips into his mouth, unable to help herself. It was like he'd shocked her with electric current, and her body could only react. The muscles of her stomach contracted, and he doubled his efforts, his tongue stroking quickly, and she nearly came off the sofa as another orgasm swept up and over her. Stronger than the first one, it seemed to go on and on, a never-ending cascade of ecstasy that she was powerless to stop.

When the peak ebbed, she sagged into the couch, boneless. Her throat ached from her cries. He nibbled her folds and the crease of her thigh, his finger still embedded in her channel, and he pumped his hand lazily, mimicking what his cock would do. God, she couldn't wait.

"Please," she said, her hands scrabbling at him, trying to bring him closer.

"One more, I think." He began giving her those drugging, open-mouthed deep kisses again and her eyes rolled back in her head.

"No, Lucien. It's too much."

"You can take it, my clever girl."

He didn't let up, and she could only whine, too far gone to form words as he gave her one more orgasm. When it was over, she couldn't open her eyes, her body sore and heavy, and he finally released her. She winced as his finger withdrew, but there was a strange emptiness now, a sense that part of her was missing.

"Sleep, my darling," he said, his lips brushing her forehead.

He never found his release, was her last thought before the blackness tugged her down.

7

Eliza awoke wrapped in a warm and soft cocoon, not a stitch of clothing on her body. How long had she been asleep? Dying afternoon light streamed through large bay windows she didn't recognize. An unfamiliar painted ceiling stared down, while strange furniture surrounded her.

Lucien. Ledger books. Sofa.

Ah, yes. Relaxing, she pulled the blanket tighter around her nakedness. That had been remarkable, though not quite what he'd paid for. Interesting that during his thorough ministrations, he hadn't lost control. He hadn't been overcome with need, like last night.

He hadn't come close to taking her virginity.

Was this her fate? To have the one man she'd been obsessed with for years pleasure her beyond reason, but never claim her?

He was at his desk, and she watched through her lashes as he reviewed the ducal accounting books, his hair mussed and sleeves rolled high on his forearms. He'd discarded his collar, revealing the thick column of his throat, and on his face sat a pair of thin eyeglasses. Her sex quivered. He was absolutely gorgeous, concentrating so intently that a crease had formed between his brows. She wanted to smooth it away with her thumb.

When she thought of Lucien, this was what she imagined, a serious and clever man. Dedicated and responsible, not the reprobate with two mistresses and a devil-may-care attitude. She far preferred this version.

I could love this version.

No, no, no. This was not a romance. As much as the thirteen-year-old inside her begged for her to fall at his feet and worship him, that was just a fantasy. Real life had taken them in different directions and she would not become his mistress. Fanny was her responsibility now.

Lucien was hers for the next six nights, that was all.

Holding the blanket tight, she sat up. His gaze flicked toward her, and he removed his eyeglasses. "There you are," he said. "I was wondering how long you would sleep."

She rose and went around the desk to stand by his chair. "Your mouth should be outlawed."

The side of his mouth hitched as he leaned back in his chair. "I know."

Unable to keep from reaching out, she swept a lock of dark hair off his forehead. "Arrogant man."

He edged away and cleared his throat. "Eliza, we should talk."

"Excellent idea. Let's go up to your bedroom and talk in bed."

"Absolutely not." He pushed his chair back and stood, as if he needed to put space between them. "I have an idea."

"A naughty idea?"

"Dash it, no. Will you let me finish?" He sighed and pointed to the books on his desk. "This is a disaster. I need help sorting out the estate and you've already started working on the books with me. I'd like to hire you."

"I don't understand. You've already 'hired' me for six more nights."

"No, I haven't—and not for this. I want to offer you legitimate work. Here, for me. With the accounts."

"Oh." She looked at the desk, her mind turning this over.

"This way, we needn't do any more of *that*." He waved his hand in the direction of the sofa.

Her stomach dropped, her lungs tightening in disappointment. He wasn't going to bed her. She'd thrown herself at him twice and Lucien had resisted. Now he'd found a way to pay her to *not* take her virginity.

She should've been thrilled.

She should've been grateful.

Instead, she was disappointed.

"I see."

"I . . ." He dragged a hand through his hair, mussing it even more. "I thought you'd be relieved. This way, you needn't lose your virginity. You can still marry a decent man and have a family. You needn't sleep with me for money."

But I want to sleep with you, Lucien. Badly.

It wasn't one sided, either. He admitted to wanting her. Had climaxed last night, and pounced on her when she removed her clothes earlier.

You're mine, Eliza.

Had he meant it? If so, why the sudden and annoying nobility? The man had *two* mistresses! Seducing him should not prove this damn difficult.

She considered his proposition. Working on his accounts would keep her here in the house. With him. Alone. That was a plus, unless he was determined to leave her chaste, which was a colossal minus.

Admittedly, it would be nice to put her maths skills to use. Balancing her and Fanny's meager budget each month wasn't exactly taxing to her brain box. But agreeing felt like giving up on something monumental. Something she'd dreamed of for *years*.

"May I be honest with you?" she asked.

His expression wary, he folded his arms across his chest. "Of course."

"I was looking forward to more of that." She hooked a thumb at the sofa. "I was looking forward to sleeping with you."

Lips parting in surprise, he stood, frozen. "I . . .don't understand. Why? You'd be ruined."

She could only throw her head back and laugh. "Lucien, I don't care about my maidenhead or my reputation. Those things matter in Mayfair, not in the real world. And in case you haven't noticed, I like doing these things with you. I . . . " God, was she really going to confess this? "I had a crush on you as a girl. This is actually fulfilling some of my fantasies."

He dragged both hands through his hair, appearing aggravated at her revelation. "Do not tell me these things. Your brother would cut off my bollocks with a rusty knife, Eliza."

"He's not here, but I am. I'll help you with your accounts, but I want to do the rest, too."

"Why are you insisting on this? I thought you would be grateful."

"Do you desire me, Lucien?"

"I shouldn't answer that."

Which was an answer unto itself. Still, she had to push. One thing Eliza had learned in the last five years was to take charge of her life, not to let an obstacle in her path deter her.

And right now, that obstacle was Lucien's nobility.

She dropped the blanket. "Do you want to fuck me, Lucien?"

The air in the room turned heavy and thick, making it impossible to breathe. He hardly moved, and the hunger in his expression sent a torrent of heat along her veins, causing her core to pulse with desire.

"You know I do," he growled.

"Then prove it."

ROBERT WOULD PUNCH Lucien in the face were he still alive.

Lucien tried to resist, but he inhaled and caught the scent of Eliza's arousal, and he was lost, drowning in a sea of longing. He hadn't washed his face from earlier, either, and the taste of her lingered on his tongue, on his skin. Christ, he wanted her.

She stood there patiently, as bare as the day she was born, waiting for him to make up his mind. The curve of her hip beckoned, the perfect place to hold onto whilst he explored her body. Then he studied the slope of her breast, the swell of her belly. His cock throbbed in his trousers, insistent and annoying, and the temptation was more than he could bear.

This was terrible. *He* was terrible—spoiled and selfish, used to getting what he wanted—and his body hated to be denied. After all, he'd paid for her innocence. The idea of stretching her virgin cunt with his cock . . .

He closed his eyes briefly. Goddamn it, this was Robert's sister, and it was Lucien's fault she was in this predicament to begin with. Why wouldn't she take the hundred thousand pounds, buy a house in

Mayfair, and everything could return to the way it was before? The last five years would disappear. Why did she insist on torturing him like this?

Why must she insist on giving him her virginity?

His body didn't care about the reasons at present. She was naked and asking him to fuck her, and he didn't think he was capable of refusing her a damn thing. His fingers curled into fists.

I shouldn't.

She deserves better.

She will hate me when she learns what happened to her brother.

The devil in him, however, began rationalizing.

One night. Afterwards, she would help him with his accounts. He would give her the money and ease his conscience. She would restart her life like nothing ever happened.

"You'll help me with the accounts? After we sleep together once?"

"Yes."

"And you'll accept the money?"

"In exchange for my virginity and five days of accounting, yes."

"Five days! This will take longer than that."

"I agreed to only seven nights, Lucien. You'll get no more than that." She stretched her arms toward the ceiling, her perfect apple-shaped breasts rising. Her nipples were hard little points begging for his mouth.

Distracted, he lost his train of thought. "Wait, why?"

"Because I have a life and responsibilities outside of you. Shocking, I know."

"But . . . ."

"But, nothing. You already have two mistresses. You don't require a third."

He hadn't seen those two mistresses in days, had lost interest in them because of Eliza, who at the moment was moving toward him, her hips swaying and breasts bouncing. The urge to bite all that perfect skin, to mark her as his own, had his hands shaking.

When she reached him, she trailed her finger down his throat, between his collarbones. "You claim my virginity tonight, then we move on to business tomorrow. Everyone wins."

"No taking it back once it's done," he warned.

"I won't regret it. Deep down, I always wanted it to be you."

Jesus Christ.

Hesitation evaporated like morning dew in the hot sun. Spinning, he found his topcoat on the chair. In a flash, he wrapped her in it, covered her, then lifted her in his arms. She clutched him, laughing. "Where are we going?"

"Upstairs."

Then they were in the corridor, his leather shoes slapping the marble floor on their way to the staircase. The footman in the front hall quickly averted his eyes, expression unchanging, as if his employer held a naked woman in his arms every day. Despite his reputation, though, this was a first. Lucien never fucked women here.

Just Eliza, apparently.

She'd grown bolder these last few years, nothing like the young girl who used to blush when he stared at her a few seconds too long from across a dining table. Yet she was still so innocent.

A combination that hardened his cock beyond reason, apparently.

Once in his bedroom, he strode to the bed and tossed her on top. She bounced, chuckling, and he began tearing off his clothing, desperate to feel her bare skin against his own. Coming to her knees, she shuffled forward to help, her eager fingers starting with his trousers.

They worked together until he was naked, then he let her look her fill. His erection stood out proudly, eagerly, and he half-expected her to change her mind. "Are you sure, Eliza?"

She looked at his cock and reached a tentative hand toward it, all wide-eyed curiosity and fascination. "Very."

Oh, God. If she touched him, he wouldn't last.

He pointed to the bed. "On your back. Spread your legs."

She hurried to comply, limbs scrambling in her haste. Now it was his turn to look his fill, never wishing to forget the way she appeared in his bed. No lover had ever visited his home before, and he anticipated smelling her on his sheets afterward.

One night. That was all.

He crawled onto the mattress, up between her thighs, which he shoved wider to make room for himself. Her pussy gleamed in the fire-light, her slickness like a sweet treat just waiting to be devoured. "I'm going to prepare you, so relax. Understand?"

"Yes," she said on an exhale of breath.

Without waiting another second, he lowered his head and nuzzled her. This couldn't be rushed. He teased the edges of her sex with his nose and lips. When she shifted impatiently, he gave a gentle lick through her seam, stopping just below her clitoris.

Then he applied himself to the task, using his tongue in creative ways —back and forth, circling, pressing—until she was panting. Her fingers found their way into his hair and she held on, her hips rocking, churning, seeking . . .and it took everything he had not to surge up and ram his cock inside her. He had to go gently.

A mewling sound escaped her throat, while her nails dug into his scalp. "Now, Lucien. Please."

The need in his body doubled, tripled, and he had to close his eyes before he began humping the bed in desperation. He sucked her clitoris between his lips and flicked it with his tongue. Gasping, she tensed and let out a moan, the sweetest sound he'd ever heard.

"It's not enough, Lucien. I need you."

Moving a finger toward her channel, he pushed gently inside, the walls sucking him in greedily. Fuck, she was tight. Hot. Slick. He growled into her flesh, every muscle clenched in agony as he tried to stem the hunger clawing inside him. Sweet Eliza, with her spine of steel and mind for numbers. He could get used to her taste, the way she swelled on his tongue. How she gripped his hair in her fist to keep his mouth where she wanted.

He could do this for the rest of his life and die a happy man.

"More, Lucien. Please."

He rose up over her as he slid another finger inside her. "Yes, my lovely girl. You're so very tight, but I'm going to fill you up, stretch you until I'm all you can feel."

Remembering her reaction on the sofa, he crooked his fingers inside her, and she jolted, letting out a loud moan. "There we go, angel," he crooned. "That's my favorite spot."

Soon, he wedged a third finger in her channel. This was a tighter squeeze, so he distracted her with a deep kiss, until he had the digits seated inside her. Damn, she was snug. He imagined all that heat strangling his shaft and nearly came right then.

"Oh, God. Please, now. Lucien, I'm ready." Her hands pulled at him. "Please."

He reached for the drawer next to the bed and found the package containing a shield. It took only a second or two to roll the thick rubber onto his shaft. Then he took a vial out of the drawer.

"What is that?" she panted.

"Oil. It will help me slide inside you."

He poured a small amount into his hands, set the vial down, then smeared the oil on his rubber-covered shaft, trembling at the sensation. He wasn't certain how long he could last.

Clenching his jaw to keep from spending, he lined up at her entrance and pushed forward, making certain to watch the slow invasion. His hands held her hips steady as her entrance gave way and sucked the crown inside. "That's it, darling. Take me in. Be my very good girl and take my cock inside you."

When she tensed, his gaze darted to hers. "Easy," he said, stroking her thigh. "I'm going to take care of you."

Using his thumb, he drew circles over her clitoris and her muscles eased, relaxed, which allowed Lucien to sink deeper into her sex. They both groaned. This gentle advance went on for several minutes as he invaded and conquered, stroked and petted. Wet heat surrounded him, strangled his shaft, and his brain struggled to keep up.

"Corblimey," she whispered and tilted her hips higher. "More, please. I need you deep inside me, where I ache."

Gritting his teeth against the need to ram inside her, he said, "I don't want to hurt you."

She wrapped her arms around his waist, then slid them lower, grabbing his buttocks. Then she sunk her nails into his backside, hard.

He hissed at the exquisite pain and his hips snapped, driving her into the mattress, their bodies fully joined. She squeaked, almost recoiling, and guilt slammed through him. "Goddamn it, Eliza. I'm sorry." He held perfectly still, his lids squeezed tightly against the absolute bliss of being fully sheathed. "I didn't mean to enter you so quickly. Are you all right?"

"I'm fine. Stop worrying." She wriggled slightly beneath him. "It was a pinch but now it's done."

"I should pull out." He started to shove up off the mattress, but she clutched him harder, digging those nails into his skin once more. He shivered.

"Don't you dare, duke. Teach me, Lucien. Tell me what you like, what makes you come."

Groaning, he shoved his face into the soft skin of her throat. "No, no, no. Stop talking." His hips began rocking, pleasure coursing down his spine. "Fuck, Eliza. I need to make this last. I need to make this good for you."

"This isn't about me," she whispered, the vixen. "You bought me, paid for my virginity. I'm yours to do with whatever you please."

Goddamn it. Lust shot through his groin and along his cock. This was wrong. All of this was so bloody wrong.

He began thrusting then, sweat gathering on his skin, and the bed rocked with the force of his movements. "It's so good . . .you feel so good. Tight. Oh, God, so bloody tight."

"*Yes,*" she moaned near his ear. "Keep going. I'm yours, Lucien. Only yours."

Whatever restraint he'd been clinging to deserted him. Pushing up, he grabbed her hands and pinned them to the mattress, holding her down as he continued to pound into her. He felt like an animal, a beast mindlessly rutting. "Do you like it? Do you like the way a cock feels inside you?"

Her walls clenched around his length, giving him her answer. "Yes, yes, yes," she chanted, her face awash in pleasure, making him feel like the most powerful man on earth. "Just yours, Lucien."

Satisfaction filled him. He was the first man to fuck this glorious creature, the first to see her expression twist in euphoria as he thrust inside her. He made certain to brush her clitoris with his pelvic bone on every stroke. His hands kept her where he wanted her, but she didn't try to pull free, as if she liked being at his mercy.

A million pricks of fire exploded in his veins. "You're mine now," he said, his voice thick. "Mine to fuck whenever I want. Perhaps I'll tie you to my bed, naked, spread open so you'll always be ready for me. Ready to take my cock."

She must've liked that because her core spasmed around his length, as if she were trying to pull him deeper inside. Her shout filled the room as she came.

"Goddamn it." He couldn't hold out any longer. His hips stuttered, grew uncoordinated, and he threw his head back to roar at the ceiling.

Jets of spend filled the rubber and every muscle twitched in blissful agony. When his thoughts realigned moments later, he stared down at her gorgeous face and saw her satisfied expression. His stomach instantly sank.

Oh, shit. What had he done?

8

Eliza floated for a bit after, contentment rippling throughout her limbs as they lay there, still joined. Lucien panted, his face relaxed, making him appear younger, more like the man she once knew. The man she'd once dreamt about marrying. Her heart turned over in her chest, and a girlish giddiness she'd long buried resurfaced. She had the sudden urge to wrap around him and never let go.

Oh, no.

No, this was terrible. These feelings were both inappropriate and inconvenient. She'd tried to maintain control of this afternoon, bargaining with him for her virginity. Seducing him instead of letting him relegate her to the position of secretary.

Yet somewhere along the way, her plan had backfired.

Sharing his bed had been so much more than she imagined, like he'd taken her apart and rearranged her, an equation that no longer made sense. One only he could solve. And, she craved more of him, of their intimacies.

Damn and blast.

She pushed his shoulder and he obliged, falling to his back on the mattress with a thud. The shield still covered his softening erection, and his spend was making a mess of him and the bedclothes. Apt, considering how the afternoon had gone. She'd made a mess of everything.

Worse, she'd agreed to return tomorrow. How could she keep from seducing him once more?

She had to resist the temptation, because this affection, this blooming emotion towards him would only grow worse. What happened at the end of the seven days? Would she fall in love with him? Agree to be his mistress, anything for another crumb of his attention?

She absolutely couldn't risk it. The money was for Fanny's treatment, for the two of them to start a new life. She didn't wish to be tied to a man for the rest of her days, not when she'd worked so hard for independence. Giving it up would destroy her.

Yes, he'd taken her virginity, which was the fulfillment of so many of her girlhood dreams. Now she would straighten out the ducal accounts and help him set things to rights. Then, she would disappear from his life with her heart intact.

"I should go," she blurted and shoved up off the bed.

"Wait." He reached for her. "Let me take care of you. Clean you up and make sure you're not hurt."

Dread clogged her throat. Any hint of tenderness would do her in right now. The walls between this man and her heart had taken a beating moments ago, nearly crumbling, and she needed time and space to rebuild and reinforce them.

"I'm right as rain, duke." She removed her arm from his grasp and lunged for his silk dressing gown on the chair. "You needn't fuss over me."

"Eliza, goddamn it." He sat up and dealt with the shield. "Don't rush out of here again. I want to talk about this."

Crikey, that was almost a worse idea than the bloody tenderness.

Besides, she had to get home to her sister.

Throwing her arms into the oversized sleeves, she started babbling on her way to the door. "Lovely time, must run. You were amazing. The stuff of poetry, really. Talk more later. Sweet dreams. Good night."

"Do not dare—"

She closed the door behind her and hurried toward the stairs. Humiliating that her clothing was in his study, but there was no help for it now. She had to quickly dress and find a hack. Fanny would be worried sick if Eliza wasn't home before dark.

Lucien had collected her things into a pile, bless him, so she began dragging the pieces on. Just as she fastened her corset, the door opened and the duke stormed in, his face a picture of unhappiness. He wore trousers, shirt, and waistcoat, a pair of shoes and topcoat in his hands. "So you were planning on sneaking out again? Is that it?"

"I said goodbye. I was hardly sneaking."

"I know someone desperate for escape when I see it, Eliza." He dragged on his coat. "Shall I tie you to my bed, or are you going to answer me honestly right here?"

Her mouth went dry and she had to drag in a deep breath, the words appealing to her in ways she would never have guessed two hours ago. "I must return home to my sister." It was true, after all.

He studied her face as if searching for a lie. "I called for my carriage already, so I will take you."

"No, I'd rather—"

"You'd rather take a hack or a tram. I know, but I won't allow it. So short of poisoning or stabbing me, that won't happen."

"You should return to your books. They need your help far worse than I do."

"The books may wait. I will ensure you get home safely first."

And I must put distance between us before I fall in love with you.

She tried to reason with him as she fastened her skirts. "I'll allow your driver to see me home if you stay here."

"Absolutely not. I'm not letting you go all the way to Shoreditch alone. End of discussion."

"You're being absurd."

"And you're being stubborn." Once he shoved his feet into his shoes, he folded his arms, blocking her only path to escape with his body. "I'll gladly carry you to the carriage. Your choice."

She glared at him as she buttoned her shirtwaist. "Are you like this with all your lovers, or merely me?"

"Just you, it appears. Ready?"

There was no getting out of it that she could see, so she followed him to the large fancy carriage and piled in. He sat across from her, their knees touching, and heat curled in her belly. The smell of their love-making hung thick in the air, every bounce of the springs reminding her that Lucien had just taken her virginity.

She must've winced, because he asked, "Are you sore?"

Her chest expanded, like her heart was swelling. The urge to crawl into his lap and let him hold her roared inside her. Lord, what was happening to her? "I'm fine. Just a bit tired. Mind if I sleep?"

His gaze narrowed as if he didn't believe her. "You wouldn't be trying to ignore me, would you?"

"No," she lied. The nap she'd taken today was more sleep than she'd had in years. "I'm exhausted. You've worn me out."

"Then sleep. I'll wake you once we're there.'

She thought to close her eyes for a few moments, but she must've truly fallen asleep because Lucien was suddenly shaking her awake. The carriage had stopped.

"We've arrived," his deep voice said, the expression in his eyes so soft and adoring that she nearly kissed him.

No, that wouldn't do. No more kisses, no more adoration. She was his accountant from here on out.

Pushing up, she straightened. He'd ordered the carriage directly to her lodgings, which meant . . . "You discovered where I live. How?"

"I've been waiting for you to ask me that all day. I had a man waiting outside my home last night, just in case someone came to collect one of her evenings."

Damn. She'd led Lucien right to her. "Bully for you, then." She reached over him to push the latch on the carriage door. "I'll see you in the morning."

He stepped down and held out his hand. Confusion furrowed her brows. "What are you doing?"

"Escorting you inside."

She barely stifled her gasp. She couldn't imagine his reaction to her humble apartment. It would mortify her beyond belief. "Absolutely not."

"If you want to make it inside, it will be with me at your side. Come, Eliza."

"You needn't worry over my virtue. You've taken care of that already, duke."

"This has nothing to do with your virtue or reputation. This is about your safety. Now, must I carry you?"

"Stop threatening to carry me," she snapped. "It's tiresome."

In a flash, he grabbed her forearms, yanked her forward, and hauled her over his shoulder. "I'll return shortly," he called to his driver.

She was draped over him like a carpet, her legs dangling while he cradled the backs of her thighs. "You obnoxious toff. Put me down this bloody instant."

He had the nerve to smack her bottom. "Quiet, impudent baggage."

"That's the way, guv!" some female voice shouted out from a window above them.

"You're welcome to slap my bottom, sir," another woman called.

Thankfully, they were soon inside her building. "Which floor?" he asked, his voice clipped.

"Four—and there's no elevator, so have a jolly time carrying me up all those steps."

"I've carried pillows that were heavier than you."

Lucien proved his excellent physical condition by taking the four flights easily, not even sounding winded. "Which one?"

"Second on the right."

After he stomped over, jostling her, he knocked on the door.

"This is humiliating," she muttered.

"I told you I wanted to take care of you," he said. "I saw your wince in the carriage."

Her skin heated, partly embarrassment but mostly pleasure. This caring and possessive side of him was nearly irresistible.

The door opened.

"Is that . . . ." Fanny sounded confused. "Is that my sister over your shoulder?"

"Lady Fanny," Lucien said. "If you'll allow me in, I'll drop off this parcel and be on my way."

Parcel? Eliza huffed. So much for the caring and possessive Lucien. "Put me down, you oaf."

"Your Grace," Fanny said, a hint of disapproval in her voice. "Come in."

"Thank you." He strode in, bent down, and put Eliza on her feet.

"Was that necessary?" she asked him.

"I think so, yes."

Fanny's worried gaze looked the duke over first, then Eliza, and Eliza could see the wheels turning in her sister's head, putting the pieces in place. Of course, with Lucien half-dressed, higher level reasoning wasn't exactly required.

"Is Your Grace planning to stay for dinner?" Fanny asked. "We have soup."

Eliza didn't give him a chance to answer. "No, he's leaving. Good night, Lucien. I will see you in the morning."

"Ladies," he said with a perfectly executed bow. "I'll leave you to your evening."

Then he departed and the silence in the apartment was deafening. The sisters stared at one another for so long, they heard Lucien's carriage pull away.

"You have feelings for him," Fanny finally said.

"That's absurd." Though Eliza suspected it wasn't.

"We should rethink this plan, because I will never forgive myself if my illness forces you to become some toff's mistress."

"I'm not going to become his mistress. It's only five days and I'm only helping him with some accounting matters. No intimacy required. Furthermore, we agreed on this. It's the best way to get the money and then sail to America."

Before that happened, Eliza had to earn her hundred thousand pounds.

Fanny narrowed her eyes and opened her mouth—to continue arguing, no doubt—but she coughed instead. Deep wracking coughs that crackled in her chest. Even though it was warm in the apartment, Eliza closed the window, trying to keep the dirty London air out for the moment. Fanny needed clean air, which was scarce in the city.

When Fanny caught her breath, she continued their conversation as if the coughing fit never happened. "Just promise me you won't fall in love with him."

"I promise."

For the rest of the night, Eliza feared she'd already broken that promise.

THE DUCAL BOOKS were even worse off than Eliza first believed. That Lucien allowed things to get this bad was absolutely appalling.

And quite unlike the man she remembered from all those years ago.

What happened to him?

She hadn't seen the duke in three and a half days. Instead, she came to his home, sat in his office, and poured through the accounting ledgers. The books hadn't been updated in some time, and there were strange entries she didn't understand. Those she noted on a separate piece of paper to ask him about.

She tried not to think about him, but it was hard when she was surrounded by reminders of him all day long.

You're mine now. Mine to fuck whenever I want.

Heat suffused her, as it did every time she considered Lucien's words. She dared not tell Fanny any of the details. Hearing how gloriously rough and filthy Lucien was in bed wouldn't reassure Fanny about Eliza's vow never to become his mistress.

And honestly, Eliza wasn't certain she wanted to tell anyone. Not right now, at least. There were lonely years ahead of her in which she could try to make sense of him and the last few days.

In the meantime, she'd enjoy the work, the challenge to her brain, while sitting in a fine Mayfair home again, where it was warm and smelled nice. She wasn't on her knees scrubbing, or leaning over to sew in candlelight. Perhaps Lucien could write her a letter of recommendation, too, one that would allow her to find employment in an American accounting firm.

Where was he anyway? Was he intending not to see her at all before the end of the five days?

The possibility sent a pang through her chest. She hadn't expected that. When she agreed to help him with the books, she assumed they would be side-by-side, laughing and talking as they worked. Not with her cooped up alone while he did whatever it was he did all day.

Was he with his mistresses?

The pang sounded again, the pressure on her sternum like a boulder had been dropped there. She tried to remind herself that she held no claim over him. *I cannot be jealous. He is not mine.*

Besides, tomorrow was her last day here.

Afterwards, they'd both return to their lives, and Eliza would focus on Fanny's recovery. They would find an American sanitarium to accept

Fanny and help her get better. Then they would buy a house and settle somewhere with plenty of fresh air and sunshine.

So it shouldn't bother her if Lucien wished to ignore her. The more time they spent together would make it harder to separate tomorrow.

And yet, she couldn't stop glancing at the door every few minutes, waiting for it to pop open and reveal his handsome face.

Then the door did open. Eliza straightened, a hopeful smile twisting her lips . . .which dimmed when a footman appeared with a tray. She swallowed her disappointment.

"Your lunch, my lady."

"Michael, as I told you yesterday and the day before, you may call me Eliza. Or Miss Hartsford."

He shook his head. "His Grace's orders. We address you properly, as befitting your station."

Oh, that dratted annoying man.

"Can you tell me, is His Grace here today?"

"Yes, miss."

"I see."

He was here, yet he hadn't stopped in to say hello. Were they no longer friends now that he'd taken her virginity? Was her hymen all he'd wanted, like some sort of trophy or prize? Hurt and anger swirled in her belly, twisting and turning, until the urge to yell at him rose to a fever pitch. "Where is he?"

The skin above the footman's collar turned a deep red. "I probably shouldn't say, my lady. His Grace asked to be left alone."

"I understand. I wouldn't like for you to lose your position." Finding work was a miserable endeavor, and as much as she wished to see Lucien, she wouldn't do it at an employee's expense. "Thank you for the tray."

"Your ladyship is most welcome."

When the footman left, Eliza waited a few minutes, then set off exploring. It shouldn't be terribly hard to find Lucien. The townhouse was large, but it wasn't a labyrinth. She would conduct a systematic search of every floor, avoiding the areas reserved for the staff.

She decided to start on the ground floor, then work her way up. Moving quickly and quietly, she explored but found only empty rooms. On the first floor, his bedroom was quiet and still. Same for the other bedrooms. As she passed the ballroom, however, a thumping sound caught her notice.

Carefully, she cracked the door and peered inside. Her lips parted on a surprised exhale. A bare-chested Lucien was pummeling a large canvas bag, his hands wrapped in cloth. Sweat rolled down his skin, his muscles popping with his rapid movements.

Sweet heavens. She couldn't tear her gaze away. He was stunning, a Greek god come to life to make mortal men appear like flabby, inconsequential fools. Arousal tightened her nipples into points, the area between her legs tingling as she watched. The minutes dragged on and she began to worry she'd melt into a puddle on the floor. All that would be left was some threadbare clothing and hair pins.

She desired him. Right now.

It wasn't easy to admit, considering this wasn't an affair and she'd vowed to keep her distance.

But Eliza knew when she'd been beaten. Her resistance crumbled like grains of sand. What was one more time when her heart already belonged to him?

She closed the door behind her, which caused him to pause midpunch and glance over. His chest heaved as he panted. "What are you doing here?"

"Coming to find you."

"Why?" He wiped his forehead with the back of his hand. "Is there a problem downstairs?"

There was a problem all right, and it had to do with the ache inside her that only he could satisfy.

"Are you avoiding me?" As she approached, he went over to pick up a cloth from the floor. "Because I haven't seen you in three and a half days."

"I'm busy, Eliza." He wiped his face with the cloth. "You've been making excellent progress, though."

"You've been looking at the books after I leave, then."

"Yes."

"Why not look at them with me? Then we may discuss any questions I have."

His hands rested on his hips, making his bare chest appear impossibly wide. "Just leave the questions and I'll get to them when I can."

Why was he being so cagey?

Ignoring his deep frown, she closed the distance between them. The heat from his body was like a furnace, and she longed to touch all that sweat and strength. "I was thinking . . ." She licked her lips as a bead of sweat trickled down the center of his chest. "Tomorrow is our last day together."

"And?"

"And it would be a shame to waste it, hiding in the ballroom."

"I'm not hiding," he said, his voice sounding strangled as she caught a bead of his sweat on her fingertip before it could reach his stomach. "And you shouldn't be in here, Eliza."

"Am I still yours, Lucien?"

The whispered question echoed in the empty room, and a muscle worked in his jaw as they stared at one another. *Say yes,* she thought. *Please say yes.*

"Eliza—"

"It's a simple question. Am I still yours?"

"It doesn't matter. I cannot keep you. It's best if we maintain our distance until you finish tomorrow."

"It does matter. It matters at this moment."

"Why? Because you're trying to torture me?"

She placed her palm on his jaw and stroked the heavy whiskers he hadn't shaved off today. "Because I want you to take me to your bed one more time."

9

SURPRISINGLY, LUCIEN DIDN'T PUT UP A FIGHT. HE MERELY GRABBED HER hand and tugged her through his house as if they'd done this a hundred times. She didn't bother hiding in embarrassment. What was the point? He'd taken her virginity already and her body was burning alive, desperate for him. Let the servants talk. She'd never see them again after tomorrow anyway.

You're mine now.

How she wished it were true. To wake up with him every day, roll over into his arms and find his warm hard body. To laugh with him and discuss maths at the dinner table. To have days and months and years together, their memories and hearts intertwined.

But those were just fantasies.

Lucien wasn't for her. Dukes married girls from the very best families, not girls who once scrubbed privies and mopped vomit off the floor. Certainly not a girl who sold her virginity in a club full of aristocratic gentlemen.

Do not fall in love with him, Fanny had warned.

Too late. It felt like Eliza had loved Lucien for so long that it was hard to remember a time when she hadn't. Sharing his bed had caused those feelings to multiply exponentially. Leaving him was going to kill her.

Nevertheless, she planned to depart tomorrow with a bank draft and never look back. Fanny came first, always. So Eliza would make the most of every second she had left with him, starting right now.

When his bedchamber door closed, she threw herself at him, wasting no time in sealing her mouth to his. He met her kiss eagerly, and her hands skated over his bare torso. He felt divine, big and hot.

"I have to fuck you." He began walking her toward the wall while gathering her skirts in his hand. "It will be fast and hard, so please tell me you aren't too sore."

"Not sore. Please, Lucien. Hurry."

He growled and lunged for her mouth again, his tongue thrusting inside to flick and rub against hers as cool air hit her stocking-covered legs. "Put your legs around my waist," he said and lifted under her buttocks until her thighs were splayed, her knees hugging his hips.

"That's it," he crooned and, after some maneuvering with his clothing, the head of his cock nudged her entrance. "Let me in, my darling girl. I'm going to take such good care of you."

Oh, heavens. The temptation of those words. She couldn't let herself believe them.

This was all, right here. Today and tomorrow. Then they'd go their separate ways—Lucien back to his two mistresses and Eliza to America.

But while she couldn't keep him, she'd ensure he remembered her long after she'd gone.

"I like when you take care of me," she whispered. "I like when you teach me, too. Will you spank me and put me in the corner if I'm a naughty student?"

"Goddamn it," he gritted out from between clenched teeth and shoved halfway inside her, as if he couldn't help himself. "You drive me out of my bloody mind."

It was not an easy fit, and she was impatient to lose herself in him. "More," she begged. "I need all of you."

With a grunt, he flexed his hips and drove up until he was fully seated. She gasped, her nails digging into his shoulders, as her body adjusted. "Good lord, Lucien."

"Shh, you can take me." He held still, his big body pinning her to the wall, hands under her thighs. "You were made for my cock, Eliza."

She doubted it. At the moment, it felt as if he would snap her in two. Still, she loved the feeling of having Lucien inside her, his thick shaft stretching her wide and stealing her breath. A small bite of pain chased by immense pleasure.

So much pleasure.

"Please," she whispered into his throat. "Please, you have to move. I am dying to feel you."

"Is that so?" His voice was low and tight, like she wasn't the only one suffering. "Is your pussy greedy for me?"

Her lids fell as her head dropped onto his shoulder. Did all dukes speak in such a filthy manner, or just hers?

Get a grip on yourself, Eliza. He isn't yours.

While she would always belong to him, Lucien would never be hers. Her heart dropped at the thought, like the organ had grown too heavy for her chest, but she pushed those feelings aside for later. She had to remain in the present. There would be years and years ahead to miss him.

"Yes," she answered, wriggling her hips. "So greedy. I need you."

He gave a small thrust, and tiny sparkles raced along her spine. Her walls gripped him, unwilling to let him go, but he withdrew and pushed forward, rocking back and forth, until they built a steady rhythm. His mouth hovered over hers, his hot breath warming her skin, and she could feel him everywhere, inside and out, drowning her, and she never wanted to resurface. "Oh, God," she said on a moan as he ground into her, bliss echoing in every cell, every muscle.

"Would you like to learn something new?"

"Yes, please."

He carried her to the bed. "Roll over, then get up on your hands and knees."

Keeping her skirts above her waist, she did as he asked. "Like this?" She glanced over her shoulder.

With his stare locked on the slit of her drawers, he tucked his hard cock into his trousers, but didn't touch her. Instead, he went to the small secretary against the wall and opened a drawer. When she saw what he took out, her whole body quivered.

A ruler.

"You've been very bad." As he approached the bed, he smacked the hard wooden stick against his palm. "Teasing me and making me want to fuck you."

Sweet Jesus, was he truly going to spank her? She'd mentioned this in jest, but now she wasn't so sure. "What are you doing?"

His smile was sinister as he stepped just off to the side. "Giving you your punishment. Aren't you curious to know what it will feel like to have this hard ruler strike your bottom, my naughty girl?"

She hesitated. Yes, she was a bit curious, but she also wasn't keen on pain. "Will it hurt?"

"For only a second." He dragged his palm over one of her buttocks, then drew his fingers along her seam, making her squirm. "But the burn will turn into something bright and pleasurable, like your skin is shimmering. Glowing. Will you let me teach you? I think you're going to like it."

She likely would have agreed to anything in that moment, as long as he kept using that deep seductive voice. "All right."

Before she could even brace for it, he struck her backside with the wooden ruler. Fire roared across her skin. That smarted, her thin undergarment doing seemingly nothing to protect her.

He put a hand on her back, holding her still. "Good girl, there's one. Only nine more to go."

"Nine!" She tried to turn toward him, but his grip didn't budge, and another strike landed in a different spot. She inhaled sharply.

"That's it," he said. "Let the pain warm your skin. Then I'm going to fuck you and it will feel so very good."

The place where he'd first spanked her didn't hurt any longer. Instead, it pulsed, the entire area hot. She quite liked it.

"Can you take more?" When she nodded, he gave her two brisk slaps. It was over quickly, and she moaned at the resulting buzz in her veins as moisture collected between her thighs.

"Dirty girl, you cannot help yourself, can you? Taking off your clothes and begging me to give you my cock. You're so very needy, aren't you?"

After another smack, she was panting, shifting, her arousal at a fever pitch. "I do need you, Lucien. Please."

"Mmm, I can see your pussy dripping from here. You are an eager little thing, aren't you?" Another slap of the ruler, this time across the back of her thigh. She waited out the sharp pricks of misery until they eased and bloomed into something wonderful. Instead of holding her, he was petting her spine. "If you beg me properly, I might fuck you again."

"Oh, blimey. Please, please, please. Fuck me, Your Grace."

Two spanks right together. "And you're not going to tease me any longer?"

"No, Your Grace."

He gave her another hard smack. "That is for calling me Your Grace."

Before she could say anything else, he roughly pulled her hips closer with one hand. Then the head of his cock met her entrance and he was back inside her. "Jesus fuck, you're wet."

His palms slid inside her drawers to cup the red-hot abused skin. He squeezed, causing a fresh wave of pain to roll through her, but it quickly turned to a blissful throb. Finally he started moving, driving, pounding, rattling her bones with his powerful thrusts.

Whimpering, she clawed at the bedclothes. This angle brought him deeper, rubbing a certain spot with every drive of his hips, and the sound of their slapping bodies filled the room. Her skin vibrated, a reminder of what he'd done with the ruler, and it quickly became too much. "Oh, God. Don't stop . . ." The orgasm streaked through her, fierce and bright, a flash of sparks against a night sky, and she shouted, her walls clenching around his length as she trembled.

"You're so beautiful," he gasped, holding perfectly still and panting against her back. "You've always been so goddamn beautiful." He snapped his hips once. "I love the way you make me feel. Never leave me, my clever girl."

Her toes curled in blissful happiness. It was the most he'd ever revealed as far as his feelings for her, and the words sank in to fill the holes in her lonely heart. If only she could stay with him. "I'm yours, Lucien."

He began riding her fast and rough then, his cock punching into her sex until he pressed tight, his fingertips digging into her hips. "Fuck, Eliza!" he shouted to the ceiling. "You're *mine*." Suddenly, he swelled inside her, his body straining as he grunted with pleasure.

When it was over, she collapsed on the bed. Lucien's forehead rested on her back, his warm pants heating her spine through her clothing. "I forgot a shield," he said.

Oh.

The image filled her mind—a small boy or girl with his eyes and a keen ability for maths—and her heart twisted. If only. Some other lucky woman would marry him and bear his children. Watch him roll around on the floor to play with his son or daughter and hear their laughter.

It would not—could not—be Eliza.

She moved, sliding out from underneath him. "We should've been more careful."

"I'm sorry." He dragged a hand through his hair and dropped onto the mattress, disheveled and beautiful. "I don't have any diseases, if you're concerned. But Eliza, if there are consequences . . ."

She waited for him to finish. When he didn't, she knew why. There was no future between them, not in the ways that mattered.

Though it was for the best, that *hurt.*

I've survived worse. I'll survive this, too.

She willed her insides to freeze, forced her heart to toughen up. "You needn't worry about consequences," she promised, suddenly grateful for Helen's advice the night of the auction. Having a duke's bastard would add another burden onto her and Fanny's future they could scant afford, even with a hundred thousand pounds in her pocket.

"You can't know that." He grimaced. "Even with a shield, it's possible. And your brother would not have wanted that for you."

Telling that his only concern was in disappointing her long-dead brother. Why was Lucien so focused on the past when the present was what mattered?

She decided to tell him the truth. Perhaps then he would see her as an adult woman, not Robert's little sister. "There are places where a woman can procure a tonic to prevent conception. I plan to buy one after tomorrow."

A flash of surprise crossed his face before he masked it. "I see."

"I should return downstairs."

Just as she took a step toward the door, he grabbed her hand. "Why not stay and let me fuck you again?" He pressed a kiss to the inside of her wrist. "I'll remove your clothing and do it properly this time."

She shouldn't.

There were the ledgers and Fanny and the miles between Shoreditch and Mayfair . . .but bloody hell, Eliza wanted more of him. Enough to last the rest of her life.

Once more could not make things worse. She already loved him. After tomorrow, she'd never see him again, so better to gather all these memories while she could.

Stepping back, she began unfastening her bodice, giving her best attempt at a sultry smile. "Whatever Your Grace wishes."

EARLY THE NEXT MORNING, Lucien lifted the brass knocker and rapped it several times. It took longer than expected, but the door finally opened to reveal a maid. "Yes?"

"The Duke of Blackwood to see his lordship."

"His lordship is not receiving callers at the moment."

"He will see me." Lucien presented a card. "Tell him to come down or I will pull him out of bed myself."

The maid begrudgingly opened the door. "Wait in there," she said, gesturing to a front room.

Lucien entered, removed his gloves, and glanced about. Robert's former home was a pitiful sight. The once vibrant townhouse was dour, with bare walls and dirty floors. Lucien remembered flowers and laughter, family portraits and the smell of lemons. Those things were gone now.

The current earl, Lucien had learned, was a gambler and an idiot. He'd used the title to borrow funds on credit, and hadn't yet been able to pay any of it back. There were rumors of more loans through unscrupulous means, which meant serious consequences—the deadly kind—if they weren't paid back.

After what the new earl had done to Eliza and Fanny, Lucien couldn't bring himself to care. His only interest was in discovering if anything was still here for the two sisters.

Heavy feet on the front stairs caught his attention. Seconds later a bleary-eyed man entered, his necktie an absolute disgrace. "Blackwood," he said, as if they'd been introduced before. Which they hadn't. "What's this about?"

Lucien put a fair deal of menace in his voice as he said, "Justice."

"I beg your pardon?"

"By a twist of fate, you inherited this house, this title—neither of which you deserved—but you made a grave error when you turned your cousins out into the streets."

Barnett's lip curled. "You mean those two girls? They weren't my problem. Let one of the other relatives take care of them."

"Only a bloody monster would cast two young women into the streets of London without seeing them provided for, while telling everyone they went to an aunt in Scotland."

Possibly sensing Lucien's rage, Barnett edged around the back of the sofa, out of arm's reach. "Those two weren't my concern. For all I knew there was an aunt in Scotland. Besides, all they had to do was marry or find some rich man to keep them as a mistress—"

Lucien lunged. In one swift motion, he snatched Barnett's throat in his fist and pinned the earl against the wall. "You miserable piece of filth. They were mere girls—and your cousins. I am going to ruin you." He shook the other man, causing Barnett's head to bang into the plaster. "You'll be left with nothing when I am through."

Barnett had the audacity to appear affronted. "Are you mad? Release me at once, Blackwood."

"Not until we have a little chat." He tightened his grip, satisfied when the earl's face turned red. "I want to know what possessions remain from the former earl's family, what you haven't yet sold off to cover your debts, you miserable worm."

"Everything here belongs to me," he rasped.

Lucien leaned in. "While that may be true in a legal sense, I find it difficult to believe there isn't one painting, one knick-knack, one *piece of lint* left over from the former family. I suggest you think hard about it, because I'm not letting you go until I get an answer."

"You have no right—"

"The best part of being a duke is that I have every right to do as I wish with absolute impunity. That includes making men disappear. There's no one to stop me from squeezing the life out of you and dropping your body into the Thames."

Real fear seeped into Barnett's dark eyes as he clawed at Lucien's unforgiving grip on his throat. "Wait, please."

"Have you thought of something?"

"Yes," the earl squeaked. "There's a painting."

Lucien eased his grip, then cast the other man away in disgust. "Then I suggest you go retrieve it for me."

Barnett darted from the room and up the stairs. In case the earl was lying, Lucien decided to give him ten minutes, no more. If Barnet hadn't returned by then, Lucien would follow.

With two minutes to spare the earl hurried down the stairs, a canvas in hand. "Here. Take the damned thing and get out."

Lucien accepted the framed portrait. It was of a young Eliza, Fanny, Robert and their parents. Robert's unhappy expression seemed to stare out at Lucien, a judgmental glare full of resentment.

I'm sorry, Robert. I couldn't resist her.

"Satisfied now, Blackwood?"

Lucien quirked a brow at the insolent earl. "No, not in the least. I won't be satisfied until you are living on scraps, cast out of this home . . .as your cousins were forced to do five years ago. Be forewarned, Barnett. Your debts are coming due." He'd personally see to it that the moneylenders came calling as soon as possible.

Gripping the painting in his fist, Lucien stalked out of the townhouse and found his carriage. During the ride, he braced himself for the sight of Eliza again. Today was their last day together, and he had to find a way to let her go.

It was why he'd avoided her for three and a half days. The more time he spent with her, the more he wanted to keep her—and that was out of the question. Someday she'd learn what happened to her brother and she would hate Lucien for it. The best course of action would be to pay her and let her start over, return her life to some normalcy. Some luxury. Then they could all forget the last five years ever happened.

The ride to his townhouse took hardly any time at this early hour, which was why he was surprised to see people gathered on his stoop.

It was Eliza . . .and Rathbone. The marquess stood a bit too close to Eliza, as if he was using his body to intimidate her.

Lucien was out of the carriage before the wheels even stopped rolling. "Rathbone," he barked. "Move away from her."

Eliza appeared relieved to see him, which meant Rathbone had been harassing her again.

"Duke, you're just in time," Rathbone drawled.

Lucien headed straight for the pair, painting in hand. "To pulverize you into a jelly? Excellent. Been looking forward to it."

"No, to hear me inform her ladyship about her brother."

A sinking feeling bloomed in Lucien's gut, but he shoved it aside. Only a few people knew what happened that night, and none would betray him by discussing it. Rathbone was clearly referring to something else.

"My brother?" Eliza's brows arched. "What about him?"

Rathbone's voice was sharp, like a blade, cutting and clipped. "Hasn't His Grace informed you what happened the night your brother was killed?"

"Shut your mouth," Lucien snapped as panic lit up his insides. He didn't want anyone to hear this, especially Eliza. She'd never think of him the same way again. "There's no need to dredge up those old memories for her."

"No, wait," Eliza said. "I want to hear it. Please, my lord. What about my brother?"

"Eliza, go inside," Lucien ordered. "Allow me to speak with Rathbone alone."

She never even looked at him, her attention remaining on the marquess.

Malice glittered in Rathbone's dark eyes, his lips curled into a gleeful smirk. "She deserves to know, Blackwood, especially since you were determined to win her from me the other night and make me look like a fool. Or were you planning on keeping the part you played in Robert's death a secret from her forever?"

10

Eliza studied both men. She didn't trust Rathbone, but Lucien appeared on edge, his body trembling as if he might strike the marquess at any minute.

Which made her wonder—again—if he had something to hide.

Had Lucien something to do with Robert's death?

Rathbone had appeared this morning outside Lucien's house when she arrived, clearly having followed her. Without preamble, he asked how well she knew Lucien. When she tried to escape inside, Rathbone carried on, insisting on speaking with her. That was when Lucien had arrived.

So, what was really going on?

"Your Grace?" she prompted when Lucien didn't say anything. "Care to explain?"

Instead, Lucien glared at Rathbone. "Get off my property."

"Interesting what I was able to learn by digging into your life, Blackwood. Your former mistresses do like to talk."

Lucien took a threatening step forward, but the marquess held up his hands and bowed to her. "My lady, when you leave him—and you definitely will—please know you have an admirer in me. I would be more than willing to step into his shoes and set you up in a fine house—"

Bile rose in her throat at the offer, but she was spared the need to respond because Lucien shoved Rathbone toward his carriage. "Get the bloody hell out of here!"

Rathbone smiled slyly and departed, his carriage soon rolling away from Lucien's, but she didn't move. She couldn't. Her feet were rooted to the walk. "Please tell me what he's talking about."

"Come inside and we'll talk."

"Lucien, now."

He rubbed his eyes and sighed. "Eliza, please. I don't wish to do this on the street."

Because he knew it would upset her?

A knot tightened between her shoulder blades, but she marched up the walk, climbed the steps, and went inside. Lucien followed, a painting in his hands. She didn't care much about art at the moment. She'd rather hear what Lucien knew regarding Robert's death.

"We'll talk in my office." Lucien led the way, the house eerily quiet.

Once there, he set the painting on the ground by his desk. The lines on his face had deepened, making him appear older than his years, and a strange ringing started in her ears. Almost as if her body was warning her of oncoming doom.

"Tell me it isn't true," she said. "Tell me you had nothing to do with my brother's death."

"Eliza . . . ."

"I want the truth. The police were never able to give us much information. I have no idea what happened to him, other than he was robbed and dumped in an alley."

He gestured to the armchairs. "Shall we sit?"

"No, Lucien. Open your gob and speak, man. What happened to Robert?"

He dragged in a deep breath, then let it out slowly. "I was having an affair with an actress. I didn't know it, but this actress was also seeing another man, a dangerous thug who ran one of the waterfront gangs. He found out about her relationship with me and decided to kill me—a fact I was unaware of."

He stared at the wall, his tone even. Like he was reciting a lesson in class. "One night, Robert begged me to attend some dinner party with him, but I cancelled at the last minute. The men from the gang were waiting for Robert when he left the dinner party. They . . .thought he was me. He was shoved into a carriage, beaten, and killed near the docks."

Disbelief and horror washed through her, the news worse than she'd imagined. Still, it didn't make sense. "They thought he was you? Why?"

He cleared his throat as he clasped his hands. "Back then, the three of us, we frequently used different names instead of our own, especially with women. Sometimes we made up the names, sometimes we borrowed them. For me, it seemed easier than being a duke and all that came with it."

A boulder-sized lump settled in her throat. She whispered, "So, this particular woman. You told her . . .?"

"I told her my name was Robert Hartsford, Earl of Barnett."

Eliza doubled over, a hand to her stomach as she nearly crumpled to the floor. He rushed toward her, but she backed away, her palms out as if to ward off an evil spirit. "Do not touch me. God, Lucien! How could you do such a terrible thing? To your best friend? What is *wrong* with you?"

"We did it all the time, Jasper and Robert too. We laughed about it, thought it was a big joke."

"I cannot believe this." The backs of her lids burned, the betrayal slashing deep through her heart. Lucien, her kind and serious hero, was no hero at all. He didn't deserve her love, not by a long shot. "I cannot believe you kept this from me, that you would let Fanny and I struggle for years knowing you were responsible. Never once did you try to find us. He died and you went back to your two mistresses and your perfect life on Grosvenor Square."

"I've regretted it every single second, Eliza. The guilt has weighed on me for five years. But you must believe me, I had no idea you and Fanny had been turned out on the street. I thought you were in Scotland! I would have helped you, I swear."

She scrubbed her face with her hands. "There were nights we ate garbage, slept in alleys. I cleaned privies and shoveled horse shit. Washed clothes and—" She bit off the words and shook her head. "Why am I bothering? You have no idea what it's like to worry, to live without all this." She waved her hand to indicate his home. "You've never had to struggle a day in your life."

"I'm terribly, terribly sorry, Eliza. I would give anything to go back and change things. I never thought any of this would happen. I never wanted anyone to suffer."

"And yet we have." A tear escaped her lids and rolled down her cheek. "We all have, my entire family. You destroyed us." Her voice broke. God, she had *loved* this man, admired and worshipped him. Had let him inside her body. All the while he'd known this terrible secret and hadn't shared it.

"That's why I want you to take the money. Please, you needn't clean privies or shovel shit any longer. You can buy a house in Mayfair and forget all of this ever happened."

Was he serious? "I can't do that."

"Why not? You'll be independently wealthy, with a home of your own. Everything you've ever wanted."

I wanted you.

No, she'd wanted the version of Lucien that existed only in her head. The real man was cruel and selfish. No wonder he'd been so eager to pay her off and have her disappear! It was the easiest way to reduce his guilt. He thought money would fix this, would give her and Fanny the means to go back in time. To the way things were five years ago.

But life didn't work that way.

"This cannot be fixed with money. You merely want to ease your guilt —but nothing can bring my brother back or erase the last five years."

"I know it won't bring him back, but I'd like to take care of you. I want to get you out of Shoreditch and back where you belong."

And he thought she belonged in Mayfair? "Lucien, I haven't belonged here in a very long time, even when Robert was alive. When I told him my plans to attend university, he ridiculed me. Women are not supposed to be clever here. They're supposed to marry young and fade into the background of their husbands' lives. A forgotten footnote in the sands of time. I don't want that. I've never wanted that."

"Then what do you want? Why did you need the money so desperately if not to change your circumstances?"

He appeared confused, absolutely befuddled that she didn't wish to rejoin his fragile and restrictive world. Frustrated, she snapped, "Because my sister is sick. I need money to take her to a sanitarium in America and help her get better."

"America! You cannot go there. It's . . . ."

"It's, what? Too uncivilized for Your Grace? Too progressive? Too modern?"

"No, it's too far," he shouted, then he immediately closed his eyes as if he regretted the outburst. "I cannot stand the thought of you so far away from me."

"I see." Nodding in understanding, she folded her arms across her chest. "You'd prefer me in a house in Mayfair, where you'll stop by and visit. A few times a week, perhaps? And I'll give you a key to make it easier? Just admit you hoped to turn me into your third mistress, Lucien."

"No, absolutely not. I never planned to sleep with you. I wanted you to retain your virginity, if you recall."

"But then I seduced you, right? Poor Lucien, always fighting off my advances."

"I didn't say that. Stop twisting what I'm saying." He dragged his hands through his hair, disturbing the perfectly styled strands. "Eliza, I care about you a great deal. I want—I *need* to make things better for you."

But he didn't love her. He didn't even care for her as a woman, only as a cause. A way to alleviate his suffering and assuage his guilt. She would never be more than a bad reminder to him of the past he'd destroyed.

And while taking his money would help Fanny and her in countless ways, it would also ease his conscience. He didn't deserve that relief.

No, he deserved to suffer, to live with the knowledge of how he'd hurt Eliza and her sister. Forever.

As if he sensed the direction of her thoughts, he jerked open a desk drawer and held up a bank draft. "Here. It's already made out to you. A hundred thousand pounds."

Her chest squeezed at the sight of it, and her anger at him outweighed everything else. *I will not make this easy for him.*

"Keep your money. I don't want it." She turned and started for the door, the backs of her lids burning with oncoming tears.

"Eliza, don't be ridiculous. You need this money. Moreover, you earned it."

"I don't need a bloody thing from you, Lucien. Not now, not ever."

"Wait!"

Reluctantly, she paused at the door. Escape was close at hand, and she desperately longed for space from him. "What is it?"

"Please, take the check—and take this." He came toward her carrying the painting he'd brought in earlier. "I got it this morning from your old home."

Hadn't he understood her a second ago? "I don't want anything from you."

"But it's yours." He flipped to painting to face her. "It's your family's portrait."

The breath left her chest at the sight of those people, so young and so happy. With no idea of the tragedy about to befall them. She didn't even recognize herself, a pampered Mayfair princess who'd believed anything was possible if one only wanted it badly enough.

Lucien held out the frame like he expected her to take it. She shook her head sadly. "You keep it. I don't care to remember the past. I can't afford to. Goodbye, Lucien."

Two Weeks Later

Lucien sat by the fountain, a basket of walnuts on his lap and a cigar clamped between his teeth. The day stretched out in front of him like all the rest—a gauntlet of misery to endure until he could start drinking. Scotch was the only way to sleep, the only way to forget her. In the meantime, he stayed mostly outside, away from the memories.

He tossed a nut into the fountain, strangely satisfied by the plunking sound as it hit the water. It sounded like a heartbeat, not that he would know as his heart had stopped beating two weeks ago.

God's teeth, he missed her.

I don't need a bloody thing from you, Lucien. Not now, not ever.

She hated him, and rightfully so. He hated himself, too.

It should've been Lucien beaten, kidnapped, and murdered that night, not Robert. No one would have missed Lucien. He had no family, no siblings. Some distant cousin would've lucked into a dukedom and that would have been that.

Instead, his best friend had died, and Eliza and Fanny had suffered.

There were nights we ate garbage, slept in alleys. I cleaned privies and shoveled shit.

Another nut landed in the water. Everything hurt. He couldn't focus, not even on the accounting she'd started for him. Nearly every room of the house reminded him of her. He was fucking miserable.

A scratch on stone caught his attention but he didn't turn around. Likely his valet come to chastise him for not shaving and bathing. Again. "Go away."

"You'll see me—or at least listen to me."

He jolted, the cigar nearly falling from his mouth. Fanny?

Eliza's sister slid onto the stone bench next to him and tilted her chin toward the basket on his lap. "This seems like a fun game. Is there a point?"

"Why are you here?"

"I cannot talk any sense into my sister, so I thought I would try with you. By the looks of it, however, I'm probably wasting my time."

He threw another nut into the water. No doubt she'd come to hear an apology in person, something he damn well owed her. "I must beg your pardon, Lady Fanny. You have every right to hate me as much as your sister does, but please believe me. I never knew the two of you weren't being looked after."

"Just Fanny will do, and thank you for the apology." They sat in silence for a few minutes before she said, "I suppose it's difficult for you to understand why we didn't seek help after our cousin kicked us out, but young women in our world are conditioned to believe no one gives a damn about them. We're hidden away until it's time to marry, kept ignorant of things that really matter. Perhaps we could've found a distant relative to take us in or gone to an orphanage, but Eliza didn't want us separated. It was easier to stay together and find work to support ourselves. Unfortunately, I grew sick and the burden soon fell on Eliza's shoulders alone."

A sharp pain lanced his chest. "I would have given a damn. I *do* give a damn."

"Then why did you let her go?"

"What do you mean? She left."

"And you let that stop you?" She scoffed. "Your Grace, you give up far too easily. Your best friend dies, and you shirk your responsibilities to the estate. Eliza leaves you and you just let her go, willing to watch the best woman you'll ever meet move away and start a life on another continent without you. Do you never fight for anything?"

"I . . ."

The protest died on his tongue. Had he?

Life had come easily to him before Robert's death. Women, friends, the title and wealth—all of it had fallen into Lucien's lap. When the worst had happened to Robert, Lucien had retreated, horrified and embarrassed. He wasn't strong, like Eliza. He was a terrible person, selfish. A reprobate with two mistresses and money he didn't deserve.

He shook his head and threw another walnut in the water. This self-reflection was giving him a headache. "She made it very clear when she left. She doesn't care to see me again."

"Her feelings are hurt. She's angry. Surely you can understand why."

"Of course, I understand. I don't expect her to forgive me."

"So, you won't even try?"

He wouldn't even begin to know how. Hell, he couldn't forgive himself, so how could he expect Eliza to? "She's better off."

"If you could see her, you wouldn't say so."

"Why? What's wrong?" He sat straighter, angling to see Fanny's face. "Is she all right?"

"No, you idiot. She's heartbroken. She's in love with you."

In love with him? The idea was laughable. They hadn't even been reunited for a full week, and nearly all that time he'd been withholding a terrible secret. "No, she's not."

"For a smart man, you are truly thick-headed, Your Grace. *Yes*, she is in love with you. Otherwise, she wouldn't be walking around looking like a creature from a Mary Shelley novel—"

Fanny began coughing then, deep racking coughs that made his own lungs hurt in sympathy. When she quieted, he said, "Shall I fetch you water or tea?"

"No, I'm fine."

"Is it consumption?"

"No. It's some mysterious lung ailment, worsened by the dirty air." She lifted a shoulder. "But everyone fears I'm consumptive, so I try to stay at home."

"This is why she plans to take you to America."

"Yes, to a sanitarium there."

"There are places like that here, you know."

"I think Eliza prefers the idea of a fresh start. No doubt you could convince her otherwise, if you gave a damn."

Of course he gave a damn. He loved her, for God's sake. Which is why he had to let her go. She was better off without him, building her independent life without memories and judgment. He threw another walnut. "What makes you think I don't?"

"Because you're brooding here instead of telling her how you feel and trying to win her back."

"I've hurt her enough."

"Therefore your guilt is more important than a future with her?"

"Are you saying I shouldn't feel guilty?"

"You most definitely should feel guilty. You should feel awful for being a foolish young man who thought he was impervious to consequences for his selfishness."

The next nut landed in the water with more vigor, splashing them. "Then you may sleep well at night, because I do."

"We cannot change the past, Your Grace. The present is for the living, the future for our penance. What is your penance?"

"Liver disease and insomnia, if I had to guess."

"Be serious. Free of all that transpired with Robert, do you want her?"

If he hadn't ruined Eliza's life? If Robert were still alive? The answer came instantly. "Yes."

"Then fix it."

She made it sound so easy. "How?"

"That is for you to figure out. You're clever."

The nape of his neck tightened in annoyance. He chucked another nut into the fountain. "Lovely chat. Thank you for dropping by."

She merely chuckled. "I realize it's not the answer you're hoping for, but it's for you to figure out."

"Do you . . . ?" He forced himself to ask it, even if he sounded like a fool. "Do you think she can forgive me after I ruined your lives?"

"You didn't ruin our lives. Robert's death gave us a different life, but we aren't unhappy. We have freedom, while women in Mayfair do not. I think Eliza learned how strong she was, how much we love each other. We wouldn't trade the last five years for anything."

A glimmer of light took root in his dark soul, a seed of hope that Eliza might one day forgive him. That they could live in the present and not the past. "Truly?"

Waving her hand, Fanny said, "Of course, I wish my brother was still alive—I miss him terribly—and I wish I wasn't sick. Our lives, though, have vastly improved since leaving Mayfair. Had Robert lived, we each would've been married off to a man we hardly knew and started having children. Our possessions and our bodies would've belonged to our husbands. Now, though we are poor, everything we have is ours."

Eliza's fierce independence made even more sense now. Why on earth would she ever come back to Mayfair, back to him? "When you put it like that, I'm not certain I stand a chance in winning her."

She rose and shook out her skirts. "I have faith in Your Grace."

11

LETTERS BEGAN ARRIVING DAILY.

At first, Eliza stared at Lucien's seal, wary. If they were love notes, she wasn't certain she cared to read them. Two and a half weeks had passed since she saw him last, and she still felt a gnawing anger in her belly when she thought of him.

And an ache in her heart.

So she let the letters collect on the kitchen table. Each night, Fanny would ask, "Are you going to open them today?" To which Eliza would respond, "No."

Finally, when there were more than ten, Fanny apparently decided to take matters into her own hands. After dinner, she reached for one and opened it.

"What are you doing?" Eliza screeched as she dried her hands on a towel. "Leave those alone."

"I will not. I'm dying of curiosity." Fanny unfolded the paper. "Blimey. That's disappointing."

"This is an invasion of my privacy—and don't tell me what's inside. I don't want to know."

"It's not a letter. It's a maths problem."

Surprise had Eliza taking the paper out of her sister's hands. Sure enough, Lucien hadn't written a word. He'd sent her a complicated equation to solve.

How . . . clever. A smile tugged at her lips before she could hide it.

"Aha!" Fanny playfully smacked the table with her palm. "I saw that reaction—and it's the first time you've smiled in more than two weeks."

"Stop." Eliza set the paper down and returned to the dishes. "It's interesting, is all. I hadn't expected it."

As she washed their plates and cutlery, her mind turned over the problem, working it out in her head. By the time everything was dry, she'd solved it. Her impulse was to share the solution with him, but that was silly. That would require mailing the letter back, and she didn't care to start any epistolary dialogue with him, even of the mathematical kind.

I love the way you make me feel. Never leave me, my clever girl.

Damn him. Why had he said things such as that, sweet things that caused her to fall in love with him again, while hiding information about Robert's death?

The paper on the table beckoned, her hand itching to write the solution down. Of course, she could write the answer but never mail the letter back to him. Yes, that's what she'd do. She would do this for *her*, not for him.

Taking a pencil, she sat at the table and scribbled. Fanny said nothing, just watched, until Eliza finished. "Quite impressive," her sister said. "Are you going to send it to him?"

"No."

Eliza reached to open another letter. As she suspected, it contained a different problem. This one was simpler, and she was reaching for a third letter in no time.

At some point Fanny drifted away, but Eliza kept at it. When she opened and solved all ten letters, it was quite late. A familiar sense of accomplishment fluttered in her chest. It felt nice. She hadn't done that in quite awhile.

"Are you going to forgive him?" Fanny, dressed in her nightgown, strolled over and sat at the table. "Because he obviously misses you."

"I'm not certain that's true. It's not as if he poured his heart out in the letters."

"Yes, he did." Fanny rolled her eyes toward the ceiling. "Eliza, he thought up these problems, wrote them down, and sent them to you. Maths is your thing."

"Our thing?"

"Your poetry. Your flowers and valentines. Come on. Can you not see it? The man is wildly in love with you."

Eliza shook her head. "You're wrong, and I don't wish to discuss it."

"Do you hate him for the role he played in Robert's death?"

Did she? Certainly, it had been selfish on Lucien's part to pose as another, but he admitted the three friends had laughed about it. Robert and Jasper had used other names, as well.

Still, Lucien hadn't told her, not even after sleeping with her. If it weren't for Rathbone, she never would've learned what happened.

But did she hate Lucien?

No. God, no. It would be far easier if she did, if these feelings lingering inside her disappeared. Loving him was terrible, painful and awful, like a rotten tooth she wished she could extract. Instead, the ache remained, twisting her up into knots.

"I don't hate him, but he hurt me. It's unforgivable."

"Unforgivable? Really, Eliza? That seems harsh, considering."

"Considering, what? That he was responsible for Robert's death and never told me? I trusted him with my body and my heart, and he has proven unworthy of that trust."

"Yes, he should've told you before taking you to bed, but can you honestly say you gave him a chance? You said you seduced him each time."

"Believe it or not, we did have conversations outside of bed, too."

Fanny coughed, then took a moment to catch her breath. Eliza waited patiently, hating that her sister struggled. *Maybe I should've taken Lucien's money.*

No, they would find another way. They always did.

When Fanny spoke, it was quieter. "You cannot fault him for what came after Robert's death or for my illness."

"I know." Eliza rolled the pencil on the table, not wanting to meet Fanny's eye. "I shouldn't have made Lucien think I blamed him for our financial straits."

"No, you shouldn't have. You know we're happier now, together and poor, than we ever would've been as separated, married, and rich ladies."

"Yes, but your illness," Eliza said. "That's because of where we live, these conditions."

"Dr. Humphries isn't certain about that. He said I might have caught it somewhere, or I might've been born with it and it took this long to present. The truth is, we don't know."

"I suppose. Why are you pushing me to give Lucien another chance, anyway?"

"Because I want to see you happy—and you were happy during that one week. It was clearly Lucien's doing."

"I won't be his mistress, and there aren't other options for a girl like me."

"Why not? You'd make a fine duchess."

"Sure. Can't you see me in Mayfair, telling all those fine ladies about my various jobs over the years? Not to mention auctioning off my virginity. I'd fit right in over petit fours."

"You're embarrassed of how you've earned a living for us."

"No, I'm not," she snapped. "I worked my bloody tail off to support us, and neither one of us had to—"

"Sell our bodies?" Fanny finished when Eliza fell silent.

Eliza grimaced. Yes, that was what she'd been about to say.

Fanny yawned and stretched her arms. "Who cares about what people say? You never have up until now."

"You merely wish for me to end up with Lucien, like I'm Cinderella or some such nonsense. You're making it sound so easy when we both know it's not."

"It won't be easy, but you're the strongest, most determined person I know. If you want something bad enough, you'll bring it about come hell or high water. The question is, what do you want?"

Eliza considered it, but her emotions were too jumbled, too scattered to come up with an answer about Lucien. She focused on the two of them, instead. "I want you to get better. I want to take you to America so you can recover."

"At some point, you need to live for yourself. I'll be fine. Don't ruin your chance at happiness for me."

"I love you. I'm not ruining anything by taking care of you. You're my family."

Fanny reached forward to clutch Eliza's hand. "We'll always be family. But I also know we need more than just each other. You might not want them, but I do want a husband and children."

This was the first they'd ever discussed it. "So, what are you saying? You want me to send you to America by yourself?"

"Perhaps. I don't know."

It was only fair, but the prospect caused sorrow to scald the back of Eliza's throat. She couldn't imagine a life without Fanny in it.

Exhaustion weighed her down. Lord, it was after one o'clock, and such a conversation was too heavy for this hour. She stood. "I have an early morning, so I'll go to bed. Are you coming?"

"In a bit. I want to get some water first."

"All right. Good night."

Once she was in bed, Eliza told herself not to think about Lucien. Not to miss him or to wonder what he was doing.

Her resolve quickly crumbled in the darkness, however, and she fell asleep to memories of his filthy words and possessive touch.

"A LETTER ARRIVED FOR YOU TODAY," Fanny said as soon as Eliza walked in the door from work. Fanny grinned. "Several letters, actually."

Eliza didn't want to admit it, but her heart leapt at the news. The letters from Lucien had continued, even a week later, and she looked forward to them. One might even have said they were the highlight of her day.

She strove for nonchalance. "Oh?"

"And they're not all from Lucien."

That got Eliza's attention. "Please don't tell me it's from a bill collector."

"Don't be absurd. We're current on all of our payments." Fanny held up a very fancy looking letter. "This is from Somerville College."

"At Oxford?" Eliza's brows climbed as high as they could go. "Who is it for?"

"You, silly." Fanny rushed over and handed Eliza the letter. "I didn't open it. I wanted to, very, very badly, but I didn't."

"Thanks, Fan," Eliza drawled. There was no privacy between two sisters who lived together.

"Open it!"

Eliza opened the letter and then gaped. "It's from Mrs. Maitland, the principal."

"Gorblimey," Fanny whispered. "What does she say?"

Eliza read quickly. Apparently, Mrs. Maitland had reviewed the maths solutions Eliza had sent and invited her to sit for Somerville's entrance exam next term.

"Oh, my God," Eliza breathed. "I've been invited to sit for the entrance exam at Somerville College."

"You're going to Oxford?" Fanny screamed.

Eliza looked at Mrs. Maitland's words again. Wait, what maths solutions? And she'd never written to Somerville. "This doesn't make any sense."

A guilty look crossed Fanny's face as she twined her fingers together. A sure sign of nerves. "What have you done?" Eliza asked her sister.

"Nothing! I returned those solutions to Blackwood. After that, I never saw them again. You'll have to ask him what he did with them."

Eliza pinched the bridge of her nose between her thumb and forefinger. "Lucien. I should've known."

The man couldn't help himself.

Even though she'd refused his money and assistance, he'd gone and done *this*. He must've sent those sheets of paper to Mrs. Maitland and begged the principal to take Eliza on. How embarrassing.

"Wait, why are you frowning? This is exciting, Liza."

"I suppose, but I can't go." She folded the principal's letter and set it on the table.

"Whyever not?"

"First, no doubt Lucien has paid the woman to make the offer to me. Second, we cannot afford it. Third, I cannot leave you to fend for yourself."

"Lucien wouldn't do that, and there are charity societies who could cover your costs. And if you're concerned about me, you needn't worry any longer." Fanny held out another letter, this one addressed to her.

"What's this?"

"Read it," Fanny urged.

Eliza took the paper. Her breath caught at the name on the outside. "The Royal National Hospital for Chest Diseases?"

Fanny's grin took up almost her entire face. "They've accepted me. I'm leaving for the Isle of Wight tomorrow."

"Tomorrow!" To mask her rioting emotions, Eliza quickly read the letter. Sure enough, Fanny had been given a treatment bed there and they would send someone to escort her to the hospital tomorrow. "I can't believe this."

"It's a bleedin' miracle. They only take thirty or so patients a year. And my fees have been paid."

"It's not a miracle. It's the Duke of Blackwood."

"I don't care. I'm not stupid enough to turn down an opportunity like this."

The comment dug under Eliza's ribs like a sharp knife. "And you think I am? Stupid enough to turn down Oxford, that is?"

Fanny sighed. "I don't think you're stupid. I think you're proud and stubborn, and in the past I've always agreed with you. Someone without your best interests at heart will try to take advantage, but that isn't the case here. Lucien has your best interests at heart. Can't you see? He's in love with you. He's trying to make things better for you without gaining anything in return."

In love with her? The idea was ludicrous. "Wrong. No doubt he expects me to . . . ."

"To what? Go to Oxford and study until your brain melts? He's not even trying to keep you in London, Liza. He's giving you a life without him in it. How is that possibly serving his own interests?"

"He's doing this because he feels guilty."

"And? Why do you think rich nobs give to charities? To ease their guilt." Fanny shook her head, clearly frustrated. "Do you think for one second I am going to turn down the opportunity to recuperate at this prestigious hospital because I'm worried about easing Lucien's guilt?"

"No, and I wouldn't let you. This is a tremendous opportunity for you."

Fanny gestured to the letter from Mrs. Maitland. "This is no different."

"Wrong. Going to study at Oxford isn't life or death."

"Isn't it? If you stay here, you'll work yourself to the bone for the rest of your days. If you go off to school, everything will change for the better. This will change the course of your life."

"For which I will owe him."

"Who solved those maths problems every night? Who will have to pass the entrance exams?"

"That is hardly—"

"Who?" Fanny repeated.

"Me, but—"

"There is no but. You proved your worth on those pieces of paper. You deserve this. You deserve to go. You owe no one for your intelligence. He merely helped you illustrate it to the right people."

Ever so slowly, the heaviness sitting on her chest began to lift. Was Fanny right? Did Eliza deserve this? Biting her lip to contain her hopeful smile, she stared at Mrs. Maitland's letter. Could she really sit for the entrance exams?

It seemed almost too good to be true.

Was it more than guilt on Lucien's part? Fanny thought the duke was in love with Eliza, but he'd barely hinted at deeper feelings whilst they were together.

I cannot stand the thought of you so far away from me.

Yet he was helping her leave London to study in Oxford.

She couldn't think about this right now. Apparently, Fanny was departing in the morning and Eliza needed to help her sister prepare. There would be time to contemplate her own life later.

12

"I don't care what it costs," Lucien snapped at Mr. Paulson, the architect. "We cannot throw these people out on the streets. Offer them twice the fair market value and do not bully them."

"Your Grace," Paulson started. "With all due respect, this sets a terrible precedent for other—"

"That is not my problem. If these families won't sell, we'll find another property."

"Very well. I'll see to it personally." He started to collect the plans, but Lucien held out a hand.

"I'd like to review those drawings. Leave them with me and I'll see them returned tomorrow."

The architect blinked several times behind his spectacles. "You wish to review the plans?" At Lucien's nod, Paulson said, "Shall I explain them to you first? They can be rather complicated to the untrained eye."

"I'll manage." Lucien struggled to keep his tone polite in the face of the architect's condescension. "My man will see you out."

Lucien's new secretary rose from where he'd been taking notes and escorted Paulson out of the office. Standing, Lucien spread the plans for the settlement house on his desk. Hartsford Hall would be a place to offer food, shelter, and education to poor women and girls. They were searching for the right location, though he was leaning toward the Old

Nichol, a notorious slum situated between Shoreditch and Bethnal Greene.

"Your Grace, a visitor."

Lucien glanced up to tell his butler to refuse any caller—and the words died in his throat.

Eliza.

She was there, standing tall and beautiful, a vision straight out of one of his dreams. His mouth dried out and he couldn't think of a thing to say, lest he scare her off somehow. Was she truly here?

He drank in her fine features and golden hair. The lithe curves barely visible under her garments. Her cheeks held a slight flush, her lips plump and red, as if she had been biting them. Goddamn, he missed her.

She nodded at his butler and came closer, her skirts rustling, and his butler pulled the door shut. "Hello, Your Grace."

He hated the formality, loathed the distance between them, but he had no one to blame but himself. Though he ached to take her into his arms and kiss the living hell out of her, he forced a smile and folded his hands behind his back. "Lady Eliza. To what do I owe the pleasure?"

"May I sit?"

"Of course." He came forward to help assist her, but she waved him away. Foolish of him, really. Eliza was entirely self-reliant. She didn't need him.

I don't need a bloody thing from you, Lucien. Not now, not ever.

His chest twisted, the insides raw and tattered. He'd screwed everything up from the start, and he deserved the misery now permanently lodged in his heart.

Clearing his throat, he lowered himself into his chair. "You look well."

"I've come to thank you."

Straight and to the point, as always. He wanted to grin, but his face hadn't attempted one in six weeks. He wasn't certain he was capable of it any longer.

Besides, she was only here to thank him for Fanny and the Royal Hospital. A small sliver of disappointment dug under his skin, but he pushed it aside. What had he expected? That she'd missed him, as he'd missed her?

He held her gaze. "That wasn't necessary."

"Indeed, it is. You've given Fanny the very best hope for recovery. I'm entirely grateful."

"She's left already?"

"Yes, yesterday."

He nodded once. Good. The hospital was the best in Europe and if anyone could heal Eliza's sister, it was those doctors. "I'm happy to hear it."

"I admit, it wasn't easy to let her go." She gave a small laugh, as if she knew it was silly. "We haven't been apart for five years. I felt like a mama bird watching her baby leave the nest."

"They'll take very good care of her."

"I know. Whatever your reasons for helping us, I cannot begin to thank you enough."

He didn't want her gratitude. He wanted her laughter and kisses. The touch of her hand across his bare skin. He wanted to roll over every morning and see her face beside him, then finish the day by solving problems together before taking her to bed.

I love you, he almost said. *I would do anything for you.*

But she would never believe his motives were pure. She would always think he was trying to control her through privilege and money.

He nodded once, unable to think of anything more brilliant to say other than, "You're welcome."

"I leave for Oxford next month. I thought you'd like to know."

Straightening, he blurted, "Oxford?"

"Come now. Surely you were aware."

"Aware of what, exactly?"

"I've heard from Mrs. Maitland. About sitting for the entrance exams."

"At Somerville College? Eliza, that's tremendous. Congratulations."

"I have you to thank for that, as well."

"Why? Because I sent her the problems you solved?"

"Yes, and asked her to take me on as a student."

"I did no such thing." When her expression didn't change, he leaned forward. "Eliza, I didn't bribe her or pay her off to offer you a spot. I merely sent her the problems along with your address. I didn't even affix my seal to the letter."

Her mouth parted. "You didn't wield your ducal influence?"

"Not with Mrs. Maitland. I admit I did so with the Royal Hospital, however."

"You mean . . . ."

"You did that all on your own, Eliza. Because you're brilliant and tenacious. I couldn't be prouder."

"I can't believe it," she murmured, rubbing her forehead. "I thought for certain it was because of you."

Remaining silent, he let the truth of it sink in while his own thoughts turned darker. She would go away to study and live apart from him. Build a life free from the horrors of her past, including Lucien. It was what he'd always wanted for her, except he hadn't expected it to hurt this badly.

When she finally looked up, her eyes were moist. "I don't know what to say."

"It's very happy news." For her, anyway. "You're allowed to be overwhelmed."

"No, that's not what I meant." She exhaled slowly. "To you. I don't know what to say to you."

"Oh." He lifted his shoulders and let them fall. "I don't quite know what to say to you, either, other than I'm dashed proud of you and I wish you all the very best. You're going to have a marvelous time."

"Part of me doesn't want to go."

"Why on earth not? You no longer have Fanny to look after. You may do anything you like now."

"I don't want to go because . . .well, because you won't be there."

His muscles jolted, the words hitting him square in the chest. Had she missed him? Was she entertaining the idea of a future with him? "What are you saying?"

"I can't stop thinking about you. About us. I miss you."

"God, Eliza." He closed his eyes briefly. "I miss you so much. I'm miserable without you."

"Then why haven't you told me?"

"I did. With the letters. I thought . . . ." He thought she'd understand what he was doing.

"I knew you were thinking of me and trying to get my attention, but I want to hear what's in your heart. I need the words, Lucien."

Do you never fight for anything?

Remembering Fanny's words, Lucien swallowed his nerves and stood. In a few steps, he reached Eliza's chair, where he took her arm, pulled her to her feet, and cupped her face in his hands. "I love you madly, Eliza. I love everything about you, from your clever brain to your stubborn will. I want you here with me, by my side, until I draw my last breath."

A tear slipped free from the corner of her eye. "Even after everything I've done for the last five years? After offering up my virginity to a room full of strangers?"

He gently brushed the tear away with his fingers. "Do you still want me after everything I've done to you, to your family? I kept it a secret from you, and let you suffer on the streets."

"Yes, I do. We can't change the past, and my brother deserves his fair share of the blame for not providing for Fanny and me. But you need to be sure about how you feel, because the whispers will dog me for the rest of my life if I stay in London."

"Let them whisper. It's because of all you've done that I love you. There's no one stronger than you, no one who needs rescuing less than you. You don't need me, but I hope like hell that you want me, because I need you so desperately, angel."

"I love you. And I do want you, but I'm not certain this world is one in which I fit any longer."

He shook his head. "You'll fit in wherever you go. And besides, I thought we were moving to Oxford."

"You would move to Oxford for me?"

"You make that sound like a hardship. I wasn't jesting, Eliza. I need you by my side, day in and day out. I don't care where."

"Even if we never come back to Mayfair?"

"I don't give a fuck about Mayfair."

A spark flashed through her blue gaze at his profanity. Then she rose up on her toes and sealed her lips to his. He wasted no time in kissing her deeply, the sensation washing over him like rain on a barren desert. He'd missed the feel of her mouth, the soft stroke of her tongue. He would never get enough.

When they broke for air, she whispered, "There's that filthy mouth I like so much."

"You may have it whenever you desire. It's entirely at your disposal."

"What about now?"

A blast of heat bored through his system, filling every pore and cell with lust for her. "Sit on my desk and lift your skirts so I may lick you and make you come on my tongue. Then you'll agree to marry me."

Her hooded gaze darkened. "Yes, Your Grace."

Edging around his desk, she looked down and paused. "What's this?" She was staring at the plans for the settlement house. "Hartsford Hall?"

He removed his topcoat and tossed it onto an armchair. "A settlement house I'm building in Shoreditch."

"You . . .what?" Head lowered, she trailed her fingers over the plans. "This is amazing, Lucien."

"It's nothing. The very least I can do." After removing his cufflinks, he began unbuttoning his vest. "On the desk, my sweet girl."

The edge of her mouth lifted as she took him in. "Sit down, Your Grace."

"What?"

She pointed to his chair. "Right now."

He liked this bossy side of her. Crossing to his heavy leather armchair, he asked, "Why?"

After he sat, she lowered herself to her knees. Lucien's lungs seized as she reached for the fastenings on his trousers, her fingers skimming his hard cock. "I feel like I need another lesson. And I promise to be a very diligent student for you."

"Oh, Jesus," he gasped, her palm pressing hard on the ridge of his shaft and sending a jolt of pleasure down to his toes. "You're sure?"

"Very." She bit her lip and stared up at him through her lashes. "And you know what studying at Somerville College means, don't you?"

He swallowed. "No, what?"

"I will have access to many, many rulers."

The End.

Looking for more daring historical romance from Joanna Shupe?

Check out My Dirty Duke, a forbidden romance about a wallflower
and her father's best friend...

Violet knows that her father's best friend, the Duke of Ravensthorpe,
is the most powerful man in all of London with a reputation for sin.

But nothing can stop Violet from wanting to shed her wallflower ways
and fulfill her darkest, most forbidden desires...even if it means
seducing a man twice her age.

Find My Dirty Duke Here!

ALSO BY JOANNA SHUPE

My Dirty Duke

ABOUT THE AUTHOR

Award-winning author **Joanna Shupe** has always loved history, ever since she saw her first Schoolhouse Rock cartoon. Since 2015, her books have appeared on numerous yearly "best of" lists, including Publishers Weekly, The Washington Post, Kirkus Reviews, Kobo, and BookPage.

Sign up for Joanna's Gilded Lilies Newsletter for book news, sneak peeks, reading recommendations, historical tidbits, and more!

www.joannashupe.com

CPSIA information can be obtained
at www.ICGtesting.com
Printed in the USA
BVHW041649300323
661467BV00016B/162

9 781949 364194